YOU THOUGHT YOU WERE A *STAR TREK* FAN, BUT DID YOU KNOW . . .

— Picard has an artificial heart because he was stabbed by Nausicaans while at the Academy.

— Martin Luther King, Jr. told Nichelle Nichols— Uhura on Classic *Trek*—that she shouldn't quit the show because she provided such a valuable role model for black women.

— Q has an IQ level of 2005.

— The voice of the *Enterprise* computer on all three *Treks* is provided by Majel Barrett— Gene Roddenberry's second wife (who also played Nurse Chapel on the Classic *Trek* episodes).

Discover all these facts and more in this unauthorized *Trek* encyclopedia, covering the original *Star Trek*, *Star Trek: The Next Generation*, *Deep Space 9*, and all six movies.

TREK:
THE
UNAUTHORIZED
A-Z

BY HAL SCHUSTER
AND WENDY RATHBONE

HarperPrism
An Imprint of HarperPaperbacks

Star Trek, Star Trek: The Next Generation, and Star Trek: Deep Space Nine are registered trademarks of Paramount Pictures Corporation.

This book was not prepared, approved, licensed, or endorsed by any entity involved in creating or producing the Star Trek television series or films.

HarperPaperbacks   A Division of HarperCollinsPublishers
                    10 East 53rd Street, New York, N.Y. 10022

A trade paperback edition of this book was published in 1994 by Pioneer Books, Inc.

Cover photograph by Rob Atkins/The Image Bank

First HarperPaperbacks printing: February 1995

Printed in the United States of America

HarperPaperbacks, HarperPrism, and colophon are trademarks of HarperCollinsPublishers

❖ 10 9 8 7 6 5 4 3 2 1

ACKNOWLEDGMENTS

I want to thank Andy Rathbone for assisting me in computer format, which often eludes me. Also, James Van Hise was of great assistance with research material. Also thanks to: Della Van Hise, Tina Rathbone, Rhett Rathbone, Alice Rathbone, Alayne Gelfand, Marge Simon, Ann Schwader, Kym Hansen, Linda Berez, and Taerie Bryant for assistance and support above and beyond the call of duty.

FOREWORD

This encyclopedia covers all the *Star Trek* series: Classic, *The Next Generation*, *Deep Space 9*, the films, and the animated series. I have included not only names of actors, writers, and other people involved with *Star Trek*, but characters, ships, events, locations, and terminology. Since the series is still ongoing, I have covered material through the sixth season, but not beyond. *DS9* is covered for its first, short season only.

As I did the research for this book, I encountered numerous ways to spell certain lesser-known terms, planets, races, and characters. I chose the spellings I thought best described the word. Often, I used spellings from *Starlog* magazine, when that information was available. I also used many different fan encyclopedias, as well as books by James Van Hise, John Peel, and Ed Gross to locate specialized information, spelling, and relevant details.

I have attempted, with the materials on hand, to make this as complete a reference manual as possible, including entries for everything I could find in every source at hand. A bibliography at the end of this book gives credit to those sources which were invaluable.

Names of episodes and people (both real and fictional) appear in uppercase. Other references appear in lowercase. One appendix gives an episode guide to each series, which I hope will be helpful for quickly locating an exact title to look up. A second appendix gives a list of *Star Trek* novels through the summer of '93, of note for those who collect the books.

This is an A to Z guide. Everything is alphabetized for your convenience, and nothing is set off in any special category to confuse you.

Live long and prosper,
Wendy Rathbone

TREK:
THE UNAUTHORIZED
—A-Z—

A&P Parisian Grand Premier — alcoholic drink in *TNG* episode "Datalore" that Lore gives Data to knock him out.

A-7 Computer Rating — Spock has an A-7 computer rating, which means he's an expert in computer science.

Aaron, Admiral — character in the *TNG* episode "Conspiracy," played by Ray Reinhardt. He is controlled by parasites.

Abatemarco, Frank — scriptwriter of *TNG* episodes "Chain of Command, Parts I and II," and "Man of the People."

Abbott, Jon — the actor who played Ayleborne in Classic *Trek* episode "Errand of Mercy." Born 1905 in London, England, he moved to Hollywood in 1941. He has appeared in the films *Mrs. Miniver* ('42), *Gigi* ('58), and *The Black Bird* ('75).

Abrom — character played by William Wintersole on Classic *Trek* episode "Patterns of Force." He is a native of Zeon, and the elder brother of Isak.

absorbed — term used on Classic *Trek* episode "The Return of the Archons" for placing a person under the mental control of the computer, Landru, that runs the society. When a person is "absorbed," s/he becomes of the "body," and possesses almost zombielike qualities. They have no free will of their own.

Academy of Sciences — mentioned in the animated episode "The Pirates of Orion." The school is located on Deneb V and is associated with Starfleet.

Acadian Star System — mentioned on the animated episode "Mudd's Passion." This region contains the mining planet Motherlode.

Acamar III — Picard visits Acamar III in *TNG* episode "The Vengeance Factor" in order to reunite the Acamarians with the Gatherers. Acamar III is ruled by Sovereign Marouk.

Acamarian brandy — served in *TNG* episode "The Vengeance Factor."

Acamarians — inhabitants of Acamar III, they are encountered in *TNG* episode "The Vengeance Factor." They have iron-copper composite blood. They are related to the Gatherers who split off from them a century before.

Accolan — character in *TNG* episode "When the Bough Breaks," played by Dan Mason. He is Harry Bernard's adoptive father.

Aceton Assimilators — referred to in *TNG* episode "Booby Trap," they are used by the Menthars as booby traps to catch ships. They feed on raw power, convert the power to radiation, then throw it back to the source.

acetylcholine test — in the Classic *Trek* episode "The Immunity Syndrome," Spock gives the amoebalike creature this test while he is on the shuttlecraft.

Achilles — a gladiator in the Classic *Trek* episode "Bread and Circuses." Achilles beats McCoy down until he is saved by Spock who gives Achilles the neck pinch.

Achrady VII — referred to in *TNG* episode "Captain's Holiday," this is the world Lwaxana Troi was visiting for a conference before meeting the *Enterprise* at Starbase 12.

Acker, Sharon — actress who appeared in the Classic

Trek episode "The Mark of Gideon" as Odona. Born 1936 in England, she has had roles in the series *The Senator*, *The New Perry Mason*, and *Executive Suite*. Films: *Lucky Jim* ('57), *Point Blank* ('67), *Threshold* ('83).

Acost, Jared — in *TNG* episode "Devil's Due," he is the leader of Ventax II. He was played by Marcelo Tubert.

Actos IV — referred to in *TNG* episode "Manhunt," this world is an oligarchy.

Acts of Cumberland — referred to in *TNG* episode "The Measure of a Man," this is the Starfleet precedent that makes Data "owned" by Starfleet.

Adam — character from the Classic *Trek* episode "The Way to Eden." Played by Charles Napier, Adam is a follower of Dr. Sevrin looking for the mythical planet Eden. He is the son of an admiral.

Adams, Marc — the actor who played Hamlet in Classic *Trek* episode "The Conscience of the King."

Adams, Phil — a stunt man who was Kirk's double in Classic *Trek* episode "Amok Time." He has done stunt work on *The Wackiest Ship in the Army*, and *The Christmas Coal Mine Miracle* ('77).

Adams, Stanley — scriptwriter and actor, 1915–77. Wrote, with George F. Slavin, Classic *Trek* episode "The Mark of Gideon," and performed as Cyrano Jones in Classic *Trek* episode "The Trouble with Tribbles," and as the voice of Cyrano in the animated episode "More Tribbles, More Troubles." He also appeared in the SF series *Lost in Space* and *The Atomic Kid* ('54), as well as in *Nevada Smith* ('66). He committed suicide in 1977.

Adams, Tristan, Dr. — character from Classic *Trek* episode "Dagger of the Mind." He is the head doctor of the Tantalus penal colony. He invents a machine called a neural neutralizer with which he can brainwash and control his patients. The machine empties the mind. Adams eventually dies of loneliness under the ray of the neutralizer. He was played by James Gregory.

Adele, Aunt — mentioned in *TNG* episode "Cause and Effect" as Picard's aunt who served him steamed milk to combat insomnia.

Adelphi, **USS** — ship in *TNG* episode "Tin Man" commanded by Captain Darson.

Adelphous IV — destination of the *Enterprise* at the end of *TNG* episode "Data's Day."

Adini Star Cluster — in *TNG* episode "Too Short a Season," the *Enterprise* passes through here on her way to Mordan IV.

Adler, Alan J. — scriptwriter who penned *TNG* episode "The Loss."

Agamemnon, **USS** — one of the ships being led in an attack against the Borg in *TNG* episode "Descent."

Age of Ascension — a Klingon term referring to a rite of manhood. It is referred to in *TNG* episode "Sins of the Father."

Age of Inclusion — a Klingon term referring to age. Worf has not yet reached the age of inclusion when he is orphaned in *TNG* episode "Heart of Glory."

Agmar — character on the animated episode "The Infinite Vulcan." He is a plant being. His voice is the voice of James Doohan.

agonizer — a weapon used in the Classic *Trek* "Mirror, Mirror" episode. In the "mirror" universe, the device is used for punishment. When it is attached to a person's body, it gives great pain.

agony booth — used in the Classic *Trek* episode "Mirror, Mirror," it is a booth about the size of a phone booth in which a person is placed for punishment. When the controls are turned on, great pain is experienced by the victim. One of the victims is Chekov who screams when placed in the booth.

Ahart, Kathy — actress who appeared as an elite crew woman in Classic *Trek* episode "Space Seed."

ahn-woon — a Vulcan weapon like a long band, which is used to trip, strangle, or tie up an opponent. Spock uses the *ahn-woon* to strangle Kirk in Classic *Trek* episode "Amok Time" and believes he has killed him.

Air Police Sergeant — character played by Hal Lynch in Classic *Trek* episode "Tomorrow Is Yesterday." He is the one who gets to taste chicken soup in the transporter room.

Ajax, USS — ship referred to in *TNG* episode "Where No One Has Gone Before" as being a part of the Kosinski experiments.

Ajur — character from *TNG* episode "Captain's Holiday" and played by Karen Landry. She is a Vorgon security agent from the 27th century.

Akaar, Leonard James — in Classic *Trek* episode "Friday's Child," Eleen has a baby boy. Because Kirk and McCoy help deliver him, he is named after them. The child becomes the new ruler of Capella IV.

Akaar — character played by Ben Gage in Classic *Trek* episode "Friday's Child." He is the *teer*, the leader on Capella IV. He has a wife, Eleen, and is killed by Maab.

Akagi, USS — one of the ships mentioned as being used in a blockade in the Klingon civil war in *TNG* episode "Reunion."

Akharin — the original name of Flint, played by James Daly, from the Classic *Trek* episode "Requiem for Methuselah." Akharin is a soldier born on Earth, in Mesopotamia, in 3834 B.C. who falls in battle with an arrow through the heart but does not die. His tissues are regenerated every time he is injured or killed. He takes on other personas as he enjoys a life of immortality, until he meets the *Enterprise* crew in the 23rd century. (See entry for Flint.)

Akuta — character in Classic *Trek* episode "The Apple," played by Keith Andes. He is the leader on Gamma Trianguli VI, also known as "the eyes of Vaal." Vaal is a ruling computer, and only Akuta can interpret its demands and orders through a set of antennae behind his ears.

Alaimo, Marc — actor who played Commander T'Bok in the *TNG* episode "The Neutral Zone," guest starred in *TNG* "The Wounded," "Time's Arrow," and guest starred in *DS9* "Emissary."

Alans — a specialist in Vulcanology and geomechanics, he is a member of Wesley's Secundi Drema team in *TNG* episode "Pen Pals." He is married to Hildebrandt, and is played by Whitney Rydbeck.

Alar — a character referred to in the animated episode "Jihad." He is a religious teacher of the Skorr.

Alaynan singer stone — a gift that Data leaves with the memory-erased Sarjenka at the end of *TNG* episode "Pen Pals." She finds it in Pulaski's office and plays with it. It sings a different song for every person, but will not sing for Data.

"Albatross" — written by Dario Finelli, this animated Classic *Trek* episode aired 9/28/74. McCoy is accused of infecting a planetful of people with a virus that killed most of them nineteen years before. When the *Enterprise* visits the planet, McCoy is jailed. Meanwhile, when a senility plague hits the *Enterprise* crew, McCoy must be released to find an antidote. They discover that an aurora, and not McCoy, is responsible for the plague, and McCoy discovers the cure. Guest voices: James Doohan (Kol-tai, Supreme Prefect).

Albeni meditation crystal — in *TNG* episode "Angel One," Riker gives this item to Beate as a gift.

Albert, Edward Lawrence — actor who guest starred in *DS9* episode "A Man Alone."

Albert, Joshua, Cadet — the cadet who is killed in the Kolvoord Starburst performed by Wesley and his classmates in *TNG* episode "The First Duty."

Albert, Lieutenant Commander — father of Cadet Joshua Albert who is killed in an illegal Academy ship maneuver in *TNG* episode "The First Duty."

Albright, Budd — actor who played Rayburn in Classic *Trek* episode "What Are Little Girls Made Of?"

Alcyone — The inhabitants of this planet kill the plague-carrying Tarellian refugees in *TNG* episode "Haven."

Aldea — planet mentioned in *TNG* episode "When the Bough Breaks." It is located in the Epsilon Mynos system.

Aldebaran III — planet mentioned in Classic *Trek* episode "The Deadly Years," where Dr. Janet Wallace and her husband, Dr. Theodore Wallace, experiment on plants to slow their aging process.

Aldebaran Colony — planet where Dr. Elizabeth Dehner from Classic *Trek* episode "Where No Man Has Gone Before" has lived.

Aldebaran exchange — a chess move Riker makes to win against Nibor in *TNG* episode "Ménage à Troi."

Aldebaran serpent — in *TNG* episode "Hide and Q," Q assumes this form in front of Picard and the crew.

Aldebaran whiskey — Mr. Scott and Picard share some in *TNG* episode "Relics." It is green. Guinan gives it to Picard.

Aldrich, Rhonda — actress who played the secretary Madeline in the *TNG* episodes "The Big Goodbye," "Manhunt," and "Clues."

Aldron IV — referred to in *TNG* episode "Coming of Age" as the *Enterprise*'s destination after leaving Relva.

Alert B–2 — Kirk gives this order in Classic *Trek* episode "The Naked Time" to signify that the main sections of the ship should be sealed off.

Alexander — character on Classic *Trek* episode "Plato's Stepchildren," played by Michael Dunn. He is a dwarf who is also the only person on Platonius who does not have the power of psychokinesis. He eventually leaves Platonius with Kirk, Spock, and McCoy.

Alexander — Worf's son, played by Brian Bonsall. He has a recurring role on *TNG*. His last name is Rozhenko. His mother was K'Ehleyr. He was born on the 23rd day of *Maktag*, on the Klingon calendar.

Alexander, David — director of the Classic *Trek* episodes "The Way to Eden" and "Plato's Stepchildren." He also directed episodes of *The Man from U.N.C.L.E.*

Alexandra — girl who is kidnapped in *TNG* episode "When the Bough Breaks," played by twins Jessica and Vanessa Bova.

Alfa 177 — planet in Classic *Trek* episode "The Enemy Within" that contains a strange ore that causes the transporter to malfunction and split Kirk into two people. The rest of the landing party is marooned on Alfa 177 during its long, freezing night while the *Enterprise* crew tries to fix the transporter.

Algeron, Treaty of — established 180 years before, it created the Neutral Zone between the Federation and the Romulans. It is mentioned in *TNG* episode "The Defector."

Algolian Ceremonial Rhythms — in *TNG* episode "Ménage à Troi," these are chimes played to signal the end to a Trade Agreements Conference held on board the *Enterprise*.

Alice — character in Classic *Trek* episode "Shore Leave." Played by Marcia Brown, she is a little blonde girl that only McCoy sees. She is dressed like Alice in Wonderland and is chasing a large white rabbit. Alice is also the name of a character in the Classic *Trek* episode "I, Mudd," played by twins Rhae and Alyce Andrece. She is an android, and there are 500 of her, all identical.

"All Our Yesterdays" — written by Jean Lisette Aroeste, directed by Marvin Chomsky, this third-season Classic *Trek* episode aired 3/14/69. On the planet Sarpeidon, Kirk, Spock, and McCoy discover a library where there is a doorway which is a time machine called an atavachron. The inhabitants' sun is about to go nova, and all have escaped to the past except Mr. Atoz, the librarian. He thinks Kirk, Spock, and McCoy are there to escape, and pushes them through the doorway. Spock and McCoy end up in a snowy ice age, while Kirk is deposited in a society obsessed with witch-hunting. Spock falls in love with a lonely woman named Zarabeth as he mentally reverts 5000 years into the past, at a time when Vulcans were emotional, barbaric creatures. Guest stars: Mariette Hartley, Ian Wolfe, Anna Karen, Johnny Haymer, Ed Bakey, Kermit Murdock, Al Cavens, and Stan Barrett. Of note: This episode prompted a sequel by novel writer Ann Crispin, who wrote *Yesterday's Son* based on this episode, as well as the sequel to it, *Time For Yesterday*.

allasomorph — a shapeshifter. The Daledi of *TNG* episode "The Dauphin" are allasomorphs. Odo of *DS9* is a shapeshifter, but he is very different in his natural state and so seems unrelated to the Daledi.

"Allegiance" — this third-season *TNG* episode was written by Hans Beimler and Richard Manning, directed by Winrich Kolbe. Aliens replace Captain Picard in the *Enterprise* with a duplicate, and the real Picard is held with three other hostages who face problems varying from hunger to mistrust when they believe one among them is involved in the kidnapping itself. Guest stars: Stephen Markle, Reiner Schone, Joycelyn O'Brien, Jerry Rector, and Jeff Rector.

Allen, Chad — actor who played Jono/Jeremiah Rossa in *TNG* episode "Suddenly Human." He was a regular in the TV series *Our House*, and is currently a regular on *Dr. Quinn, Medicine Woman*. He has a twin sister.

Allen, Corey — director of *TNG* episodes "Encounter At Farpoint," "Homesoil," "Final Mission," and "The Game," and *DS9* episode "Captive Pursuit."

Allen, George E. — actor who played the engineer in Classic *Trek* episode "Devil in the Dark."

Allen, Philip Richard — actor who played Captain Esteban in the Classic *Trek* movie *The Search for Spock*. He also appeared in the film *Mommie Dearest* and the series *Get Christie Love!*

Allen, Richard — actor who played Kentor in *TNG* episodes "The Ensigns of Command" and "Darmok."

Allenby, Tess, Ensign — conn officer on the *Enterprise* in *TNG* episode "Final Mission." She is played by Mary Kohnert.

Alley, Kirstie — born 1955 in Wichita, Kansas, Alley is the actress who played Saavik in the movie *The Wrath of Khan*, her first feature-film role. Another actress, Robin Curtis, took up the role in *The Search for Spock* and *The Voyage Home* after Alley asked for too much money. This didn't hurt her career, however. Known for her character Rebecca on *Cheers*, for which she's won an Emmy award for best actress in a comedy series. Her other film credits are numerous. She is married to actor Parker Stevenson, and is a Scientologist.

Allin, Jeff — actor who guest starred in *TNG* episode "Imaginary Friend."

Alondra — a planet mentioned in the animated episode

"One of Our Planets Is Missing." This world is uninhabited, and is eaten by a cosmic cloud creature.

Alpha VI — a known dead world, where Kirk reencounters Khan in the second Classic *Trek* feature film, *The Wrath of Khan.* How he missed the fact that Ceti Alpha V wasn't where it was supposed to be is a mystery.

Alpha Carinae II — mentioned in Classic *Trek* episode "The Ultimate Computer," this planet is approached by the *Enterprise* and analyzed by the M-5 computer, which notes it is a class M planet and then begins making landing-party recommendations.

Alpha Carinae V — mentioned in Classic *Trek* episode "Wolf in the Fold," it is where the Drella comes from.

Alpha Centauri — mentioned in the Classic *Trek* episodes "Tomorrow Is Yesterday" and "Metamorphosis." In the former, Kirk tells his captors that Alpha Centauri "is a beautiful place, you ought to see it." In the latter, Zefrem Cochrane is said to be a native of that world. Also mentioned by Geordi in *TNG* episode "Elementary, Dear Data."

Alpha Cygnus IX — referred to in *TNG* episode "Sarek" as the location of a treaty negotiation which Sarek attended in the past.

Alpha Cygnus IX, Treaty of — something Sarek helped create, mentioned in *TNG* episode "Sarek."

Alpha Leonis — in *TNG* episode "The Vengeance Factor," this is the *Enterprise*'s destination after they seal the Gatherer treaty.

Alpha Leonis System — where the *Enterprise* is headed in *TNG* episode "The Vengeance Factor." They are bringing much-needed drugs to this sector.

Alpha Majoris I — mentioned in Classic *Trek* episode "Wolf in the Fold." It is said the cloud creature, the Mellitus, is from that world.

Alpha Omicron System — where the Galaxy's Child is found in the *TNG* episode of the same name.

Alpha Onias III — in *TNG* episode "Future Imperfect," this is the world where Riker supposedly contracted Altairian encephalitis while on an away team mission. An alien boy lives there.

Alpha Proxima II — mentioned in Classic *Trek* episode "Wolf in the Fold." On this planet, there was a series of murders similar to the Jack the Ripper murders on Earth.

Alpha Quadrant — the quadrant of the galaxy that is most known and explored by the Federation and Starfleet. The Gamma Quadrant is the unknown section of the galaxy that can be reached through the wormhole near which *DS9* is located.

Alrik — in *TNG* episode "The Perfect Mate," he is the Chancellor of Valt Minor, betrothed to Kamala. He is played by Mickey Cottrell.

Altair III — referred to in "Encounter at Farpoint" by Riker who visited this world when he was stationed on the USS *Hood*.

Altair VI — this planet is mentioned over and over again in Classic *Trek* episode "Amok Time." The *Enterprise* is headed there for a presidential inaugural dedication, but is diverted to Vulcan when Spock goes into *Pon farr*.

Altairian encephalitis — Riker is wrongly supposed to have contracted this while on an away team to Alpha Onias III in *TNG* episode "Future Imperfect."

Altar of Tomorrow — in Classic *Trek* episode "Devil in the Dark," the horta refers to her nest as "The Altar of Tomorrow" and "The Chamber of the Ages."

Altek — planet of the Coalition of Medina. It has a twin planet named Streleb. Both are located in the Omega

Sagitta XII system. It is referred to in the *TNG* episode "The Outrageous Okona."

"Alternative Factor, The" — written by Don Ingalls, directed by Gerd Oswald, this first-season Classic *Trek* episode aired 3/30/67. A traveler from a parallel universe threatens the Enterprise and the entire universe when his ship rips a hole in the fabric of existence. Guest stars: Robert Brown, Janet MacLachlen, Richard Derr, and Eddie Paskey.

alternative warp — mentioned in Classic *Trek* episode "The Alternative Factor," it is a negative magnetic corridor where universes come together. In order to avert annihilation, the corridor is not supposed to be breached.

Altine Conference — destination of the alien scientists aboard the *Enterprise* in *TNG* episode "Suspicions."

Altor VII — mentioned in *TNG* episode "Birthright," it is the world Beverly says she is looking forward to recreating on a *DS9* holosuite.

Alva — in the *TNG* episode "Manhunt," she is a murder victim found in a river. The character is never seen.

Alvin — old man's dead body which Chekov finds in Classic *Trek* episode "The Deadly Years."

Alwanna Nebula — in *TNG* episode "Rightful Heir," the *Enterprise* passes and scans this phenomenon.

Amanda — character played by Jane Wyatt in Classic *Trek* episode "Journey to Babel," and the fourth movie *The Voyage Home*. Her full name is Amanda Grayson. The character reappears in the animated episode "Yesteryear," but the voice is that of Majel Barrett. She is Spock's human mother, the wife of Ambassador Sarek. She met Sarek on Earth when she was a teacher and he was visiting in his role of ambassador from Vulcan. She is the person from whom Spock learned compassion and a love for the arts. She is not a little perturbed by the fact that Spock seems to have turned his back on his human heritage and she confronts him about it in "Journey to Babel."

Amarie — character in *TNG* episode "Unification, Part II" who has multiple arms and plays a keyboard. Riker encounters her at the Qualor II bar. She is played by Harriet Leider.

***Ambassador*-class ship** — the *Enterprise* C from *TNG* episode "Yesterday's Enterprise" is of this class. *Enterprise* D is *Galaxy* Class. The first *Enterprise* starship was a *Constitution*-class ship.

ambergris — referred to in the animated "The Ambergris Element," this substance is produced by sperm whales. A similar chemical is used to make Kirk and Spock water-breathers on the planet Argo.

"Ambergris Element, The" — Written by Margaret Armen, this animated Classic *Trek* episode aired 12/1/73. Kirk and Spock become water-breathers on the water planet Argo, and when rescued cannot survive in the air.

American Continent Institute — referred to in Classic *Trek* pilot "The Cage," it is the agency which sent the original expedition to Talos IV.

Amick, Mädchen — actress who played the teenage girl in *TNG* "The Dauphin." She is best known for her role in *Twin Peaks*, and also appeared in the film *Sleepwalkers*.

Amigosa Diaspora — a globular cluster the *Enterprise* charts in *TNG* episode "Schisms."

amoeba — a single-celled creature. In Classic *Trek* episode "The Immunity Syndrome," a giant galactic amoeba which is eleven thousand miles in length is encountered by the *Enterprise*. The optical special effects for this creature were created by Frank Van Der Veer (see entry). The all-Vulcan manned starship *Intrepid* is destroyed by this creature before the *Enterprise* kills it. The amoeba looks exactly like the *Amoeba dubia* variety, now known as *Polychaos dubia*, with the exception of its size.

"Amok Time" — Written by award-winning science-fiction author Theodore Sturgeon (who also wrote the episode "Shore Leave") and directed by Joseph Pevney, this Classic *Trek* episode began the second season and aired 9/15/67. Spock must return to Vulcan as he enters *Pon farr*, a shameful Vulcan physiological condition which forces him to mate or die. This episode is famous for addressing the delicate subject of Vulcan sexuality. Guest stars: Arlene Martel, Celia Lovsky, Lawrence Montaigne, and Byron Morrow. Of note: Here we are first introduced to the Vulcan salute invented by Leonard Nimoy, *Pon farr*, plomeek soup, and Finagle's Law. It is the only episode in which Spock's home planet is shown, though the first, third, and fourth Classic *Trek* movies give us further glimpses of this "desert" world. Also, this episode marks Walter Koenig's first appearance as Ensign Pavel Chekov. This episode was nominated for a Hugo Award for Best Dramatic Presentation of 1967.

Amos, Gregory — scriptwriter who penned *TNG* script "A Matter of Honor."

ampheon — referred to in the animated episode "The Counter-Clock Incident," it is the term used for a dead star in an antimatter universe.

Amritraj, Vijay — actor who played the role of Starship Captain in *The Voyage Home*. Born in India, Vijay was a member of the team that won the Davis Cup in tennis. Acting credits include: *Octopussy* ('83), and the TV series *Fantasy Island*.

Anan 7 — character from Classic *Trek* episode "A Taste of Armageddon," played by David Opatoshu. He is the first councilman of Eminiar VII.

anastazine — in *TNG* episode "The Hunted," this is a gas used to flood the cargo bays on the *Enterprise* in order to put Danar to sleep.

anbo-jytsy — a martial art practiced with armor and

long sticks. Riker fights in the anbo-jytsy ring in the *Enterprise* gymnasium on deck 12 with his father, Kyle, in *TNG* episode "The Icarus Factor."

Anchilles fever — in *TNG* episode "Code of Honor," Anchilles Fever sweeps planet Styris IV.

"And the Children Shall Lead" — written by Edward J. Lakso, directed by Marvin Chomsky, this third-season Classic *Trek* episode aired 10/11/68. On the planet Triacus, an evil entity called Gorgan controls five children whose parents he killed. The children use their alien powers to take over the *Enterprise*. Guest stars: Melvin Belli, Craig Hundley, James Wellman, Pamelyn Ferdin, Brian Tochi, Caesar Belli, and Mark Robert Brown. Of note: Famous attorney Melvin Belli got the role because he was a *Star Trek* fan. He also managed to get the role of one of the kids, Stevie, for his son, Caesar.

Anderson, Barbara — actress who played Lenore Karidian in Classic *Trek* episode "The Conscience of the King." She also played Ironside's assistant, Eve, in the *Ironside* series from 1967 to 1971, for which she won an Emmy. She has been in *Mission: Impossible, The Six Million Dollar Man*, and other TV series.

Anderson, Erich — actor in *TNG* episode "Conundrum."

Anderson, John — actor who played Kevin Uxbridge in *TNG* episode "The Survivors."

Anderson, Judith — actress (1898–1992) who played the Vulcan High Priestess in the second Classic *Trek* film *The Search for Spock*. Dame Judith Anderson was born in Australia, and has appeared on stage and screen numerous times. She was given the title Dame Commander of the British Empire in 1960 for her excellent work. She won an Emmy award, and appeared in films including *The Ten Commandments* ('56) and *A Man Called Horse* ('70). She also appeared on the soap opera *Santa Barbara*.

Anderson, Sam — actor who played the assistant manager of the Hotel Royale in the *TNG* episode "The Royale."

Anderson, Steve — actor who guest starred in *TNG* episode "First Contact."

Andes, Keith — actor who played Akuta in Classic *Trek* episode "The Apple." Born in New Jersey in 1920, Andes has done radio, stage, movie, and TV work. He is in the films: *Clash By Night* ('52), *Tora! Tora! Tora!* ('70), and the TV series *Glynis* and *Search*.

Andonesian encephalitis — a noncontagious disease in *TNG* episode "The Dauphin."

Andonian tea — in *TNG* episode "Conspiracy," Picard drinks Andonian tea while on Earth.

Andor — home of the Andorian race and mentioned in Classic episode "Journey to Babel."

Andorian — an Andorian is a being with blue skin, white hair, and antennae. They are traditionally warriors with a somewhat violent nature. Andorians are first encountered in Classic *Trek* episode "Journey to Babel," though the character Thelev (William O'Connell) turns out to be an Orion in Andorian disguise. Shras (Reggie Nalder) is an Andorian in that episode. There is an Andorian (Dick Crockett) in "The Gamesters of Triskelion." An Andorian (Richard Geary) also appears in "Whom Gods Destroy" as a patient in the penal colony on Elba II. In the animated episode "Yesteryear," an Andorian, Thelin, (voice provided by James Doohan) is first officer of the *Enterprise* when Vulcan history is changed and Spock died as a young boy. Andorians also appear in the animated episode "Time Trap." They are mentioned in *TNG*, but are not seen.

Andorian Sivalthu — a horse.

Andrea — character from Classic *Trek* episode "What

Are Little Girls Made Of?" played by Sherry Jackson. She is an android created by Dr. Korby on Exo III. While trying to learn of emotion, she falls in love with Dr. Korby and he destroys himself and her with a single, suicidal phaser blast as they embrace.

Andrece, Alyce and Rhae — twin actresses who appeared as the Alices in "I, Mudd." They also appeared in *Batman.* They were hired when the *Trek* casting director saw them walking down the street and asked them if they wanted to be on TV.

Andrews, Bunny — music editor of the *Trek* Classic film *The Undiscovered Country.*

Andrews, Tige — actor who played Kras in Classic *Trek* episode "Friday's Child." He was the star of *The Mod Squad* (1968–73). Other credits: *The Detectives* (1959–62), *Mr. Roberts* ('55), *The Last Tycoon* ('76), *Raid on Entebbe* ('77), *The Return of the Mod Squad* ('79).

android — androids are mechanical beings who are made in human form. They are first encountered in Classic *Trek* episode "What Are Little Girls Made Of?" Andrea, Ruk, Brown, and Dr. Korby are all advanced forms of androids made from a thousand-year-old superior technology left by an alien race. Androids also appear in "I, Mudd," another race of machines created by a long-dead (1,743,912 years dead), technologically advanced race called "the makers." In "Return to Tomorrow," Sargon, Thalessa, and Henoch unsuccessfully work to create android bodies for their energies to inhabit. In "Requiem for Methuselah," Flint created Reena (a.k.a. Rayna) to be his perfect mate. Because of his immortality, all his other brides had too-brief lifespans, which made it hard for him to form relationships. Reena was supposed to live forever with him on the planet Holberg 917G. However, when she experienced conflicting emotions by falling in love with both Kirk and Flint at the same time, the power of her feelings destroyed her. Mr. Atoz has android replicants which help him tend the library on Sarpeidon in "All Our Yesterdays." On *The Next Generation*, Data and Lore are androids created by Dr. Noonian Soong, as seen in the episode "Brothers." Data (see entry), one of the most popular main characters in the series, is always trying to learn more about the nature of humans. Although it often gets him into deep trouble, at other times it is a positive experience, and he seems on the verge of becoming human, of evolving. He is, as stated in "The Naked Now," a fully functional male android who can, if he chooses, be sexually compatible with a human. In the episode "The Offspring," Data creates his child, a female android named Lal, whose emotions ultimately destroy her. In the Classic *Trek* film *Star Trek: The Motion Picture*, the Ilia probe sent to the *Enterprise* by Vejur is an android. Her curiosity of humans and desire to seek emotion send her and Decker to another plane of existence.

Andromeda — referred to in Classic *Trek* episode "By Any Other Name," it is the galaxy from which the invaders, the Kelvans, come. It is the galaxy closest to our galaxy, the Milky Way. It is also referred to in "I, Mudd" as the galaxy where the "makers" of the androids are from.

Angel One — in the *TNG* episode "Angel One," this world is seen as a matriarchal planet where men are inferior.

"Angel One" — This first-season *TNG* episode was written by Patrick Barry and directed by Michael Rhodes. The *Enterprise* finds survivors of the missing *Odin* on Angel One, where they are fugitives. On this world, women rule and men are subservient. Guest stars: Karen Montgomery, Sam Hennings, Patricia MacPherson, and Leonard John Crowfoot.

Angela — character played by Barbara Baldavin. Her full name is Angela Martine, and appears in the Classic *Trek* episodes "Balance of Terror" (wherein she loses the husband whom she marries in that episode) and "Shore Leave."

Angosia — in *TNG* episode "The Hunted," this world is up for Federation membership. Prime Minister Nayrok tells the *Enterprise* crew that his people have dedicated themselves to developing intellectual interests for centuries. However, they have imprisoned veterans from the recent Tarsian War, and when the veterans escape and take over, the government is threatened. The *Enterprise* leaves them behind, as the Prime Directive stipulates, to sort out their differences and we never find out what happens to the world.

Angosian alteration — used in *TNG* episode "The Hunted" to turn ordinary men into perfect killing machines for war. The process alters cell structure using cryptobiolin, triclenidil, macrospentol, and other substances which are unrecognized by the *Enterprise* crew.

Angosian Senate — in *TNG* episode "The Hunted," this group is responsible for the decison to isolate the Angosian veterans left over from the Tarsian War.

Angosian transport — in *TNG* episode "The Hunted," this ship is captured by Roga Danar, a war veteran. He uses it to escape Lunar V.

Anka — character on Classic *Trek* episode "The Cloud Minders," played by Fred Williamson. He is a Troglyte, and also a "disruptor," or terrorist.

Ansara, Michael — actor who played Kang in Classic *Trek* episode "The Day of the Dove." Born in Lowell, Mass. in 1922, his credits are numerous, including *Broken Arrow* (1956–58), *The Law of the Plainsman* (1959–62), *Buck Rogers in the 25th Century* (1979–80), *Voyage to the Bottom of the Sea* ('60), *Guns of the Magnificent Seven* ('69), and *The Manitou* ('78).

Ansata — in *TNG* episode "The High Ground," the Ansata are terrorist separatists fighting for autonomy on Rutia IV. Kyril Finn leads them. They have been fighting for 70 years.

Antarean brandy — beverage served in Classic *Trek* episode "Is There in Truth No Beauty?" It is blue, and served on special occasions.

Antarean glow water — in Classic *Trek* episode "The Trouble with Tribbles," Cyrano Jones has Antarean glow water to sell, as well as tribbles. It appears to be something like perfume, though it could be simply merchandise of a decorative nature.

Antares, **USS** — referred to in Classic *Trek* episode "Charlie X," it is a science vessel with a crew of 20. Captain Ramart is her commander, and she is destroyed by Charlie's mental powers after they rescue him and turn him over to the *Enterprise*.

Antares-**class freighter** — freighters that carry cargo, mentioned in *TNG* episodes "Face of the Enemy" and "Ensign Ro."

Antede III — in *TNG* episode "Manhunt," this world's inhabitants are fishlike beings. They are afraid of space travel, and travel in a self-induced catatonia. When the *Enterprise* transports two of these beings to Pacifica, they turn out to be assassins.

Antedian Delegate — character played by Mick Fleetwood in *TNG* episode "Manhunt." He represents Antede III, but is an assassin in disguise.

Anthony, Larry — actor who played Ensign Berkeley in Classic *Trek* episode "Dagger of the Mind." His credits include *The Man from U.N.C.L.E.*

Anthony, Richard — actor who played Rider in Classic *Trek* episode "Spectre of the Gun."

Antica — mentioned in *TNG* episode "Lonely among Us," its inhabitants are caninelike. The planet, located in the Beta Renner system, is at war with its neighbor, Selay.

anticontamination suit — seen in Classic *Trek* episode "The Naked Time," this suit is worn by Spock and Tormolen. It is red and pliant, like a plastic coverall.

antigravity — something that defies gravity despite its weight and mass. This term often refers to devices that can be attached to a heavy object to move or lift it. Antigravity devices are used to carry Nomad in Classic *Trek* episode "The Changeling," and to bring Kollos aboard the *Enterprise* in "Is There in Truth No Beauty?" In the Classic *Trek* episode "The Cloud Minders," Stratos City uses antigravity elevation. Antigravity chambers are seen on board the *Enterprise* in the Classic *Trek* episodes "Space Seed" and "The Lights of Zetar." Antigravity gurneys are used in the movies and on *TNG* and *DS9* to move patients to sick-bay, as well as for antigravity handles which are attached to heavy cargo for ease of movement. These are sometimes referred to as "antigravs."

antimatter — a dangerous and mysterious substance used along with matter for warp propulsion in all *Star Trek* series. In the animated episode "The Counter-Clock Incident," the *Enterprise* enters an antimatter universe.

Antonio, Lou — actor who played Lokai in the Classic *Trek* episode "Let That Be Your Last Battlefield." He was also in *The Snoop Sisters* ('73), *Dog and Cat* ('77), and *Makin' It* ('79). His films include *Hawaii* ('66) and *Partners in Crime* ('73). He is also a producer.

Antos IV — a planet mentioned in Classic *Trek* episode "Whom Gods Destroy." It was on this world that Garth learned the talent of cellular metamorphosis.

Anya — character in *TNG* episode "The Dauphin" who is an allasomorph, a shapeshifter whose natural state is pure light. Anya is the guardian of future leader Salia and is from Daled IV's third moon. She appears as an older woman played by Paddi Edwards, as a teenage girl played by Mädchen Amick, and as a beast played by Cindy Sorenson.

Apella — character in Classic *Trek* episode "A Private Little War," played by Arthur Bernard. He is the headman of a village.

Apgar, Manua — character from *TNG* episode "A Matter of Perspective," played by Gina Hecht. The wife of Dr. Nel Apgar, she is a Tanugan who accuses Riker of trying to rape her.

Apgar, Nel, Dr. — Tanugan scientist and creator of a Krieger wave converter from *TNG* episode "A Matter of Perspective." His wife is Manua. He destroys himself when he blows up the space station he lives on. Apgar is played by Mark Margolis.

aphasia — the diagnosis of what seems to be affecting the people of *DS9* in the episode "Babel." Aphasia victims suffer from a condition that leaves the thought processes unaffected but redirects all aural and visual stimuli. The victims in "Babel" begin speaking using nonsense words.

Apnex Sea — located on Romulus, it is mentioned by Jarok as where his home is located in *TNG* episode "The Defector."

Apollo — character in Classic *Trek* episode "Who Mourns for Adonais?" played by Michael Forest. He is one of the mythical Greek gods, apparently really a highly advanced alien being, who wants the *Enterprise* crew to settle on Pollux IV and worship him. He dies by spreading himself upon the wind and disintegrating.

Appel, Ed — character on Classic *Trek* episode "Devil in the Dark," played by Brad Weston. He is a chief engineer on Janus VI.

"Apple, The" — written by Max Ehrlich and Gene L. Coon, directed by Joseph Pevney, this second-season Classic *Trek* episode aired 10/13/67. The landing party beams down to a seemingly idyllic planet only to find it filled with poisonous plants that throw darts, and inhabited by humanoid beings whose lives are controlled by an entity called Vaal. The beings never age, never reproduce, and never die. Guest stars: John Winston, Keith Andes, Celeste Yarnall, Shari Nims, David Soul, Mal Friedman, Jerry Daniels, Jay Jones, and Dick Dial.

April, Robert, Commodore — the first captain of the *Enterprise*. He appears in the animated "The Counter-Clock Incident," and has a wife, Sarah.

April, Sarah, Dr. — the first medical officer of the *Enterprise*. She appears in the animated "The Counter-Clock Incident," and is married to Commodore Robert April.

Apter, Harold — scriptwriter of *TNG* episode "Data's Day."

Aquans — water-breathing beings on the planet Argo seen in the animated episode "The Ambergris Element." They have webbed feet and hands, green hair, and dorsal fins.

aquashuttle — a shuttlecraft aboard the *Enterprise* that can be piloted underwater. It is seen in the animated episode "The Ambergris Element."

Aquiel — see entry under Uhnari, Aquiel, Lt.

"Aquiel" — this sixth-season *TNG* episode was written by Brannon Braga, Ronald D. Moore, and Jeri Taylor, directed by Cliff Bole. The Klingons have picked up Lt. Aquiel Uhnari in a shuttle she used to leave Subspace Relay Station 47. She left because she feared for her life when her coworker Rocha tried to kill her and then killed himself on the station. She is suspected of murdering him. The only person who believes her story is Geordi, who has been reading the journals and letters she left behind. He has grown very fond of her. Guest star: Renée Jones.

Aran — character in *TNG* episode "When the Bough Breaks" who was supposed to be Alexandra's Aldean father.

Arboretum — a place on board the *Enterprise* where there is parklike scenery.

Arcanis — planet referred to in Classic *Trek* episode "Arena."

arch — mentioned in *TNG* episode "Elementary, Dear Data," it is a computer-interface system within the holodeck that contains a fantasy scenario.

Archer IV — at the end of *TNG* episode "Yesterday's Enterprise," this is the *Enterprise*'s destination.

***Archon*, USS** — a starship that has been missing for one hundred years before the *Enterprise* finds out she has been pulled into the atmosphere of the planet Beta III in Classic *Trek* episode "The Return of the Archons."

Archons — what the survivors of the destroyed ship USS *Archon* are called by the inhabitants of Beta III in Classic episode "The Return of the Archons." It becomes a general term to refer to anyone who comes from outside the world to resist the hypnotic control of Landru. The *Enterprise* crew are, thus, Archons.

Archos — a civilian ship of the Federation mentioned as lost in *TNG* episode "Legacy."

Arcturian — alien on the recreation deck in *Star Trek: The Motion Picture*, played by an extra.

Arcturian fizz — in *TNG* episode "Ménage à Troi," Lwaxana refers to this drink as having aphrodisiac qualities.

Arcturus — referred to in Classic *Trek* episode "The Conscience of the King" as a culture from which the actors borrowed their props and costuming. They stage the play *Macbeth* as if it occurred in that culture.

Ardan — character who is never seen in *TNG* episode "Too Short a Season." He is a dead Mordanite terrorist.

Ardana — a mining planet in Classic *Trek* episode "The

Cloud Minders," over which Stratos City presides. The planet is the only known source of zienite.

Ardra — the devil of Ventax II in *TNG* episode "Devil's Due." Myth says the people struck a bargain with Ardra to have a millennium of peace.

"Arena" — written by Gene L. Coon and Frederick Brown, directed by Joseph Pevney, this first-season Classic *Trek* episode aired 1/19/67. The *Enterprise* is chasing a Gorn ship when it is stopped in space by all-powerful beings called Metrons who are appalled at the violence of both ships. Kirk and the Gorn captain are then transported to the surface of a planet to battle to the death. Guest stars: Carole Shelyne, Jerry Ayres, Grant Woods, Tom Troupe, James Farley, and Sean Kenney. Of note: This episode is, like the Theodore Sturgeon episode "Shore Leave," based on a science-fiction short story. The story, "Arena" by Frederick Brown, was first published in *Astounding* in 1944. An *Outer Limits* episode called "Fun and Games" was also based on this story.

Arenberg, Lee — actor who guest starred in *DS9* episode "The Nagus."

Aresco, Joey — actor who played Brull in *TNG* episode "The Vengeance Factor."

Arex, Lieutenant — recurring character in the animated series. He is a navigator with three arms and three legs. The Edoan is orange-skinned with an oddly shaped (by human standards) head. James Doohan provided the voice for the character.

Argelius II — a planet visited by the *Enterprise* in Classic *Trek* episode "Wolf in the Fold." It is a popular shore-leave planet because the inhabitants are hedonists and live for pleasure. There is little crime on this world and no jealousy.

Argo — a water planet visited by the *Enterprise* in the animated episode "The Ambergris Element." It has underwater cities inhabited by Aquans (see entry), a water-breathing alien species.

Argolis Cluster — a region of space the *Enterprise* charts in *TNG* episode "I, Borg." It is also mentioned in "True Q."

Argus River — referred to in Classic *Trek* episode "Wolf in the Fold." It is a river on Rigel IV with carvings done by hill people that are famous throughout the galaxy.

Argus Subspace Telescope Array — automated installation that has been malfunctioning, which the *Enterprise* visits in *TNG* episode "The Nth Degree."

Argus X — this planet is where Kirk meets the vampire cloud creature for the second time in Classic *Trek* episode "Obsession."

Argyle, Blake — engineering officer on board the *Enterprise* in *TNG* episodes "Where No One Has Gone Before" and "Datalore." He is played by Biff Yeager.

Ariana — a dying Tarellian refugee in *TNG* episode "Haven." She is played by Danitza Kingsley.

Ariannus — planet referred to in Classic *Trek* episode "Let That Be Your Last Battlefield" which the *Enterprise* saves from a bacterial invasion by spraying decontaminants.

Ariel — a science ship containing a crew of six in the animated episode "The Eye of the Beholder."

Ariel — in *TNG* episode "Angel One," she is the assistant to Beate in love with Captain Ramsey. She is played by Patricia MacPherson.

Aries, USS — Riker is offered command of this ship in *TNG* episode "The Icarus Factor."

Arkaria — planet where Riker and crew are briefly held in *TNG* episode "Starship Mine." According to Data, the Arkaria is an egalitarian culture.

Arkarian horn — flocks of this bird sometimes darken the sky over Arkaria, mentioned in *TNG* episode "Starship Mine."

Arloph IX — referred to in *TNG* episode "The Neutral Zone."

Armagnal, Gary — actor who played McNary in *TNG* episode "The Big Goodbye."

Armen, Margaret — scriptwriter whose credits include Classic *Trek* episodes "The Gamesters of Triskelion," "The Paradise Syndrome," "The Cloud Minders" (with David Gerrold and Oliver Crawford), and animated episodes "The Lorelei Signal" and "The Ambergris Element." She's also written for *The Rifleman*, *The Big Valley*, and *Barnaby Jones*.

Armenian, Dawn — actress who played Miss Gladstone in *TNG* episode "The Child."

Armor, Gene — actor who played the Bajoran bureaucrat in *DS9* episode "Emissary."

Armstrong, Dave — actor who played Kartan in "Operation: Annihilate!" His other credits include *Sex and the Married Woman* ('77) and *The Man from U.N.C.L.E.*

Armstrong, Vaughn — actor who played Korris in *TNG* episode "Heart of Glory."

Armus, Burton — scriptwriter who wrote *TNG* episodes "The Outrageous Okona" and "A Matter of Honor." Also a producer.

Armus — creature that looked like a puddle of tar in *TNG* episode "Skin of Evil." The sadist killed Tasha Yar. Armus was played by Mart McChesney, with the voice of Ran Gans.

Armus IX — referred to in *TNG* episode "Angel One" as the place where Riker wore feathers to honor the leaders.

Arndt, John — actor who played crewmen in Classic

Trek episode "Miri," "Dagger of the Mind," "Balance of Terror" (crewman Fields), and "Space Seed."

Arneb — a star that can be seen from Aucdet IX, mentioned in the *TNG* episode "The Child."

Arnett, Cameron — actor in *TNG* episode "Disaster."

Arnold, Kacey Ince — scriptwriter who wrote *TNG* episode "Final Mission."

Arnold, Steve — actor who played Zabo in Classic *Trek* episode "A Piece of the Action."

Aroeste, Jean Lisette — scriptwriter of Classic *Trek* episodes "Is There in Truth No Beauty?" and "All Our Yesterdays."

Aron, Michael — actor who played Jack London in *TNG* episode "Time's Arrow."

Aron — character in *TNG* episode "The Dauphin," played by Peter Neptune. He is an *Enterprise* officer.

Arrants, Rod — actor who played Rex in *TNG* episode "Manhunt."

Arret — the planet where Kirk, Spock, and McCoy discover the spheres containing the energy essences of Sargon, Thalessa, and Henoch in Classic episode "Return to Tomorrow." Its atmosphere was ripped away half a million years before in a terrible war. In the antimatter universe of the animated "The Counter-Clock Incident," Arret is a planet where people age backward, and the sky darkens when the sun rises.

Arridor, Dr. — character from *TNG* episode "The Price," played by Dan Shor. He is a Ferengi scientist who is lost on the other side of an unstable wormhole.

"Arsenal of Freedom, The" — This first-season *TNG* episode was written by Maurice Hurley, Bob Lewin, Richard Manning, and Hans Beimer, directed by Les

Landau. The *Enterprise* encounters the planet Minos whose people destroyed themselves in a terrible war, but whose weapons still exist. Guest stars: Vincent Schiavelli, Marco Rodriguez, Vyto Ruginis, Julia Nickson, and George De La Peña.

Artemis, SS— in *TNG* episode "The Ensigns of Command," this is the ship that transported colonists to Tau Cygna V, though its original destination was Septimis Minor. The ship's guidance system failed, and 15,253 Artemis ancestors have ended up on Tau Cygna V.

Arthurs, Bruce D. — scriptwriter who wrote *TNG* episode "Clues."

Artonian Lasers — referred to in *TNG* episode "The Vengeance Factor," these are weapons found at a Gatherer camp.

Ashmore, Kelly — actress who played Francine in *TNG* episode "We'll Always Have Paris."

Asimov, Isaac — (1920–92) science consultant for Classic *Trek* film *Star Trek: The Motion Picture*. Born in Russia, he immigrated to the USA at age four. He wrote over 400 books, both fiction and nonfiction books explaining science, religion, and literature to the lay reader. Asimov is most famous for his Robot series and Foundation series, and won numerous awards for his work, including science fiction's Hugo and Nebula awards. His wife, Janet Asimov, is a doctor and, now, also a writer. He has a son and daughter. *Asimov's SF*, a magazine, was named after him. He never pretended the science of *Star Trek* was possible but offered valuable advice nonetheless.

Asmodeus — a demon referred to by Megan in the animated "The Magicks of Megas-Tu." He claims he was once Asmodeus.

Asoth — character in *DS9* episode "Past Prologue," played by Bo Zenga.

Asphia — referred to in *TNG* episode "Angel One" as the planet where the SS *Odin* crash-landed.

Assael, David — scriptwriter who wrote *TNG* episode "The Icarus Factor."

"Assignment: Earth" — written by Art Wallace and Gene Roddenberry, directed by Marc Daniels, this final second-season Classic *Trek* episode aired 3/29/68. This episode was a pilot for a new series that never got off the ground. Gary Seven is an operative from a highly advanced alien society which recruits humans and trains them as agents to interfere with potential planetary disasters before they happen. Kirk and Spock go back in time to observe Earth history and get in Seven's way. Guest stars: Robert Lansing, Teri Garr, Don Keefer, Morgan Jones, and Lincoln Demyan. Of note: Barbara Babcock provides the voice for the cat Isis. Majel Barrett's voice is used for the incredible Beta 5 computer which Seven uses to help him thwart disaster.

Assistant Manager, The — character in *TNG* episode "The Royale" who is the desk clerk of the Hotel Royale. He was played by Sam Anderson.

Astar, Shay — actress who guest starred in *TNG* episode "Imaginary Friend."

Aster, Jeremy — character in *TNG* episode "The Bonding," played by Gabriel Damon. He is a 12-year-old boy whose mother was killed in a landing party mishap. This leaves him orphaned, but he does have an aunt and uncle on Earth.

Aster, Marla, Lieutenant — *Enterprise* archeologist from *TNG* episode "The Bonding," played by Susan Powell. She is the mother of Jeremy Aster who dies while on a landing party commanded by Worf. Her husband had died five years earlier of a Verustin infection. The energy beings called Koinonians re-create her image for her son, Jeremy, in order to get him to agree to accompany them to their planet where they will raise him. They do not succeed.

Astral V annex — a Federation cataloguing terminal referred to in *TNG* episode "Booby Trap."

Astral Queen — the ship in Classic *Trek* episode "The Conscience of the King" that is supposed to transport the Karidian players to Benecia. The *Enterprise* transports them instead, and that ship is never seen.

Atalia VII — in *TNG* episode "The Chase," the *Enterprise* is supposed to attend a diplomatic conference there, but Picard has other plans.

atavachron — device used in Classic episode "All Our Yesterdays" to "prepare" a time-traveler's biochemistry to the time he wishes to visit on the planet Sarpeidon. Without it, he will die in a matter of hours.

Atienza, Frank — actor who played the executioner in Classic *Trek* episode "The Omega Glory."

Atkins, Doris, Yeoman — character who appears in Classic episode "The Deadly Years." She is played by Carolyn Nelson.

Atlek ship — a ship mentioned in *TNG* episode "The Outrageous Okona." The Class-7 ship carries a crew of 26. Debin is its commander.

Atoz, Mr. — character on Classic episode "All Our Yesterdays" who is the Sarpeidon "time-travel" librarian. Played by Ian Wolfe, he has made android replicants of himself to help tend the library.

Atwater, Barry — actor who played Surak in Classic *Trek* episode "The Savage Curtain." Atwater died in the '70s. He played the vampire in the movie *The Night Stalker* ('72). Other credits include *The Man from U.N.C.L.E.*, *Voyage to the Bottom of the Sea*, and *One Step Beyond*.

Auberjonois, René — actor who plays Odo on *DS9*. He was also in Classic *Trek* film *Star Trek VI: The Undiscovered Country*. Born in 1940, he has done much stage work, including *Coco* with Audrey Hepburn, winning a Tony Award for that performance. His film debut was the movie *M*A*S*H*. He has also starred in the movies *Pete 'n' Tillie*, *The Hindenburg*, *King Kong* ('76), and *Police Academy 5*, among others. He won an Emmy twice for his work in *The Legend of Sleepy Hollow*. René also won an Emmy for best supporting actor in a comedy for his work on the TV series *Benson*, in which he played regular Clayton Endicott III. He has also been seen on *L.A. Law*, *Matlock*, and *Civil Wars*. He is the voice of the chef in Disney's *The Little Mermaid*. In the *Trek* Classic film *The Undiscovered Country* he played the assassin, Colonel West. He has a bachelor of arts degree in drama from Carnegie-Mellon University.

Aucdet IX — a Federation Medical Collection Station mentioned in *TNG* episode "The Child."

Aurelan — see Kirk, Aurelan.

Aurelia — a planet referred to in the animated episode "Yesteryear" that has birdlike natives.

Aurora — the small stolen ship containing Dr. Sevrin and his followers in Classic episode "The Way to Eden." It is destroyed when its engines overload, just as the *Enterprise* beams its crew aboard.

autodestruct sequence — this is used throughout the series. Kirk uses it to destroy the *Enterprise* with a Klingon boarding party on board in the Classic *Trek* film *The Search for Spock*. It is also used, and aborted, several times in *Star Trek* and *TNG*. In *TNG* episode "The Defector," Jarok uses it on his ship before he leaves so he will not leave behind top-secret Romulan information.

Auxiliary Control — a part of the ship in the center of the saucer where, in a state of emergency, complete control of the ship can be transferred. In Classic *Trek* "The Immunity Syndrome," it is said to reside on deck 8. In *TNG*, it is referred to as a Battle Bridge.

Avadney IV — in *TNG* episode "Clues," this is the destination of the *Enterprise* after leaving Ngame Nebula.

Avari, Erick — actor in *TNG* episode "Unification, Part I."

Aveda III — referred to in *TNG* episode "The Arsenal of Freedom" as a colony world where Beverly Crusher lived for awhile with her grandmother as a child. A disaster on the planet threatened colonists' lives, and Beverly's grandmother saved many people with her knowledge of the Avedan plants.

Avian — a birdlike creature seen in the animated "Mudd's Passion."

away team — term used in *TNG* for a landing party. This term is not used in Classic *Trek*, just as the term "landing party" is not used in *TNG*. However, the two terms seem interchangeable.

Axanar — referred to in Classic episode "Court-Martial," it is a planet where there was a war. Kirk took part in the peace mission to Axanar and was awarded the Palm Leaf of the Axanar Peace Mission. The planet is also referred to by Garth in "Whom Gods Destroy."

Ayleborne — character in Classic episode "Errand of Mercy," played by Jon Abbott. He is the chairman of the elders on Organia, and is actually an energy being, though he appears humanoid until the end of the episode.

Ayres, Jerry — actor who played O'Herlihy in "Arena" and Rizzo in "Obsession." His credits include *Message to My Daughter* ('73), *Attack on Terror*, *The FBI versus the Ku Klux Klan* ('75), and *Disaster on the Coastliner* ('79).

Babcock, Barbara — actress who appeared in many Classic *Trek* episodes. She was the voice of Trelane's mother in "The Squire of Gothos," Mea 3 in "A Taste of Armageddon," the voice of Isis the cat in "Assignment: Earth," and Philana in "Plato's Stepchildren." She won an Emmy for her role in *Hill Street Blues*. She was also on *Dallas,* and in the movies *Salem's Lot* ('79) and *Lords of Discipline* ('83).

Babel — planet mentioned in Classic *Trek* episode "Journey to Babel." It is the destination of the ambassadors on board the *Enterprise.* There they will attend the Babel Conference which will decide if Coridan will be admitted to the Federation.

"Babel" — first-season *DS9* episode written by Michael McGreevey, Naren Shankar, Sally Caves, and Ira Stephen Behr, directed by Paul Lynch. Something is wrong with the food replicators on *DS9.* People are catching aphasia, a disease that affects the brain so speech becomes nonsense and they cannot communicate. Eventually, the condition attacks the nervous system, leaving the victims only 12 hours to live. Guest stars: Jack Kehler, Matthew Faison, Ann Gillespie, Geraldine Farrell, Bo Zenga, Kathleen Wirt, Lee Brooks, Richard Ryder, Frank Novak, and Todd Feder.

Bachelin, Franz — art director of original Classic *Trek* pilot "The Cage."

Badar N'D'D — leader of the Antican party on *TNG* episode "Lonely among Us."

Bader, Dietrich — actor who played Tactical Crewman in *TNG* episode "The Emissary."

Bader, Hillary — scriptwriter of *TNG* episodes "The Loss" and "Hero Worship."

Ba'el — half-Romulan, half-Klingon girl whom Worf meets at the Romulan camp in *TNG* episode "Birthright, Parts I and II."

Bailey, Dennis — scriptwriter of *TNG* episodes "Tin Man" and "First Contact."

Bailey, Dave, Lieutenant — character in Classic *Trek* episode "The Corbomite Maneuver," played by Anthony Hall. He is the *Enterprise* navigator who stays with Balok as a human ambassador on a first-contact mission to the First Federation.

Bajor — homeworld of the Bajorans. This world has recently been at war with the Cardassians, who tried to conquer Bajor with superior technology. The Bajorans have their world back now, but are still reeling from the effects of the war. Bajor is an Earth-like world not yet a member of the Federation, but well on its way. It is very close to a newly discovered wormhole which is used to travel to the Gamma Quadrant, a neighbor to the space station *Deep Space 9*.

Bajoran death chant — two-hour-long ritual mentioned in *TNG* episode "The Next Phase."

Bajorans — native to the planet Bajor, they are humanoid with ridges on the bridge of the nose. They are a highly spiritual race, whose religion and culture involves mysterious orbs that show selected people scenes from the future. These orbs come from the wormhole itself. They mystify scientists. Nearly all Bajorans wear a decorative earring on their right ear that is a a cuff chained to a post or ring. This piece of jewelry seems to denote pride in their race, a kind of brotherhood. Ensign Ro of *TNG* is Bajoran, as is Major Kira Nerys of *DS9*.

Baker — character played by Barbara Baldavin in Classic episode "Space Seed."

Bakey, Ed — actor who played the role of first fop in "All Our Yesterdays." He also appeared in *Dead and Buried* ('81), *Zapped!* ('82), and *The Philadelphia Experiment* ('84).

Bakke, Brenda — actress who played Rivan in *TNG* episode "Justice."

Bal, Jeanne — actress who played the older Nancy Crater in the Classic *Trek* episode "The Man Trap." Her credits include *Love and Marriage* (1959–60), *Bachelor Father* ('61), and *Mr. Novak* (1964–65).

"Balance of Terror" — written by Paul Schneider and directed by Vince McEveety, this first-season Classic *Trek* episode aired 12/15/66. The *Enterprise*'s first encounter with warlike Romulans shows how much like Vulcans they appear. Bigotry is one theme, with Spock its unfortunate victim. Guest stars: Mark Lenard (who later plays Sarek, Spock's Vulcan father), Paul Comi, Lawrence Montaigne (who later plays Stonn in "Amok Time"), John Warburton, Stephen Mines, and Barbara Baldavin. Of note: The introduction of the famous Romulan cloaking device.

Balcer, René — scriptwriter of *TNG* episode "Power Play."

Baldavin, Barbara — actress who played Angela Martine in the Classic *Trek* episodes "Balance of Terror" and "Shore Leave," Baker in "Space Seed," and the communications officer in "Turnabout Intruder." Her credits include *Medical Center* and *The Bionic Woman*.

Ballard, Lieutenant — character in *TNG* episode "The Offspring," played by Judyann Elder. She is a teacher on the *Enterprise*.

Ballerina — an Enterprise crewwoman on *TNG* episode "Where No One Has Gone Before" who fantasizes a dance on the holodeck. She was played by Victoria Dillard.

Balok — character from Classic *Trek* episode "The Corbomite Maneuver," played by Clint Howard. He is a small, almost childlike alien encountered by the *Enterprise*. He hides behind a monstrous mask when communicating with unknown ships. His flagship, the *Fesarius*, tests the *Enterprise* for hostile intentions.

Balthazar's Syndrome — Klingon malady suffered by J'Dan in *TNG* episode "The Drumhead."

Bandi — people who live on Deneb IV, also known as Farpoint, in *TNG* episode "Encounter at Farpoint."

Bandi Shopkeeper — played by David Erskine in *TNG* episode "Encounter at Farpoint."

Banks, Emily — actress who played Tonia Barrows on "Shore Leave." Credits include *The Tim Conway Show* and *When Hell Was in Session* ('79).

Bar-David, S. — pen name for scriptwriter Shimon Wincelberg. He wrote the Classic *Trek* episodes "Dagger of the Mind" and "The Galileo Seven" (with Oliver Crawford).

Barash — alien boy abandoned on Alpha Onias III in *TNG* episode "Future Imperfect." He was also known as Jean-Luc and Ethan. He was played by Chris Demetral.

Barbara — one of the android series in Classic episode "I, Mudd," played by twins Maureen and Colleen Thornton.

Barclay, Endicott Reginald, III, Lieutenant — character in *TNG* episodes "Hollow Pursuits," "The Nth Degree," and "Realm of Fear." He is called Reg by his friends, and also bears the unflattering nickname "Broccoli." He is an expert engineer. Socially, however, he lacks many skills. He stutters around his peers, acts nervous, and fails to join in group activities. His favorite drink in Ten Forward is warm milk. A self-taught fencer, he is a man with a vivid imagination seen in his holodeck fantasies.

Baris, Nilz — character in Classic *Trek* episode "The Trouble with Tribbles," played by William Schallert. He is in charge of agricultural affairs on Space Station K–7 and Sherman's Planet. He is the one who sends the *Enterprise* a priority distress signal, though his station is not apparently under any threat.

Barlow, Jennifer — actress who played Ensign Gibson in *TNG* episode "The Dauphin."

Barnett, Gregory — stunt man who was Spock's double in the Classic *Trek* films *The Voyage Home* and *The Final Frontier*.

Barnhart — crewman in Classic *Trek* episode "The Man Trap" who is killed by the salt vampire.

Barolians — mentioned in *TNG* episode "Unification," they are a race who conducted trade negotiations with the Romulans prior to Spock going to Romulus.

Baron, Michael — scriptwriter of *TNG* episode "Code of Honor."

Barona — in Classic *Trek* episode "Errand of Mercy," Kirk goes by the Organian name of Barona in hopes the Klingons won't recognize him as a Starfleet officer.

Barrett, Majel — also known as M. (Majel) Leigh Hudec, the actress played Nurse Christine Chapel in the original series, and the voice of Christine and M'Ress and numerous other characters in the animated series, as well as Number One in the Classic *Trek* pilot "The Cage." Majel reappeared as Chapel in the movies *Star Trek: The Motion Picture*, and *The Voyage Home*. Majel also plays Lwaxana Troi, Deanna Troi's mother, in *TNG* and the voice of the computer in the Classic *Trek* movies, *TNG*, and *DS9*. Born in Columbia, Ohio, she married Gene Roddenberry. They have a son together, Gene. The much-accomplished actress and businesswoman has appeared in other Roddenberry productions and runs Lincoln Enterprises, which sells many types of merchandise associated with *Star Trek*. She was born Feb. 23.

Barrett, Stan — actor who played the jailor in "All Our Yesterdays."

Barrett, Lieutenant — she is an officer on *Enterprise* D in *TNG* episode "Yesterday's Enterprise."

Barrier, Michael — actor who played DeSalle in the Classic *Trek* episodes "The Squire of Gothos," "This Side of Paradise," and "Catspaw." He played a guard in *The City on the Edge of Forever*. He was also in *Voyage to the Bottom of the Sea*.

Barron, Dr. — in *TNG* episode "Who Watches the Watchers," he is the chief scientist of the Mintakan Anthropological Station, played by James Greene.

Barrows, Tonia, Yeoman — character in the Classic *Trek* episode "Shore Leave" who is Dr. McCoy's girlfriend. She is played by Emily Banks.

Barry, Carolyn — actress who plays the female engineer in the *TNG* episode "Home Soil."

Barry, Patrick — scriptwriter of *TNG* episode "Angel One."

Barstow, Commodore — in Classic *Trek* episode "The Alternative Factor," Barstow orders the *Enterprise* to investigate what he thinks is a massive invasion from another universe. He is played by Richard Derr.

Bartholomew, Regina, Countess — partner and love interest for Professor Moriarty in *TNG* episode "Ship in a Bottle."

baryon particles — in *TNG* episode "Starship Mine,"

the *Enterprise* goes to Arkaria to be swept clear of baryon particles that build up from the ship's warp drive over time.

Barzan II — world whose inhabitants own the Barzan wormhole. This world is hostile to all life except the native inhabitants. It is seen in the *TNG* episode "The Price."

Barzan wormhole — only stable wormhole known to exist at this point, noted in *TNG* episode "The Price." It appears every 233 minutes and leads to the Gamma Quadrant. It is a galactic phenomenon located by the world Barzan II.

Basch, Harry — actor who played Dr. Brown in "What Are Little Girls Made Of?" Credits: *Falcon Crest* (1982–84).

Bashir, Julian, Dr. — doctor of station *Deep Space 9*. A human male about 28 years old, he has just graduated from the Starfleet Medical Academy before taking the *DS9* assignment. He is enthusiastic about everything, a man who dreams of adventure. An expert in alien species medicine, Julian loves his work. His curiosity helps solve problems on *DS9*. It also gets him into trouble. He has a crush on Dax, who thinks he's cute but she's not interested in romance. Sisko is a good calming influence on him, and they get along, but Kira and O'Brien still don't completely trust him. He may be naïve and a little arrogant, but his heart is in the right place. He sees everything as a challenge to surmount. The character has great potential, his puppy-dog energy and slight immaturities countered by obvious genius and overall good nature. When he's working on a medical problem, he's all business. Dark hair, dark eyes, and a lean body add to his attraction. His British accent is icing on the cake.

Basotile — priceless piece of art in *TNG* episode "The Most Toys."

Bass, Bobby — actor who played a crewman in the Classic *Trek* episodes "Space Seed" and "This Side of

Paradise," and a Klingon guard in "Errand of Mercy." His credits include *Megaforce* ('82), *Blood Beach* ('81), and *Star 80* ('83).

Bass Player — member of the holodeck band in *TNG* episode "11001001," played by Abdul Salaam El Razzac.

Batanides, Arthur — actor who played D'Amato in Classic *Trek* episode "That Which Survives." Credits include: *Cry Tough* ('59), *The Feminist and the Fuzz* ('71), *The Heist* ('73), *Lost in Space, The Man from U.N.C.L.E.,* and *The Rifleman.*

Batanides, Marta, Ensign — one of Picard's friends at the Academy he meets again courtesy of Q while reliving his Academy days in *TNG* episode "Tapestry."

Batareal — Hahliian holiday spot Aquiel mentions to her sister, Sheana, in *TNG* episode "Aquiel."

Bates, Russell — scriptwriter of the animated "How Sharper Than a Serpent's Tooth" (written with David Wise).

Bates, John, Brother — character in *TNG* episode "The Defector" who is in Data's Henry V holodeck simulations. He is played by S. A. Templeton.

Bates, Hannah, Dr. — chief physicist on Moab IV who leaves her society to join the Federation in *TNG* episode "The Masterpiece Society." She was played by Dey Young.

Bateson, Morgan, Captain — captain of the USS *Bozeman* which had been lost for 80 years in a time-space continuum in *TNG* episode "Cause and Effect." He was played by Kelsey Grammer.

Batris — Telarian ship commandeered by Klingons and found by the *Enterprise* in *TNG* episode "Heart of Glory."

bat'tehl — Klingon sword Worf uses to teach Alexander in *TNG* episode "Rightful Heir."

"Battle, The" — first-season *TNG* episode written by Larry Forrester and Herbert Wright, directed by Rob Bowman. Ferengi Commander DaiMon Bok gives Picard his lost ship, the *Stargazer*. On board is a mind-control device which takes Picard back to the past on the ship. Guest stars: Frank Corsentino, Doug Warhit, and Robert Towers.

Battle of Maxia — first battle between the Federation and the Ferengi in *TNG* episode "The Battle." Picard's ship, the *Stargazer*, is destroyed.

Batur — one of Duras's scheming sisters, a Klingon, who appears in the *TNG* episode "Redemption," and returns in *DS9* episode "Past Prologue." Her sister is Lursa. She is played by Gwynyth Walsh.

Bauer, Robert — actor who played Kuivas in *TNG* episode "Heart of Glory."

Baxley, Paul — stunt man who played Kirk's double in the Classic *Trek* episodes "What Are Little Girls Made Of?" and "Amok Time," the Black Knight in "Shore Leave," Ensign Freeman in "The Trouble with Tribbles," a patrol leader in "A Private Little War," a trooper in "Patterns of Force," and the security chief in "Assignment: Earth." His credits also include *The Man from U.N.C.L.E.*

Baxter, George — actor who played David in *TNG* episode "Unnatural Selection."

Bay, Susan — actress who played the admiral in *DS9* episode "Past Prologue." She is Leonard Nimoy's wife.

Bayer, John — actor who played the policeman in "The City on the Edge of Forever." Credits include *The Life and Legend of Wyatt Earp* (1955–56).

Bayle, Hayne — actor who played one of the Ten Forward crew in *TNG* episode "The Offspring."

Baylor, Hal — actor who played the guard in the Classic *Trek* episode "Elaan of Troyius."

Beach — crewmember on the *Reliant* in the Classic *Trek* film *The Wrath of Khan*, played by Paul Kent.

Beacham, Stephanie — actress who played Countess Regina Bartholomew in *TNG* episode "Ship in a Bottle."

Beagle, Peter S. — scriptwriter of *TNG* episode "Sarek."

Beagle, USS — ship destroyed in Classic episode "Bread and Circuses" after Captain Merik had his crew beam to Planet 892–IV. Six years later, the *Enterprise* encountered the debris, visited the world, and discovered the few survivors.

Bear, Greg — author who wrote Pocket Classic *Trek* novel *Corona*. He is a science-fiction writer of repute who has won several awards for his novels.

Beate — official of Angel One on *TNG* episode "Angel One," played by Karen Montgomery.

Beaumont, Gabrielle — director of the *TNG* episodes "The Booby Trap," "The High Ground," "Suddenly Human," "Disaster," "Imaginary Friend," and "Face of the Enemy."

Beauregard — plant in Sulu's botanical garden in Classic episode "The Man Trap." It is a pet that responds to humans by swaying and singing. Sulu calls it Gertrude; Rand calls it Beauregard.

Beck, Nurse — obstetrics specialist who comes aboard the *Enterprise* from Starbase 218 in *TNG* episode "Lessons."

Becker, James — actor who played Ensign Youngblood in many *TNG* episodes.

Becker, Robert — director of *TNG* episodes "We'll Always Have Paris" and "The Outrageous Okona." He died in a tragic car accident on May 6, 1993.

Beecher, Bonnie — actress who played Sylvia in the Classic *Trek* episode "Spectre of the Gun."

Beecroft, Gregory — actor who played Mickey D in *TNG* episode "The Royale."

Beggs, Hagen — actor who played Lt. Hanson in the Classic *Trek* episodes "The Menagerie" and "Court-Martial." Film credits: *I Love a Mystery* ('73), *Hey I'm Alive* ('75), and *Star 80* ('83).

Behan, Johnny — character in Classic *Trek* episode "Spectre of the Gun," played by Bill Zuckert. He appears to be the sheriff of Cochise County but is actually a Melkot in disguise.

Behar, Eli — actor who played the therapist in the Classic *Trek* episode "Dagger of the Mind."

Behr, Ira Stephen — scriptwriter of *TNG* episodes "Yesterday's Enterprise," "Captain's Holiday," and "Qpid." He also wrote the story for *DS9* episode "Babel" (with Sally Caves) and the teleplay for "The Nagus." He is also a producer.

Beimler, Hans — scriptwriter of *TNG* episodes "The Arsenal of Freedom," "Symbiosis," "The Schizoid Man," "The Emissary," "Shades of Gray," "Allegiance," "Who Watches the Watchers," and "Yesterday's Enterprise." He is also coproducer with Richard Manning.

Belanoff, Adam — scriptwriter of "The Masterpiece Society."

Bele — character in the Classic *Trek* episode "Let That Be Your Last Battlefield," played by Frank Gorshin. He is the hunter of Lokai, whom he blames for the destruction of his civilization. The left side of his face is white, the right side black.

Belgrey, Thomas — actor who played a crewman in *TNG* episode "Realm of Fear."

Bell, Dan — character in *TNG* episode "The Big Goodbye," played by William Boyett. He is the police chief in 1941 San Francisco on the holodeck.

Bell, Felecia M. — actress who guest starred in *DS9* episode "Emissary."

Bell, Michael — actor who played Groppler Zorn in the *TNG* episode "Encounter at Farpoint."

Bell Boy — character in *TNG* episode "The Royale." He was played by Leo Garcia. He dies defending the honor of his love, Rita.

Bellah, John — actor who played a crewman in the Classic *Trek* episodes "Charlie X" and "The Naked Time." Credits include: *The Man From U.N.C.L.E.*, *The Amazing Howard Hughes* ('77), *A Few Days in Weasel Creek* ('81), *Ghost Dancing* ('83).

Belli, Caesar — actor who played Stevie in the Classic *Trek* episode "And the Children Shall Lead." His father, attorney Melvin Belli, appears as Gorgon in the same episode.

Belli, Melvin — actor who played Gorgon in the Classic *Trek* episode "And the Children Shall Lead." He is a famous attorney whose brief acting career included stints in *Wild in the Streets* ('68), *Gimme Shelter* ('70), *The Lady of the House* ('78), and the game show *Whodunnit?* ('79). Born in Sonora, CA, in 1907, Belli defended Jack Ruby, the man who shot Lee Harvey Oswald, after Oswald was accused of assassinating President John F. Kennedy. He has also defended other notables, including Jim and Tammy Bakker.

Beltane IX — mentioned in *TNG* episode "Coming of Age" as the place to which Jake Kurland will escape.

Belzoidian flea — Q mentions this in *TNG* episode "Déjà Q."

Bem, Ari bn, Commander — character in animated episode "Bem." A native of Pandro, he can break his body into small, independent parts. James Doohan provided the voice of Bem.

"Bem" — written by David Gerrold, this animated episode aired 9/14/74. Commander Ari bn Bem is a guest of the *Enterprise* from the planet Pandro. After he beams down with a landing party to investigate Delta Theta III, the *Enterprise* crewmen learn he can split his body into several parts that operate independently of each other. The natives of the planet are supervised by a planet intelligence that demands the landing party leave and not interfere. They want to comply, but Bem runs away and they can't leave before they find him. Guest voices: Majel Barrett (M'Ress, Alien), James Doohan (Arex, Commander Ari bn Bem). Of note: David Gerrold admits to naming his alien Bem because the initials stand for *B*ug-*E*yed-*M*onster. This is just one of many in-jokes *Trek* episodes contain.

Benbeck, Marcus — keeper of the customs and traditions of the Moab colony in *TNG* episode "The Masterpiece Society," played by Ron Canada.

Bender, Slade — thug who tried to kill Dixon Hill in *TNG* episode "Manhunt," played by Robert Costanzo.

Bendii Syndrome — disease afflicting Sarek in *TNG* episode "Sarek." The rare malady affects Vulcans over the age of 200, forcing the victim to project emotions instead of suppressing them. There is no cure.

Benecia Colony — mentioned in Classic episode "The Conscience of the King," as the destination of the Karidian players after they leave Planet Q. It is also the planet where Janice Lester wants to maroon Kirk, whose essence is trapped in her body, in "Turnabout Intruder."

benjisidrine — heart medication Sarek secretly takes in "Journey to Babel."

Benko, Tom — director of the *TNG* episodes "Transfigurations" and "Devil's Due."

Bennett, Fran — actress in *TNG* episode "Redemption, Part II."

Bennett, Harve — scriptwriter/producer on the Classic *Trek* films *The Wrath of Khan*, *The Search for Spock*, and *The Voyage Home*. He also supplied the voice of the flight recorder in *The Search for Spock*, and had a walk-on role as a Starfleet chief of staff in *The Final Frontier*. He won an Emmy as executive producer of *A Woman Called Golda* (which starred Leonard Nimoy), and produced TV series including *The Six Million Dollar Man*, *The Bionic Woman*, *The Gemini Man*, and *The Powers of Matthew Starr*.

Bennett, Ensign — *Enterprise* conn officer in *TNG* episode "Captain's Holiday."

Bensmiller, Kurt Michael — scriptwriter of the *TNG* episode "Time Squared" and *DS9* episode "The Storyteller."

Benson, Björn — chief engineer of the terraforming project on Velara III in *TNG* episode "Home Soil," played by Gerard Prendergast.

Benton — lithium miner in Classic episode "Mudd's Women," played by Seamon Glass.

Benton, Craig — actor in *TNG* episode "Violations."

Benzali, Daniel — actor who played the surgeon who operates on Picard in *TNG* episode "Samaritan Snare."

Benzan — son of Kushell of Streleb in love with Yanar in *TNG* episode "The Outrageous Okona," played by Kieran Mulroney.

Benzar — home planet of the Benzites in *TNG* episode "A Matter of Honor." The world is a member of the Federation.

Benzite — Mordok in *TNG* episode "Coming of Age" is a Benzite. He has a breathing apparatus and gray skin and is larger than a human. Mordok is the first of his race to attend Starfleet Academy.

Beratis — in Classic episode "Wolf in the Fold," this name is applied to the Jack the Ripper entity by Sybo.

Berel — member of the medical staff at the hospital Riker is taken to in *TNG* episode "First Contact," played by George Hearn.

Berengaria VII — planet Spock mentions to Leila in Classic *Trek* episode "This Side of Paradise." He says he's seen dragons there.

Bergere, Lee — actor who played Abraham Lincoln in the Classic *Trek* episode "The Savage Curtain." Credits include: *One Step Beyond*, *The Man from U.N.C.L.E.*, *Hotel Baltimore*, *Dynasty*, and *Evening in Byzantium* ('78).

Bergman, Alan — actor who played Lal in the Classic *Trek* episode "The Empath." His credits include *Welcome Home Johnny Bristol* ('72) and *Cannon*.

Berkeley, Ensign — young transporter officer in Classic *Trek* episode "Dagger of the Mind," played by Larry Anthony.

***Berlin*, USS** — starship patrolling the Neutral Zone in *TNG* episode "The Neutral Zone."

Berman, Rick — Executive producer of *TNG* and creator and executive producer (with Michael Piller) of *DS9*. His other credits include work on *MacGyver*, *Cheers*, and *Family Ties*. He won an Emmy for his work on *The Big Blue Marble* (1977–82). He was scriptwriter of the *TNG* episodes "Brothers," "Ensign Ro," "A Matter of Time," "Unification, Parts I and II," and "Brothers." He also wrote, with Michael Piller, the *DS9* episode "Emissary."

Bernard, Harry, Dr. — *Enterprise* doctor in *TNG*

episode "When the Bough Breaks" who has a son named Harry. He is played by Dierk Torsek.

Bernard, Harry, Jr. — character played by Philip N. Waller on *TNG* episode "When the Bough Breaks" whose father is an *Enterprise* doctor, Dr. Harry Bernard. He is kidnapped by the Aldeans.

Bernard, Joseph — actor who appeared as Tark in the Classic *Trek* episode "Wolf in the Fold." Credits include *The Immortal* ('69), *The Challenge* ('70), *The Winds of Kitty Hawk* ('78), and *The Man Who Loved Women* ('83).

Bernheim, Robin — scriptwriter of the *TNG* episode "The Hunted."

Bernsen, Corbin — actor who played Q2 in *TNG* episode "Déjà Q."

Berryman, Michael — actor who played the Starfleet display officer in the Classic *Trek* film *The Voyage Home* and Captain Rixx of the USS *Thomas Paine* in the *TNG* episode "Conspiracy." Credits: *Doc Savage, Man of Bronze* ('75), *Deadly Blessing* ('81), *Invitation to Hell* ('84).

Bersallis III — world swept by firestorms every seven years. The *Enterprise* loses eight crewmembers in the rescue of these colonists in *TNG* episode "Lessons."

Berthold rays — in Classic *Trek* episode "This Side of Paradise," these rays would be deadly to humans if it weren't for the protection of the spores on Omicron Ceti III. They are mentioned again in *TNG* episode "Déjà Q" as being part of a Calamarain probe.

Besch, Bibi — actress who played Dr. Carol Marcus in the Classic *Trek* film *The Wrath of Khan*. She has numerous credits, including an appearance on *Northern Exposure* that led to her winning an Emmy in '92.

"Best of Both Worlds, The" — first part was a third-season *TNG* episode written by Michael Piller and directed by Cliff Bole; the second part a fourth-season *TNG* episode written by Michael Piller and directed by Cliff Bole. A Borg vessel, the advance ship of a vast invading armada, is engaged by the *Enterprise*. The Borg kidnap Picard and turn him into their leader, a Borg named Locutus. The Borg continue to attack Starfleet, then head toward Earth. The only way to defeat them is to command them to go into a regenerative cycle and sleep. Picard is brought back aboard ship and his Borg "parts" are surgically removed. Guest stars: Elizabeth Dennehy, George Murdock, Whoopi Goldberg, Todd Merrill, and Colm Meaney (last two, second part only).

Beta III in Star System 6–11 — planet where the USS *Archon* was lost in Classic episode "The Return of the Archons." This is where Landru rules.

Beta V computer — computer Gary Seven keeps in his apartment in Classic episode "Assignment: Earth." The voice of the computer is provided by Majel Barrett.

Beta VI — the *Enterprise* I's destination before being detained by Trelane in Classic episode "The Squire of Gothos."

Beta XIIA — mentioned in Classic episode "Day of the Dove" where supposedly a hundred Federation citizens were murdered by Klingons. The story is not true.

Beta Agni II — in *TNG* episode "The Most Toys," Kivas Fajo contaminates this planet's water supply with tricyanite to lure the *Enterprise* to him so he can kidnap Data. It is a Federation colony world.

Beta Antares IV — in Classic *Trek* episode "A Piece of the Action," Kirk says this planet is where he learned to play Fizzbin. He is, of course, making up this story.

Beta Aurigae — in Classic *Trek* episode "The Ultimate Computer," the binary system toward which the *Enterprise* heads to join the *Potemkin* and study gravitational effects.

Beta Canopus — in animated episode "The Pirates of Orion," the drug strobolin can be found on this planet.

Beta Cassius system — Haven from *TNG* episode "Haven" is in this system.

Beta Geminorum — mentioned in Classic episode "Who Mourns for Adonais?," it is in the system of the planet Pollux IV where Apollo lives.

Beta Kupsik — the *Enterprise*'s destination after they leave Starbase *Montgomery* in *TNG* episode "The Icarus Factor."

Beta Lyrae — conglomerate of stars of different colors and sizes, considered one of the wonders of the universe. It is seen in the animated episode "The Slaver Weapon."

Beta Magellan system — Bynaus from *TNG* episode "11001001" is located here.

Beta Niobe — star that is about to go nova and destroy all life on Sarpeidon in Classic episode "All Our Yesterdays." It is also encountered in the animated "The Counter-Clock Incident."

Beta Portalan system — in Classic *Trek* episode "Operation: Annihilate!" this is the location of the flying parasites' first victims, an ancient civilization that died of insanity many centuries before.

Beta Renner system — the worlds Antica and Selay from *TNG* episode "Lonely among Us" are located in this system.

Beta Stromgren — in *TNG* episode "Tin Man," the probe Vega Nine returns from here with evidence the star will go supernova.

Betazed — Troi and Lwaxana are natives of this world. (Troi is half human.) Inhabitants are called Betazoids (see entry). The planet is a member of the Federation.

Betazoid kitten — Deanna owned one as a child as mentioned in *TNG* episode "Pen Pals." Her mother did not get along with it.

Betazoids — natives of the planet Betazed. They look human. Deanna Troi and Lwaxana Troi are Betazoids, though Troi is half human. They can read each other's thoughts and communicate telepathically but are limited to reading emotions of alien species. They cannot read Ferengi emotions. Betazoids usually develop their abilities in adolescence, but in *TNG* episode "Tin Man," Tam Elbrun was born telepathic and found the mental "noise" too painful to endure. In the *TNG* episode "Manhunt" it is shown that one of their customs is to ring a chime during a meal to give thanks for their food. In *TNG* episode "The Child," it is revealed that a Betazoid gestation period is ten months. Betazoids are a matriarchal society, and believe men to be a commodity.

Beth Delta I — in *TNG* episode "Evolution," the character Stubbs tells Troi he will show her "New Manhattan on Beth Delta I" as she has never seen it.

Bethune, Ivy — actress who played Duana, Wesley's "adopted mother" on Aldea, in *TNG* episode "When the Bough Breaks."

"Beyond Antares" — song Uhura sings in Classic episodes "The Conscience of the King" and "The Changeling."

"Beyond the Farthest Star" — written by Samuel A. Peeples, this animated Classic *Trek* episode aired 12/22/73. The *Enterprise* is pulled by the gravity of a negative star mass to discover a giant ship that makes their ship look like a mere speck. On board the alien ship is a dead crew of an insectile race that destroyed themselves because they were invaded by a deadly life-form. It is still alive, and invades the *Enterprise*. Kirk pretends to destroy his ship to trick the alien into vacating the *Enterprise*.

Guest voice: James Doohan (Kyle, engineer, Commander of Alien Starship, Alien).

Bezaride — planet of the Pallas 14 system mentioned in animated episode "One of Our Planets Is Missing."

Bhavani, Premier — planetary leader of Barzan II in *TNG* episode "The Price," played by Elizabeth Hoffman.

Bickell, Andrew — actor who played Wagnor in *TNG* episode "The Hunted."

bi-dyttrium — powerful energy source sought by the Cardassians in *DS9* episode "Past Prologue."

"Big Goodbye, The" — first-season *TNG* episode written by Tracy Torme and directed by Joseph L. Scanlan. On the *Enterprise* holodeck, Picard and crew visit 1940s San Francisco. A computer mishap leaves them stranded in a very real, very deadly scenario. Guest stars: Mike Genovese, Dick Miller, Carolyn Alport, Rhonda Aldrich, Eric Cord, Lawrence Tierney, Harvey Jason, William Boyett, David Selburg, and Gary Armagnal. This episode won the Peabody Award.

Bikel, Theodore — actor who guest starred in *TNG* episode "Family."

Biko, USS — in *TNG* episode "A Fistful of Datas," the *Enterprise* is delayed on its way to meet the *Biko*.

Bilana III — location of the wave propulsion method test in *TNG* episode "New Ground."

Bilar — character from Classic episode "The Return of the Archons," played by Ralph Maurer. He directs the *Enterprise* crew to a place to stay.

Billings, Earl — actor in *TNG* episode "The Drumhead."

Billy, Michele Ameen — actress who played the Epsilon Lt. in the Classic *Trek* film *Star Trek: The Motion Picture*. She was assistant to Harold Livingston at the time.

Bingham, Michael J. — scriptwriter of the *TNG* episode "The Naked Now."

Binney, Geoffrey — actor who played Compton in Classic *Trek* episode "Wink of an Eye." Credits include: *The Appearances of Pretty Boy Floyd* ('74), *Once an Eagle* ('77), *Swan Song* ('80).

biobeds — beds used in the medical ward in *TNG* episode "Contagion."

biocomputer — portable one was used in Classic episode "Miri."

biofilter — filter for harmful bacteria used in the transporter. It is referred to by Dr. Pulaski in *TNG* episode "Shades of Gray."

Biomolecular Specialist — doctor who operates on Picard in *TNG* episode "Samaritan Snare," played by Tzi Ma.

bioplast sheeting — Data is composed of this element, as stated in *TNG* episode "The Most Toys."

Bird-of-Prey — Romulan ships in Classic *Trek*; both Romulan and Klingon ships in the Classic movies, *TNG*, and *DS9*.

biridium pellet — implant in Worf's neck inserted at the Carraya prison colony in *TNG* episode "Birthright, Part II."

Birk, Raye — actor who played Wrenn in the *TNG* episode "Haven."

Birkin, David Tristan — actor who guest starred in *TNG* episode "Rascals."

"Birthright, Parts I and II" — sixth-season *TNG* episode written by Brannon Braga (part I) and René Echevarria (part II), directed by Winrich Kolbe (part I) and Dan Curry (part II). Worf visits *Deep Space 9* and meets a Yridian named Shrek who tells him he can help Worf find his father, a prisoner in a Romulan-run camp holding refugees from the Khitomer massacre. Meanwhile, Data hallucinates when he is knocked unconscious, and the visiting Dr. Bashir tells him he experienced a dream. Worf finds the camp and discovers it is more of a village than a prison, and that Romulans and Klingons are living together in peace, even marrying and having families. Worf is appalled. He tries to convince the Klingons born in the camp, now young adults, that they must embrace the Klingon way to be true to their heritage. Guest stars: Siddig El Fadil, James Cromwell, Alan Scarfe, Richard Herd, Christine Rose, Sterling Macer, Jr., and Jennifer Gatti.

Bischoff, David — scriptwriter of the *TNG* episodes "Tin Man" and "First Contact." He also wrote Pocket *TNG* novel *Grounded*.

Bishop, Ed — actor who was the voice of the Megan Prosecutor in the animated "The Magicks of Megas-Tu." Bishop is famous to SF fans for his role as Ed Straker in the British TV series *UFO*.

Bissell, Whit — actor who played Lurry in "The Trouble with Tribbles." Born in 1919, he died in 1981. His credits include *The Time Tunnel*, *Creature from the Black Lagoon* ('54), *Invasion of the Body Snatchers* ('56), *The Time Machine* ('60), and *Soylent Green* ('73).

Bixby, Jerome — scriptwriter who penned the Classic *Trek* episodes "Mirror, Mirror," "By Any Other Name" (with D. C. Fontana), "Day of the Dove," and "Requiem for Methuselah."

Black, John D. F. — scriptwriter/producer who wrote "The Naked Time" and produced *Star Trek*'s first season. He also wrote the *TNG* episode "The Naked Now," and early drafts of "Justice." He has won the Edgar award for *Thief*, was nominated for an Emmy, wrote the original *Wonder Woman*, and wrote and produced *A Shadow in the Streets* ('75) and *The Clone Master* ('78).

Black Cluster — uncharted part of the galaxy mentioned in *TNG* episode "Hero Worship." The Black Cluster reflects deflector shield power back at a ship when it tries to enter the area.

Black Knight — synthetic character in Classic episode "Shore Leave" that attacks and kills McCoy.

Blackburn, Bill — stunt double who played The White Rabbit in the Classic *Trek* episode "Shore Leave," an extra in "A Taste of Armageddon," a guard in "The Alternative Factor," Lt. Hadley in "A Piece of the Action," and a storm trooper in "Patterns of Force."

blackjack — card game Data plays at the Royale in *TNG* episode "The Royale."

Blackman, Robert — *TNG* and *DS9* costume designer.

Blanton, Arell — actor who played Lt. Dickerson in "The Savage Curtain." Credits include *Pennies from Heaven* ('81). He also works in soft-core porn films.

Blish, James — author who wrote *Star Trek 1–12* (#12 was written with his wife, J. A. Lawrence, who finished the book after he died in 1975), and *Spock Must Die!*.

Bloch, Robert — scriptwriter who penned the Classic *Trek* episodes "What Are Little Girls Made Of?," "Catspaw," and "Wolf in the Fold." A horror writer of great repute, his episodes are darker than most *Trek*. Born in 1917, he is most famous for his script *Psycho* directed by Alfred Hitchcock. He also wrote *The Cabinet of Caligari* ('62) and *The House That Dripped Blood* ('71), as well as many short stories and novels.

Bloom, John — actor who played the behemoth alien in the Classic *Trek* film *The Undiscovered Country*.

Bloom, Commander — person Riker meets at the asylum in *TNG* episode "Frame of Mind." She claims to be the commander of the *Yorktown*, but her real name is Jaya.

Blue Parrot Café — in *TNG* episode "We'll Always Have Paris," this café is on Sarona VIII. It serves the famous Blue Parrot.

Bluejay 4 — code name of Captain Christopher's jet in Classic episode "Tomorrow Is Yesterday."

Blum, Katherine — actress who played the Vulcan Child in the Classic *Trek* film *The Search for Spock*. This ended up on the cutting-room floor.

Bochra — Romulan Centurion who survives a crash on Galorndon Core in *TNG* episode "The Enemy," played by John Snyder.

Body, The — term used in Classic *Trek* episode "The Return of the Archons." A person who has been "absorbed" and controlled by Landru, the computer that runs the planet, is considered 'of the Body.'

Boen, Earl — actor who played Nagilum in *TNG* episode "Where Silence Has Lease."

Bok, DaiMon — Ferengi commander on *TNG* episode "The Battle." His son was killed by Picard nine years before. He is played by Frank Corsentino.

Bolan — one of these blue-skinned people appears in *DS9* episode "Emissary." He is the tactical officer on the USS *Saratoga* who drags Sisko to safety when the ship is attacked by the Borg. He is played by Stephen Davies.

Bolder, Cal — actor who played Keel in "Friday's Child." His credits include *The Man from U.N.C.L.E.*

Bole, Cliff — director of the *TNG* episodes "Lonely among Us," "Hide and Q," "Conspiracy," "The Royale," "The Emissary," "The Ensigns of Command," "The Hunted," "A Matter of Perspective," "Hollow Pursuits," "The Best of Both Worlds Part 1 and 2," "Remember Me," "First Contact," "Qpid," "Redemption Part 1," "Silicon Avatar," "Unification, Part 2," "The Perfect Mate,"

"Realm of Fear," "Aquiel," "Starship Mine," and "Suspicions."

Bolians — natives of Bolius IX, humanoid with green skin and a ridge in the middle of the head (like Klingons). They appear in *TNG* episodes "Conspiracy" and "Allegiance."

Boma, Lieutenant — astrophysicist in Classic episode "The Galileo Seven," played by Don Marshall. He is one of the survivors of the *Galileo*'s crash landing on Taurus II.

Bonanno, Margaret Wander — author of the Classic *Trek* novels *Probe*, *Strangers From the Sky*, and *Dwellers in the Crucible*.

Bonaventure — mentioned in animated episode "Time Trap" as the first ship to be fitted with the warp drive.

Bonaventure, Ruth — one of the three women, the brunette, whom Harry Mudd is transporting to Rigel XII in Classic episode "Mudd's Women." She is played by Maggie Thrett.

Bond, Nancy — scriptwriter of *TNG* episode "Silicon Avatar."

Bond, Timothy — director of the *TNG* episodes "The Vengeance Factor" and "The Most Toys."

"Bonding, The" — third-season *TNG* episode written by Ronald D. Moore, directed by Winrich Kolbe. A young boy's mother is killed on an away team mission, but she returns to comfort him and try to get him to come away with her. She is really an alien who wants to raise the boy. Guest stars: Susan Powell, Gabriel Damon, and Colm Meaney.

Bones — nickname Kirk uses to address his friend Dr. Leonard H. McCoy (see entry).

Bonestell Recreation Facility — in *TNG* episode "Samaritan Snare," this facility is located at Starbase *Earhart*.

Bonne, Shirley — actress who played Ruth in "Shore Leave." Credits: the TV series *My Sister Eileen* (1960–61).

Bonney, Gail — actress who played the second witch in "Catspaw." Her credits include *One Step Beyond, The Priest Killer* ('71), *The Devil's Daughter* ('73), *Death Scream* ('75), and *Kingston: The Power Play* ('76).

Bonsall, Brian — actor who played Alexander, Worf's son, in *TNG* episodes "New Ground," "Ethics," "Cost of Living," "Imaginary Friend," "A Fistful of Datas," and "Rascals." He also starred as Andrew in the last couple of seasons of the hit series *Family Ties*.

"Booby Trap" — third-season *TNG* episode written by Michael Wagner, Ron Roman, Michael Piller, and Richard Danus, directed by Gabrielle Beaumont. The *Enterprise* gets caught in a 1000-year-old booby trap left behind by a war, and discovers a derelict Promelian ship also from that war. Geordi reconstructs an image of Dr. Leah Brahms, designer of the *Enterprise* propulsion systems, on the holodeck to help escape the trap. Guest stars: Susan Gibney, Whoopi Goldberg, Albert Hall, Julie Warner, and Colm Meaney.

Book of the People — term for a book of history and knowledge to be given to the people of Yonada when they arrive at their destination in Classic *Trek* episode "For the World Is Hollow and I Have Touched the Sky."

Boone, Walker — actor who played Leland T. Lynch in *TNG* episode "Skin of Evil."

Booth, Jimmie — actor who played a Klingon in Classic *Trek* film *Star Trek: The Motion Picture*.

Boothby — groundskeeper of Starfleet Academy in *TNG* episode "The First Duty," played by Ray Walston.

Boratis — character played by Michael Champion in *TNG* episode "Captain's Holiday." Apparently a Vorgon security agent from the 27th century, he is really a thief trying to steal the Tox-Uthat.

Boratis system — system of thirteen colonies, all new. In *TNG* episode "The Emissary," the *Enterprise* picks up Special Emissary K'Ehleyr from this system.

Boreth — frozen Klingon world mentioned in *TNG* episode "Rightful Heir" where Kahless is supposed to reappear someday.

Borg — cybernetically enhanced being that looks human but with lots of mechanical parts. Borgs have a mission to destroy and/or absorb all life in the galaxy. They possess a hive mind and are the Federation's most ruthless enemy until Picard sends Hugh back to them with a virus in his programming. They are responsible for destroying Guinan's home system. They appear in several *TNG* episodes, beginning with "Q Who."

Borgia plant — in Classic episode "The Man Trap," it is a poisonous plant found on planet M–113. It is thought to have killed Darnell.

Borgolis Nebula — destination of the *Enterprise* when they are called to Bersallis III in *TNG* episode "Lessons."

boridium — in Classic episode "Wolf in the Fold," the knife used by the killer has a boridium blade.

borkaas — what Bajorans call "ghosts" in *TNG* episode "The Next Phase."

Bortas — Klingon ship seen in *TNG* episode "The Defector" and later an attack cruiser of the same name used by Gowron in "Reunion Part I."

Boryer, Lucy — actress who played Janeway in *TNG* "Man of the People."

Botany Bay, USS — ship enountered in Classic

episode "Space Seed" that carries Khan's people in sleep stasis.

Botsford, Diana Dru — scriptwriter of *TNG* episode "Rascals."

Botsford, Ward — scriptwriter of *TNG* episode "Rascals."

Bouchet, Barbara — actress who played Kelinda in "By Any Other Name." She was born in Germany and has been a model in commercials. Credits include: *Casino Royale* ('66), *Sweet Charity* ('69).

Bounty — name McCoy gives to the Klingon ship Kirk and crew have inherited in the Classic *Trek* film *The Voyage Home*. He names the ship after the *Bounty* in *Mutiny on the Bounty*.

Bova, Vanessa and Jessica — twin actresses who played Alexandra, a girl kidnapped from the *Enterprise* in the *TNG* episode "When the Bough Breaks."

Bowers, Antoinette — actress who played Sylvia in "Catspaw." Her credits include *The Man From U.N.C.L.E.*, *Perry Mason*, and *Mission: Impossible*, plus the films *The Scorpio Letters* ('67), *Death of Innocence* ('71), *First You Cry* ('78), *Blood Song* ('81), *The Thorn Birds* ('83), and *The Evil That Men Do* ('84).

Bowman, Rob — director of the *TNG* episodes "Where No One Has Gone Before," "The Battle," "Datalore," "Too Short a Season," "Heart Of Glory," "The Child," "Elementary, Dear Data," "A Matter of Honor," "The Dauphin," "Q Who," "Manhunt," "Shades of Gray," and "Brothers."

Box, Talking — in *TNG* episode "Haven," this device is a box that has a face and speaks. It speaks with the voice of Armin Shimerman.

Boy — 12-year-old Ansata separatist in *TNG* episode "The High Ground," played by Christopher Pettiet.

Boyce, Phillip, Dr. — ship's doctor in Classic pilot "The Cage," played by John Hoyt. He is a surgeon as well as an amateur psychologist/philosopher.

Boyer, Katy — actress who played a citizen of Bynus, a Bynar, in *TNG* episode "11001001."

Boyett, William — actor who played police chief Dan Bell in *TNG* episode "The Big Goodbye," and played a police man in "Time's Arrow, Part 2."

Bozeman, **USS** — commanded by Captain Morgan Bateson, this ship was lost 80 years before in a time/space continuum in *TNG* episode "Cause and Effect."

Brack, Mr. — man who bought the planet Holbert 917G. This name is an alias for Flint in Classic episode "Requiem for Methuselah."

Bractor, DaiMon — leader of the Ferengi ship *Krik'ta* in *TNG* episode "Peak Performance," played by Armin Shimerman.

Bradbury, **USS** — in *TNG* episode "Ménage à Troi," Wesley is supposed to board this ship for a trip to Starfleet Academy. He misses his ride.

Braden, Kim — actress who guest starred in *TNG* episode "The Loss."

Bradley, Arthur Glinton — unseen husband of Jessica Bradley in *TNG* episode "The Big Goodbye."

Bradley, Jessica — murder victim in the Dixon Hill holo-projection in *TNG* episode "The Big Goodbye," played by Carolyn Allport.

Bradley, Paul — actor who played Ensign Freeman in "The Trouble with Tribbles."

Braga, Brannon — scriptwriter for *TNG* episodes "Identity Crisis," "Power Play," "The Game," "Schisms," "Realm of Fear," "A Fistful of Datas," "Aquiel," "Cause and Effect," "Imaginary Friend," "Birthright, Part I," "Reunion," "Frame of Mind," and "Timescape."

Brahms, Johannes — one of Flint's past identities from Classic episode "Requiem for Methuselah."

Brahms, Leah, Dr. — character in *TNG* episode "Booby Trap" who is a propulsion engineer and a graduate of the Daystrom Institute Theoretical Propulsion Group. She is Geordi's personal hero. He programs her image in a holo-fantasy to help solve the ship's problems. She is played by Susan Gibney.

Bralver, Robert — stunt man who played Grant in the Classic *Trek* episode "Friday's Child" and who appeared in the Classic *Trek* film *Star Trek: The Motion Picture.* He also served as stunt driver of the car in *Knight Rider,* and appeared in *The Bionic Woman* and *The Man from U.N.C.L.E.*

Bramley, William — actor who played the policeman in the Classic *Trek* episode "Bread and Circuses." His credits include the movies *Jaws 3-D* ('83) and *The Wild Life* ('84) as well as the TV series *The Girl from U.N.C.L.E., Iron Horse, Petrocelli,* and *Barnaby Jones.*

Branagh, Kenneth — mentioned in *TNG* episode "The Defector," he is an actor/director Data wants to study.

Branch, Commander — Epsilon station commander in the Classic *Trek* film *Star Trek: The Motion Picture.*

Brand, Admiral — superintendent of Starfleet Academy in *TNG* episode "The First Duty," played by Jacqueline Brookes. A Vulcan, Captain Satelk, is her assistant.

Brandt, Victor — actor who played Watson in the Classic *Trek* episode "Elaan of Troyius" and Tongo Rad in "The Way to Eden." Credits: *Nobody's Perfect* ('80), *Strange Homecoming* ('74), *The Deadly Triangle* ('77), *Zuma Beach* ('78), *Wacko* ('83).

Brannen, Ralph — actor who played a crewman in the Classic *Trek* film *Star Trek: The Motion Picture*.

Braslota system — location of the Starfleet battle simulation between the USS *Hathaway* and the *Enterprise* shown in *TNG* episode "Peak Performance." It is located in the Oneamisu sector. Its worlds include Kei, Yuri, and Totoro.

Brattain, USS — science ship of Starfleet found by the *Enterprise* with all but one of its crew dead in *TNG* episode "Night Terrors."

"Bread and Circuses" — written by Gene Roddenberry, Gene L. Coon, and John Kneubuhl, directed by Ralph Senensky, this second-season Classic *Trek* episode aired 3/15/68. The wrecked ship *S.S. Beagle* is found orbiting planet 892–IV. The world below exhibits 20th-century technology, but ancient Roman culture, complete with gladiatorial fights to the death. Claudius Marcus, the proconsul of the Empire, controls those left alive of the *Beagle*'s crew, and attempts to gain control of the *Enterprise*. Guest stars: William Smithers, Logan Ramsey, Ian Wolfe, Rhodes Reason, and Lois Jewell. Of note: Introduction of Hodgkin's Law of Parallel Planets, which conveniently explains why many aliens speak English but not why they have Earth gods and customs.

Brechtian Cluster — where the *Enterprise* meets for the second time with the crystalline entity in *TNG* episode "Silicon Avatar."

Bre'el IV — world threatened by a falling asteroid in *TNG* episode "Déjà Q." Q intervenes and saves the world.

Breen — race with attack ships that use disruptors and cloaking devices encountered in *TNG* episode "The Loss" and mentioned in "Hollow Worship."

Brekka — this planet, the fourth world of the Delos system, holds felicium, a cure for a plague on Ornara in *TNG* episode "Symbiosis."

Brenner, Eve — actress who guest starred in *TNG* episode "Violations."

Brenner, Faye — script supervisor for *The Undiscovered Country*.

Brent, Lieutenant — minor character on the bridge in Classic *Trek* episode "The Naked Time," played by Frank da Vinci.

Breton, Brooke — associate producer of the Classic *Trek* film *The Voyage Home*.

Brevelle, Ensign — member of LaForge's away team to Tarchannen III absorbed by the group of indigenous humanoid life-forms in *TNG* episode "Identity Crisis." He was played by Paul Tompkins.

Briam, Ambassador — envoy from Krios to Valt Minor, played by Tim O'Connor, in *TNG* episode "The Perfect Mate."

Brian, David — actor who played John Gill in Classic *Trek* episode "Patterns of Force." Born in 1914, his credits include *Mr. District Attorney* (1954–55), *The Immortal* ('70), *Million Dollar Mermaid* ('52), and *How the West Was Won* ('62).

Brianon, Kareen — ward of Dr. Ira Graves in *TNG* episode "The Schizoid Man," played by Barbara Alyn Woods. He is in love with her.

Briggs, Bob — head of the Cetacean Institute in the Classic *Trek* film *The Voyage Home*, played by Scott DeVenney.

Brill, Charlie — actor who played Arne Darvin in the Classic *Trek* episode "The Trouble with Tribbles." He also appeared on *Rowan and Martin's Laugh-In* and *Supertrain*, and in the films *Young Love, First Love* ('79), and *Your Place or Mine* ('83).

Brincas V — in *TNG* episode "The Loss," Geordi remembers skin-diving on this world.

Bringloid — colony in the Ficus Sector in *TNG* episode "Up the Long Ladder." Bringloid is Gaelic for *dream*. The inhabitants are Irish humans who left Earth to develop their own independent world in 2123.

Brislane, Mike — actor who played the *Saratoga* science officer in *The Voyage Home*.

Brocco, Peter — actor who played Claymare in "Errand of Mercy." Credits include films *Alias Smith and Jones* ('71), *Raid on Entebbe* ('77), *Jeckyl and Hyde: Together Again* ('82), *Twilight Zone: The Movie* ('83), and TV credits *Chase*, *Voyage to the Bottom of the Sea*, and *The Man from U.N.C.L.E.*

Brocksmith, Roy — actor who played Sirna Kolrami in *TNG* episode "Peak Performance."

Brody, Larry — scriptwriter of the animated episode "The Magicks of Megas-Tu." He has also written scripts for *Cannon* and *Barnaby Jones*, and several TV movies.

Bronken, Trenka — mentioned in *TNG* episode "The Ensigns of Command," he is a concert violinist whose style Data emulates.

Bronson, Fred — scriptwriter of the *TNG* episodes "Ménage à Troi" and "The Game."

Brookes, Admiral — mentioned in *TNG* episode "Suspicions" as the senior officer Beverly will have to report to for a formal inquiry after Dr. Reyga, the Ferengi scientist, is murdered.

Brooks, Avery — actor who plays Commander Benjamin Sisko in *DS9*. Born and raised in Indiana, Brooks graduated from Oberlin College and performed on the stage. His TV credits include being a regular on *Spenser: for Hire* as the character Hawk, and starring in the short-lived series spin-off *A Man Called Hawk*. He plays jazz, and often teaches. He is a tenured professor at Rutgers University, where he has taught for 20 years. He is married and currently lives in Los Angeles with his wife, a daughter, and two sons.

Brooks, Jacqueline — actress in *TNG* episode "The First Duty."

Brooks, James E. — scriptwriter who wrote the story for *TNG* episode "Rightful Heir."

Brooks, Joel — actor who guest starred in *DS9* episode "Move Along Home."

Brooks, Lee — actor who played the aphasia victim in *DS9* episode "Babel."

Brooks, Rolland M. — art director of Classic *Star Trek*'s first season.

Brooks, Stephen — actor who played Garrovick in "Obsession." His other TV credits include *The Nurses*, *The FBI*, and *The Interns*.

Brophy, Brian — actor who played Commander Bruce Maddox in *TNG* episode "The Measure of a Man."

"Brothers" — fourth-season *TNG* episode written by Rick Berman, directed by Rob Bowman. Data meets his creator, his father, Dr. Soong, played by Brent Spiner. Soong wants to give Data feelings, but gives the special chip to Lore instead, who becomes crazed, assaults Soong, and runs away. Data is rescued just as his father dies. Guest stars: Cory Danziger, Adam Ryen, James Lashly, and Colm Meaney.

Browder IV — world being terraformed in *TNG* episode "Allegiance;" the *Enterprise* is en route to rendezvous with the USS *Hood*.

Brown, Caitlin — actress who guest starred in *DS9* episode "The Passenger."

Brown, Dr. — Dr. Korby's android assistant in Classic episode "What Are Little Girls Made Of?" played by Harry Basch.

Brown, Frederick — writer whose original story, "Arena," published in *Astounding Science Fiction Stories* in 1944, was the foundation for the Classic *Trek* episode "Arena." The original story was republished in *Starlog #4*.

Brown, Georgia — actress who starred in *TNG* episode "Family."

Brown, Marcia — actress who played Alice in the Classic *Trek* episode "Shore Leave."

Brown, Mark Robert — actor who played Don in the Classic *Trek* episode "And the Children Shall Lead."

Brown, Robert — actor who played Lazarus in the Classic *Trek* episode "The Alternative Factor." He also starred in *Here Come the Brides* and *Primus*.

Brown, Roger Aaron — actor who played the Epsilon tech in the Classic *Trek* film *Star Trek: The Motion Picture*. His film credits include *McNaughton's Daughter* ('76), *Death on the Freeway* ('79), *Don't Cry, It's Only Thunder* ('82), and *Sins of the Past* ('84).

Brown, Ron — actor who played Drummer in the holodeck band in *TNG* episode "11001001."

Brown, Wren T. — actor who played the transport pilot in *TNG* episode "Manhunt."

Browne, Kathie — actress who played Deela in Classic *Trek* episode "Wink of an Eye." TV credits include *Slattery's People* and *Hondo*, with film credits for *Berlin Affair* ('70). She is married to actor Darren McGavin, best known as Kolshak of *The Night Stalker*.

Bruck, Karl — actor who played King Duncan in "The Conscience of the King." Born in 1906, he died in 1987. His film credits include *Escape of the Birdmen* ('71) and *Escape from the Planet of the Apes* ('71.) He is a survivor of the Holocaust, and was a regular on *The Young and the Restless*.

Brull — leader of the Gatherers on Gamma Hromi II in

TNG episode "The Vengeance Factor," played by Joey Aresco.

Brute, The — character in the prison who fights Kirk in the Classic *Trek* film *The Undiscovered Country*, played by Tom Morga. Apparently his genitals are where his knees should be.

Bry, Ellen — actress who guest starred in *TNG* episode "The Quality of Life."

Bryant, Ursaline — actress who played Captain Tryla Scott of the USS *Renegade* in the *TNG* episode "Conspiracy."

Bryce, Randi — biologist in animated episode "The Eye of the Beholder," with voice played by Majel Barrett.

B'tardat — Kaelon administrator and scientist in *TNG* episode "Half a Life." He was played by Terence McNally.

Buckland, Marc — actor who played Katik Shaw in *TNG* episode "The High Ground."

Budron, Admiral — mentioned in *TNG* episode "Frame of Mind" as the person who denied Riker was a member of Starfleet.

buffers — information processors worn by the Bynars around their waists in *TNG* episode "11001001."

Bulgalian sludge rat — what Rondon calls Wesley when he meets him in *TNG* episode "Coming of Age."

Bundy, Brooke — actress who plays Sarah MacDougal, chief of engineering in *TNG* episode "The Naked Now."

buoy, Melkotian — the *Enterprise* encounters this buoy in Classic episode "The Spectre of the Gun." It supposedly speaks telepathically and in the native language of each listener. James Doohan supplied the voice.

Burdette, Marlys — actress who played Krako's Gun Moll in the Classic *Trek* episode "A Piece of the Action."

Burke, Ensign — tactical officer on the *Enterprise* who takes Worf's place when Worf goes to the *Hathaway* in *TNG* episode "Peak Performance." He was played by Glenn Morshower.

Burke, John — mentioned in Classic episode "The Trouble with Tribbles" as the person who mapped Sherman's Planet.

Burns, Elkanah J. — actor who played Temarek in *TNG* episode "The Vengeance Factor."

Burns, Judy — scriptwriter for Classic *Trek* episode "The Tholian Web" (with Chet Richards). She has also written for *Mission: Impossible*, *Toma*, and uncounted others.

Burns, Tim — actor who played Russ in "The Doomsday Machine." Film credits include: *Gargoyles* ('72), *Monkey Grip* ('83).

Burnside, John — actor who was an extra in "A Taste of Armageddon."

Burton, LeVar — actor who plays Geordi LaForge on *TNG*. Born Feb. 16, 1957, in Landsthul, West Germany, he played Kunta Kinte in the epic *Roots*. Film credits include *Looking for Mr. Goodbar*, *The Hunter*, and *The Supernaturals* (which also starred Nichelle Nichols). He hosts *Reading Rainbow*, a PBS show for children. His TV movies include *Dummy*, *One in a Million: The Ron LeFlore Story*, *Grambling's White Tiger*, *The Guyana Tragedy: The Story of Jim Jones*, *Battered*, *Billy: Portrait of a Street Kid*, and the mini-series *Liberty*. He was a *Star Trek* fan long before landing the role, and entered a Catholic seminary at age 13, his goal: to become a priest. His interest in philosophy led him to read Lao Tzu, Kierkegaard, and Nietzsche by the time he was fifteen. After he left the seminary, he won a scholarship to USC, where he was when at age 19 he landed the grand role in *Roots*. He got an Emmy nomination for his portrayal of Kinte. Burton lives in Los Angeles with his German

Shepherd, Mozart. His character is named after a real *Star Trek* fan who died of muscular dystrophy in 1975. Burton also directed *TNG* episode "Second Chances."

Buruk — Klingon Bird of Prey commanded by Gowron in *TNG* episode "Reunion."

Butler, Megan — actress who starred as a lieutenant in *DS9* episode "Emissary."

Butler, Nathan — psuedonym of scriptwriter and SF writer Jerry Sohl who wrote the Classic *Trek* episode "This Side of Paradise."

Butler, Robert — director of the Classic *Trek* episodes "The Cage" and "The Menagerie, Part II." His directing credits include Disney's *The Computer Wore Tennis Shoes* ('69) and *Now You See Him, Now You Don't* ('71). He won an Emmy in 1973 for Director of the Year, and another for his work on *Hill Street Blues*. He is cocreator of *Remington Steele*.

Butrick, Merritt — actor who played David Marcus, Kirk's son, in the Classic *Trek* films *The Wrath of Khan* and *The Search for Spock*. He played T'Jon in *TNG* episode "Symbiosis." Before he died of AIDS in 1990, he starred in many TV series, including *Beauty and the Beast*, and as a regular on the series *Square Pegs*, where he played Johnny Slash. His film credits include *Zapped!*, *When Your Lover Leaves*, and *Shy People*.

"By Any Other Name" — written by D. C. Fontana and Jerome Bixby, directed by Marc Daniels, this second-season Classic *Trek* episode aired 2/23/68. Aliens from the galaxy Andromeda, as a prelude to invasion, hijack the *Enterprise* for the 300-year journey back to their home. They reduce everyone but the command crew to compressed, minerallike hexagonal boxes. The command crew must find a way to take back control of the ship. Guest stars: Warren Stevens, Barbara Bouchet, Stewart Moss, Robert Fortier, Carol Byrd, Leslie Dalton, and Julie Cobb.

Byers, Ralph — actor who played a crewman in *Star Trek: The Motion Picture*. Film credits: *Blind Ambition* ('79), *The Cradle Will Fall* ('83.)

Bynars, The — characters in *TNG* episode "11001001" who are linked by an organic computer and work in pairs. The small beings are named 11, 00, 10, and 01. They steal the *Enterprise* from Starbase 74. They are played by Katy Boyer, Alexandra Johnson, Iva Lane, and Kelly Ann McNally.

Bynaus — homeworld of the Bynars from *TNG* episode "11001001." They are a race who exist as part of an organic computer.

Byram, Amick — actor who guest starred in *TNG* episode "Identity Crisis."

Byram, Cassandra — actress who played the communications officer in *DS9* episode "Emissary."

Byrd, Carl — actor who played Lt. Shea in the Classic *Trek* episode "By Any Other Name."

Cabot, Ensign — *Enterprise* junior officer who wants a transfer in *TNG* episode "Lessons."

Cadiente, Dave — played a Klingon in *The Search for Spock.*

Cairo, **USS** — *Excelsior*-class ship from *TNG* episode "Chain of Command" commanded by Captain Edward Jellicoe.

Caitian — feline people covered with fur, bearing tails. M'Ress from the animated series is a Caitian.

Calamarain — Q torments these people, a race comprised of ionized gas, in *TNG* episode "Déjà Q."

Calder, Thomas — scriptwriter of the *TNG* episode "The Emissary."

Caldonians — beings committed to pure research in *TNG* episode "The Price."

Calenti, Vince — actor who played a security guard in the Classic *Trek* episode "The Alternative Factor."

Call, Anthony — actor who played Lt. Dave Bailey in the Classic *Trek* episode "The Corbomite Maneuver."

Cameron, Laura — actress who played Bajoran Woman in *DS9* episode "Q Less."

Campbell, William — actor who played Captain Koloth in Classic *Trek* episode "The Trouble with Tribbles," and Trelane in the episode "The Squire of Gothos." Campbell was born in 1926 and has many TV credits, including *Gunsmoke*, and the Gene Roddenberry–produced movie *Pretty Maids All in a Row*.

Campbell, William O. — actor who played Captain Thaddiun Okona in *TNG* episode "The Outrageous Okona."

Campio — third minister of the conference of judges on Kostolain who is going to marry Lwaxana Troi until they discover incompatibilities, in *TNG* episode "Cost of Living." Campio is played by Tony Jay.

Camus II — planet in Classic *Trek* episode "Turnabout Intruder" where Janice Lester and her team of scientists explored the ruins of a dead civilization and discovered the device that switched her essence with Kirk's. In *TNG* episode "Legacy," the *Enterprise* bypasses this world.

Canada, Ron — actor in *TNG* episode "Masterpiece Society."

Canar — Hahliian device used to augment a telepathic link with others. It is seen in *TNG* episode "Aquiel."

Canon, Peter — actor who played the Gestapo lieutenant in the Classic *Trek* episode "Patterns of Force." TV credits include: *The Wackiest Ship in the Army*.

Canopus — in Classic *Trek* episode "Where No Man Has Gone Before," Gary Mitchell quotes from a poem called "Nightingale Woman" which was written by Phineas Tarbolde, who was from Canopus.

Canopus III — place where Kirk saw a beast that resembled the fire-breathing iguana of Lactra VII mentioned in animated episode "Eye of the Beholder."

Cansino, Richard — actor who played Dr. Garin in *TNG* episode "Déjà Q."

Cantaba Street — where Morla lives in Classic *Trek* episode "Wolf in the Fold."

Capella IV — small world with red seas, valued for its deposits of topaline, a substance used in life-support systems on planetoid colonies in Classic episode "Friday's Child." The Federation and the Klingons compete for the allegiance of the planet. This planet is also mentioned in the animated episode "Counter-Clock Incident" as the location of one of the most beautiful flowers in the galaxy.

Capellan Power Cat — fiercest beast in the galaxy, mentioned in the animated episode "How Sharper Than a Serpent's Tooth." The untamable animal is like a bobcat with red fur and gold eyes with brown spines down its back. It possesses a white, glowing aura of electricity and can throw jolts at its victims.

Capellan Salute — shown in Classic episode "Friday's Child," it consists of forming the right hand into a fist, holding it against the center of the chest, then extending it outward with the palm up.

Capellans — tall, humanlike warriors seen in Classic episode "Friday's Child." They believe only the strong should survive and hold little value for medicine. They enjoy combat and interpret any show of force as a challenge to battle.

Capra, Frank, III — assistant director of the Classic film *The Voyage Home*. He is the grandson of director Frank Capra. He also worked on the film *Zapped!*

"Captain's Holiday" — third-season *TNG* episode written by Ira Stephen Behr, directed by Chip Chalmers. Picard takes a holiday on Risa, which turns out to be anything but restful. He first meets Vash in this episode. Together they search for the *Tox Uthat*, which the Ferengi and two Vorgons from the 27th century are also after. Guest stars: Jennifer Hetrick, Max Grodenchik, Karen Landry, Michael Champion, Deirdre Impershein.

Captain's Woman — see entry for Moreau, Marlena.

"Captive Pursuit" — first-season *DS9* episode written by Jill Sherman Donner and Michael Piller, directed by Corey Allen. A reptilian alien from the Gamma Quadrant visits *DS9* with a damaged spacecraft. O'Brien befriends him only to learn that Tosk is bred to be prey in a great chase to the death, and is being pursued. Guest stars: Gerrit Graham, Scott MacDonald, and Kelly Curtis.

Carabatsos, Stephen W. — writer and producer who scripted the Classic *Trek* episodes "Court-Martial" and "Operation: Annihilate!" He was a producer during Classic *Trek*'s first season.

Carapledes, Una — character mentioned as having been killed in an accident by Starfleet in *TNG* episode "Conspiracy."

Carbon Cycle Life-Form — creature on Excalbia in Classic episode "The Savage Curtain" is one.

Cardassians — members of a hostile race whose leaders love to conquer, they are involved in a bitter war with Bajor. Ridges seem to attach their necks to their shoulders and make them look awkward. Except for their somewhat ridged foreheads, they are otherwise humanoid in appearance with hair on top of their heads. They appear often on *DS9* as the resident villains. In *TNG* episode "Chain of Command," their leader shows a sadistic side when they torture and attempt to brainwash the captured Picard. Occasional episodes show that not all Cardassians are inherently evil, although they live under a barbaric regime.

Caretaker, The — character on Classic episode "Shore Leave" who oversees the recreational facilities on the planet. He is played by Oliver McGowan. He dies in the animated episode "Once upon a Planet."

Carey, Diane — author of *TNG* novel *Ghost Ship*, Classic *Trek* novels *Best Destiny*, *Final Frontier*, *Dreadnought!*, *Battlestations!*, and *The Great Starship Race*.

Carhart, Timothy — actor in *TNG* episode "Redemption, Part II."

Carlisle, Lieutenant — security officer in Classic *Trek* pilot "The Cage," played by Arnold Lessing.

Carlyle, Richard — played Karl Jaeger in the Classic *Trek* episode "The Squire of Gothos." TV credits include: *One Step Beyond* and *Cannon*.

Carmel, Roger C. — played Harcourt Fenton Mudd in "Mudd's Women," "I, Mudd," and the voice of Mudd in the the animated episode "Mudd's Passion." His TV credits include being a regular on *The Mothers-In-Law* and *Fitz and Bones*, as well as guest starring in such shows as *I Spy*, *The Man From U.N.C.L.E.*, *The Alfred Hitchcock Show*, and *Voyage to the Bottom of the Sea.* He is famous as the voice of Señor Naugles (for a Mexican fast-food restaurant chain) and Smokey the Bear. He died in 1986 of an apparent drug overdose. Before his death he made several convention appearances.

Carmichael, Mrs. — landlady in 19th-century San Francisco who keeps demanding the rent from Picard in *TNG* episode "Time's Arrow, Part II." She is played by Pamela Kosh.

Carnel — world where Picard and Tasha first met, mentioned in *TNG* episode "Legacy."

Carolina, USS — vessel mentioned in Classic episode "Friday's Child" as the supposed origin of a second distress signal that draws Scotty away from the planet where the landing party remains. He does not heed this signal when he decides the Klingons are tricking him.

Carr, Paul — played Lee Kelso in "Where No Man Has Gone Before." His TV credits include *The Rifleman*, *Voyage to the Bottom of the Sea*, *The Green Hornet*, *The Six Million Dollar Man*, *Buck Rogers in the 25th Century*, and *Highway to Heaven*.

Carraya IV — location of the Romulan prison camp that Worf invades in *TNG* episode "Birthright."

Carrel — viewing area in the library on Sarpeidon in Classic episode "All Our Yesterdays."

Carren, David Bennett — scriptwriter of the *TNG* episode "Future Imperfect."

Carrigan-Fauci, Jeanne — scriptwriter of *DS9* episode "Move Along Home."

Carroll, Larry J. — scriptwriter of the *TNG* episode "Future Imperfect."

Carson, David — director of *TNG* episodes "The Enemy," "Yesterday's Enterprise," "Redemption, Part II," and "The Next Phase." He also directed *DS9* episodes "The Emissary" and "Move Along Home." His other directing credits include *Northern Exposure, Alien Nation, Homefront, Doogie Howser, M.D.,* and *L.A. Law.* He moved his family from England to the U.S. only a few years ago.

Carson, Fred — played First Denevan in the Classic *Trek* episode "Operation: Annihilate!"

Carter, Carmen — author of *TNG* novels *The Children of Hamlin, Doomsday World, The Devil's Heart,* and *Dreams of the Raven.*

Carter, Dr. — doctor of the *Exeter* who died from the disease the landing party brought back from Omega IV on Classic episode "The Omega Glory." Played by Ed McCready.

Cartwright, Admiral — member of Starfleet Command, played by Brock Peters, in *The Voyage Home* and *The Undiscovered Country.* Cartwright is one of the traitors involved in the conspiracy to assassinate the Klingons.

Caruso, Anthony — played Bela Oxmyx in Classic *Trek* episode "A Piece of the Action." Born in 1915, his career includes singing as well as acting. He is well known for his portrayal of gangsters in various TV shows.

Carver — security guard who beams down to Taurus II with the landing party in the animated episode "The Lorelei Signal."

Carver, Stephen James — actor in *DS9* episode "A Man Alone."

Cary, Hiroyuki — played Mandarin Bailiff in *TNG* "Encounter at Farpoint."

Cascone, Nicholas — played Ensign Davies in *TNG* episode "Pen Pals."

Cassel, Seymour — played Hester Dealt in *TNG* episode "The Child."

Cassidy, Ted — played Ruk in the Classic *Trek* episode "What Are Little Girls Made Of?" He also provided the voice of Balok in "The Corbomite Maneuver" and the voice of the Gorn in "Arena." Born in 1932, he is best known for his portrayal of Lurch in the TV series *The Addams Family*. He died in 1979.

Castillo, Richard, Lieutenant — helmsman and later senior officer of *Enterprise* C in *TNG* episode "Yesterday's Enterprise." He is in love with Tasha. He is played by Christopher McDonald.

Catching, Bill — stunt double for Spock in the Classic *Trek* episode "This Side of Paradise," as well as stunt double for Lazarus in "The Alternative Factor." He also appears in "Operation: Annihilate!"

Catron, Jerry — played Second Denevan in the Classic *Trek* episode "Operation: Annihilate!" and Montgomery in "The Doomsday Machine." His career includes playing henchmen and monsters on various TV shows of the '60s.

"Catspaw" — written by famous horror writer Robert

Bloch, directed by Joseph Pevney, this second season Classic *Trek* episode aired 10/27/67. The *Enterprise* investigates a ghostly, haunted planet where alien creatures have the power to generate illusions. Guest stars: Michael Barrier, Antoinette Bower, Theo Marcuse, and Jimmy Jones. Of note: This was obviously planned as a Halloween episode, and not one of the best.

Cattrall, Kim — played Valeris in the Classic *Trek* film *The Undiscovered Country*. Her film debut was *Mannequin*, and she has recently appeared in many theatrical and TV movies, including the surreal, virtual reality miniseries *Wild Palms*, and *Big Trouble in Little China*.

Catullan Ambassador — mentioned in Classic episode "The Way to Eden" as being the father of Tongo Rad, one of the group of "space hippies" the *Enterprise* brings aboard.

"Cause and Effect" — fifth-season *TNG* episode written by Brannon Braga, directed by Jonathan Frakes. The *Enterprise* is caught in a time loop and keeps repeating the same day over and over and over and over. Guest stars: Kelsey Grammer and Michelle Forbes.

Cavens, Al — played Second Fop in the Classic *Trek* episode "All Our Yesterdays."

Caves, Sally — scriptwriter of the *TNG* episode "Hollow Pursuits."

Cavett, Jon — played a guard in the Classic *Trek* episode "Devil in the Dark."

celebium — type of radiation Janice Lester was exposed to on Camus II, in Classic episode "Turnabout Intruder." She deliberately exposed the rest of her team to get the *Enterprise* to rescue them. Her team died.

Celestial Temple — term the Bajorans use for their rough equivalent of heaven. They believe the Orbs come from the Celestial Temple.

cellular casting — what the creatures on the recreational planet in Classic episode "Shore Leave" are made of.

Centauri VII — mentioned in Classic episode "Requiem for Methuselah" as the home planet of Taranallus, a lithographer. Flint collects his work. Spock sees one titled "The Creation" displayed on a wall in Flint's living room.

Centurion — older Romulan man who appears to be second in rank, "centurion," to the commander in Classic episode "Balance of Terror," played by John Warburton. He dies when the debris from an attack falls on him.

Cepheus — Arachna sun with one planet orbiting it, mentioned in animated episode "The Terratin Incident."

Cerberan youth drug — drug invented by Admiral Jameson to reverse the aging process in *TNG* episode "Too Short a Season."

Cerberus — location of the school McCoy's daughter attended, mentioned in animated episode "The Survivor."

Cerberus II — world on which Admiral Jameson developed a rejuvenation process in *TNG* episode "Too Short a Season."

Cestus III — world of the Federation colony attacked by the Gorns in Classic episode "Arena."

Ceti Alpha V — planet where Khan and his people are exiled by Kirk in Classic episode "Space Seed." Chekov mistakes this planet for Ceti Alpha VI (which was unknowingly destroyed) in *The Wrath of Khan*, and, with Captain Terrell, runs into the survivors of Khan's party.

Ceti Alpha VI — world that blew up and affected the orbit of Ceti Alpha V, making it nearly unlivable. Chekov thinks he's on Ceti Alpha VI in *The Wrath of Khan*.

Ceti Eels — sluglike creatures indigenous to Ceti Alpha V that destroyed many of Khan's people. Their young enter a person's body through the ear and wrap themselves around the cerebral cortex. As they feed and grow, the person experiences pain and insanity, then death.

Cha'dich — term for a Klingon attorney. Kurn is Worf's *Cha'dich* in *TNG* episode "Sins of the Father."

Chadwick, Robert — played Romulan Scope Operator in Classic *Trek* episode "Balance of Terror."

"Chain of Command, Parts I and II" — sixth-season *TNG* episode written by Ronald D. Moore (part I) and Frank Abatemarco (parts I and II), directed by Robert Scheerer (part I) and Les Landau (part II). Picard, Crusher, and Worf go on a secret mission to learn if the Cardassians have a hidden base on Celtris III, but they walk into a trap. Worf and Crusher escape, but Picard is captured by the Cardassians, one of whom, Gul Madred, tortures him mercilessly for his own sadistic pleasure. Guest stars: Ronny Cox and David Warner.

Chalice of Rixx — clay pot growing mold which belongs to Lwaxana in *TNG* episode "Ménage à Troi."

Chalmers, Chip — director of *TNG* episodes "Captain's Holiday," "The Loss," "The Wounded," and "Ethics." He is also assistant director of various episodes.

Chalna — homeworld of the Chalnoth people, a race of warriors, including Esoqq. Picard visited while captain of the *Stargazer* in *TNG* episode "Allegiance."

Chalnoth — anarchists, warrior inhabitants of the world Chalna. Esoqq in *TNG* episode "Allegiance" is a Chalnoth, and, in their language, his name means "fighter."

Chamber of the Ages — in Classic episode "The Devil in the Dark," the Horta refers to her "nest" of silicon eggs as "The Chamber of the Ages" and "The Altar of Tomorrow."

chameleon rose — flower presented by Wyatt to Deanna in *TNG* episode "Haven." This flower changes color according to the mood of the person holding it.

Champion, Michael — played Boratis in *TNG* "Captain's Holiday."

Chandler, Estée — played Mirren Oliana in *TNG* episode "Coming of Age."

Chandra, Captain — member of Kirk's trial board when Kirk is tried for the murder of Ben Finney in Classic episode "Court-Martial." He is played by Reginald Lalsingh.

Chandra — Child that talks in riddles, telling pieces how to get past obstacles during game Quark plays with the Waddi in *DS9* episode "Move Along Home." She is played by Clara Bryant.

Chandra V — planet mentioned in *TNG* episode "Tin Man." Tam Elbrun is the only Federation delegate assigned there.

Chandrans — peaceful inhabitants of Chandra V encountered in *TNG* episode "Tin Man." For them, saying "hello" can involve a three-day ritual.

Chang — Klingon warrior in the Classic *Trek* film *The Undiscovered Country*, played by Christopher Plummer. He frames Kirk for the murder of Gorkon and attacks the *Enterprise* at Khittomer.

Chang, Lieutenant — tactical officer in *TNG* episode "Coming of Age" who is Wesley's proctor for his Academy exam. He was played by Robert Ito.

Changeling — term used in Classic episode "The Changeling," which refers to the term for a fairy child substituted for human child. The machine Nomad is called a "changeling" because it is not the same as when Earth sent it off to explore life in the year 2002. It merged with a machine called *Tan ru* and became a murdering machine. The term is also used to describe Odo in *DS9* episode "Vortex." Crodon calls him a changeling since he's met the race in the Gamma Quadrant and they are shapeshifters. He is lying, retelling a myth, but Odo could still be related to changelings. It is a mystery he has been trying to solve all his life.

"Changeling, The" — written by John Meredyth Lucas, directed by Marc Daniels, this second-season Classic *Trek* episode aired 9/29/67. Nomad is a probe that merged with another machine, *Tan ru*, altering its programming from that of seeking out life to that of destroying it. It believes Kirk is its creator because Kirk's name resembles that of its maker, and so does not immediately destroy the *Enterprise*. Guest stars: Blaisdell Makee, Barbara Gates, Arnold Lessing, and Vic Perrin (voice of Nomad). Of note: The plot of the Classic film *Star Trek: The Motion Picture* derives much from this episode.

Channel E — channel Nilz Baris uses to contact the *Enterprise* in Classic episode "The Trouble with Tribbles."

Channing, Dr. — dilitium theorist whom Wesley studies, mentioned in *TNG* episode "Lonely among Us."

chant — in Classic episode "And the Children Shall Lead," the five kids chant: "Hail, hail, fire and snow,/call the angel we will go/far away for to see/friendly angel come to me." They stand in a circle with their hands placed in the center, one on top of the other. After they finish the chant, Gorgon appears to tell them what to do.

Chao, Rosalind — actress who played Keiko in *TNG* episodes "Data's Day," "The Wounded," "Night Terrors," "In Theory," "Disaster," "Violations," and "Power Play." She is also a regular on *DS9*. Her character is married to Miles O'Brien; they have a small daughter.

Chapel, Christine, Nurse (later Doctor) — recurring character on Classic *Trek*, played by Majel

Barrett. She is the head nurse on the *Enterprise*, and by *Star Trek: The Motion Picture* has become a doctor. She has a secret, unrequited crush on Spock. Her fiancé, Dr. Roger Korby, died on Exo III in Classic episode "What Are Little Girls Made Of?," the first episode to present Chapel. After that incident, she becomes McCoy's head nurse. Although recurring, she remains a minor character. Little else is known of her.

Chapman, Lanei — actress who played Rager in *TNG* "Galaxy's Child," "Night Terrors," and "Relics."

***Charleston*, USS** — this ship was to rendezvous with the *Enterprise* in *TNG* episode "The Neutral Zone."

"Charlie X" — first-season, Classic *Trek* episode aired 9/15/66 penned by D. C. Fontana and Gene Roddenberry. Larry Dobkin directs a story involving an orphan, Charlie Evans, marooned on an alien planet and raised by psychokinetic energy beings who teach him their powers. Guest star: Robert Walker, Jr. Of note: In this episode, Uhura sings a song to/about Spock, Janice Rand gets smacked on the behind, and Spock first plays his Vulcan harp (or lyre, or lytherette).

Charno, Sara — scriptwriter of *TNG* episodes "The Wounded," "New Ground," and "Ethics" (with Stuart Charno).

Charno, Stuart — scriptwriter of *TNG* episodes "The Wounded" (with Cy Chermak), "New Ground," and "Ethics" (with Sara Charno).

Charnoks' Comedy Cabaret — club simulated by Data on the holodeck in *TNG* episode "The Outrageous Okona."

Charybdis — lost NASA exploratory ship launched July 23, 2037, from America. Mentioned in the *TNG* episode "The Royale."

"Chase, The" — sixth-season *TNG* episode written by

Joe Menosky and Ronald D. Moore, directed by Jonathan Frakes. An old archeology professor of Picard's, Galen, comes aboard the *Enterprise* with knowledge of a rare discovery on a microscopic level. He dies when his shuttle is attacked by Yridians in an attempt to steal his information, which is of galactic significance. It is a message from a long-dead race who seeded many worlds, hoping that by the time the offspring of their seedings had the technology to unravel the message, they would be living in a world of peace and fellowship. Guest stars: Norman Lloyd, Linda Thorson, John Cothran, Jr., Maurice Roeves, and Salome Jens.

Chattaway, Jay — composer of music in *TNG* "Tin Man."

Chaya VII — place Leah Brahms visited mentioned in *TNG* episode "Booby Trap."

chech'tluth — Klingon drink seen in *TNG* episode "Up the Long Ladder."

Chekov, Pavel, Ensign — major character in Classic *Trek*, played by Walter Koenig. He appears in second season beginning with the episode "Who Mourns for Adonais?" A Russian, the *Enterprise* navigator is supposedly only 22 when first seen. He is very proud of his Russian heritage, and often jokes that Russians invented almost everything good in Earth history. Little is known of his family. He is apparently single, and becomes close friends with Sulu. They take leave together in *The Final Frontier*, only to get lost hiking through a forest on Earth. They are beamed back to the ship by Uhura. Chekov achieves the rank of "commander" by the time of the *Star Trek* movies, and is the first officer of the ship *Reliant* under the command of Captain Terrell in *The Wrath of Khan*. In *The Motion Picture* he is the *Enterprise* weapons officer. In the later films, he is restationed on the *Enterprise*. In "Mirror, Mirror," Chekov is an assassin.

Chekov, Piotr — mentioned in Classic episode "Day Of the Dove," he is supposedly Chekov's brother who was killed by Klingons in a raid on an outpost. This is not a true memory as Chekov never had a brother, according to Sulu.

Cheney, Ensign — in *TNG* episode "Lessons," she plays in a chamber music trio with Data and Lt. Commander Nella Daren.

Chermak, Cy — scriptwriter of *TNG* episode "The Wounded" (with Sara and Stuart Charno).

Cheron — homeworld of Lokai and Bele in Classic episode "Let That Be Your Last Battlefield" which was completely destroyed by race wars.

Cheron, Battle of — battle in which the Federation humiliated the Romulans, mentioned in *TNG* episode "The Defector."

Chess, Joe — camera operator on *DS9*.

Chess, 3-D — Kirk and Spock's favorite pastime is a three-dimensional form of chess. They are good opponents for each other as Kirk often wins utilizing intuition rather than formal logic, easily fooling Spock. Kirk uses a chess move code to communicate to the *Enterprise* from Elba II in the Classic *Trek* episode "Whom Gods Destroy."

Chicago Mobs of the Twenties — title of the book left behind on Iotia by the *Horizon* that directed their whole culture in Classic episode "A Piece of the Action."

Chief Officer, Commission of Political Traitors — Bele's official title in Classic episode "Let That Be Your Last Battlefield."

Chilberg, John E. — art director of the Classic *Trek* film *The Search for Spock*.

"Child, The" — second-season *TNG* episode written by Jaron Summers, Jon Povill, and Maurice Hurley and directed by Rob Bowman. New chief of surgery Kate Pulaski comes aboard the *Enterprise* to replace Dr. Crusher for a season, and Troi becomes mysteriously pregnant by an energy alien. Her gestation lasts two days and the alien boy who is born ages extraordinarily rapidly. Guest stars: Seymour Cassel, R. J. Williams, Dawn Arnemann, Zachary Benjamin, and Dore Keller. Whoopi Goldberg appears for the first time as Guinan.

Childress, Ben — character played by Gene Dynarski in Classic episode "Mudd's Women," he is a lithium miner on Rigel XII. He marries Eve McHuron.

chime, Betazoid — chime customarily used during a Betazoid meal as a means for giving thanks, seen in the *TNG* episode "Haven."

Chiya VII — mentioned in *TNG* episode "Booby Trap" as a site for many intergalactic caucuses.

Chomsky, Marvin — director of Classic *Trek* episodes "And the Children Shall Lead," "Day of the Dove," and "All Our Yesterdays." Born in 1929, he directed *Assault on the Wayne* ('70, starring Leonard Nimoy), *Holocaust* ('78), *Attica*, and *Inside the Third Reich* ('81), winning an Emmy each time.

Chorgon — leader of the Gatherers in *TNG* episode "The Vengeance Factor," played by Stephen Lee.

chorus — group of people—a woman, a scholar, a warrior—who are a team that communicates for Riva, a famous mediator in *TNG* episode "Loud as a Whisper." The chorus translates his emotions but are later killed in an accident, leaving Riva uncommunicative.

Christina — O'Brien's pet tarantula, which he found on Titus IV and mentioned in *TNG* episode "Realm of Fear."

Christopher, John, Captain — twentieth-century Air Force pilot beamed aboard the *Enterprise* in Classic *Trek* episode "Tomorrow Is Yesterday," played by Roger Perry. The action threatens to change history because Christopher's future son, Shaun Geoffrey, is destined to man an

Earth–Saturn probe significant in the exploration of space. The *Enterprise* must return him to Earth without affecting history. At the time, Christopher has a wife and two children, both daughters, as he tells Spock he has no son.

Christopher, Shaun Geoffrey, Colonel — future son of Captain John Christopher, who will head the Earth–Saturn probe, a significant moment in space exploration history mentioned in Classic *Trek* episode "Tomorrow Is Yesterday."

Christopher, Dr. — subspace theoretician whose wife, Dr. T'Pan, and he criticize Dr. Reyga's theories in *TNG* episode "Suspicions."

Chrysalians — peaceful race encountered in *TNG* episode "The Price."

Chuft, Captain — leader of the Kzin in animated episode "The Slaver Weapon."

Chula, Valley of — mentioned as being on the planet Romulus in *TNG* episode "The Defector."

Cignoni, Diana — actress who plays Dabo Girl in *DS9*.

Circausian plague cat — pet Geordi had when he was eight, mentioned in *TNG* episode "Violations."

Circonea — world having a dispute with the Rekkags, mentioned in *TNG* episode "Man of the People."

"City on the Edge of Forever, The" — first-season Classic *Trek* scripted by award-winning author Harlan Ellison, directed by Joseph Pevney, aired 4/6/67. McCoy, delirious from an accident, beams down to the mysterious planet the *Enterprise* is investigating. The landing party discovers The Guardian of Forever portal, and McCoy jumps through to a different time. Somehow his actions change the future and the *Enterprise* no longer orbits. Kirk and Spock follow to save the future they all know. Guest stars: David L. Ross, Hal Boylor, Joan Collins, John Harmon, and John Winston. Of note: The original, uncut version of Ellison's script is published in *Six Science Fiction Plays*, edited by Roger Elwood. Ellison never approved of Gene Roddenberry's changes to his script, and never hid that his *Star Trek* experience was an unhappy one. The episode won the Hugo Award for Best Dramatic Presentation in 1967.

Claiborne, Billy — member of the Clanton gang Chekov is supposed to be in Classic episode "Spectre of the Gun."

Clancy, Ensign — assistant engineer on the *Enterprise* who later became the ops officer in *TNG* episodes "Elementary, Dear Data" and "The Emissary." She is played by Anne Elizabeth Ramsey.

Clanton, Billy — member of the Clanton gang Scotty is supposed to be in Classic episode "Spectre of the Gun."

Clanton, Ike — leader of the Clanton gang Kirk is supposed to be in Classic episode "Spectre of the Gun."

Clapp, Gordon — actor in *DS9* episode "Vortex."

Clark, Bob — actor who played the Gorn in the Classic *Trek* episode "Arena." He also was a stunt man in "Return of the Archons," an extra in "Mirror, Mirror," and a native in "The Apple." His other TV credits include *Bonanza* and *Gunsmoke*.

Clark, Josh — actor who played bridge position in *TNG* episode "Justice."

Clark, Howard, Doctor — head of the Federation science team on Ventax II in *TNG* episode "Devil's Due," played by Paul Lambert.

class 1 probe — mentioned in *TNG* episodes "Time Squared," "Yesterday's Enterprise," "The Defector," and "Pen Pals." They are used to get information at a distance.

class 2 probe — launched from the *Enterprise* in *TNG* episode "The Most Toys" to deliver hytritium to the water source contaminated by tricyanate.

class 3 probe — machine with a neutrino beacon sent to the Galorndon Core in *TNG* episode "The Enemy."

class 8 probe — can travel at warp 9 and is seen in *TNG* episode "The Emissary."

class J cargo ship — referred to in Classic episode "Mudd's Women" as the size of Harry Mudd's ship.

class J starship — older vessels used for trainees mentioned in Classic episode "The Menagerie."

class M planet — Earth-like world suitable for human survival, also known on *TNG* as a class M atmosphere.

Claudius Marcus — see entry for Marcus, Claudius.

Claymare — Organian elder in Classic episode "Errand Of Mercy," played by Peter Brocco.

Cleary, Lieutenant — crew member of the *Enterprise*, played by Michael Roygas in the Classic *Trek* film *The Motion Picture*.

Clemons, L. Q. ("Sonny") — cryonically frozen human from *TNG* episode "The Neutral Zone," played by Leon Rippy. The character died of drug abuse and was brought back to life in the 24th century.

Cleponji — thousand-year-old Promellian battlecruiser, commanded by Galek Sar, found by the *Enterprise* in *TNG* episode "Booby Trap." It is trapped in the Menthar booby trap.

Cliffs of Heaven — place from which an officer of the *Enterprise* jumps in a holodeck re-creation, straining her shoulder, in *TNG* episode "Conundrum."

cloaking device — invisibility shield used by Romulans, first encountered in Classic episode "Balance of Terror."

Kirk and Spock later steal the technology in a complex undercover plot in "The *Enterprise* Incident."

cloth, Mintakan — ornament given as a gift to Picard by Nuria and Haki in *TNG* episode "Who Watches the Watchers." Seen again in "Sarek."

Cloud City — see entry for Stratos.

cloud creature — several cloudlike creatures are encountered in the series. Kirk encounters the vampire cloud in the Classic *Trek* episode "Obsession." In *TNG* episode "Lonely among Us" the *Enterprise* and several of its crew are taken over by another cloud creature.

"Cloud Minders, The" — written by Margaret Armen, David Gerrold, and Oliver Crawford, this third-season Classic *Trek* episode aired 2/28/69. The *Enterprise* pays a visit to Ardana, a world with a vast cloud city. The ship needs to shuttle the zienite from Ardana's mines to a nearby world where it is the only known cure for a plague. Kirk and Spock become embroiled in a struggle between the cloud city dwellers and the miners on the planet below, and the ship and millions of people awaiting the shipment are threatened. Guest stars: Jeff Corey, Diana Ewing, Charlene Polite, Fred Williamson, and Ed Long.

Cloud William — a Yang, one of the group fighting the Kohms, played by Roy Jenson in Classic *Trek* episode "The Omega Glory."

Clow, Chuck — stunt man in the Classic *Trek* episode "Friday's Child."

Clowes, Carolyn — author of Classic *Trek* novel *The Pandora Principle*.

"Clues" — fourth-season *TNG* episode written by Bruce D. Arthurs and Joe Menosky, directed by Les Landau. The crew discovers that 24 hours of their lives have been lost, and they investigate. Data interferes with the investigation, even lying to Picard. Guest stars: Whoopi Goldberg,

Rhonda Aldrich, Pamela Winslow, Colm Meaney, and Thomas Knickerbocker.

Coalition of Madina — twin planets, Atlek and Streleb, mentioned in *TNG* episode "The Outrageous Okona."

coalsack — term for a dark spot in the galaxy used in Classic episode "Let That Be Your Last Battlefield." Cheron is located near a coalsack.

Cobb, Julie — actress who played Yeoman Leslie Thompson in the Classic *Trek* episode "By Any Other Name." She held regular roles in the TV series *A Year at the Top, The DA,* and *Charles in Charge.* TV movies include: *The Death Squad* ('74), *Salem's Lot* ('79), and *Brave New World* ('80).

Coburn, David — actor in *TNG* episode "The Nth Degree."

Cochrane, Zefrem — inventor of the warp drive in Classic episode "Metamorphosis," played by Glenn Corbett. He has been marooned on an asteroid with the "companion," a cloud creature that keeps him young, healthy, and immortal. When Kirk, Spock, and McCoy encounter him, he is over 200 years old, and has been alone for a long time. The "companion" brought the shuttlecraft to the asteroid so Cochrane could have human company.

Cochrane deceleration maneuver — battle maneuver mentioned by Spock in Classic episode "Whom Gods Destroy." In *TNG* episode "Ménage à Troi," Riker refers to a Cochrane distortion.

coco-no-no — drink Geordi offers Christy in *TNG* episode "Booby Trap."

Code 1 — warning used when war or invasion will occur. It appears in the Classic episodes "The Alternative Factor" and "Errand of Mercy."

Code 2 — code the Romulans break in Classic episode "The Deadly Years." A forgetful, aging Kirk mistakenly orders this code used to send messages.

Code 3 — code the Romulans do not break in Classic episode "The Deadly Years."

Code 47 — emergency transmission for captain's eyes only, mentioned in *TNG* episode "Conspiracy."

Code 710 — term used by the planet Eminiar VII which means under no circumstances to approach their world in Classic episode "A Taste of Armageddon."

"Code of Honor" — first-season *TNG* episode written by Kathryn Powers and Michael Baron, directed by Russ Mayberry. Yar is kidnapped by the leader, Lutan, on a planet named Ligon II. She is forced to fight a death duel. Guest stars: Jessie Lawrence Ferguson, Karole Selmon, James Louis Watkins, and Michael Rider.

Code One, Alpha Zero — code for a Federation starship in distress in *TNG* episode "Relics."

Coe, George — actor in *TNG* episode "First Contact."

Coffey, Gordon — actor who played a Romulan soldier in the Classic *Trek* episode "The *Enterprise* Incident."

Cogan, Rhodie — actress who played First Witch in Classic *Trek* episode "Catspaw."

Cogley, Samuel T. — Kirk's lawyer in Classic episode "Court-Martial," played by Elisha Cook, Jr. He loves books and is a brilliant defender. When Kirk is acquitted of killing Finney, Cogley defends Finney against charges brought against him for trying to frame Kirk.

Cogswell, Theodore R. — author of the Classic *Trek* novel *Spock Messiah!* (with Charles A. Spano, Jr.)

Cole, Megan — actress in *TNG* episode "The Outcast."

Coleman, Arthur, Dr. — character in Classic *Trek*

episode "Turnabout Intruder," played by Harry Landers. He is in love with Janice Lester, and helps her try to take over Kirk's body and the *Enterprise*. He also helps her murder a scientific team by exposing them to celebium radiation.

Colicos, John — actor who played Kor, the Klingon commander in the Classic *Trek* episode "Errand of Mercy." He also was a regular in the science-fiction TV series *Battlestar Galactica*. He was born in Canada in 1928.

Colla, Richard — director of *TNG* episode "The Last Outpost."

Colleena — young woman Picard makes a date with in *TNG* episode "Tapestry." She later slaps him.

Collins, Christopher — actor who plays Grebnedlog in *TNG* episode "Samaritan Snare" and Captain Kargan in "A Matter of Honor." He is also in the *DS9* episode "The Passenger."

Collins, Joan — actress who played Edith Keeler in the Classic *Trek* episode "The City on the Edge of Forever." Born in London in 1933, her credits are numerous. She is most famous for her role as a villainous woman on the TV series *Dynasty*. Her sister Jackie Collins is a best-selling author.

Collins, Sheldon — actor who played the young boy in the Classic *Trek* episode "A Piece of the Action."

Collins, Stephen — actor who played Commander Will Decker in Classic *Trek* film *Star Trek: The Motion Picture*. The character is the son of Matt Decker ("The Doomsday Machine"). The actor was born in 1947 in Iowa and appeared on Broadway and guest starred in many TV shows, including *The Waltons* and *Charlie's Angels*. His TV series include *Tales of the Gold Monkey*. One of his best performances is opposite Whoopi Goldberg in the film *Jumpin' Jack Flash*.

Collis, Jack T. — production designer of the Classic

Trek film *The Voyage Home*. Other credits include: *The Four Seasons* ('81), *Paternity* ('81), *Tex* ('82), *Night Shift* ('82), *National Lampoon's Vacation* ('83), and *Splash* ('84).

Collison, Frank — actor in *TNG* "Ensign Ro."

Colony V — the *Enterprise*'s destination for Charlie in Classic episode "Charlie X." Apparently Charlie has relatives there.

Colt, J. M., Yeoman — young woman with a crush on Captain Pike in Classic pilot "The Cage" ("The Menagerie") played by Laurel Goodwin.

Coltair IV — planet that experiences the time distortion mentioned in *TNG* episode "We'll Always Have Paris."

***Columbia*, USS** — ship in Classic pilot "The Cage" from which Vina, horribly crippled, was the only survivor.

Columbus — shuttlecraft onboard the *Enterprise*, first seen in Classic episode "The Galileo Seven."

Combs, David Q. — actor who played a mediator in *TNG* episode "Justice."

Comi, Paul — actor who played the centurion in the Classic *Trek* episode "Balance of Terror." His TV credits include *Voyage to the Bottom of the Sea* and *Barnaby Jones*. Films include *Warlock* ('59), *Pork Chop Hill* ('59), and *Cry Rape!* ('73).

Comic — character played by Joe Piscopo on Data's holodeck re-creation in *TNG* episode "The Outrageous Okona."

"Coming of Age" — first-season *TNG* episode written by Sandy Fries and directed by Michael Vejar. Wesley takes the Starfleet Academy entrance exam on Relva VII while an investigation is undertaken to test Picard's loyalties to Starfleet. Guest stars: Estée Chandler, Daniel Riordan, Brendan McKane, Wyatt Knight, Ward Costello, Robert Schekkan, Robert Ito, John Putch, Stephan Gregory, and Tasia Valenza.

Command Level — reference to the level of *DS9* that holds the ops center.

common cold — by the time of *Star Trek*, the cure for the common cold has been found. This is mentioned in *TNG* episode "Angel One."

communicator — device like a futuristic walkie-talkie or cellular phone. In Classic *Trek*, it is a square box with a grid that flips up. In *The Motion Picture* it is a wrist bracelet. On *TNG* and *DS9* it is the insignia pin on the Starfleet uniforms.

Companion, The — misty cloud-being in Classic episode "Metamorphosis" who takes care of "the man," Zefrem Cochrane, maintaining his health and youth for 150 years and communicating by surrounding him with its energy. It exists on the asteroid remnant of the destroyed planet Gamma Canaris N. It directs the shuttlecraft to the asteroid against its will to provide human companionship for the lonely Cochrane. Voice is provided by Majel Barrett.

Complete Klingon Culture Index — book Wesley reads to find out about the Klingon custom the Age of Ascension in *TNG* episode "The Icarus Factor."

Compton, Richard — actor/director who played Washburn in Classic *Trek* episode "The Doomsday Machine" and the technical officer in "The *Enterprise* Incident." He also directed *TNG* episode "Haven."

Compton, Crewman — character played by Geoffrey Binney in Classic episode "Wink of an Eye." He is accelerated to the level of the Scalosians only to die of a minor injury that causes his cellular structure to age and decompose.

comptronics — computer technology invented by Dr. Richard Daystrom in Classic episode "The Ultimate Computer."

computer — the *Enterprise* computer is a vast voice-command system that helps run the ship. The voice is provided by Majel Barrett. Other computers run the society in Classic episode "The Return of the Archons," the Bynars in *TNG* episode "11001001," and the Borg on *TNG*. In Classic *Trek* "For the World Is Hollow and I Have Touched the Sky," Yonada is run by a computer. In "A Taste of Armageddon," Eminiar and Vendikar conduct war by computers. There are portable computers, desk computers, diagnostic computers, library computers, and many others mentioned throughout all three series and movies.

Con — command of the bridge; short for "consoles."

Condition Green — code Kirk uses in Classic episode "Bread and Circuses" that means the landing party is in danger but the *Enterprise* must not interfere.

Conley, Lawrence V. — scriptwriter of *TNG* episode "Silicon Avatar."

Conor, Aaron — Troi's lover and leader of the Moab IV colony in *TNG* episode "The Masterpiece Society," played by John Snyder.

Conrad, Bart — played Captain Krasnowsky in the Classic *Trek* episode "Court-Martial." His TV credits include *Perry Mason*.

"Conscience of the King, The" — first-season Classic *Trek* episode written by Barry Trivers and directed by Gerd Oswald aired 12/8/66. A troupe of actors comes aboard the *Enterprise* and Kirk thinks the star is really the infamous Kodos the Executioner of Tarsus IV, who killed thousands of people to prevent all from dying of starvation. Kirk was on Tarsus as a child when this happened, and he and Lt. Kevin Riley are two of only three survivors still alive. Guest stars: Arnold Moss, Barbara Anderson, Bruce Hyde, Eddie Paskey, and William Sargent. Of note: The return of Kevin Thomas Riley delighted fans, *Hamlet* by Shakespeare is performed for the crew, and Uhura sings "Beyond Antares" (words written by Gene L. Coon) to Riley.

"Conspiracy" — first-season *TNG* episode written by Robert Sabaroff and Tracy Torme, directed by Cliff Bole. Picard is warned by his old friend Walker Keel that there is a conspiracy by top officials to undermine Starfleet. Walker's ship is then destroyed, leading Picard on a journey during which he discovers an invasion via parasites into the bodies of some very powerful Starfleet officials. Guest stars: Michael Berryman, Ursaline Bryant, Henry Darrow, Robert Schenkkan, and Jonathan Farwell.

Constantinople — Federation transport ship in distress in *TNG* episode "The Schizoid Man."

***Constellation*, USS** — starship attacked by the doomsday device in Classic episode "The Doomsday Machine." All hands are lost after Captain Decker beams them down to a nearby world, supposedly to save them, only to watch in horror as the machine eats the world. The ship is damaged, used in conjunction with the *Enterprise* to destroy the deadly war device, and, ultimately, destroyed.

***Constellation*-class starship** — the USS *Stargazer* commanded by Picard was one of this class of starship with four warp nacelles.

***Constitution*-class starship** — the first *Enterprise* from Classic *Trek* is of this class of starship.

"Contagion" — second-season *TNG* episode written by Steve Gerber and Beth Woods, directed by Rob Bowman. A computer virus that is transmitted to the *Yamato* destroys it, and the *Enterprise* becomes infected. Meanwhile, a Romulan ship is in orbit about Iconia, where the virus seems to originate. Guest stars: Thalmus Rasulala, Carolyn Seymour, Dana Sparks, Folkert Schmidt, and Colm Meaney.

control coils — integral parts of Ornaran freighters mentioned in *TNG* episode "Symbiosis."

Controller, The — in Classic episode "Spock's Brain" the Eymorgs refer to Spock's brain as the Controller.

"Conundrum" — fifth-season *TNG* episode written by Paul Schiffer, Barry M. Schkolnick, and Joe Menosky, directed by Les Landau. The Lysians wipe the minds of the *Enterprise* crew, who awaken to find themselves in the middle of a war. Nobody recognizes the new bridge crewman. Guest stars: Erich Anderson, Kieran MacDuff, Michelle Forbes, Liz Vassey, and Erick Weiss.

Conway, James L. — director of *TNG* episodes "Justice," "The Neutral Zone," and "Frame of Mind."

Conway, Kevin — played the cloned Kahless in *TNG* episode "Rightful Heir."

Cook, Elisha, Jr. — played Samuel T. Cogley, attorney-at-law in the Classic *Trek* episode "Court-Martial." Born in San Francisco in 1906, his film credits include *The Maltese Falcon*, *The Big Sleep*, *Shane*, *Rosemary's Baby*, and *Carny*. TV credits: *The Bionic Woman* and *The Man from U.N.C.L.E.*, among others.

Coombs, Gary — stunt man in Classic *Trek* episodes "The Galileo Seven," "Arena," "Errand of Mercy," "Space Seed," "The Alternative Factor," and "Operation: Annihilate!"

Coon, Gene L. — writer/producer of Classic *Trek* who also wrote under the name Lee Cronin. He wrote "Arena," "Space Seed," "A Taste of Armageddon," "Devil in the Dark," "Errand of Mercy," "The Apple," "Metamorphosis," "A Piece of the Action," "Bread and Circuses," "Spock's Brain," "Spectre of the Gun," "Wink of an Eye," and "Let That Be Your Last Battlefield." He also worked with Gene Roddenberry on the movie *The Questor Tapes*, and died in 1974.

Cooper, Charles — played K'mpec on *TNG* episode "Sins of the Father," and acted in "Reunion."

Cooper, Sonni — author of the Classic *Trek* novel *Black Fire*.

Copage, John — played Elliot in Classic *Trek* episode "The Doomsday Machine."

Copernicus — shuttlecraft on the *Enterprise* first referred to in animated episode "The Slaver Weapon."

Cor Caroli V — world cured of a phyrox plague in *TNG* episode "Allegiance."

coradrenalin — medication for treating frostbite and exposure McCoy needs in Classic episode "All Our Yesterdays."

Corbett, Glenn — played Zefrem Cochrane in Classic *Trek* episode "Metamorphosis." Born in 1934, his many credits include *Midway*, *Route 66*, *The Road West*, and *Dallas*.

corbomite — imaginary substance Kirk fantasizes to delay the people of the First Federation from attacking the *Enterprise* in Classic episode "The Corbomite Maneuver." Kirk says it is a substance that is contained in the ship's hull that will blow up when the ship is destroyed and reflect the energy back on the attacker.

"Corbomite Maneuver, The" — written by Jerry Sohl and directed by Joe Sargent, this Classic *Trek* first-season episode aired 11/10/66. The *Enterprise* encounters a space buoy that blocks them and then threatens to destroy them. The word "corbomite" refers to a nonexistent substance Kirk makes up to "bluff" aliens into a less hostile approach. Guest stars: Anthony Call and Clint Howard (Ron Howard's younger brother).

Cord, Erik — played a thug in *TNG* episode "The Big Goodbye."

cordrazine — miracle drug that can save or kill a deathly ill person, depending upon the dosage and problem.

McCoy accidentally injects himself with cordrazine in Classic episode "The City on the Edge of Forever," goes insane, and leaps through the Guardian of Forever into Earth's past, changing all of history.

Corey, Jeff — played Plasus in Classic *Trek* episode "The Cloud Minders." Born in 1914, he also taught acting. His films include *The Man Who Wouldn't Die*, *Seconds*, and *Beneath the Planet of the Apes*.

Coridan — system of worlds that wishes admission to the Federation. In Classic episode "Journey to Babel," the Babel Conference is being held to decide this issue. Orion mining pirates have, in the past, raided the Coridan system because its worlds are rich in minerals.

Corinth IV — location of a starbase mentioned in Classic episode "Metamorphosis."

Cornelian system — destination of the *Enterprise* when it is trapped in a void in *TNG* episode "Where Silence Has Lease."

Correll, Charles — director of photography of *The Search for Spock*. Other credits include *Cheech and Chong's Nice Dreams* and *The Joy of Sex*.

Correllium fever — disease on Nahmi IV in *TNG* episode "Hollow Pursuits."

Correy, Lee — author of the Classic *Trek* novel *The Abode of Life*.

Corrigan — old friend of Kirk's who turns his back on him when Kirk walks into the bar on the starbase in Classic episode "Court-Martial."

Corsentino, Frank — played Bok in *TNG* episode "The Battle," and DaiMon Tog, Ferengi captain of the *Krayton*, in *TNG* episode "Ménage à Troi."

cortropine — stimulant McCoy uses to keep the crew alive in animated episode "The Lorelei Signal."

Corvallens — mercenary race that Troi senses will betray the Romulans in *TNG* episode "Face of the Enemy."

Cory, Donald — character played by Keye Luke in Classic *Trek* episode "Whom Gods Destroy," who runs the penal colony on Elba II.

"Cost of Living" — fifth-season *TNG* episode written by Peter Allan Fields, directed by Winrich Kolbe. Parasites are eating the *Enterprise*. Meanwhile, Lwaxana takes a lonely Alexander under her wing and entertains him on the holodeck. Guest stars: Majel Barrett, Brian Bonsall, Tony Jay, Carel Struycken, Patrick Cronin, Albie Setznick, David Oliver, Tracy D'Arcy, George Edie, and Christopher Halste.

Costanzo, Robert — played Slade Bender in *TNG* "Manhunt."

Costello, Ward — played Admiral Gregory Quinn in *TNG* episodes "Coming of Age" and "Conspiracy."

Coster, Nicolas — played Admiral Anthony Haftel in *TNG* episode "The Offspring." He has numerous acting credits, including recurring roles on *The Facts of Life* and in movies such as *Little Darlings*. (In 1993, he showed up on *As the World Turns*.)

Cothran, John, Jr. — played Klingon Captain Nu'Daq in *TNG* episode "The Chase."

Cottrell, Mickey — actor in *TNG* episode "The Perfect Mate."

Couch, Chuck — stunt man in Classic *Trek* episode "Space Seed."

Couch, William — stunt man in *Star Trek: The Motion Picture*. Has also worked on the films *Dead and Buried* and *Brainstorm*.

Council of Elders — head leaders of Organia from Classic episode "Errand of Mercy."

Council of Nobles — ruling class of Elas from Classic episode "Elaan of Troyius."

"Counter-Clock Incident, The" — written by John Culver, this animated Classic *Trek* episode aired 10/12/74. The first captain of the *Enterprise*, Commodore Robert April and his wife, Sara April, are being transported by the ship to Babel. En route, they encounter a ship heading straight for a nova, Beta Niobe. They lock onto the ship trying to save it but are pulled into the nova and an antimatter universe where the sky is white, the stars are black, and time flows backward. There they encounter a race of beings on the planet Arret. The crew rapidly ages backward until they are toddlers and cannot run the ship. April and his wife must save the day, since they were older to begin with and are now young adults who can still remember how to run the ship.

Courage, Alexander — composer who scored the original series theme. He also wrote much of the music for the episodes. Born in 1919, his credits include *Voyage to the Bottom of the Sea* and *Lost in Space*, and the musicals *Porgy and Bess*, *Doctor Doolittle*, and *Fiddler on the Roof*. Gene Roddenberry wrote the words to the *Star Trek* theme as the poem "Star Trek."

"Court-Martial" — first-season Classic *Trek* episode written by Don M. Mankiewicz and Stephen W. Carabatsos, directed by Marc Daniels, which aired 2/2/67. Kirk stands accused of the death of a crewman. He will lose everything unless he can prove he did not make the error, but the video records (as we have learned almost 30 years later in the '90s) are very damning. Guest stars: Percy Rodriguez, Elisha Cook, Jr., Joan Marshall, Richard Webb, Alice Rawlings, and Hagen Beggs. Of note: Kirk kisses his old flame on the bridge of the *Enterprise*, showing he has no grudge against her, even though she was the prosecutor in the trial.

Courtney, Chuck — played Davod in the Classic *Trek* episode "Patterns of Force."

Cousins, Brian — actor in *TNG* "The Next Phase."

Cox, Nikki — played Sarjenka in *TNG* "Pen Pals." She has done movies and TV commercials.

Cox, Richard — played Kyril Finn in *TNG* "The High Ground."

Cox, Ronny — guest star in *TNG* episode "Chain of Command."

Craig, Yvonne — played Marta in Classic *Trek* episode "Whom Gods Destroy." Born in 1941, her numerous credits include Batgirl in the *Batman* series.

Crandell, Melissa — author of Classic *Trek* novel *Shell Game*.

Crater, Nancy — McCoy's old girlfriend who apparently reappears in Classic episode "The Man Trap." Actually it is a creature that has taken her shape from McCoy's and Professor Crater's minds to fool the *Enterprise* crew. The real Nancy actually died at the hands of the creature. She called McCoy by the nickname "Plum."

Crater, Robert, Professor — archeologist on planet M–113, played by Alfred Ryder in Classic episode "The Man Trap," who is protecting a creature that killed his wife.

Crawford, John — played Commissioner Ferris in Classic *Trek* episode "The Galileo Seven." Born in 1926, his credits include *Satan's Satellites* (with Leonard Nimoy), *Voyage to the Bottom of the Sea*, and a semiregular stint on *The Waltons*.

Crawford, Oliver — scriptwriter who penned Classic *Trek* episodes "The Galileo Seven," "Let That Be Your Last Battlefield," and "The Cloud Minders." He also wrote scripts for TV shows including *Voyage to the Bottom of the Sea*, *The Rifleman*, *The Bionic Woman*, and *Perry Mason*.

Crazy Horse, USS — attack ship in *TNG* episode "Descent."

Creaghan, Dennis — actor in *TNG* episode "Family."

credit — monetary unit of the Federation in all three series, though gold-pressed latinum seems to be favored on *DS9*.

crimson force field — term Riker makes up in *TNG* episode "Samaritan Snare" to describe the exhaust of the hydrogen collectors he pretends is a force field.

Crisalians — race of beings negotiating on the bidding for the Barzan wormhole in *TNG* episode "The Price."

Crispin, A. C. — author of Classic *Trek* novels *Yesterday's Son*, *Time for Yesterday*, and *TNG* novel *The Eyes of the Beholders*.

Crist, Paula — played a crewmember in *Star Trek: The Motion Picture*. She has also done stunt and extra work in such films as *Logan's Run*.

Crockett, Dick — stunt director who played Kirk's double in Classic *Trek* episode "Where No Man Has Gone Before," and an Andorian in "The Gamesters of Triskelion." He was also a Klingon in "The Trouble with Tribbles."

Crodon — character, played by Cliff DeYoung, who kills one of the Miradorn twins in self-defense in *DS9* episode "Vortex" and is then jailed and tried for murder.

Cromwell — launch director at McKinley Rocket Base, played by Don Keeferin, in Classic episode "Assignment: Earth."

Cromwell, James — played Prime Minister Nayrock in *TNG* episode "The Hunted," and Yaglom Shrek in "Birthright, Part I."

Cronin, Lee — scriptwriter credited for Classic episodes "Spock's Brain," "Spectre of the Gun," "Wink of an Eye," and "Let That Be Your Last Battlefield." Pen name of Gene L. Coon.

Cronin, Patrick — actor in *TNG* episode "Cost of Living."

cronitron field — Data tracks this throughout the *Enterprise* to help determine whether Ro and Geordi are still alive in *TNG* episode "The Next Phase."

Crosby, Denise — played Tasha Yar in *TNG*'s first season, then returned in "Yesterday's Enterprise," and as Yar's daughter Sela in "Redemption," "The Mind's Eye," and "Unification." Film credits include *48 Hours, Miracle Mile,* and *The Eliminators.* She also has numerous television credits. She is the granddaughter of Bing Crosby, and has also been a model, which she did not enjoy, and worked on the stage.

Crosis — Borg captured in *TNG* episode "Descent."

Crucis, Jud — scriptwriter who wrote the story for Classic *Trek* episode "A Private Little War."

Crucis system — located near Romulan space, it is mentioned in *TNG* episode "Disaster."

Crusher, Beverly C., Dr. — regular character in *TNG,* played by Gates McFadden. She is the *Enterprise* head doctor. Her husband, Jack Crusher, died under Picard's first command, when he was on an away team from the *Stargazer.* Her son, Wesley, is a genius who becomes an ensign on the *Enterprise* even before he leaves to attend Starfleet Academy. She left the *Enterprise* for one year with no explanation and was replaced by Dr. Pulaski, then returned in the third season. She and Picard are very good friends, even though she once blamed him for the death of her husband. They have breakfast together every morning, and though they seem to be attracted to one another, they rarely act on that attraction. Beverly lived on Aveda III when she was a child.

Crusher, Wesley — regular character in the first episode of *TNG,* played by Wil Wheaton. He is a child genius who helps solve many problems and is made acting ensign and then full ensign. He left the *Enterprise* to attend Starfleet Academy where he ran into trouble when involved in a cover-up of the death of a classmate. He returns to visit the *Enterprise* every once in awhile. In the *TNG* episode "Hide and Q," he becomes an adult played by actor William A. Wallace.

Crusher, Jack R., Lieutenant Commander — first officer of the *Stargazer* and husband of Dr. Beverly Crusher, he died under Picard's command. He is the father of Wesley Crusher.

cryonetrium — gaseous substance flooded into the injector pathway conduits to lower their temperature in *TNG* episode "Hollow Pursuits."

cryptobiolin — one of the elements used to create perfect soldiers in *TNG* episode "The Hunted."

Crystalline Entity — destructive entity that feeds off energy emanations of life-forms encountered in *TNG* episode "Datalore." It destroyed many planets in its path until it was killed in *TNG* episode "Silicon Avatar."

Cueller system — system in which the *Enterprise* investigates the destruction of a Cardassian station in *TNG* episode "The Wounded."

Culbreath, Myrna — author (with Sondra Marshak) of the Classic *Trek* novels *The Price of the Phoenix, The Fate of the Phoenix, Triangle, The Prometheus Design,* and editor of *Star Trek: The New Voyage* and *Star Trek: The New Voyages 2.* She also wrote (with Sondra Marshak and William Shatner) *Shatner: Where No Man,* a biography of the actor long out of print. It will never see print again because William Shatner, not liking how it turned out, bought all the rights to it.

Culea, Melinda — actress in *TNG* episode "The Outcast."

Cullum, J. D. — actor in *TNG* "Redemption."

Culver, John — scriptwriter who penned the animated "The Counter-Clock Incident."

Cummings, Bob — played Klingon Gunner in *The Search for Spock*.

Cupo, Patrick — played Bajoran Man in *DS9* episode "A Man Alone."

Curry, Dan — visual effects supervisor on various *TNG* episodes, as well as director of *TNG* episode "Birthright, Part II."

Curtis, Kelly — actress in *DS9* episode "Captive Pursuit."

Curtis, Robin — played Saavik (after Kirstie Alley did not return) in *The Search for Spock* and *The Voyage Home*. She also appeared in a seventh-season *TNG* episode as a Vulcan disguised as a Romulan.

Curzon — best friend and mentor of Benjamin Sisko whose body Dax occupied before becoming Jadzia Dax. Curzon's memories continue to be a part of Jadzia Dax. Curzon lived a long life, and died an old man. He is seen in *DS9* episode "Emissary," played by Frank Owen Smith. See entries for Trill and Dax.

Cushman, Marc — scriptwriter of *TNG* episode "Sarek."

Custodian, The — supercomputer built by progenitors on Aldea in *TNG* episode "When the Bough Breaks."

Cygnet XIV — all-female world where the *Enterprise* had its computer system overhauled. The computer was given a personality that caused it to fall in love with Kirk in Classic episode "Tomorrow Is Yesterday."

Cygnia Minor — mentioned in Classic episode "The Conscience of the King" as a world which is regularly threatened by famine.

cylodin — poison self-inflicted by the Starnes expedition under the influence of the Gorgon in Classic episode "And the Children Shall Lead." Only the children survive.

Cytherians — Barclay inadvertently becomes the Cytherians' emissary when they temporarily make him the most intelligent human in the universe in *TNG* episode "The Nth Degree." The curious humanoid Cytherians meant no harm.

D'Abo, Olivia — guest starred in *TNG* "True Q." Best known for her recurring role as Karen in *The Wonder Years*, D'Abo has also starred in several films, including *Beyond the Stars*.

dabo — gambling game played in Quark's bar on *DS9*.

Dachlyds — culture of stubborn people for whom Picard mediated a trade dispute mentioned in *TNG* episode "Captain's Holiday."

"Dagger of the Mind" — first-season Classic *Trek* episode written by Shimon Wincelberg (who also writes under the name S. Bar David) which aired 11/3/66. Directed by Vince McEveety, the story involves an asylum, or penal colony, on Tantalus V, where criminals and the mentally ill receive treatment. A new device, the neural neutralizer, which empties the brain of all thought and memory and allows the victim to be open to new suggestions, gives the head doctor Tristan Adams full control over his patients as well as his staff. Guest stars: James Gregory, Morgan Woodward (who later plays Captain Tracy in "Omega Glory"), Marianna Hill, and Suzanne Wasson. Of note: This is the first time we see the famous Vulcan mind meld performed, an invention attributed as much to Leonard Nimoy as to the show's writers.

dahk'ta — Klingon dagger Worf sees rusting in a drawer at the Carraya prison camp in *TNG* episode "Birthright."

Daily, Jon, Captain — captain of the *Astral Queen*, ship originally designated to transport the Karidian players to Benecia in Classic episode "Conscience of the King."

Daled IV — homeworld of Salia, the shapechanger from *TNG* episode "The Dauphin."

Dalton, Leslie — played Drea in Classic *Trek* "By Any Other Name."

Daly, James — played Flint in Classic *Trek* "Requiem for Methuselah." Also famous for his regular role in the TV series *Medical Center*.

Daly, Jane — played Varria in *TNG* "The Most Toys."

D'Amato, Ensign — is put on report by Worf in *TNG* episode "Sarek."

D'Amato, Lieutenant — *Enterprise* geologist, played by Arthur Batanides, killed by Losira in Classic episode "That Which Survives."

Damian, Leo — played Warrior/Adonis in *TNG* "Loud as a Whisper."

Damon, Gabriel — played Jeremy Aster in *TNG* "The Bonding."

Danar, Gul — commander of the Cardassian warship in *DS9* "Past Prologue."

Danar, Roga — perfect soldier and an Angosian veteran of the Tarsian War who yearns for his freedom. Played by Jeff McCarthy in *TNG* "The Hunted."

Danese, Connie — played Toya in *TNG* "When the Bough Breaks."

Dang, Timothy — played main bridge security in *TNG* "Encounter at Farpoint."

Daniels, Jerry — played Marple in Classic *Trek* "The Apple."

Daniels, Marc — directed Classic *Trek* episodes "The Man Trap," "The Naked Time," "The Menagerie," "Court-Martial," "Space Seed," "Who Mourns for Adonais?" "The Changeling," "Mirror, Mirror," "The Doomsday Machine," "I, Mudd," "A Private Little War," "By Any Other Name," "Assignment: Earth," "Spock's Brain," and Roddenberry's pilot "Planet Earth." He also wrote the script for the animated "One of Our Planets Is Missing" and has directed numerous other TV shows.

Dano, Kal — scientist from the 27th century who invents the *Tox Uthat* and hides it on Risa in *TNG* episode "Captain's Holiday." He later dies in the 22nd century.

Dante, Michael — played Maab in "Friday's Child." Often cast in Native American roles because of his dark looks, his films include *Kid Galahad*, *Willard*, *Shining Star*, and *Winterhawk*. He is also a writer.

Danula II — planet on which Cadet Picard won a marathon as mentioned in *TNG* episode "The Best of Both Worlds."

Danus, Richard — wrote *TNG* episodes "Déjà Q" and "Booby Trap" and became the show's executive story editor during its third season.

Danzinger, Cory — appears in *TNG* episode "Brothers."

Dara — Dr. Timicin's daughter, played by Michelle Forbes, who wants him to accept his honorable, but early death, as is the Kaelon custom in *TNG* episode "Half a Life." Forbes also played Ensign Ro (see entry).

Darabin V — planet where Lt. Uhnari was posted prior to her job on Subspace Relay Station 47 in *TNG* episode "Aquiel."

Daran V — in danger of being hit by the spaceship world Yonada, if its course is allowed to continue, in Classic episode "For the World Is Hollow and I Have Touched the Sky."

Daras — member of the Ekosian underground, played by Valora Noland, who poses as a hero of the Fatherland in Classic episode "Patterns of Force."

Darby, Kim — played Miri in Classic *Trek* episode "Miri." Born in 1948, some of her other credits include *True Grit* (with John Wayne) and *The People* (with William Shatner).

D'Arcy, Tracy — actress in *TNG* "Cost of Living."

Daren, Nella, Lieutenant Commander — head of Stellar Cartography on the *Enterprise*, and a pianist, she and Captain Picard have a brief liaison but part, still very much in love, when they realize a shipboard romance is impossible without jeopardizing their professional concerns. She asks for a transfer, and they agree to see each other during shore leaves and continue a long-distance friendship.

Daren herbal tea #3 — drink Lt. Commander Nella Daren programs into the food replicators in *TNG* episode "Lessons." Picard doesn't like the tea.

Daris, James — played a savage in Classic *Trek* "Spock's Brain."

dark matter — exists in the Mar Obscura Nebula and can cause depressurization on board starships as their hulls phase in and out of existence. Mentioned in *TNG* episode "In Theory."

"Darmok" — fifth-season *TNG* episode written by Philip Lazebnik and Joe Menosky, directed by Winrich Kolbe. A ship manned by a species which calls itself the Children of Tama is met by the *Enterprise*, but communication is nearly impossible because the Tamans speak in metaphors alluding to their own history and myth, which the *Enterprise* and its universal translator know nothing about, but must learn. Guest stars: Paul Winfield, Richard Allen, Colm Meaney, and Ashley Judd.

Darnay's disease — illness afflicting Graves in *TNG* episode "The Schizoid Man."

Darnell — crewman, played by Michael Zaslow, killed by the salt vampire in Classic episode "The Man Trap" and found with a piece of borgia plant in his mouth.

Daro, Glenn — member of the Cardassian delegation, played by Tim Winters, who comes aboard the *Enterprise* in *TNG* episode "The Wounded."

Darrow, Henry — played Admiral Savar in *TNG* episode "Conspiracy."

Darson, Captain — commander of the ship *Adelphi*, who died in the Ghorusda disaster in *TNG* episode "Tin Man."

Darvin, Arne — Klingon, played by Charlie Brill, disguised as an assistant to Nilz Baris on Space Station *K-7* in Classic episode "The Trouble with Tribbles."

Data, Lieutenant Commander — android operations officer of the *Enterprise*, played by Brent Spiner, in *The Next Generation*. Created by Dr. Noonian Soong on Omicron Theta IV, he is first found by the ship USS *Tripoli* and later attends Starfleet Academy. When a Turing Test declares him sentient, he is awarded several different posts on Starfleet vessels before coming aboard the *Enterprise*. Data and his twin, Lore, are designed in their father Soong's image. Data and Lore, who is created first, have very pale skin, yellow eyes, and are physically human in every way, except for off switches on their backs. Data's fondest wish is to know what it is like to be mentally and emotionally human. He comes close many times to attaining feeling, but each attempt results in disaster. His hobbies include music; acting; writing poetry; his cat, Spot; painting; stand-up comedy; solving mysteries (his favorite sleuth is Sherlock Holmes); and playing poker. He says he cannot speak in contractions, yet he does so easily when imitating a human or acting out a role. An accomplished engineer, often assisting Geordi with mechanical problems, Data is also an expert on many subjects, and can pilot the *Enterprise* out of tough situations with ease. Although designed to be completely rational, he is one of the most compassionate crewmembers on the *Enterprise*. He even breaks the Prime Directive in *TNG* episode "Pen Pals," going against command orders to save a little girl calling for help from a doomed world. (For more, see entry on Androids.)

"Datalore" — first-season *TNG* episode written by Bob Lewin, Maurice Hurley, and Gene Roddenberry, directed by Rob Bowman, in which Data discovers he has a twin brother, named Lore. (Both characters are played by Brent Spiner.) Created before Data, Lore does have emotions but no conscience, a combination which makes him selfish and deadly. Guest star: Biff Yeager.

"Data's Day" — fourth-season *TNG* episode written by Harold Apter and Ronald D. Moore, directed by Robert Wiemer. The camera follows Data on the start of a typical day, which ends up highly unusually. First, Data is to give Keiko away in the O'Briens' wedding, until Keiko calls the wedding off. Then, a Vulcan ambassador beams aboard on a mission of utmost secrecy. Guest stars: Rosalind Chao, Sierra Pecheur, Alan Scarfe, Colm Meaney, V'Sal, and April Grace.

Dathon, Captain — Tamarian ship captain, played by Paul Winfield in *TNG* episode "Darmok," who is killed on the world of El-Adrel.

Daugherty, Herschel — director of Classic *Trek* episodes "Operation: Annihilate!," "The Savage Curtain," and numerous other TV shows.

"Dauphin, The" — second-season *TNG* episode written by Scott Rubenstein and Leonard Mlodinow, directed by Rob Bowman. Salia, future ruler of Daled IV, comes aboard the *Enterprise* for transport and falls for Wesley, who doesn't know she is a shapechanger. Guest stars: Paddi Edwards, Jamie Hubbard, Mädchen Amick, Cindy Sorenson, Jennifer Barlow, and Peter Neptune.

David — child, played by George Baxter, whom Pulaski beams aboard the shuttlecraft in *TNG* episode "Unnatural Selection."

David, Deborah Dean — wrote script for *TNG* episode "We'll Always Have Paris."

David, Peter — wrote the Classic *Trek* novel *The Rift*, *TNG* novels *Imzadi*, *Vendetta*, *Strike Zone*, *Doomsday World*, *Q-In Law*, *A Rock and a Hard Place*, and the *DS9* novel *The Siege*. Also wrote a number of *TNG* comic book stories.

Davies, Ensign — played by Nicholas Cascone, assists Wesley in solving the Secundi Drema system problem in *TNG* episode "Pen Pals."

Davies, Stephen — plays tactical officer in *DS9*.

Davila, Carmen — official on Melona IV, played by Susan Diol, who is attracted to Riker and is killed by the Crystalline Entity in *TNG* episode "Silicon Avatar."

Da Vinci, Frank — played Lt. Brett in Classic *Trek* "The Naked Time" and a crewmember in "The Lights of Zetar."

Davis, Daniel — played Professor James Moriarty in *TNG* shows "Elementary, Dear Data" and "Ship in a Bottle."

Davis, Joe W. — played the young Spock in the film *The Search for Spock*.

Davis, Teddy — played a transporter technician in *TNG* "Sins of the Fathers."

Davis, Walt — played a therapist in Classic *Trek* "Dagger of the Mind," a Romulan crewman in "Balance of Terror," and a Klingon soldier in "Errand of Mercy." Other credits include *Alias Smith and Jones* and *The Bionic Woman*.

Davod — Zeon, played by Chuck Courtney, on Classic episode "Patterns of Force."

Dawson, Bob — special effects supervisor in films *The Wrath of Khan* and *The Search for Spock*.

"Dax" — in this first-season *DS9* episode, written by D. C. Fontana and Peter Allen Fields, Dax is accused of a murder he allegedly committed while occupying his former host, Curzon. Should Jadzia stand trial for crimes committed when she was essentially another person? Guest stars: Gregory Itzin, Anne Haney, Richard Lineback, and Fionnula.

Dax, Jadzia — regularly featured character on *DS9* made up of two different species. Dax is a member of the symbiotic species known as the Trill. Jadzia, a 28-year-old female humanoid with a series of intricate, frecklelike markings from her temples down to her shoulders, is the host body. As a symbiote, Dax resembles a large worm, and Jadzia is his seventh host, meaning he has lived seven lifetimes and is over 300 years old. Jadzia shares his many lives' memories once they are physically fused and become one being. Dax is a brilliant scientist. Jadzia is also brilliant, with several doctorates and degrees in exobiology, zoology, astrophysics, and exoarchaeology, studying all her life in order to be chosen as a host, which is the greatest honor a Trill can give.

"Day of the Dove, The" — written by Jerome Bixby and directed by Marvin Chomsky, this third-season Classic *Trek* episode aired 11/1/68. An entity which feeds off violent thoughts and actions causes the *Enterprise* crew and a Klingon crew to misunderstand each other and fight. No one, however, dies in these skirmishes. When deadly blows instantly heal, both crews realize an alien influence is at work. Guest stars: Michael Ansara, Susan Johnson, David L. Rose, and Mark Tobin.

Daystrom Annex — located on Galor IV, part of the Daystrom Institute (see entry).

Daystrom Institute — major Federation/Starfleet research facility named after Dr. Daystrom from Classic episode "The Ultimate Computer."

Daystrom Institute Theoretical Propulsion Group — school from which Dr. Brahms graduated, mentioned in *TNG* episode "Booby Trap."

Daystrom, Richard, Dr. — computer science genius, played by William Marshall, and winner of the Nobel Prize and the Z Magnees Prize, he creates the M–5 computer which takes over the *Enterprise* and kills the crew of the *Excalibur*. At the end of Classic episode "The Ultimate Computer," he suffers a mental breakdown.

Dayton, Charles — played a crewmember in *TNG* "Where No One Has Gone Before."

De La Peña, George — played Solis in *TNG* "The Arsenal of Freedom."

De Vries, Jon — played Wilson Granger in *TNG* "Up the Long Ladder."

"Deadly Years, The" — written by David P. Harmon, directed by Joseph Pevney, this second-season Classic *Trek* episode aired 12/8/67. *Enterprise* crewmembers visit Gamma Hydra IV and are infected by a disease which prematurely ages them. Kirk loses command when he begins to act senile. Guest stars: Charles Drake, Sarah Marshall, Beverly Washburn, Felix Locher, Laura Wood, and Carolyn Nelson. Of note: *TNG* episode "Unnatural Selection" involves a similar plotline.

Deadrick, Vince — played Matthews in Classic "What Are Little Girls Made Of?"; a Romulan crewman in "Balance of Terror"; a native in "The Apple"; as well as doing stunt work for McCoy in "Mirror, Mirror" and stunts in "Shore Leave" and "The Doomsday Machine." Film credits include *Romancing the Stone*.

Deadwood, South Dakota — location of

Alexander and Worf's holodeck simulation of the Wild West in *TNG* episode "A Fistful of Datas."

Dealt, Hester — Lieutenant Commander and medical trustee of the Federation Medical Collection Station, played by Seymour Cassel, in *TNG* episode "The Child."

Dean, Lieutenant — character played by Dan Kern in *TNG* episode "We'll Always Have Paris," with whom Picard fenced.

Debin — leader of the planet Atlek, played by Douglas Rowe, in *TNG* episode "The Outrageous Okona."

Decius — Romulan warship which transports Ambassador Tomalak, Picard, and Troi to the *Enterprise* in *TNG* episode "Future Imperfect."

Decius — Romulan officer, played by Lawrence Montaigne, in Classic episode "Balance of Terror."

Decker, Matthew, Commodore — captain of the *Constellation*, played by William Windom, and sole survivor of the destructive device in Classic episode "The Doomsday Machine," who later dies trying to destroy the device. He is the father of Will Decker who appears in *The Motion Picture*.

Decker, Willard, Commander — captain of the *Enterprise*, played by Stephen Collins, from whom Kirk takes control during an emergency in *The Motion Picture*. The son of Commodore Matt Decker, Willard is in love with the Deltan navigator Ilia, and ends up dissipating into a higher being at the end of the movie. Supposedly *TNG* character Riker is patterned after Willard, as *TNG*'s Deanna is patterned after Ilia.

Deela — queen of the Scalosians who falls in love with Kirk. Deela, played by Kathie Brown, and her people live in an accelerated time frame in Classic episode "Wink of an Eye."

Deep Space 4 — space station mentioned in *TNG* episode "The Chase," where Professor Galen wanted to start his micropaleontology search.

Deep Space 9 — space station located in the Bajor sector which aided the Bajoran government in repairs after their system was pillaged by the Cardassians. Worf visits *DS9* in *TNG* episode "Birthright." *DS9*, located near the only connecting wormhole through which travel to the distant, virtually unexplored Gamma Quadrant is possible, became the setting for the series of the same name and is commanded by Benjamin Sisko.

"Defector, The" — third-season *TNG* episode written by Ronald D. Moore, directed by Robert Scheerer. A Romulan defector claims the Romulans are about to wage war, but Picard does not trust him. Guest stars: James Sloyan, Andreas Katsulas, John Hancock, and S. A. Templeman.

Defiant, USS — starship lost in interphase between universes in Classic episode "The Tholian Web." Kirk is a member of the landing party on the ship when he disappears and is presumed dead.

Deflectors — force shield which protects starships from attack.

DeHaas, Tim — scriptwriter of *TNG* episode "Identity Crisis."

Dehner, Elizabeth, Dr. — ship's psychiatrist, who, along with Gary Mitchell, develops heightened telepathic powers when the *Enterprise* hits the barrier rim at the edge of the galaxy. Played by Sally Kellerman, she dies defending Kirk against Mitchell.

Deighan, Drew — scriptwriter of *TNG* episodes "Sins of the Father" and "Reunion."

"Déjà Q" — third-season *TNG* episode written by Richard Danus and directed by Les Landau. Q, deprived of his powers as punishment by his own people, visits a populated world threatened by an asteroid and learns what it's like to be human. Guest stars: John deLancie, Whoopi Goldberg, Richard Cansino, Betty Muramoto, and Corbin Bernsen.

Dekyon Field — field used by Data to transmit a message to his alternate self in *TNG* episode "Cause and Effect."

Del Arco, Jonathan — guest starred as Hugh in *TNG* "I, Borg."

DeLancie, John — plays Q in *TNG* episodes "Encounter at Farpoint," "Hide and Q," "Q Who," "Déjà Q," "QPid," "True Q," "Tapestry," and the *DS9* episode "Q Less." He also appears in the Peter Weir movie *Fearless* with Jeff Bridges.

Delano, Lee — played Kalo in Classic *Trek* "A Piece of the Action." Film credits include *Blood Sport*, *In the Glitter Palace*, and *Splash!*

DeLaure Belt — mentioned in *TNG* episode "The Ensigns of Command" as an area, located in the Tau Cygna V region, of hyperonic radiation.

Delos IV — location of Dr. Crusher's medical residency under Dr. Dalen Quaice as mentioned in the *TNG* episode "Remember Me."

Delos System — location of the planets Brekka and Ornara, as mentioned in the *TNG* episode "Symbiosis." Also the site of a sun which had an unstable magnetic field for a short period.

Delphi Ardu — outpost world of the Tkon Empire, which became extinct thousands of years before, in *TNG* episode "The Last Outpost."

Delta 05 — science station, bordering the destroyed Neutral Zone, mentioned in the *TNG* episode "The Neutral Zone."

Delta Quadrant — part of the galaxy 200 light years

away from the Alpha Quadrant, where the shuttle and Ferengi craft come out on the other side of the wormhole in the *TNG* episode "The Price."

Delta Rana system — location of the planet Rana IV mentioned in the *TNG* episode "The Survivors."

Delta rays — injured Captain Pike while on a cadet training vessel, as mentioned in the Classic episode "The Menagerie."

Delta Theta — class M world visited in animated episode "Bem."

Delta Triangle region — region of the galaxy where many starships have disappeared in the animated episode "Time Trap."

Delta Vega — desolate world and site of an automated lithium-cracking station in Classic episode "Where No Man Has Gone Before." Kirk hopes to strand Gary Mitchell on Vega, where the ore freighters call only once every twenty years. Instead, both Mitchell and Elizabeth Dehner die there.

Deltans — hairless race from Delta IV, of which Ilia is a member, which projects pheromones, causing male sexual arousal. First introduced in *The Motion Picture*, they are also empaths, and when mated, bond mentally as well as physically. A bonded Deltan pair working with Dr. Marcus on Regula is killed by Khan in *The Wrath of Khan*.

Deltived Asteroid Belt — Q2 mentions he misplaced this galactic anomaly in the *TNG* episode "Déjà Q."

Delugo, Winston — played Timothy in Classic *Trek* "Court-Martial."

Dement, Carol Daniels — played Zora in Classic *Trek* episode "The Savage Curtain."

Demetral, Chris — actor in the *TNG* episode "Future Imperfect."

Demos — head of security police on planet Dramia in animated episode "Albatross."

Dempsey, Mark — played the Air Force captain in Classic *Trek* "Tomorrow Is Yesterday."

Demyan, Lincoln — played Sgt. Lipton in Classic *Trek* "Assignment: Earth."

Denasian — Iconian language of Deneus III mentioned in the *TNG* episode "Contagion."

Denberg, Susan — played Maggie Kovas in Classic *Trek* "Mudd's Women." Film credits include *The Wackiest Ship in the Army*.

Deneb II — Jack the Ripper entity, named Kesla, struck this world in Classic episode "Wolf in the Fold."

Deneb IV — planet inhabited by the Bandi and site of the Farpoint Station from the *TNG* episode "Encounter at Farpoint." Deneb IV, also referred to as "Farpoint" after the space station, is mentioned in the Classic episode "Where No Man Has Gone Before" as the place where Kirk once shared a wild shore leave with Gary Mitchell.

Deneb V — planet where Harry Mudd sold the rights to a Vulcan fuel synthesizer he did not own; an act for which he was subsequently sentenced to death in the Classic episode "I, Mudd."

Denebian Alps — programmed into the holodeck by Wesley in *TNG* episode "Angel One" so he and a friend can go skiing.

Denebian slime devil — Korax's unflattering description of Kirk in the Classic episode "The Trouble with Tribbles."

Deneva — considered one of the most beautiful colony planets in the Federation and home to Kirk's brother Sam and his family before a parasitic invasion in the Classic episode "Operation: Annihilate!"

Dengel, Jake — played the Ferengi Mordoc in the *TNG* episode "The Last Outpost."

Denis, William — played Ki Mendrossen in the *TNG* episode "Sarek."

Denius III — world in the *TNG* episode "Contagion" where Captain Varley of the *Yamato* discovered evidence which led him to the ruined Iconian homeworld.

Denkiri Arm — located in the Gamma Quadrant, the final home of the Barzan probe featured in the *TNG* episode "The Price."

denkirs — unit of measurement used by the Fajo in the *TNG* episode "The Most Toys."

Dennehy, Elizabeth — played Lt. Commander Shelby in the *TNG* episode "The Best of Both Worlds."

Dennis, Charles — played Sunad in the *TNG* episode "Transfigurations."

Denorios Belt — area of heavy neutrino activity mentioned in *DS9* episode "Emissary," where most of the Bajoran Orbs were found.

Denver, Maryesther — played Third Witch in the Classic *Trek* "Catspaw."

Denver — ship which hits a mine in the *TNG* episode "Ethics." The *Enterprise* saves most of the people on board.

DePaul, Lieutenant — *Enterprise* navigator in Classic episodes "Arena" and "A Taste of Armageddon."

deridium — valuable element necessary to the survival of a dying race in the *DS9* episode "The Passenger."

Derr, Richard — played Commodore Barlow in Classic *Trek* episode "The Alternative Factor" and Admiral Fitzgerald in "The Mark of Gideon." Other TV credits include *Perry Mason, Barnaby Jones,* and *Cannon.*

DeSalle, Vincent, Lieutenant — relief navigator, played by Michael Barrier, in Classic episodes "The Squire of Gothos" and "This Side of Paradise," who is later promoted to assistant chief of engineering in "Catspaw."

"Descent, Part I" — sixth-season *TNG* episode written by Ronald D. Moore and Jeri Taylor. A new breed of Borg, led by Data's twin Lore, ambush a Federation outpost on Ohniaka III. A stranded *Enterprise* landing party bands together with an underground Borg resistance group of which Hugh is a part and attempt to stop Lore. Guest stars: Jim Norton and Stephen Hawking.

DeSeve, Stefan, Ensign — defected to the Romulan empire 20 years before working with Spock in the Romulan underground in the Classic episode "Face of the Enemy."

DeSoto, Jeremiah, Captain — commander of the USS *Hood,* and Riker's former commanding officer, mentioned in the *TNG* episode "Encounter at Farpoint."

Detrian system — the *Enterprise* goes to this system to watch the birth of a new star in the *TNG* episode "Ship in a Bottle."

deuterium gas — element leaked from a reactor on the planet Battress in the *TNG* episode "Heart of Glory."

Devenny, Scott — played Klingon Chancellor Azetbur in *The Undiscovered Country.*

Devereaux, Terry — scriptwriter of the *TNG* episode "Manhunt."

Devidia II — Data's head is found in a cave on this world, located in the Marrab sector, in the *TNG* episode "Time's Arrow." Also mentioned in "Timescape."

"Devil in the Dark, The" — written by Gene L. Coon and directed by Joseph Pevney, this first-season Classic *Trek* episode aired 3/9/67. Miners, working in a resource-rich planet, are being killed by a mysterious beast. The *Enterprise* investigates and discovers the miners are inadvertently destroying the creature's eggs. The creature is later determined to be intelligent and refers to herself as a Horta. Guest stars: Ken Lynch, Barry Russo, Brad Weston, John Cavett, Janos Prohaska, Biff Elliot, and Dick Dial. Of note: While filming this episode, William Shatner learned of his father's death but insisted filming continue.

"Devil's Due" — fourth-season *TNG* episode written by Philip Lazebnik and William Douglas Lansford, directed by Tom Benko. The Ventaxians made a deal with a type of metaphysical devil named Ardra for 1,000 years of peace and prosperity. Now the 1,000 years are up and the being is thought to have returned to collect. Picard, however, doesn't believe Ardra is what the Ventaxians think it is. Guest stars: Marta Dubois, Paul Lambert, Marcelo Tubert, William Glover, Thad Lamey, and Tom Magee.

Devisor — Klingon battlecruiser featured in animated episode "More Trouble, More Tribbles."

Devna — Orion woman marooned on the planet Elysia in animated episode "Time Trap."

Devo — Ferengi ship encountered in *TNG* episode "The Last Outpost."

Devor — member of a team trying to steal trilithium from the *Enterprise* in *TNG* episode "Starship Mine."

Devos, Alexana — police director on the planet Rutia, played by Kerrie Keane, in *TNG* episode "The High Ground."

Dewan — Iconian language mentioned in *TNG* episode "Contagion."

DeWeese, Gene — authored Classic *Trek* novels *Renegade, Chain of Attack, The Final Nexus*, and the *TNG* novel *The Peacekeepers*.

DeYoung, Cliff — played Crodon in *DS9* episode "Vortex."

diagnostic panel — located above sick-bay beds.

diagnostic scanner — hand-held scanner used to diagnose a patient.

Dial, Dick — stuntman who played Sam in Classic *Trek* "Devil in the Dark," Kaplan in "The Apple," and Kirk's double in "Arena." Also appears in "Friday's Child" and "The Immunity Syndrome." Other TV credits include several shows of the 1960s, including *The Man from U.N.C.L.E.*

diburnium-osmium alloy — alloy used to build the Kalandan outpost in Classic episode "That Which Survives."

Dickerson, Lieutenant — *Enterprise* security officer, played by Arell Blanton, in Classic episode "Savage Curtain."

Dickson, Lance — scriptwriter of *TNG* episode "The Outrageous Okona."

dicosilium — element delivered to Dr. Apgar by the *Enterprise* in *TNG* episode "A Matter of Perspective."

Dieghan, Liam — philosopher mentioned in *TNG* episode "Up the Long Ladder" who preached getting "back to nature" and founded the 22nd-century neo-transcendentalists.

***Dierdre*, SS** — subject of a fake distress call made by the Klingons asking for emergency assistance in Classic episode "Friday's Child."

Dierkop, Charles — played Morla in Classic *Trek* "Wolf in the Fold." Also appeared regularly on *Police Woman,* and has numerous other TV credits.

DiFalco, Chief — relief navigator of the *Enterprise,* played by Marcy Lafferty (William Shatner's wife) in *The Motion Picture.*

dikironium — elemental ingredient in planet Tycho IV's vampire cloud in Classic episode "Obsession."

Dilinea IV — planetary home to scientists who designed a transporter modification to eliminate transporter psychosis, mentioned in *TNG* episode "Realm of Fear."

dilithium — rare crystal which powers Starfleet starships' warp drives.

Dillard, J. M. — authored Classic *Trek* novels *Mindshadow*, *Bloodthirst*, *Demons*, *The Final Frontier*, *The Undiscovered Country*, *The Lost Years*, and the *DS9* book *Emissary*.

Dillard, Victoria — played ballerina in *TNG* episode "Where No One Has Gone Before."

dimensional shifter — device used by the Ansata to transport anywhere on the planet Rutia in *TNG* episode "The High Ground." The device's major side effects involve DNA breakdown and accelerated cellular aging.

Dimorus — mentioned in Classic episode "Where No Man Has Gone Before," as a world visited by Kirk and Gary Mitchell where the inhabitants attacked them, and Mitchell shielded Kirk from a poison dart, saving his life.

Dinonicus VII — planet where the *Enterprise* schedules a rendezvous with the *Biko* in *TNG* episode "A Fistful of Datas."

Diomidian scarlet moss — substance Dr. Crusher is growing in her lab when she notices a time difference in its growth patterns in *TNG* episode "Clues."

Dion, Susan — actress in *TNG* "Silicon Avatar."

Dioyd — young-looking Platonian with black hair, played by Derek Patridge, in Classic episode "Plato's Stepchildren."

Dirgo, Captain — shuttle pilot, played by Nick Tate, who dies after his shuttle crashes on a nearby moon while taking Picard and Wesley to Pentarus V in *TNG* espisode "Final Mission."

"Disaster" — fifth-season *TNG* episode written by Ron Jarvis, Philip A. Scorza, and Ronald D. Moore, directed by Gabrielle Beaumont. After the ship is nearly wrecked hitting a cosmic string fragment, Picard finds himself trapped in the turbolift with three panicky *Enterprise* school kids and Keiko goes into labor while trapped in Ten Forward. Guest stars: Rosalind Chao, Colm Meaney, Michelle Forbes, Erika Florews, John Christian Graas, Max Supera, Cameron Arnett, and Jana Marie Hupp.

disruptor — weapon carried on Klingon ships. They also use hand-held versions. The Eminian weapons in Classic episode "A Taste of Armageddon" are also referred to as disruptors.

Disruptors — name the Stratos dwellers use for terrorist Troglytes in Classic episode "The Cloud Minders."

Ditmars, Ivan — music composer in Classic *Trek* episode "Requiem for Methuselah."

Divok — young Klingon who has a vision of Kahless in *TNG* episode "Rightful Heir."

Dobkin, Larry — director of the Classic *Trek* episode "Charlie X." Also an actor and writer, he guest starred in *TNG* episode "The Mind's Eye." TV credits include *Streets of San Francisco* and *The Rifleman*.

Doe, John — transforming Zalkonian played by Mark LaMura in *TNG* episode "Transfigurations."

Dohlman — ruler and warlord of Elas. Elaan in Classic episode "Elaan of Troyius" is also a dohlman.

Dokachin, Klin — Zakdorn administrator, played by Graham Jarvis, of the Zed 15 surplus depot at Qualor II in *TNG* episode "Unification."

Dolak, Gul — Cardassian, played by Frank Collison, in on a conspiracy with Admiral Kennelly in *TNG* episode "Ensign Ro."

Dolinsky, Meyer — scriptwriter of the Classic *Trek* "Plato's Stepchildren."

dom-jot — game similar to pool played by Academy cadets in *TNG* episode "Tapestry."

Dominguez, José, Commander — friend of Kirk's mentioned in Classic episode "The Man Trap" as the commander of a starbase on Corinth IV.

Don — one of the little boys in "And the Children Shall Lead" (see entry for Linden, Don).

Don Juan — Yeoman Tonia Barrows runs into a version of the famous romancer, played by James Grusaf, on the recreational planet in Classic episode "Shore Leave."

Donahue, Elinor — played Commissioner Nancy Hedford in Classic *Trek* "Metamorphosis." A regularly featured character on TV series *Father Knows Best*, she also guest starred in many other series and TV movies.

Donald, Juli — played Tayna in *TNG* "A Matter of Perspective."

Donatu V — disputed territory, mentioned in Classic episode "The Trouble with Tribbles," over which a battle was fought with the Klingons.

Donner, Jack — played Subcommander Tal in Classic *Trek* episode "The *Enterprise* Incident."

Donner, Jill Sherman — scriptwriter for *DS9* episode "Captive Pursuit."

Doohan, James — played Lt. Commander (later promoted to Commander and Captain) Montgomery Scott, the engineer of the Classic *Trek Enterprise*. Voice-over credits for aliens include father's voice in "The Squire of Gothos,"

Sargon, the Melkot buoy, M–5 in "The Ultimate Computer," and Lt. Arex in the animated series. Born in Vancouver, Canada, he started his career doing voices on the radio. His TV credits include *Bonanza, Hazel, The Virginian, Blue Light, Daniel Boone, The FBI, The Gallant Men, Gunsmoke, The Man from U.N.C.L.E., Outer Limits, Peyton Place, Shenandoah, Then Came Bronson, The Twilight Zone, Voyage to the Bottom of the Sea, The Fugitive, Iron Horse, Ben Casey,* and *Bewitched*. He also appeared in the Saturday morning series *Space Academy* (with "And the Children Shall Lead" actors Brian Tochi and Pamelyn Ferdin), and had a recurring role in *Jason of Star Command*. Doohan appeared in the Roddenberry-produced movie *Pretty Maids All in a Row*, and is an accomplished carpenter and wood carver. He has also appeared in all six *Trek* movies, as well as the *TNG* episode "Relics," reprising his role of Scotty. He has four children from his first marriage. His second wife, Anita Yagel, was a Paramount secretary he met on the lot. He recently wrote his memoirs, to be published by Pocket Books, which were untitled when this encyclopedia went to press. In the late 1980s he suffered a heart attack but has completely recovered.

doomsday machine — planet and starship killing device referred to as a doomsday machine by Spock in the Classic episode of the same name.

"Doomsday Machine, The" — written by noted science-fiction author and critic Norman Spinrad and directed by Marc Daniels, this second-season Classic *Trek* episode aired 10/20/67. A device which devours planets for fuel is discovered after the *Enterprise* encounters the USS *Constellation* empty and adrift, with only the captain, Matthew Decker, left on board. Guest stars: William Windom, Elizabeth Rogers, John Copage, and Richard Compton. Of note: Captain Decker, who dies in this episode, is the father of Will Decker who later shows up in *Star Trek: The Motion Picture* (and "dies"). This episode was nominated for a Hugo Award for Best Dramatic Presentation of 1967.

Doraf I — mentioned as a world scheduled for terraforming in *TNG* episode "Unification."

Doran — character, played by Lynnda Fergusson, who appeared in *DS9* episode "Emissary."

Dorian — ship Ambassador Olcar leaves to come aboard the *Enterprise* in *TNG* episode "Man of the People."

Dorn, Michael — an avid *Star Trek* fan, Dorn was very excited to land the role of the Klingon Worf on *The Next Generation* series. Prior to *TNG*, he was a regular on the series *C.H.I.P.S.*, a background extra (a writer in the newsroom) on the last two years of *The Mary Tyler Moore Show*, and appeared in *Days of Our Lives* and *Capitol*. His film credits include *Demon Seed*, *Rocky*, and *The Jagged Edge*. Born in Liling, Texas, Dorn grew up in Pasadena, California, and performed in a rock band during high school and college. He also played a Klingon public defender in the Classic episode *The Undiscovered Country* (he does his best to defend McCoy and Kirk, who are being tried for murder), and has done voice-overs for the TV series *Dinosaurs*. Still interested in rock music, he does occasional studio work as a bass player and writes music in his spare time.

Dornisch, William P. — film editor on *The Wrath of Khan*.

doublejack — form of solitaire Eve is playing with round cards in Classic episode "Mudd's Women."

Douglas, Pamela — scriptwriter of *TNG* episode "Night Terrors."

Douglas, Phyllis — played Yeoman Mears in Classic *Trek* "The Galileo Seven," and Girl in "The Way to Eden."

Douglass, Charles — played Haskell in *TNG* "Where Silence Has Lease."

Douwd — immortal who can take on any form and is

thousands of years old when the *Enterprise* encounters it in the form of Kevin Uxbridge in *TNG* episode "The Survivors."

Downey, Deborah — played Girl in Classic *Trek* "The Way to Eden."

Downey, Gary — played a Tellerite in Classic *Trek* "Whom Gods Destroy," and did stunt work as Kirk's double in "Catspaw."

Draconians — natives of Sigma Draconis who steal Spock's brain in the Classic episode of the same name. Women run the society and control the men, who are reduced to savages, with a pain-inducing device.

Drake, Charles — played Commodore George Stocker in Classic *Trek* "The Deadly Years."

Drake, Laura — played the Klingon Vekma in *TNG* "A Matter of Honor."

Drake, USS — captained by Paul Rice, this ship was destroyed by a weapon called Echo Papa 607 in *TNG* episode "The Arsenal of Freedom."

Draken IV — home of a Starfleet base near the Kaleb sector in *TNG* episode "Face of the Enemy."

Drea — Kelvin, played by Leslie Dalton, in Classic episode "By Any Other Name."

Dream of the Fire, The — title of a book, written by the Klingon Karatok, Worf gives Data in *TNG* episode "The Measure of a Man."

Drella — the Jack the Ripper entity, which feeds off fear, is compared to a Drella, an entity which lives off love, in the Classic episode "Wolf in the Fold."

Dresden, John — played a security officer in *Star Trek: The Motion Picture*. Other TV credits include *Barnaby Jones*.

drill thralls — slaves on the planet Triskelion in Classic episode "The Gamesters of Triskelion."

Dromm, Andrea — played Yeoman Smith in Classic *Trek* "Where No Man Has Gone Before."

Droxine — Diana Ewing plays the spoiled aristocratic daughter of Plasus, high advisor to the city of Stratos, who becomes fascinated with Spock in Classic episode "The Cloud Minders."

drubidium calamus — plant Keiko brings back with her from Marlonia in *TNG* episode "Rascals."

"Drumhead, The" — fourth-season *TNG* episode written by Jeri Taylor and directed by Jonathan Frakes. Admiral Satie comes aboard the *Enterprise* to investigate a Klingon exchange student charged with treason. Satie is so paranoid, however, that she sees conspiracy everywhere, to the point of putting Picard on trial as well as an innocent Vulcan ensign who hid the fact he is part Romulan to avoid prejudice. Guest stars: Jean Simmons, Bruce French, Spencer Garrett, Earl Billings, Henry Woronicz, and Ann Shea.

Drusilla — slave, played by Lois Jewell, given to Kirk for the night in Classic episode "Bread and Circuses."

dryworm — creature mentioned in Classic episode "Who Mourns for Adonais?" which, if it grows to its largest size, can control energy outside its body as Apollo does.

D'Sora, Jenna, Ensign — *Enterprise* engineering officer who plays the flute and is courted by Data in *TNG* episode "In Theory." Data finds he cannot give Jenna, played by Michele Scarabelli, what she needs, and the relationship ends.

Duana — Wesley's adoptive mother, played by Ivy Bethune, in *TNG* episode "When the Bough Breaks."

Duane, Diane — author of the Classic *Trek* novels *The*

Wounded Sky, *The Romulan Way*, *My Enemy, My Ally*, *Doctor's Orders*, *Spock's World*, and the *TNG* novel *Dark Mirror*. Also wrote the script for *TNG* episode "Where No One Has Gone Before."

Dubois, Marta — actress in *TNG* "Devil's Due."

Duffy — an engineer, played by Charley Lang, in Geordi's crew in *TNG* episode "Hollow Pursuits."

Dukat, Gul — Cardassian leader who became the administrator of Bajor when the Cardassians conquered the planet.

Dumont, Suzanne, Ensign — girl with whom Wesley has a date in *TNG* episode "Sarek."

Duncan — played by Karl Bruck, character who plays King Duncan from *Macbeth* in Classic episode "The Conscience of the King."

Duncan, King — member of the Karidian players, played by Karl Bruck, in Classic episode "The Conscience of the King."

Duncan, Lee — played Evans in Classic *Trek* "Elaan of Troyius."

Dunn, Michael — played Alexander in Classic *Trek* "Plato's Stepchildren." He was most well known for his recurring role as Dr. Lovelace in the TV series *Wild, Wild West*.

Dunsel, Captain — term used to refer to Kirk, meaning someone who is useless, in Classic episode "The Ultimate Computer."

duotronics — computer technology, mentioned in Classic episode "The Ultimate Computer," Daystrom used to develop the M–5 computer and the Starfleet computer system.

Durand, Judi — plays the computer voice on *DS9*.

duranium — element used in the bulkheads of the *Enterprise* as mentioned in *TNG* episode "A Matter of Perspective." Also used as an alloy in shuttlecrafts as mentioned in Classic episode "Metamorphosis."

Duras — son of Worf's father's greatest enemy in *TNG* episode "Sins of the Father." Although he sits on the Klingon High Council, it is actually his father who was the traitor on Khitomer, not Worf's father.

Durbin, John — played Bada N'D'D' in *TNG* episode "Lonely among Us."

Durenia IV — destination of the *Enterprise* when Dr. Crusher disappears into Wesley's warp field in *TNG* episode "Remember Me."

Durkin, Avill, Chancellor — leader of Malcoria III, played by George Coe, who thinks his world is not ready for Federation or outside contact in *TNG* episode "First Contact."

Durnham, Brett — played the security chief in Classic *Trek* "The Menagerie."

Durock, Dick — played an Elasian guard in Classic *Trek* "Elaan of Troyius."

Duryea, Peter — played José Tyler in Classic *Trek* "The Menagerie."

Dusay, Marj — played Kara in Classic *Trek* "Spock's Brain." Dusay has appeared in several TV shows, including *Facts of Life*, and does stage work.

Duur — Capellan warrior, played by Kirk Raymone, who is killed by Klingon Kras in Classic *Trek* episode "Friday's Child."

Dvorkin, Daniel — authored the *TNG* novel *The Captain's Honor* (with David Dvorkin).

Dvorkin, David — wrote the Classic *Trek* novels *The*

Trellisane Confrontation, Timetrap, and the *TNG* novel *The Captain's Honor* (with Daniel Dvorkin).

D'Voris — Romulan ship under command of Admiral Mendak in *TNG* episode "Data's Day."

DY 100 — class of ship from the late 1990s. The sleeper ship *Botany Bay* from Classic episode "Space Seed" is of this class.

DY 500 — class of ship from the 21st century mentioned in Classic episode "Space Seed."

Dylaplane — governor of Pacifica, mentioned in *TNG* episode "Conspiracy."

dylovene — drug McCoy uses on Sulu who was bitten by a poisonous retlaw in animated episode "The Infinite Vulcan."

Dynarski, Gene — played Ben Childress in Classic *Trek* "Mudd's Women," Krodak in "The Mark of Gideon," and base commander Orfil Quinteros in *TNG* episode "11001001." Other TV credits include *Voyage to the Bottom of the Sea* and *Iron Horse.* Film credits include *Duel, The Sound of Anger, Double Indemnity,* and *Sins of the Past.*

Dyson sphere — structure built around a G type star named after the 20th-century American engineer and theorist who first came up with the idea of building one in *TNG* episode "Relics."

Dytalix Mining Corporation — company which mines the world Dytalix B mentioned in *TNG* episode "Conspiracy."

Dytalix B — fifth of six planets located in the Mira system, it is mined by the Dytalix Mining Corporation and is the site of a Starfleet conspiracy in *TNG* episode "Conspiracy."

Earl Grey — Picard's favorite brand of tea.

Earp, Morgan — character, played by Rex Holman, known historically as "the man who kills on sight" and who "kills" Chekov in Classic episode "Spectre of the Gun."

Earp, Virgil — character in Classic episode "Spectre of the Gun," played by Charles Maxwell. Historically, he was the town marshall of Tombstone, but not in this episode.

Earp, Wyatt — marshall of Tombstone, played by Ron Soble, who is knocked down by Kirk at the O.K. Corral in Classic episode "Spectre of the Gun."

Earth — class M planet.

Earth–Saturn Probe — pivotal mission in space exploration to be manned by Captain John Christopher's son, Shaun Christopher, as mentioned in Classic episode "Tomorrow Is Yesterday."

Earther — Klingons use this term to refer to Terrans, also called Earthlings, in Classic episode "The Trouble with Tribbles."

Easton, Robert — played the Klingon judge in *The Undiscovered Country*.

Echevarria, René — scriptwriter of *TNG* episodes "The Offspring," "Transfigurations," "The Mind's Eye," "The Perfect Mate," "True Q," "I, Borg," "Face of the

Enemy," "Ship in a Bottle," "Birthright, Part II," and "Second Chances."

Echo Papa 607 — weapon designed by the Minos which a salesman tries to sell to Picard in *TNG* episode "The Arsenal of Freedom."

Ecklar, Julia — science-fiction writer nominated for several writing awards and author of Classic *Trek* novel *The Kobayashi Maru*.

Ed — Tombstone barkeep, played by Charles Seel, in Classic episode "Spectre of the Gun."

Ede, George — appeared in *TNG* "Cost of Living."

Edelman Neurological Institute — school from which Dr. Toby Russel graduated in *TNG* episode "Ethics."

Eden — mythical planet sought by a gang from Classic episode "The Way to Eden." Spock thinks he finds its location in Romulan space, only to discover that the beautiful world's plant life is acid-based and poisonous to non-indigenous life.

Edo — inhabitants of the planet Rubicam III encountered by the *Enterprise* in *TNG* episode "Justice." The Edo are guided by a superior energy force.

Edoans — species featured in the animated episodes with three arms and three legs, and orange skin. Lt. Arex, a navigator for the *Enterprise*, is an Edoan.

Edouard — maître d', played by Jean-Paul Vignon, of the Parisian café re-created in the holodeck in *TNG* episode "We'll Always Have Paris."

Edwards, Paddi — played Anya in *TNG* "The Dauphin."

Edwards, Tony — played the helicopter pilot in *The Voyage Home*. He also appeared in *Starman*.

Edwell, Captain — mentioned in *TNG* episode "Starship Mine" as an amazing officer, born on Gaspar VII, to whom Picard is compared by Hutchison.

eel birds — in Classic episode "Amok Time," Spock refers to the giant eel birds of Regulus V when trying to explain to Kirk the nature of *Pon farr*. The eel birds must return every eleven years to mate in the caverns in which they were hatched, or die trying.

Efros, Mel — coproducer of *The Final Frontier*.

Egg, The — probe invented by Dr. Paul Stubbs to examine the Kavis Alpha system in *TNG* episode "Evolution."

Ehrlich, Max — scriptwriter of Classic *Trek* "The Apple." His other writing credits include *Voyage to the Bottom of the Sea*.

Eichner radiation — radiation emitted by subspace phase inverters. The creature Ian in *TNG* episode "The Child" is a source of this kind of radiation.

Eight Eleven East 68th Street, Apartment 12B — Gary Seven's New York address in Classic episode "Assignment: Earth."

Eisenberg, Aron — plays the recurring character of the young Ferengi Nog in *DS9*. He appears in the pilot, "Emissary," as well as several other episodes.

Eisenmann, Ike — played Peter Preston in *The Wrath of Khan*. He also appeared in the Disney movies *Escape to Witch Mountain* and *Return to Witch Mountain*, and in the science-fiction TV series *Fantastic Journey*.

Eitner, Don — played the navigator in Classic *Trek* "Charlie X," and Kirk's double in "The Enemy Within." Also appeared in *Lost in Space*.

Eklund, Gordon — author of Classic *Trek* novels *The Starless World* and *Devil World*.

Ekor — Scalosian, played by Eric Holland, in Classic episode "Wink of an Eye."

Ekos — planet in the M43 Alpha sector at war with its peace-loving neighbor, Zeon, in Classic episode "Patterns of Force."

Elaan — name of the Dohlman of Elas, played by France Nuyen, sent to marry the ruler of Troyius so their worlds can at last have peace in Classic episode "Elaan of Troyius." She does not want to marry him, but must fulfill her duty. Elasian women's tears are supposed to have a biochemical effect on men. It is said that once a man touches an Elasian woman's tears, he falls in love with her and can refuse her nothing.

"Elaan of Troyius" — written and directed by John Meredyth Lucas, this third-season Classic *Trek* episode aired 12/20/68. The *Enterprise* must transport the spoiled princess Elaan, the Dohlman of Elas, to Troyius for her marriage to the Troyian leader, insuring peace between the two historically hostile people. Elaan has a substance in her tears that can make a man fall in love with her, and uses her "weapon" on Kirk when he becomes impatient with her while teaching her manners. A Klingon ship also gives the *Enterprise* trouble. Guest stars: France Nuyen, Jay Robinson, Tony Young, Victor Brandt, K. L. Smith, and Lee Duncan.

El Adrel IV — in *TNG* episode "Darmok," Picard and Dathon beam down to this world to try to gain an understanding of their peoples.

Elas — world located in the Tellan system and ruled by the Dohlman Elaan and a Council of Nobles, who decide Elaan should marry the ruler of Troyius in the interests of peace, in Classic episode "Elaan of Troyius."

Elba II — planet with a poisonous atmosphere and site of an insane asylum which an inmate, Garth of Izar, takes over in Classic episode "Whom Gods Destroy."

The asylum is contained within a large dome and covered by a force field to protect it from the planet's air.

El Baz — *Enterprise* shuttle pod five, named after NASA geologist Farouk El Baz, in which Picard is found unconscious in *TNG* episode "Time Squared." The shuttle pod also appears in "Transfigurations."

Elbrun, Tam — Betazoid telepath, played by Harry Groener, who is a specialist in first contact. Born with telepathy (most Betazoids develop it in adolescence), he is highly sensitive and is hospitalized for stress resulting from his abilities in the *TNG* episode "Tin Man."

Elder, Judyann — played Lt. Ballard in *TNG* "The Offspring."

Elected One — Beate is the Elected One, or head of state, of Angel One in the *TNG* episode of the same name.

electromagnetic synthomometer — tool used by Soong to construct Data and Lore in *TNG* episode "Datalore."

Eleen — pregnant Capellan wife, played by Julie Newmar, of the ruler the Teer Akaar in Classic episode "Friday's Child."

"Elementary, Dear Data" — second-season *TNG* episode written by Brian Alan Lane and directed by Rob Bowman. When Data, Pulaski, and Geordi reenact a Sherlock Holmes mystery in the holodeck, one of the characters, Moriarty, takes on consciousness and a will of his own, taking over the *Enterprise* using the holodeck computer. Guest stars: Daniel Davis, Alan Shearman, Biff Manard, Diz White, Anne Ramsay, and Richard Merson.

El Fadil, Siddig — stars as Dr. Julian Bashir in *DS9*. He also appeared in *TNG* episode "Birthright, Part I." El Fadil was born in the Sudan, but grew up in London, England. He began to study acting out of a desire to become a director and has acted in and directed several stage plays. His

British television debut was as a Palestinian in the six-part miniseries *Big Battalions*. He later landed the small role of King Faisal in the British production of *A Dangerous Man: Lawrence after Arabia*. The role did not attract much attention, but by luck Rick Berman, coexecutive producer of *DS9* saw it and considered the then 24-year-old El Fadil for the role of Commander Sisko. Berman, however, thought El Fadil was older than he actually was because he was aged with makeup for the King Faisal role. Although the producers wanted an older actor to play Commander Sisko, they were impressed enough with the now 26-year-old El Fadil to give him the role of the 27-year-old doctor. He currently resides in West Hollywood.

Elias, Louis — played the first technician in Classic *Trek* "And the Children Shall Lead."

Elig, Dekon, Dr. — thought to be the creator of a virus which causes a form of aphasia in *DS9* episode "Babel." When he cannot be found, it is his assistant, Surmak Ren, who finds the cure for the virus and admits that Elig did create it.

Eline — Kamin's wife, played by Margot Rose, in *TNG* episode "The Inner Light." Picard is Kamin in another reality and has two children with Eline, Meribor and Batai.

Ellenstein, David — played a doctor in *The Voyage Home*.

Ellenstein, Robert — played the Federation Council President in *The Voyage Home*, and the character Stephen Miller in *TNG* "Haven." His other acting credits include *The Man from U.N.C.L.E.*, *One Step Beyond*, and *Bonanza*.

Elliott, Biff — played Schmitter in Classic *Trek* "Devil in the Dark." His credits include *Voyage to the Bottom of the Sea*, *Planet of the Apes*, and *Cannon*.

Elliott, Kay — played Stella Mudd in Classic *Trek* "I, Mudd." Other credits include *The Man from U.N.C.L.E.*

Ellis, Mr. — mentioned, but never seen, as the first officer of the *Antares*, in Classic episode "Charlie X."

Ellison, Harlan — scriptwriter of Classic *Trek* "The City on the Edge of Forever." Famous in science-fiction circles and winner of several Hugo and Nebula awards, Ellison also wrote under the pen name Cordwainer Bird. He has written many film scripts, including *A Boy and His Dog*, TV teleplays, novels, and short stories. TV script credits include *The Voyage to the Bottom of the Sea*, *The Starlost*, *The Man from U.N.C.L.E.*, *The Outer Limits*, and *Twilight Zone*. Also a noted reviewer and critic, Ellison is a popular speaker at science-fiction conventions and has done some quite elegant car commercials. His relationship with Hollywood has been rocky, however. Several of Ellison's story ideas have been stolen in the past, but he has successfully sued for compensation. He is married to Susan Ellison and lives in the Los Angeles area.

El Razzac, Abdul Salaam — played the bass player in *TNG* "11001001."

Elway Theorem — theorem which helps the *Enterprise* crew understand how the Ansata rebels are transporting themselves from location to location in *TNG* episode "The High Ground."

Elysia — located in the Delta Triangle region, where many ships are reported lost, the *Enterprise* visits this planet in the animated episode "Time Trap."

Em/3/Green — green-skinned character in the animated episode "Jihad" whose voice was played by David Gerrold.

Emila II — destination of the *Enterprise* at the end of *TNG* episode "A Matter of Perspective."

Eminiar VII — planet ruled by Anan 7 and located in star cluster NGC 321 which has warred for 500 years with its neighbor, Vendikar. The struggle is carried on via computer when the *Enterprise* visits the two planets in Classic episode "A Taste of Armageddon."

"Emissary" — first-season *DS9* episode written by Michael Piller and Rick Berman, directed by David Carson. Sisko comes aboard *DS9* as its new commander and meets his crew for the first time. Additionally, he must deal with memories of losing his wife in the Borg attack at Wolf 359, and with the fact that he is the emissary for whom the Bajorans are waiting. The wormhole is also discovered. Guest stars: Patrick Stewart, Camille Saviola, Felecia M. Bell, Marc Alaimo, Joel Swetow, Aron Eisenberg, Stephen Davies, Max Grodenchik, Steve Rankin, Lily Mariye, Cassandra Byram, John Noah Hertzler, April Grace, Kevin McDermott, Parker Whitman, William Powell Blair, Frank Owen Smith, Lynnda Fergusson, Megan Butler, Stephen Power, Thomas Hobson, Donald Hotton, Gene Armor, and Diana Cignoni.

"Emissary, The" — second-season *TNG* episode written by Thomas H. Calder, Richard Manning, and Hans Beimer, directed by Cliff Bole. K'Ehleyr, a half-human, half-Klingon emissary and Worf's past lover, comes aboard ship to meet with a group of Klingons stuck in suspended animation for 100 years who are still set on attacking and conquering the Federation. Guest stars: Suzie Plakson, Georgann Johnson, Colm Meaney, Anne Elizabeth Ramsay, and Dietrich Bader.

Emmis I — Federation colony under Borg attack in *TNG* episode "Descent."

"Empath, The" — written by Joyce Muskat and directed by John Erman, this third-season Classic *Trek* episode aired 12/6/68. When the *Enterprise* arrives to evacuate researchers from the planet Minara II, they are unable to find them. Landing party members then begin to vanish, one by one, reawakening in an underground chamber where creatures called Vians torture them, and they meet Gem, a mute empath. Guest stars: Kathryn

Hays, Willard Sage, Alan Bergmann, David Roberts, and Jason Wingreen.

Empathic Metamorph — Kamala is an empathic metamorph with the ability to bond with only one person and become his or her perfect mate in *TNG* episode "The Perfect Mate."

Empath — being with a talent for reading or feeling another's emotions. Gem, from Classic episode "The Empath," is an example, but one who additionally can heal physical wounds on another by touching them and taking the wound onto herself. Deanna Troi of *TNG* is an empath who can sense feelings in others with the exception of Ferengis but who is a full telepath with her own species, Betazoid (see entry). Ilia, the Deltan (see entry) from *The Motion Picture* also has empathic powers to some extent.

Enberg, Alexander — played a reporter in *TNG* "Time's Arrow, Part II."

"Encounter at Farpoint" — first-season *TNG* episode written by Dorothy Fontana and Gene Roddenberry. Directed by Corey Allen, it is shown in two parts and involves the *Enterprise*'s maiden voyage to Deneb IV, or Farpoint. They encounter Q for the first time while trying to solve the mystery of the Bandi, builders of Farpoint. Guest stars include: John DeLancie, Michael Bell, DeForest Kelley, Colm Meaney, Cary Hiroyuki, Timothy Dang, David Erskine, Evelyn Guerrero, Chuck Hicks, and Jimmy Ortega. Of note: McCoy from Classic *Trek* appears, though his name is never spoken. This show was made in both a two-part TV and a movie format although the episodes made for TV are cut down and some scenes heavily edited. The unedited versions are available from Paramount on video or laser disc.

Endar, Captain — Talarian, played by Sherman Howar, who adopts a human son in *TNG* episode "Suddenly Human."

Endeavor, USS — ship used as a blockade in the Klingon civil war mentioned in *TNG* episode "Reunion." In "The Game," the *Endeavor*'s crew is one of the first to become addicted to the Ktaran game.

Endicor system — destination of the *Enterprise* before it is picked up by the time vortex and almost destroyed in *TNG* episode "Time Squared."

endroki — another game mentioned in reference to billiards in *TNG* episode "Tapestry."

Eneg — played by Robert Horgan, a member of the underground on Ekos on Classic episode "Patterns of Force."

"Enemy, The" — third-season *TNG* episode written by David Kemper and Michael Piller, directed by David Carson. Geordi is stranded on the Galorndan Core with a Romulan crash victim and the two must learn to trust each other in order to survive. Guest stars: John Snyder, Andreas Katsulas, Steven Rankin, and Colm Meaney.

"Enemy Within, The" — first-season Classic *Trek* episode written by science-fiction author Richard Matheson and directed by Leo Penn, which aired 10/6/66. A transporter malfunction divides Kirk into twins, one evil, one good. Guest stars: Jim Goodwin (who also shows up as Farrell in "Mudd's Women," "Miri," and others), Edward Madden, and Garland Thompson. An alien unicorn dog, played by DeForest Kelley's dog, appears as well. Fans find the plot flawed because it never occurs to the characters to send a shuttle to the planet below to rescue the freezing men, but the shuttlecraft had not yet been conceived by *Trek* writers. Of note: This is the first time Spock uses his Vulcan neck pinch, invented by William Shatner and Leonard Nimoy in their spare time.

Energy Barrier — potent energy field which surrounds the entire galaxy at its rim and destroys most ships that attempt to cross it. It is first discovered in Classic episode (and second pilot) "Where No Man Has Gone Before," and again in "By Any Other Name" and "Is There in Truth No Beauty?"

Engelberg, Leslie — actress appeared in *DS9* "Vortex."

Ennan VI — in *TNG* episode "Time Squared," Pulaski says the ale she brings to dinner comes from Ennan VI.

Ensign, Michael — played Krola in *TNG* "First Contact."

Ensign Ro — fifth-season *TNG* episode written by Rick Berman and Michael Piller, directed by Les Landau. Ro Laren, a Bajoran who was court-martialed for disobeying her commanding officer's orders and causing deaths, has served her prison sentence and is assigned aboard the *Enterprise*. She must figure out the mysterious destruction of a colony near Cardassian territory. Guest stars: Michelle Forbes, Cliff Potts, Whoopi Goldberg, Ken Thorley, Jeffrey Hayenga, Frank Collison, Scott Marlowe, and Harley Venton.

"Ensigns of Command, The" — third-season *TNG* episode written by Melinda M. Snodgrass and directed by Cliff Bole. Human settlers on Tau Cygna V are in violation of a treaty with the Sheliak, and must be evacuated before the Sheliak come to destroy them. Guest stars: Eileen Seeley, Grainger Hines, Mark L. Taylor, Richard Allen, Mart McChesney, and Colm Meaney.

Enterprise, USS — *Constitution*-class starship first commanded by Robert April. Its various commanders include Christopher Pike, James Kirk, Will Decker, Spock, and Jean-Luc Picard (though Picard's ship is referred to in *TNG* as a *Galaxy*-class ship). It was destroyed in *The Search for Spock* but rebuilt by the end of *The Voyage Home*. It has gone through many stages of revision. The *Enterprise* of *The Next Generation* looks very different from the original version in "The Cage." In Classic *Trek* it housed 432 crewmembers. In *TNG* it holds over one thousand, many of them crewmembers' families. A legendary ship in Starfleet history, it is the only starship to come back from its first five-year mission relatively intact. Her call numbers are NCC 1701. Other versions are identified with additional letters, such as NCC 1701C, an *Ambassador*-class ship, captained by Rachel Garrett, from an alternate timeline that was supposedly destroyed in Picard's ship's timeline 22 years ago, in *TNG*'s "Yesterday's Enterprise." NCC 1701D is the streamlined, modernized starship Picard commands in *TNG*. This fifth starship *Enterprise* is said to have been manufactured at the Utopia Planetia shipyards on Mars.

Enterprise, ISS — pirate starship from a mirror universe captained by James Kirk and owned and run by the Empire in Classic episode "Mirror, Mirror."

"Enterprise Incident, The" — written by D. C. Fontana and directed by John Meredyth Lucas, this third-season Classic *Trek* episode aired 9/27/68. Kirk and Spock get secret orders to infiltrate the Romulan Neutral Zone, allow themselves to be captured, and sneak aboard the Romulan vessel to steal the infamous cloaking device. Guest stars: Joanne Linville, Jack Donner, and Richard Compton. Of note: In this episode Spock's ability to lie is tested and he admits to having another, unpronounceable name.

Enwright, Commodore — unseen character who orders the *Enterprise* to test the M–5 computer in Classic episode "The Ultimate Computer."

epidermal mold — material Soong used to construct Data and Lore in *TNG* episode "Datalore."

Epperson, Van — played Bajoran Clerk in *DS9* "Q Less" and the morgue attendant in "Time's Arrow, Part II."

Epsilon Canaris III — planet on the verge of war and destination of peace-keeper Commissioner Nancy Hedford in Classic episode "Metamorphosis" before the shuttlecraft is diverted to an asteroid housing Zefrem Cochrane and the Companion.

Epsilon Indi — system in which the planet Triacus is located, home of the Gorgon which caused the scientific team to kill themselves in Classic episode "And the Children Shall Lead." The *Enterprise* rescues the children from Triacus, unaware they are bringing the Gorgon on board with them. The planet Andor is also located in the system as stated in *TNG* episode "The Child."

Epsilon IX Sector — the *Enterprise*'s destination in *TNG* episode "Samaritan Snare."

Epsilon Monitoring Station — station which monitored the progress of the ship *Vejur*'s attack on the Klingon ships and reported back to Starfleet in *The Motion Picture*. It was eventually destroyed by the Vejur.

Epsilon Mynos system — planet where Aldea from *TNG* episode "When the Bough Breaks" is located.

Epstein, Terence, Professor — mentioned in *TNG* episode "11001001" as Dr. Crusher's favorite instructor who teaches at Starbase 74.

Eraclitus — character, played by Ted Scott, who played psychokinetic chess with Alexander from Classic episode "Plato's Stepchildren."

Erb, Stephanie — played Liva in *TNG* "Man of the People."

Erko — played by Patrick Cronin, aide and master of protocol to Campio in *TNG* episode "Cost of Living."

Erman, John — director of Classic *Trek* "The Empath," as well as many other movies and TV series.

"Errand of Mercy" — written by Gene L. Coon and directed by John Newland, this first-season Classic *Trek* episode aired 3/23/67. Kirk and Spock beam down to Organia to get permission from the inhabitants to build a

Federation base on the planet. Tensions erupt, however, when the Klingons decide they want to build there as well. Guest stars: David Hillary Hughes, Jon Abbott, John Colicos, Peter Brocco, Victor Lundin, George Sawaya, and Walt Davis. Of note: This episode results in the famous Organian Peace Treaty and introduces the Klingon mind sifter. First appearance, as well, of Kirk and Spock in tights.

Ersalrope Wars — the planet Ersalrope was destroyed in these wars by weapons made by the Minos in *TNG* episode "The Arsenal of Freedom."

Erskine, David — played a Bandi Shopkeeper in *TNG* "Encounter at Farpoint."

Erstwhile, SS — class 9 cargo freighter captained by Thaddiun Okona in *TNG* episode "The Outrageous Okona."

Erwin, Bill — played Dr. Dalen Quaice in *TNG* "Remember Me."

Erwin, Lee — scriptwriter of Classic *Trek* "Whom Gods Destroy."

Erwin, Libby — played a technician in Classic *Trek* "The Lights of Zetar."

Esoqq — Chalnoth warrior, played by Reiner Schone, in *TNG* episode "Allegiance" who is kidnapped along with Picard, Tholl, and Haro.

Espinoza, Richard — second assistant director on *The Wrath of Khan*. His other film credits include *Vice Squad* and *Yellowbeard*.

Essex, USS — ship lost 200 years ago in *TNG* episode "Power Play." The *Enterprise* finds it, apparently haunted by its dead crew, but they are not ghosts, simply the Ux Mal prisoners trying to escape and take over the *Enterprise*.

Estragon, Samuel, Professor — legendary archeologist, mentioned in *TNG* episode "Captain's Holiday," who searched for the *Tox Uthat* and tracked it to Risa, but died before he could find it. Vash was his assistant.

Ethan — another name the boy Barash (see entry) calls himself in *TNG* episode "Future Imperfect."

"Ethics" — fifth-season *TNG* episode written by Stuart and Sara Charno and Ronald D. Moore, directed by Chip Chalmers. Worf has an accident that severs his spinal cord and could leave him permanently paralyzed. A new doctor, however, has been experimenting with a procedure that could help him. Meanwhile Worf considers ritualistic suicide. Guest stars: Caroline Kava, Brian Bonsall, and Patti Yasutake.

Eugenics Wars — occurred in Earth's late 20th century (the 1990s) and resulted in the last World War on Earth. The "supermen," who were genetically created and bred for the war, took over Earth for awhile, until they were chased out of power. Khan, of Classic episode "Space Seed" and who reappears in *The Wrath of Khan*, is a "superman" left over from the Eugenics Wars.

Evadne IV — destination of the *Enterprise* when they meet the "forgettable" Paxans in *TNG* episode "Clues."

Evans, Richard — played Isak in Classic *Trek* "The Patterns of Force" and was also a regular on *Peyton Place*.

Evans, Charlie — orphan with undisciplined and deadly mind powers, marooned on Thasus after a colony ship crashed on the planet. He attempts to take over the *Enterprise* in Classic episode "Charlie X."

Evans — crewman, played by Lee Duncan, in Classic episode "Elaan of Troyius."

Evers, Jason — played Rael in Classic *Trek* "Wink of an Eye." Born in 1922, Evers's numerous TV credits include guest spots on *Gunsmoke* and *Fantastic Journey*.

"Evolution" — third-season *TNG* episode written by

Michael Piller and Michael Wagner, directed by Winrich Kolbe. Wesley accidentally lets loose some Nanites he has been experimenting with, which infest the ship and cause many malfunctions. Guest stars: Ken Jenkins, Whoopi Goldberg, Mary McCusker, Randall Patrick, Scott Grimes, and Amy O'Neill.

Ewing, Diana — played Droxine in Classic *Trek* "The Cloud Minders."

Excalbia — world where the rock creature Yarnek, of Classic episode "The Savage Curtain," brings Kirk and crew to fight with heroic and evil figures of the past. A patch of Earth-like territory is created to protect the humans from the planet's poisonous atmosphere.

Excalibur, USS — commanded by Captain Harris, this starship is attacked by the M–5 computer in Classic episode "The Ultimate Computer," and the entire crew is killed. Another version of this ship is commanded by Riker in *TNG* episode "Redemption."

Excelsior, USS — this is a fat-bellied version of a starship seen in *The Search for Spock*, captained by Stiles. Later, in *The Undiscovered Country*, Sulu is captain of the *Excelsior*. His yeoman is a young man who closely resembles Christian Slater (see entry). Another officer aboard the ship is Commander Rand.

Exeter, USS — ship, commanded by Captain Ronald Tracey, which the *Enterprise* finds adrift about the planet Omega IV in Classic episode "The Omega Glory."

Exo III — cold, frozen world where Dr. Korby and his androids are found living in underground caves in Classic episode "What Are Little Girls Made Of?"

"Eye of the Beholder, The" — written by David P. Harmon, this animated Classic *Trek* episode aired 1/5/74. Giant, intelligent slug-beings of the planet Lactra put Kirk, Spock, and McCoy into a zoo. The telepathic

Lactrans don't understand that humans are intelligent because the officers cannot communicate on their level. Spock finally communicates with them using his rudimentary Vulcan telepathy on a Lactran child. Guest voices: James Doohan (Lt. Arex, Lt. Commander Tom Markel) and Majel Barrett (Randi Bryce).

Eymorgs — name the mentally childlike females of Sigma Draconis call themselves. The men, called Morgs by the women, refer to the women as the "Givers of Pain and Delight" in Classic episode "Spock's Brain."

Fabrina — sun of the Fabrini system which once had eight planets before it went nova. The people of Yonada are the survivors, as mentioned in Classic episode "For the World Is Hollow and I Have Touched the Sky."

Fabrini — people of Fabrina who now live on the spaceship world Yonada in Classic episode "For the World Is Hollow and I Have Touched the Sky." The Fabrini records contain a cure for xenopolycythemia, the disease from which McCoy is dying when he meets Natira.

"Face of the Enemy" — sixth-season *TNG* episode written by Naren Shankar and René Echevarria, directed by Gabrielle Beaumont. Troi awakens to find herself on board a Romulan vessel, disguised as a Romulan. She has been kidnapped by N'Vek who wants her to impersonate Rakal of the Tal Shiar of Imperial Romulan Intelligence to help him get three members of the Romulan underground, held in stasis in the ship's cargo bay, to Federation space. Guest stars: Carolyn Seymour and Scott MacDonald.

Faga, Gary — played the airlock technician who gets neck pinched by Spock in *Star Trek: The Motion Picture*. He also played one of the prison guards watching McCoy in *The Search for Spock*.

Fairmont Hotel — mentioned by Dixon Hill's secretary in *TNG* episode "The Big Goodbye."

Faison, Matthew — guest starred in *DS9* "Babel."

Fajo, Father — wealthy thief and Kivas Fajo's father, mentioned in *TNG* episode "The Most Toys."

Fajo, Kivas — Zibalian trader from *TNG* episode "The Most Toys." A collector of rare objects, played by Saul Rubinek, who steals Data for his collection.

Fallow — leader of the Waddi who is in charge of the game Quark plays in which the pieces are really Sisko, Kira, Julian, and Dax in *DS9* episode "Move Along Home."

Famen — *Enterprise* shuttlecraft in *TNG* episode "Chain of Command."

"Family" — fourth-season *TNG* episode written by Ronald D. Moore from a premise by Susanne Lambdin and Bryan Stewart, directed by Les Landau. Still recovering from his experience as a Borg, Picard takes a leave on Earth and visits his family in Labarre, France. Worf also sees his parents, and Wesley sees a message from his long-dead father. Guest stars: Jeremy Kemp, Samantha Eggar, Theodore Bikel, Georgia Brown, Whoopi Goldberg, Colm Meaney, Dennis Creaghan, David Tristan Birken, and Doug Wert.

Fancy, Richard — appeared in *TNG* "The First Duty."

Farek, Dr. — Ferengi doctor on the ship *Krayton* in *TNG* episode "Ménage à Troi."

Farley, James — played Lt. Lang in Classic *Trek* "Arena."

Farley, Morgan — played Hacom in Classic *Trek* "Return of the Archons" and Marak Scholar in "The Omega Glory." Film credits include *A Killing Affair*, *Orphan Train*, and *Charlie and the Great Balloon Race*.

Farpoint — complex built and inhabited by the Bandi, but discovered to be a life-form all its own in *TNG* episode "Encounter at Farpoint."

Farr, Kimberly — played Lango in *TNG* "Symbiosis."

Farragut, USS — commanded by Captain Garrovick, the ship Kirk first served on as a lieutenant during his first deep-space assignment, when the ship ran into the vampire cloud that killed Garrovick. Kirk meets up with the cloud creature again eleven years later in Classic episode "Obsession."

Farralon, Dr. — director of the mining facility at Tyrus VIIA in *TNG* episode "The Quality of Life."

Farrell, Brioni — played Tula in Classic *Trek* "Return of the Archons." Her movie credits include *Keefer* and *My Tutor*. She also guest starred on the TV shows *The Man from U.N.C.L.E.* and *The Bionic Woman*.

Farrell, Geraldine — guest starred in *DS9* "Babel."

Farrell, Terry — stars as Jadzia Dax on *DS9*. Born in Cedar Rapids, Iowa, Farrell signed on with the Elite modeling agency at 16 and has appeared on the covers of *Mademoiselle* and *Vogue*. Her first TV role was the short-lived series *Paper Dolls* (with Jonathan Frakes). She also appeared in an episode of the reincarnated *The Twilight Zone*, and guest starred on *The Cosby Show*, *Family Ties*, and *Quantum Leap*. Films include *Back to School* (with Rodney Dangerfield), *Beverly Hills Madam* (with Faye Dunaway), *The Deliberate Stranger* (as a victim of Ted Bundy, who was played by Mark Harmon), and *Hellraiser III: Hell on Earth* (in which she was spotted by *TNG* producers Rick Berman and Michael Piller). She was a *Star Trek* fan when she was a little girl, and even owned a tribble. Other coincidences: She knew Michael Dorn prior to getting the role, and she and Marina Sirtis have a mutual friend. She lives in Los Angeles with her dog, Freckles.

Farrell, John, Lieutenant — ship's navigator, played by Jim Goodwin, in Classic episodes "The Enemy Within," "Miri," and "Mudd's Women."

Farrell — Kirk's personal guard, played by Pete Kellert, in mirror universe in Classic episode "Mirror, Mirror."

Farspace Starbase *Earhart* — location of the Bonestell Recreation Facility and mentioned in *TNG* episode "Samaritan Snare" as the only frontier outpost before the Klingons joined the Federation.

Farwell, Jonathan — played Captain Walker Keel in *TNG* "Conspiracy."

***Fearless*, USS** — *Excelsior*-class starship seen in *TNG* episode "Where No One Has Gone Before."

Feder, Todd — played Federation Man in *DS9* "Babel."

Federation — United Federation of Planets, founded in 2161, as mentioned in *TNG* episode "The Outcast."

Federation Undersecretary for Agricultural Affairs — Nilz Baris's title in Classic episode "The Trouble with Tribbles."

Feinburger — medical scanner used by McCoy and named after Irving Feinburg, a famous 20th-century technician.

Fek'lhr — Klingon demon in *TNG* episode "Devil's Due."

felicium — narcotic, mentioned in *TNG* episode "Symbiosis," which cured the Breckans and the Ornarans of a deadly plague 200 years before.

feline supplement 127 — food Data gives his cat which shows up in the replicators on several decks in *TNG* episode "A Fistful of Datas."

Fellini, Colonel — man, played by Ed Peck, who captures Kirk at the Omaha Air Force Base on 1960s Earth in Classic episode "Tomorrow Is Yesterday."

felodesine chip — orange wafer that contains poison in *TNG* episode "The Defector."

Felton, Ensign — *Enterprise* con officer, played by Sheila Franklin, who appears in several *TNG* episodes.

Fento — Mintakan wise man, played by John McLiam, in *TNG* episode "Who Watches the Watchers."

Ferdin, Pamelyn — played Mary Janowski in Classic *Trek* "And the Children Shall Lead." As a child, she was a familiar face in television shows of the 1960s and '70s. Her credits include Disney movies as well as a regular character on the Saturday morning TV series *Space Academy*.

Ferengi — small, bald, and large-eared species, driven by greed and immature relative to their technology, which was stolen. The women are considered inferior, are not educated, and never wear clothing. Ferengi are hostile to the Federation, though more like irritating, dangerous children than threatening enemies. Quark of *DS9* is a Ferengi, and though motivated by greed, he seems to show some integrity in certain situations as the series progresses, giving his character more depth. Their ears are their most sensitive spot. They refer to their "lobes" as one of their most erogenous zones when sexually aroused. They also rate another Ferengi's courage or masculinity by the size of his "lobes." Betazoids can read most alien beings' emotions, but not those of Ferengis.

Ferguson, Brad — wrote Classic *Trek* novels *Crisis on Centaurus*, and *A Flag Full of Stars*.

Ferguson, Jessie Lawrence — played Lutan in *TNG* "Code of Honor."

Fergusson, Lynnda — played Doran in *DS9* "Emissary."

Fermi — *Enterprise* shuttle seen in *TNG* episode "True Q" and later destroyed in "Rascals."

Ferrer, Miguel — played first officer of the *Excelsior* in *The Search for Spock*. He has guest starred on *Miami Vice*, *Magnum P.I.*, and many other TV series. His film credits include *Deep Star Six* and *Robocop*. He was a regular in the acclaimed TV series *Twin Peaks* and returned to play the same role in the *Twin Peaks* movie *Fire Walk with Me*. He is the son of José Ferrer. He is also the drummer in a rock band whose lead singer is Bill Mumy (from *Lost in Space*).

Ferris, High Commissioner — Federation official on his way to Makus III, played by John Crawford, who wants Kirk to abandon his search for the *Galileo* in Classic episode "The Galileo Seven."

Fesarius — name of Balok's First Federation flagship in Classic episode "The Corbomite Maneuver."

Festival — celebrated by the people of Beta III, also called Red Hour, during which they go wild for twelve hours and riot in the streets as seen in Classic episode "Return of the Archons."

Feynman — shuttlepod seen in *TNG* episode "The Nth Degree."

FGC 13 — cluster scanned by the *Enterprise* in *TNG* episode "Schisms."

FGC 47 — nebula studied by the *Enterprise* in *TNG* episode "The Icarus Factor."

Ficus Sector — mentioned in *TNG* episode "Up the Long Ladder" as a system with severe sunflares and the location of two Earth colonies, although there is no record of them. The inhabitants of Planet Five, a class M world in the system, have no modern technology.

Fiedler, John — played Hengist in Classic *Trek* "Wolf in the Fold." His numerous film credits include *True Grit*, *Double Indemnity*, *Woman of the Year*, and *The Cannonball Run*. He was a regular on *The Bob Newhart Show*, and has appeared in *Kolchak: The Night Stalker* and *Buffalo Bill*. He continues to guest star in various TV series.

Fiedling, Jerry — music composer of Classic *Trek* episodes "The Trouble with Tribbles" and "Spectre of the Gun." His other scores include *The Bionic Woman* and

Hogan's Heroes, as well as the movies *The Wild Bunch*, *The Enforcer*, and *The Gauntlet*.

Fields, Jimmy — played a guard in Classic *Trek* "The Cloud Minders."

Fields, Peter Allen — scriptwriter and story editor of *TNG* "Half a Life," "Silicon Avatar," "The Inner Light," and "Cost of Living." He also wrote *DS9* episode "Dax" with D. C. Fontana. He is now coproducer of *DS9*, which he enjoys more than writing for *TNG*. He likes the fact that the characters don't all get along and believes Gene Roddenberry made *TNG* too perfect. He was quoted in *Starlog* as saying, "For me as a writer, as someone who likes character conflict, this show is very exciting."

Finagle's Folly — green drink McCoy tells Kirk he makes well in Classic episode "The Ultimate Computer."

Finagle's Law — "Any port chosen for leave or liberty should not be one's own home port," Kirk quotes in Classic episode "Amok Time."

"Final Mission" — fourth-season *TNG* episode written by Kacey Arnold Ince and Jeri Taylor, directed by Corey Allen. Wesley is leaving the ship to enter Starfleet Academy, but before he leaves, he accompanies Picard in a shuttle to Pentarus V. The shuttle crashes, however, and Wesley must use all his knowledge to save Picard from death. Guest stars: Nick Tate, Kim Hamilton, and Mary Kohnert.

Finelli, Dario — scriptwriter of the animated episode "Albatross."

Finn, Kyril — artist and leader of the Ansata terrorists, he uses dimensional-shift devices to attack their enemy, the Rutians, and kidnaps Dr. Crusher in *TNG* episode "The High Ground." Played by Richard Cox, he dies in the episode.

Finnegan — practical joker, played by Bruce Mars, who plagued Kirk at the Academy and whom Kirk meets again on a recreational planet in Classic episode "Shore Leave."

Finnerman, Gerald Perry ("Jerry") — director of Classic *Trek* photography, he also worked on *Planet of the Apes*, *Moonlighting*, and others.

Finney, Benjamin, Lieutenant Commander — *Enterprise* records officer who frames Kirk for his own murder as revenge for Kirk's reporting him for negligence on duty. Finney, played by Richard Webb, turns out to be alive and later suffers a nervous breakdown in Classic episode "Court-Martial."

Finney, Jamie — daughter of Kirk's good friend Ben Finney and Kirk's namesake, played by Alice Rawlings. She thinks Kirk killed her father in Classic episode "Court-Martial."

Finoplak — salve that dissolves Data's uniform in *TNG* episode "The Most Toys."

Fionnula — appears in *DS9* as "Dax."

First Citizen — title of Merik (or Mericus), Lord of the Games and Chief Magistrate of the Condemned, on Planet 892 IV in Classic episode "Bread and Circuses."

"First Contact" — fourth-season *TNG* episode written by Marc Scott Zicree, Dennis Russell Bailey, David Bischoff, Joe Menosky, Michael Piller, and Ronald D. Moore, directed by Cliff Bole. Riker is injured while on a first contact mission on Malkor and taken to a local hospital, where the inhabitants discover he is an alien. Meanwhile, Picard and Troi reveal themselves to top officials, who aren't sure their world is ready for outside contact, with the exception of one scientist who has dreamed for years of making first contact. Guest stars: George Coe, Carolyn Seymour, Michael Ensign, George Hearn, Steven Anderson, Sachi Parker, and Bebe Neuwirth.

"First Duty, The" — fifth-season *TNG* episode written by Ronald D. Moore and Naren Shankar, directed by Paul Lynch. Wesley's Nova Squadron is responsible for the death of one of their own when they participate in a forbidden flying formation. Fearing punishment or possible expulsion from Starfleet Academy, they attempt to cover their tracks but their lies get more exaggerated. Guest stars: Wil Wheaton, Ray Walston, Jacqueline Brooks, Robert Duncan McNeill, Ed Lauter, Richard Fancy, Walker Brandt, Shannon Fill, and Richard Rothenberg.

First Electorine — title of the administrator on the planet Haven in the *TNG* episode of the same name.

First Federation — Balok in Classic episode "The Corbomite Maneuver" is from the First Federation.

First Security Guard — played by Colm Meaney in *TNG* episode "Lonely among Us."

Fisher, Technician — geologist, played by Edward Madden, and a member of the landing party on Alfa 177 who falls and hurts himself in Classic episode "The Enemy Within." He is beamed up before Kirk, but the ore on his uniform causes the transporter to malfunction.

"Fistful of Datas, A" — sixth-season *TNG* episode written by Robert Hewitt Wolfe and Brannon Braga, directed by Patrick Stewart. During a layover at a starbase, Worf goes to the holodeck with Alexander to play out a Western with his son, but things go wrong when the computer locks the program and pits Data against them in a deadly game of kidnapping and murder. Guest star: Brian Bonsall.

Fitts, Rick — guest starred in *TNG* "Violations."

Fitzgerald, Admiral — admiral, played by Richard Derr, on whom Spock calls for help when he runs into trouble searching for the missing Kirk in Classic episode "Mark of Gideon."

Fitzpatrick, Admiral — admiral, played by Ed Reimer, who orders Kirk to protect the quadro triticale on Space Station *K–7* in Classic episode "The Trouble with Tribbles."

Fix, Paul — played Dr. Mark Piper in Classic *Trek* "Where No Man Has Gone Before." Born in 1901, his many credits include the movie *Night of the Lepus* with DeForest Kelley. A regular character in the TV series *The Rifleman*, Fix died in 1983.

fizzbin — game Kirk creates to distract the guards in Classic episode "A Piece of the Action." It has very odd rules such as: Each player gets six cards except the player on the dealer's right who gets seven. The second card is turned up except on Tuesdays (though Kirk turns all the cards up as he deals). Two jacks is a half fizzbin, but three is a sralk which disqualifies the player. The player then needs a king or deuce, except at night when he needs a queen or four. It is excellent if another jack is dealt, unless the next card is a six, in which case the player must forfeit a card to the dealer, unless it's a black six in which case the player gets another card. The object of the game is to get a royal fizzbin, but the odds against that happening are astronomical. The last card dealt is called a kronk. Kirk doesn't get to finish explaining the rest.

Flaherty, Commander — *Ares* first officer who speaks 40 languages, as mentioned in *TNG* episode "The Icarus Factor."

Flanagan, Kellie — played the little blond girl in Classic *Trek* "Miri."

Flavius, Maximus — worshipper of the "Son," played by Rhodes Reason, who is killed defending Kirk in the arena in Classic episode "Bread and Circuses."

Fleck, John — played Commander Taibak in *TNG* "The Mind's Eye."

Fleetwood, Mick — lead singer of the famous musical group "Fleetwood Mac," he played the Andedian Delegate in *TNG* "Manhunt."

Fletcher, Robert — costume designer for *Star Trek:*

The Motion Picture, The Wrath of Khan, The Search for Spock, and *The Voyage Home.* His other costume credits include *Caveman* and *The Last Starfighter.*

flex coordinating sensor — device Wesley studies in preparation for his Academy exams in *TNG* episode "Coming of Age."

Fliegel, Richard — scriptwriter of *TNG* "Imaginary Friend."

Flint — immortal human who is six thousand years old when found by the crew in Classic episode "Requiem for Methuselah." Born Akharin, he realized he was immortal when he was struck through the heart in battle and didn't die. He claims to have been Leonardo da Vinci and Johannes Brahms, and to have known Alexander the Great and Galileo. He created Reena as his perfect wife. He also uses the name Mr. Brack (see entry).

Flood, Eloise — author of *TNG* novel *Chains of Command.*

Flores, Marissa — played by Erika Flores, the child winner of the primary school science fair aboard the *Enterprise* who is given the temporary title of Ensign by Picard because of her proven leadership skills in *TNG* episode "Disaster."

Flux Capacitor — term borrowed as a joke from *Buckaroo Banzai* and mentioned as a system on the *Enterprise* in *TNG* episode "Hollow Pursuits."

Flynn, Michael J. — played Zayner in *TNG* "The Hunted."

Foley, Lieutenant — found evidence that the three people the *Enterprise* is looking for were kidnapped, in *TNG* episode "Ménage à Troi."

Folsom point — Spock thinks the weapons used by the creatures in Classic episode "The Galileo Seven" are

Folsom points, reminiscent of those used by the old Folsom culture found on Earth in New Mexico.

Fontana, D. C. ("Dorothy") — scriptwriter of Classic *Trek* episodes "Charlie X," "Tomorrow Is Yesterday," "This Side of Paradise," "Journey to Babel," "Friday's Child," "By Any Other Name," "The Ultimate Computer," "The *Enterprise* Incident," and the animated episode "Yesteryear." Her other writing credits include the TV series *Logan's Run, Fantastic Journey, Buck Rogers,* and *Dallas.* She has written the novelization of the movie *The Questor Tapes* (scripted by Gene Roddenberry and Gene L. Coon), and the Classic *Trek* novel *Vulcan's Glory.* She also cowrote the *TNG* pilot, "Encounter at Farpoint," and episodes "Heart of Glory" and "Too Short a Season." Her most recent addition to the *Trek* trilogy is the script for *DS9* episode "Dax" (with *TNG* writer Peter Allen Fields).

food synthesizers — machines, later called *replicators* in *TNG* and *DS9,* that make and deliver food in Classic *Trek.*

foolie — in Miri's world, a game or trick played on someone, in Classic episode "Miri."

"For the World Is Hollow and I Have Touched the Sky" — written by Rick Vollaerts and directed by Tony Leader, this third-season Classic *Trek* episode aired 11/8/68. Yonada, a completely enclosed spaceship world, is on a collision course which must be corrected without violating the Prime Directive. McCoy, suffering from a rare incurable disease, decides he wants to stay on the world and marry its leader, Natira. A cure for his disease is found in the vast Fabrini library on this spaceship world and its course is corrected. Guest stars: Kate Woodville, Byron Morrow, and Jon Lormer.

Forbes, Michelle — played Dara in *TNG* "Half a Life." She also played Ensign Ro in "Ensign Ro," "Disaster," "Power Play," "Cause and Effect," and "The Next Phase." The role of Kira Nerys in *DS9* was originally created for her, but was altered when she announced she could not be in the series.

force field — invisible barrier used in the brig and in certain spots on *DS9* for sealing off an area.

Forchion, Raymond — played Ben Prieto in *TNG* "Skin of Evil."

Ford, John M. — author of Classic *Trek* novels *The Final Reflection* and *How Much for Just the Planet?*

Forest, Michael — played Apollo in Classic *Trek* "Who Mourns for Adonais?" His TV credits include *Gunsmoke, Branded,* and *The Rifleman.*

formazine — McCoy, who says it is a vitamin supplement, gives Hanar this drug which makes him edgy, in Classic episode "By Any Other Name."

Forrest, Brad — played an ensign in Classic *Trek* "That Which Survives."

Forrester, Larry — scriptwriter of *TNG* "The Battle."

Fortier, Robert — played Tomar in Classic *Trek* "By Any Other Name."

Foster — trainee on board the *Enterprise,* played by Phil Morris (son of Greg Morris), in *The Search for Spock.* Father and son starred in *Mission: Impossible* and *The New Mission: Impossible,* respectively.

Foster, Alan Dean — scriptwriter on *Star Trek: The Motion Picture.* He is also the author of numerous science-fiction books, as well as novelizations of movies such as *Aliens, The Last Starfighter,* and *Clash of the Titans.* He also wrote all the Log Books, which novelize the animated *Trek* series' scripts.

Foster, Stacie — played Bartel in *TNG* "Relics."

Fox, Robert, Ambassador — ambassador to Eminiar VII, played by Gene Lyons, who wants to help the planet make peace with Vendikar in Classic episode "A Taste of Armageddon."

Frakes, Jonathan — stars as William Riker, also called Number One, on *TNG*. His other acting credits include *Falcon Crest*, *Paper Dolls*, *Bare Essence*, and regular appearances on the soap opera *The Doctors*. A stage actor both on and off Broadway, he also appeared in the TV movie *The Nutcracker* and in the miniseries *Dream West* and *North and South*. Born in Pennsylvania, he attended Penn State and Harvard, where he studied psychology. He currently lives in Los Angeles and is married to actress Genie Francis (Laura, of Luke and Laura fame on *General Hospital*, and a regular on *Days of Our Lives*). He has also directed the *TNG* episodes "The Offspring," "The Drumhead," "Reunion," "Cause and Effect," "The Quality of Life," and "The Chase."

"Frame of Mind" — sixth-season *TNG* episode written by Brannon Braga and directed by Jim Conway. Riker keeps phasing out from reality and finding himself in a mental institution, where he is told his entire life is a mental hallucination and that he is very ill. Guest stars: Andrew Prine, Gary Werntz, David Selburg, and Susanna Thompson.

Francine — Gabrielle's friend, played by Kelly Ashmore, in *TNG* episode "We'll Always Have Paris."

Francis, Al — director of photography for many third-season Classic *Trek* episodes.

Francis, John H. — played science crewman in *TNG* "Sarek."

Frankenstein — doctor Guinan once knew, with whom she compares Wesley in *TNG* episode "Evolution."

Frankham, David — played Lawrence Marvick in Classic *Trek* "Is There in Truth No Beauty?" He has also appeared in the films *The Return of the Fly*, *Winter Kill*, *Eleanor: First Lady of the World*, and *Wrong Is Right*.

Franklin — *Enterprise* security guard killed when Borg beam aboard the bridge in *TNG* episode "Descent."

Franklin, Matt — unseen officer who dies from a pattern degradation when teleported with Scotty to the transport ship *Jenolan*, in *TNG* episode "Relics."

Franklin, Sheila — guest starred in *TNG* "A Matter of Time," "The Masterpiece Society," and "Imaginary Friend."

Fredericks — officer on *Enterprise* C in *TNG* episode "Yesterday's Enterprise."

Freeman, Ensign — *Enterprise* officer, played by Paul Bradley, given a Tribble by Uhura in Classic episode "The Trouble with Tribbles."

French, Bruce — played Sabin in *TNG* "The Drumhead."

Frewer, Matt — guest starred as Professor Berlinghoff Rasmussen in *TNG* "A Matter of Time." A well-known comedian and actor, he starred in the series *Max Headroom* and other TV shows, and has also made many film appearances.

"Friday's Child" — written by D. C. Fontana and directed by Joseph Pevney, this second-season Classic *Trek* episode aired 12/1/67. The Federation and the Klingons are vying for control of Capella IV. The *Enterprise* crew is forced to retreat to the hills and fight for their lives when their ship doesn't answer. Guest stars: Julie Newmar, Tige Andrews, Michael Dante, Cal Bolder, and Ben Gage. Of note: In an unusual move, this episode was obviously shot in real California country (probably the back lot), not on a sound stage using fake plants and painted skies.

Fried, Gerald — music composer for the Classic *Trek* episodes "Shore Leave," "Amok Time," "The Apple," "Catspaw," "Journey to Babel," "Friday's Child," "Wolf in the Fold," and "The Paradise Syndrome." He also worked on *The Man from U.N.C.L.E.*, *The Cabinet of Caligari*, *Soylent Green*, and *Roots*.

Friedman, Mal — played Hendorff in Classic *Trek* "The Apple."

Friedman, Michael Jan — wrote *TNG* novels *A Call to Darkness*, *Doomsday World*, *Fortune's Light*, *Reunion*, *Relics*, and the Classic novel *Faces of Fire*.

Fries, Sandy — scriptwriter of *TNG* "Coming of Age."

Froman, David — played Captain K'Nera on *TNG* "Heart of Glory."

fusing pitons — used by Worf, Crusher, and Picard in *TNG* episode "Chain of Command" to climb to the secret Cardassian base on Seltris III.

fusion bombs — kind of bomb supposedly used in the war between Eminiar VII and Vendikar, but they are really imaginary bombs in a war being fought by a computer in Classic episode "A Taste of Armageddon."

"Future Imperfect" — fourth-season *TNG* episode written by J. Larry Carroll and David Bennett Carren, directed by Les Landau. Riker wakes up to find himself captain of the *Enterprise* sixteen years in the future and is told he had a virus which wiped out all his memories of the last sixteen years. Guest stars: Andreas Katsulas, Chris Demetral, Carolyn McCormick, April Grace, Patti Yasutake, Todd Merrill, and George O. Hanlon, Jr.

Gabrielle — played by Isabel Lorca, reminds Picard of Jenice Manheim in the Paris holoimage in *TNG* episode "We'll Always Have Paris."

Gaetano — *Enterprise* radiation technician, played by Peter Marko, who is the second member of the shuttlecraft to be killed on Taurus II in Classic episode "The Galileo Seven."

Gagarin IV — location of the Darwin Genetic Research Station mentioned in *TNG* episode "Unnatural Selection."

Gage, Ben — played Akaar in Classic *Trek* "Friday's Child." He was a guest star in many TV shows of the 1960s, including *Iron Horse.*

gakh — "serpent worms," a Klingon delicacy, served up in *TNG* episode "A Matter of Honor."

Gal Ga'thong — area on Romulus where firefalls occur, mentioned in *TNG* episode "The Defector."

Galactic Cultural Exchange Project — organization mentioned as sponsoring the Karidian players in Classic episode "The Conscience of the King."

Galaxy-class — the Federation's most powerful class of ship. The *Enterprise* is of this class.

"Galaxy's Child" — fourth-season *TNG* episode written by Maurice Hurley and Thomas Kartozian, directed by Winrich Kolbe. Dr. Leah Brahms comes aboard the ship but is not what Geordi expected. Meanwhile an alien life-form, believing the *Enterprise* to be its mother, attaches itself to the ship and drains its power. Guest stars: Susan Gibney, Whoopi Goldberg, Jana Marie Hupp, April Grace, and Lanei Chapman.

Galen, Richard, Professor — famed archeologist and one of Picard's past teachers who tries to get the captain to accompany him on a micropaleontology quest. He is later killed in *TNG* episode "The Chase."

Galen IV — the Talarians attacked this Federation colony ten years before, where Jeremiah Rossa, whose Talarian father is Endar, was raised by Talarians. Galen IV is mentioned in *TNG* episode "Suddenly Human."

Galileo, NCC 1701/7 — *Enterprise* shuttlecraft which breaks up in orbit over Taurus II in Classic episode "The Galileo Seven." It is later replaced and seen again in "Metamorphosis." Supposedly the real, life-sized model of the shuttle sits in a fan's garage in Los Angeles.

"Galileo Seven, The" — written by Oliver Crawford and S. Bar David, directed by Robert Gist, this first-season Classic *Trek* episode aired 1/5/67. Spock's first command mission, of a shuttle called *Galileo*, crash lands on Taurus II where large creatures threaten the crew and kill two members. Guest stars: Don Marchall, Peter Marko, Reese Vaughn, Grant Woods, Phyllis Douglas, and John Crawford. Of note: The shuttlecraft is destroyed in this episode, but is later replaced and used in "Metamorphosis."

Gallegos, Joshua — played a security officer in *Star Trek: The Motion Picture*. Other film credits include *Survival of Diana* and *The Mystic Warrior*.

Gallian, The — title of a magazine seen on Planet 892 IV in Classic episode "Bread and Circuses."

Galliulin, Irini — played by Mary Linda Rapelye, member of a gang of "space hippies" from Classic episode

"The Way to Eden." She and Chekov met previously at the Academy and appear to share a strong attraction for each other.

Galloway, Lieutenant — *Enterprise* security officer, played by David L. Ross, in Classic episodes "Miri," "A Taste of Armageddon," and "The Omega Glory," in which he is killed by Captain Tracey.

Galor IV — location of an annex of the Daystrom institute and a Starfleet research center. Also the birthplace of Haftel from *TNG* episode "The Offspring."

Galorndon core — referred to in *TNG* episode "The Defector" as well as the site of a Romulan scout vessel crash landing in *TNG* episode "The Enemy."

Galt — master thrall, played by Joseph Ruskin, in Classic episode "The Gamesters of Triskelion."

Galvan V — world where, according to Data in *TNG* episode "Data's Day," a marriage is successful only if children are produced within one year.

Galway, Arlene, Lieutenant — member of the landing party and chief biologist on the *Enterprise,* played by Beverly Washburn. In Classic episode "The Deadly Years," she contracts the deadly Gamma Hydra IV radiation which ages her prematurely, and she dies of old age before a cure is found.

"Game, The" — fifth-season *TNG* episode written by Susan Sackett, Fred Bronson, and Brannon Braga, directed by Corey Allen. Riker brings a game from Risa aboard the *Enterprise,* and soon the entire crew is addicted to it and neglecting its duties. Guest stars: Wil Wheaton, Ashley Judd, Colm Meaney, Katherine Moffat, and Diane M. Hurley.

Gamelan V — a world subjected to deadly radiation from an abandoned garbage scow, in *TNG* episode "Final Mission." Gamelan's leader is Songi.

"Gamesters of Triskelion, The" — written by Margaret Armen and directed by Gene Nelson, this second-season Classic *Trek* episode aired 1/5/68. Kirk, Uhura, and Chekov are kidnapped and transported to Triskelion as slaves to entertain three powerful mind beings called "The Providers." Guest stars: Joseph Ruskin, Angelique Pettyjohn, Steve Sandor, Mickey Morton, Victoria George, Jane Ross, and Dick Crockett.

Gamma II — world to which Kirk, Uhura, and Chekov are beaming when they are snatched by the Providers' long-range transport beam and brought to Triskelion to become thralls in Classic episode "The Gamesters of Triskelion."

Gamma VII Sector — where the USS *Lantree* was patrolling in *TNG* episode "Unnatural Selection."

Gamma 7A solar system — system wiped out by the giant space amoeba in Classic episode "The Immunity Syndrome."

Gamma 400 system — mentioned as the location of Starbase *12* in Classic episode "Space Seed."

Gamma Arigulon — site of radiation anomalies the *Enterprise* is studying in *TNG* episode "Reunion."

Gamma Canaris N — small planetoid much like Earth, inhabited by Zefrem Cochrane, to which the shuttle is steered by the Companion in Classic episode "Metamorphosis."

Gamma Erandi Nebula — area where the *Enterprise* is incommunicado when Riker, Deanna, and Lwaxana are kidnapped in *TNG* episode "Ménage à Troi."

gamma field — force which kills the Nanites in *TNG* episode "Evolution."

Gamma Hromi II — location of the Gatherer encampment in *TNG* episode "The Vengeance Factor."

Gamma Hydra IV — class M world, close to the neutral zone and within the jurisdiction of Starbase 10, where a deadly radiation from a comet's tail killed the colonists by causing them to age rapidly, in Classic episode "The Deadly Years."

Gamma Quadrant — virtually unexplored section of the galaxy only accessible since the discovery of the wormhole near Bajor and *Deep Space 9*, located in the Alpha Quadrant. The Barzan wormhole leads there as well, but is an unstable wormhole.

Gamma Sequence — evasive maneuver used by the *Enterprise* in *TNG* episode "Yesterday's Enterprise."

Gamma Tauri IV — planet from which the Ferengi stole a K 9 converter, mentioned in *TNG* episode "The Last Outpost."

Gamma Trianguli VI — visited by the *Enterprise* crew in Classic episode "The Apple," a very warm, jungle-like planet where the inhabitants are ruled by a machine called Vaal.

Gamma Vertis IV — Gem's planet in Classic episode "The Empath" where the inhabitants are mutes with the empathic healing powers to survive great catastrophes.

***Gandhi*, USS** — ship on which the second Riker, created by a transporter field distortion and still a lieutenant, accepts a position in *TNG* episode "Second Chances."

Ganges — runabout used on *Deep Space 9*.

Ganino, Trent Christopher — scriptwriter who penned *TNG* "Yesterday's Enterprise."

Gans, Ron — the voice of Armus in *TNG* "Skin of Evil."

Ganymede — Jupiter moon where Scotty claims he got his "green" drink in Classic episode "By Any Other Name."

Garadius IV — destination of the *Enterprise* after it

answers a Romulan ship's distress call in *TNG* episode "The Next Phase."

Garaman sector — destination of the *Enterprise* in *TNG* episode "Rightful Heir" when Worf tries to have a vision of the Klingon "god" Kahless.

Garcie, Leo — played the bellboy in *TNG* "The Royale."

Gardeners of Eden — terraforming project on Velara mentioned in *TNG* episode "Home Soil."

Garin, Dr. — leader, played by Richard Cansino, of Bre'el's research team in *TNG* episode "Déjà Q."

Garion, Buddy — played Krako's gangster in Classic *Trek* "A Piece of the Action." His other credits include *The Death Squad* ('74).

Garrison, C.P.O. — *Enterprise* officer, played by Adam Roarke, under the command of Captain Pike in Classic episode "The Menagerie."

Garner, Shay — played a scientist in *TNG* "A Matter of Time."

Garo VII system — location of Pandro, Commander Ari Bem's homeworld from animated episode "Bem."

Garon II — planet mentioned in *TNG* episode "Ensign Ro" where, as a member of an away team, Ensign Ro disobeyed orders, causing eight people to die; an act for which she went to prison.

Garr, Teri — played Roberta Lincoln in Classic *Trek* "Assignment: Earth." Garr has guest starred on many TV series including *The Ken Berry Wow Show*, *The Burns and Schreiber Comedy Hour*, *The Girl with Something Extra*, and *The Sonny and Cher Comedy Hour*. Her most famous film credits are *Young Frankenstein*, *The Black Stallion*, *Tootsie*, and *Mr. Mom*. She is a favorite guest of David Letterman, appearing regularly on his talk show, and recently appeared on *Murphy Brown*.

Garretson, Katy E. — second assistant director on *The Undiscovered Country.*

Garrett, John — played a lieutenant in *TNG* "Loud As a Whisper."

Garrett, Rachel, Captain — captain of the *Enterprise* C, played by Tricia O'Neil, who is killed in a Klingon attack in *TNG* episode "Yesterday's Enterprise."

Garrett, Spencer — played Simon Tarses in *TNG* "The Drumhead."

Garrovick, Captain — captain of the *Farragut,* and the commander during Kirk's first deep-space assignment, who dies when the vampire cloud creature attacks his ship.

Garrovick, Ensign — *Enterprise* security officer, played by Stephen Brooks, and the son of Captain Garrovick (Kirk's first deep-space commander), who blames himself for the deaths of the men killed by the vampire cloud creature when it attacks the *Enterprise.*

Garth of Izar — brilliant starship commander and tactician, played by Steve Inhat, who is an Academy hero. He suffers from a mental breakdown and is sent to the asylum on Elba II, which he then takes over and where he tortures Kirk, Spock, and the asylum's governor, Cory, in Classic episode "Whom Gods Destroy." He has learned cellular metamorphosis from an alien race, which further complicates matters. When finally cured, he has no memory of his aberrant behavior.

Garum — Roman condiment served with roasted sparrows on Planet 892 IV in Classic episode "Bread and Circuses."

Gates, Barbara — played the astrochemist in Classic *Trek* "The Changeling." Her other credits include *The Young Country* ('70).

Gatherers — nomadic raiders, led by Chorgon, who

left Acamar III because of blood feuds, in *TNG* episode "The Vengeance Factor."

Gatti, Jennifer — guest starred in *TNG* episode "Birthright."

Gault — farm world where Worf was raised by human parents along with a human stepbrother after he was found at the Khitomer Outpost as mentioned in *TNG* episode "Heart of Glory."

Gautreaux, David — played Commander Branch in *Star Trek: The Motion Picture.* He was originally hired to play Xon in the new *Star Trek* TV series before Nimoy agreed to return as Spock and the first movie was made.

Gav — Tellerite, played by John Wheeler, who opposes Coridan's entry to the Federation in Classic episode "Journey to Babel" and is later murdered by an Orion.

Geary, Richard — played an Andorian in Classic *Trek* "Whom Gods Destroy." His other credits include *The Man from U.N.C.L.E.* and *Perry Mason.*

Gedeon, Conroy — played the agent at the bar in *The Search for Spock.*

Geer, Ellen — played Dr. Kila Marr in *TNG* "Silicon Avatar."

Gehring, Ted — played a police officer in Classic *Trek* "Assignment: Earth." His credits include *The Intruders, The Rockford Files, Captains and the Kings, The Legend of the Lone Ranger, The Night the Bridge Fell Down, Little House on the Prairie, Alice,* and *Dallas.* He was a regular on the TV series *The Family Holvak.*

Gem — empath named by Dr. McCoy, played by Kathryn Hays, who has a special ability by which she can heal severe wounds in another with a touch of her hand. The Minarans, who can save only one planet as their sun goes nova, choose to save Gem's world, Gamma Vertis IV in the Minara system, in the Classic episode "The Empath."

Gemarians — people for whom Picard mediated a dispute, mentioned in *TNG* episode "Captain's Holiday." Their neighbors are the Dachlyds.

Gemaris V — mentioned in *TNG* episode "Captain's Holiday" as a world where Picard mediated a dispute.

Gendel, Morgan — scriptwriter of *TNG* "The Inner Light," "Starship Mine," and of *DS9* "The Passenger."

General Order Number One — another term for the Prime Directive (see entry).

General Order Number Seven — order, quoted in Classic episode "The Menagerie," which allows no vessel under any circumstances to approach Talos IV.

General Order Number Six — supposedly a ship's self-destruct sequence automatically activated 24 hours after the entire crew has died as mentioned in animated episode "The Albatross."

General Order Number Twenty-Four — directs an entire world to be destroyed if the galaxy is threatened. Kirk gives this order to Scotty in Classic episode "A Taste of Armageddon."

Genesis — device, developed by the science team headed by Dr. Carol Marcus on Regula I in *The Wrath of Khan*, which creates a living world from a lifeless planet.

Genesis Planet — unstable world created when Khan activated the Genesis wave in an attempt to destroy the *Enterprise*. Because David Marcus had put proto-matter into the device, against Dr. Carol Marcus's wishes, the world aged too quickly and was breaking up even as the *Enterprise* and the *Grissom* arrived on it, in *The Search for Spock*.

genetronic replicator — experimental device that creates a new spinal column for Worf in *TNG* episode "Ethics."

Genghis Khan — considered the most ruthless of military geniuses, played by Nathan Jung, he is encountered in Classic episode "The Savage Curtain," but is really an image taken from Kirk's mind.

Genovese, Mike — played the desk sergeant in *TNG* "The Big Goodbye."

Gentile, Robert — played the Romulan technician in Classic *Trek* "The *Enterprise* Incident."

George, Victoria — played Ensign Jana Haines in Classic *Trek* "The Gamesters of Triskelion."

George — the male humpback whale the *Enterprise* transports to the 23rd century in *The Voyage Home*.

Gerber, Steve — scriptwriter of *TNG* "Contagion."

Gerrold, David — scriptwriter for Classic *Trek* "I, Mudd," "The Trouble with Tribbles," "The Cloud Minders," and the animated "More Tribbles, More Troubles" and "Bem." He also scripted the *TNG* episode "Encounter at Farpoint" and helped create the show and its characters. He provided the voice of two characters in the animated series: Korax in "More Tribbles, More Troubles" and M 3 Green in "Jihad." He has written scripts for other TV series including *Logan's Run* and *The New Twilight Zone*. He is the author of the books *The Trouble with Tribbles*, *The World of Star Trek*, the Classic *Trek* novel *The Galactic Whirlpool*, and the *TNG* novel *Encounter at Farpoint*. A noted science-fiction writer outside the *Trek* genre as well, he has many short stories and novels to his credit, including his most recent *War Against the Chtorr* series. He lives with his son in the Los Angeles area.

Gettysburg, USS — ship once commanded by Admiral Mark Jameson mentioned in *TNG* episode "Too Short a Season."

Ghaimon — exotic language Flaherty speaks in *TNG* episode "The Icarus Factor."

Ghorusda — Tam Elbrun's destination in *TNG* episode "Tin Man" where an apparently very alien, very complex culture lives.

Ghorusda Disaster — first contact situation in which 47 people were killed, including the captain of the *Adelphi* and two friends of Riker's, as mentioned in *TNG* episode "Tin Man."

Gibney, Susan — played Dr. Leah Brahms in *TNG* "Booby Trap" and "Galaxy's Child."

Gibson, Ensign — *Enterprise* officer, played by Jennifer Dauphin, in *TNG* episode "The Dauphin."

Gideon — world where overpopulation, due to a lack of disease and the long life span of the people, has become such a problem that the government is willing to infect their own biosphere with a deadly disease to control it. Kirk is kidnapped and held on the planet in Classic episode "Mark of Gideon."

Gierasch, Stefan — played Dr. Hal Moseley in *TNG* "A Matter of Time."

Gilden, Mel — author of *TNG* novel *Boogeymen* and Classic *Trek* novel *The Starship Trap.*

Giles Belt — mentioned in *TNG* episode "The Most Toys."

Gill, John — historian and Kirk's former teacher, played by David Brian, who goes to Ekos as a cultural observer but ends up violating the Prime Directive when he tries to help bring the people together. His attempts result in the creation of a Nazi-type regime he cannot control in Classic episode "Patterns of Force."

Gillespie, Ann — played Hildebrandt in *TNG* "Pen Pals" and also appeared in *DS9* "Babel."

Gillespie, Ensign — *Enterprise* officer, played by Duke Moosekian, in *TNG* episode "Night Terrors."

Gilman, Sam — played Doc Holliday in Classic *Trek* "Spectre of the Gun." He was a regular in the TV series *Shane*, and also guest starred on many shows of the 1960s, including *The Rifleman*.

Gilnor — dead terrorist mentioned in *TNG* episode "Too Short a Season."

Gimpel, Sharon — played the creature, a salt vampire, in Classic *Trek* "The Man Trap."

gin'tak — Klingon warrior spear seen in *TNG* episode "Birthright, Parts I and II."

Giotto, Lieutenant Commander — head of the Janus VI security in Classic episode "The Devil in the Dark," played by Barry Russo.

Gi'ral — Klingon female, captured at Khitomer, whose daughter, Ba'el, is half Klingon, half Romulan. Her husband is the Romulan commander of the Carraya System colony in *TNG* episode "Birthright, Parts I and II."

Gisborne, Sir Guy of — adversary Picard is forced to duel in the Robin Hood scenario Q creates in *TNG* episode "Qpid."

Gist, Robert — director of Classic *Trek* episode "The Galileo Seven."

Givers of Pain and Delight — name the Morgs give the Eymorgs (see entry) in Classic episode "Spock's Brain."

Gladstone, Miss — nursery attendant, played by Dawn Armenian, onboard the *Enterprise* in *TNG* episode "The Child."

Glass, Seamon — played Benton in Classic *Trek* "Mudd's Women." Credits include *Buck Rogers in the 25th Century* and the films *The Other Side of Hell*, *She's Dressed to Kill*, *Gideon's Trumpet*, and *Partners*.

glavyn — Ligonian weapon which looks like a bird worn over the hand, in *TNG* episode "Code of Honor."

Gleason, Captain — captain of the USS *Zhukov*, Barclay's old ship, who gives Barclay a very high performance rating as mentioned in *TNG* episode "Hollow Pursuits."

Glee, Mona — scriptwriter of the original *TNG* story "The Neutral Zone."

glob fly — Klingon fly with an unpleasant buzzing sound mentioned in *TNG* episode "The Outrageous Okona."

Globe Illustrated Shakespeare, The — title of book shown to Q by Picard who keeps it in his ready room in *TNG* episode "Hide and Q."

glommer — the tribbles' only natural enemy, seen in animated episode "More Tribbles, More Troubles."

Glover, Edna — played one of the Vulcan masters in *Star Trek: The Motion Picture.*

Glover, Kirstin — camera operator for *The Undiscovered Country.*

Glover, William — played Marley in *TNG* "Devil's Due."

Goddard, USS — ship with which the *Enterprise* is to rendezvous in *TNG* episode "The Vengeance Factor."

Gol — area on Vulcan, seen in *The Motion Picture,* where a temple exists for the acolytes of *Kolinahr.* The students learn to purge all emotion from their minds and live like monks or hermits.

Golas, Thaddeus — played Controller in *The Voyage Home.*

gold-pressed latinum — currency used on *DS9* by gamblers. Quark deals in gold-pressed latinum which is made in the form of heavy bars.

Goldberg, Whoopi — stars semiregularly as Guinan on *TNG*. She started her career as a highly successful comedienne, then went on to win an Oscar nomination for her role in *The Color Purple*. She also starred in the movies *Jumpin' Jack Flash, Burglar, Fatal Beauty, Clara's Heart, Ghost* (for which she won an Oscar for best supporting actress), *The Long Walk Home, Soapdish, Sister Act,* and *Sarafina*. She starred in the TV series *Bagdad Café* (with Jean Stapleton) and won an Emmy for her guest role on *Moonlighting*. A former talk-show host as well, she is one of the stars of Comic Relief (along with Billy Crystal and Robin Williams), an annual telethon which raises money for the homeless. A *Star Trek* fan as a child, (her hero was Nichelle Nichols), the role of Guinan was created specifically for her after producers found out she really wanted to be a part of the series.

Golden, Murray — director of Classic *Trek* "Requiem for Methuselah." He also directed an episode of *The Rifleman* and *The Wackiest Ship in the Army*.

Goldin, Stephen — author of Classic *Trek* novel *Trek To Madworld*.

Goldsmith, Jerry — composer who wrote the theme and score for *Star Trek: The Motion Picture*. The same theme is now used in *The Next Generation*. Born in Los Angeles in 1930, he composed scores for such TV series as *Climax!*, *Playhouse 90*, and *Gunsmoke*. He also wrote the famous theme from *The Man from U.N.C.L.E.*, as well as for the movies *Planet of the Apes, Papillon, The Omen* (for which he won an Oscar), and *The Secret of NIMH*.

Goldstone, James — director of Classic *Trek* episodes "Where No Man Has Gone Before" and "What Are Little Girls Made Of?" Born in 1931, his directing credits include *Iron Horse* (which he created with Stephen Kandel), *They Only Kill Their Masters, The Day the World Ended, Earth Star Voyager, Voyage to the Bottom of the Sea,* and *Kent State*, for which he won an Emmy.

Gomez, Mike — played DaiMon Taar in *TNG* "The Last Outpost."

Gomez, Sonya, Ensign — recent Academy graduate, played by Lycia Naff, who was handpicked by Geordi from Rayna VI. She appears in *TNG* episodes "Q Who" and "Samaritan Snare."

Goodhartz, Shari — scriptwriter of *TNG* episodes "The Most Toys," "Night Terrors," and "Violations."

Goodwin, Jim — played Lt. John Farrell in Classic *Trek* episodes "The Enemy Within," "Mudd's Women," and "Miri." His character was played by a different actor during the show's second season. His TV and film credits include *Perry Mason* and *Ten Seconds to Hell* ('59).

Goodwin, Laurel — played Yeoman Colt in Classic *Trek* pilot "The Cage" and appears in "The Menagerie."

Gordon, Barry — appeared in *DS9* "The Nagus."

Gordon, Jay — boy, played by John Christian Graas, who wins the primary school science fair on the *Enterprise* in *TNG* episode "Disaster."

Gorgon — alien entity, played by the famous attorney Melvin Belli, which thrives on negative energy. It attempts to take control of the *Enterprise,* and ultimately the galaxy, using five children whose parents it killed. The last inhabitant of an ancient race from the planet Triacus, he ends up being destroyed by the children's positive thoughts of love, happiness, and grief over the memories of their parents.

Gorkon — Klingon chancellor, played by John Warner, who wants peace in *The Undiscovered Country*. He is assassinated by his own general, Chang, and Kirk is framed for the murder.

Gorkon, USS — ship commanded by Vice Admiral Alina Nechayev during an attack on the Borg in *TNG* episode "Descent, Part I."

Gorla — colony that exists in the mirror universe in Classic episode "Mirror, Mirror."

Gorn — alien species resembling a gigantic lizard, which appears in Classic episode "Arena," played by both Garry Coombs and Bobby Clark. It has green skin, speaks with a hissing sound, and is bred for fighting. Gorns are also encountered in the animated episode "Time Trap."

Goro — father, played by Richard Hale, of Miramanee in Classic episode "The Paradise Syndrome."

Gorsheven — leader of Tau Cygna V, played by Grainger Hines (whose name does not appear in the credits) in *TNG* episode "The Ensigns of Command."

Gorshin, Frank — played Bele in Classic *Trek* "Let That Be Your Last Battlefield." Gorshin guest starred in many TV series, including *Batman*.

Goss, DaiMon — Ferengi leader, played by Scott Thomson, in *TNG* episode "The Price."

gossamer mice — transparent mice McCoy keeps in his lab in animated episode "The Terratin Incident."

Gossett, Herb — miner, played by Jon Kowal, on Rigel XII in Classic episode "Mudd's Women," who ends up marrying one of the women.

Gotell, Walter — played Kurt Mandl in *TNG* "Homesoil."

Gothos — Trelane's moveable planet, located in space where no sun or stars exist, which follows the *Enterprise* and where he keeps Kirk and crew after kidnapping them in Classic episode "The Squire of Gothos."

Gouw, Cynthia — played Caitlin Dar in *The Final Frontier*.

Gowans, John D. — played transporter assistant in *Star Trek: The Motion Picture*.

Gowron — Klingon warrior, played by Robert O'Reilly, who sits on the Klingon High Council. The character is regularly featured in *The Next Generation*.

Graas, John Christian — played Jay Gordon in *TNG* "Disaster."

Grace, April — Hubbell in "Future Imperfect," and a transporter technician in *TNG* "Reunion," "Data's Day," "Galaxy's Child," and "The Perfect Mate." She also played the transporter chief in *DS9* "Emissary."

Gracie — the pregnant female whale the *Enterprise* transports to the 23rd century in *The Voyage Home*.

Graf, Kathryn — played Bajoran woman in *DS9* "A Man Alone."

Graf, L. A. — author of Classic *Trek* novels *Ice Trap* and *Death Count*.

Graffeo, Charles M. — set decorator for *The Wrath of Khan*.

Graham, Gerrit — appeared in *DS9* "Captive Pursuit."

Grak Tay — composer Data reprogrammed himself to sound like in *TNG* episode "Sarek."

Grammer, Kelsey — played Captain Bateson in *TNG* "Cause and Effect." Most famous for his portrayal of Frasier Crane in the sitcom *Cheers* and its spin-off show *Frasier*.

Granger — Granger clones, played by Jon de Vries, made from a combined archetype of Wilson Granger, Prime Minister of Maripose, and Victor Granger, Minister of Health, in *TNG* episode "Up the Long Ladder."

Grant — security guard, played by Robert Bralver, and member of the landing party to Capella IV, who is killed when he sees the Klingon Kras and automatically reaches for his weapon in Classic episode "Friday's Child."

Graves, David Michael — played one of the Edo Children in *TNG* "Justice."

Graves, Ira, Dr. — cyberneticist and Dr. Noonian Soong's teacher, played by W. Morgan Sheppard, living on Graves' World with his assistant in *TNG* episode "The Schizoid Man."

Graves' World — home and research center of Dr. Ira Graves and Kareen Brianon in *TNG* episode "The Schizoid Man."

gravitic mine — the *Denver* hits a gravitic mine left over from the Federation–Cardassian war in *TNG* episode "Ethics."

Grax, Reittan — Betazoid conference director and Deanna's father's friend, played by Rudolph Willrich, who tells Picard that Deanna, Lwaxana, and Riker have been kidnapped in *TNG* episode "Ménage à Troi."

Gray, Mike — scriptwriter of *TNG* episodes "Unnatural Selection" and "Violations." Also a producer.

Gray, Pamela — scriptwriter of *TNG* "Violations."

Grayson, Amanda — see entry for Amanda.

Grebnedlog — captain, played by Christopher Collins, of the Pakled ship *Mondor*, who takes Geordi hostage in *TNG* episode "Samaritan Snare."

Green, Colonel — supposedly a ruthless military man responsible for a genocidal war on Earth in the 21st century. His image, taken from Kirk's mind and played by Phillip Pines, is encountered in Classic episode "The Savage Curtain."

Green, Crewman — character, played by Bruce Watson, killed by the salt vampire on planet M–113 in Classic episode "The Man Trap." The creature then assumes Green's appearance to gain access to the *Enterprise*.

Green, Gilbert — played the SS Major on Classic *Trek* "Patterns of Force." His appearances include the pilot for the TV series *Starsky and Hutch.*

Greenberger, Robert — coauthor of *TNG* novel *Doomsday World* and sole writer of Classic novel *The Disinherited.*

Greene, James — played Dr. Barron in *TNG* "Who Watches the Watchers."

Greene, Vanessa — scriptwriter of *TNG* "The Loss."

Gregory, James — played Dr. Tristan Adams in Classic *Trek* "Dagger of the Mind." Born in 1911, his credits include *The Naked City, The Sons of Katie Elder,* and *Beneath the Planet of the Apes.* An actor with extensive stage experience, he also appeared regularly on *The Paul Lynde Show, Barney Miller,* and *Detective School.*

Gregory, Stephen — played Jake Kurland in *TNG* "Coming of Age."

Grenthamen water hopper — type of vessel mentioned in *TNG* episode "Peak Performance."

Grimes, Scott — played Eric (in scenes later cut) in *TNG* "Evolution."

Grissom, SS — science ship, commanded by Captain Esteban, destroyed by Kruge in *The Search for Spock.* Another *Grissom* is mentioned in *TNG* episode "The Most Toys" as sought by the *Enterprise* for help obtaining hytritium, but it is unable to aid the *Enterprise* although it is the closest ship in the quadrant.

Grist, Robert — director of Classic *Trek* episode "The Galileo Seven."

Grizellas — beings named as arbiters by Picard in the Treaty of Armens because of their long hibernation period which gives the *Enterprise* time to rescue people in *TNG* episode "The Ensigns of Command."

Grodenchik, Max — played Sovak in *TNG* "Captain's Holiday" and Par Lenor in "The Perfect Mate." He also played the Ferengi Pit Boss in *DS9* "Emissary" and appeared in *DS9* "A Man Alone," "The Nagus," and "Vortex."

Groener, Harry — played Tam Elbrun in *TNG* "Tin Man."

Gromek, Admiral — Starfleet Admiral, played by Georgann Johnson, in *TNG* episode "The Emissary."

grubs — favorite food of the Ferengi who eat them live in *DS9* episode "The Nagus."

Grudt, Mona — Graham in *TNG* "Identity Crisis."

grum'ba — Nausicaan word that means "guts" or "courage," in *TNG* episode "Tapestry."

grup — name the children on Miri's planet use for adults—a contraction of "grown ups"—in Classic episode "Miri."

Gruzaf, James — played Don Juan in Classic *Trek* "Shore Leave."

GSK 783, Subspace Frequency 3 — Aurelan Kirk uses this private communication wave to call the *Enterprise* for help from Deneva in Classic episode "Operation: Annihilate!"

Guardian of Forever — gateway to the past on a ruined, windblown world seen in Classic episode "The City on the Edge of Forever" and in the animated "Yesteryear."

Guernica system — destination of the *Enterprise* when Dr. Leah Brahms comes aboard in *TNG* episode "Galaxy's Child."

Guerra, Castulo — played Seth Mendoza in *TNG* "The Price."

Guerrero, Evelyn — played an ensign in *TNG* "Encounter At Farpoint."

Guerz, Karl — scriptwriter of *TNG* "Homesoil."

Guest, Nicholas — played a cadet in *The Wrath of Khan*. A stage actor as well, he has appeared in the movies *Trading Places* and *Cloak and Dagger*.

Guinan — recurring character, played by Whoopi Goldberg, in *The Next Generation*. A member of a mysterious race that doesn't seem to age, Guinan is over 1,000 years old. She has had many children and husbands but her family was wiped out by the Borg. She knew Q prior to his visits to the ship, but something unknown about their relationship is the reason she is currently aboard the *Enterprise* as head of the bar in Ten Forward. She and Picard share a very strong bond, they have a trust and an understanding that surpasses normal friendship and hints, in some episodes, at possible intimacy. In *TNG* episode "Booby Trap," she says she's attracted to bald men. She is the only one who can challenge Picard's orders, question them, even get him to change his mind. Data believes her perception goes beyond linear time, which is why she knew the timeline was altered in "Yesterday's Enterprise."

Gul — Cardassian command title, roughly the equivalent of "captain."

Gunning, Charles — played Miners in *TNG* "The Perfect Mate."

Gunton, Bob — played Captain Ben Maxwell in *TNG* "The Wounded."

Gustafson, Fleet Admiral — officer whom Picard is to meet after a magnetic wave survey of the Parvenium sector in *TNG* episode "The Inner Light."

Haakona — Romulan ship onto which Picard steps when he goes through the Iconian teleporter in *TNG* episode "Contagion."

Hacom — rabid elderly Landru follower, played by Morgan Farley, in Classic episode "The Return of the Archons."

Haden, Admiral — commander, played by John Hancock, of the Starfleet station on Lya III in *TNG* episode "The Defector."

Hadley, Lieutenant — *Enterprise* officer, played by William Blackburn, who takes over Spock's station in Classic episode "A Piece of the Action."

Haftel, Anthony, Admiral — officer, played by Nicolas Coster, who serves at research facility on Galor IV and wants to take Lal away from Data in *TNG* episode "The Offspring."

Hagan, Andrus, Counselor — catatonic Betazoid, played by John Vickery, who speaks to Deanna in dreams, in *TNG* episode "Night Terrors."

Hagerty, Michael G. — played Larg in *TNG* "Redemption, Part II."

Hagler, Lieutenant — *Enterprise* officer whose blood is turned into liquid polymer in *TNG* episode "Schisms."

Hagon — played by James Louis Watkins, holds the title

of Primary and First One To Yareena, in *TNG* episode "Night Terrors."

Hahliia — world inhabited by partially telepathic aliens of which Lieutenant Aquiel Uhnari is one in *TNG* episode "Aquiel."

Hahn, Admiral — mentioned in *TNG* episode "Ménage à Troi."

Haig, Sid — played First Lawgiver in Classic *Trek* "Return of the Archons." His other credits include *Who Is the Black Dahlia?*, *The Return of the World's Greatest Detective*, *Evening in Byzantium*, *Death on the Freeway*, *Chu Chu and the Philly Flash*, and *Galaxy of Terror*.

Haight, Wanda M. — scriptwriter of *TNG* "A Matter of Honor."

Haines, Jana, Ensign — *Enterprise* navigator, played by Victoria George, in Classic episode "The Gamesters of Triskelion."

Hajar, Cadet Second Class — member, played by Walter Brandt, of Wesley's Nova Squadron in *TNG* episode "The First Duty."

Haki — Mintakan child who gives Picard a piece of cloth as a gift in *TNG* episode "Who Watches the Watchers."

Haldeman, Jack C., II — author of Classic *Trek* novel *Perry's Planet*.

Haldeman, Joe — science-fiction writer and author of Classic *Trek* novels *Planet of Judgment* and *World Without End*.

Hale, Doug — played computer voice in *Star Trek: The Motion Picture*. He appeared in the film *Charleston* and plays voices in *Terror at Alcatraz* and *Mothers Against Drunk Drivers*.

Hale, Richard — played Goro in Classic *Trek* "The Paradise Syndrome." Born in 1893, his credits include

Julius Caesar and *Ben Hur*. He guest starred (mostly as Native American characters) in *Cheyenne* and *Iron Horse*. He died in 1981.

"Half a Life" — fourth-season *TNG* episode written by Peter Allan Fields and Ted Roberts, directed by Les Landau. A Kaelon scientist has dedicated his entire life to experimenting with a process for reenergizing a dying star because his own world's sun is dying. Lwaxana Troi meets him just as he is about to turn 60, an age when he must, according to his culture, submit himself to death. In love with him, she tries to persuade him to leave his homeworld and continue his experiments. Guest stars: Majel Barrett, David Ogden Stiers, Michelle Forbes, Terence McNally, Colm Meaney, and Carel Struycken. Of note: When Lwaxana walks away from the mirror, the boom microphone can be observed.

Hali — hellish place, mentioned in *TNG* episode "Heart of Glory."

Hali — Mintakan, played by James McIntyre, in *TNG* episode "Who Watches the Watchers."

Halkans — peaceful people with whom the *Enterprise* is trying to negotiate dilithium mining rights when Kirk, Scott, McCoy, and Uhura are transported to another universe in Classic episode "Mirror, Mirror."

Hall, Kevin Peter — played Leyor in *TNG* "The Price."

Hall, Lois — played Mary Warren in *TNG* "Who Watches the Watchers."

Hall of Audiences — place where people come to see Landru in Classic episode "The Return of the Archons."

Halloway, Thomas, Captain — commander of the *Enterprise* in an alternate future in *TNG* episode "Tapestry."

Halperin, Michael — scriptwriter of *TNG* episode "Lonely among Us."

Halste, Christopher — played First Learner in *TNG* "Cost of Living."

Hambly, Barbara — author of Classic *Trek* novels *Ishmael* and *Ghost Walker*.

Hamilton, Kim — played Chairman Sonji in *TNG* "Final Mission."

Hamilton, Laurell K. — wrote *TNG* novel *Nightshade*, and has authored a fantasy novel and a three-book vampire series.

Hamlet, Prince — role a Karidian actor, played by Marc Adams, assumes in Classic episode "The Conscience of the King."

Hamner, Robert — scriptwriter of Classic *Trek* "A Taste of Armageddon" and episodes of *The Man from U.N.C.L.E.* and *Voyage to the Bottom of the Sea*. He also wrote *You Lie So Deep My Love*, *Dallas Cowboys Cheerleaders*, and *The Million Dollar Face*. He is also a producer.

Hanar — Kelvin invader, played by Stewart Moss, to whom McCoy gives formazine in Classic episode "By Any Other Name."

Hancock, John — played Admiral Haden in *TNG* episodes "The Defector" and "The Wounded."

Haney, Anne — appeared in *DS9* "Dax."

Hanlon, George O., Jr. — played the transporter chief in *TNG* "Future Imperfect."

Hanolin Asteroid Belt — location near Vulcan where a Ferengi shuttle crashes in *TNG* episode "Unification."

Hansen, Lieutenant — *Enterprise* helmsman, played by Hagan Beggs, in Classic episodes "Court-Martial" and "The Menagerie."

Hanson, Commander — commander, played by

Garry Walberg, of Outpost IV, which is destroyed by the Romulans in Classic episode "Balance of Terror."

Hanson, J. P., Admiral — Starfleet tactical officer, played by George Murdock, in *TNG* episode "The Best of Both Worlds."

Hanson's Planet — mentioned in Classic episode "The Galileo Seven" as another world inhabited by furry creatures like those on Taurus II.

Harder, Richard — played Joe in *The Voyage Home*.

Hardin, Jerry — played Radue on *TNG* "When the Bough Breaks," and Samuel Clemens in "Time's Arrow, Parts I and II."

Haritath — played by Mark L. Taylor, character who supports Data and Ard'rian as they try to evacuate Tau Cygna V in *TNG* episode "The Ensigns of Command."

Harmon, David P. — scriptwriter of Classic *Trek* episodes "The Deadly Years," "A Piece of the Action," and the animated "The Eye of the Beholder." His TV scripts include *Honeymoon with a Stranger*, *Killer by Night*, *Rescue from Gilligan's Island*, and *The Harlem Globetrotters on Gilligan's Island*.

Harmon, John — played Rodent in Classic *Trek* "The City on the Edge of Forever," and Tepo in "A Piece of the Action." Other credits include a semiregular part on *The Rifleman*.

Haro, Mitena — Bolian cadet and spy, played by Joycelyn O'Brien, kidnapped with Thool, Esoqq, and Picard in *TNG* episode "Allegiance."

Harod IV — world from which the *Enterprise* rescues several miners in *TNG* episode "The Perfect Mate."

Harold, Lieutenant — survivor, played by Tom Troups, of the Gorn attack on Cestus III in Classic episode "Arena."

Harper, Ensign — engineer, played by Sean Morgan, who is killed by the M–5 computer when he tries to shut it down in Classic episode "The Ultimate Computer."

Harper, James — appeared in *DS9* "The Passenger."

Harper, Robert — played Lathal in *TNG* "The Host."

Harrakis V — planet where the *Enterprise* finishes its work early in *TNG* episode "Clues."

Harris, Joshua — played Timothy in *TNG* "Hero Worship."

Harris, Leon — art director on *Star Trek: The Motion Picture* who also worked on the movie *The Devil and Max Devlin.*

Harris, Captain — unseen captain of the *Excalibur* who is killed with his crew by the M–5 computer in Classic episode "The Ultimate Computer."

Harrison, Dr. — tagger, played by John Bellah, who paints "Sinner Repent" and "Love Mankind" on the bulkheads of the *Enterprise* in Classic episode "The Naked Time."

Harrison, Gracie — played Clare Raymond in *TNG* "The Neutral Zone."

Harrison, Technician — character on the bridge when Khan takes over in Classic episode "Space Seed."

Harrison, William B. — last of Captain Merik's men to die in the arena during gladiatorial combat in Classic episode "Bread and Circuses."

Hart, Harvey — director of Classic *Trek* episode "Mudd's Women." A producer of several low-budget movies, most of his work as a director is limited to television.

Hartley, Mariette — played Zarabeth in Classic *Trek* "All Our Yesterdays." Born in 1940, Hartley made guest appearances in many TV series of the 1960s, including *The Twilight Zone,* and was a regular on *Peyton Place, The Hero,* and *Goodnight, Beantown* (costarring with Bill Bixby and Tracey Gold). She also starred in Roddenberry's *Genesis II*, and won an Emmy for her guest star performance in *The Incredible Hulk* (again with Bill Bixby).

Haskell — *Enterprise* crewman, played by Charles Douglass, killed in *TNG* episode "Where Silence Has Lease."

Haskins, Theodore, Dr. — one of the survivors, played by Jon Lormer, on Talos IV in Classic episodes "The Menagerie" and "The Cage." Also has a role in "For the World Is Hollow and I Have Touched the Sky."

Hatae, Hana — played Molly in *DS9* "A Man Alone."

***Hathaway*, USS** — 80-year-old derelict ship over which Riker is given command with 40 officers in order to participate in a simulated battle, in *TNG* episode "Peak Performance."

Havana — ship with which *Enterprise* has orders to rendezvous in *TNG* episode "Lessons."

Haven — paradise world located in the Beta Cassius system and governed by First Electorine Valeda Innis in *TNG* episode "Haven."

"Haven" — Troi's mother, Lwaxana, is introduced in this first-season *TNG* episode written by Tracy Torme and Lian Okun, directed by Richard Compton. Wyatt Miller, to whom Troi has been promised in a Betazoid arranged marriage, also comes aboard, but he constantly sees images of another young woman who he believes is his true love. Guest stars: Danzita Kingsley, Carel Struycken, Anna Katarina, Raye Birk, Michael Rider, Majel Barrett, Rob Knepper, Nan Martin, and Robert Ellenstein.

Hawke, Simon — author of *TNG* novel *The Romulan Prize*.

Hawking — *Enterprise* shuttle, named after quantum physicist Stephen Hawking (who makes an appearance in *TNG*'s seventh season) in *TNG* episode "The Host."

Hawking, Stephen — famous quantum physicist who made a cameo appearance in *TNG* episode "Descent."

Hawkins, Ambassador — leader of the diplomatic party on Mordan IV in *TNG* episode "Too Short a Season."

Hayashi system — location from which the *Enterprise* is called in *TNG* episode "Tin Man."

Hayenga, Jeffrey — played Orta in *TNG* "Ensign Ro."

Haymer, Johnny — played the constable in Classic *Trek* "All Our Yesterdays." His credits include feature roles on *M*A*S*H* and *Madame's Place*. Film work includes *Mongo's Back In Town*, *Ring of Passion*, and *The Best Place To Be*.

Hayne — leader of the faction on Turkana IV, played by Don Mirrault in *TNG* episode "Legacy."

Haynes, Lloyd — played Communications Officer Lt. Alden in Classic *Trek* "Where No Man Has Gone Before." Most famous for his starring role in the TV series *Room 222*, his other credits include *Assault on the Wayne* (with Leonard Nimoy), *Look What's Happened to Rosemary's Baby*, and *Born to Be Sold*. He died in 1986.

Hays, Kathryn — actress who played Gem in Classic *Trek* "The Empath." Her credits include a regular role on *The Road West* and guest roles on *The Man from U.N.C.L.E.* and *Circle of Fear*. She has appeared regularly as Kim on the soap opera *As the World Turns* for over 20 years.

"Heading out to Eden" — song Adam sings in Classic episode "The Way to Eden."

Hearn, George — played Berel in *TNG* "First Contact."

"Heart of Glory" — first-season *TNG* episode written by Maurice Hurley, Herbert Wright, and D. C. Fontana, directed by Rob Bowman. Klingons board the *Enterprise* and try to turn Worf against his fellow crewmembers in an attempt to capture the ship. Guest stars: Vaughn Armstrong, Robert Bauer, Brad Zerbst, Dennis Madalone, and Charles H. Hyman.

Hecht, Gina — played Manua in *TNG* "A Matter of Perspective."

Hedford, Nancy — commissioner, played by Elinor Donahue, on her way to negotiate peace on Epsilon Canaris III when her shuttle is taken off course by the Companion in Classic episode "Metamorphosis."

Hedrick, Chief — transporter officer, played by Dennis Madalone, in *TNG* episode "Identity Crisis."

Heinemann, Arthur — scriptwriter of Classic *Trek* episodes "Wink of an Eye," "The Way to Eden," and "The Savage Curtain." He has also written scripts for the TV series *Cannon*.

Hektah — Klingon ship commanded by Kurn, Worf's brother, in *TNG* episode "Redemption."

Held, Christopher — played Lindstrom in Classic *Trek* "Return of the Archons."

Helglenian shift — method used by Ligon transporters in *TNG* episode "Code of Honor."

Heller, Chip — played a warrior in *TNG* "Loud As a Whisper."

Hendorf — security guard, played by Mal Friedman, who is killed by thorns shot from a beautiful flower in Classic episode "The Apple."

Hengist — administrator, played by John Fiedler, on Argelius II and a native of Rigel, who is eventually discovered to be the murdering entity in Classic episode "Wolf in the Fold."

Hennessy — Dr. Pulaski's patient in *TNG* episode "The Dauphin."

Hennings, Sam — played Ramsey in *TNG* "Angel One."

Henoch — energy being which takes over Spock's body and decides it does not want to give it up in Classic episode "Return to Tomorrow."

Henriques, Darryl — played The Portal in *TNG* "The Last Outpost" and Nanclus in *The Undiscovered Country*.

Henry, Thomas, Admiral — officer, played by Earl Billings, who closes down Sadie's witch hunt in *TNG* episode "The Drumhead."

Hensel, Karen — played Admiral Brackett in *TNG* "Unification, Part I."

Henshaw, Christy — character, played by Julie Warner, whom Geordi tries and fails to romance in *TNG* episodes "Transfigurations" and "Booby Trap."

Henteloff, Alex — played Nichols in *The Voyage Home*. His other credits include regular roles on TV series *Pistols 'n' Petticoats*, *The Young Rebels*, *Needles and Pins*, and *The Betty White Comedy Show*. He also appeared in the films *Partners in Crime*, *The Invisible Man* ('75), *The Bastard*, *Victims*, *The Red*, and *Light Sting*.

Herbarium — name of the Arboretum on the *Enterprise* in Classic *Trek* "Is There in Truth No Beauty?"

Herbert, Ensign — transporter officer, played by Lance Spellerberg, in *TNG* episodes "We'll Always Have Paris" and "The Icarus Factor."

Hercos III — Devinoni Ral's adopted world in *TNG* episode "The Price."

Herd, Richard — guest starred in *TNG* episode "Birthright." He is a popular character actor who has appeared on many TV series and movies.

Herman — series of androids, played by twin actors Tom and Ted LeGarde, created by Harry Mudd in Classic episode "I, Mudd."

Hermes, **USS** — Starfleet ship participating in the Klingon blockade in Classic episode "Redemption."

"Hero Worship" — fifth-season *TNG* episode written by Hilary J. Bader and Joe Menosky, directed by Patrick Stewart. A young survivor of a terrible starship accident blames himself and tries to block his emotions by emulating Data in an attempt to become a robot himself. Guest stars: Joshua Harris and Steven Einspahr.

Herron, Robert — played Pike's stunt double in Classic *Trek* pilot "The Cage" and Kahless in "The Savage Curtain."

Hertzler, John Noah — played Vulcan Captain in *DS9* "Emissary."

Het'ba — Klingon suicide ceremony Worf considers performing when he suffers paralysis in *TNG* episode "Ethics."

Hetrick, Jennifer — played Vash in *TNG* "Captain's Holiday," "Qpid" and *DS9* "Q Less."

"Hey Out There" — gang song in Classic episode "The Way to Eden."

Hibishan civilization — built elaborate tombs, later plundered by the Cardassians in *TNG* episode "Chain of Command."

Hickman, Paul, Lieutenant — officer, played by Amick Byram, on the USS *Victory* who steals a shuttlecraft in *TNG* episode "Identity Crisis."

Hicks, Catherine — played Gillian Taylor in *The Voyage Home*. TV credits include regular roles in the series *Ryan's Hope* and *The Bad News Bears*. She also won an Emmy for her portrayal of Marilyn Monroe in *Marilyn: The Untold Appearances*. Film credits include *The Razor's Edge* and *Peggy Sue Got Married*.

Hicks, Chuck — played Military Officer in *TNG* "Encounter at Farpoint."

"Hide and Q" — first-season *TNG* episode written by C. J. Holland and Gene Roddenberry, directed by Cliff Bole. Q gives Riker Q powers, but Riker turns down Q's offer to make him a Q permanently. Guest stars: John deLancie, Elaine Nalee, and William A. Wallace.

"High Ground, The" — third-season *TNG* episode written by Melinda Snodgrass and directed by Gabrielle Beaumont. Dr. Crusher is kidnapped by terrorists on Rutia IV who need a doctor to help them combat a DNA breakdown caused by the use of their strange teleport device, the *Invertor*, which leads to death if overused. Finn, her kidnapper, also uses Crusher in an attempt to lure the *Enterprise* into the planet's conflict. Guest stars: Kerrie Keane, Richard Cox, Marc Buckland, Fred G. Smith, and Christopher Pettiet.

Highway 949 — road leading to McKinley Rocket Base and on which agents 201 and 347 die in a car crash in Classic episode "Tomorrow Is Yesterday."

Hildebrandt — member, played by Ann H. Gillespie, of the Secundi Drema team, who is married to Alans in *TNG* episode "Pen Pals."

Hill, Marianna — played Dr. Helen Noel on Classic *Trek* "Dagger of the Mind." Other TV credits include *Perry Mason* and the movies *Death at Love House*, *Relentless*, *Blood Beach*, and *Invisible Strangler*.

Hill, Dixon — role Picard assumes during his holodeck mystery recreations in *TNG* episode "Manhunt."

Hillyer, Sharon — played one of the "girls" in Classic *Trek* "A Piece of the Action." She appeared regularly in the third season of *The Man from U.N.C.L.E.*

Hines, Grainger — played Gosheven in *TNG* "The Ensigns of Command."

Hobson, Thomas — played young Jake in *DS9* "Emissary."

Hobson, Christopher, Lieutenant Commander — first officer, played by Timothy Carhart, of the USS *Sutherland*, who gives Data a hard time in *TNG* episode "Redemption."

Hock, Allison — scriptwriter of *TNG* "Rascals."

Hockridge, John — first assistant director on *The Search for Spock.*

Hodgkin's Law of Parallel Planet Development — theory, mentioned in Classic episode "Bread and Circuses," on why so many humanoid beings and cultures resembling Earth exist throughout the galaxy.

Hodin — Odona's father, played by David Hurst, who risks his daughter's life to solve the planet Gideon's population problem in Classic episode "Mark of Gideon."

Hoffman, Elizabeth — played Bhavani in *TNG* "The Price."

Holberg 917G — ryetaliyn-rich planet, located in the Omega system, visited by the *Enterprise* in search of a cure for the Rigelian fever sweeping the ship, and where they meet Flint and Reena in Classic episode "Requiem for Methuselah."

Holland, C. J. — scriptwriter who penned *TNG* "Hide and Q."

Holland, Erik — played Ekor on Classic *Trek* "Wink of an Eye." TV credits include *The Man from U.N.C.L.E.* and

Voyage to the Bottom of the Sea. Film credits include *Friendly Persuasion, The French Atlantic Affair, Little House: Look Back to Yesterday*, and *Table for Five*.

Hollander, Eli — young gun hostile to Worf in *TNG* episode "A Fistful of Datas."

Holliday, Doc — Melkotian alien, played by Sam Gilman, in Classic episode "Spectre of the Gun."

Hollis — *Enterprise* security officer in *TNG* episode "Descent."

"Hollow Pursuits" — third-season *TNG* episode written by Sally Caves and directed by Cliff Bole. Engineer Reginald Barclay, addicted to the holodeck because of his shyness and inability to socialize with others, is needed to help solve the ship's problems. Guest stars: Dwight Schultz, Whoopi Goldberg, Charley Lang, and Colm Meaney.

Holloway, Roger — played Mr. Lemli on Classic *Trek* "Turnabout Intruder."

Holman, Rex — played Morgan Earp in Classic *Trek* "Spectre of the Gun" and J'Onn in *The Final Frontier*. His other film credits include *The Bounty Man, The Legend of the Golden Gun*, and *The Wild Women of Chastity Gulch*.

Holmes, Sherlock — role Data assumes in holodeck mystery re-creations in *TNG* episode "Elementary, Dear Data."

holodeck — recreation facility that creates crewmembers' fantasies in virtual reality.

holodiction — addiction to the holodeck, to the point where reality is shunned. Barclay falls victim to holodiction in *TNG* episode "Hollow Pursuits."

holosuites — sex fantasy programs run by Quark on *Deep Space 9*.

"Home Soil" — first-season *TNG* episode written by Robert Sabaroff, Karl Guerz, and Ralph Sanchez, directed by Corey Allen. A rare life-form, called a "microbrain," living in the soil of Velara III, attempts to save itself from a Federation terraforming project by killing the scientists involved. Guest stars: Walter Gotell, Elizabeth Lindsey, Gerard Pendergast, Mario Roccuzzo, and Carolyn Barry.

Homeier, Skip — played Melakon in Classic *Trek* "Patterns of Force" and Dr. Sevrin in "The Way to Eden." Born in 1930 as George Vincent Homeier, he made regular appearances on radio and on TV, including starring roles in *Dan Raven* and *The Interns*. His film credits include *The Gunfighter, Comanche Station,* and *The Greatest.*

Homn, Mr. — Lwaxana Troi's mute aide, played by Carel Struycken, first seen in *TNG* episode "The Big Goodbye."

Hood, USS — ship, commanded by Captain DeSoto, on which Riker served as first officer before transferring to the *Enterprise,* as mentioned in *TNG* episode "Encounter at Farpoint." The ship, encountered in several future episodes, is also involved in war games with the M–5 computer in Classic episode "The Ultimate Computer."

hook spiders, Talarian — insects with half-meter-long legs which supposedly infested Zera IV, as mentioned by O'Brien in *TNG* episode "Realm of Fear."

Hooks, Robert — played Commander Morrow in *The Search for Spock*. Born in 1937, his credits include *Hurry Sundown, Airport '77,* and a starring role in the 1960s series *NYPD.*

Horan, James — guest starred in *TNG* episode "Suspicions."

Horatio, USS — ship, commanded by Captain Walker Keel, destroyed in *TNG* episode "Conspiracy."

Horga'hn — symbol of sexuality on Risa, a stone statue

that Riker asks Picard to bring him from the captain's trip to that planet in *TNG* episode "Captain's Holiday."

Horgan, Patrick — played Eneg in Classic *Trek* "Patterns of Force." TV credits include the miniseries *George Washington* and a starring role in the series *Casablanca*.

***Horizon*, USS** — ship which made first contact with Iotia and left behind the book *Chicago Mobs of the Twenties*, altering the culture, in Classic episode "A Piece of the Action."

hornbuck — Mintakan animal native mentioned in *TNG* episode "Who Watches the Watchers."

Horner, James — composed themes for *The Wrath of Khan* and *The Search for Spock*. His other film scores include *Battle beyond the Stars* (his first), *Aliens*, and *Brainstorm*.

***Hornet*, USS** — starship working with the Klingon blockade in *TNG* episode "Redemption."

Horta — intelligent rock creature whose nest the miners inadvertently disturb in Classic episode "Devil in the Dark."

Horvat, Michel — scriptwriter of *TNG* "The Host."

"Host, The" — fourth-season *TNG* episode written by Michel Horvat and directed by Marvin V. Rush. Dr. Crusher falls in love with a Trill, a being hosting a symbiotic life-form. When the body is injured beyond repair, another body is ordered for him but the host turns out to be female, a turn of events Crusher cannot come to terms with. Guest stars: Franc Luz, Barbara Tarbuck, William Newman, Nicole Orth-Pallavicini, Robert Harper, and Patti Yasutake.

Hotton, Donald — played Monk #1 in *DS9* "Emissary."

hoverball — sport Picard is not particularly fond of in *TNG* episode "Captain's Holiday."

"How Sharper Than a Serpent's Tooth" — written by Russell Bates and David Wise, this animated Classic *Trek* episode aired 10/5/74. The *Enterprise* encounters a ship which looks like a Kulkukan from Mayan or Aztec legend. The entity ship, angry at being forgotten by humans, gives the crew a puzzle to solve. Kirk, McCoy, Scott, and Ensign Dawson Walking Bear are then transported to a city where they end up saving the entity's life. James Doohan guest stars as Arex the Kulkukan.

Howard, Clint — played Balok in Classic *Trek* "The Corbomite Maneuver." Brother of actor/producer/director Ron Howard, he had regular starring roles in the TV series *The Baileys of Balboa*, *Gentle Ben*, and *The Cowboys*. His films include *Evilspeak*, *Night Shift*, *Splash!*, and *Backdraft*.

Howard, Leslie C. — played a yeoman in *Star Trek: The Motion Picture*.

Howard, Sherman — played Endar in *TNG* "Suddenly Human."

Howard, Susan — played Mara in Classic *Trek* "Day of the Dove." Other credits include *Quarantined*, *Indict and Convict* (with William Shatner), *Superdome*, and *The Power Within*. She also appeared regularly in *Petrocelli* and *Dallas*.

Howard, Vince — played "Uhura's Crewman" in Classic *Trek* "The Man Trap." He was featured regularly on the TV series *Mr. Novak* and appeared in the films *Vanished*, *Love Is Not Enough*, and *The Red Light Sting*.

Howden, Mike — played Lt. Rowe in Classic *Trek* "I, Mudd," and a Romulan guard in "The *Enterprise* Incident."

Hoy, Ensign — character in *TNG* episode "Who Watches the Watchers."

Hoyt, Clegg — played Transporter Chief Pitcairn in Classic *Trek* pilot "The Cage." His other TV credits include *The Man from U.N.C.L.E.* and *The Rifleman*.

Hoyt, John — played Dr. Philip Boyce in Classic *Trek* pilot "The Cage." Born in 1905, his film credits include *When Worlds Collide*, *Duel at Diablo*, and *Flash Gordon*. A regular on the TV series *Tom, Dick and Mey* and *Gimme A Break*, he appeared in *The Man from U.N.C.L.E.*, *Planet of the Apes*, and *Voyage to the Bottom of the Sea*.

Hromi Cluster — location of the Gatherer camp in *TNG* episode "The Vengeance Factor."

Hubbard, Jamie — played Salia in *TNG* "The Dauphin."

Hubbell, J. P. — played an ensign in *TNG* "Man of the People."

Hubble, Chief — transporter tech, played by April Grace, in *TNG* episodes "Reunion," "Future Imperfect," "Galaxy's Child," and "The Perfect Mate."

Hudec, M. Leigh — see entry for Barrett, Majel.

Hugh — Borg captured by the *Enterprise*, given individuality, and then sent back to the other Borgs with a virus in his system. Played by Jonathan del Arco, he appeared in *TNG* episode "I, Borg" and "Descent."

Hughes, David Hillary — played Trefayne in Classic *Trek* "Errand of Mercy."

Hughes, Wendy — guest starred as Nella Daren in *TNG* episode "Lessons."

Humbolt, Chief — chief of the computer section, played by George Sawaya, on Starbase 11 in Classic episode "The Menagerie."

Hummel, Sayra — played the engine room technician in *Star Trek: The Motion Picture*.

Hundley, Craig — played Peter Kirk in Classic *Trek* "Operation: Annihilate!" and Tommy Starnes in "And the Children Shall Lead."

Hungerford, Michael — played Roughneck in *TNG* "Time's Arrow, Part I."

Hunt, Marsha — played Anne Jameson on *TNG* "Too Short a Season."

Hunt, The — official contest of an alien race from the Gamma Quadrant which hunts prey bred solely for the game. The *Enterprise* encounters a hunted creature, named Tosk, who is to be pursued until he dies in *DS9* episode "Captive Pursuit."

Hunter, Jeffrey — played Captain Christopher Pike in Classic *Trek* pilot "The Cage." Born in New Orleans in 1925, his credits include *Red Skies of Montana*, *King of Kings*, *The Longest Day*, and a regular role in the series *Temple Houston*. He died in 1969 from a brain injury while filming in Spain.

"Hunter, The" — third-season *TNG* episode written by Robin Bernheim and directed by Cliff Bole. Genetically superior soldiers, created by the government during a civil war on Angosia, are being held in prison during peace time. One of the soldiers, Roga Danar, escapes and asks the *Enterprise* for help but the ship refuses, leaving the society to resolve its own problems. Guest stars: Jeff McCarthy, James Cromwell, J. Michael Flynn, Andrew Bicknell, and Colm Meaney.

Hupp, Jana Marie — played Ensign Pavlik in *TNG* "Galaxy's Child" and Ensign Monroe in "Disaster."

Hurkos III — world to which Ral relocates at age 19 as mentioned in *TNG* episode "The Price."

Hurley, Craig — played Peeples in *TNG* "Night Terrors."

Hurley, Diane M. — played "woman" in *TNG* "The Game."

Hurley, Maurice — scriptwriter of *TNG* "Datalore," "11001001," "Heart of Glory," "The Arsenal of Freedom,"

"The Neutral Zone," "The Child," "Time Squared," "Q Who," "Shades of Gray," "Galaxy's Child," and "Power Play."

Huron, SS — dilithium cargo freighter commanded by Captain O'Shea in animated episode "The Pirates of Orion."

Hurst, David — played Hodin in Classic *Trek* "The Mark of Gideon."

Husnock — race of 50 billion people mentally destroyed by Kevin Uxbridge after they kill his wife in *TNG* episode "The Survivors."

Husnock vessel — gigantic spectre ship five times the size of the *Enterprise* and fully armed in *TNG* episode "The Survivors."

Hutchison, Calvin, Commander ("Hutch") — incredibly boring Starfleet officer assigned to Arkaria who hosts a party, which Picard orders the entire crew to attend, in *TNG* episode "Starship Mine." The commander is killed by thieves attempting to steal the *Enterprise*'s trilithium at the end of the episode.

Hutzel, Gary — responsible for visual effects in *DS9*.

Hyde, Bruce — played Lt. Kevin Thomas Riley in Classic *Trek* "The Naked Time" and "The Conscience of the King."

hydrogen collectors — red areas located on the front of the warp nacelles which project hydrogen, referred to in *TNG* episode "Samaritan Snare."

Hyman, Charles — played Konmil in *TNG* "Heart of Glory."

hyperacceleration — time realm inhabited by the Scalosians who cannot be seen or heard, except for a faint buzzing sound, in Classic episode "Wink of an Eye."

hyperonic radiation — level of toxicity which interferes with phasers, sensors, and transporters and is deadly to humans. The colonists of Tau Cygna adapted to the radiation after it killed a third of them as mentioned in *TNG* episode "The Ensigns of Command."

hypo — syringe without a needle, also called hypospray in *TNG*, used in Sick Bay.

hyronalin — drug that cures the disease which causes rapid aging in Classic episode "The Deadly Years."

hytritium — substance the *Enterprise* uses to cleanse the water supply, contaminated with tricyanate, on Beta Agni II, in *TNG* episode "The Most Toys."

"I, Borg" — fifth-season *TNG* episode written by René Echevarria and directed by Bob Lederman. A young and impressionable survivor from a crashed Borg ship is brought aboard the *Enterprise*, befriended by Geordi (who names him Hugh), and is taught about independence. Guest stars: Jonathan del Arco and Whoopi Goldberg.

"I, Mudd" — written by Stephen Kandel and David Gerrold, directed by Marc Daniels, this second-season Classic *Trek* episode aired 11/3/67. The plot, centered on the return of Harry Mudd, makes for a very humorous script involving a world of androids. Guest stars: Roger C. Carmel, Kay Elliot, Richard Tatro, Rhae and Alyce Andrece, Tom and Ted LeGarde, Maureen and Colleen Thornton, Tamara and Starr Wilson, Mike Howden, and Michael Zaslow.

Ian — alien entity to which Deanna Troi gives birth, born as a glowing white pulse of energy which then takes the form of a human boy so it can experience humanoid life, in *TNG* episode "The Child." He ages rapidly and dies when he learns he is emitting deadly Eichner radiation. Zachary Benjamin plays the younger Ian, and R. J. Williams plays the older.

Ibodan — Bajoran murderer and black marketeer who is murdered, and Odo is accused of the crime, in *DS9* episode "A Man Alone."

I'Chaya — Spock's *sehlat* (see entry) in the animated episode "Yesteryear." The *sehlat* is also referred to, but not by name, in "Journey to Babel."

Icarus IV — comet through which the Romulan ship intentionally passes to throw the *Enterprise* off its track in Classic episode "Balance of Terror."

"Icarus Factor, The" — second-season *TNG* episode written by David Assael and Robert L. McCullough, directed by Robert Iscove. Riker's father, Kyle, comes aboard to tell his son that Will Riker has been promoted to command the starship *Ares*. Guest stars: Mitchell Ryan, Colm Meaney, and Lance Spellerberg.

Icobar — Iconian language mentioned in *TNG* episode "Contagion."

Iconia — lost civilization's homeworld located in the Neutral Zone, mentioned in *TNG* episode "Contagion."

Icor IX — location of a symposium on Rogue Star Clusters, mentioned in *TNG* episode "Captain's Holiday."

"Identity Crisis" — fourth-season *TNG* episode written by Tim DeHaas and Brannon Braga, directed by Winrich Kolbe. Five years before, Geordi and a friend visited a planet on which all the colonists have since disappeared; and they may be experiencing the same phenomenon. Guest stars: Maryann Plunkett, Patti Yasutake, Amick Byram, Mona Grudt, Dennis Madalone, and Paul Tompkins.

IDIC — Vulcan philosophy, meaning Infinite Diversity in Infinite Combinations, symbolized by a circle with a triangle sticking through it. Spock wears the symbol on a necklace in Classic episode "Is There in Truth No Beauty?" Gene Roddenberry created the theory, and its symbol, so he could sell the necklaces through the mail and make more money.

Idini Star Cluster — location through which the *Enterprise* passes in *TNG* episode "Too Short a Season."

Igo — star system to which the *Enterprise* is sent to find the *Yosemite* in *TNG* episode "Realm of Fear."

Ilia — Deltan navigator and Will Decker's old flame, played by Persis Khambatta, who comes aboard the *Enterprise* in the film *Star Trek: The Motion Picture.* She is attacked by the Vejur probe. The Vejur later sends a probe in her image to the *Enterprise* in order to learn about the humans on board.

ilium 629 — isotope in dilithium mentioned in *TNG* episode "Pen Pals."

"I'll Take You Home Again, Kathleen" — a song Kevin Riley sings in Classic episode "The Naked Time" after he has commandeered Engineering.

Illicon — mentioned in *TNG* episode "We'll Always Have Paris" as a world that feels the time distortion.

Ilyra IV — a charming world where Mudd sold Starfleet Academy, mentioned in animated episode "Mudd's Passion."

"Imaginary Friend" — fifth-season *TNG* episode written by Ronald Wilderson, Jean Matthias, Richard Fliegel, Edithe Swenson, and Brannon Braga, directed by Gabrielle Beaumont. The imaginary friend of an *Enterprise* officer's daughter forms into a real being with superpowers and deliberately causes dangerous accidents on the ship. Guest stars: Noley Thornton, Shay Astar, Brian Bonsall, Jeff Allin, Patti Yasutake, and Sheila Franklin.

Iman — famous model who played Martia in the film *The Undiscovered Country.* Her film work includes a Michael Jackson video and the movie *L.A. Story* (with Steve Martin). She is married to the actor/rock star David Bowie.

"Immunity Syndrome, The" — written by Robert Sabaroff and directed by Joseph Pevney, this second-season Classic *Trek* episode aired 1/19/68. The *Enterprise* enters a dark rift in space and finds itself being pulled toward an amoebalike creature that is miles long. They must find a way out or die. No guest stars. Of note: The USS *Intrepid*, a ship commanded by an all-Vulcan crew, is lost with all hands, a loss Spock telepathically feels.

Imodene system — system mentioned as the place where Geordi's father studied invertebrates in *TNG* episode "The Icarus Factor."

Impershein, Dierdre — played Joval in *TNG* "Captain's Holiday."

impulse power — secondary, very slow propulsion used by the *Enterprise* when moving away from space docks or planets, and when the warp drive is out.

Imzadi — Betazoid term meaning a "beloved" person, mentioned in *TNG* episode "Shades of Gray." Troi refers to Riker with this form of endearment on occasion.

"In Theory" — fourth-season *TNG* episode written by Ronald D. Moore and Joe Menosky, directed by Patrick Stewart. Data becomes involved romantically with a young ensign who has just broken up with her lover. Later, as the *Enterprise* moves into a nebula cloud, things start going wrong, as if a poltergeist is on board. Guest stars: Michele Scarabelli, Rosalind Chao, Whoopi Goldberg, Pamela Winslow, and Colm Meaney. Of note: During filming of this episode, a member of the set renamed a shuttlepod *Pontiac* to play a joke on Patrick Stewart. Patrick Stewart, of course, does Pontiac commercials.

Inad — Ullian historian, played by Eve Brenner, whose son, Jev, is a mind rapist in *TNG* episode "Violations."

Indri VIII — world destroyed by Klingon Captain Nu'Daq to stop anyone from finding the key to Professor Galen's micropaleontology mystery in *TNG* episode "The Chase."

Industrial Light and Magic — company responsible only for the special effects in "Encounter at Farpoint," but which continued to get credit throughout the *TNG* series because stock footage from the two-hour episode is used universally.

"Infinite Vulcan, The" — written by Walter Koenig, this animated Classic *Trek* episode aired 10/20/73. On the planet Phylos the crew encounters plantlike beings and a giant human, Dr. Stavos Keniclius, whom the beings refer to as Master or Savior. Keniclius kidnaps Spock and clones him in his laboratory into a giant immortal Vulcan. Guest voices: James Doohan (Dr. Keniclius 5, Agmar, Lt. Arex) and Nichelle Nichols as the computer.

Ingalls, Don — scriptwriter of Classic *Trek* "The Alternative Factor." He also wrote the scripts for the films *A Matter of Wife and Death*, *Flood*, *The Initiation of Sarah*, and *Captain America*.

Ingledew, Rosalind — played Yanar in *TNG* "The Outrageous Okona."

Ingraham B — world invaded by parasites which destroy the inhabiting civilization two years before the invasion on Deneva in Classic episode "Operation: Annihilate!"

Inhat, Steve — played Captain Garth in Classic *Trek* "Whom Gods Destroy." Born in Czechoslovakia in 1934, his credits include *The Chase* and *Fuzz* as well as several appearances in Westerns such as *Iron Horse*. He died in 1972.

"Inner Light, The" — fifth-season *TNG* episode written by Morgan Gendel and Peter Allan Fields, directed by Peter Lauritson. A strange, alien probe knocks Picard unconscious and installs in his conciousness memories of a native of Katan, a now dead world. While unconscious, Picard lives an entire life on Katan as a man named Kamin, who marries, fathers two children, and dies an old man. When he wakes up, he is told he has been out for only minutes. Guest stars: Margot Rose, Richard Riehle, Scott Jaeck, Jennifer Nash, Daniel Stewart (Patrick Stewart's son), and Patti Yasutake. Of note: This episode won the Hugo award in 1993 for best science-fiction dramatic presentation.

Innis, Valeda — a First Electorine of Haven played by Anna Katarina in *TNG* episode "Haven."

inoprovaline — drug given to John by Dr. Crusher in *TNG* episode "Transfigurations."

Insomok, Admiral — an officer to whom Wesley is to report when he arrives at Starfleet Academy in *TNG* episode "Final Mission."

Inspector General's Officer — branch of Starfleet which insures Starfleet's integrity mentioned in *TNG* episode "Coming of Age."

Instrument of Obedience — implant placed by the Oracle in the temple of the people of Yonada to control them from asking too many questions about the nature of their world, which is contained within an asteroid, in Classic episode "For the World Is Hollow and I Have Touched the Sky." The Oracle monitors the implants and can administer a severe dose of pain to questioners or even cause death.

interceptor — type of airplane piloted by Captain John Christopher in Classic episode "Tomorrow Is Yesterday."

interium — element used on Vulcan ships mentioned in *TNG* episode "Unification."

intermix chamber — part of the ship's engines mentioned in Classic episode "The Naked Time."

interphase — rip in the fabric of space through which the *Defiant* disappears and reappears at certain intervals, which can be charted through spacetime waves in Classic episode "The Tholian Web."

Intrepid, USS — ship docked at the Starbase for repairs in Classic episode "Court-Martial." Mentioned as first on the site of the Khitomer disaster in *TNG* episode "Sins of the Father," it is later destroyed by the giant amoeba in "The Immunity Syndrome."

invidium — packing substance used by the Mikulaks, which causes the technical systems of the *Enterprise* to malfunction in *TNG* episode "Hollow Pursuits."

ion propulsion — Eymorg's ship uses this propulsion system in Classic episode "Spock's Brain."

ion storm — caused Kirk, Scotty, McCoy, and Uhura to be sent to an alternative universe in Classic episode "Mirror, Mirror." An ion storm also occurred in "Court-Martial" and was supposedly responsible for Ben Finney's death.

Iotia — planet where the intelligent, humanoid inhabitants' culture was based upon the book *Chicago Mobs of the Twenties*, left behind by the *Horizon* in Classic episode "A Piece of the Action."

Iraatan V — where Kivas Fajo claims he was educated in *TNG* episode "The Most Toys."

Ireland, Jill — played Leila Kalomi in Classic *Trek* "This Side of Paradise." Born in London in 1936, she died in 1991 after a long battle with cancer. Her credits include several roles in husband Charles Bronson's films, including *Hell Drivers*, *Breakheart Pass*, and *Love and Bullets*. A regular character on *Shane*, she guest starred several times in *The Man from U.N.C.L.E.* (with her first husband, David McCallum).

Iresine Syndrome — disease *Enterprise* crewmembers who have been mind raped by Jev are thought to be suffering from in *TNG* episode "Violations."

irillium — substance which renders ryetalyn (see entry) useless when mixed with it, mentioned in Classic episode "Requiem for Methuselah."

Irish Unification of 2024 — referred to by Data in *TNG* episode "The High Ground."

"Is There in Truth No Beauty?" — written by Jean Lissette Aroeste and directed by Ralph Senensky, this third-season Classic *Trek* episode aired 10/18/68. The *Enterprise* transports the Medusan ambassador Kollos and his blind assistant back to his home planet. The assistant must be blind to work with Kollos, who is kept in a box, because it is said anyone who looks at the Medusan will go insane. In order to protect the ambassador from attempted murder, Spock inadvertently looks at him. Guest stars: Diana Muldaur and David Frankham. Of note: In this episode, the Vulcan philosophical symbol, IDIC, makes its first appearance. Roddenberry wrote the symbol into the script because he wanted to sell the newly invented medallion through his company, Lincoln Enterprises.

Isak — Zeon native, played by Richard Evans, whose brother is named Abrom in Classic episode "Patterns of Force."

Iscove, Robert — director of *TNG* "The Icarus Factor."

Ishikawa, Keiko — see entry for O'Brien, Keiko.

Isis — Gary Seven's sleek black cat, with which he seems to have some kind of mental telepathy, in Classic episode "Assignment: Earth." At the end of the episode, Roberta Lincoln sees the cat change into a woman for a few seconds, but the cat's natural form remains a mystery.

Isis III — destination of the *Enterprise* in *TNG* episode "Too Short a Season."

isolinear chips — computer storage used by *Enterprise* in *TNG* episode "The Drumhead."

Ito, Robert — played Tactical Officer Chang in *TNG* "Coming of Age."

Itzkowitz, Howard — played the cargo deck ensign in *Star Trek: The Motion Picture*. His credits include a regular role in the variety show *Marie* and the movie *Amateur Night at the Dixie Bar and Grill*.

Iverson's Disease — disease for which Admiral Mark Jameson takes Cerberan youth drugs, which eventually kill him, in *TNG* episode "Too Short a Season."

Izar — home of Garth of Izar in Classic episode "Whom Gods Destroy."

J-25 system — location to which Q sends the *Enterprise* in *TNG* episode "Q Who" where they first encounter the Borg.

Jack the Ripper — an entity which feeds off fear and possesses people on various worlds, making them commit serial murders. It is called Redjac, Kesla, and Beratis on the worlds it has visited. It inhabits the body of Hengist on Argelius II in Classic episode "Wolf in the Fold."

Jackson — member, played by Jimmy Jones, of the landing party on Pyris VII who is killed and beamed back to the ship as a warning for others to stay away, in Classic episode "Catspaw."

Jackson, Sherry — played Andrea in Classic *Trek* "What Are Little Girls Made Of?" Her credits include a regular role as one of the children in *The Danny Thomas Show* and appearances in *Lost in Space* and *Gunsmoke*. Her films include *Wild Woman, The Girl on the Late, Late Show, Returning Home,* and *Casino.*

Jacobs, Jake — scriptwriter for *TNG* "Sarek."

Jacobsen, Jill — played Vanessa in *TNG* "The Royale."

Jaeger, Karl, Lieutenant — member, played by Richard Carlyle, of the landing party on Gothos in Classic episode "The Squire of Gothos."

Jaglom Shrek — character in *TNG* episode

"Birthright" who takes Worf to Carraya in search of his father.

Jahil, Captain — captain of an alien ship in *DS9* episode "Babel."

Jahn — Miri's paranoid and conniving friend, played by Michael J. Pollard, the oldest boy in Classic episode "Miri."

jakmanite — element which can break down glass, mentioned in *TNG* episode "Hollow Pursuits."

jamaharohn — reference to sex on Risa in *TNG* episode "Captain's Holiday."

Jamal, Zahra, Yeoman — member, played by Maurisha Taliferro, of the landing party on Deneva in Classic episode "Operation: Annihilate!"

James, Anthony — played Thei in *TNG* "The Neutral Zone."

James, Loren — stunt man for Norman in Classic *Trek* "I, Mudd."

James, Richard D. — production designer of *TNG*.

Jameson, Anne — wife, played by Marsha Hunt, of Admiral Mark Jameson in *TNG* episode "Too Short a Season."

Jameson, Mark — a Starfleet Admiral, played by Clayton Rohner, who dies of a Cerberan rejuvenation drug overdose in *TNG* episode "Too Short a Season."

Janaran Falls — Betazoid location where Riker and Troi last met before Riker was stationed on the *Potemkin* in *TNG* episode "Second Chances."

Janowsky, Mary — young girl, played by Pamelyn Ferdin, whose parents commit suicide because of the Gorgon's influence in Classic episode "And the Children Shall Lead."

Janssen, Famke — played Kamala in *TNG* "The Perfect Mate."

Janus VI — mineral treasure house which had been mined by the Federation for fifty years before encountering the Horta in Classic episode "Devil in the Dark."

Jarada — mentioned by Riker in *TNG* episode "Samaritan Snare" and described as a new Federation ally with insectoid people obsessed by protocol In "The Big Goodbye."

Jaris — prefect of Argelius II whose wife, Sybo, is murdered by the entity inhabiting Hengist in Classic episode "Wolf in the Fold."

Ja'rod — Duras's father in *TNG* episode "Sins of the Father."

Jarok, Alidar, Admiral — officer, played by James Sloyan, who poses as Sublieutenant Setal in order to defect to the Federation but eventually commits suicide in *TNG* episode "The Defector."

Jaros II — location of the Starfleet prison facility where Ensign Ro was confined in *TNG* episode "Ensign Ro."

Jarvis, Graham — played Klin Dokachin in *TNG* "Unification, Part I."

Jarvis, Ron — scriptwriter for *TNG* "Disaster."

Jasal, Gul — Cardassian character, played by Joel Swetow, in *DS9* episode "Emissary."

Jason, Harvey — played Felix Leech in *TNG* "The Big Goodbye."

Jat'yln — Klingon word meaning "taking the living by the dead," mentioned in *TNG* episode "Power Play."

Jay, Tony — played Campio in *TNG* "Cost of Living."

Jaya — asylum inmate who claims to be Commander Bloom of the *Yosemite* in *TNG* episode "Frame of Mind."

J'Ddan — Romulan spy, played by Henry Woronicz, who masquerades as a Klingon exchange exobiologist during a visit to the *Enterprise* in *TNG* episode "The Drumhead."

Jedda — researcher on Regula I, played by John Vargas, who is killed in *The Wrath of Khan*.

Jefferies tube — tunnellike area on the *Enterprise* through which crewmembers access various delicate parts of the ship for repair.

Jellico, Edward, Captain — takes command of the *Enterprise* when Picard is captured by the Cardassians in *TNG* episode "Chain of Command." He immediately decorates the ready room with his young son's artwork depicting elephants and does not get along well with Riker.

Jemison, Mae — guest starred in *TNG* episode "Second Chances."

Jenkins, Ken — played Paul Stubbs in *TNG* "Evolution."

Jennings, Joseph R. — production designer on *The Wrath of Khan*. He has also done work on the movies *Yellowbeard* and *Johnny Dangerously*.

Jennings, Junero — played an engine-room technician in *Star Trek: The Motion Picture*. She has had other small roles, including an appearance in *Stone*.

jenok — Klingon necklace given to a girl who has come of age in *TNG* episode "Birthright."

Jenolan — transport ship which has been missing for 75 years and is found by the *Enterprise* crashed into the Dyson sphere in *TNG* episode "Relics." Montgomery Scott, preserved in a transporter pattern, is found on the ship.

Jens, Salome — actress who guest starred in *TNG* episode "The Chase."

Jensen, Keith L. — stunt man in *Star Trek: The Motion Picture.*

Jenson, Len — scriptwriter of the animated episode "Once upon a Planet."

Jenson, Roy — played Cloud William in Classic *Trek* "The Omega Glory." His film credits include *Ride Lonesome, Powderkeg, Hit Lady, Nightside, Honkytonk Man,* and *Last of the Great Survivors.* He has also appeared on the TV shows *The Man from U.N.C.L.E.* and *Voyage to the Bottom of the Sea.*

Jeter, K. W. — author of *DS9* novel *Bloodletter.*

Jev — character from Ullian, played by Ben Lemon, who mind rapes some of the *Enterprise* crew in *TNG* episode "Violations."

Jewel of Thesia — the prized possession of the planet Streleb (in the Coalition of Medina), thought to have been stolen by Captain Okona in *TNG* episode "The Outrageous Okona." It was actually taken by Benzan, the son of Streleb leader Kushell, for a wedding gift.

Jewell, Austen — unit production manager for *Star Trek: The Motion Picture.* He has also worked on the 1950s films *Gunfight at Dodge City* and *Cast a Long Shadow.*

Jewell, Lois — played Drusilla in Classic *Trek* "Bread and Circuses."

"Jihad" — written by Stephen Kandel, this animated Classic *Trek* episode aired 1/13/74. Kirk and Spock, along with other members of alien ships, are chosen for a secret mission to find the Soul of Skorr and stop the breakout of a holy war. Guest voice: David Gerrold (Em/3/Green).

Jilestra, Sabin — Admiral Satie's Betazoid aide, played by Bruce French, in *TNG* episode "Chain of Command."

Jil Orra — see entry for Orra, Jil.

J'naii — androgynous race which does not allow its members to act as a single gender in *TNG* episode "The Outcast."

J'onn — man on Nimbus III, played by Rex Holman, who joins Sybok in his search for ShaKaRee in the film *The Final Frontier*.

Joaquim — Khan's right-hand man, played by Judson Scott (whose name does not appear in the credits), in the film *The Wrath of Khan*.

Joaquin — Khan's right-hand man, played by Mark Tobin, in Classic episode "Space Seed."

Jo'Bril, Dr. — Takaran scientist who fakes his own death but comes back to life while on a shuttle with Crusher who kills him in *TNG* episode "Suspicions."

Jochim, Anthony — played a survivor in the Classic *Trek* pilot "The Cage." He has appeared in *The Big Fisherman* ('59) and *One Step Beyond*.

Johnson, Alexandra — played One Zero in *TNG* "11001001."

Johnson, Elaine — old woman, played by Laura Wood, who is dying in Classic episode "The Deadly Years."

Johnson, Georgann — played Admiral Gromek in *TNG* "The Emissary."

Johnson, George Clayton — scriptwriter of Classic *Trek* "The Man Trap" and often a featured speaker at *Star Trek* conventions. A science-fiction writer and the author of the movie and book *Logan's Run*, he also wrote for *The Twilight Zone*, among other TV shows.

Johnson, Joan — played a guard in Classic *Trek* "Space Seed."

Johnson, Julie — stunt woman who doubled for Yeoman Landon in Classic *Trek* "The Apple."

Johnson, Katie Jane — played the "child Martia" who led Kirk and McCoy through small tunnels and out of prison in *The Undiscovered Country.*

Johnson, Lieutenant — man, played by David L. Ross, who is wounded in battle but heals quickly and rejoins the fray in Classic episode "Day of the Dove."

Johnson, Robert — old man, played by Felix Locher, in Classic episode "The Deadly Years" who is really 29 years old.

Joining — Betazoid marriage ceremony performed in the nude, mentioned in *TNG* episode "Haven."

Jol, Etana — leader of the Ktarans who gives an addictive game to Riker in *TNG* episode "The Game."

Jones, Cyrano — con man, played by Stanley Adams, who will sell anything to anyone. He is responsible for the tribble infestation onboard the *Enterprise* and on Space Station *K-7* in Classic episode "The Trouble with Tribbles." Adams was also a *Trek* scriptwriter. (See entry for Adams, Stanley.)

Jones, Jay — played Ensign Mallory in Classic *Trek* "The Apple" and Mirt in "A Piece of the Action." He was also a stunt man in several episodes, including as a double for Scotty in "Who Mourns for Adonais?" His other credits include *Man on the Outside* and *The Man from U.N.C.L.E.*

Jones, Jimmy — played Jackson in Classic *Trek* "Catspaw."

Jones, Judith — played one of the Edo children in *TNG* "Justice."

Jones, Miranda, Dr. — blind, telepathic aide, played by Diana Muldaur, to Kollos. Her jealousy, pride, and bitterness about her handicap threaten the lives of others in Classic episode "Is There in Truth No Beauty?"

Jones, Morgan — played Colonel Nesvig in Classic

Trek "Assignment: Earth." He also starred in the TV series *Blue Angels* in 1960. His film credits include *Doctors' Private Lives*, *Advice to the Lovelorn*, and *The Red Light Sting*.

Jones, Renée — played Lt. Aquiel Uhnari in *TNG* episode "Aquiel."

Jones, Ron — composer of incidental music for dozens of *TNG* episodes.

Jordan, Ensign — android, played by Michael Zaslow, controlled by Harry Mudd, who takes over the *Enterprise* in Classic episode "I, Mudd."

Josephs, Lieutenant — officer, played by James X. Mitchell, who finds Ambassador Gav's body in Classic episode "Journey to Babel."

Jouret IV — site of a colony completely wiped out by the Borg in *TNG* episode "The Best of Both Worlds."

"Journey to Babel" — written by D. C. Fontana and directed by Joseph Pevney, this second-season Classic *Trek* episode aired 11/17/67. Spock's parents, Amanda and Ambassador Sarek, who is dying from a heart condition, board the *Enterprise* which is shuttling ambassadors and their families to the important Babel Conference. Meanwhile someone is killing the ambassadors. Guest stars: Mark Lenard, Jane Wyatt, William O'Connell, Reggie Nalder, and John Wheeler. Of note: Spock's childhood pet, a large, furry beast with six-inch fangs called a *sehlat*, is mentioned in this episode.

Joval — flirtatious character, played by Dierdre Imershein, who tells Picard how to display the Horga'hn on Risa in *TNG* episode "Captain's Holiday."

Jovis — Kivas Fajo's ship in *TNG* episode "The Most Toys."

Judd, Ashley — played Robin Lefler in *TNG* "Darmok" and "The Game." She is Naomi's younger daughter and Wynonna's sister, of the former country superstar team the Judds.

Judge Advocate General's Corps — Starfleet legal affairs branch mentioned in *TNG* episode "The Measure of a Man."

Julian, Heidi — production coordinator of *DS9*.

Jung, Nathan — played Genghis Khan in Classic *Trek* "The Savage Curtain."

Jupiter Eight — car seen in a magazine in Classic episode "Bread and Circuses."

"Justice" — first-season *TNG* episode written by Worley Thorne and Ralph Willis, directed by James L. Conway. The inhabitants of Rubicam III welcome the crew openly but their "god," orbiting overhead, does not want the *Enterprise* interfering with her children. Guest stars: Josh Clark, David Q. Combs, Richard Lavin, Judith Jones, Eric Matthew, Brad Zerbst, and David Michael Graves.

Justman — *Enterprise* shuttlecraft upon which Dr. Reyga's experimental metaphasic shielding is tested. The shuttle is piloted into the star Vaytan in *TNG* episode "Suspicions."

Justman, Robert — associate producer of Classic *Trek*'s first two seasons and supervising producer on *Star Trek: The Next Generation*. He also worked on the show *Stoney Burke* and produced *Then Came Bronson*, as well as the pilot for the series *The Man from Atlantis* (with Herb Solow) and *Planet Earth* (with Gene Roddenberry).

K–7, Space Station — located near Sherman's planet, the site of the battle of Donatu V, mentioned in Classic episode "The Trouble with Tribbles."

Kabatris — world where Riker wore fancy robes to impress its leaders, mentioned in *TNG* episode "Angel One."

Kaelon II — planet threatened by its dying star, where the inhabitants believe in suicide at age 60, performed in a ceremony called the Resolution. Dr. Timicin, a Kaelon scientist who is about to turn 60, develops a theory to relight his home-world's star but his people insist he must fulfill the death ritual in *TNG* episode "Half a Life."

Kaferian apples — Mitchell creates Kaferian apple trees on Delta Vega with his newfound talents in Classic episode "Where No Man Has Gone Before."

Kagen, Janet — noted science-fiction author of Classic *Trek* novel *Uhura's Song* and winner of the Hugo award for science fiction.

Kahless — famous ancient Klingon, known as "The Unforgettable," responsible for bringing Klingon culture together into a warrior society. Klingon myth says he will reappear one day to lead Klingons into a new, greater era. He appears in Classic episode "The Savage Curtain," played by Robert Herron, and in *TNG* episode "Rightful Heir," in which he is a clone of himself.

Kahlest — Worf's nurse, played by Thelma Lee, and only survivor from the massacre at the Khitomer Outpost. She appears again after a long silence to help Worf in the *TNG* episode "Sins of the Father."

Kahn, James — scriptwriter of *TNG* "The Masterpiece Society."

kahs'wan — Vulcan test of manhood taken by all seven-year-old boys, during which they must journey alone into the desert and learn how to survive for ten days, mentioned in the animated episode "Yesteryear."

Kai — Bajoran term for an elder or revered member of society, in *DS9*.

Kail, James — makeup artist on *The Search for Spock*.

Kalandans — dead civilization which succumbed to an unknown disease, leaving behind only an outpost and the computer-generated vision of Losira in Classic episode "That Which Survives."

Kaldra IV — world to which the *Enterprise* is delivering an Ullian delegation of telepathic historians in *TNG* episode "Violations."

Kaleb Sector — location for a rendezvous between the Romulan warbird *Khazara* and a Corvallen ship in *TNG* episode "Face of the Enemy."

Kali — female Klingon in animated episode "Time Trap."

kalifee — Vulcan term meaning "challenge" used in Classic episode "Amok Time."

Kalin Trose — see entry for Trose, Kalin.

Kallisko — ship whose crew is killed by the Crystalline Entity in *TNG* episode "Silicon Avatar."

Kalo — one of Oxmyx's gunmen, played by Lee Delano, in Classic episode "A Piece of the Action."

Kalomi, Leila — colony botanist, played by Jill Ireland, on Omicron Ceti III and Spock's friend six years before he has a "spore-induced" love affair with her in Classic episode "This Side of Paradise."

Kamal, Jon — played the Vulcan Sonak in *Star Trek: The Motion Picture.*

Kamal, Stanley — played Kosinski in *TNG* "Where No One Has Gone Before."

Kamala — empathic metamorph from Krios, played by Famke Janssen, promised to be Chancellor Alrik of Valt's wife but who accidentally bonds with Picard. She carries out her duty, however, and marries the Chancellor although he can no longer be her perfect mate in *TNG* episode "The Perfect Mate."

Kamin — Picard's name on Katan where, according to a memory installed in his subconscious, he plays the flute and has a son, Batai; a daughter, Meribor; and a wife, Eline, in *TNG* episode "The Inner Light."

Kandel, Stephen — scriptwriter of Classic *Trek* "Mudd's Women," "I, Mudd," and the animated episodes "Mudd's Passion" and "The Jihad." A cocreator of the series *Iron Horse,* he also wrote for *Green Hornet* and *Wonder Woman* and was producer of the series *MacGyver.*

Kang — captain of a Klingon ship, played by Michael Ansara, in Classic episode "Day of the Dove."

Kanutu — one of a tribe of Neural hill people who have knowledge of herbs and roots that can cure sickness, in Classic episode "A Private Little War."

Kapec, Reena — Flint's android ward, played by Louise Sorel, who dies from emotional overload when she is forced to choose between her newfound love for Kirk and her loyal love for Flint in Classic episode "Requiem for Methuselah."

Kaplan, Sol — composer for Classic *Trek* episodes "The Enemy Within," "The Doomsday Machine," "The Deadly Years," "Obsession," "The Immunity Syndrome," and "The Ultimate Computer." He has also written scores for such movies as *Tales of Manhattan* and *The Spy Who Came in from the Cold*.

Kaplan — security guard, played by Dick Dial, killed by a lightning bolt in Classic episode "The Apple."

Kara — café dancer, played by Tania Lemani, on Argelius II in Classic episode "Wolf in the Fold." In "Spock's Brain," a woman named Kara, played by Marj Dusay, is the Eymorg who steals Spock's brain. Her planet is Sigma Draconis VI.

Karapleedeez, Onna — Starfleet officer who was a victim of a Starfleet conspiracy in *TNG* episode "Conspiracy."

Karas, Greg — played the intern in *The Voyage Home*.

Karatok — author of *The Dream of the Fire*, a book given to Data in *TNG* episode "The Measure of a Man."

Kareel — female body, played by Nicole Orth-Pallavicini, which hosts the Trill Ambassador Odan, who was Dr. Crusher's lover while hosted in a male body in *TNG* episode "The Host."

Karelkie — *Enterprise* security officer on the away team to Ohniaka in *TNG* episode "Descent."

Karema III — world mentioned as a mining possibility in *TNG* episode "The Quality of Life."

Karen, Anna — played "woman" in Classic *Trek* "All Our Yesterdays."

Karf — gunman, played by Buddy Garion, for Krako in Classic episode "A Piece of the Action."

Kargan, Captain — commander, played by

Christopher Collins, of the Klingon ship *Pagh* in *TNG* episode "A Matter of Honor."

Karidian, Anton — actor, played by Arnold Moss, who heads the Karidian players, and who Kirk thinks is really Kodos the Executioner (see entry), who was responsible for the execution of half the population of Tarsus IV during a famine. Karidian is later accidentally killed by his own daughter, Lenore, in Classic episode "The Conscience of the King."

Karidian, Lenore — nineteen-year-old member, played by Barbara Anderson, of the Karidian company of players and daughter of Anton Karidian. She went insane as a child when she secretly found out her father was responsible for a mass genocide. She accidentally phasers him to death in Classic episode "The Conscience of the King."

Karidian Players — traveling troupe of actors, sponsored by the Galactic Cultural Exchange Program, who have been performing together for nine years in Classic episode "The Conscience of the King."

Karl 4 — Karla 5's son from animated episode "The Counter-Clock Incident" who is from Arret, where time runs backward.

Karla 5 — character from Arret who ages backward in the animated episode "The Counter-Clock Incident."

Karnas — governor of Mordan IV, played by Michael Pataki, who kidnaps a group of Starfleet people as revenge against Admiral Jameson in *TNG* episode "Too Short a Season."

Karst Topography — planet filled with sinkholes, underground caverns, and rivers that confuse the *Enterprise* sensors in *TNG* episode "Who Watches the Watchers."

Kartan — Denevan native, played by Dave Armstrong, in Classic episode "Operation: Annihilate!"

Kartozian, Thomas — scriptwriter of *TNG* "Galaxy's Child."

Katan — world where Picard lives an entire life in virtual reality while inside a probe in *TNG* episode "The Inner Light." His experience makes him the foremost authority on the dead civilization.

Katarina, Anna — played Valeda Innis in *TNG* "Haven."

Katie — one of the children, played by Jandi Swanson, kidnapped by the Aldeans in *TNG* episode "When the Bough Breaks."

katra — Vulcan term for the soul that they can supposedly transfer to another person at death, as seen in *The Search for Spock*.

Katsulas, Andreas — played Commander Tomalak in *TNG* "The Enemy" and "Future Imperfect."

Kava, Caroline — played Dr. Toby Russell in *TNG* "Ethics."

Kavis Alpha IV — site of the new Nanite colony in *TNG* episode "Evolution."

Kavis Alpha Sector — location to which the *Enterprise* travels to study a stellar explosion that happens once every 196 years in *TNG* episode "Evolution."

Kayron — Ferengi, played by Tracey Walter, under command of DaiMon Tarr in *TNG* episode "The Last Outpost."

Kaz — Klingon officer, second-in-command to Kor in animated episode "Time Trap."

Kazago — Ferengi first officer, played by Doug Warhit, under command of DaiMon Bok in *TNG* episode "The Battle."

Kazanga — genius as big as Einstein or the Vulcan Sikar, mentioned in Classic episode "The Ultimate Computer."

Kazis Binary system — location where an Earth capsule is found mentioned in *TNG* episode "The Neutral Zone."

Keefer, Don — played Cromwell in Classic *Trek* "Assigment: Earth." Other credits include *Angel, The Guns of Will Sonnett*, and *Iron Horse*. His films include *The Bait, The Immigrants, Marathon, The Five of Me*, and *Creepshow*.

Keel — Capellan, played by Cal Bolder, who kills the Klingon Kras in Classic episode "Friday's Child."

Keel, Anne and Melissa — sisters of Walker Keel who never appear but are mentioned in *TNG* episode "Conspiracy."

Keel, Walker, Captain — officer, played by Jonathan Farwell, who warns Picard of a Starfleet conspiracy in *TNG* episode "Conspiracy." He served with Picard and Jack Crusher aboard the *Stargazer* and introduced Beverly to Jack.

Keeler, Edith — social worker, played by Joan Collins, on Earth during the 1920s with whom Kirk falls in love in Classic episode "The City on the Edge of Forever." McCoy changes history when he saves her life but her eventual death when she is hit by a truck restores history as we know it.

Keeper — Talosian zookeeper, played by Meg Wyllie, in Classic episodes "The Menagerie" and "The Cage." Malachi Throne plays the zookeeper's voice.

Keeve, Falor — Bajoran member of the underground in *TNG* episode "Ensign Ro."

Kehler, Jack — appeared in *DS9* "Babel."

K'Ehleyr — half-Klingon, half-human woman, played by Suzie Plakson, who had an affair with Worf six years prior to appearing as an emissary for the *T'Ong* situation in *TNG* episode "The Emissary."

Kehoe, Patrick — first assistant director on *The Voyage Home*. He was also assistant director on *Poltergeist*, *Things Are Tough All Over*, *Bad Boys*, *Twilight Zone: The Movie*, and *The Philadelphia Experiment*.

Keiko O'Brien — see entry for O'Brien, Keiko.

Kelinda — Kelvin female, played by Barbara Bouchet, and Rojan's apparent love interest, whom Kirk tries to distract by seducing her in Classic episode "By Any Other Name."

Kell, Ambassador — Klingon official in league with the Romulans who brainwashes LaForge into attempting the assassination of Governor Vagh in *TNG* episode "The Mind's Eye."

Keller, Dore — played a crewman in *TNG* "The Child."

Kellerman, Sally — played Dr. Elizabeth Dehner on Classic *Trek* "Where No Man Has Gone Before." Born in 1938, her other film credits include *M*A*S*H*, *Reform School Girl*, *Lost Horizon*, *Serial*, and others. She studied under actor Jeff Corey, who played Plasus in "The Cloud Minders."

Kellett, Pete — played Kirk's henchman in Classic *Trek* "Mirror, Mirror." He had a recurring role on *Branded* and *The Man from U.N.C.L.E.*

Kelley, DeForest — starred as Dr. Leonard ("Bones") McCoy in the Classic and animated series and all six *Trek* movies. He also appeared as the old doctor in *TNG* "Encounter at Farpoint." Born in Atlanta, Georgia, in 1920, the son of a Baptist minister, he moved to California at age seventeen after graduating from high school. He did radio work before signing on with Paramount in the 1940s, after which he worked as a stage and TV actor in both New York and Los Angeles. His TV credits include *Schlitz Theatre*, *Playhouse 90*, *Gunsmoke*, *You Are There*, *Navy Log*, *Science*

Fiction Theatre, Zane Grey Theatre, Rawhide, and *Bonanza*. He appeared in the films *Fear in the Night, Canon City, Gunfight at Comanche Creek, Illegal, Marriage on the Rocks, The Men, Variety Girl, View from Pompey's Head, Waco, Duke of Chicago, House of Bamboo, Tension at Table Rock, Gunfight at the O.K. Corral, Raintree Country, The Law and Jake Wade, Black Spurs, Town Tamer, Warlock, Gunfight, Johnny Reno, Apache Uprising,* and *Where Love Has Gone*. Roddenberry originally wanted Kelley for the role of Mr. Spock, but Kelley refused, taking instead the small role, his first, of a lieutenant in the series. He did two other (non-*Trek*) pilots for Roddenberry before the producer decided to give him the role of the doctor (after a series of other doctor characters failed to work out). A fortune teller once told Kelley during the 1940s that his greatest success would not occur until after he reached 40, and she was right. However, Kelley, who likes to be called "De," had a difficult time playing second fiddle to William Shatner and Leonard Nimoy. Kelley claims a *Star Trek* producer once wrote an episode which did not include him and the writer later apologized, explaining that Kelley's exclusion was an oversight. His favorite episode is "The Deadly Years," because of the challenge involved playing an aging McCoy. It is a well-known Classic *Trek* tradition that McCoy gets the best, and often the last, lines in each episode.

Kelley, Irene — played Sirah in Classic *Trek* "The Omega Glory."

Kellick, Robin — stand-in in the movie *The Search for Spock*.

Kelly — security guard killed by the Horta in Classic episode "Devil in the Dark."

Kelly, Chief Engineer — officer of the *Yosemite* killed while trying to take cover in a transporter stream in *TNG* episode "Realm of Fear."

Kelowitz, Lee, Lieutenant — security guard, played by Grant Woods, who searches for the shuttle on the wrong world in Classic episode "The Galileo Seven." Kelowitz also appears in "Arena" and "This Side of Paradise."

Kelsey — leader who dies, along with her team, while trying to steal trilithium from the *Enterprise* in *TNG* episode "Starship Mine." Devor, Kiros, Neil, and Pompet are the other members of the team.

Kelso, Chief — *Enterprise* transporter tech in *TNG* episode "The Quality of Life."

Kelso, Lee, Lieutenant — helmsman, played by Paul Carr, who is strangled by Gary Mitchell with a cord in Classic episode "Where No Man Has Gone Before."

Kelvans — multitendriled creatures from Kelva, a planet ruled by the Kelvan empire in the Andromeda Galaxy, who disguise themselves as humans and try to take over the *Enterprise* in Classic episode "By Any Other Name." They want to conquer the Milky Way because their own Andromeda Galaxy will not be able to support life in the future.

Kelven, Max — played Maximus in Classic *Trek* "Bread and Circuses."

Kemp, Jeremy — played Robert Picard in *TNG* "Family."

K'Mpec — leader of the Klingon Council, played by Charles Cooper, in *TNG* episode "Sins of the Father."

Kemper, David — scriptwriter of *TNG* "Peak Performance" and "The Enemy."

Keniclius, Stavos, Dr. — scientist, whose voice is played by James Doohan, responsible for the Eugenics Wars when people were cloned into superhumans. He traveled to the planet Phylos where he cloned himself several times before the *Enterprise* encounters him in the animated episode "The Infinite Vulcan."

Kennelly, Admiral — Starfleet officer, played by Cliff Potts, who conspires with the Cardassian Gul Dolak to kill the Bajoran rebel leader Orta in *TNG* episode "Ensign Ro."

Kenner, Commander — mentioned in Classic episode "Mirror, Mirror," as a man who plans to temporarily take Marlena, the captain's woman, after she moves out of Kirk's cabin.

Kenney, Sean — played the injured Captain Pike in Classic *Trek* "The Menagerie, Parts I and II" and Lt. DePaul in the episodes "Arena" and "A Taste of Armageddon."

Kent, Paul — played Beach in *The Wrath of Khan*. Other film credits include *The Astronaut, Pray for the Wildcats* (with William Shatner), *The Night They Took Miss Beautiful*, and *If Things Were Different*. He also appeared on the TV series *The Man from U.N.C.L.E., Alias Smith and Jones*, and *Griff*.

Kentor — played by Richard Allen, a supporter of Data in *TNG* episode "The Ensigns of Command."

Kenwith, Herb — director of the Classic *Trek* "The Lights of Zetar."

Keppler, Werner — makeup artist on *The Wrath of Khan*.

Kepros, Nicholas — played Movar in *TNG* "Redemption, Parts I and II."

Kern, Dan — played Lt. Dean in *TNG* "We'll Always Have Paris."

Kesla — one of several names used to refer to the Jack the Ripper entity in Classic episode "Wolf in the Fold."

Kevas — dealer in kevas and trillium, which are never defined, mentioned in Classic episode "Errand of Mercy."

Khambatta, Persis — starred as Ilia in *Star Trek: The Motion Picture*. Born in Bombay, India, in 1950, she first worked as a model and was crowned Miss India at age 16. Her film credits include *The Wilby Conspiracy, Conduct Unbecoming, Nighthawks,* and *Megaforce.* She has also guest starred on the TV series *Hunter, MacGyver,* and *The New Mike Hammer.*

Khan — see entry for Singh, Khan Noonian.

Khazara — name of the Romulan ship on which Troi awakens in *TNG* episode "Face of the Enemy."

Khitomer — mentioned as the site of Worf's father's death during a Romulan attack called the Khitomer Massacre in *TNG* episode "Sins of the Father." It is also the location of a peace conference between the Federation and the Klingons, during which an attempt to assassinate the Federation president is thwarted by Kirk in *The Undiscovered Country.*

khoth'va — Klingon term meaning "ritual hunt," mentioned in *TNG* episode "Birthright."

Kim, Luisa, Dr. — assistant director, played by Elizabeth Lindsey, of the Gardeners of Eden on Velara III in *TNG* episode "Home Soil."

Kingsbridge, John — scriptwriter of Classic *Trek* "Return to Tomorrow."

Kingsley, Danitza — played Ariana in *TNG* "Haven."

Kingsley, Sara, Dr. — chief researcher, played by Patricia Smith, at the Darwin Genetic Research Station in *TNG* episode "Unnatural Selection."

Kino, Lloyd — played Wu in Classic *Trek* "The Omega Glory." His credits include *Seizure: The Appearance of Kathy Morris* (with Leonard Nimoy), *Hammett,* and *Forced Vengeance.* Other TV appearances include *The Man from U.N.C.L.E.* and *Voyage to the Bottom of the Sea.*

Kir — Scalosian extra in Classic episode "Wink of an Eye."

Kira, Major — see entry for Nerys, Kira, Major.

Kirk, Aurelan — played by Joan Swift, wife of George Samuel ("Sam") Kirk, James Kirk's brother, both of whom die when infected by the stinger of the parasites in Classic episode "Operation: Annihilate!" Her son, Peter, survives.

Kirk, George Samuel ("Sam") — James Kirk's older brother, a research biologist, who dies with his wife, Aurelan, in Classic episode "Operation: Annihilate!" All that is known about him is that Kirk calls him "Sam" and he had (according to *The Making of Star* Trek) three sons. One son, Peter, survives the parasite attack and is rescued from Deneva but the other two are never mentioned. Sam's only appearance is as a corpse and the actor who played him is not credited.

Kirk, James Tiberius — captain of the *Enterprise* in Classic *Trek* and the six films. He is promoted to Admiral by the *The Motion Picture* but in *The Voyage Home* he is reduced back to captain as punishment for going against orders in order to rescue Spock from Genesis. The youngest captain in Starfleet when he took command of the *Enterprise* at age 34, his heroes include Abraham Lincoln and Garth of Izar. He seems well versed in literature, sometimes quoting famous poetry, and he loves books, antiques, Earth history, and sports. He is very ambitious, a natural leader with a great imagination and a tendency to use it to get what he wants. Kirk does not want to grow old gracefully and resents age, although in the films it does not seem to hamper his ability to command. His best friends are Spock and McCoy. He had a son with Carol Marcus, David, who was killed by Kruge in *The Search for Spock*. Kirk's only other child died unborn when the child's mother, Miramanee, was killed in Classic episode "The Paradise Syndrome." However, Kirk may have other, unknown children since he has had several affairs with women in the past. Kirk is excited by challenge; even while on vacation he will find risky things to do (such as free climbing in Yosemite in *The Final Frontier*). He is excellent in hand-to-hand combat, and has a quick mind and a great sense of humor, qualities which have made him a great Starfleet hero and a legend across the galaxy.

Kirk, Peter — son-in-law of James Kirk and son of Sam Kirk, he is the only Kirk, played by Craig Hundley (who also played Tommy Starnes in "And the Children Shall Lead") mentioned as a survivor of the parasite attack on Deneva in Classic episode "Operation: Annihilate!"

Kirok — name Miramanee calls Kirk when she can't remember his entire name in Classic episode "The Paradise Syndrome."

kironide — substance, found in Platonian food, which affects the pituitary gland, allowing the Platonians to experience psychokinesis in Classic episode "Plato's Stepchildren."

Kiros — member of a team trying to steal trilithium from the *Enterprise* in *TNG* episode "Starship Mine."

kithara — musical instrument given to Spock as a gift by the Platonians in Classic episode "Plato's Stepchildren."

Kivel, Barry — played the doorman in *TNG* "Time's Arrow, Part I."

Klag, Lieutenant — second-in-command, played by Brian Thompson, of the Klingon ship *Pagh* in *TNG* episode "A Matter of Honor."

Klass, Judy — author of Classic *Trek* novel *The Cry of the Onlies*.

Klavdia III — planet on which Anya and Salia, born on Daled IV, have lived for 16 years in *TNG* episode "The Dauphin."

kligat — Capellan weapon, much like a sharp-edged boomerang, seen in Classic episode "Friday's Child."

Kline, Richard H. — director of photography on *Star Trek: The Motion Picture*. His other credits include *The Andromeda Strain, Battle for the Planet of the Apes,* and *King Kong* ('76).

Kling — also known as Klinzhai, the Klingon homeworld, mentioned in *TNG* episode "Heart of Glory."

Klingon death ritual — involves opening the eyes of the dead person, lifting the head, and loudly crying out, performed in *TNG* episode "Heart of Glory."

Klingon oath — part of the Klingon marriage ceremony.

Klingon pain sticks — long rods which inflict pain, in *TNG* episode "The Icarus Factor."

Klingon sark — horse.

Klingon tea ceremony — ceremony during which Klingon love poetry is recited. The tea is said to be deadly to humans and has ill effects on Klingons as well. Pulaski and Worf share the tea, but Pulaski first takes an antidote to the poison in *TNG* episode "Up the Long Ladder."

Klingonese — language of the Klingons, also known as Klingoni.

Klingons — alien race whose culture is based on a warrior code honoring strength, combat, and ritual. They seem very violent and aggressive in Classic *Trek* but by the *TNG* era they are allies of the Federation, an alliance first introduced in *The Motion Picture*. In Classic *Trek*, Klingons appear dark and swarthy but are later given more alien distinctions in the films and *TNG*, appearing with ridged foreheads and long hair.

Kloog — thrall, played by Mickey Morton, on Triskelion in Classic episode "The Gamesters of Triskelion."

Klothos — name of a Klingon battlecruiser in animated episode "Time Trap."

Klunis, Tom — appeared in *DS9* "A Man Alone."

Klystron IV — where Dax, at the time Curzon Dax, was allegedly responsible for the murder of a famous military commander in *DS9* episode "Dax."

Knepper, Rob — played Wyatt Miller in *TNG* "Haven."

K'Nera, Captain — commander, played by David Froman, of the Klingon vessel in *TNG* episode "Heart of Glory."

Kneubuhl, John — scriptwriter of Classic *Trek* "Bread and Circuses."

Knickerbocker, Thomas — played the gunman in *TNG* "Clues."

Knife of Kirom — knife, stained with the blood of the real Kahless, used to test the authenticity of Kahless in *TNG* episode "Rightful Heir."

Knight, William — played the singing crewman in Classic *Trek* "The Naked Time."

Knight, Wyatt — played a technician in *TNG* "Coming Of Age."

Knowland, Joe — played the antique storeowner in *The Voyage Home.*

Koch, Kenny — played the kissing crewman in *TNG* "The Naked Now."

Kodos the Executioner — also known as Anton Karidian, Kodos was the governor on Tarsus IV who invoked martial law during a famine and executed half the colonists, supposedly choosing people thought to be inferior, in order to save the rest. However, a supply ship arrived just after the incident and Kodos was held morally responsible for the deaths. He was supposedly burned to death but actually escaped with his daughter, Lenore, and created

the Karidian company of actors as a disguise. Kirk and
Kevin Riley, who witnessed his entire family killed, were
the only two witnesses left who could identify Kodos, since
they were children on Tarsus when the incident occurred.

Koenig, Walter — starred as Pavel Chekov in Classic
Trek during its second and third seasons. He also wrote
the animated script "The Infinite Vulcan," and has starred
in all the *Trek* movies. Born in Chicago, Illinois, on
September 4, 1936, Koenig grew up in Manhattan and
attended Grinnell College in Iowa, where he studied pre-
med and performed in summer productions. He later
transferred to U.C.L.A. where he graduated with a B.A. in
psychology while studying theatre with Arthur Friedman.
He later moved to New York where he worked as a hospi-
tal orderly, and did off-Broadway work for two years. His
TV credits include *Day in Court; Mr. Novak; The Great
Adventure; Gidget; Jerrico; The Lieutenant; Ben Casey; Combat;
The Great Adventure; Ironside; Mannix; Medical Center; The
Men from Shiloh; The Untouchables; I Spy;* and *Alfred
Hitchcock Presents* in an episode titled "Memo from
Purgatory," written by Harlan Ellison. (Koenig and Ellison
remained good friends after the show.) His role on *Star
Trek* was not meant to be permanent at first. When George
Takei took ten weeks off to star in the John Wayne movie
The Green Berets, however, Koenig's character got the lines
originally written for Sulu. It wasn't until the series' third
season that he was signed on as a permanent character.
His favorite episodes include "Spectre of the Gun," "I,
Mudd," and "The Trouble with Tribbles." After *Trek* was
cancelled, he had bit roles in *Columbo* (with William
Shatner), *Goodbye Raggedy Ann* (with Martin Sheen and
Mia Farrow), and *The Questor Tapes* (with Mike Farrell and
produced by Gene Roddenberry). He also appeared in two
episodes of *The Starlost,* created by Harlan Ellison. He did
more stage work, appeared at many *Trek* conventions, and
began concentrating on writing and selling scripts to the
TV series *Family, Class of '65, The Powers of Matthew Star,*

and the Saturday-morning show *Land of the Lost*. He now writes a comic book, *Raver*, for Malibu Comics. His recent acting appearances include a starring role in the film *Moontrap* (a film which may have a sequel) and an appearance in the film *Deadly Honeymoon*. His wife, son, and daughter are actors as well. His son appeared as a semiregular character, Boner, on the sitcom *Growing Pains* and was billed both as Josh A. Koenig and Andrew Koenig. His daughter, Danielle, appeared in two episodes of *Life Goes On*, and the short-lived series *The Fanelli* Boys. His wife, Judy Levitt, appeared with him and actor Mark Lenard (Sarek, The Romulan Commander, etc.) in a one-act play. She also appeared in *The Voyage Home* as a doctor. Koenig also works as an acting teacher and continues to write. His book *Chekov's Enterprise* was recently updated and rereleased.

Kohms — term referring to the Asian-looking villager people in Classic episode "The Omega Glory."

Kohnert, Mary — played Ensign Tess Allenby in *TNG* "Final Mission" and "The Loss."

Koinonia — planet on which the Koinonians wiped themselves out in a war, leaving a second native species of energy beings to live alone on the world in *TNG* episode "The Bonding."

Kol — Goss's second aide, who, along with the first aide, Arridor, is marooned in *TNG* episode "The Price."

Kolbe, Winrich — director of *TNG* episodes "Where Silence Has Lease," "Pen Pals," "Up the Long Ladder," "Evolution," "The Bonding," "Allegiance," "Identity Crisis," "Darmok," "The Masterpiece Society," "Cost of Living," "Man of the People," "Birthright," "Rightful Heir," and of *DS9* episodes "Past Prologue" and "Vortex."

kolem — Romulan unit of measure, mentioned in *TNG* episode "The Next Phase."

Kolinahr — Vulcan rite which supposedly purges participants of all emotion and gives them total logic. Spock attempts to complete the rite successfully for two years on Gol on Vulcan prior to *The Motion Picture* and fails.

Kollos, Ambassador — member of the telepathic Medusan race who is transported in a box because his appearance drives humans insane in Classic episode "Is There in Truth No Beauty?" He appears as a creature made up of a kaleidoscope of multicolored flashing lights.

Koloth, Captain — Klingon, played by William Campbell, whose ship visits Space Station *K-7* in Classic episode "The Trouble with Tribbles."

Kolrami, Sirna — Zakdornian Starfleet strategist, played by Roy Brocksmith, in *TNG* episode "Peak Performance."

Kolvoord Starburst — illegal and dangerous maneuver which killed Wesley's classmate when they and their friends decided to try it during graduation rehearsals in *TNG* episode "The First Duty."

Komack, Admiral — head of Starfleet Command, played by Byron Morrow, who orders Kirk to go to Altair VI for the inauguration ceremonies instead of to Vulcan in Classic episode "Amok Time."

Komack, James — director of Classic *Trek* "A Piece of the Action." A well-known TV director, he also starred in the series *The Courtship of Eddie's Father* (which he produced).

Konmel — Klingon lieutenant who dies trying to escape from the *Enterprise* brig in *TNG* episode "Heart of Glory."

Konsav — Romulan lecturer silenced for his dissident statements, mentioned in *TNG* episode "Face of the Enemy."

Koo-nut Kal-ifee — Vulcan word for a marriage or a challenge in Classic episode "Amok Time."

Kopache, Thomas — played Mirok in *TNG* "The Next Phase."

Kor, Commander — Klingon commander, played by John Colicos, who tries to conquer Organia in Classic episode "Errand of Mercy." In the animated episode "Time Trap," he is the commander of the Klingon ship *Klothos*.

Korak, Glin — aide to Gul Lemec in *TNG* episode "Chain of Command."

Korax — Captain Koloth's second, played by Michael Pataki, who starts a fight with Scotty on Space Station *K-7* by insulting Kirk and the *Enterprise* in Classic episode "The Trouble with Tribbles."

Korby, Roger, Dr. — Christine Chapel's fiancé who had been missing for years before an android in his likeness is found on Exo III. It is discovered that the real Korby, an exobiologist and an expert in archeological medicine, played by Michael Strong, is dead.

Korob — warlock character, played by Theo Marcuse, on Pyris VII who is really a tiny crablike creature killed by Sylvia in Classic episode "Catspaw."

Koroth — leader of the monastery Klingons visit to conjure up a vision of Kahless in *TNG* episode "Rightful Heir."

Korris — leader, played by Vaughn Armstrong, of a rebel group of Klingons, who dies fighting Worf in *TNG* episode "Heart of Glory."

Kosh, Pamela — played Mrs. Carmichael in *TNG* "Time's Arrow, Part II."

Kosinski — one of the Starfleet Corps of Engineers, played by Stanley Kamel, who is really a fraud in *TNG* episode "Where No One Has Gone Before."

Kostolain — home of Campio, Lwaxana Troi's fiancé in *TNG* episode "Cost of Living."

Kovack, Nancy — played Nona in Classic *Trek* "A Private Little War." Born in 1935, her credits include several TV shows of the 1960s as well as *Jason and the Argonauts* and *Tarzan and the Valley of Gold*.

Kovas, Magda — short-haired, blonde android, raised at a helium experimental station, played by Susan Denberg, who is one of Mudd's women in the Classic episode of the same name.

Kowal, Jon — played Gossett in Classic *Trek* "Mudd's Women." His credits include guest stints on *The Wackiest Ship in the Army* and *Voyage to the Bottom of the Sea*.

Krag, Inspector — member, played by Craig Richard Nelson, of the Tanugan security force who is ordered to take Riker into custody for the murder of Dr. Apgar in *TNG* episode "A Matter of Perspective."

Krako, Jojo — boss, played by Victor Tayback, of the southside territory on Iotia in Classic episode "A Piece of the Action."

Kramer, Joel — played a Klingon in *Star Trek: The Motion Picture*.

Kras — Klingon, played by Tige Andrews, who is trying to prevent Capella from joining the Federation in Classic episode "Friday's Child."

Krasnowsky, Captain — member, played by Bart Conrad, of Kirk's trial board in Classic episode "Court-Martial."

Krayton — name of the Ferengi ship captained by Tog in *TNG* episode "Ménage à Troi."

Kreechta — Ferengi ship commanded by DaiMon Bractor in *TNG* episode "Peak Performance."

Krell — Klingon agent, played by Ned Romeo, who arms the villagers in Classic episode "A Private Little War."

Kreos — Klingon colony world whose leader is Vagh in *TNG* episode "The Mind's Eye."

Krieger Waves — new source of power Dr. Apgar is working to harness at the Tanuga Research Station before he dies in *TNG* episode "A Matter of Perspective."

Krikes, Peter — scriptwriter of *The Voyage Home*.

Krios — world locked in a war with Valt Minor and home of the empathic metamorph Kamala in *TNG* episode "The Perfect Mate."

Krodak — member of the planet Gideon, played by Gene Dynarski, who beams aboard the *Enterprise* in Classic episode "Mark of Gideon."

Krola — security minister, played by Michael Ensign, of Malcoria III in *TNG* episode "First Contact."

Krotus — mentioned by Garth as a famous ruler in Classic episode "Whom Gods Destroy."

kroykah — Vulcan term for silence, used in Classic episode "Amok Time."

Kruge — Klingon commander, played by Christopher Lloyd, who kills Kirk's son, David, and almost succeeds in killing Spock in *The Search for Spock*.

Kryton — one of Elaan's attendants, played by Tony Young, whose love for her causes him to turn traitor to the Klingons in order to stop her marriage to the ruler of Troyius. He ends up committing suicide in Classic episode "Elaan of Troyius."

Krzemian, Richard — scriptwriter of *TNG* "The Last Outpost."

K'Tarans — race which attempts to take over Starfleet by using an addictive game to control the officers in *TNG* episode "The Game."

K'Temoc — Klingon leader of the T'Ong, played by

Lance LeGault, who had been in cryonic sleep for 75 years in *TNG* episode "The Emissary."

Ku'vat — Klingon ship under the command of Morag patrolling near Starfleet Subspace Relay Station 47 in *TNG* episode "Aquiel."

Kuda, Ving — author of the book *Ethics, Sophistry and the Alternate Universe*, which Picard is reading in *TNG* episode "Captain's Holiday."

Kukulkan — alien who visited Earth as a feathered serpent in the past and became the basis of many legends. He appears, played by James Doohan, in the animated episode "How Sharper Than a Serpent's Tooth."

Kunivas — Klingon, played by Robert Bauer, who dies in *TNG* episode "Heart of Glory."

Kurak — female Klingon warp-field specialist who thinks Dr. Reyga's theories will never work in *TNG* episode "Suspicions."

Kuri, Commander — Klingon in the animated episode "Time Trap."

Kurlan Naikous statue — rare, 1,200-year-old bowl with statues decorating its sides, made by the extinct Kurlan race and given to Picard by Professor Galen in *TNG* episode "The Chase."

Kurland, Jake — young student, played by Stephen Gregory, who loses to Wesley for an opportunity to take the Academy entrance exam in *TNG* episode "Coming of Age."

Kurn, Commander — Worf's younger brother, played by Tony Todd, also orphaned at Khitomer and raised by Lorgh.

Kusatsu, Clyde — played Admiral Nakamura in *TNG* "The Measure of a Man."

Kushell — played by Albert Stratton, leader of the planet Streleb's Legation of Unity. He is searching for Okona, believed to have stolen Streleb's Jewel of Thesia, in *TNG* episode "The Outrageous Okona."

kut'luch — Klingon assassin's ceremonial weapon in *TNG* episode "Sins of the Father."

K'Vada, Captain — Klingon captain who takes Picard and Data to the Romulan homeworld in *TNG* episode "Unification."

K'vort-**class battlecruisers** — class of ship named after Klingon birds of prey in *TNG* episode "Yesterday's Enterprise."

Kyle, Lieutenant — British transporter chief, played by John Winston, who appeared in many Classic *Trek* episodes as well as *The Wrath of Khan*.

Kyushu, **USS** — ship destroyed by the Borg at Wolf 359 in *TNG* episode "The Best of Both Worlds." Benjamin Sisko's ship in *DS9* episode "Emissary" was also destroyed there.

Kzinti — alien race of felinoid beings who are eight feet tall and have two hearts, in the animated episode "The Slaver Weapon." They will eat humans if given the opportunity.

L374 III — planet on which Commodore Decker left his crew, to protect them from a monolithic ship-eating machine, in Classic episode "The Doomsday Machine." The machine attacks the planet, however, leaving it in rubble.

Labarre, France — location of Picard's family estate and vineyard in *TNG* episode "Family."

Lactra VII — location of a gigantic zoo in which *Enterprise* members are confined in animated episode "The Eye of the Beholder."

lacunar amnesia — type of selective amnesia the children of the Starnes expedition experience in Classic episode "And the Children Shall Lead."

Lafferty, Marcy — played Chief DeFalco on *Star Trek: The Motion Picture*. She is married to William Shatner, with whom she also appeared in *T.J. Hooker* and in stage play *Otherwise Engaged*. Her other stage work includes *Cat on a Hot Tin Roof*. She met Shatner while working on the set of *The Andersonville Trial*. She and her husband also show horses.

LaForge, Geordi, Lieutenant Commander — chief engineer of the *Enterprise*, played by LeVar Burton, in *The Next Generation*. Born blind, he wears a special visor which enables his brain to detect objects in minute detail, allowing him to "see" better than humans. Geordi has trouble forming romantic relationships with women because he lacks confidence in himself, but he is a genius in the engine room. He has saved the ship countless times thanks to his quick imagination and diligence. Geordi gets along with everyone well but has developed an actual friendship only with Data. Geordi's mother is a starship captain who disappeared in a seventh-season episode. He has several siblings in his close-knit family.

Laid, Lamont — played the Native American boy in Classic *Trek* "The Paradise Syndrome."

Lakso, Edward J. — scriptwriter of Classic *Trek* "And the Children Shall Lead." He also wrote for *The Guns of Will Sonnett* and the pilot for *The Pigeon*.

Lal — Data's daughter, played by Hallie Todd, whom he constructs in *TNG* episode "The Offspring." Data creates her with an ability to feel emotion and use contractions (which Data claims he cannot do, although he can when mimicking someone else). Lal dies from emotional overload when facing possible separation from her "father" by a man who wants to take her away to study her, and Data cannot resurrect her. Lal means "beloved" in Hindi. The sexless, faceless version of the android was played by Leonard John Crowfoot.

Lal — one of the Vians, played by Alan Bergmann, who tortures Kirk, Spock, and McCoy in Classic episode "The Empath."

Lalo, USS — freighter attacked by the Borg and never heard from again in *TNG* episode "The Best of Both Worlds." It is also mentioned in "We'll Always Have Paris," an episode which takes place before its destruction.

Lalsingh, Reginald — played Captain Chandra in Classic *Trek* "Court-Martial."

lambda field generator — part of Dr. Apgar's work with Krieger wave equipment mentioned in *TNG* episode "A Matter of Perspective."

Lambdin, Susanne — writer of *TNG* story premise "Family."

Lambert, Paul — played Melian in *TNG* "When the Bough Breaks," and Dr. Howard Clarke in "Devil's Due."

Lamey, Thad — played the devil in *TNG* "Devil's Due."

La Mura, Mark — played John Doe in *TNG* "Transfigurations."

Landau, Les — director of *TNG* "The Schizoid Man," "Samaritan Snare," "The Survivors," "Déjà Q," "Sins of the Father," "Sarek," "Family," "Future Imperfect," "Clues," "Night Terrors," "Half a Life," "Ensign Ro," "Unification, Part I," "Conundrum," "Time's Arrow, Parts I and II," "Chain of Command," and "Tapestry."

Lander, David L. — played a tactician in *TNG* "Peak Performance."

Landers, Harry — played Dr. Coleman on Classic *Trek* "Turnabout Intruder." He was also a regular on the series *Ben Casey*.

Lando, Joe — played a shore patrolman in *The Voyage Home*. Formerly a regular character on *All My Children*, he currently plays Sully in the hit series *Dr. Quinn, Medicine Woman*.

Landon, Martha, Yeoman — Chekov's girlfriend, played by Celeste Yarnall, in Classic episode "The Apple."

Landor, Rosalyn — played Brenna O'Dell in *TNG* "Up the Long Ladder."

Landris II — archeology dig headed by Professor Mowray, which Picard wants to visit in *TNG* episode "Lessons."

Landru — ruler of the planet Beta III, played by Charles MacAulay, who is actually an image generated by the computer which has controlled the populace for six thousand years in Classic episode "The Return of the Archons."

Landry, Karen — played Ajur in *TNG* "Captain's Holiday."

Landsburg, David — scriptwriter of *TNG* "The Outrageous Okona."

Lane, Brian Alan — scriptwriter of *TNG* "Elementary, Dear Data."

Lane, Iva — played one of the bridge crew in *Star Trek: The Motion Picture*, and Zero Zero in *TNG* "11001001." Her movie credits include *10 to Midnight*.

Lanel — medical staff person, played by Bebe Neuwirth, who demands Riker have sex with her before she'll help him escape in *TNG* episode "First Contact."

Lang, Charlie — played Duffy in *TNG* "Hollow Pursuits."

Lang, Lieutenant — gunnery officer, played by James Farley, who dies on Cestus III at the hand of the Gorns in Classic episode "Arena."

Lang cycle fusion engines — propulsion system of the Promellian ship *Cleponji* in *TNG* episode "Booby Trap."

Langford, Dr. — archeologist from whom Picard has a standing invitation to join him at his dig in *TNG* episode "Rascals."

Langor — Brekkan salesperson, played by Kimberly Farr, trying to sell felicium to the Ornarans in *TNG* episode "Symbiosis."

Lansford, William Douglas — scriptwriter of *TNG* "Devil's Due."

Lansing, Robert — played Gary Seven in Classic *Trek* "Assignment: Earth." Other TV credits include *Gunsmoke*, *One Step Beyond*, *The Twilight Zone* (in an episode with Mariette Hartley), and regular roles in *87th Precinct*, *Twelve*

O'Clock High, The Man Who Never Was, and *Automan.* Film credits include *The 4–D Man* and *Empire of the Ants.* He is currently a regular on *The New Kung Fu* series (starring David Carradine).

Lantree, USS — class 6 supply ship, captained by L. Iso Tolaka, whose crew is exposed to Darwinian antibodies which cause them to age rapidly and die in *TNG* episode "Unnatural Selection."

lapling — sand-burrowing creature, and the last of her species, owned by Fajo in *TNG* episode "The Most Toys."

Lappa IV — Ferengi world mentioned in *TNG* episode "Ménage à Troi."

Lara — character in animated episode "Jihad."

Laren, Ro, Ensign — see entry for Ro Laren.

Large, Norman — played Proconsul Neral in *TNG* "Unification, Parts I and II."

LaRouque, Frederick — character in *TNG* episode "Time's Arrow" who discovers Data has abilities surpassing normal humans'.

Larroquette, John — comedian who played Maltz in *The Search for Spock.* His film credits include *Stripes, Cat People, Bare Essence, The Last Ninja,* and *Meatballs II.* His first regular series was *Black Sheep Squadron* and later *Doctor's Hospital,* but he is most famous for playing Dan Fielding in *Night Court.* He also recently starred in his own TV series named after him.

Lars — drill thrall, played by Steve Sandor, specially assigned to Uhura in Classic episode "The Gamesters of Triskelion."

Larson, Majliss — author of Classic *Trek* novel *Pawns and Symbols.*

La Rue, Bartell — played the voice of the Guardian of

Forever in Classic *Trek* "The City on the Edge of Forever," the newscaster in "Patterns of Force," and the announcer on "Bread and Circuses."

LaSalandra, John — (S.M.E.) music editor of *TNG*.

LaSalle, USS — ship which reports radiation anomalies in the Gamma Arigulon system in *TNG* episode "Reunion."

Lashly, James — played Ensign Kopf in *TNG* "Brothers" and appeared in *DS9* episodes "The Passenger" and "Move Along Home."

"Last Outpost, The" — first-season *TNG* episode written by Richard Krzemian and Herbert Wright and directed by Richard Colla. The *Enterprise* and a Ferengi ship become trapped by the last outpost of the Tkon Empire. A gnome appears, challenging them to solve a riddle. Guest stars: Darryl Henriques, Armin Shimerman, Jake Dengel, Tracy Walter, and Mike Gomez.

Lathal — representative, played by Robert Harper, of the Beta moon of Peliar Zel in *TNG* episode "The Host."

Latimer — navigator, played by Ress Vaughn, on the *Galileo* and the first crewmember killed on Taurus II in Classic episode "The Galileo Seven."

latinum, gold-pressed — see entry for "credit."

Lauritson, Peter — director and coproducer of *TNG* "The Inner Light."

Lauter, Ed — played Albert in *TNG* "The First Duty."

Lavin, Richard — played one of the mediators in *TNG* "Justice."

Lavinius V — location of an ancient civilization destroyed by the Denevan parasites, mentioned in Classic episode "Operation: Annihilate!"

Lawgiver, First — played by Sid Haig, member of

Landru's brainwashing enforcement organization in Classic episode "The Return of the Archons." Anyone who does not cooperate is shot with a hollow tubelike weapon.

Lawmim Galactopedia — rare artifact owned by Fajo in *TNG* episode "The Most Toys."

Lawrence, J. A. — coauthor of *Star Trek 12* with James Blish, also her husband, and sole author of Classic novel *Mudd's Angels.*

Lawton, Tina, Yeoman — played by Patricia McNulty, character turned into an iguana by Charlie in Classic episode "Charlie X."

Lazarus — time traveler, played by Robert Brown, who has met his double from a negative universe. The two Lazarus are trying to kill one another in Classic episode "The Alternative Factor."

Lazebnik, Philip — scriptwriter of *TNG* "Devil's Due" and "Darmok."

Leader, Tony — director of Classic *Trek* "For the World Is Hollow and I Have Touched the Sky" and episodes of *Lost In Space.*

Leda — Harry Bernard's "adopted mother," played by Michele Marsh, in *TNG* episode "When the Bough Breaks."

Leder, Reuben — scriptwriter of *TNG* "The Perfect Mate."

Lederman, Bob — director of *TNG* "I, Borg."

Lee, Bill Cho — played the male patient in *TNG* "Time's Arrow, Part II."

Lee, Everett — played the café owner in *The Voyage Home.*

Lee, Stephen — played Chorgon in *TNG* "The Vengeance Factor."

Lee, Thelma — played Kahlest in *TNG* "Sins of the Father."

Leech, Felix — played by Harvey Jason, assistant to Cyrus Redblock, a crime boss in the Dixon Hill scenario on the holodeck in *TNG* episode "The Big Goodbye."

Lefler, Robin, Ensign — junior officer, played by Ashley Judd, on the *Enterprise* and Wesley's friend in *TNG* episodes "The Game" and "Darmok."

"Legacy" — fourth-season *TNG* episode written by Joe Menosky and directed by Robert Scheerer. Tasha's sister, Ishara, comes aboard the *Enterprise* when the ship travels to Turkana IV to answer a distress signal. Data befriends her, only to discover she has ulterior motives behind her diplomacy. Guest stars: Beth Toussaint, Don Mirrault, Colm Meaney, Vladimir Velasco, and Christopher Michael.

Legara IV — world for which Sarek hopes to negotiate a treaty and which he visits prior to coming aboard the *Enterprise* in *TNG* episode "Sarek."

Legarans — race which exists in a slimy residue at 150º Celsius and for which Sarek is negotiating a treaty in *TNG* episode "Sarek."

Le Garde, Tom and Ted — twin actors who played the Hermans in Classic *Trek* "I, Mudd."

Legato, Rob — director of *TNG* "Ménage à Troi" and "The Nth Degree," and visual effects supervisor on *DS9*.

LeGault, Lance — played K'Temoc in *TNG* "The Emissary."

Leider, Harriet — played Amarie in *TNG* "Unification, Part II."

Leighton, Sheila — played Luma in Classic *Trek* "Spock's Brain." Her TV credits include *The Man from U.N.C.L.E.*

Leighton, Thomas, Dr. — Kirk's friend, played by William Sargent, who sees the Karidian players perform and believes Anton is Kodos the Executioner. He is later murdered in Classic episode "The Conscience of the King."

Leighton, Martha — wife, played by Natalie Norwick, of Dr. Thomas Leighton in Classic episode "The Conscience of the King."

Leitjen, Susanna, Lieutenant Commander — officer, played by Maryann Plunkett, who met Geordi while aboard the USS *Victory*. Both are affected by a parasitic alien metamorphosis in *TNG* episode "Identity Crisis."

Lemani, Tania — played Kara in Classic *Trek* "Wolf in the Fold." Her TV credits include *The Man from U.N.C.L.E.* and *The Wackiest Ship in the Army*.

Le'Matya — deadly mountain creature native to Vulcan. It has poisonous teeth and claws, in the animated episode "Yesteryear."

Lemec, Gul — Cardassian representative in *TNG* episode "Chain of Command." He is not the one who captures Picard.

Lemli, Mr. — *Enterprise* officer, played by Roger Holloway, who appears in Classic episodes "Return to Tomorrow," "The Way to Eden," and "Turnabout Intruder."

Lemon, Ben — played Jev in *TNG* "Violations."

Lenard, Mark — played the Romulan Commander in Classic *Trek* "Balance of Terror" and the Klingon commander in *Star Trek: The Motion Picture*. He is known, however, as Sarek in the Classic episode *Journey to Babel*, the movies *The Search for Spock*, *The Voyage Home*, and *The Undiscovered Country*, TNG episodes "Sarek," and "Unification Part I," and the animated "Yesteryear." Lenard was a stage actor before he was cast as Sarek, his first role on television. He later guest starred in various TV shows and movies and regularly appeared in "Here Comes the Brides" and "Planet of the Apes."

Lenarians — alien race which fires on the *Enterprise*, almost killing Picard, who has a near-death experience with Q as his guide in *TNG* episode "Tapestry."

Leone, Maria — played one of the Ten Forward crew in *TNG* "The Offspring."

Leong, Page — played April Anaya in *TNG* "The Nth Degree."

lepton — substance which, when combined with mesons, builds up and causes wormholes to become unstable, in *TNG* episode "The Price."

Leslie, Lieutenant — officer, played by Eddie Paskey, who appears in many Classic episodes as an *Enterprise* relief helmsman, a participant on landing parties, and as a security guard. (One of the few of such extras who survive.)

Lessing, Arnold — played a security guard in Classic *Trek* "The Changeling."

"Lessons" — sixth-season *TNG* episode written by Ronald Wilderson and Jean Louise Matthias and directed by Robert Wiemer. Picard and a stellar cartologist, Nella Daren, fall in love but find their romance interferes with their professional lives. They part as friends, hoping to see each other on shore leave, and Nella transfers to another ship. Guest star: Wendy Hughes.

Lester, Janice — Kirk's old friend and lover, played by Sandra Smith, who exchanges bodies with him on Camus II in Classic episode "Turnabout Intruder." She is insane after deliberately murdering her science team by exposing them to radiation.

Lester, Jeff — played the FBI agent in *The Voyage*

Home. He played a regular role in *Walking Tall* and starred in the film *The Little Drummer Girl.*

Lestrade, Inspector — infamous Victorian London lawman, played by Alan Shearman, who appears in a holodeck projection in *TNG* episode "Elementary, Dear Data."

Letek — Ferengi played by Armin Shimerman in *TNG* episode "The Last Outpost."

Lethe — very hollow, unemotional woman, played by Suzanne Wasson, encountered in the Tantalus penal colony in Classic episode "Dagger of the Mind."

"Let me help" — Kirk tells Edith these three words are revered over "I love you" as suggested by a novelist who lived on a planet orbiting a star in Orion's belt in Classic episode "The City on the Edge of Forever."

"Let That Be Your Last Battlefield" — written by Oliver Crawford and Lee Cronin, directed by Jud Taylor, this third-season Classic *Trek* episode aired 1/10/69. The *Enterprise* picks up an alien named Lokai who is fleeing the planet Cheron. The man pursuing him, Bele, is of the same race, and yet because he is black on the right side and white on the left, he and others like him believe they are superior to Lokai's type who are black on the left side and white on the right. Guest stars: Lou Antonio and Frank Gorshin.

Lettian — Aldean musician, played by Paul Lambert, who "adopted" Katie, a young girl from the *Enterprise* and encouraged her to seek music.

Leutscher virus — compared to the Nanites in *TNG* episode "Evolution."

levetric pulse — phaser energy level used against Data in *TNG* episode "Descent."

Levitt, Judy — stage actress, married to Walter Koenig, she played Doctor #2 in *The Voyage Home.*

Lewin, Bob ("Robert") — scriptwriter of *TNG* "Datalore," "11001001," "The Arsenal of Freedom," and "Symbiosis."

Lewis, Shari — scriptwriter of Classic *Trek* "The Lights of Zetar" and famous for her puppeteering, especially with her sidekick Lambchop.

***Lexington*, USS** — ship, commanded by Commodore Wesley, damaged severely by the M–5 computer in Classic episode "The Ultimate Computer."

Leyor — Caldonian, played by Kevin Peter Hall, who is part of the Barzan negotiations in *TNG* episode "The Price."

Liator — played by Jay Louden, a member of the council of Edo looking into Wesley's violation of the law in *TNG* episode "Justice."

Library — place on Sarpeidon that people visit to pick a past time in which they would like to live, in Classic episode "All Our Yesterdays."

lidugeal gold — supposedly the purest form of gold known in the galaxy, with which the Ferengi try to bribe Ambassador Briam in *TNG* episode "The Perfect Mate."

Lieutenant, S. S. — played by Ralph Maurer, man from whom Spock steals a police uniform in Classic episode "Patterns of Force."

Ligana Sector — location four months away to which the *Gandhi* is sent on a terraforming mission in *TNG* episode "Second Chances."

"Lights of Zetar, The" — written by Jeremy Tarcher and Shari Lewis and directed by Herb Kenwith, this third-season Classic *Trek* episode aired 1/31/69. The "Lights" are the mental energy of a group of aliens who take over Lt. Mira Romaine's body, Scotty's new love, after destroying all life-forms and vast computer stores of knowledge on Memory Alpha. Guest stars: Jan Shutan, John Winston, and Libby Erwin.

Ligillium, Ruins of — archeological site where the famous Zatteral Emerald is hidden in *TNG* episode "Devil's Due."

Ligon II — planet where inhabitants know the cure for Anchilles Fever, a disorder plaguing Styris IV in *TNG* episode "Code of Honor."

Ligos VII — planet where the Ferengi capture a Federation science team in *TNG* episode "Rascals."

Liko — Mintakan, played by Ray Wise, who is saved by the *Enterprise* and returns to his people talking of worshipping "The Picard" in *TNG* episode "Who Watches the Watchers."

Lima Sierra system — location of a planet with an irregular orbit mentioned by Picard in *TNG* episode "Loud as a Whisper."

Lin, Kenny, Ensign — *Enterprise* junior officer, played by veteran *Trek* actor Brian Tochi, in *TNG* episode "Night Terrors."

linar — batlike creature that lives in caves on Seltris III in *TNG* episode "Chain of Command."

Lincoln, Abraham — Kirk's hero. An image of him, played by Lee Bergere, appears in Classic episode "The Savage Curtain."

Lincoln, Roberta — Gary Seven's secretary, played by Teri Garr, who has no idea what her boss uses his powerful computers and transporters for in Classic episode "Assignment: Earth."

Linden, Don — child, played by Mark Robert Brown, in Classic episode "And the Children Shall Lead."

Lindesmith, John — played an Engineer in Classic *Trek* "The Paradise Syndrome."

Lindsey, Elizabeth — played Luisa Kim in *TNG* "Home Soil."

Lindstrom — played by William Meader, a member of Kirk's trial board in Classic episode "Court-Martial." Another Lindstrom, a sociologist played by Christopher Held, stays behind on Beta III to help its people in "The Return of the Archons."

Linear Models of Viral Propagation — supposedly the first definitive book on its subject written by Dr. Katherine Pulaski and mentioned in *TNG* episode "Unnatural Selection."

Lineback, Richard — played Romas in *TNG* "Symbiosis." He also appears in *DS9* "Dax."

Ling — one of Khan's followers in Classic episode "Space Seed."

Linke, Dr. — one of the researchers, played by Jason Wingreen, killed by the Vians in Classic episode "The Empath."

Linville, Joanne — played the Romulan commander in Classic *Trek* "The *Enterprise* Incident." Her many TV credits include *Gunsmoke*, *Dan August*, and a starring role in the 1981 series *Behind the Screen*. She has also appeared in the films *Secrets*, *The Critical List*, *The Users*, and *The Seduction*.

Lipton, Police Sergeant — security guard, played by Lincoln Demyan, at McKinley Rocket Base in Classic episode "Assignment: Earth."

lirpa — deadly Vulcan weapon which is sharp and hatchet-like on one end and blunt on the other, like a club. Kirk and Spock fight with these weapons in Classic episode "Amok Time."

Liska, Stephen — played Torg in *The Search for Spock*.

Little Boy — Jahn's sidekick, played by John Megna, in Classic episode "Miri."

Livingston, David — director of *TNG* "The Mind's Eye" and "Power Play" and line producer of the series. He also wrote and directed *DS9* episode "The Nagus."

Livingston, Harold — scriptwriter for *Star Trek: The Motion Picture*. Known for his TV work, he also wrote *Escape to Mindanao*, and worked on *The Barbary Coast*.

Liyang — member of the Kohm race about to execute a Yang in Classic episode "The Omega Glory."

L'Kor — head of the Klingons in the Carraya IV Romulan prison camp in *TNG* episode "Birthright."

L'Langon Mountains — high desert range on Vulcan where children take their *kahs'wan* tests as mentioned in animated episode "Yesteryear." Also, the location of Vulcan's Forge.

Lloyd, Christopher — played Kruge in *The Search for Spock*. He is famous for his *Taxi* role as Reverend Jim from 1978 to '83, and for his professorial role in the *Back to the Future* films. He also appeared in the films *The Legend of the Lone Ranger*, *Clue*, and *To Be or Not to Be*.

Lloyd, Norman — guest starred in *TNG* episode "The Chase."

lobes — Ferengi erogenous zone. Also, a term the Ferengi frequently use as a synonym for strength, courage, and masculinity as in, "I didn't think you had the lobes!"

Locarno, Nicholas, Cadet First Class — leader, played by Duncan McNeill, of the Nova Squadron in *TNG* episode "The First Duty."

Locher, Felix — played Robert Johnson in Classic *Trek* "The Deadly Years." His TV guest appearances include *The Man from U.N.C.L.E.*, *Branded*, and *One Step Beyond*.

Lockwood, Gary — played Gary Mitchell in Classic *Trek* "Where No Man Has Gone Before." Born in Van Nuys, CA, in 1937, he got his start as a stunt man and

Anthony Perkins' stand-in. He went on to star in the series *The Lieutenant* (produced by Gene Roddenberry) and was a regular on *Follow the Sun*. His films include *The Magic Sword* and *2001: A Space Odyssey*. He was once married to actress Stefanie Powers.

Locutus — name of the person Picard becomes when he is integrated with the Borg in *TNG* episode "The Best of Both Worlds."

Lodge, Suzanne — played a serving girl in Classic *Trek* "Wolf in the Fold."

Loftin, Gary — stunt driver in Classic *Trek* "The City on the Edge of Forever."

Lofton, Cirroc — stars as Jake Sisko in *DS9*. Born in Los Angeles, Cirroc started acting at age 9 in the educational program *Agency for Instructional Technology* and appeared in commercials for McDonald's, Tropicana Orange Juice, and Kellogg's Rice Krispies. His big break was an appearance in the movie *Beethoven*. He aspires to be a doctor when he grows up and loves to play basketball. He lives with his sister and mother.

Logan — *Enterprise* engineer, played by Vyto Ruginis, who tries to take command in *TNG* episode "The Arsenal of Freedom."

Lokai — native of the planet Cheron, played by Lou Antonio, where the inhabitants killed themselves in race wars mentioned in Classic episode "Let That Be Your Last Battlefield." Black on the left side and white on the right, he is pursued as a fugitive by Bele, also from Cheron and the only other native still living, who has reversed coloring.

London Kings — 21st-century baseball team which included a player who broke Joe DiMaggio's hitting record, mentioned in *TNG* episode "The Big Goodbye."

"Lonely among Us" — first-season *TNG* episode written by D. C. Fontana and Michael Halperin, directed by Cliff Bole. A cloudlike being takes over the computer and Picard. Guest stars: Colm Meaney, Kavi Raz, and John Durbin.

Long, Ed — played Midro in Classic *Trek* "The Cloud Minders."

Lonka Pulsar — rotating neutron star to which the fake Picard brings the *Enterprise* as a test of the crew in *TNG* episode "Allegiance."

Loomis, Rod — played Paul Manheim in *TNG* "We'll Always Have Paris."

Lopez, Ensign — *Enterprise* junior officer criticized by a distracted Worf for incorrectly preparing the duty roster in *TNG* episode "Birthright."

Lopez, Perry — played Lt. Esteban Rodriquez in Classic *Trek* "Shore Leave." Born in 1931, his credits include *Voyage to the Bottom of the Sea* and *Hec Ramsey*.

Lora — woman, whose voice is played by Majel Barrett, to whom Harry Mudd gives his love potion in animated episode "Mudd's Planet."

Lorca, Isabelle — played Gabrielle in *TNG* "We'll Always Have Paris."

Lore — Data's twin brother, also played by Brent Spiner, created before Data by Dr. Noonian Soong. Lore, who was given emotions but no conscience, is very cruel. He is first seen in "Datalore" and in several later *TNG* episodes.

"Lorelei Signal, The" — written by Margaret Armen, this animated Classic *Trek* episode aired 9/29/73. Kirk, Spock, McCoy, and a security man are imprisoned on a planet populated only by women, and are drained of their energy, causing them to age rapidly. An all-female landing party, with Uhura in command, rescues them. Guest voices: Majel Barrett (Theela) and Nichelle Nichols (Dara, Computer, and Security Officer Davison).

Loren III — only world located in the Kurlan sector which supports life, mentioned in *TNG* episode "The Chase."

Lorenze Cluster — location of the planet Minos in *TNG* episode "The Arsenal of Freedom." It is also said this star group can be seen from the planet Aucdet IX in "The Child."

Lorgh — Klingon who raised Kurn, Worf's younger brother, after their parents were killed in the Khitomer Massacre mentioned in *TNG* episode "Sins of the Father."

Lormer, Jon — played Dr. Theodore Haskins in Classic *Trek* pilot "The Cage" and "The Menagerie," Tamar in "Return of the Archons," and Old Man in "For the World Is Hollow and I Have Touched the Sky." His other TV credits include *One Step Beyond*, *Voyage to the Bottom of the Sea*, and *Perry Mason*. His film credits include *Rally 'round the Flag Boys*, *Frankenstein*, *Conspiracy of Terror*, *The Golden Gate Murders*, and *Creepshow*.

Lornack Clan — people known to have massacred the Tralestas in *TNG* episode "The Vengeance Factor."

Lorrah, Jean — science-fiction author of several books including the Classic *Trek* novels *The Vulcan Academy Murders*, *The IDIC Epidemic*, and *TNG* novels *Survivors* and *Metamorphosis*.

Los, Tana — injured fugitive who asks for political asylum on *Deep Space 9* in *DS9* episode "Past Prologue."

Losira — Kalandan projection of a long-dead Kalandan leader, played by Lee Meriwether, who severely injures Sulu with her deadly touch in Classic episode "That Which Survives."

Loskene, Commander — heard but unseen commander of a Tholian ship who asks the *Enterprise*, which is on a rescue mission for the missing Captain Kirk, to leave their space immediately in Classic episode "The Tholian Web."

"Loss, The" — fourth-season *TNG* episode written by Hilary J. Bader, Alan J. Adler, and Vanessa Greene, directed by Chip Chalmers. Two-dimensional life-forms, on their way toward a cosmic string fragment, catch the *Enterprise* in their path, causing Troi to temporarily lose her empathic powers. Guest stars: Kim Braden, Whoopi Goldberg, and Mary Kohnert.

Lou, Cindy — played the nurse in Classic *Trek* "Return to Tomorrow."

"Loud As a Whisper" — second-season *TNG* episode written by Jacqueline Zambrano and directed by Larry Shaw. Ambassador Riva, the great deaf mediator, is brought to Soleis IV to mediate a dispute between the world's peoples but the three-member chorus through whom he communicates is accidentally killed and he is at a loss as to how to communicate on his own. Guest stars: Howie Seago, Marnie Mosiman, Thomas Oglesby, and Leo Damian. Of note: Data translates sign language in this episode but sometimes makes the mistake of translating the words before the signer has "spoken" them.

Louis — Picard's old friend, played by Dennis Creaghan, who wants Picard to work with him on the Atlantis deep-sea colonization project in *TNG* episode "Family."

Louise — Miri's friend, who reaches maturity and succumbs to the virus that killed all the adults. She attacks Kirk and is killed by a phaser stun blast.

Louvois, Philipa, Captain — played by Amanda McBroom, the senior officer of Starbase 173 Judge Advocate General's office who prosecuted the *Stargazer* court-martial ten years before and presides over the hearing concerning Data's sentience in *TNG* episode "The Measure of a Man."

Lovsky, Celia — played T'Pau in Classic *Trek* "Amok Time."

Lowry-Johnson, Junie — in charge of casting for *TNG* and *DS9*.

Lucas, John Meredyth — scriptwriter/ director/ producer who wrote Classic *Trek* episodes "The Changeling," "Patterns of Force," "Elaan Of Troyius," and "That Which Survives," directed "The Ultimate Computer," "The *Enterprise* Incident," and "Elaan of Troyius," and produced the series' second season. He also directed *Planet of the Apes* and wrote for the TV series *Logan's Run* as well as the pilot for *City Beneath the Sea/One Hour to Doomsday*.

Lucia, Chip — played Ambassador Ramid Ves Alkar in *TNG* "Man of the People."

Lucien — satyr, played by James Doohan, in animated episode "The Magicks of Megas-Tu" who appears on the *Enterprise* bridge. He is a magician who claims to love humans and has visited Earth.

Luckinbill, Laurence — played Sybok in *The Final Frontier*. Born in 1934, his credits include *The Boys in the Band*, *Winner Take All*, and *The Lindbergh Kidnapping Case*. He is married to actress Lucie Arnaz.

lucrovextitrin — toxic substance which can alter glass in *TNG* episode "Hollow Pursuits."

Luke, Keye — played Cory in Classic *Trek* "Whom Gods Destroy." Born in Canton, China in 1904, his credits include *The Painted Veil*, many *Charlie Chan* films, several *Dr. Kildare* movies, and the role of Kato in some *Green Hornet* serials. He appeared regularly in the TV series *Kentucky Jones*, *Anna and the King*, *Kung Fu* (1972–75), and *Harry O* ('76). He also played the Chinese man who had the gremlin in the movie *Gremlins*.

Lum, Benjamin W. S. — played Jim Shimoda in *TNG* "The Naked Now."

Luma — Eymorg, played by Sheila Leighton, of Sigma

Draconis VI who is overpowered by Kirk and his landing party in Classic episode "Spock's Brain."

Lumar Café — where Beverly, Worf, and Data are when the Rutian bomb goes off in *TNG* episode "The High Ground."

Lumo — Native American warrior, played by Peter Virgo, Jr., who rescues the drowned boy from the lake in Classic episode "The Paradise Syndrome."

Luna, Barbara — played Marlena Moreau in Classic *Trek* "Mirror, Mirror." Born in New York in 1939, her credits include *Mission: Impossible* and *Buck Rogers in the 25th Century* (in which she played Hawk's wife, Koori). Her films include *Five Weeks in a Balloon* and *The Gatling Gun*. She is the former wife of actors Doug McClure and Alan Arkin.

Lunar V — moon orbiting Angosia and the location of a penal colony housing supersoldiers from a past war in *TNG* episode "The Hunted."

Lund, Jordan — played Kulge in *TNG* "Redemption, Part II."

Lundin, Victor — played a Klingon lieutenant in Classic *Trek* "Errand of Mercy." His credits include *Voyage to the Bottom of the Sea*.

Lupo, Tom — played a security guard in Classic *Trek* "The Alternative Factor."

lura-mag — siren device used by the women of Taurus II to lure men in animated episode "The Lorelei Signal." They are not from the same Taurus II featured in "The Galileo Seven."

Lurian, DaiMon — Ferengi renegade leader who tries to take over the *Enterprise* in *TNG* episode "Rascals."

Lurry — manager, played by Whit Bissell, of Space Station *K-7* in Classic episode "The Trouble with Tribbles."

Lursa — played by Barbara March, a Klingon who, with her sister, is attempting to make an illegal sale on *Deep Space 9* in episode "Past Prologue." Lursa also appears in *TNG* episode "Redemption, Part II."

Lutan — Primary of Ligon, played by Jessie Lawrence Ferguson, who kidnapped Tasha Yar in *TNG* episode "Code of Honor."

Luz, Franc — played Odan in *TNG* "The Host."

Lya III — planet from which Admiral Haden's transmission originates, mentioned in *TNG* episode "The Defector," and the destination of the *Enterprise* after leaving Angosia in "The Hunted."

Lya IV — planet Fajo orbits for half a day after kidnapping Data in *TNG* episode "The Most Toys."

Lya Station Alpha — where the *Enterprise* takes refuge from the Cardassian attack on Solarion IV in *TNG* episode "Ensign Ro."

Lynch, Hal — played an air police sergeant in Classic *Trek* "Tomorrow Is Yesterday." His other TV credits include *Cannon*.

Lynch, Ken — played Chief Engineer Vanderberg in Classic *Trek* "Devil in the Dark." His credits include the films *Anatomy of a Murder*, *Run, Simon, Run*, *Poor Devil*, *The Winds of War*, and regular roles on *The Plainclothesman* and *McCloud*.

Lynch, Leland T., Lieutenant Commander — *Enterprise* engineer, played by Walker Boone, in *TNG* episode "Skin of Evil."

Lynch, Paul — director of *TNG* "The Naked Now," "11001001," "Unnatural Selection," and "A Matter of Time" as well as *DS9* episodes "A Man Alone," "Babel," "Q Less," and "The Passenger."

Lyon, Bob — played a villager in Classic *Trek* "A Private Little War."

Lyons, Gene — played Ambassador Robert Fox in Classic *Trek* "A Taste of Armageddon." His other credits include *One Step Beyond* and a regular role on *Ironside*.

lyre, Vulcan — autoharp-type of instrument, also called a lytherette, which Spock plays in several episodes, including "Charlie X" and "The Way to Eden."

Lysian Alliance — enemies of the Sartaarans. The *Enterprise* is told the Federation is at war with the Lysians in *TNG* episode "Conundrum."

Lytian System — location where Worf and Beverly rendezvous with the *Enterprise* after the two officers, raid on the Cardassian base at Seltris III in *TNG* episode "Chain of Command."

M–4 — hovering robot created by Flint in Classic episode "Requiem for Methuselah" to do all his chores and act as a security guard that can kill.

M–5 multitronic unit — computer designed by Dr. Richard Daystrom which takes over the *Enterprise* in Classic episode "The Ultimate Computer." James Doohan provides the voice until Kirk talks it into sentencing itself to death for murder and releasing control of the ship.

M24 Alpha — name of Triskelion's sun mentioned in Classic episode "The Gamesters of Triskelion."

M–33 Galaxy — galaxy beyond Triangulum, 2.7 million light years from the Milky Way, mentioned in *TNG* episode "Where No One Has Gone Before." The Traveler accidentally propels the *Enterprise* to this galaxy.

M43 Alpha — name of the star around which the planets Ekos and Zeon orbit in Classic episode "Patterns of Force."

M–113 creature — salt vampire in Classic episode "The Man Trap" that can take the form of anyone it sees, but actually looks like a hairy, elephant-nosed creature with suction cups on the ends of its fingers.

M–113, Planet — Professor Crater and his wife Nancy lived and studied archeological digs on this homeworld of the salt vampire in Classic episode "The Man Trap."

Ma, Tzi — played the biomechanical specialist in *TNG* "Samaritan Snare."

Maab — Akaar's man, played by Michael Dante, who takes over when Akaar is killed by the Klingon Kras in Classic episode "Friday's Child."

Mab Bu IV — giant, gaseous planet seen in *TNG* episode "Power Play," its class M moon holds a penal colony for Ux-Mal prisoners.

MacCauley, Charles — played Landru in Classic *Trek* "The Return of the Archons," and Jaris in "Wolf in the Fold." Other TV credits include *Griff* and *Shannon*. Films include *A Case of Rape*, *The Return of the World's Greatest Detective*, and *The Munsters' Revenge*.

MacDonald, Scott — actor in *DS9* "Captive Pursuit," he also guest starred in *TNG* episode "Face of the Enemy."

MacDougal, Sarah — *Enterprise*'s chief engineer in *TNG* episode "The Naked Now," played by Brooke Bundy.

Macer, Sterling, Jr. — appeared in *TNG* episode "Birthright."

Macet, Gul — Cardassian, played by Marc Alaimo, who comes aboard the *Enterprise* to help search for Captain Benjamin Maxwell in *TNG* episode "The Wounded."

MacKenzie, Ard'rian — cyberneticist and resident of Tau Cygna V, played by Eileen Seeley, who falls in love with Data in *TNG* episode "The Ensigns of Command."

MacLachlan, Janet — played Lt. Charlene Masters in Classic *Trek* "The Alternative Factor." TV credits include *Ghost Appearances*, *Griff*, and regular roles on *Love Thy Neighbor*, *Friends*, and *All in the Family*.

Madalone, Dennis — played Ramos in *TNG* "Heart of Glory" and Hedwick in *TNG* "Identity Crisis."

Madden, Edward — played a geologist in Classic *Trek* pilot "The Cage" ("The Menagerie") and Technician Fisher in "The Enemy Within."

Maddox, Bruce, Commander — assistant chairman of robotics at the Daystrom Institute, played by Brian Brophy, who wants to take Data apart and see what makes him tick in *TNG* episode "The Measure of a Man."

Madeline — secretary, played by Rhonda Aldrich, of Dixon Hill in the holodeck simulation in *TNG* episodes "Manhunt," "Clues," and "The Big Goodbye."

Madeline II — planet from which Lt. Commander Nella Daren says she bought a small keyboard. She plays it in a duet with Picard, playing his Resican flute, in *TNG* episode "Lessons."

Madison — Regula I scientist working with Dr. Carol Marcus in *The Wrath of Khan.*

Madred, Gul — Cardassian on Seltris III who tortures Picard in *TNG* episode "Chain of Command." Jil Orra is his daughter.

Maffei, Buck — played the creature in Classic *Trek* "The Galileo Seven." He was also in the movie *Cheech and Chong's Nice Dreams.*

Magee, Tom — played the Klingon monster in *TNG* "Devil's Due."

Magellan — *Enterprise* shuttlecraft from *TNG*. The shuttle is destroyed in an explosion in "The Outcast." In "Starship Mine," there is a reference to a starship of this name.

Magnaspanner — Ensign Zweller uses this tool to tamper with the dom'jot table, a game like pool, in *TNG* episode "Tapestry."

magnesite-nitron tablets — McCoy has them in his medi-kit. When struck, they burn with a bright light, as seen in Classic episode "Friday's Child."

magnetometric-guided charges — type of "depth charge" used by the Borg in *TNG* episode "The Best of Both Worlds."

Maht-H'a — attack ship under the command of Captain Nu'Daq in *TNG* episode "The Chase."

"Maiden Wine" — song Spock sings in Classic episode "Plato's Stepchildren." It was written by Leonard Nimoy.

Maisie — series of androids created by Harry Mudd and played by twins Tamara and Starr Wilson in Classic episode "I, Mudd."

"Magicks of Megas-Tu, The" — written by Larry Brody, this animated Classic *Trek* episode aired 10/27/73. The *Enterprise* is caught in an energy whirlwind which carries it somewhere they cannot determine because the ship's instruments do not work. As they drift toward a nearby planet, a satyr appears on the bridge, calling himself Lucien and taking part of the crew down to the magic world of Megas-Tu. The natives become angry at Lucien for bringing strangers and put him on trial. Guest voices: James Doohan (Lucien), Ed Bishop (Megan Prosecutor), and George Takei (voice).

Major, S.S. — officer of Ekos played by Gilbert Green in *TNG* episode "Patterns of Force."

MajQa — Klingon rite consisting of meditation followed by exposure to great heat, inducing hallucinations and, it is hoped, a vision of the ancient fathers. In *TNG* episode "Birthright," it is mentioned that Worf underwent the rite as a child.

Makee, Blaisdell — played Lt. Spinelli in Classic *Trek* "Space Seed" and Mr. Singh in "The Changeling." TV credits include *Iron Horse*.

Makers, The — mysterious, now extinct, race who made the androids on Mudd's Planet in Classic episode "I, Mudd."

makho root — ugly root used in medicinal/magical healing by Nona, a Kanutu witch woman, on Kirk to cure him of the Mugato's poison in Classic episode "A Private Little War."

Makora — Sayana's boyfriend, played by David Soul, in Classic episode "The Apple."

Maktag — in *TNG* episode "New Ground," it is learned that Alexander, Worf's son, was born on the 23rd of this Klingon month on Stardate 43205.

Makus III — destination of the the *Enterprise* when delayed by the loss of the shuttlecraft in Classic episode "The Galileo 7." They are transporting medical supplies to Makus III.

Malad — transport ship in *TNG* episode "New Ground."

Malcoria III — world receiving first-contact team from the *Enterprise* in *TNG* episode "First Contact." Malcoria's leader, Chancellor Durken, thinks that though his people are scientifically advanced, they are too traditional and closed to face alien contact. He plans to cover up the *Enterprise*'s visit.

Malencon, Arthur — hydraulic specialist, played by Mario Roccuzzo, working on the terraforming project on Velara III when the laser drill malfunctions, killing him, in *TNG* episode "Home Soil."

Maleran system — home of Amanda Rogers's adoptive parents, Starfleet marine biologists, mentioned in *TNG* episode "True Q."

Maliamanda tapestry — rare item owned by Fajo in *TNG* episode "The Most Toys."

Malkis IX — home of the Lairons, people who developed the written word before developing sign or spoken language, mentioned in *TNG* episode "Loud As a Whisper."

Mallon — in *TNG* episode "The Vengeance Factor," he is left in charge of the Hromi.

Mallory, Ensign — security officer, played by Jay Jones, killed by tripping over an exploding rock on Gamma Trianguli VI in Classic episode "The Apple."

Maltz — Klingon, played by John Larroquette, who worked under Kruge and is the only survivor of the Klingon party that attacked the ship and people on Genesis in *The Search for Spock*.

Malurian system — the four planets of Omega Cygni destroyed by Nomad after it deemed four billion inhabitants "imperfect biological units" in Classic episode "The Changeling."

"Man Alone, A" — first-season *DS9* episode written by Michael Piller and Gerald Sanford and directed by Paul Lynch. Odo is accused of the murder of a Bajoran black marketeer on the Promenade. Guest stars: Rosalind Chao, Edward Lawrence Albert, Max Grodenchik, Peter Vogt, Aron Eisenberg, Stephen James Carver, Tom Klunis, Scott Trost, Patrick Cupo, Kathryn Graf, Hana Hatae, and Diana Cignoni.

"Man of the People" — sixth-season *TNG* episode written by Frank Abatemarco, directed by Winrich Kolbe. An alien ambassador tries to use Troi as a receptacle for his evil thoughts and emotions, drastically changing Troi's personality. Guest stars: Chip Lucia, Susan Rench, Stephanie Erb, Rick Scarry, J. P. Hubbell, Lucy Boryer, and George D. Wallace.

"Man Trap, The" — this first-season Classic *Trek*, written by George Clayton Johnson and directed by Marc Daniels, aired 9/8/66. A creature fans have dubbed a Salt Vampire morphs into human forms but actually looks like a fuzzy swamp beast with suction cups on its elongated fingers and a megaphone for a mouth. Guest stars: Jeanne Bal and Alfred Ryder. Of note: First introduction of Saurian brandy and the phrase "Great Bird of the Galaxy" (which is how fans later affectionately refer to Gene Roddenberry).

Manark IV — home of "sandbats" which, when resting, appear to be rock crystals, mentioned in Classic episode "The Empath."

Mancour, T. L. — author of *TNG* novel *Spartacus*.

Mandarin Bailiff — played by Cary-Hiroyuki, he assists Q at the *Enterprise's* trial in *TNG* episode "Encounter at Farpoint."

Mandel, Johnny — stunt double for Sulu in Classic *Trek* "Mirror, Mirror."

Mandl, Kurt — director of the Gardeners of Eden, a terraforming project on Valara III, played by Walter Gotell in *TNG* episode "Home Soil."

Manheim, Janice — Picard's old flame, married to Dr. Paul Manheim, who comes aboard the *Enterprise* in *TNG* episode "We'll Always Have Paris."

Manheim, Paul, Dr. — scientist who created an uncontrollable experiment with time on Vandor IV, played by Rod Loomisseen, in *TNG* episode "We'll Always Have Paris" and mentioned in "Time Squared."

Manheim Effect — time distortion created by Dr. Paul Manheim on Vandor IV in *TNG* episode "We'll Always Have Paris."

"Manhunt" — second-season *TNG* episode written by Terry Devereaux and directed by Rob Bowman. Lwaxana Troi boards ship while experiencing "the phase," a kind of menopause that makes Betazoid women highly sexed, and Picard hides on the holodeck in a Dixon Hill story. Guest stars: Majel Barrett, Rod Arrants, Carel Struycken, Rhonda Aldrich, Robert Costanzo, Mick Fleetwood, Wren T. Brown, Colm Meaney, and Robert O'Reilly.

Manitoba Journal of Interplanetary Psychology — publication which contacts Deanna Troi for research purposes in *TNG* episode "The Price."

Mankiewicz, Don — scriptwriter of Classic *Trek* "Court-Martial." Writing credits include *I Want to Live*, *One Step Beyond*, and *Ironside*.

Manley, Stephen — played Spock at age 17 in *The Search for Spock*. TV credits include regular roles on *Married: The First Year* and *Secret of Midland Heights*.

Manners, Kim — director of *TNG* episode "When the Bough Breaks."

Manning, Richard — story editor of first and second season and scriptwriter of *TNG* "The Arsenal of Freedom," "Symbiosis," "The Schizoid Man," "The Emissary," "Shades of Gray," "Who Watches the Watchers," "Yesterday's Enterprise," and "Allegiance." He was coproducer of *TNG*'s third season.

Mar Obscura Nebula — the *Enterprise* fires photon torpedoes into this dark area to illuminate it in *TNG* episode "In Theory."

Mara — Klingon woman, Kang's wife and science officer, played by Susan Howard in Classic episode "Day of the Dove."

Marajeritus VI — inhabited by people known as Ulans in *TNG* episode "Manhunt."

Marcelino, Mario — played the communications officer on USS *Grissom* in *The Search for Spock*. TV credits include a regular role on *Falcon Crest*, and the film *Losin' It*.

March — scientist, played by Kevin Sullivan, on Regula I working with Dr. Carol Marcus in *The Wrath of Khan*.

March, Barbara — played Lursa in *TNG* "Redemption, Parts I and II," and guest starred in *DS9* "Past Prologue."

Marcoffian snow lizard — Q mentions that he could have taken this form instead of appearing human during his exile from the Continuum in *TNG* episode "Déjà Q."

Marcos XII — planet to which the Gorgon wants the children to lead him. The monster plans to enslave the world's supposed millions of inhabitants in Classic episode "And the Children Shall Lead."

Marcus, Carol, Dr. — Kirk's past lover and head of the scientific team that invented Genesis on Regula I, played by Bibi Besch in *The Wrath of Khan*. She has brought up their son, David.

Marcus, David, Dr. — son of Dr. Carol Marcus and James Kirk, he was instrumental in the development of the Genesis device in *The Wrath of Khan*. Kruge kills him when he tries to protect Saavik and Spock in *The Search for Spock*. He was played by Merritt Butrick.

Marcus, Claudius — proconsul, played by Logan Ramsey, who presides over planet 892-IV's version of the Roman empire in Classic episode "Bread and Circuses."

Marcus II — Sten, a famous artist known to Spock, lived on this planet in Classic episode "Requiem for Methuselah." Flint might have been Sten.

Marcuse, Theo — played Korob on Classic *Trek* "Catspaw." Born in 1920 and died in 1967, his TV credits include *Voyage to the Bottom of the Sea* and *The Man from U.N.C.L.E.* Films include *The Cincinnati Kid* and *Last of the Secret Agents*.

Margan — Ornaran leader who needs felicium in *TNG* episode "Symbiosis."

Margolis, Mark — played Dr. Apgar in *TNG* "A Matter of Perspective."

Mariposa — class M planet in the Ficus Sector, one light year from the Bringloidi system, inhabited by a race of slowly dying clones in *TNG* episode "Up the Long Ladder." The Spanish word *mariposa* means "butterfly."

Mariposa, SS — DY0–500 class Earth ship, commanded by Captain Walter Granger, sent from Earth November 27, 2183 with the ultimate destination of Ficus Sector. It is mentioned in *TNG* episode "Up the Long Ladder."

Mariye, Lily — played the ops officer in *DS9* "Emissary."

"Mark of Gideon, The" — written by George F. Slavin and Stanley Adams, directed by Jud Taylor, this third-season Classic *Trek* episode aired 1/17/69. Kirk is unknowingly transported to a duplicate *Enterprise* and believes his crew has disappeared. He meets a mysterious woman apparently connected to the secretive planet Gideon, which the *Enterprise* was investigating. Guest stars: Sharon Acker, David Hurst, Gene Dynarsky, and Richard Derr.

Markle, Stephen — played Kover Tholl in *TNG* "Allegiance."

Marko, Peter — played Gaetano in Classic *Trek* "The Galileo Seven."

Marlo, Steve — played Zabo in Classic *Trek* "A Piece of the Action." Credits include *Branded* and several other Westerns, including the films *The Young Captives* and *The Hanged Man*.

Marlonia — mentioned by Guinan as the most beautiful planet in the quadrant in *TNG* episode "Rascals."

Marlowe, Scott — played Keeve Falor in *TNG* "Ensign Ro."

Marouk, Sovereign — leader on Acamar III, played by Nancy Parsons, who tries to make peace with the Gatherers in *TNG* episode "The Vengeance Factor." Yuta, her chef, is a traitor.

Marple — unseen security guard in Classic episode "The Apple" who, on Gamma Triguli VI, is killed when one of the natives bashes his head in with a club.

Marplon — Landruite technician and member of the underground, played by Torin Thatcher in Classic episode "The Return of the Archons," who helps Kirk and Spock stop the machine on Beta III.

Marquez, Lieutenant — helps Lt. Commander Nella

Daren coordinate the evacuation of the Bersallis III colonists in *TNG* episode "Lessons."

Marr, Kila, Dr. — *Enterprise* xenologist, played by Ellen Geer, who finds the journal of her son, who was killed by the Crystalline Entity on Omicron Theta, carried within Data in *TNG* episode "Silicon Avatar."

Marrab Sector — location of Devidia II mentioned in *TNG* episode "Time's Arrow." A ciliated life-form from this world is found along with Data's head in a cave in San Francisco.

Mars — fourth planet of Sol system. The *Enterprise* was constructed on this world at the Utopia Planetia shipyards.

Mars, Bruce — played Finnegan in Classic *Trek* "Shore Leave" and a police officer on "Assignment: Earth." His credits include *Voyage to the Bottom of the Sea* and *Then Came Bronson*.

Mars defense perimeter ships — automated ships mentioned in *TNG* episode "The Best of Both Worlds." Three are destroyed by the Borg.

Mars Toothpaste — advertised in a magazine on Planet 892-IV in Classic episode "Bread and Circuses."

Marsh, Michele — played Leda in *TNG* "When the Bough Breaks."

Marshak, Sondra — author of Classic *Trek* novels *The Price of the Phoenix*, *The Fate of the Phoenix*, *The Prometheus Design*, *Triangle*, and the nonfiction book *Shatner: Where No Man*, and editor of *The New Voyages I* and *II* with Myrna Culbreath. She also cowrote *Star Trek Lives!*

Marshall, Booker — played Dr. M'Benga in Classic *Trek* "A Private Little War" and in "That Which Survives." He is also a writer.

Marshall, Don — played Lt. Boma in Classic *Trek* "The Galileo Seven." He also starred in the TV series *Land of the*

Giants and has appeared on other shows, including *The Bionic Woman*.

Marshall, Joan — played Lt. Areel Shaw in Classic *Trek* "Court-Martial."

Marshall, Sarah — played Dr. Janet Wallace in Classic *Trek* "The Deadly Years." She was a regular on *Miss Winslow and Son*, guested on *Perry Mason*, and has been in the films *Scruples*, *The Bunker*, and *The Letter*.

Marshall, William — played Dr. Richard Daystrom in Classic *Trek* "The Ultimate Computer." Born 1924, he is a Shakespearean actor whose film credits include *Blacula*, *The Boston Strangler*, and *Twilight's Last Gleaming*. He had a regular role on *Rosetti and Ryan*.

Marta — Orion woman, played by Yvonne Craig, kept at the asylum on Elba II with Garth of Izar, who kills her by forced exposure to Elba's poisoned atmosphere, in Classic episode "Whom Gods Destroy."

Martel, Arlene — played T'Pring in Classic *Trek* "Amok Time." She guest starred in such TV series as *Iron Horse*, *The Man from U.N.C.L.E.*, and *Petrocelli*, and in the films *The Adventures of Nick Carter*, *Indict and Convict*, and *Conspiracy of Terror*. She was sometimes credited under the name Tasha Martel.

Martia — shapeshifting alien assassin played as an adult by Iman in *The Undiscovered Country*. When she appears as a little girl, she is played by Katie Jane Johnson.

Martian Colonies, Fundamental Declaration of — mentioned in Classic episode "Court-Martial" as a precedent-setting document in interstellar law. A Mars colony is mentioned in *TNG* episode "The Drumhead" as the birthplace of Crewman First Class Simon Tarses.

Martian Colony III — home of Mira Romaine in Classic episode "The Lights of Zetar."

Martin, Dr. — *Enterprise* medical doctor played by Rick Fitts in *TNG* episode "Violations."

Martin, Jeffrey — played an electronic technician in *The Voyage Home.*

Martin, Meade — played an engineer in Classic *Trek* "The Changeling."

Martin, Nan — played Victoria Miller in *TNG* "Haven."

Martine, Angela — specialist in life sciences, played by Barbara Baldavin, who married Robert Tomlinson just before he died in an accident on the *Enterprise* in Classic episode "Balance of Terror." She reappears in "Shore Leave."

Marvick, Lawrence, Dr. — coworker, played by David Frankham, infatuated with Miranda Jones in Classic episode "Is There in Truth No Beauty?" Jealous of the Medusan Kollos, he attempts to kill him, but instead glimpses him, which drives him insane. The doctor then takes the *Enterprise* beyond the galaxy energy barrier, nearly stranding them.

masiform D — drug McCoy uses on Spock, making him sick to his stomach, after he is attacked by poison darts from a plant on Gamma Trianguli VI in Classic episode "The Apple."

Mason — one of the kidnapped *Enterprise* children in *TNG* episode "When the Bough Breaks."

Mason, Dan — played Accolan in *TNG* "When the Bough Breaks."

Mason, John — producer and scriptwriter of *TNG* "Unnatural Selection."

Massett, Patrick — played Duras in *TNG* "Sins of the Father" and "Reunion."

"Masterpiece Society, The" — fifth-season *TNG*

episode written by James Kahn, Adam Belanoff, and Michael Piller, directed by Winrich Kolbe. A stellar core fragment is heading for a planet inhabited by human colonists who have constructed a utopian world and do not want outside interference. Their lives are in danger without the intervention of the *Enterprise*, which in turn causes disruption and entices some colonists to leave. The changes will ultimately destroy the perfect society even though the stellar core fragment is diverted. Guest stars: John Snyder, Dey Young, Ron Canada, and Sheila Franklin.

Masters, Charlene, Lieutenant — officer in charge of some engineering sections on the *Enterprise*, played by Janet MacLachlan in Classic episode "The Alternative Factor."

Matheson, Richard — scriptwriter of Classic *Trek* "The Enemy Within." Born in 1926, he is a famous horror author who wrote scripts for *The Incredible Shrinking Man*, *The Night Stalker*, and *Ghost Appearances/Circle of Fear*, as well as many print stories.

Matlovsky, Alisa — second assistant director in *DS9* "Emissary."

Matlovsky, Samuel — composer of music in Classic *Trek* "I, Mudd." His other score credits include the movie *Fish Hawk*.

Matson, Lieutenant — crewmember in the rec room, played by David Troy in Classic episode "The Conscience of the King," when Uhura sings "Beyond Antares" to Riley.

"Matter of Honor, A" — second-season *TNG* episode written by Wanda M. Haight, Gregory Amos, and Burton Armus, directed by Rob Bowman. In an officer exchange program, Riker is sent to serve on the Klingon ship *Pagh*. Then the captain decides to attack the *Enterprise*. Guest stars: John Putch, Christopher Collins,

Brian Thompson, Laura Drake, Colm Meaney, and Peter Parros.

"Matter of Perspective, A" — third-season *TNG* episode written by Ed Zuckerman and directed by Cliff Bole. Riker is accused of murdering Dr. Apgar when the research station orbiting Tanuga IV explodes just as he beams off it to return to the *Enterprise*. Different versions of the events on the station are played out according to the testimony of different witnesses. Guest stars: Craig Richard Nelson, Gina Hecht, Mark Margolis, Juli Donald, and Colm Meaney.

"Matter of Time, A" — fifth-season *TNG* episode written by Rick Berman and directed by Paul Lynch. A time traveler, Dr. Rasmussen, visits the *Enterprise* from the future, but is actually from the past, stealing future technology to sell for profit before it is actually discovered. Guest stars: Matt Frewer, Stefan Gierasch, Sheila Franklin, and Shay Garner. Of note: This episode was supposedly written with Robin Williams in mind, but when he could not play the role, Matt Frewer was hired. Robin Williams is a *Star Trek* fan and has always wanted to act in an episode.

Matter/Energy Scrambler — transporterlike device used by the Minarans in Classic episode "The Empath."

Matthew — child on the *Enterprise* in *TNG* episode "The Last Outpost."

Matthews — one of the security officers, killed by Ruk, who accompany Kirk and Chapel to Exo III in Classic episode "What Are Little Girls Made Of?"

Matthews, Eric — played one of the Edo children in *TNG* "Justice."

Matthews, Todd — mentioned in *TNG* episode "The Royale" as the author of the novel *The Hotel Royale*.

Matthias, Jean Louise — scriptwriter for *TNG* "Imaginary Friend," "Lessons," and "Schisms."

Maura — Lt. Aquiel Uhnari's dog in *TNG* episode "Aquiel."

Maurer, Ralph — played Bilar in Classic *Trek* "The Return of the Archons," and the SS Lieutenant in "Patterns of Force."

Mavek — attendant at the Tilonus Institute for Mental Disorders who insists Riker stabbed another man in *TNG* episode "Frame of Mind."

Mavig — played by Deborah Downey, a young blonde woman who wore her hair in a ponytail in Classic episode "The Way to Eden."

Maxia Zeta — site of a battle between the *Stargazer* and a Ferengi vessel mentioned in *TNG* episode "The Battle." It was supposedly the first Ferengi contact, though the ship's origin was unknown at the time.

Maxwell, Benjamin, Captain — Starfleet captain who lost his family to a Cardassian raid, played by Bob Gunton in *TNG* episode "The Wounded."

Maxwell, Charles — played Virgil Earp in Classic *Trek* "Spectre of the Gun." His TV credits include *I Led Three Lives* and *Branded*.

Mayama, Miko — played Yeoman Tamura in Classic *Trek* "A Taste of Armageddon."

Mayberry, Russ — director of *TNG* "Code of Honor."

Maylor, Sev — 93-year-old believed to be the mother of Ambassador Olcar in *TNG* episode "Man of the People."

Maynard, Biff — played Ruffian in *TNG* "Elementary, Dear Data."

M'Benga, Dr. — *Enterprise* doctor of African descent, and a specialist in Vulcan medicine, who appears in Classic episodes "A Private Little War" and "That Which Survives."

McAllister C–5 Nebula — gaseous cloud which hides an entire Cardassian fleet in *TNG* episode "Chain of Command."

McBroom, Amanda — played Philipa Louvois in *TNG* "The Measure of a Man."

McCarthy, Jeff — played Roga Danar in *TNG* "The Hunted."

McCartny, Dennis — composer of incidental music in a dozen first-season *TNG* episodes, and at least that many more during the second and third seasons. He also scored the main title theme for *DS9* and the music for "Emissary."

McCauley, Danny — assistant director on *Star Trek: The Motion Picture*. His other directing credits include *Zorro: The Gay Blade, Jinxed,* and *Blue Thunder.*

McCay, Bill — author of *TNG* novel *Chains of Command.*

McChesney, Mart — played Armus in *TNG* "Skin of Evil," and Sheliak in *TNG* "The Ensigns of Command."

McConnell, Judy — played Yeoman Tankris in Classic *Trek* "Wolf in the Fold." TV credits include *The Beverly Hillbillies, Green Acres,* and the movie *Gidget Gets Married.*

McCormick, Carolyn — played Minuet in *TNG* "11001001" and "Future Imperfect."

McCoy, James L. — makeup artist on *The Search for Spock.*

McCoy, Joanna — unseen daughter of Dr. Leonard McCoy. Trained in the medical field, she communicates with her father often. In the animated episode "The Survivor," she is mentioned as attending school on Cerberus.

McCoy, Leonard H., Dr. — ship's doctor in Classic *Trek* played by DeForest Kelley. "An old country doctor" from Georgia, nicknamed Bones, he is Kirk's good friend and Spock's friendly adversary. He is divorced and has a daughter named Joanna (who is never seen). McCoy appears in *TNG* at age 137 in "Encounter at Farpoint," though his name is never officially spoken. Prior to *The Motion Picture*, he tried to retire but Kirk had him called back to duty. A cynic with a good heart, he hates transporters (he's afraid of them). He always gets some of the best lines, including his famous "I'm a doctor, not a . . ." statements. In "Court-Martial," the computer reads off his commendations as including "Legion of Honor, Awards of Valor, decorated by Starfleet Surgeons."

McCoy, Matt — played Devinoni Ral in *TNG* "The Price."

McCready, Ed — actor and stunt man who played both the male and female creature in Classic *Trek* "Miri," an inmate in "Dagger of the Mind," an SS trooper in "Patterns of Force," Dr. Carter in "The Omega Glory," and the barber in "Spectre of the Gun." His other credits include *Today's FBI* and the film *Partners*.

McCullough, Robert L. — producer, and scriptwriter of *TNG* "The Icarus Factor" and "Samaritan Snare."

McCusker, Mary — played the nurse in *TNG* "Evolution."

McDermott, Kevin — played the alien baseball player who goes up to bat in *DS9* "Emissary."

McDonald, Christopher — played Castillo in *TNG* "Yesterday's Enterprise."

McDougall, Don — director of Classic *Trek* "The Squire of Gothos." He has also directed episodes of *Ghost Appearances*, *Planet of the Apes*, *The Gemini Man*, and *The Bionic Woman*. He has also directed the films *The Aquarians*, *The Heist*, and *The Mark of Zorro*.

McDuff. Kieran, Commander — identity

assumed by a Sartaaran provocateur, played by Erich Anderson, to control the *Enterprise* and make them attack the Lysian Alliance in *TNG* episode "Conundrum."

McEveety, Steven — played the red-haired boy in Classic *Trek* "Miri." He is the son of director Vincent McEveety.

McEveety, Vincent — director of Classic *Trek* episodes "Miri," "Dagger of the Mind," "Balance of Terror," "Patterns of Force," "The Omega Glory," and "Spectre of the Gun." He has also directed episodes of the TV series *Petrocelli*, and the Disney films *Million Dollar Duck* and *Herbie Goes Bananas*.

McFadden, Gates — stars as Dr. Beverly Crusher in *TNG*. Before landing the *TNG* role, the actress did stage work and studied dance. She attended Brandeis University where she graduated with a B.A. in theater arts, and studied acting under Jack LeCoq in Paris. She starred in several New York plays, directed the choreography and puppet movement for the film *Labyrinth*, and assisted in stage fantasy sequences for *Dreamchild*. McFadden was dropped from *TNG* after the first season for reasons unknown to her, then was re-assigned the role in the third season. During the second season of *TNG* Diana Muldaur played the ship's doctor, a completely different character from that of Beverly Crusher. During the year she was not on *TNG*, Gates had a small role in the film *The Hunt for Red October*.

McGinnis, Scott — played "Mr. Adventure" in *The Search for Spock*. His TV credits include a regular role in *Operation: Petticoat*, and the films *Survival of Dana* and *Joysticks*.

McGivers, Marla, Lieutenant — ship's historian, played by Madlyn Rhue, who falls in love with Khan and ends up going into exile on Ceti Alpha V with him in Classic episode "Space Seed."

McGonagle, Richard — played Dr. Ja'Dar in *TNG* "New Ground."

McGowan, Oliver — played the caretaker in Classic *Trek* "Shore Leave."

McGreevey, Michael — scriptwriter of *DS9* "Babel."

McHuron, Eve — one of Mudd's women, played by Karen Steele in Classic episode "Mudd's Women," who marries Ben Childress.

McIlvain, Randy — art director of *DS9*.

McIntyre, Deborah — writer of *TNG* "The Neutral Zone." (The original story was written with Mona Glee).

McIntyre, James — played Hali in *TNG* "Who Watches the Watchers."

McIntyre, Vonda — author of Classic *Trek* novels *The First Adventure*, *The Entropy Effect*, *The Wrath of Khan*, *The Voyage Home*, and *The Search for Spock*.

McKane, Brendan — played a technician in *TNG* "Coming of Age."

***McKinley*, Earth Station** — repair facility which orbits Earth in *TNG* episodes "Family" and "The Drumhead." The *Enterprise* goes here after suffering damage during an attack by the Borg.

McKinley Rocket Base — houses the rocket Gary Seven sabotages in Classic episode "Assignment: Earth."

McKinney — crewmember killed in an accident mentioned in *TNG* episode "Conspiracy."

McKnight, Ensign — played by Pamela Winslow, an *Enterprise* officer in *TNG* episodes "Clues" and "In Theory."

McLeister, Tom — played Kolos in *TNG* "Q Less."

McLiam, John — played Fento in *TNG* "Who Watches the Watchers."

McLowery, Frank — one of the Clanton gang in Classic episode "Spectre of the Gun." This is also the name the people of Tombstone call Spock.

McLowery, Tom — member of the Clanton gang and the role given to McCoy by the Melkotians in Classic episode "Spectre of the Gun."

McNally, Kelly Ann — played One One in *TNG* "11001001."

McNally, Terence — played B'Tardat in *TNG* "Half a Life."

McNamara, Patrick J. — played Captain Taggert in *TNG* "Unnatural Selection."

McNary — Police Chief Dan Bell's lieutenant, played by Gary Armagnal, in a hologram simulation in *TNG* episode "The Big Goodbye."

McNary, Sharon — Lt. McNary's wife in *TNG* episode "The Big Goodbye."

McNeill, Robert Duncan — played Nicholas Locarno in *TNG* "The First Duty."

McNulty, Patricia — played Yeoman Tina Lawton in Classic *Trek* "Charlie X." Her other TV credits include a regular role on *The Tycoon*.

McPherson — one of the "supermen" in Classic episode "Space Seed."

McTosh, Bill — played a Klingon in *Star Trek: The Motion Picture.*

Mea 3 — native of Eminiar VII, played by Barbara Babcock, in Classic episode "A Taste of Armageddon."

Meader, William — played Space Command Representative Lindstrom in Classic *Trek* "Court-Martial."

Meaney, Colm — stars as Chief Miles Edward

O'Brien in both *TNG* and *DS9*. Born in Dublin, Ireland, he appeared in the BBC programs *Z Cars* and *Strangers* before relocating to New York in 1978. He worked off Broadway and in regional theatre before moving to Los Angeles in the mid–1980s to do film and TV work. His many credits include TV guest spots on *Moonlighting, Remington Steele, Tales from the Dark Side,* and the pilot for *Dr. Quinn, Medicine Woman.* His films include *Dick Tracy, Come See the Paradise, Die Hard II, The Gambler III, Far and Away* (in which he helped Tom Cruise with his accent), *The Last of the Mohicans, Under Siege,* and *The Commitments.* He was in the first three episodes of *TNG,* then took a role in the soap opera *One Life To Live* before finally getting the more permanent *TNG* role, although he does not appear in every episode. Meaney jumped at the chance to be transferred to a starring role on *DS9*. He has a wife, Barbara, and a young daughter, Brenda, a *Star Trek* fan herself.

Mears, Yeoman — one of the survivors when the shuttlecraft, with seven aboard, crashes on Taurus II, played by Phyllis Douglas in Classic episode "The Galileo Seven."

"Measure of a Man, The" — second-season *TNG* episode written by Melinda M. Snodgrass and directed by Robert Scheerer. A cyberneticist, who believes Data to be an object and not a being, wants to take him apart to learn how to make more Datas. A trial ensues to prove that Data has rights as an individual and can deny this man's request to take him away from the *Enterprise*. Guest stars: Amanda McBroom, Clyde Kusatsu, Brian Brophy, Colm Meaney, and Whoopi Goldberg. Of note: This episode got Melinda Snodgrass the attention of *TNG*'s producers and more assignments. She ended up moving to Hollywood to become *TNG*'s executive script consultant for the third through fifth seasons.

mecklinite — substance which interferes with the *Enterprise*'s sensors in *TNG* episode "Galaxy's Child."

Medal of Honor — medal which reminds Kirk of his real life as he is packing to leave the *Enterprise* and join his crew on Omicron Ceti III. The shock of his remembrances throws off the spores' effect in Classic episode "This Side of Paradise."

medallion — piece of jewelry containing a shapeshifting element that may be a distant "cousin" to Odo in *DS9* episode "Vortex."

Mediators — two Mediators, played by David Q. Combs and Richard Lavin, sentence Wesley to death on Rubicam III, in *TNG* episode "Justice."

Medina — star system and location of Atlek and Streleb in *TNG* episode "The Outrageous Okona."

Medlock, Michael A. — scriptwriter who wrote *TNG* "Second Chances."

Medusans — race whose members resemble a rainbow spectrum of lights. It is said that their appearance drives humans insane. Medusans are telepaths and empaths. Kollos of Classic episode "Is There in Truth No Beauty?" is a Medusan.

Meerson, Steve — played "Fat Little Boy" in Classic *Trek* "Miri." Film credits include *The Boy in the Plastic Bubble*, *Skag*, and *The Cannonball Run*.

Megas-Tu — magical planet in animated episode "The Magicks of Megas-Tu."

Meier, John — stunt double for William Shatner in *The Voyage Home*. He also did work on the film *Cannery Row*.

Mek'ba — name of the court trial Worf must go through to clear his father's name of treason in *TNG* episode "Sins of the Father."

melakol — Romulan unit of pressure mentioned in *TNG* episodes "The Defector" and "The Next Phase."

Melakon — in Classic episode "Patterns of Force," the deputy Führer, who is truly in charge. He is played by Skip Homeier (who also plays Dr. Sevrin in "The Way to Eden").

Melanoid slimeworm — insult Rondon calls Wesley in *TNG* episode "Coming of Age."

Melbourne, USS — one of the ships involved with the Borg at the same time as the *Saratoga* in *DS9's* first episode "Emissary." It is also seen in *TNG* episode "11001001." The ship is offered to Riker in "The Best of Both Worlds."

Melkotians — species mistrustful of strangers who test the *Enterprise* command crew by putting them through the motions of acting out the Battle at the O.K. Corral in Classic episode "Spectre of the Gun."

Mell, Joseph — played the Orion trader in Classic *Trek* pilot "The Cage" (scenes of which appeared in "The Menagerie" which was actually released). Film credits include *City of Fear* and *The Delphi Bureau*. He has also guest starred on the TV series *Adventures of Superman*.

Mellis II — in *TNG* episode "Ship in a Bottle," this is the destination (in virtual reality) of Moriarty and Countess Bartholomew.

Mellitus — cloud creature of Alpha Majoris I mentioned in Classic episode "The Wolf in the Fold." It is solid at rest and gaseous in motion.

Melona IV — new Federation colony attacked by the Crystalline Entity in *TNG* episode "Silicon Avatar."

Meltasion Asteroid Belt — area through which the *Enterprise* tows a 300-year-old garbage scow leaking radiation to dump it in the Gamelan system in *TNG* episode "Final Mission."

Memory Alpha — central library storage and research

facility which is damaged by "The Lights of Zetar" in the third season of Classic *Trek*. Mira Romaine goes to Memory Alpha at the end of the episode to help start restoring its computers' knowledge banks.

Mempa Sector — in *TNG* episode "Redemption," Gowron attacks Duras's supply bases located in this sector.

"Ménage à Troi" — third-season *TNG* episode written by Fred Bronson and Susan Sackett, directed by Rob Legato. The Ferengi kidnap Riker, Troi, and Lwaxana while the *Enterprise* is on shore leave at Betazed. Guest stars: Majel Barrett, Frank Cosentino, Ethan Phillips, Peter Slutsker, Rudolph Willrich, and Carel Struycken.

"Menagerie, The, Parts I and II" — written by Gene Roddenberry, this first-season Classic *Trek* episode aired 11/17/66 and 11/24/66. Part I was directed by Marc Daniels and Part II by Robert Butler. Interspersed with scenes from *Star Trek*'s original pilot "The Cage," this ingenious script brings back Captain Pike and sets Spock on an illegal journey to the off-limits world of Talos IV, a trip which reveals a lot of the history of the *Enterprise*. Guest stars, which include both those who appeared in "The Cage" as well as in the later sequel: Malachi Throne, Sean Kenney (Pike in wheelchair), Julie Parrish, Jeffrey Hunter (original Pike), John Hoyt, Susan Oliver, Majel Barrett (when she played Number One her stage name was M. Leigh Hudec), Laurel Goodwin, Peter Duryea, Meg Wyllie, and Jon Lormer. Of note: The Keepers were all played by older women. The early Spock behaves uncharacteristically, smiling and yelling a lot because "The Cage" scenes were filmed before much was known about Vulcans, their behavior, and their philosophy. Leonard Nimoy notes that he was at a loss as to how to play his role opposite the brooding, stoic, and standoffish Jeffrey Hunter (both characters, Pike and

Spock, were too alike to allow for much contrast). When William Shatner was brought in to play a more impulsive and brash young captain, everything clicked into place. This episode won the Hugo Award for Best Dramatic Presentation of 1966.

Menchen, Les — scriptwriter of *TNG* "The Outrageous Okona."

Mendak, Admiral — Romulan commander of the *D'Voris* in *TNG* episode "Data's Day." He was played by Alan Scarfe.

Mendez, José I., Commodore — commander of Starbase *11* in Classic episodes "The Menagerie" and "The Cage." He was played by Malachi Throne.

Mendon, Ensign — Benzite junior officer, played by John Putch, on the *Enterprise* as part of an exchange program in *TNG* episode "A Matter of Honor."

Mendoza, Seth — Federation representative to Barzan in *TNG* episode "The Price." He is played by Castulo Guerra.

Mendrossen, Ki — Chief of Sarek's staff, played by William Denis, who shields Sarek from others to hide Sarek's disease in *TNG* episode "Sarek."

Menges, James — played the jogger in *The Voyage Home*.

Menosky, Joe — scriptwriter of *TNG* "Legacy," "Clues," "First Contact," "The Nth Degree," "In Theory," "Darmok," "Hero Worship," "Conundrum," "Time's Arrow, Parts I and II," "The Chase," and "Suspicions."

Menthars — in *TNG* episode "Booby Trap," dead race known to be very innovative at one time who built the booby traps in the debris of Orelious IX.

Menville, Chuck — scriptwriter of the animated

episodes "Once upon a Planet" (with Len Jenson) and "Practical Joker."

Menyuk, Eric — played the Traveler in *TNG* "Where No One Has Gone Before" and "Remember Me."

Merak II — planet plagued by a disease that is destroying all its vegetation in Classic episode "The Cloud Minders." The *Enterprise* goes to Ardana to get the zienite which will stop the spread of this scourge.

Merculite rockets — Koras says the Klingons warded off the Ferengi with these weapons in *TNG* episode "Heart of Glory."

Meret, Vice Proconsul — Romulan high official defector in *TNG* episode "Face of the Enemy."

Merik, R. M., Captain — commander of the *Beagle*, played by William Smithers, which the *Enterprise* finds empty and orbiting Planet 892 IV in Classic episode "Bread and Circuses." Merik, who has become Merikus, First Citizen of the Roman Empire, is killed by Claudius when he tries to help the *Enterprise* crew escape Claudius' prison.

Merikus — see entry for Merik, R.M., Captain.

Meriwether, Lee — played Losira in Classic *Trek* "That Which Survives." Born in 1935, the former Miss America had regular roles on *The Time Tunnel*, *The New Andy Griffith Show*, *Mission: Impossible*, and *Barnaby Jones*. She also played Catwoman in the 1960s movie *Batman*. Most recently, she has appeared in commercials for Uncle Ben's Rice among other products.

Merrifield, Richard — played Technician Webb in Classic *Trek* "Tomorrow Is Yesterday."

Merrill, Todd — played Gleason in *TNG* "The Best of Both Worlds, Part II" and "Future Imperfect."

Merrimac, USS — ship that will transport Sarek and Perrin to Vulcan at the end of *TNG* episode "Sarek."

Merson, Richard — played the pie man on *TNG* "Elementary, Dear Data."

Meruvian tea — in *TNG* episode "The Child," Guinan makes this drink in Ten Forward.

Meseroll, Kenneth — played McDowell in *TNG* "The Next Phase."

meson — substance which, combined with leptons, builds up in the Barzan wormhole, making it unstable, in *TNG* episode "The Price."

Messalina system — destination of the *Enterprise* after *TNG* episode "Cost of Living."

metagenic weapon — genetic virus that can destroy an entire biosphere. These kinds of weapons are outlawed by the Federation because they are so deadly. It is believed the Cardassians have one in *TNG* episode "Chain of Command," but it is only a lure to get Picard, Worf, and Crusher to check it out.

"Metamorphosis" — written by Gene L. Coon and directed by Ralph Senensky, this second-season Classic *Trek* episode aired 11/10/67. In this alien love story, Kirk, Spock, McCoy, and Nancy Hedford's shuttle is forced to land on an asteroid where they discover a marooned man, Zephrem Cochrane, inventor of the warp drive, and a cloudlike creature he calls The Companion. Guest stars: Elinor Donahue and Glenn Corbett. Of note: Majel Barrett provides the voice for The Companion. A universal translator is used to communicate with the alien entity.

metaphasic shield — invented by Ferengi scientist Dr. Reyga, a type of force field which allows a ship to enter, unharmed, the core of a star. Reyga is killed for his theories in *TNG* episode "Suspicions."

Metaphysics, First Law of — philosophical theory which comes up on Spock's computer in *The Voyage Home* as he is reeducating himself. It states, simply, "Nothing unreal exists."

metathalmus — Vulcan brain organ mentioned in *TNG* episode "Sarek."

Metrons — advanced race of beings resembling young, angelic boys who can stop ships with their minds and are encountered in Classic episode "Arena." The Metron we see is played by Carole Shelyne.

mev yap — Klingon for "that is enough," heard in *TNG* episode "Sins of the Father."

Meyer, Nicholas — director/scriptwriter. He directed *The Wrath of Khan* and *The Undiscovered Country* and cowrote the scripts for *The Voyage Home* and *The Undiscovered Country*. His other film scripts include *The Seven Percent Solution* and *Time after Time* as well as some movies made for TV.

Michael, Christopher — played Man #1 in *TNG* "Legacy."

Michaelian, Michael — scriptwriter of *TNG* "Too Short a Season."

Michaels, Mickey S. — set decorator on *DS9*.

Michelson, Harold — production designer on *Star Trek: The Motion Picture*. He also did work on the film *Mommie Dearest*.

Mickey D. — character who kills the Bell Boy in *TNG* episode "The Royale." He is played by Gregory Beecroft.

microbrain — inorganic but intelligent life-form on Velara III which declares war on the *Enterprise* in *TNG* episode "Home Soil."

Micromius — mentioned in *TNG* episode "11001001" as the location of a medical disaster which Dr. Crusher studied under Dr. Epstein.

Midos V — world mentioned by the Kirk android in Classic episode "What Are Little Girls Made Of?" as the location of the first experiments involving Dr. Korby's androids.

Midro — troglyte, played by Garry Evans, in Classic episode "The Cloud Minders."

Mikat — Cardassian city where Gul Madred grew up, mentioned in *TNG* episode "Chain of Command."

Mikulaks — race that donated tissue samples to help cure Correllium Fever on Nahmi IV in *TNG* episode "Hollow Pursuits."

Milan — transport ship carrying Worf's parents in *TNG* episode "New Ground."

Miles, Bob — actor and stunt man who played McCoy's double in Classic *Trek* "Miri" and played a Klingon in "The Trouble with Tribbles."

Miles, Joanna — played Perrin in *TNG* "Sarek," and "Unification, Part I."

Milika III — mentioned in *TNG* episode "Tapestry" as a world where Picard led an away team which saved an ambassador's life, a major event in his career.

Milkis, Edward K. — assistant producer of Classic *Trek*'s second season and the producer of third season as well as the producer of *TNG*. He also produced the series *Petrocelli*, and the movies *Women in Chains* and *The Devil's Daughter*.

Miller, Allan — played the "Alien in the Bar" in *The Search for Spock*. TV credits include regular roles on *AES Hudson Street*, *Soap*, *Nero Wolfe*, and *Knots Landing*. He also had guest roles on such shows as *Battlestar Galactica*.

Miller, Stephen — Wyatt Miller's elderly father in *TNG* episode "Haven." He was played by Robert Ellenstein.

Miller, Victoria — Wyatt Miller's elderly mother in *TNG* episode "Haven." She was played by Nan Martin.

Miller, Wyatt — doctor who is engaged to Deanna in *TNG* episode "Haven." He left the *Enterprise* to save some Tarellian refugees dying from a plague. He was played by Rob Knepper.

Mills, Keith — scriptwriter of *TNG* "The Royale."

Milnos IV — mentioned as the world where Lt. Commander Nella Daren studied thermal geysers early in her career in *TNG* episode "Lessons."

Mimas — moon of Saturn where Wesley's Nova Squadron team is taken by an emergency transporter after evacuating them from their ships in *TNG* episode "The First Duty."

Minara — sun about to go nova. It has several satellites, including the world where Gem lives and the Vians' homeworld in Classic episode "The Empath."

Minara II — second planet in the Minaran system and apparently the Vians' homeworld in Classic episode "The Empath."

"Mind's Eye, The" — fourth-season *TNG* episode written by Ken Schafer and René Echevarria, directed by David Livingston. Geordi is kidnapped on his way to Risa and brainwashed by the Romulans using his visor, to kill a Klingon governor. Guest stars: Larry Dobkin, Edward Wiley, John Fleck, Colm Meaney, and Denise Crosby.

mind meld — Vulcan technique of joining minds with another by placing their hands at various pressure points on the face of the person they are melding with. The minds join and thoughts can be exchanged as well as feelings and personality. Spock uses the meld for the first time in the Classic episode "Dagger of the Mind" when he joins minds with Van Gelder. He melds with McCoy in "Mirror, Mirror," Kirk in "The Paradise Syndrome" and

"Requiem for Methuselah," and Kirk, Scotty, and McCoy
in "Spectre of the Gun." He uses the meld in the movie
The Wrath of Khan to give McCoy his *katra* for safe-keep-
ing. A meld restores him in *The Search for Spock*. In *The
Voyage Home* he melds with the humpback whale Gracie
and ascertains that she is pregnant. In *The Undiscovered
Country* he melds with Valeris to get information from
her. Sarek melds with Kirk in *The Search for Spock*, and
with Picard in "Sarek." In short, a nifty Vulcan talent that
makes for some good drama.

mind-sifter — Klingon device mentioned in Classic
episode "Errand of Mercy." Supposedly a way to empty a
mind of valuable information, its side effects include brain
damage.

mind sphere — in *TNG* episode "The Battle," a Ferengi
mind-control tool that DaiMon Bok uses to convince
Picard he is back on the *Stargazer*.

Mines, Stephen — played Specialist Robert Tomlinson
in Classic *Trek* "Balance of Terror."

Minnerly, Lieutenant — mentioned in *TNG* episode
"Skin of Evil" as Tasha's martial arts opponent.

Minor, Michael — art director on *The Wrath of Khan*.
He has also done work for the Classic *Trek* series and on
the movies *The Man Who Saw Tomorrow* and *Spacehunter:
Adventures in the Forbidden Zone*.

Minos — located in the Lorenze Cluster, planetary home
of a humanoid race which sold weapons to both sides in
the Ersalrope Wars mentioned in *TNG* episode "The
Arsenal of Freedom." Their own weapons wiped them
out.

Minos Corva — mentioned in *TNG* episode "Chain
of Command" as a world fought over in the
Federation/Cardassian war and eventually ceded to the
Federation although the Cardassians still want it. Picard

is tortured when he won't reveal Starfleet's defense plans for the world. It is eleven light years from McAllister C–5 Nebula (see entry).

Mintaka III — in *TNG* episode "Who Watches the Watchers," world inhabited by Vulcanoids. The world is again encountered in "Allegiance."

Mintakans — Vulcanoid inhabitants of the planet Mintaka III who are at a primitive age in their development in *TNG* episode "Who Watches the Watchers."

Minuet — in *TNG* episode "11001001," an image, played by Carolyn McCormick, created by the Bynars to distract Riker.

Mira System — location of the planet Dytalix B in *TNG* episode "Conspiracy."

Miradorn — bad-tempered race in *DS9* episode "Vortex."

Miramanee — Native American woman, one of two who see Kirk emerge from the temple and believe he is a god. Later, she and Kirk marry and she becomes pregnant with his child. She dies when her people shower her and Kirk with rocks in the belief that Kirk is a false god when he cannot make the beam come from the temple. Miramanee is played by Sabrina Scharf in Classic episode "This Side of Paradise."

Miranda, John — played a garbageman in *The Voyage Home*. He has also appeared on the TV series *The Paper Chase*.

Mirat, Penny — student from Rigel who studied at the Academy with Picard. She and Picard never had an affair but always wanted to. Picard gets a chance to change that when Q makes him relive this episode in his life in *TNG* episode "Tapestry."

"Miri" — this first-season Classic *Trek* episode aired 10/27/66 and was directed by Vince McEveety and written by Adrian Spies. The *Enterprise* visits a planet where all the adults died as a result of a virus which also makes children age just one month for every 300 years. As the children enter puberty, they go insane and die. Guest stars: Kim Darby, Michael J. Pollard, Jim Goodwin (Farrell in several *Trek* episodes), John Megna, and Ed McCready. Of note: Several of the children in this episode are the children of cast members. Grace Lee Whitney's sons are included, as well as William Shatner's two older daughters, Leslie and Lisabeth, around seven and five years old at the time. Director Vince McEveety's son Steven McEveety had the role of the "red-headed boy," while Dawn Roddenberry, Gene's daughter from his first marriage, played another extra.

Miri — young girl played by Kim Darby in Classic episode "Miri." She is on the verge of adolescence and contracts the aging disease. She helps Kirk find the other children so he can help them and develops a crush on him in the process.

Mirich, Ernie — played the waiter in *TNG* "Relics."

Mirok — Romulan science officer, played by Thomas Kopache, in *TNG* episode "The Next Phase."

Mirrault, Don — played Hayne in *TNG* "Legacy."

Mirren, Oliana — one of the students, played by Estée Chandler, competing with Wesley to take the Academy exam in *TNG* episode "Coming of Age."

"Mirror, Mirror" — written by Jerome Bixby and directed by Marc Daniels, this second-season Classic *Trek* episode aired 10/6/67. Kirk, McCoy, Scott, and Uhura are accidentally transported to a parallel universe where their crewmates are barbaric and the *Enterprise* is part of a violent empire. Meanwhile, their savage counterparts are transported aboard the real ship and all must find a way to get back to where they belong. Guest stars: Barbara Luna, Vic Perrin, Pete Kellett, Garth

Pillsbury, and John Winston. Of note: The savage Spock sports a slick beard, Sulu has a long facial scar and the hots for Uhura, and Chekov screams. This episode was nominated for a Hugo Award for Best Dramatic Presentation of 1967.

Mirt — one of Oxmyx's hoods in Classic episode "A Piece of the Action." He was played by Jay Jones.

Mishiama wrist lock and break — martial arts strategy Tasha mentions she wants to learn for the competition in *TNG* episode "Skin of Evil."

Mitchell, Admiral — mentioned in *TNG* episode "Starship Mine" as an official in Starfleet for whom Commander Hutchinson worked.

Mitchell, Dallas — played Tom Nellis in Classic *Trek* "Charlie X." TV credits include *Voyage to the Bottom of the Sea*. Films include *Any Second Now*, *Hijack!*, and *Tail Gunner Joe*.

Mitchell, Gary, Lieutenant Commander — science officer of the *Enterprise* who experiences an electrical shock when the ship tries to cross the galaxy's energy barrier in Classic episode "Where No Man Has Gone Before." He is Kirk's best friend and attended Starfleet Academy with him. He is killed by Dr. Elizabeth Dehner when the heightened mental powers he gains from the shock cannot be controlled and he turns evil. He was played by Gary Lockwood.

Mitchell, James X. — played Lt. Josephs in Classic *Trek* "Journey to Babel."

Mitchell, V. E. — author of *TNG* novel *Imbalance* and Classic *Trek* novels *Windows on a Lost World* and *The Enemy Unseen*.

Mizar II — mentioned in *TNG* episode "Allegiance" as the homeworld of Kova Tholl which has been conquered six times in 300 years.

Mizarians — inhabitants of Mizar II who have been conquered six times in 300 years because they do not resist attack. This is how they've survived, as mentioned in *TNG* episode "Allegiance."

Mlodinow, Leonard — story editor and scriptwriter of *TNG* "The Dauphin."

Moab IV — name of the closed colony that has had no outside contact for over 200 years in *TNG* episode "The Masterpiece Society."

Module L–73 — module affected by Eichner radiation in *TNG* episode "The Child." It carries a plasma plague that begins to mutate and grow after being exposed to the radiation.

Moffat, Katherine — played Etana in *TNG* "The Game."

Mogh — mentioned in *TNG* episode "Sins of the Father" as Worf and Kurn's father. He was denounced as a Romulan spy in the Khitomer massacre, where he died, but it was really Duras's father, Ja'rod, who was the traitor.

mok'ba — Klingon exercises mentioned in *TNG* episodes "Birthright" and "Second Chances."

Molecular Cybernetics — Dr. Noonian Soong's specialty mentioned in *TNG* episode "The Schizoid Man."

molybdenum-cobalt alloy — substance out of which Data is made, mentioned in *TNG* episode "The Most Toys."

Monak, Gary — responsible for special effects on *DS9*.

Mondor — Pakled ship in *TNG* episode "Samaritan Snare." Captained by Captain Grebnedlog, it has few armaments and Romulan-designed shields.

***Monitor*, USS** — in *TNG* episode "The Defector," ship on its way to the Neutral Zone to help the *Enterprise*, but it doesn't arrive in time.

Monroe, Lieutenant — *Enterprise* bridge officer, played by Jana Marie Hupp, killed in an explosion in *TNG* episode "Disaster," leaving Deanna in charge as the next highest-ranking officer.

Montaigne, Lawrence — played Decius in Classic *Trek* "Balance of Terror" and Stonn in "Amok Time." TV credits include *The Man from U.N.C.L.E.*, *Voyage to the Bottom of the Sea*, and *The Feather and Father Gang*. Films include *The Underground Man* and *Deadly Blessings*.

Montalban, Ricardo — played Khan Noonian Singh in Classic *Trek* "Space Seed" and in the film *The Wrath of Khan*. Born November 25, 1920, in Mexico City, his credits in the U.S. include the films *Neptune's Daughter*, *The Singing Nun*, and *Conquest of the Planet of the Apes*. His starring role in the *Fantasy Island* series and his Chrysler car commercials made him a household name.

Montgomery — *Enterprise* security guard in Classic episode "The Doomsday Machine." He is attacked by Decker while escorting him to sick-bay. He was played by Jerry Catron.

Moordigan, Dave — played a Klingon in *Star Trek: The Motion Picture*. Film credits include *48 Hours*.

Moore, James, Admiral — officer who tells Picard of a distress call from the Ficus Sector in *TNG* episode "Up the Long Ladder."

Moore, Ronald D. — story editor and scriptwriter of *TNG* "The Bonding," "The Defector," "Yesterday's Enterprise," "Sins of the Father," "Family," "Reunion," "First Contact," "In Theory," "Redemption, Parts I and II," "Disaster," "The First Duty," "The Next Phase," "Relics," "Aquiel," "Tapestry," "The Chase," "Rightful Heir," "Descent," and "Chain of Command."

Moosekian, Duke — played Gillespie in *TNG* "Night Terrors."

Morag, Commander — Klingon commander of the *Ku'vat* patrolling the nearby Starfleet Subspace Relay Station 47 in *TNG* episode "Aquiel."

Moran, W. Reed — scriptwriter of *TNG* "Sins of the Father."

Mordan IV — planetary member of the Federation, headed by Karnas who kidnapped a Federation diplomatic party in *TNG* episode "Too Short a Season."

Mordoc — Ferengi in *TNG* episode "The Last Outpost." He was played by Jake Dengel.

Mordock — Benzite who is the first of his people to be accepted by Starfleet Academy in *TNG* episode "Coming of Age." He was played by John Putch, the same actor who played the Benzite Ensign Mendon in "A Matter of Honor." Wesley suspects the two characters are the same person.

Mordock strategy — the Benzite Mordock becomes famous for this military theory at the Academy and greatly impresses Wesley in *TNG* episode "Coming of Age."

"More Troubles, More Tribbles" — written by David Gerrold, this animated Classic *Trek* episode aired 10/6/73 and features the return of Cyrano Jones, the tribbles, the Klingons (including Captain Koloth), and a glommer, the tribbles' natural enemy. In this story, instead of reproducing when they eat, the tribbles just get bigger and bigger. Voices: David Gerrold (Korax), James Doohan (Koloth), and Stanley Adams (Cyrano Jones).

Moreau, Marlena, Lieutenant — the captain's woman who works in the ship's chem labs in the mirror universe in Classic episode "Mirror, Mirror."

Morga, Tom — played a Klingon in *Star Trek: The Motion Picture*, and The Brute in *The Undiscovered Country*.

Morgan, Sean — played Lt. O'Neil in Classic *Trek* "The Return of the Archons" and "The Tholian Web." He also played Ensign Harper in "The Ultimate Computer" and the engineer in "The Paradise Syndrome." TV credits include *Voyage to the Bottom of the Sea* and a regular role on *The Adventures of Ozzie and Harriet*.

Morgana Quadrant — destination of the *Enterprise* after it leaves Tango Sierra in *TNG* episode "The Child," and mentioned as a destination in "Where Silence Has Lease."

Morgs — male species on Sigma Draconis in Classic episode "Spock's Brain." They are kept primitive by the women who will not let them have use of any technology. The leader of the Morgs is played by James Daris.

Mori, Jeanne — played the helmswoman on the USS *Grissom* in *The Search for Spock*. Film credits include *Night Shift*.

Moriarty, James, Professor — first seen in *TNG* episode "Elementary, Dear Data," he is played by Daniel Davis. Sherlock Holmes's famous adversary returns to the *Enterprise* via the holodeck in "Ship in a Bottle." He believes he can become a real person and not a simulation, if given the correct technology.

Morikun VII — world where Picard trained during his days at the Starfleet Academy, mentioned in *TNG* episode "Tapestry."

Morla — Kara's fiancé who lives on Cantaba Street on Argelius II and is questioned about her murder in Classic episode "Wolf in the Fold." He is played by Charles Dierkop.

Moropa — race which maintains a truce with the Bolians in *TNG* episode "Allegiance."

Morris, Joan Stuart — appeared in *TNG* episode "Suspicions."

Morris, Leslie — played Reginod in *TNG* "Samaritan Snare."

Morris, Phil — played Trainee Foster in *The Search for Spock*. He is the son of Greg Morris, who starred in *Mission: Impossible*. Phil Morris starred in the new *Mission: Impossible* as Barney's son.

Morrow, Byron — played Komack in Classic *Trek* "Amok Time" and Admiral Westervliet in "For the World Is Hollow and I Have Touched the Sky." TV credits include *Lost in Space* and *The Bionic Woman*, and regular roles on *The New Breed* and *Executive Suite*.

Morrow, Admiral — officer who appears in *The Search for Spock*, played by Robert Hooks.

Morshower, Glenn — played Burke in *TNG* "Peak Performance."

Mortae — mining tool used by the troglytes in Classic episode "The Cloud Minders."

Morton, Mickey — played Kloog in Classic *Trek* "The Gamesters of Triskelion." TV credits include *The Bionic Woman*, *The Man from U.N.C.L.E.*, and *Iron Horse*.

Morway, Professor — mentioned as an archaeologist working at the Landris digs in *TNG* episode "Lessons."

Morwood, Peter — author of Classic *Trek* novel *Rules of Engagement*.

Moser, Diane — played a member of the Ten Forward crew in *TNG* "The Offspring."

Mosiman, Marnie — played "woman" in *TNG* "Loud As a Whisper."

Mosley, Hal, Dr. — scientist on Penthara IV assisting the *Enterprise* in cooling the planet's atmosphere in *TNG* episode "A Matter of Time." He was played by Stefan Gierasch.

Moss, Arnold — played Anton Karidian in Classic *Trek* "The Conscience of the King." Born January 28, 1910, in Brooklyn, his TV credits include *The Man from U.N.C.L.E.* and *The Girl from U.N.C.L.E.* His film credits include *My Favorite Spy* and *Caper of the Golden Bulls.*

Moss, Stewart — played Joe Tormolen in Classic *Trek* "The Naked Time" and Hanar in "By Any Other Name." TV credits include a regular stint on *Fay* and guest spots on *Cannon.* Film credits include *Live Again, Die Again, Conspiracy of Terror,* and *Women in White.*

"Most Toys, The" — third-season *TNG* episode written by Shari Goodhartz and directed by Timothy Bond. Kivas Fajo, a collector of rare items, kidnaps Data for his collection, but Data refuses to cooperate. Guest stars: Saul Rubinek, Jane Daly, Nehemiah Persoff, and Colm Meaney.

Mot — Bolian barber who works in the *Enterprise* and appears in *TNG* episodes "Ensign Ro" and "Starship Mine." He is played by Ken Thorley.

Movar, General — Romulan officer under Commander Sela in *TNG* episode "Redemption." He was played by Nicholas Kepros.

"Move Along Home" — first-season *DS9* episode written by Frederick Rappaport, Lisa Rich, Jeanne Carrigan Fauci, and Michael Piller, directed by David Carson. Beings who call themselves the Waddi visit *DS9* and introduce Quark to a new game. Unknown to Quark, however, his players are actually Sisko, Kira, Dax, and Bashir, who experience the life-threatening events of the game as if they are really happening. Guest stars: Clara Bryant, Joel Brooks, and James Lashly.

M-Rays — Spock uses them to neutralize Apollo's force field holding the *Enterprise* in Classic episode "Who Mourns for Adonais?"

M'Rel — Gowron's father, who heads the Klingon high council mentioned in *TNG* episode "Redemption."

M'Ress — felinoid alien bridge personnel/communications officer from the planet Cait in the Lynx system in the animated series. Majel Barrett provided the voice.

Mudd, Harcourt Fenton — swindler, liar, cheat, and rogue encountered by the *Enterprise* in Classic episodes "Mudd's Women," "I, Mudd," and the animated "Mudd's Planet." Leo Francis Walsh is one of his aliases. He had a wife named Stella who apparently tormented him until he left her. He was played by Roger C. Carmel.

Mudd, Stella — Harcourt Fenton Mudd's wife of whom he made an android duplicate in Classic episode "I, Mudd." She was played by Kay Elliott.

"Mudd's Passion" — written by Stephen Kandel, this animated Classic *Trek* episode aired 11/10/73. Yet another sequel to the Harry Mudd series. This time Mudd has a love potion which gets released on the *Enterprise* and affects the crew. It has a side-effect, however. Once the potion has run its course, the victims go through a few hours of hating each other. Guest voices: Majel Barrett (M'Ress, Lora), James Doohan (Lt. Arex, human miner), Roger C. Carmel (Mudd), and Nichelle Nichols (female Ursinoid).

"Mudd's Women" — first-season Classic *Trek* written by Stephen Kandel and Gene Roddenberry, directed by Harvey Hart, this episode aired 10/13/66, and features the first appearance of Harry (Harcourt Fenton) Mudd (later seen in "I, Mudd"). Shuttling women to sell as brides to men on a mining colony on Rigel XII is only one of Mudd's jobs. He also possesses an illegal drug from Venus which exaggerates an individual's physical attractiveness. Guest stars: Roger C. Carmel, Karen Steele, Susan Denberg, Maggie Thrett, Gene Dynarski, and Jim Goodwin (who appears as Farrell in "The Enemy Within," "Miri," and others). Dilithium crystals are a big deal in this episode. Round playing cards are also featured when Eve McHuron (one of the brides to be) plays a version of solitaire called doublejack.

Mudie, Leonard — played a survivor in Classic *Trek* pilot "The Cage" and in "The Menagerie." Born in 1894 and died in 1965, his film credits include *The Mummy* ('32), *Dark Victory* ('39), and *The Magnetic Monster* ('53). TV credits include *Adventures of Superman*.

Mudor V — planet on which the *Enterprise* just completed a mission at the beginning of *TNG* episode "Disaster."

Mugato — apelike creature from planet Neural with white fur and a horn like a unicorn sticking out from the center of its forehead. One attacks Kirk in Classic episode "A Private Little War." Later, another one attacks Nona. They have poisonous fangs, mate for life, and are very territorial. Kirk refers to it once as a gumato, which could have just been a slip of the tongue.

Muktok Plants — plant which sings or emits music. Riker and Troi planted one on Betazed when they met and which is still there, mentioned in *TNG* episode "Ménage à Troi."

Muldaur, Diana — played Dr. Ann Mulhall in Classic *Trek* "Return to Tomorrow," Dr. Miranda Jones in "Is There in Truth No Beauty?" and Dr. Katherine Pulaski during the second season of *TNG*. She also had regular roles on *The Survivors*, *McCloud*, *Born Free*, *The Tony Randall Show*, *Hizzoner*, *Fitz and Bones*, and *L.A. Law*. She has also guest starred in numerous TV series.

Mulhall, Anne, Dr. — astrobiologist whose body is used by the entity Thalessa in Classic episode "Return to Tomorrow." She is played by Diana Muldaur.

Mull, Penthor — mentioned in *TNG* episode "The

Vengeance Factor" as an Acamarian Gatherer who died because of Yuta's vengeance.

Mullendore, Joseph — composer of the score for Classic *Trek* "The Conscience of the King." He also scored episodes of *Lost in Space* and *Voyage to the Bottom of the Sea.*

Mulroney, Kieran — played Benzan in *TNG* "The Outrageous Okona."

multitronics — technology used on the M–5 computer invented by Dr. Daystrom in Classic episode "The Ultimate Computer."

M'Umbha — Uhura's mother, mentioned in Classic episode "The Man Trap."

Muramoto, Betty — played the scientist on *TNG* "Déjà Q."

Murasaki 312 — electromagnetic, quasarlike phenomenon the shuttlecraft *Galileo* is on its way to study when it is swept off course and crashes on Taurus II in Classic episode "The Galileo 7."

Murdock, George — played the god creature in *The Final Frontier* and Admiral Hanson in *TNG* "The Best of Both Worlds, Parts I and II."

Murdock, John M. — played the beggar in "Time's Arrow, Part I."

Murdock, Kermit — played the prosecutor in Classic *Trek* "All Our Yesterdays." Film credits include *The Lonely Profession, The Godchild,* and *Captains and the Kings.*

Murdock, M. S. — author of the Classic *Trek* novel *Web of the Romulans.*

Murinite — mineral found on Rigel IV. Hengist's knife is made of this material as mentioned in the Classic episode "Wolf in the Fold."

Muskat, Joyce — scriptwriter of Classic *Trek* "The Empath."

Muskinseed punch — Hahliian drink Lt. Uhnari enjoys in *TNG* episode "Aquiel."

Mustin, Tom — played an intern in *The Voyage Home*.

Myers — one of Geordi's diagnostic engineers in *TNG* episode "Hollow Pursuits."

M-Zed V — false destination of the ship *Batris* mentioned in *TNG* episode "Heart of Glory." Actually a Federation outpost.

Naab, Captain — captain of the *Ajax*, mentioned in *TNG* episode "Tapestry."

Naff, Lycia — played Sonya Gomez in *TNG* "Q Who" and "Samaritan Snare."

Nagel, Ensign — in *TNG* episode "Peak Performance," crewmember who accompanies Riker to the *Hathaway* and helps create the "false image" defense maneuver. She was played by Leslie Neale.

Nagilum — alien scientist who studies life and death and captures the *Enterprise* in *TNG* episode "Where Silence Has Lease." He was played by Earl Boen.

"Nagus, The" — first-season *DS9* episode written by Ira Steven Behr and David Livingston, directed by David Livingston. The Ferengi high ruler, the Nagus, visits Quark on *DS9* in the hope that the Ferengi can use the wormhole to do business in the Gamma Quadrant, where their reputation does not precede them as it does in the Alpha Quadrant. Guest stars: Wallace Stevens, Max Grodenchik, Lou Wagner, Tiny Ron, Barry Gordon, Lee Arenberg, and Aron Eisenberg.

Nagus, Grand — Ferengi high official who rules the race. In *DS9* his name is Zek, played by Wallace Shawn.

Nahmi IV — world which has an outbreak of Correllium Fever in *TNG* episode "Hollow Pursuits."

Nakamura, Admiral — commander of Starbase *173*

in *TNG* episode "The Measure of a Man," played by Clyde Kusatsu.

"Naked Now, The" — first-season *TNG* episode written by John D. F. Black and J. Michael Bingham, directed by Paul Lynch. In a story very similar to the Classic episode "The Naked Time," the *Enterprise* encounters the Psi 2000 virus from another ship, the *Tsiolkovsky*, which causes victims to lose all inhibitions. Guest stars include: Brooke Bundy, Benjamin W. S. Lum, Michael Rider, David Renan, Skip Stellrecht, and Kenny Koch. Of note: Tasha manages to successfully seduce Data and it apparently has a very positive effect on both of them. In this episode, an image on the computer screen appears: A picture of a bird with nacelles wearing a Starfleet shirt with insignia. Could this be the Great Bird?

"Naked Time, The" — first-season Classic *Trek* episode written by John D. F. Black and directed by Marc Daniels which aired 9/29/66. An alien virus infects the crew and exposes their most private longings. This plot was reused in a first-season *Next Generation* episode called "The Naked Now." Guest stars: Bruce Hyde and Stewart Moss. Lieutenant Kevin Riley makes his first appearance, later returning in "Conscience of the King." Nurse Christine Chapel (Majel Barrett) also makes her first appearance, of many. Spock cries, Sulu chases people with a sword and Kirk professes an almost psychotic love for his ship.

Nalder, Reggie — played Shras in Classic *Trek* "Journey to Babel." Film credits include: *The Dead Don't Die*, *Salem's Lot*, and *The Devil and Max Devlin*. He has also done TV guest appearances on shows such as *The Man from U.N.C.L.E.*

Nalee, Elaine — played the female Klingon in *TNG* "Hide And Q."

Nanites — little robots created by Wesley who run amok on the *Enterprise* in *TNG* episode "Evolution."

Napier, Charles — played Adam in Classic *Trek* "The Way to Eden." He had regular starring roles on the TV series *Outlaws* and *The Oregon Trail*. Film credits include *Wacko* ('82).

Naradzay, Joseph — played First Sergeant USMC in *The Voyage Home*.

Nardino, Gary — executive producer of *The Search for Spock* and *The Undiscovered Country*.

Narenda III — Klingon outpost mentioned as having been destroyed in an alternate timeline in *TNG* episode "Yesterday's Enterprise."

Narsu, Uttan, Admiral — superior officer to Captain Shumar on the *Exeter* in *TNG* episode "Power Play."

Nash, Jennifer — played Maribor in *TNG* "The Inner Light."

Natira — high priestess of Yonada in Classic episode "For the World Is Hollow and I Have Touched the Sky." She and McCoy fall in love and want to marry. She was played by Kate Woodville.

Nausicaans — three thugs who attacked Cadet Picard and pierced his heart with a knife as mentioned in *TNG* episode "Samaritan Snare" and who are seen in "Tapestry."

Nayrock, Prime Minister — in *TNG* episode "The Hunted," the leader of the Angosians. He was played by James Cromwell.

Nazreldine — mentioned as the *Enterprise*'s last stop in *TNG* episode "The Icarus Factor," where a crewman picks up the flu.

Neale, Leslie — played Nagel in *TNG* "Peak Performance."

***Nebula*-class starship** — ships of this class include the *Phoenix* and the *Sutherland*, which appeared in *TNG* episodes "The Wounded" and "Redemption" in that order.

Nechayev, Alina, Vice Admiral — in *TNG* episode "Chain of Command" she allows Picard to take a commando team into Cardassian space. She also appears in "Descent."

neck pinch — see entry for Vulcan neck pinch.

Needham, Hal — actor/director/stuntman who played Mitchell's double in Classic *Trek* "Where No Man Has Gone Before." Born in 1931, his directing credits include *Smokey and the Bandit*, *The Cannonball Run*, and *Megaforce*.

negatron hydrocoils — a drop of jellylike substance which makes robotic muscles work like real muscles in the android bodies Sargon, Henoch, and Thalessa are constructing in Classic episode "Return to Tomorrow."

Neil — member of the team trying to steal trilithium from the *Enterprise* in *TNG* episode "Starship Mine."

Neinmann — mentioned in *TNG* episode "When the Bough Breaks" as a lost civilization, much like Atlantis, which disappeared on Xerxes VII.

Nel — in *TNG* episode "Violations," telepathic rapist Jev previously visited this world.

Nel Bato system — mentioned in *TNG* episode "The Most Toys" as a place where *Jovis* might have gone.

Nellen — silent aide to Admiral Satie in *TNG* episode "The Drumhead." She was played by Ann Shea.

Nellis, Tom — *Enterprise* crewman in Classic episode "Charlie X." He was played by Dallas Mitchell.

Nelson, Carolyn — played Yeoman Atkins in Classic

Trek "The Deadly Years." Film credits include: *Man on a String*, *Freedom*, and *Memorial Day*.

Nelson, Gene — director of Classic *Trek* "The Gamesters of Triskelion." Born in 1920, he also worked as an actor. He has directed the movies *Kissin' Cousins* and *Washington Behind Closed Doors*, as well as episodes of *Get Christie Love!* and *The Wackiest Ship in the Army*.

Nelvana III — in *TNG* episode "The Defector," Jarok says the Romulans are building a base on this world so they can have an advantage in a first-strike attack against the Federation.

Nenebek — miner Captain Dirgo's shuttle in *TNG* episode "Final Mission."

Neptune, Peter — played Aron in *TNG* "The Dauphin."

Neptune bath salts — advertised in a magazine on Planet 892 IV in Classic episode "Bread and Circuses."

Neral — Romulan proconsul when Picard last visited the Romulan homeworld, mentioned in *TNG* episode "Unification."

Nervala IV — earthquake-prone world on which a duplicate Riker is stranded for eight years in *TNG* episode "Second Chances."

Nerys, Kira, Major — regular character in *DS9* played by Nana Visitor. She is a Bajoran who grew up fighting the Cardassians. A young woman whose mistrust of others' motives has made her both strong and naive, she became an underground terrorist at a very early age but quit when she didn't agree with their tactics. Although she works for the Federation she doesn't agree with every decision they make. A capable pilot, her fighting abilities are equal to a man's and she has proven herself capable of commanding *DS9* when Sisko is away. Despite her violent nature, she is a woman of compassion and intellect but who has a lot of trouble relating to others on a personal level. She hates the Cardassians, although she understands her view is prejudiced since not all Cardassians are represented by the evil few in charge.

Nestorial III — in *TNG* episode "Time's Arrow," the planet where Guinan was living when picked up by the *Enterprise* to begin running Ten Forward.

Nesvig, Colonel — head of McKinley Rocket Base who captures Kirk and Spock in Classic episode "Assignment: Earth." He was played by Morgan Jones.

Neural — planet of hill people and villagers who used to be peaceful but are learning about weapons and killing due to Klingon interference in Classic episode "A Private Little War."

neural field — weapon the Kelvans use to paralyze their opponents in Classic episode "By Any Other Name."

neural neutralizer — machine which can empty the mind and is used on the Tantalus penal colony in Classic episode "Dagger of the Mind." The device appears to be much like the Klingon mind-sifter (see entry).

neural paralyzer — drug McCoy gives Kirk when he is fighting Spock on Vulcan in Classic episode "Amok Time." It puts the body in a deathlike state.

neural scanners — in *TNG* episode "Future Imperfect," Riker is told the Romulans used these machines on him to find out everything about him.

"Neutral Zone, The" — first-season *TNG* episode written by Maurice Hurley, Deborah McIntyre, and Mona Glee and directed by James L. Conway. Three 20th-century humans in cryonic suspension are discovered on an old Earth satellite. They are brought aboard the *Enterprise* as the ship heads to a meeting with the Romulans to try to find out why Earth outposts are being mysteriously destroyed. Guest stars: Marc Alaimo, Anthony James, Leon Rippy, and Gracie Harrison. In this episode Clare

Raymond's family tree includes references to the TV series *Dr. Who*, *M*A*S*H*, and *Gilligan's Island*.

Neutral Zone, Romulan — area of space that is a no-man's-land of sorts. Federation and Romulan ships agree not to cross it, protecting their territories from each other.

neutrino beacon — device used to find Geordi in *TNG* episode "The Enemy."

neutrino beam — used in *TNG* episode "A Matter of Honor" to remove ship-eating parasites from the *Enterprise* and the *Pagh*.

neutronium — mentioned in Classic episode "The Doomsday Machine" as the element used to make the hull of the out-of-control weapon.

Neuwirth, Bebe — played Lanel in *TNG* "First Contact." She is best known for her recurring role in *Cheers* and has done both theatrical films and TV.

New Berlin — Federation colony which thinks it's being attacked by the Borg when Ferengi ships show up in *TNG* episode "Descent."

"New Ground" — fifth-season *TNG* episode written by Stuart and Sara Charno and Grant Rosenberg, directed by Robert Scheerer. Worf's son, Alexander, comes to live with Worf on board the ship. Meanwhile, the *Enterprise* is to participate in an experiment involving a new means of propulsion called a Soliton Wave. Guest stars: Brian Bonsall, Georgia Brown, Jennifer Edwards, and Richard McGonagle.

Newland, John — director of Classic *Trek* "Errand of Mercy." He hosted and directed the series *One Step Beyond* and directed episodes of *The Man from U.N.C.L.E.*, and many other 1960s shows.

Newman, William — played Kalin Trose in *TNG* "The Host."

New Manhattan — located on Beth Delta I, mentioned in *TNG* episode "Evolution."

Newmar, Julie — played Eleen in Classic *Trek* "Friday's Child." Born in 1935, her TV credits include *Batman* (she played Catwoman), *The Twilight Zone*, *The Bionic Woman*, and *My Living Doll*. Her film credits include *Seven Brides for Seven Brothers* and *McKenna's Gold*.

New Martim Vaz — aquatic city on Earth mentioned in *TNG* episode "The Survivors."

New Paris — colony suffering from a plague. The *Enterprise* is en route there when the *Galileo* is lost in Classic episode "The Galileo Seven."

New Providence — colony mentioned in *TNG* episode "The Best of Both Worlds" as located on Jouret IV.

New United Nations — referred to by Data in *TNG* episode "Encounter at Farpoint" as having been active since 2036.

"Next Phase, The" — fifth-season *TNG* episode written by Ronald D. Moore and directed by David Carson. It appears that Ro and Geordi are killed when they return from a rescue mission, but they have actually phased into another space where they can see the crew but the crew cannot see them. Guest stars: Michelle Forbes, Thomas Kopache, Susanna Thompson, Kenneth Meseroll, Shelly Leverington, and Brian Cousins.

N'Game Nebula — planet inhabited by the Paxans in *TNG* episode "Clues."

Nibor — Ferengi who plays chess with Riker in *TNG* episode "Ménage à Troi." He was played by Peter Slutsker.

Nichols, Nichelle — starred as Uhura in Classic *Trek* and all the movies, and provided the voice for Uhura and many other characters in the animated series. Born in Robbins, Illinois, she has done stage work, writing, singing, and dancing. She was twice nominated for the Sara Siddon Award as best actress of the year for her work in the plays *Kicks & Co.* and *The Blacks*. She also toured as a vocalist with Duke Ellington and the Lionel Hampton bands. Her TV credits before *Trek* include *The Lieutenant* and *CBS Repertory Theatre*. When she was on *The Lieutenant*, she met and had a love affair with Gene Roddenberry, but they had parted as friends before she landed her role as Uhura. She almost quit *Trek* after its first season because of her lack of lines but met Martin Luther King, Jr., who told her that she had to stay on because her character was treated as an equal by her shipmates, providing a great role model for blacks and black women. Her film credits include *Mister Buddwing*, *Three for the Wedding*, *Truck Turner*, *Made in Paris*, *Porgy and Bess* (with Sammy Davis, Jr.), and *Doctor, You've Got to Be Kidding*. One of her more recent films is *The Supernaturals*. She has made frequent appearances at *Star Trek* conventions, sung at many night clubs and released an album, *Dark Side of the Moon*. She is also involved in the recruitment of minorities for NASA. She recently sold her memoirs, *Beyond Uhura*, to Putnam. She also sold an idea for a science-fiction novel which she is currently writing. In her spare time she paints, sculpts, designs clothing, and writes poetry (some of which was published in the magazine *All about Star Trek Fan Clubs* during the late 1970s).

Nickson, Julia — played Lian T'su in *TNG* "The Arsenal of Freedom."

Nigala IV, Station — destination of the *Enterprise* in "Déjà Q."

"Night Terrors" — fourth-season *TNG* episode written by Shari Goodhartz, Pamela Douglas, and Jeri Taylor and directed by Les Landau. The crew experiences dream deprivation which makes them hallucinate while stranded in Tyken's Rift, a tear in space. Troi may resolve their dire straits if she can communicate with the only survivor of the *Brittain*, a comatose Betazoid man. Guest stars: Rosalind Chao, John Vickery, Duke Moosekian, Colm Meaney, Deborah Taylor, Lanei Chapman, Brian Tochi, and Craig Hurley.

night-blooming throgni — mentioned in *TNG* episode "Angel One" as a Klingon plant that has an odor like the virus plaguing the ship.

"Nightingale Woman" — poem Gary Mitchell quotes in Classic episode "Where No Man Has Gone Before." It was written in 1996 by Phineas Tarbolde on Canopus and is considered one of the most passionate sonnets ever written. The excerpt Gary quotes reads: "My love has wings, slender-feathered things with grace and upswept curve and tapered tip."

Nilrem — medical personnel working at the hospital to which Riker is taken on Malcoria III in *TNG* episode "First Contact."

Nimbus III — planet of Galactic Peace in *The Final Frontier*. It is on this world that Sybok takes his hostages, one human, one Klingon, one Romulan, to lure the *Enterprise* (or any starship) into his clutches so he can use it to seek ShaKaRee.

Nimoy, Adam — director of *TNG* episodes "Rascals" and "Timescape." He has a degree in law and is the son of actor/director/writer/producer Leonard Nimoy.

Nimoy, Leonard — actor/writer/director/producer who starred as Mr. Spock in *Star Trek*, all the movies, played the voice of Spock in the animated series, and an older Spock in *TNG* "Unification." He also directed *The Search for Spock*, and directed and cowrote *The Voyage Home*. Nimoy is also responsible for inventing the Vulcan salute, the Vulcan neck pinch (with the help of Shatner), and the Vulcan mind meld. Born March 26, 1931 in Boston, he married actress Sandi Zober in 1954. They have two children, Julie and Adam (who went on to direct two episodes of *TNG*). He studied acting under Jeff Corey (who played Plasus on "The Cloud Minders). In the early part of his career, Nimoy also taught and worked in a pet shop and as a movie theater usher. His first roles, other than on the stage, include *Zombies of the Stratosphere*, *Queen for a Day*, and *Kid Monk Baroni*. He also had walk-on and bit parts in movies such as *Them!* His TV roles included small stints on *Rawhide*, *The Virginian*, *The Outer Limits*, *The Twilight Zone*, *Profiles in Courage*, *Dr. Kildare*, *The Lieutenant*, *Sea Hunt*, and *The Man from U.N.C.L.E.* (with Shatner), not all of them starring roles. After Trek was cancelled, Nimoy landed the starring role as Paris in *Mission: Impossible* where he remained for two years. He was offered roles in other series but declined them. He hosted the long-running series *In Search of . . .* and *Lights, Camera, Action!* and did Broadway work, playing Tevye in *Fiddler on the Roof*, Holmes in the play *Sherlock Holmes*, and Dr. Martin Dysart in *Equus*. He appeared on many game shows, including *The 20,000 Dollar Pyramid* with Shatner. He appeared in the films *Catlow* (in which he has a seminude scene, mostly in shadow), *The Alpha Caper*, and *The Missing are Deadly* all while going to Antioch college where he finally obtained a Masters in education. He also produced several albums on which he sang hit songs of the 1960s much to his embarrassment today (his voice is weak). He wrote several poetry books, and the autobiography of his early *Trek* days called *I Am Not Spock*. He also starred in the remake of *Invasion of the Body Snatchers*, and following that, starred in his one-man play *Vincent* (which he also wrote and directed). Nimoy refused to sign on as Spock for *Star Trek: The Motion Picture* until he came to an agreement with Paramount to receive royalties on the merchandising of his likeness. Spock was a popular face, and Nimoy received no money for any merchandising after the series. He finally got a $2.5 million settlement from Paramount as part of his agreement to play Spock in the film. He also starred in the film *Seizure* around the same time. Though Nimoy denies it now, he was the one who came up with the idea to kill Spock in *The Wrath of Khan*. He was tired of the role and didn't think it was furthering his career. Now that he's changed his mind, he denies any culpability in the "killing" of Spock. He had some more great roles in the 1980s, including *A Woman Called Golda*, and the miniseries *Marco Polo*. He has also directed the feature films *Three Men and a Baby*, *The Good Mother*, and *Funny about Love*. During the filming of *The Voyage Home*, Nimoy met his second wife, Susan Bay. They are currently married and living in Los Angeles. (Bay, a studio production executive, recently had a small part in an episode of *DS9*.) His first wife, Sandi, from whom he separated in 1986 and then divorced, has appeared on some TV talk shows discussing their long marriage and quick divorce. She claims she had no warning and to this day they do not speak. Nimoy, in his turn, discussed the divorce on *The Whoopi Goldberg Show*, explaining that the marriage had been rocky for many years, but that he was waiting for his children to "grow old and die" before he took on the difficult task of breaking up with his wife of over 30 years. His most recent starring role (other than *Trek*) is in the 1991 film *Never Forget*, which he also produced. He is currently working on possible future stage and television projects with William Shatner. The two, who have stayed in touch since the 1960s and have developed a close friendship, recently successfully toured the country in a two-man show discussing their *Star Trek* years. Of Shatner's directing on *The Final Frontier*, Nimoy professes only admiration. Though the movie was not as successful as the other *Trek* movies, Nimoy blames a poor script for its lukewarm reception, the same reason, he says, for his own flop, *Funny about Love*. When not acting or directing, Nimoy's hobbies include photography and writing.

Nims, Shari — played Sayana in Classic *Trek* "The Apple."

ni'pok — Klingon word meaning "déjà vu," in *TNG* episode "Cause and Effect."

nitrium — in *TNG* episode "Cost of Living," the *Enterprise* involuntarily picks up parasites that feed off this substance and disable the ship.

Niven, Larry — scriptwriter of the animated episode "The Slaver Weapon." He is a well known science-fiction writer and coauthor of several bestsellers with Jerry Pournelle such as *The Mote in God's Eye* and *Lucifer's Hammer*, among others. He won the Hugo for his novel *Ringworld*, which spurred many sequels. The Kzin characters in the animated episode are an alien race he invented in his novels.

Noel, Helen, Dr. — psychiatrist who investigates the Tantalus penal colony with Kirk. He is forced by the neural neutralizer to fall in love with her in Classic episode "Dagger of the Mind." She is played by Marianna Hill.

Nog — young Ferengi who is Jake Sisko's friend on *DS9*. He is the son of Rom and Quark's nephew. He is played by Aron Eisenberg.

Nomad — machine that was once an Earth space probe but, through an accident, merged with a machine called *Tan ru* in Classic episode "The Changeling." Its mission, to secure and sterilize soil samples, changed to "seek out and sterilize biological life-forms" as a result. The voice of Nomad is Vic Perrin's.

nome — a part of Vulcan philosophy mentioned in Classic episode "The Savage Curtain" as meaning "all."

Nona — Kanutu woman who has great knowledge (or magical powers) in healing and heals Kirk's Mugato bite with a makho root. She is Tyree's wife but has her eye on Kirk. She dies when she is stabbed with her own knife by the villagers. She was played by Nancy Kovack.

noranium alloy — substance found on Gamma Hromi II at the Gatherers' camp in *TNG* episode "The Vengeance Factor."

Nored, Anne, Lieutenant — in animated episode "The Survivor," an *Enterprise* security woman engaged to Carter Winston. Her voice is Nichelle Nichols'.

norep — drug Dr. Crusher uses on Warren in *TNG* episode "Who Watches the Watchers" without result. Dr. Crusher also uses this drug, referred to as "noreph," when trying to save Tasha in "Skin of Evil."

Noress, Susan, Dr. — said to be the creator of the plasma plague held in module L–73 in *TNG* episode "The Child."

Norkan outposts — site of a massacre for which Admiral Jarok is responsible, mentioned in *TNG* episode "The Defector."

Norland, Victoria — played Daras in Classic *Trek* "Patterns of Force." TV credits include *The Man from U.N.C.L.E.*

Norman — the only coordinator of the androids on Mudd's planet in Classic episode "I, Mudd." He is played by Richard Tatro.

Norphin V — mentioned in *TNG* episode "Relics" as a beautiful retirement world for former Starfleet officers.

Norton, Jim — played Einstein in *TNG* "The Nth Degree" and "Descent."

Norwick, Natalie — played Martha Leighton in Classic *Trek* "The Conscience of the King."

Nova Squadron — name of Wesley's cadet group in *TNG* episode "The First Duty."

Novachron — Wesley tells Guinan that he, and everyone else, thinks she's from this world in *TNG* episode "The Child."

Novak, Frank — played the businessman in *DS9* "Babel."

Nowell, David — camera operator on *The Search for Spock.*

"Nth Degree, The" — fourth-season *TNG* episode written by Joe Menosky and directed by Robert Legato. Reginald Barclay is back after having been exposed to an alien probe that elevates his intelligence to near omnipotence. He takes control of the ship to increase the warp capacity in the engines and creates a distortion in space. Guest stars: Dwight Schultz, Saxon Trainor, Jim Norton, Page Leong, and David Coburn.

Nu'Daq, Captain — Klingon officer commanding the attack ship *Maht H'a* in *TNG* episode "The Chase."

Null G Ward — mentioned in *TNG* episode "Yesterday's Enterprise" as the place to which Dr. Selar is ordered.

Number 4 Shield — shield protecting the starboard side of the ship and that always seems to go out first.

Number One — first officer of the *Enterprise* under Captain Pike in Classic pilot "The Cage" and "The Menagerie." She was played by Majel Barrett under the name M. Leigh Hudec.

Number One — name Picard often calls Riker in *TNG.*

Numerian — Ambassador Olcar of *TNG* episode "Man of the People" is a member of this empathic species, whose powers work only within their own race.

Nuria — leader of the primitive Vulcans on Mintaka, in *TNG* episode "Who Watches the Watchers," she thinks Picard and his crew are gods. She was played by Kathryn Leigh Scott.

nus'ra — Tilonus IV blade used for ceremonial bartering. Worf accidentally cuts Riker with one in *TNG* episode "Frame of Mind."

Nuyen, France — played Elaan in Classic *Trek* "Elaan of Troyius." Born in 1939, her credits include *South Pacific,*

A Girl Named Tamiko, *Battle for the Planet of the Apes*, and a regular role on *St. Elsewhere*. She is married to actor Robert Culp.

N'Vek, Subcommander — second-in-command on the Romulan warbird *Khazara* who kidnaps Troi in *TNG* episode "Face of the Enemy." He is killed when his plot is discovered.

Oath — Klingon term for marriage.

Obelisk — structure in Classic episode "The Paradise Syndrome" supposedly built by the Preservers as an asteroid deflector. Kirk falls inside it when his communicator inadvertently replicates the sound code that opens it up.

Obi VI — world mentioned in *TNG* episode "The Child" where Dr. Susan Nuuress tested a virus similar to the plasma plague.

Obi system — where the plasma plague contained in Module L 73 was developed by Dr. Susan Noress as mentioned in the *TNG* episode "The Child."

O'Brian — mentioned as an officer Mudd captures, but who is never seen in Classic episode "I, Mudd."

O'Brien, Joycelyn — played Mitana Haro in *TNG* episode "Allegiance."

O'Brien, Keiko Ishikawa — recurring character in *TNG* and *DS9*. She is married to Miles O'Brien and they have a young daughter, Molly (played by Hana Hatae). A botanist aboard the *Enterprise* in *TNG*, on *DS9* she teaches the diverse group of children living at the station. She is played by Rosalind Chao.

O'Brien, Miles Edward, Ops Chief — a regular on *DS9* and a recurring character on *TNG*. Miles, played by Colm Meaney, is married to Keiko and they have a small daughter, Molly (played by Hana Hatae). He served aboard the USS *Rutledge* under Captain Benjamin Maxwell, where he fought against the Cardassians, and has traumatic memories of when he was forced to kill one. He has a deep-seated prejudice against them. He met Keiko Ishikawa after joining the *Enterprise* crew. He loves gambling, is a wizard with hardware, and an excellent technician. On *DS9* he has settled down somewhat, a devoted family man and a valued worker.

O'Brien, Molly — young daughter of Keiko and Miles O'Brien, played by Hana Hatae. She has appeared in a *TNG* episode and a few *DS9* episodes in very small roles. She is preschool age at the beginning of *DS9*'s run. She was born literally into the hands of Worf when no doctor was available to aid the laboring Keiko.

"Obsession" — written by Art Wallace and directed by Ralph Senensky, this second-season Classic *Trek* episode aired 12/15/67. A vampiric cloud creature Kirk once encountered on Tycho IV, where it killed Garrovick, his friend and captain, is rediscovered on Argus X. Kirk becomes obsessed with destroying it. Guest stars: Stephen Brooks and Jerry Ayers.

Oceanus IV — in *TNG* episode "The Game," the *Enterprise* is en route to this world on a diplomatic mission.

Ocett, Gul — female Cardassian in command of two warships in *TNG* episode "The Chase." She attacks the *Enterprise* as soon as she thinks she has the last clue to Professor Galen's micropaleontology mystery.

O'Connel, Steve — young boy in Classic episode "And the Children Shall Lead" whose parents are influenced to commit suicide by the Gorgon. He is played by Caesar Belli.

O'Connell, William — played Thelev in Classic *Trek* "Journey to Babel." His other credits include the film *The Dead Don't Die* ('72).

O'Connor, Terrance — played Chief Ross in *Star Trek: The Motion Picture*. TV credits include *Barnaby Jones*.

O'Connor, Tim — played Briam in *TNG* episode "The Perfect Mate."

Odan, Ambassador — Trill (see entry) who falls in love with Dr. Crusher while hosted in his male body, played by Franc Luz, in *TNG* episode "The Host." He is a symbiote being whose true form looks like a slug. He comes aboard to mediate a dispute between Peliar Zel's moons, Alpha and Beta. His new female body, Kareel, is played by Nicole Orth-Pallavicini.

O'Dell, Brenna — real leader of the Bringloidi colony in the Ficus Sector whose father is Danilo O'Dell, in *TNG* episode "Up the Long Ladder." She is played by Rosalyn Landor.

O'Dell, Danilo — puppet leader whose daughter, Brenna, is the real ruler of the Bringloidi colony in *TNG* episode "Up the Long Ladder." His title is Shan'a'kee. He is played by Barrie Ingham.

Odet IX — planet visited by the *Enterprise* and mentioned in *TNG* episode "The Child."

Odin, SS — freighter of which Captain Ramsey is in command when it crashes into Asphia in *TNG* episode "Angel One."

Odo, Security Chief — shapechanging alien, the only one of his race, who is a regular on *DS9*. He doesn't know what race he is because he was raised by Bajorans. He is played by René Auberjonois. Odo was found 50 years before the *DS9* series begins in a spacecraft found drifting near the Denorios Belt near Bajor but has no memory of how he got there. Once a day, Odo must change from his humanoid form to his true form, a liquid, to sleep. His bed is a bucket. When the Cardassians were in charge of *DS9*, they made Odo into a sort of circus act, forcing him to shape-change to entertain them. He worked as security for the Cardassians on the station as well, though he had no loyalties to them. Under the Federation, he is the chief of security, working for Sisko.

Odona — young woman from Gideon who befriends Kirk on the fake *Enterprise* in Classic episode "Mark of Gideon." She has contracted vegan choriomeningitis, which is deadly to her species, from Kirk's blood. This was done to her on purpose to test whether or not Gideons are susceptible to the disease, which will later be used for population control. Odona was played by Sharon Acker.

O'Ferren, Marty — mentioned in the Dixon Hill scenario in *TNG* episode "Manhunt" as having been "greased."

Offenhouse, Ralph — wealthy, fifty-five-year-old man whose body was preserved in cryonic suspension in *TNG* episode "The Neutral Zone." He is revived and played by Peter Mark Richman.

"Offspring, The" — third-season *TNG* episode written by René Echevarria and directed by Jonathan Frakes. Data creates his own child, Lal, whom he allows to choose her own form and race. She chooses to be a human female but the emotions involved with becoming human are so trying that they destroy her, coming to a head when a Starfleet official wants to take her away from Data to study her, a move she, in her relative youth, cannot handle. Guest stars: Hallie Todd, Nicolas Coster, Judyann Elder, Leonard John Crowfoot, Diane Moser, Hayne Bayle, Maria Leone, and James G. Becker.

Offzel, Mark — artist who sculpted a vase Fajo owns mentioned in *TNG* episode "The Most Toys."

Ogawa, Alyssa, Nurse — assists Dr. Crusher in sick-bay in various *TNG* episodes. She is played by Patti Yasutake.

Oglesby, Thomas — played the scholar in *TNG* "Loud As a Whisper."

Oglethorpe, Viscount — man to whom the Countess Bartholomew compares Picard in *TNG* episode "Ship in a Bottle."

O'Herlihy, Lieutenant — character killed on Cestus III by the Gorns in Classic episode "Arena." He was played by Jerry Ayers.

O'Herlihy, Michael — director of Classic *Trek* "Tomorrow Is Yesterday." Born in Ireland in 1929, his credits include Disney films such as *The Fighting Prince of Donegal* ('66) and *The One and Only Genuine Original Family Band* ('68). TV directing credits include episodes of *Today's FBI* and *The Guns of Will Sonnett*.

Oji — Mintakan and young daughter of Liko. She was played by Pamela Segall in *TNG* episode "Who Watches the Watchers."

O.K. Corral — famous gunfight scene between the Clantons and the Earps, set up by the Melkotians for Kirk, Spock, McCoy, and Scotty to relive in Classic episode "Spectre of the Gun."

Okona, Thaddiun, Captain — captain of the freighter *Erstwhile* in *TNG* episode "The Outrageous Okona." He was played by William O. Campbell.

Okrand, Marc — Vulcan language translator in *Star Trek: The Wrath of Khan*.

Okuda, Michael — technical consultant and scenic art supervisor for *TNG*. He created a lot of the ship models, and ships designed by Okuda, Greg Jein, and Robert McCall all appear in "Unification," many of them formerly featured in *Star Trek* movies and brought out from storage.

okudagram — name of the computer graphic displays

on the *Enterprise*. Obviously, this word is a tribute to *TNG*'s technical consultant, Michael Okuda.

O'Kun, Lan — scriptwriter of *TNG* story "Haven."

Olcar, Vas, Ambassador — Numerian diplomat who keeps himself young by putting his negative thoughts into another person he chooses as a receptacle. This practice prematurely ages and kills his assistant, Sev. He tries to do the same to Troi, but fails. When a second attempt to get another woman to be his psychic receptacle fails, he suddenly ages rapidly and dies. He appears in *TNG* episode "Man of the People."

Old Ones — referred to in Classic episode "What Are Little Girls Made Of?" as being the long-dead creators of the androids found on Exo III.

Oliver, Susan — played Vina in Classic *Trek* pilot "The Cage" and "The Menagerie." Born in 1937, her TV credits include a regular role on *Peyton Place*, and guest roles on *The Man from U.N.C.L.E.*, *Alias Smith and Jones*, and *Circle of Fear*. Film credits include *Green-Eyed Blonde* ('57) and *Looking for Love* ('64).

Omag — Ferengi played by William Batiani in *TNG* episode "Unification."

Omaha Air Base — where Captain John Christopher is from in Classic episode "Tomorrow Is Yesterday."

Omega IV — planet where the Yangs and Kohms are fighting a civil war, aided by Captain Ronald Tracey in Classic episode "The Omega Glory." The native inhabitants have developed a culture surprisingly parallel to American culture on Earth, down to a battered American flag.

Omega Cygni — the Malurian system is located here, as mentioned in Classic episode "The Changeling."

"Omega Glory, The" — written by Gene Roddenberry and directed by Vince McEveety, this second-season Classic

Trek episode aired 3/1/68. On the planet Omega IV, Captain Ronald Tracey of the USS *Exeter* remains the only survivor of a virus which the rest of his landing party brought back to his ship. The planet acts as a natural immunity to the virus and Tracey also believes it holds the secret to extended life. Kirk and Spock must stop his interference with the native society, a society which parallels American origins and is in the middle of a civil war. Guest stars: Morgan Woodward, Roy Jensen, Irene Kelley, David L. Ross, Eddie Paskey, Ed McCready, Lloyd Kino, and Morgan Farley.

Omega Sagitta 12 System — location of the Coalition of Medina in *TNG* episode "The Outrageous Okona."

Omicron IV — mentioned by Gary Seven as a world that was almost destroyed by nuclear arms in Classic episode "Assignment: Earth." He compares Earth to this world.

Omicron Ceti III — where an agricultural colony lived under spore influence and amid deadly Berthold Rays in Classic episode "This Side of Paradise."

Omicron Delta Region — location of the shore-leave world in Classic episode "Shore Leave."

Omicron Pascal — the *Enterprise* stayed here in *TNG* episode "11001001."

Omicron Theta IV — mentioned in *TNG* episode "Datalore" as the world where Dr. Soong lived at the time he created Data and Lore.

"Once upon a Planet" — written by Len Jenson and Chuck Menville, this animated Classic *Trek* episode aired 11/3/73. The crew return to the "Shore Leave" planet which seems to have gone out of control and produces harmful illusions. Guest voices: James Doohan (Lt. Arex, Gabler, White Rabbit), Majel Barrett (Lt. M'Ress), George Takei (computer), and Nichelle Nichols (Alice).

"One of Our Planets Is Missing" — written by Marc Daniels, this animated Classic *Trek* episode aired 9/22/73. A giant planet-eating cloud threatens heavily populated planets. The *Enterprise* makes a journey through its "insides" and Spock finally manages to communicate with it through a Vulcan mind meld. The cloud understands it is killing people and agrees to leave the galaxy and return to its "home." Guest voices: all the original cast. James Doohan supplies the voice for Lt. Arex.

Oneamisu Sector — where the Braslota system is located in *TNG* episode "Peak Performance."

O'Neil, Lieutenant — one of the officers "absorbed" with Sulu, in the first landing party sent to Beta III in Classic episode "The Return of the Archons." He was played by Sean Morgan, who also plays the transporter officer in "The Tholian Web."

O'Neil, Tricia — played Captain Rachel Garrett on *TNG* "Yesterday's Enterprise" and "Suspicions."

O'Neill, Amy — played Annette in *TNG* "Evolution" but all of her scenes were cut.

O'Neill, Ensign — member of the landing party searching on the wrong world for the crashed shuttle in Classic episode "The Galileo Seven."

Onizuka — *Enterprise* shuttlepod seen in *TNG* episodes "The Ensigns of Command" and "The Mind's Eye." The shuttle was named for one of the astronauts who died on the *Challenger* space shuttle.

onkians — Romulan temperature measurement mentioned in *TNG* episode "The Defector."

oomox — Ferengi word for "pleasure." Giving someone *oomox* means you give them great pleasure, as mentioned in *TNG* episode "Ménage à Troi."

Opaka, Kai — spiritual leader of Bajor. She shows Sisko

the celestial orb which takes him back to his past to relive meeting his wife.

Opatoshu, David — played Anan 7 in Classic *Trek* "A Taste of Armageddon." Born in 1918, his TV credits include *The Man from U.N.C.L.E.*, *Voyage to the Bottom of the Sea*, *The Bionic Woman*, and regular roles on *Bonino* and *The Secret Empire*. Film credits include: *Exodus* ('60) and *Tarzan and the Valley of Gold* ('66). He also did theater work.

"Operation: Annihilate!" — written by Stephen W. Carabatsos and directed by Herschel Daugherty, this final first-season Classic *Trek* episode aired 4/13/67. Mass insanity seems to have overtaken the inhabitants of Deneva. The *Enterprise* investigates and finds that horrible aliens which resemble flying, flat, rubbery pancakes have invaded the world. Kirk's only brother, George Samuel Kirk, dies along with his wife, Aurelean. Their son, Peter, survives. Guest stars: Dave Armstrong, Craig Hundley, Joan Swift, and Maurishka Talifero. Of note: In this episode the Vulcan inner eyelid is revealed.

Operation Support Services — branch of Starfleet which runs the Federation's starbases, mentioned in *TNG* episode "11001001."

Ophiuchus VI — where Harry Mudd was headed with his "women" in Classic episode "Mudd's Women" before taking the side trip with the *Enterprise* to Rigel XII.

Opraline — destination of the *Enterprise* after it leaves Ornara in *TNG* episode "Symbiosis."

Ops — the command center is referred to as Ops on *Deep Space 9*. On *TNG* the station often manned by Data is referred to as Ops.

Oracle — name of the computer which runs the world of Yonada in Classic episode "For the World Is Hollow and I Have Touched the Sky." It uses an implant at the temple to control its populace.

Orange, David — played the "sleepy" Klingon in *The Final Frontier*.

Ordek Nebula — the Wogneers live here in *TNG* episode "Allegiance."

O'Reilly, Robert — played Kuzo in *TNG* "Manhunt," and Gowron in "Redemption, Parts I and II" and "Rightful Heir."

Orelious IX — in *TNG* episode "Booby Trap," this world was destroyed during a war between the Promellians and the Menthars.

Organia — planet over which the Klingons and the Federation are fighting in Classic episode "Errand of Mercy." The Organians who inhabit it are actually advanced life-forms of pure energy who are disgusted by the fighting between the two races.

Organian Peace Treaty — when the Organians in Classic episode "Errand of Mercy" have had enough of the fighting between the Federation and the Klingons, they impose this treaty: If the fighting continues, the Organians will intervene, rendering all weapons useless on both sides.

Oriega, Stan — mentioned in *TNG* episode "The Outrageous Okona" as a 23rd-century comedian who joked about quantum mathematics.

orientine acid — element in animated episode "The Survivor" which eats through everything except the crystal container it is kept in.

Orion — planet known for its green slave women, who are said to be irresistible to men. A neutral world located in the Rigel system, it is mentioned in Classic episodes "The Menagerie," "What Are Little Girls Made Of?" (Dr. Korby worked on an immunization project with information from Orion ruins), "Journey to Babel" (in a reference to Orion smugglers; Thelev, an Andorian, is actually an Orion agent), "Whom Gods Destroy" (Marta is an Orion), and several animated episodes including "The Pirates of Orion."

Orion Trader — character seen in Captain Pike's fantasy in Classic episode "The Menagerie." He was played by Joseph Mell.

Orion wing slugs — Lwaxana refers to these creatures, saying she would rather eat them than face Tog in *TNG* episode "Ménage à Troi."

Ormeny, Tom — played the Klingon first officer in *TNG* episode "Redemption, Part I."

Ornara — located in the Delos System, this world thinks it suffers from a chronic disease for which they need felicium, but they are actually drug addicts, in *TNG* episode "Symbiosis."

Ornaran plague — mentioned in *TNG* episode "Symbiosis" as the disease from which the Ornaran claim to be suffering, when in actuality their world was cured of the disease 200 years before. Their symptoms are actually those of drug addiction.

Orra, Jil — young daughter of Picard's Cardassian tormentor, Gul Madred, in *TNG* episode "Chain of Command."

Orta — leader of a Bajoran resistance group. He speaks with a voice box and is disfigured because of Cardassian tortures in *TNG* episode "Ensign Ro." He was played by Jeffrey Hayenga.

Ortega, Jimmy — played Torres in *TNG* "Encounter at Farpoint."

Orth-Pallavicini, Nicole — played Kareel in *TNG* episode "The Host."

Ortiz, Ensign — mentioned as a replacement violin player for Data in *TNG* episode "The Ensigns of Command."

Orton — administrator of Arkaria in *TNG* episode "Starship Mine" who is working with the mercenaries trying to steal trilithium from the *Enterprise.*

Osborne, Lieutenant — head of security on the *Enterprise* in Classic episode "The Devil in the Dark." He is also a member of the landing party in "A Taste of Armageddon."

O'Shea, Captain — captain of the *Huron* in animated episode "The Pirates of Orion."

oskoid — type of Betazed food served by Lwaxana in *TNG* episode "Ménage à Troi." It is served with sap.

Oswald, Gerd — director of Classic *Trek* episodes "The Conscience of the King" and "The Alternative Factor." Born in 1916, he was a child actor before becoming a director. His TV directing credits include *The Outer Limits, Bonanza,* and *Voyage to the Bottom of the Sea.* He also directed the films *A Kiss before Dying* ('56) and *Agent for Harm* ('56).

Otar II — destination of the *Enterprise* at the end of *TNG* episode "The Offspring."

"Outcast, The" — fifth-season *TNG* episode written by Jeri Taylor and directed by Robert Scheerer. Riker falls for a hermaphrodite alien whose world forbids its inhabitants from preferring themselves as one gender or another. This alien, however, feels very feminine when she's with Riker, a fact which causes her people to take her away against her will to be "corrected" despite Riker's protests. Guest stars: Melinda Culea, Callan White, and Megan Cole.

Outpost 23 — hidden Starfleet base mentioned in *TNG* episode "Future Imperfect."

Outpost Delta 05 — located in the Neutral Zone, this outpost was destroyed in *TNG* episode "The Neutral Zone." In "Q Who" it is hinted that the outpost was destroyed by the Borg.

Outpost Sera VI — outpost near the Neutral Zone in *TNG* episode "The Defector."

Outpost Seran T1 — Dr. Leah Brahms worked here designing a dilithium crystal chamber as mentioned in *TNG* episode "Booby Trap."

Outposts — planets which can travel through space, made by the ancient, dead Tkon Empire. One was named the Delphi Ardu in *TNG* episode "The Last Outpost."

"Outrageous Okona, The" — second-season *TNG* episode written by Les Menchen, Lance Dickson, David Landsburg, and Burton Armus, directed by Robert Becker. Captain Okona, pursued by the warring planets Atlek and Streleb, is granted immunity by the *Enterprise*, while Data gets a lesson in humor from Guinan. Guest stars: William O. Campbell, Douglas Rowe, Albert Stratton, and Joe Piscopo.

Overdiek, Diane — production coordinator of *TNG*.

Overseer — all-powerful deity worshipped by the Mintakans in *TNG* episode "Who Watches the Watchers."

Overton, Frank — played Elias Sandoval in Classic *Trek* "This Side of Paradise." His TV credits include a regular role on *Twelve O'Clock High*, and guest star roles on *Perry Mason* and *One Step Beyond*. Film credits include *The Last Mile* ('59).

Owan eggs — type of food mentioned in *TNG* episode "Time Squared." Pulaski and Geordi don't like them.

Oxmyx, Bela — one of the bosses in Classic episode "A Piece of the Action." He runs the northside territory and is played by Anthony Caruso.

Ozaba, Dr. — one of the researchers who disappeared from the research station on Minara II, in Classic episode "The Empath." He dies after the Vians apparently torture him. He was played by David Roberts.

Ozols-Graham, Venita — first assistant director on *DS9* "Emissary."

P

Pacara VI — world where Troi was attending a neuropsychology seminar when Romulan Subcommander N'Vek abducted her in *TNG* episode "Face of the Enemy."

Pacifica — the *Enterprise* is en route to this ocean planet in *TNG* episode "Conspiracy." In "Manhunt" it is referred to as a conference planet.

Pagh — Riker serves on this Klingon ship as part of an officer-exchange program in *TNG* episode "A Matter of Honor." It is commanded by Captain Kargan. It also appears in "Sins of the Father."

Pakleds — humanoid race in *TNG* episode "Samaritan Snare." They want to tap the *Enterprise*'s computers, having stolen from others, including the Klingons and Romulans, in the past.

Palamas, Carolyn — archaeology and anthropology officer of the *Enterprise* who joins the landing party in Classic episode "Who Mourns for Adonais?" She falls in love with Apollo but betrays him to save the ship. She was played by Leslie Parrish.

Pallas 14 system — from animated episode "One of Our Planets Is Missing," this system contains Alondra, Bezaride, and Mantilles and is located on the fringe of the galaxy. Alondra is destroyed by a cosmic cloud that ingests it for food/energy.

Palmer, Charles — played a Vulcan litterbearer in

Classic *Trek* "Amok Time." His credits include *Little Gloria: Happy at Last* ('82).

Palmer, Dr. — member of the Mintakan station who escapes with Riker in *TNG* episode "Who Watches the Watchers." He is played by Tim Trella.

Palmer, Lieutenant — communications officer who relieves Uhura in Classic episodes "The Doomsday Machine" and "The Way to Eden." She is played by Elizabeth Rogers. Another Lt. Palmer, played by Dr. Mae Jemison, appears in the *TNG* episode "Second Chances."

Pandro — located in the Garo VII system and home-world of Commander Ari bn Bem as mentioned in animated episode "Bem." This world is very advanced in medical technology.

Par Lenor — one of the Ferengi representatives of the Ferengi Trade Mission who sneaks aboard the *Enterprise* in *TNG* episode "The Perfect Mate." He was played by Max Grodenchik.

Paradise Syndrome, The — written by Margaret Armen and directed by Jud Taylor, this third-season Classic *Trek* episode aired 10/4/68. On an idyllic planet, Kirk inadvertently activates an alien device, falls through the ground door, and is knocked unconscious. Meanwhile, an asteroid is hurtling toward the world, populated by peaceful Native American–type people. The *Enterprise*, unable to find Kirk, is forced to leave him behind and attempts to destroy the asteroid, a move which disables the ship. Kirk lives on the world with the native people for about two months while suffering total amnesia. He even marries a woman named Miramanee. (It is the first time Kirk is known to marry. The second time occurs prior to *Star Trek: The Motion Picture* when Kirk marries Vice Admiral Lori Ciani in a contractual marriage that lasts temporarily. Lori later dies in a transporter malfunction.) Guest stars: Sabrina Scharf, Rudy Solari, Richard Hale,

Sean Morgan, and Lamont Laird. Of note: There is a fairly intense mind meld between Kirk and Spock at the end of the episode.

Parallax Colony — colony on Shereleus VI which has mud baths, jugglers, dancers, and other interesting entertainments. Lwaxana Troi re-creates this world on the holodeck in *TNG* episode "Cost of Living."

Pardek, Senator — Romulan statesman in *TNG* episode "Unification." He was supposedly working with Spock on peace between the Romulans and the Federation but was really a spy for the Romulan government. He was played by Malachi Throne.

Parker, Sachi — played Krola in *TNG* episode "First Contact."

Parliament — destination of *Enterprise* in *TNG* episode "Lonely among Us." It is a planet comparable to Babel and belongs to the Federation.

Parmen — leader of the Platonians who is dying from a simple cut which became infected in Classic episode "Plato's Stepchildren." When McCoy cures him, he wants to keep him on Platonius as their doctor. He was played by Liam Sullivan.

Parrises Squares — Tasha and Worf play this game in *TNG* episode "11001001."

Parrish, Julie — played Miss Piper in Classic *Trek* "The Menagerie." TV credits include a regular role on *Good Morning, World*. Film credits include: *The Time Machine* ('78), *When She Was Bad . . .* ('70), and *The Devil and Max Devlin* ('81).

Parrish, Leslie — played Lt. Carolyn Palamas in Classic *Trek* "Who Mourns for Adonais?" Film credits include *Li'l Abner* ('59) and *Banyon*. TV credits include *Perry Mason* and *The Man from U.N.C.L.E.*

Parros, Peter — played the tactics officer in *TNG* "A Matter of Honor."

***Parrot's Claw* case** — mentioned in *TNG* episode "Manhunt" as a Dixon Hill case on the holodeck.

Parsons, Lindsley, Jr. — executive in charge of production on *Star Trek: The Motion Picture*. He also worked on the films *Al Capone* and *The Purple Gang*.

Parsons, Nancy — played Marouk in *TNG* "The Vengeance Factor."

parsteel — in *TNG* episode "The Measure of a Man," Data bends a rod made of this substance. It has a tensile strength of 40 kilobars.

parthus — green vegetable from Acamar III. Yuta cooks with it in *TNG* episode "The Vengeance Factor."

particle fountain — experimental mining technology used at Tyrus VIIA in *TNG* episode "Quality of Life."

Parton, Regina — stunt double for Nona in Classic *Trek* "A Private Little War."

Partridge, Derek — played Dionyd in Classic *Trek* "Plato's Stepchildren." His film credits include *The Ivory Ape* and *Savage Harvest*.

Parvenium system — system being scanned by the *Enterprise* when they encounter the Katan probe in *TNG* episode "The Inner Light."

Paskey, Eddie — played Lt. Leslie in Classic *Trek* "The Conscience of the King," "The Return of the Archons," "This Side of Paradise," "The Alternative Factor," and "The Omega Glory." He also played a security guard in "Where No Man Has Gone Before" and an Eminiar guard in "A Taste of Armageddon."

"Passenger, The" — first-season *DS9* episode written by Morgan Gendel, Robert Hewitt Wolfe, and Michael

Piller, directed by Paul Lynch. An alien named Vantakar, who was guilty of using his science illegally and was sought as a murderer, is found dead but his entity takes over Bashir. Meanwhile, Odo must contend with a Starfleet security officer he is ordered to work with. Guest stars: Caitlin Brown, James Lashly, Christopher Collins, and James Harper.

"Past Prologue" — first-season *DS9* episode written by Kathryn Powell and directed by Winrich Kolbe. A Bajoran terrorist and a member of the group to which Kira used to belong boards *DS9* asking for asylum from the Cardassians. The terrorist, however, continues to wage war against the Cardassians, and when Kira refuses to help him murder people, he tells her she is not a true patriot. They fight when she tries to stop him. Guest stars: Jeffrey Nordling, Andrew Robinson, Gwynyth Walsh, Barbara March, Susan Bay, Vaughn Armstrong, and Richard Ryder.

pasta à la fiarella — food Geordi serves to Worf on *DS9* in *TNG* episode "Birthright," but the replicators make it taste wrong. Worf, however, loves it.

Patakh — Romulan who survives the crash on the Galorndon Core and needs a transfusion of ribosomes from Worf, who refuses, in *TNG* episode "The Enemy." He is played by Steve Rankin.

Pataki, Michael — played the Klingon Korax in Classic *Trek* "The Trouble with Tribbles" and Karnas in *TNG* "Too Short a Season." His TV credits include a regular role on *Paul Sand in Friends and Lovers, Get Christie Love!, The Amazing Spiderman*, and *Phyl and Mikhy* as well as guest roles in *Voyage to the Bottom of the Sea* and others. Film credits include *Dead and Buried* and *Sweet Sixteen*.

Patches — Jeremy Aster's calico cat, who disappears in *TNG* episode "The Bonding."

Patrick, Christian — played the transporter technician in Classic *Trek* "The Alternative Factor."

Patrick, Randall — played crewman #1 in *TNG* "Evolution."

"Patterns of Force" — written by John Meredyth Lucas and directed by Vince McEveety, this second-season Classic *Trek* episode aired 2/16/68. On the planet Ekos, a Nazi-like culture has developed due to the interference of cultural observer John Gill. Gill acts as Führer of the planet but turns out to be drugged, his image used as a puppet by a more evil man, Melakon. Kirk and Spock must try to stop Ekos from warring against another planet, Zeon. Guest stars: David Brian, Skip Homeier, Richard Evans, Valora Norland, William Wintersole, Patrick Horgan, Ralph Maurer, and Gilbert Green.

Paul, Barbara — author of Classic *Trek* novel *The Three-Minute Universe*.

Paulson Nebula — in *TNG* episode "The Best of Both Worlds," the *Enterprise* enters this nebula to avoid the Borg. The nebula consists of 82 percent dilithium hydroxyls, magnesium, and chromium.

Pavlik, Ensign — *Enterprise* junior officer in *TNG* episodes "Galaxy's Child" and "Disaster." She is played by Jana Marie Hupp.

Paxans — xenophobic race encountered in *TNG* episode "Clues." They cause a memory loss in the *Enterprise* crew so the race will not be discovered by other people. They also contemplate destroying the ship if this tactic does not work.

Paz, Joe — played a Vulcan litterbearer in Classic *Trek* "Amok Time." He also appears in the 1959 movie *Never Steal Anything Small*.

"Peak Performance" — second-season *TNG* episode written by David Kemper and directed by Robert Scheerer. The *Enterprise* is involved in war games with the *Hathaway* that turn real when a Ferengi vessel arrives.

Guest stars: Roy Brocksmith, Armin Shimerman, Leslie Neale, Glenn Morshower, and David L. Lander.

Pecheur, Sierra — played T'Pel in *TNG* episode "Data's Day."

Peck, Ed — played Colonel Fellini in Classic *Trek* "Tomorrow Is Yesterday." He also played Officer Kirk in the TV series *Happy Days* and acted in *Major Dell Conway of the Flying Tigers*, *The Super*, and *Semi-Tough*. He was in the 1982 movie *Zoot Suit*.

Peddler — hologram salesman created by the Minosians, who peddles weapons in *TNG* episode "The Arsenal of Freedom." He was played by Vincent Schiavelli.

Peek, Russ — played a Vulcan executioner in Classic *Trek* "Amok Time."

Peeples, Ensign — *Enterprise* junior officer who appears in *TNG* episode "Night Terrors." He was played by Craig Hurley.

Peeples, Samuel A. — scriptwriter of Classic *Trek* "Where No Man Has Gone Before" and the animated episode "Beyond the Farthest Star." He also scripted episodes for *The Girl from U.N.C.L.E.* and *Rawhide* as well as the move script of the Roddenberry-produced *Spectre*. He wrote and produced the 1978 film *A Real American Hero*.

Pegos Minor system — Manheim's distress signal is relayed to this system in *TNG* episode "We'll Always Have Paris."

Peliar Zel — governed by Leka Trion, the world has two moons, Alpha and Beta, who require Ambassador Odan to mediate for them in *TNG* episode "The Host."

Pelius V — destination of the *Enterprise* in *TNG* episode "11001001."

"Pen Pals" — second-season *TNG* episode written by Melinda M. Snodgrass and Hannah Louise Shearer, directed by Winrich Kolbe. Data hears a distress signal from a child and breaks the Prime Directive to help save her life. Guest stars: Nicholas Cascone, Nikki Cox, Ann Gillespie, Whitney Rydbeck, and Colm Meaney.

Pendleton, Chief — mentioned as an *Enterprise* communications officer in *TNG* episode "Aquiel."

Penn, Leo — director of Classic *Trek* "The Enemy Within." He has also directed for the TV shows *The Bionic Woman, Lost in Space, Remington Steele,* and *Voyage to the Bottom of the Sea.*

Pentarus II — world with a moon on which the shuttle *Nenebek* crashes in *TNG* episode "The Final Mission."

Pentarus V — where Picard is headed to mediate a miners' dispute in *TNG* episode "The Final Mission."

Penthara IV — in *TNG* episode "A Matter of Time," an asteroid hits this world, causing the temperature to lower significantly. The *Enterprise* reverses the damages.

Penthor Mul — Gatherer leader who died 50 years before *TNG* episode "The Vengeance Factor."

"Perfect Mate, The" — fifth-season *TNG* episode written by René Echevarria, Reuben Leder, and Michael Piller, directed by Cliff Bole. The Kriosian ambassador's peace offering to Valt Minor turns out to be a metamorph being named Kamala, who can adjust herself to be the perfect mate for any man. She comes out of stasis, however, before her scheduled time and falls in love with Picard. Once metamorphed into his perfect mate, she cannot change, but pretends to so she can fulfill her duty to Valt Minor. Guest stars: Famke Janssen, Tim O'Connor, Max Grodenchik, Mickey Cottrell, Michael Snyder, April Grace, David Paul Needles, Roger Rignack, and Charles Gunning.

pergium — one of the minerals mined on Janius VI in Classic episode "Devil in the Dark."

Pericules — species of Ferengi flower, the Zan Periculi species, native to Lappa IV. Tog gives some to Lwaxana while trying to woo her in *TNG* episode "Ménage à Troi."

Perkins, Jack — played Master of the Games in Classic *Trek* "Bread and Circuses." His TV guest appearances include *Hart to Hart* and *The Young Rebels*. Film credits include: *Killer Bees* ('74) and *Night Shift* ('82).

Perna, Dave — stunt double for Spock in Classic *Trek* "Amok Time" and "A Private Little War."

Perrin — Sarek's wife in *TNG* episode "Sarek" and "Unification." She is human, as was his first wife Amanda. She is played by Joanna Miles.

Perrin, Vic — played the voice of Balok in Classic *Trek* "The Corbomite Maneuver," the Metron's voice in "Arena," Nomad's voice in "The Changeling," and Tharn in "Mirror, Mirror." He was in the 1969 film *Dragnet*, the 1975 films *The Abduction of Saint Anne*, and *The UFO Incident*. He has guest starred on such TV shows as *Perry Mason*.

Perry, Jo — scriptwriter of *TNG* episode "Reunion" with Thomas Perry, Drew Deighan, Ronald D. Moore, and Brannon Braga.

Perry, Joyce — scriptwriter of the animated episode "The Time Trap."

Perry, Rod — played the security officer in *Star Trek: The Motion Picture*. His TV credits include a regular role in *SWAT*. He has also appeared in the 1974 movie *The Autobiography of Miss Jane Pittman* and the 1974 film *Trapped Beneath the Sea*.

Perry, Roger — played Captain John Christopher in Classic *Trek* "Tomorrow Is Yesterday." He has guest starred on the TV shows *The Bionic Woman* and *Barnaby Jones*, and has had regular roles on such series as *Harrington and Son*, *Arrest and Trial*, *The Facts of Life*, and *Falcon Crest*. He is married to Joanne Worley of *Laugh In* fame.

Perry, Thomas — scriptwriter of *TNG* episode "Reunion" with Jo Perry, Drew Deighan, Ronald D. Moore, and Brannon Braga.

Persephone V — planet from which Admiral Mark Jameson is picked up in *TNG* episode "Too Short a Season."

Persoff, Nehemiah — played Toff in *TNG* episode "The Most Toys."

Personnel Officer — in Classic episode "Court-Martial," she testifies against Kirk. She was played by Nancy Wong.

Peterman, Donald — director of photography in *The Voyage Home*. He has also worked on the films *King of the Mountain*, *Rich and Famous*, *Kiss Me Goodbye*, and *Flashdance*.

Peterman, Keith — camera operator on *The Voyage Home*.

Peters, Brock — played Admiral Cartwright in *The Voyage Home* and *The Undiscovered Country*. Born in 1927, his film credits include *Porgy and Bess* ('59), *To Kill a Mockingbird* ('62), and *Soylent Green* ('73). He has also appeared on *The Girl from U.N.C.L.E.* and *The Bionic Woman*.

Peters, Gregg — assistant producer of third season of Classic *Trek*.

Peterson, Cassandra — played Maggie in *The Voyage Home*. She is the assistant who barges in on Scotty and McCoy as they are about to give the polymer plant manager the matrix for transparent aluminum. She is most famous for playing Elvira, Mistress of the Dark.

Peterson, Vidal — played D'Tan in *TNG* episode "Unification, Part II."

Petiet, Christopher — played "boy" in *TNG* "The High Ground."

Petri, Lord — ambassador of Troyius in Classic episode "Elaan of Troyius." Elaan stabs Petri, who swears not to have anything to do with her, forcing Kirk to take over in teaching her "manners." He was played by Jay Robinson.

Pettyjohn, Angelique — played Shahna in Classic *Trek* "The Gamesters of Triskelion." Her TV credits include *Batman* and *The Man from U.N.C.L.E.* She made many convention appearances in her Shahna costume in the 1980s and often worked in Las Vegas. She died of cancer in 1991.

Pevney, Joseph — director of Classic *Trek* "Arena," "The Return of the Archons," "A Taste of Armageddon," "Devil in the Dark," "The City on the Edge of Forever," "Amok Time," "The Apple," "Catspaw," "Journey to Babel," "Friday's Child," "The Deadly Years," "Wolf in the Fold," "The Trouble with Tribbles," and "The Immunity Syndrome." Born in 1920 in New York, he worked in vaudeville before becoming a TV actor. His directing credits include *Air Cadet* ('51), *Away All Boats* ('56), and *The Night of the Grizzly* ('66). TV directing credits include *Petrocelli*.

Phase — menopause for female Betazeds. During this "phase" their sex drive is increased four times over. Lwaxana Troi is at the height of her Phase in *TNG* episode "Manhunt."

Phase 1 Search — *Enterprise* search conducted in Classic episode "Court-Martial" to find Finney. This type of search presupposes a person is hurt or sick and cannot answer. It does not presume the person is intentionally eluding the search, which Finney was doing.

Phase 7 Survey — in *TNG* episode "Relics," this kind of survey is conducted by the *Enterprise* on the Dyson sphere.

phase inverter — tool used by Geordi in *TNG* episode "Time Squared" to get information from a shuttlepod's logs. The device is also mentioned in "The Next Phase."

phaser — weapon that looks like a laser but can be put

on stun or disintegrate modes. Hand phasers have several different settings and come in a phaser gun form, pistol form (hand phaser type 2), and the little box form (hand phaser type 1). Phasers do not seem to have changed much throughout the different series, although the hand phasers take on slightly different shapes.

phaser coolant — pink gas in Classic episode "Balance of Terror" which kills Tomlinson.

phaser range — target range on the holodeck which appears in *TNG* episode "A Matter of Honor."

Pheban System — in *TNG* episode "A Matter of Honor," the *Pagh* undergoes undesignated maneuvers here.

Phelan system — in *TNG* episode "The Outcast," the destination of the *Enterprise* to negotiate a trade agreement.

Phelps, Win — director of *TNG* episode "Symbiosis."

Philana — Parmen's wife in Classic episode "Plato's Stepchildren." She is 2,300 years old but stopped aging at 30. She was played by Barbara Babcock.

Philips, Robert — played the Orion space officer in Classic *Trek* pilot "The Cage" and "The Menagerie." TV credits include *Planet of the Apes*, and the films *Yuma*, *The Gun and the Pulpit*, and *The Ultimate Imposter*.

Phillips, Astrobiologist — recommended as a member of the landing party on Alpha Carinai II by both Kirk and the M–5 computer in Classic episode "The Ultimate Computer."

Phillips, Ethan — played Dr. Farek on *TNG* episode "Ménage à Troi."

Phillips, Fred B. — makeup artist on Classic *Trek* as well as *Star Trek: The Motion Picture*. He also worked as a makeup artist on the series *Stoney Burke*.

Phillips, Janna — makeup artist on *Star Trek: The Motion Picture*. She is the daughter of Fred Phillips.

Phillips, Michelle — played Janice Manheim in *TNG* "We'll Always Have Paris." She is a well-known actress who has done much television and film work.

Phillips, Ralph — scriptwriter of *TNG* episode "Suddenly Human."

Phillips, William F. — associate producer on *The Wrath of Khan*. He has also worked on the films *Richie Brockelman, The Night Rider,* and *Listen to Your Heart*.

Phoenix, USS — Nebula class starship NCC–55420 captained by Benjamin Maxwell in *TNG* episode "The Vengeance Factor."

Phoenix Cluster — in *TNG* episode "The Game," the *Enterprise* is conducting scientific studies here.

photon torpedoes — projectiles which the *Enterprise* has the capability of using to defend itself. They look like large blasts of light and explode on impact.

Phylos — planet where the *Enterprise* encounters Dr. Keniclius in animated episode "The Infinite Vulcan." Its natives are plantlike people.

Phyrox plague — ravaged Cor Caroli V as mentioned in *TNG* episode "Allegiance."

Pi — Romulan scout vessel which crashed on the Galorndon Core uses this code name in *TNG* episode "The Enemy."

Piano Player — one of the holodeck bands in *TNG* episode "11001001," played by Jack Sheldon.

Picard, Jean-Luc, Captain — captain of the *Enterprise* in *The Next Generation*. He is played by Patrick Stewart. His serial number is SP 937 215. His parents are Yvette and Maurice Gessard Picard, and he has a brother, Robert. Prior to duty on the *Enterprise*, Picard served 22 years on the

Stargazer. Born in Paris, France, his hobbies include history and archeology. He also likes to practice on the Resican flute he brought back with him in the episode "The Inner Light." He likes to read detective fiction, is a drama fan (especially of Shakespeare), and has been known to take an art class (part of the plot in "A Matter of Perspective"). A fair man and a decisive leader, he is very good friends with Dr. Crusher, with whom he has breakfast every morning. Another close friend is Guinan, to whom he can reveal indecision, pain, and his personal opinions, traits a captain cannot or should not reveal to his crew. He likes caviar and Earl Grey tea. He has an artificial heart because he was stabbed by Nausicaans while at the Academy (seen in "Tapestry"). He also loves horseback riding (he owns his own saddle), and won a running marathon at the Academy when he was a cadet. He is also a good fencer. He quarters are on deck 9, #3601.

Picard, Marie — Picard's sister-in-law, who has a son named René, in *TNG* episode "Family." She is played by Samantha Eggar.

Picard, Maurice — Picard's father who appears in *TNG* episode "Tapestry."

Picard, René — Picard's nephew, son of Robert and Marie Picard. He wants to go to the stars, like his uncle, in *TNG* episode "Family." He is played by David Tristan Birken.

Picard, Robert — Picard's older brother seen in *TNG* episode "Family." A farmer and vineyard owner, he is married to Marie, and has a son, René. He was played by Jeremy Kemp.

Picard, Yvette Gessard — Picard's mother.

Picard, Maman — old woman who appears in *TNG* episode "Where No One Has Gone Before" to serve Picard tea when the *Enterprise* goes into the Beyond. She was played by Herta Ware.

Pie Man — played by Richard Merson, he appears in *TNG* episode "Elementary, Dear Data."

"Piece of the Action, A" — Written by David P. Harmon and Gene L. Coon, directed by James Komack, this second-season Classic *Trek* episode aired 1/12/68. On the planet Iotia, mobs run the cities. Years ago, the USS *Horizon* inadvertently influenced the natives by leaving behind a book called *Chicago Mobs of the Twenties*. The *Enterprise* is sent to study the effects of this "infection" and becomes embroiled in the plots of some mobsters to take over the planet. Guest stars: William Blackburn, Anthony Caruso, Victor Tayback, Lee Delano, Steve Marlo, John Harmon, and Sheldon Collins. Of note: Kirk invents a complicated and ingenious card game called fizzbin.

Pike, Donald — stunt coordinator on *The Undiscovered Country*.

Pike, Christopher, Captain — captain of the *Enterprise* seen in the first Classic pilot "The Cage" and played by Jeffrey Hunter. He is from Mojave, California, and once had a horse named Tango. He wanted to leave the *Enterprise* because he was tired, and ended up retiring horribly scarred for life when he tried to rescue some cadets and was exposed to radiation. The scarred Pike was played by Sean Kenney. He is taken to Talos IV by Spock so he can live with Vina, with whom he fell in love in "The Cage," and not be encumbered by his useless body. He is mentioned as having been assassinated by Kirk in the Mirror universe in "Mirror, Mirror."

Pike — shuttlepod 12 from the *Enterprise* that explodes in *TNG* episode "The Most Toys." It is named after Captain Christopher Pike.

Pillar, Gary — played Yutan in Classic *Trek* "A Private Little War."

Piller, Michael — executive producer on *TNG*, and creator/executive producer of *DS9*. He wrote the scripts for *DS9* "Emissary," "A Man Alone," "Captive Pursuit," "The Passenger," and the story for "Move Along Home." He also wrote the *TNG* scripts "Evolution," "Booby Trap," "The Enemy," "The Best of Both Worlds, Parts I and II," "First Contact," "Ensign Ro," "Unification, Parts I and II," "The Masterpiece Society," "The Perfect Mate," and "Time's Arrow, Part I." Piller attended the Juilliard School of Music and worked for CBS News. He also wrote and produced for the TV series *Simon and Simon, Cagney and Lacey, Probe,* and *Miami Vice.*

Pillsbury, Garth — played Wilson in Classic *Trek* "Mirror, Mirror" and a prisoner in "The Cloud Minders."

Piloris Asteroid Field — metal parasites consuming the *Enterprise* are brought here in *TNG* episode "Cost of Living."

Pine, Philip — played Colonel Green in Classic *Trek* "The Savage Curtain." Born in 1925, his TV credits include *Barnaby Jones* and *Voyage to the Bottom of the Sea.* He had a regular role on *The Blue Knight,* and appeared in the 1959 film *The Big Fisherman.*

Pinson, Allen — played the policeman in Classic *Trek* "Bread and Circuses."

Piper, Dr. — doctor on board the *Enterprise* in second Classic pilot "Where No Man Has Gone Before." He was played by Paul Fix.

Piper, Miss — assistant to Commodore Mendez in Classic episode "The Menagerie." She was played by Julie Parrish.

"Pirates of Orion, The" — written by Howard Weinstein, this animated Classic *Trek* episode aired 9/7/74. Spock comes down with a deadly illness, and the only cure is on Beta Canopis, four days away. To save time, they plan to rendezvous with another ship, the *Huron,* which will have picked up the cure, but the *Huron* is attacked before the meeting. The *Enterprise* tracks down the Orion ship that attacked and stole the *Huron's* cargo, and attempts to retrieve the drug in time to save Spock's life.

Piscopo, Joe — actor/comedian who played the Comic in *TNG* "The Outrageous Okona." He is best known for his regular stint on *Saturday Night Live*. He has appeared in films and commercials.

Pistone, Martin — played Starfleet Controller in *The Voyage Home*.

Plak tow — Vulcan word for the blood fever mentioned in Classic episode "Amok Time." It usually appears with the *Pon farr*.

Plakson, Suzie — played Lt. Selar in *TNG* "Unnatural Selection" and K'Ehleyr in "The Emissary" and "Reunion."

Planet Q — where the *Enterprise* picks up the Karidian players. Dr. Tom Leighton lived there with his wife before he was murdered in Classic episode "The Conscience of the King."

plasma plague — mentioned in *TNG* episode "The Child" as a disease with several different strains being studied on Aucdet IX so antidotes can be created. A cure must be found to stop a plague on Rachelis.

Plasus — high advisor to the city in the sky, Stratos, in Classic episode "The Cloud Minders." He has a daughter, Droxine. He was played by Jeff Corey.

"Plato's Stepchildren" — written by Meyer Dolinsky and directed by David Alexander, this third-season Classic *Trek* episode aired 11/22/68. After receiving a distress signal, an *Enterprise* away team beams down to find a planet inhabited by a small group of people with incredible mind powers and long lives who do not have a doctor. They attempt to force McCoy to stay with them by using mind-control on Kirk and Spock and torturing them. Guest stars: Michael Dunn, Liam Sullivan, Barbara Babcock, Ted Scott, and Derek Partridge. Of note: Spock sings "Maiden Wine," and Kirk and Uhura kiss in what is said to be the first inter-racial kiss shown on TV. Consequently, the episode was originally banned by some network affiliate stations.

Platonius — planet where the seemingly ageless Platonians, who came there from Sandara, live. They lived on Earth before moving to Platonius.

Pleasure Haven — where Picard vacations on Risa in *TNG* episode "Captain's Holiday."

Pleiades Cluster — group of seven stars (the seven sisters) in the Taurus constellation. The *Enterprise* is mapping in this area of space before they are diverted to Velara III in *TNG* episode "Home Soil."

***plomeek* soup** — Vulcan dish Chapel brings to Spock's quarters in Classic episode "Amok Time." Supposedly humans find it vile.

Plummer, Christopher — played General Chang in *The Undiscovered Country*. Born in Montreal in 1927, his career spans TV, film, and stage. His most famous roles were in *The Sound of Music*, *International Velvet*, *Somewhere in Time*, *The Return of the Pink Panther*, and *Dragnet*. His daughter, Amanda, is also a successful actress.

Plunkett, Maryann — played Commander Susanna Leitjen in *TNG* episode "Identity Crisis."

Pola — young boy from the *Enterprise* in *TNG* episode "The Last Outpost."

Police Special — type of gun Sulu finds on the recreation planet in Classic episode "Shore Leave."

Policeman — character who catches Kirk and Spock with stolen clothing in Classic episode "The City on the Edge of Forever." Kirk gives him the famous mechanical rice picker story when trying to explain why Spock's ears are pointed. He was played by Hal Baylor.

Polite, Charlene — played Vanna in Classic *Trek*

"The Cloud Minders." She also starred in the 1971 film *Love Hate Love*.

Pollack, Naomi — played Lt. Rahda in Classic *Trek* "That Which Survives," and a Native American woman in "The Paradise Syndrome."

Pollack, Reginald Murray — Earth artist from the 20th century whose work appears in Flint's home in Classic episode "Requiem for Methuselah."

Pollard, Michael J. — played Jahn in Classic *Trek* "Miri." Born in 1939, his TV credits include *Lost in Space*. His films include the 1967 *Bonnie and Clyde*, the 1972 film *Dirty Little Billy*, and *Melvin and Howard*.

Pollux IV — four-billion-year-old Earth-like world Apollo inhabits in Classic episode "Who Mourns for Adonais?"

Pollux V — mentioned in Classic episode "Who Mourns for Adonais?" as a planet devoid of intelligent life but habitable.

Pompet — member of the team trying to steal trilithium in *TNG* episode "Starship Mine."

Pon farr — madness endured by Vulcans once every seven years. When afflicted, they must mate or die. Spock suffers from *Pon farr* in Classic episode "Amok Time."

Porman V — where Picard, Crusher, and Worf go in a shuttlecraft en route to Seltris III in *TNG* episode "Chain of Command."

Portal, The — protector of the Delphi Ardu in *TNG* episode "The Last Outpost." He is played by Darryl Henriques.

Porter, Brett — played General Stex in *The Undiscovered Country*.

positronic theory — robots in Isaac Asimov's books have positronic brains which allow them to think, learn, and react like humans. This term is borrowed, with permission, from Asimov's robot books to describe Data's brain. It is mentioned in *TNG* episode "Datalore" and "The Measure of a Man," among others.

poteen — Bringloidis like this Earth-brewed alcoholic beverage in *TNG* episode "Up the Long Ladder."

***Potemkin*, USS** — starship that plays war games with the *Enterprise* in Classic episode "The Ultimate Computer." It is also mentioned in "Turnabout Intruder" and the animated episode "The Pirates of Orion." In *TNG*, Riker served as a lieutenant aboard this starship as mentioned in "Peak Performance."

Potenza, Vadia — played Spock at age 13 in *The Search for Spock*.

Potts, Cliff — played Admiral Kennelly in *TNG* episode "Ensign Ro."

Potts, Jake — in *TNG* episode "Brothers," he plays a practical joke on his brother, which endangers his brother's life. He was played by Cory Danziger.

Potts, Willie — in *TNG* episode "Brothers," his life is endangered when his brother Jake plays a practical joke on him. He was played by Adam Ryen.

Povill, Jon — associate producer on *Star Trek: The Motion Picture* and scriptwriter of *TNG* "The Child."

Powell, Kathryn — scriptwriter of *DS9* "Past Prologue."

Powell, Susan — played Marla Aster in *TNG* "The Bonding."

Powell Blair, William — played a Cardassian officer in *DS9* "Emissary."

Power, Stephen — played the chanting monk in *DS9* "Emissary."

"Power Play" — fifth-season *TNG* episode written by

Paul Ruben, Maurice Hurley, René Balcer, Herbert J. Wright, and Brannon Braga, directed by David Livingston. Troi, O'Brien, and Data are possessed by prisoners from an alien moon and take command of the *Enterprise* by taking hostages in Ten Forward. Speaking through the officers, the prisoners demand their fellow prisoners be released from the moon where they have existed as energy forms for 500 years. Guest stars: Rosalind Chao, Michelle Forbes, and Colm Meaney.

Powers, Kathryn — scriptwriter of *TNG* "Code of Honor."

"Practical Joker" — written by Chuck Menville, this animated Classic *Trek* episode aired 9/21/74. The *Enterprise* hides in a cloud to avoid a Romulan attack, only to have the cloud invade their humidity system. All sorts of strange things occur as a result: The food processors screw up, forks bend, and Spock gets black rings around his eyes while looking into a viewer. Guest voices: James Doohan (Arex, Romulan Commander, Crewman) and Majel Barrett (M'Ress).

Praetor — title of the Romulan's leader.

P'Rang — Klingon ship following the *Enterprise* in *TNG* episode "The Emissary."

Praxillus — Dr. Timicin unsuccessfully attempts his theory for helium ignition on this star in *TNG* episode "Half a Life."

Prendergast, Gerard — played Bjorn Bensen in *TNG* "Home Soil."

Preservers, The — race of beings who seeded many worlds with humanoid species, which may be an answer to Hodgkins' Law of Parallel Development (since there are so many planets containing human life in the galaxy). They built the obelisk on the planet Amerind in Classic episode "The Paradise Syndrome." No one has ever seen or met a Preserver.

Preston, Peter — young engineering technician who is killed in Khan's first attack in *The Wrath of Khan*. He is mentioned in the novelization as being Scotty's nephew. He is mourned as a hero because he died in an attempt to save others. He was played by Ike Eisenmann.

"Price, The" — third-season *TNG* episode written by Hannah Louise Shearer and directed by Robert Scheerer. The *Enterprise* hosts a delegation convened to negotiate for rights to the Barzan wormhole, which turns out to be useless after all. Guest stars: Matt McCoy, Elizabeth Hoffman, Castulo Guerra, Scott Thomson, Kevin Peter Hall, Dan Shor, and Colm Meaney.

Prieto, Ben — in *TNG* episode "Skin of Evil," he was the pilot of shuttlepod 13 who is almost killed when the ship crashed on Veigra II. He was played by Raymond Forchion.

Prime Directive — also known as General Order Number One, it forbids anyone from interfering with the natural development of an alien civilization. It is often violated when danger to the alien people or the Federation itself is imminent, although at times even that is not considered a good enough reason to interfere.

Primmin — Starfleet security officer who comes to *DS9* to work with Odo (much to Odo's irritation) in *DS9* episode "The Passenger." He is played by James Lashly.

Prine, Andrew — guest starred in *TNG* episode "Frame of Mind."

Priority 2 Signal — used in *TNG* episode "Chain of Command" by Jellico to notify Admiral Nechayev that Picard has been captured by the Cardassians on Seltris III.

Priority A — distress call on channel 1 used in Classic episode "The Trouble with Tribbles." It puts a whole quadrant on alert.

"Private Little War, A" — Written by Gene Roddenberry and Judd Crucis, directed by Marc Daniels, this second-season Classic *Trek* episode aired 2/2/68. Spock is shot by a native on Neural, and the *Enterprise* discovers that this peaceful society, first explored 13 years before, is being interfered with by Klingons. Kirk, who was part of the initial exploration team, goes back to meet the people he knows and tries to help them. Guest stars: Michael Whitney, Nancy Kovack, Booker Marshall, Arthur Bernard, Ned Romero, Gary Pillar, and Janos Prohaska. Of note: Dr. M'Benga makes an appearance, and we learn about Vulcan healing trances.

Procedure Q — used in Classic episode "Bread and Circuses," it cautions that the planet is extremely hostile and the landing party should beam down fully armed.

Proconsul — title for a Romulan head of state in *TNG* episode "Unification."

Progenitors, The — supposedly built the Custodian on Aldea as seen in *TNG* episode "When the Bough Breaks."

progressive encryption lock — state-of-the-art device for communicating in code in *TNG* episode "Unification."

Prohaska, Janos — played the Horta in Classic *Trek* "Devil in the Dark" and the Mugato in "A Private Little War." He has played monsters on many TV shows including *Lost in Space*, *The Outer Limits*, and *Voyage to the Bottom of the Sea*. He regularly played a bear on *The Andy Griffith Show*.

Prokop, Paul — played a guard in Classic *Trek* "Mirror, Mirror."

Promellians — ancient beings who fought a war with the Menthars. The *Clepjoni*, encountered in *TNG* episode "Booby Trap," is a Promellian battlecruiser which is caught in a Menthar booby trap amid the debris of the destroyed world Orelious IX.

Promenade — level of *DS9* where Quark's bar and gambling casino are located, as well as other shops and food vendors.

promethean quartz — Vash's orange crystal, which she brought back from the Gamma Quadrant in *DS9* episode "Q Less," looks like this substance according to one of the *DS9* personnel.

Prostitute — appears on the holodeck "Holmes" simulation in *TNG* episode "Elementary, Dear Data." She was played by Diz White.

Proto Star Cloud — location, near Tanuga, where the *Enterprise* is headed in *TNG* episode "A Matter of Perspective."

Protodynoplaser — medical tool that stabilizes John's immune system in *TNG* episode "Transfigurations."

Providers — aliens who run the "games" on Triskelion in Classic episode "The Gamesters of Triskelion." They have evolved until they are mere brains contained in a glass case. They bet on the outcome of the games for entertainment.

proximity detectors — used by the gangs on Turkana IV to warn of approaching enemies in *TNG* episode "Legacy."

Psi 2000 — planet visited by the *Enterprise* in Classic episode "The Naked Time." It contains a virus that causes people's deepest desires and personas to surface. The *Enterprise* encounters this virus again in *TNG* episode "The Naked Now," calling it the Psi 2000 Virus.

psychotech — mentioned in Classic episode "Wolf in the Fold" as someone who is trained to run a psychotricorder.

psychotricorder — device which can play back a person's actions from the past. One is going to be used on Scotty in Classic episode "Wolf in the Fold," but the psychotech is killed.

psychotronic stability examination — Troi gives Data this test in *TNG* episode "The Schizoid Man" when Picard suspects something is wrong with him.

Pulaski, Katherine, Dr. — chief medical officer of the *Enterprise* during *TNG*'s second season, played by Diana Muldaur. She previously served aboard the USS *Repulse*. She wrote a book, *Linear Models of Viral Propagation* (see entry), has been married three times, and had an affair with Kyle Riker. She likes to argue emotions with Data, play poker, and is fascinated by Worf.

Pulford, Don — stunt double for Kirk in *The Final Frontier*.

Punishment Zone — forbidden zone on Rubicam III chosen randomly by the Mediators. Trespassing into this area is punishable by death.

Putch, John — played Mendon in *TNG* "A Matter of Honor."

PXK reactor — used on Janus VI as a power source in Classic episode "Devil in the Dark." The Horta steals its main circulating pump, causing the power to go out.

Pyne, Francine — played the younger Nancy Crater in Classic *Trek* "The Man Trap."

Pyris VII — class M planet where Kirk and crew meet Sylvia and Korob in Classic episode "Catspaw."

pyrocytes, blood — cells found in Ferengi blood that cause allergic reactions in other people in *TNG* episode "The Price."

Q — supposedly omnipotent being, and Picard's nemesis, who troubles the *Enterprise* with his strange sense of humor and jokes, often causing them harm in the process. He appears in many *TNG* episodes and one *DS9* episode to date. He has said he is a Klingon at heart and his I.Q. level is 2005. He comes from somewhere called the Q continuum and supposedly knows Guinan from another time. He is played by John DeLancie.

Q2 — another Q being with great powers. He appears in *TNG* episode "Déjà Q" and is played by Corbin Bernsen.

qapla — Klingon word meaning "success." It is used in *TNG* episodes "Sins of the Father" and "Aquiel."

Q Continuum — unknown place (or dimension) where the omnipotent Q beings exist. See entry for Q.

Q. E. II — cruise ship from the 20th century. The letters stand for Queen Elizabeth. Offenhouse compares this ship to the *Enterprise* in *TNG* episode "The Neutral Zone."

"Q Less" — first-season *DS9* episode written by Robert Hewitt Wolfe and Hannah Louise Shearer, directed by Paul Lynch. Vash arrives on the station with some rare archeological relics at the same time as Q, who purposely annoys Sisko. Guest stars: John deLancie, Jennifer Hetrick, Van Epperson, Tom McLeister, and Laura Cameron.

Q'Maire — Talarian warship captained by Endar in *TNG* episode "Suddenly Human."

"Qpid" — fourth-season *TNG* episode written by Randee Russell and Ira Steven Behr, directed by Cliff Bole. Q reappears and involves Picard and some of his officers in a Robin Hood scenario, making Picard play Robin and Vash play Maid Marian. Guest stars: John deLancie, Jennifer Hetrick, Clive Revill, and Joi Staton.

Q, Planet — see entry for Planet Q.

Quadra Sigma III — in *TNG* episode "Hide and Q," world on which a mining accident occurred.

Quadrant 904 — where the *Enterprise* is traveling when they discover Gothos in Classic episode "The Squire of Gothos."

quadratanium — another element from which Data and Lore were made, mentioned in *TNG* episode "Datalore."

quadrotriticale — four-lobed, hybrid grain stored on Space Station *K–7* for Sherman's planet in Classic episode "The Trouble with Tribbles."

Quaice, Dalen, Dr. — Beverly Crusher's mentor under whom she served her residency on Delos IV. He is about to retire when the *Enterprise* picks him up at Starbase *133* in *TNG* episode "Remember Me." He wife, Patricia, has just died. He was played by Bill Erwin.

"Quality of Life, The" — sixth-season *TNG* episode written by Naren Shankar and directed by Jonathan Frakes. Data believes Dr. Farallon's exocomp robots act as independent life-forms and should have the right not to be forced into deadly situations. Guest star: Ellen Bry.

Qualor II — in *TNG* episode "Unification," location of the orbital surplus depot Zed 15.

quantum filament — in *TNG* episode "Disaster," the *Enterprise* hits a quantum filament in space, supposedly a very rare thing to happen.

quantum singularity — Romulan ships' source of power mentioned in *TNG* episode "Face of the Enemy" and "Timescape."

Quark — regular character on *DS9*, played by Armin Shimerman. A greedy Ferengi, he runs the bar and gambling casino on the Promenade level of *DS9* with his brother Rom, whose son Nog is also a regular character. Quark also runs *DS9*'s holosuites, where any fantasy can be played out. He has shown himself to be a coward on a number of occasions, but has also shown some guilt for actions which might cause harm to others. He and Odo openly quarrel but are also tentative friends. He has an obvious lust for Dax and sometimes even Kira. While Dax likes the Ferengi and finds the race amusing and entertaining (she has been known to play cards and gamble with them), Kira has threatened Quark's life on a number of occasions should he ever touch her.

quatloos — monetary unit used by the Triskelions for betting on the games in Classic episode "The Gamesters of Triskelion."

Quazulu VII — Wesley and his friends picked up a virus here that infects the *Enterprise* in *TNG* episode "Angel One."

Questar M17 — negative star which pulls the *Enterprise* toward it in animated episode "Beyond the Farthest Star."

Quin'lat — ancient Klingon city referred to by Kahless in *TNG* episode "Rightful Heir."

Quinn, Gregory, Admiral — Starfleet admiral who appears in *TNG* episodes "Coming of Age" and "Conspiracy." He is possessed by parasites and is the only Starfleet officer to survive such an infliction. He was played by Ward Costello.

Quinteros, Orfil — commander of Starbase 74. He

helped design the *Galaxy*-class ships mentioned in *TNG* episode "11001001." He was played by Gene Dynarski.

quintotriticale — mutation of quadrotriticale (see entry), a five-lobed plant, resistant to most disease, developed for Sherman's Planet in animated episode "More Tribbles, More Troubles."

Quist, Gerald — makeup artist on *TNG*.

Quol — Ferengi who appears in *TNG* episode "The Perfect Mate." He is played by Michael Snyder.

"Q Who" — second-season *TNG* episode written by Maurice Hurley and directed by Rob Bowman. Q sends the *Enterprise* far into an unexplored region of the galaxy where they have their first encounter with the destructive Borg race. Guest stars: John deLancie, Whoopi Goldberg, Lycia Naff, and Colm Meaney.

Rabo — hunter from Mintaka in *TNG* episode "Who Watches the Watchers."

Rachelis system — in *TNG* episode "The Child," inhabitants of this system are suffering from a deadly plague.

Rad, Tongo — one of the gang in Classic episode "The Way to Eden." He is the son of a Catullan ambassador. He was played by Victor Brandt.

radans — jewels from Troyius which are actually raw dilithium in Classic episode "Elaan of Troyius."

Radley, Liz — video consultant on *DS9*.

Radue — in *TNG* episode "When the Bough Breaks," he is the Aldean leader who does not believe his race is dying from radiation exposure. He was played by Jerry Hardin.

Rael — Scalosian leader in love with Deela, but because of his sterility he must allow her to marry another in order to bear children and help save their dying race. He is played by Jason Evers in Classic episode "Wink of an Eye."

Rager, Ensign — *Enteprise* bridge officer in *TNG* episodes "Night Terrors," "Relics," and "Schisms." She was played by Lanei Chapman.

Rahm Izad system — mentioned by Dr. Crusher as the location of the missing clue to the micropaleontology mystery. It turns out to be a false clue, in *TNG* episode "The Chase."

Rakal, Major — Romulan in the Tal Shiar security service killed by the Romulan underground in *TNG* episode "Face of the Enemy." Troi impersonates her.

Rakar — world, located in the Gamma Quadrant, whose inhabitants are looking for the convict Crodon in *DS9* episode "Vortex."

Ral, Devinoni — representative hired by the Chrysalians to negotiate in the Barzan wormhole affair in *TNG* episode "The Price." He is 41 and is one-fourth Betazoid and an empath. He was born in Brussels as part of the European Alliance and has lived since age 19 on Hurkos III.

Ralston, Gilbert — scriptwriter of Classic *Trek* episode "Who Mourns for Adonais?"

Ralston, Ken — visual effects supervisor on *The Voyage Home*.

Ramart, Captain — captain of the *Antares* which discovered Charlie in Classic episode "Charlie X." Later, Charlie destroys the ship with his mind powers. Ramart is played by Charles J. Stewart.

Ramatis III — mediator on Riva's homeworld in *TNG* episode "Loud As a Whisper."

Ramos — *Enterprise* security officer who dies in *TNG* episode "Heart of Glory." He was played by Dennis Madalone.

Ramsay, Todd — film editor on *Star Trek: The Motion Picture*. He also worked on the films *The Thing* and *Escape from New York*.

Ramsey, Ann Elizabeth — played Clancy in *TNG* episodes "Elementary, Dear Data" and "The Emissary."

Ramsey, Captain — in *TNG* episode "Angel One," he and his crew are fugitives on Angel One. His ship, the SS *Odin*, crashed on Asphia.

Ramsey, Logan — played Claudius Marcus in Classic *Trek* episode "Bread and Circuses." Born in 1921, his TV appearances include *Petrocelli*, *The Man from U.N.C.L.E.*, *Alias Smith and Jones*, and a regular role on the series *On the Rocks*.

Ramus, Nick — played the helmsman on the USS *Saratoga* in *The Voyage Home*. He had regular roles on *Falcon Crest* and *The Chisholms* and appeared in the film *Windwalker*.

Rana IV — in *TNG* episode "The Survivor," the Husnock attacked and killed all 11,000 people on this world except one. It is mentioned that a tasty tea grew wild on the planet before it was destroyed.

Rand, Janice, Yeoman — Kirk's personal yeoman during first-season Classic *Trek*, played by Grace Lee Whitney. Rand also returns in *The Motion Picture* as the transporter chief. She has a cameo in *The Search for Spock*, and is one of Sulu's bridge crew, Commander Rand, in *The Undiscovered Country*. In first-season *Trek*, she appeared to have a crush on Kirk. Kirk liked her, too, but fought the feelings because he was "married" to his ship.

Randolph, Nancy, Lieutenant — navigator aboard the ship *Ariel* in animated episode "Eye of the Beholder."

Rankin, Steve — played Patakh in *TNG* episode "The Enemy." He also played a Cardassian officer in *DS9* episode "Emissary."

rapakh unguhr — a kind of Klingon measles cured by a ritualistic fasting mentioned in *TNG* episode "Up the Long Ladder."

rape gang — mentioned as a part of Yar's past. On her homeworld of Turkana IV, she was pursued by rape gangs, but survived, as seen in *TNG* episode "Where No One Has Gone Before."

Rapelye, Mary-Linda — played Irini Galliulin in Classic *Trek* episode "The Way to Eden."

Rappaport, Frederick — scriptwriter of *DS9* episode "Move Along Home."

"Rascals" — sixth-season *TNG* episode written by Allison Heck, Ward Botsford, Diana Dru Botsford, and Michael Piller, directed by Adam Nimoy. Picard, Guinan, Ro, and Keiko are on a shuttle which passes through a strange cloud, nearly causing it to break up. As they are beamed aboard the *Enterprise*, the cloud affects their bodies, making them age backward suddenly. All appear on the *Enterprise* in preadolescent bodies but with their adult memories intact. Meanwhile, the Ferengi invade the ship and try to take over. Guest stars: David Tristan Birkin, Brian Bonsall, and Michael Snyder. Of note: Adam Nimoy, Leonard Nimoy's son, makes his *TNG* directorial debut with this episode.

Rashella — in *TNG* episode "When the Bough Breaks," she is an Aldean and an aide to Radu. She adopts Alexander, one of the children kidnapped from the *Enterprise*. She was played by Brenda Strong.

Rasmussen, Berlinghoff — thief who claims to be from the future but is really from the past; he is trying to get future technology to sell in the past. He was played by Matt Frewer in *TNG* episode "A Matter of Time."

Rasulala, Thalmus — played Captain Donald Varley in *TNG* episode "Contagion."

Rata — Ferengi science officer aboard Bok's ship in *TNG* episode "The Battle." He was played by Robert Towers.

Rator III — planet located in the Neutral Zone in animated episode "The Survivor."

Rawlings, Alice — played Jamie Finney in Classic *Trek* episode "Court-Martial."

Rawlings, Phil — unit production manager on *Star Trek: The Motion Picture*. He also worked on the 1959 film *Al Capone*.

Rawlins — *Enterprise* geologist chosen by Kirk for the Alpha Carinae II landing party in Classic episode "The Ultimate Computer."

Rayburn — one of the numerous *Enterprise* security personnel killed on duty. Rayburn dies at the hand of Ruk on Exo III in Classic episode "What Are Little Girls Made Of?" He was played by Budd Albright.

Raymond, Clare — housewife from the 20th century who died of an embolism and was put into cryonic freeze at age 35 in *TNG* episode "The Neutral Zone." She is revived in the 24th century. She had two sons when she died, Eddie and Tommy, aged 8 and 5. She was played by Gracie Harrison.

Raymond, Eddie and Tommy — sons of Clare Raymond mentioned in *TNG* episode "The Neutral Zone." They were born in Secaucus, New Jersey.

Raymond, Guy — played the trader/bartender in Classic *Trek* "The Trouble with Tribbles." He had a regular role on *Ichabod and Me* and *90 Bristol Court* and appeared in the films *Queen of the Stardust Ballroom* and *4D Man*.

Raymond, Thomas — Clare Raymond's descendant on Earth in the 24th century, as mentioned in *TNG* episode "The Neutral Zone."

Raymone, Kirk — played Duur in Classic *Trek* "Friday's Child" and the Cloud Guide in "The Cloud Minders."

Rayna VI — in *TNG* episode "Q Who," Sonya is said to be from this world.

Raz, Kavi — played Singh in *TNG* episode "Lonely among Us."

Ready Room — Picard's office off the *Enterprise* bridge, furnished with two chairs, a couch, and a fish tank embedded in the wall. It also contains a food replicator as well as a model of his old ship, the *Stargazer*.

"Realm of Fear" — sixth-season *TNG* episode written by Brannon Braga and directed by Cliff Bole. Barclay returns to help solve the mystery of why the crew is missing from a derelict ship. The transporter, which he fears, holds the clues. Guest stars: Dwight Schultz, Colm Meaney, Patti Yasutake, Renata Scott, and Thomas Belgrey.

Reardon, Craig — makeup artist on *DS9*.

Reason, Rhodes — played Flavius in Classic *Trek* "Bread and Circuses." He was born in Berlin in 1928 and has a twin brother, Rex. He had regular TV roles on the series *White Hunter* and *Bus Stop*. His film credits include *Jungle Heat* and *King Kong Escapes*.

Reaves, Michael — scriptwriter of *TNG* episode "Where No One Has Gone Before."

Reclar — Cardassian warship under command of Gul Lemec in *TNG* episode "Chain of Command." It is later caught in an antimatter-mine booby trap.

Records Officer — Lt. Commander Ben Finney's official title in Classic episode "Court-Martial." See entry for Finney, Ben.

Rector, Jeff and Jerry — played aliens in *TNG* episode "Allegiance."

Red Alert — emergency alert requiring all officers to go to their posts.

Red Hour — time of mad partying and rioting on Landru's world, Beta III, in Classic episode "The Return of the Archons." The *Enterprise* landing party, in search of their lost crew, beams down when the Red Hour is being observed. Red Hour occurs on Festival Day once a year from six P.M. until dawn.

Redblock, Cyrus — crime boss in Picard's 1941 San Francisco holodeck program. He was played by Lawrence Tierney.

Reddin, Jan — played a crewmember in Classic *Trek* "Space Seed."

"Redemption, Part I" — fourth-season *TNG* episode, the first of a two-part story, written by Ronald D. Moore and directed by Cliff Bole. The *Enterprise* travels to the Klingon homeworld where Picard will see Gowron ascend the throne and Worf and his brother try to restore their father's good name. The Duras family, however, threatens to destroy all good feelings between the Klingons and the Federation, allying with the Romulans in an attempt to undermine Gowron. Guest stars: Robert O'Reilly, Tony Todd, Whoopi Goldberg, Barbara March, Gwynyth Walsh, Ben Slack, Nicholas Kepros, J. D. Cullum, Tom Ormeny, Clifton Jones, and Denise Crosby.

"Redemption, Part II" — fifth-season *TNG* episode, the second of a two part story, written by Ronald D. Moore and directed by David Carson. Sela, Tasha's daughter, launches a Romulan attack against the Federation, and Worf's restoration of his father's good name may be what saves Gowron. Guest stars: Denise Crosby, Robert O'Reilly, Tony Todd, Whoopi Goldberg, Barbara March, Gwynyth Walsh, J. D. Cullum, Michael G. Hagerty, Timothy Carhart, Fran Bennett, Nicholas Kepros, Jordan Lund, and Stephen James Carver.

Redjack — nickname Sybo calls the Jack the Ripper entity, the same name it was called while on Earth. She picks up this knowledge through her psychic talents in Classic episode "Wolf in the Fold."

Reena — see entry for Kapec, Reena. (Rayna is an alternate spelling.)

Reeves-Stevens, Judith and Garfield — writing team who authored Classic *Trek* novels *Prime Directive* and *Memory Prime*.

reflection therapy — therapy Riker undergoes at the Tilonus Institute for Mental Disorders in *TNG* episode "Frame of Mind." His friends appear in his imagination as aspects of himself, not real people, and Suna tries to convince him the *Enterprise* never existed.

Rega, Stano — 23rd-century comedian who jokes about quantum mechanics, mentioned in *TNG* episode "The Outrageous Okona."

Regalian ox — in *TNG* episode "The Schizoid Man," Dr. Graves claims to be as "healthy as a Regalian ox."

Reger — owner of a rooming house on Landru's planet, Beta III, in Classic episode "The Return of the Archons." He has a daughter named Tula and is a member of the underground. He was played by Harry Townes.

Reginod — engineer of the *Mondor*, a Pakled vessel in *TNG* episode "Samaritan Snare." He was played by Leslie Morris.

Regulan blood worms — animal to which the Klingon Korax compares humans in Classic episode "The Trouble with Tribbles." David Gerrold actually did a more thorough creation of these horrible creatures in an unsold script. They are worms that enter a person's blood stream and drink their blood. They are extremely contagious and invisible (according to the preliminary script).

Regulation 6.57 — Starfleet regulation that states: "At least two officers shall be present during any treaty or contract negotiation," as mentioned in *TNG* episode "When the Bough Breaks."

Reimers, Ed — played Admiral Fitzpatrick in Classic *Trek* "The Trouble with Tribbles." He was the announcer on the quiz show *Do You Trust Your Wife?* and is famous for doing Allstate commercials (the "good hands" guy).

Reinhardt, Ray — played Admiral Aaron in *TNG* episode "Conspiracy."

Rejac Crystal — another rarity in Kivas Fajo's collection in *TNG* episode "The Most Toys."

Rekkags — in *TNG* episode "Man of the People," this race is at war with the Cironeans. Their mediator is to be Ambassador Olcar.

"Relics" — sixth-season *TNG* episode written by Ronald D. Moore and directed by Alexander Singer. Scotty from Classic *Trek* is discovered in stasis in a transporter beam on board a ship that has crashed into a Dyson sphere. When the *Enterprise* enters the sphere, they become trapped and Scotty and Geordi must figure out a way, on a nearly useless ship, to save them. Guest stars: James Doohan, Lanei Chapman, Erick Weiss, Stacie Foster, and Ernie Mirich.

Relva VII — where Wesley took his Academy entrance exam. It houses a Federation starbase as seen in *TNG* episode "Coming of Age."

"Remember Me" — fourth-season *TNG* episode written by Lee Sheldon and directed by Cliff Bole. Because of Wesley's static warp field experiments, Beverly disappears into a reality which grows smaller and smaller. The Traveler returns to help Wesley and Geordi establish a gate through which they can rescue her. Guest stars: Eric Menyuk, Bill Erwin, and Colm Meaney.

Remmick, Dexter — head investigator of the Starfleet conspiracy in *TNG* episode "Conspiracy." He also appears in "Coming of Age." While working in the General Inspector's office he is taken over by parasites and later dies. He was played by Robert Schenkkan.

Remmler Array — in *TNG* episode "Starship Mine," site off Arkaria where the *Enterprise* docks for their baryon sweep.

Remus — twin world of Romulus, the Romulan home-world, mentioned in Classic episode "Balance of Terror."

Ren, Surmak — Bajoran medical assistant who helps solve the problem of the aphasia plague on *DS9* in "Babel."

Renan, David — played Conn in *TNG* episode "The Naked Now."

Rench, Susan — played Ramid Sev Maylor in *TNG* episode "Man of the People."

***Renegade*, USS** — frigate in *TNG* episode "Conspiracy." Its captain was Tryla Scott, who became infested with the parasites.

replicas — see entry for androids.

replicative fading — cloning term which refers to a process during which errors double with the creation of each new being, leading to an abnormal clone, as seen in *TNG* episode "Up the Long Ladder."

replicator — also known as a food processor in old *Trek* language. A non-food replicator can also reproduce items such as clothing and jewelry.

***Republic*, USS** — Kirk and Finney served together on this ship as mentioned in Classic episode "Court-Martial." They were good friends until Kirk reported Finney for negligence for leaving a circuit open that could have destroyed the ship. Finney was reprimanded by the *Republic*'s captain and put at the bottom of the promotion list, a punishment for which Finney blamed Kirk.

***Repulse*, USS** — seen in *TNG* episodes "The Child" and "Unnatural Selection," this ship is an *Excelsior*-class ship, NCC 2524, commanded by Captain Taggart. Dr. Pulaski comes aboard to serve on the *Enterprise* straight off this ship.

repulsor beam — mentioned in *TNG* episode "The Naked Now" as a reconfigured tractor beam. It is also called a pressor beam.

"Requiem for Methuselah" — written by Jerome Bixby and directed by Murray Golden, this third-season Classic *Trek* episode aired 2/14/69. A plague called Rigelian fever is affecting the *Enterprise* crew and they need vast amounts of ryetalyn to combat it. Holberg 917G is the nearest planet with deposits of ryetalyn, and when the *Enterprise* arrives they discover it inhabited by a man named Flint and his ward, Reena Kapec. Kirk falls in love with Reena, only to find out she is an advanced android form built by Flint, who wants a companion who will not age. Flint has a rare body chemistry that makes him virtually immortal and all his other wives have died. Guest stars: James Daly, Louise Sorel, and John Buonomo. Of note: This episode shows Spock's aptitude for the piano.

Rescher, Gayne — director of photography in *The Wrath of Khan*. Her film credits include *Claudine* and *Rachel Rachel*.

Research Station 75 — outpost on the Federation/Romulan border where the *Enterprise* picks up Ensign DeSeve, who had defected to the Romulans twenty years before. It is seen in *TNG* episode "Face of the Enemy."

Resican flute — flute Picard brought back with him from Katan, where he spent a life in virtual reality in *TNG* episode "The Inner Light." In "Lessons," he plays a duet on it with Nella Daren.

resonance tissue scan — medical device which can find infections. It is used by Dr. Crusher on Geordi in *TNG* episode "Schisms."

"Return of the Archons, The" — written by Boris Sobelman and Gene Roddenberry, directed by Joseph Pevney, this first-season Classic *Trek* episode aired 2/9/67. On a world where "absorbed" people are controlled by a computer called Landru, the *Enterprise* searches for the lost members of the crew of the *Archon*. Guest stars: Harry Townes, Torin Thatcher, Charles Macauley,

Christopher Held, Brioni Farrell, Jon Lormer, Morgan Farley, Sid Haig, Ralph Maurer, Eddie Paskey, and Sean Morgan. Of note: Kirk breaks the Prime Directive in this episode, but defends his actions by saying that it applies only to healthy, growing societies. It is also revealed in this episode that Spock sleeps with his eyes open.

"Return to Tomorrow" — written by John Kingsbridge and directed by Ralph Senensky, this second-season Classic *Trek* episode aired 2/9/68. The *Enterprise* picks up a communication from deep under the ground of the dead planet Arret and discovers three energy beings from an extinct civilization still alive. The beings appropriate Kirk, Spock, and Dr. Anne Mulhall's bodies in order to create robot bodies for themselves using their vast knowledge and the *Enterprise*'s facilities. Spock's entity, however, decides to keep Spock's body and will kill Spock's essence and anyone else who gets in his way. Guest star: Diana Muldaur. Of note: James Doohan provides the voice of Sargon.

"Reunion" — fourth-season *TNG* episode written by Thomas Perry, Jo Perry, Ronald D. Moore, Drew Deighan, and Brannon Braga, directed by Jonathan Frakes. Worf meets his son, Alexander, for the first time, and Picard tries to find out which of two Klingons has been poisoning the Klingon High Commander. Guest stars: Suzie Plakson, Charles Cooper, Patrick Massett, Robert O'Reilly, Jon Steuer, Michael Rider, April Grace, Basil Wallace, and Mirron E. Willis.

Rex — played by Rod Arrants in *TNG* episode "Manhunt," he runs Rex's Bar in the holo simulation of Dixon Hill. He and Dixon Hill team up to capture Marty O'Ferren and send him to jail.

Reyga, Dr. — in *TNG* episode "Suspicions" he is the Ferengi scientist who builds a device that can shield ships from the heat in the center of a star. He is killed for his discovery by Dr. Jo'Bril.

Rhada, Lieutenant — *Enterprise* helmsman who takes Sulu's place after he joins the landing party in Classic episode "That Which Survives." She was played by Naomi Pollack.

Rhodes, Michael — director of *TNG* episode "Angel One."

Rhue, Madlyn — played Lt. Marla McGivers in Classic *Trek* "Space Seed." Born in 1934, her TV appearances include *The Guns of Will Sonnett*, *The Man from U.N.C.L.E.*, and *Ghost Appearances*, as well as regular roles on *Bracken's World*, *Executive Suite*, *Fame*, and *Days of Our Lives*. Film credits include *Operation Petticoat* and *It's a Mad, Mad, Mad, Mad World*. She has been struggling with multiple sclerosis for many years, but continues to act in TV movies, appearing at times as a character in a wheelchair.

Rice, Paul — captain of the USS *Drake* who dies and is replicated by Echo Papa 607 (see entry) in *TNG* episode "The Arsenal of Freedom."

Rich, Lisa — scriptwriter of *DS9* episode "Move Along Home."

Richards, Chet — scriptwriter of Classic *Trek* episode "The Tholian Web."

Richards, Michael — scriptwriter of Classic *Trek* episodes "That Which Survives" and "The Way to Eden."

Richey, Stephen, Colonel — one of the people who was trapped and died 283 years before at the Hotel Royale in *TNG* episode "The Royale." He was commander of an early NASA ship, the *Charybdis*. He lived in the alien-made Royale for 38 years before his death.

Richman, Peter Mark — played Ralph Offenhouse in *TNG* episode "The Neutral Zone."

Richmond, Branscombe — played the Klingon gunner in *The Search for Spock*. A regular in *Hawaiian Heat*, his film credits include *Death Moon, Damien: The Leper Priest,* and *The Mystic Warrior.*

Richter scale of culture — scale for rating the development of societies. A B rating is equivalent to Earth in 1485. A rating of G is equivalent to Earth in 2030, as mentioned in Classic episodes "Errand of Mercy" and "Spock's Brain."

Rider, Michael — played the transporter chief in *TNG* episodes "The Naked Now," "Code of Honor," "Haven," and "Reunion."

Riehle, Richard — played Batal in *TNG* episode "The Inner Light."

Rigel II — world McCoy mentions in Classic episode "Shore Leave." He remembers a cabaret there and two girls, who instantly show up and flank him.

Rigel IV — Hengist, administrator of Argelius II, is from this world, as mentioned in Classic episode "Wolf in the Fold."

Rigel V — mentioned as the homeworld of beings who have a body chemistry not unlike Vulcans. A drug from this world is used on Spock when he gives his father, Sarek, a transfusion in Classic episode "Journey to Babel."

Rigel VII — site of a fight between Captain Pike and a Rigelian in Classic pilot "The Cage." One of these Rigelians appears in "The Gamesters of Triskelion."

Rigel XII — planet the *Enterprise* visits to pick up some dilithium in Classic episode "Mudd's Women." It is a mining world with dust storms and high winds.

Rigel Cup, The — great honor won by the Nova Squadron, Wesley's team, in *TNG* episode "The First Duty."

Rigelian fever — contagious disease plaguing the *Enterprise* in Classic episode "Requiem for Methuselah." Ryetalyn is the only known antidote and Holberg 917G,

Flint's planet, has deposits of it. By the end of the episode, nearly the entire crew has the disease and three people have died of it.

Rigelian Kassaba fever — McCoy tells the Kelvans that Spock is suffering from this disease, much like malaria. He says Spock will die if he isn't treated soon in Classic episode "By Any Other Name."

Rigelian phaser rifles — the Gatherers use these weapons on Gamma Hromi II in *TNG* episode "The Vengeance Factor."

"Rightful Heir" — sixth-season *TNG* episode written by Ronald D. Moore and James E. Brooks, directed by Winrich Kolbe. Worf begins questioning his Klingon beliefs and travels to Boreth, the site of a Klingon temple. Worf undergoes ritual and ceremony there in an attempt to have a vision of Kahless, when suddenly Kahless actually appears. He has been cloned from residual cells left over from the actual Kahless, but believes he is the real Kahless. Guest stars: Kevin Conway and Robert O'Reilly.

Rignack, Roger — played one of the miners in *TNG* episode "The Perfect Mate."

Riker, William Thomas, Commander — first officer of the *Enterprise* in *The Next Generation* and played by Jonathan Frakes. Often called "Number One" by Picard, he is not only second-in-command, but commands the away team missions from the ship. He was born in Valdez, Alaska, to Kyle Riker and was supposedly 32 years old by the fourth season of *TNG*. His mother died when he was very young so he never knew her. He and Deanna Troi were once lovers, when he was a psychology student and junior officer, but are now only friends. He came to serve aboard the *Enterprise* when it picked him up at Farpoint Station in "Encounter at Farpoint." His quarters are located on Deck 8, 0912. He has been offered command of his own ship several times and turned it down because he enjoys working on the *Enterprise* too much. Riker's code is "Theta Alpha 2737 Blue, Enable." He served as first officer under Captain DeSoto on the *Hood*. He is a master poker player.

Riker, Jean-Luc — in *TNG* episode "Future Imperfect," Riker is told he has a son, Jean-Luc, but it is an illusion.

Riker, Kyle — William Riker's father, played by Mitchell Ryan, who appeared in *TNG* episode "The Icarus Factor." He and Will Riker had not seen each other for fifteen years prior to this episode. He is a civilian adviser to Starfleet. He was the only survivor in Starfleet's conflict with the Tholians.

Riker, Thomas, Lieutenant — in *TNG* episode "Second Chances," a second Riker is discovered, who has been stranded on Nervala IV eight years before by a transporter accident that split Riker into two people. He is not a clone, but a real person who still has deep feelings for Troi, since he spent eight years stranded, pining after her. He consummates his love with an affair with Troi, takes on his legal middle name, and resumes his career by joining the crew of the *Gandhi*.

Riley, Kevin, Lieutenant — *Enterprise* navigator who appeared in Classic episodes "The Naked Time" and "The Conscience of the King." He is an energetic young man with a great sense of humor. He was born on Tarsus IV, where Kodos the Executioner killed his entire family. An Irishman, and very proud of it, he was brilliantly played by Bruce Hyde.

Rings of Tautee — Q mentions that Amanda could walk on these because she is all-powerful in *TNG* episode "True Q."

Rio Grande — one of the runabouts on *DS9* in "Emissary."

Riordan, Daniel — played Rondon in *TNG* episode "Coming of Age."

Rippy, Leon — played Sonny Clemons in *TNG* episode "The Neutral Zone."

Risa — resort world, very like a paradise, in *TNG* episode "Captain's Holiday." The *Tox Uthat* (see entry) is located here. Weapons are not permitted on this world.

Rishium cheese pastry — Commander Hutchison serves this at his party on Arkaria in *TNG* episode "Starship Mine."

Riva, Ambassador — deaf mediator from Ramatis III in *TNG* episode "Loud As a Whisper." He was played by Howie Seago.

Rivan — one of the council of Edo who comes aboard the *Enterprise* and sees Edo's "god" in *TNG* episode "Justice." She was played by Brenda Bakke.

Rixx, Captain — commander of the *Thomas Paine* who had met Picard before at an Altarian conference in *TNG* episode "Conspiracy." He was played by Michael Berryman.

Rizzo, Ensign — *Enterprise* officer killed on Tycho IV by the vampire cloud in Classic episode "Obsession." He was played by Jerry Ayers.

Ro Laren, Ensign — Bajoran who is responsible for the deaths of eight people while on a landing party because she disobeyed orders. She was imprisoned for her crime, as mentioned in *TNG* episode "Ensign Ro." After getting out of prison she joined the *Enterprise*. She likes to draw, grew up in a refugee camp, and hates the Cardassians because they tortured and killed her father in front of her when she was seven. She also appears in the episodes "Conundrum," "Violations," "Rascals," "Disaster," and "The Next Phase." She was played by Michelle Forbes. The part of Kira on *DS9* was originally written for Ro Laren, but Forbes had other plans.

Roarke, Adam — played C.P.O. Garrison in Classic *Trek* pilot "The Cage." He had a regular role on the TV series *The Keegans* and guest starred on such shows as *The Man from U.N.C.L.E.*

Robbiana dermal optic test — psychological test McCoy gives Kirk/Janice in Classic episode "Turnabout Intruder" because of Kirk's strange behavior.

Roberts, David — played Dr. Ozaba in Classic *Trek* episode "The Empath." His TV appearances include *The Feather and Father Gang*, *The Man from U.N.C.L.E.*, and *Branded*. His films include *The Challenge*, *Return to Earth*, and *The Winds of War*.

Roberts, Jeremy — played an *Excelsior* officer in *The Voyage Home*.

Roberts, Ted — scriptwriter of *TNG* episode "Half a Life."

Robinson, Andrew — appeared in *DS9* "Past Prologue."

Robinson, Jay — played Lord Petri in Classic *Trek* episode "Elaan of Troyius." Born in 1930 in New York, his TV appearances include *Planet of the Apes* and *Voyagers!* and the films *The Robe* and *Shampoo*.

Rocco, Tony — played a Klingon in *Star Trek: The Motion Picture*.

Rocha, Keith, Lieutenant — commander of the Starfleet Subspace Relay Station 47 in *TNG* episode "Aquiel." He had an excellent record but went crazy and tried to kill Aquiel. Instead, he kills himself, and Aquiel becomes a suspect in his murder. He turns out not to be the real person, but a coalescent organism that took on his form.

Rockow, Jill — makeup artist on *DS9*.

Roddenberry, Gene — creator/producer/writer of the *Star Trek* series and concept, as well as *The Next*

Generation. Born in El Paso, Texas, in 1921, he died on October 24, 1991. He grew up with one brother and one sister. His full name is Wesley Eugene Roddenberry. (He based the character of Wesley Crusher on the character he wanted to be as a child. In Classic *Trek*, Commodore Wesley is also a tribute to his name.) His scripts include Classic *Trek* episodes "The Cage," "Charlie X," "Mudd's Women," "The Menagerie, Parts I and II," "The Return of the Archons," "A Private Little War," "The Omega Glory," "Bread and Circuses," "Assignment: Earth," "The Savage Curtain," and "Turnabout Intruder." He also wrote *TNG* episodes "Encounter at Farpoint," "Hide and Q," and "Datalore" and the novel *Star Trek: The Motion Picture.* Roddenberry was a WW II pilot and a Los Angeles police officer before becoming a writer. He wrote speeches for the chief of police and poetry, some of which was published in the *New York Times.* He began writing for TV shows such as *Have Gun Will Travel, Highway Patrol, Dragnet, The Virginian, Alias Smith and Jones, Naked City, Dr. Kildare, Two Faces West, June Allyson Show, The Detectives, Highway Patrol,* and *West Point Story,* many of which were written under the pen name Robert Wesley. He also created the series *The Lieutenant.* He created the pilots for *Genesis II, Spectre, Planet Earth,* and *The Questor Tapes,* and produced the movie *Pretty Maids All in a Row.* He was married at the time of his death to his second wife, Majel Barrett, with whom he had a son, Gene, Jr., nicknamed "Rod." With his first wife, Eileen, he has two daughters, Darlene Incopero and Dawn Compton. Roddenberry was given, by the fans and cast, the affectionate nickname Great Bird of the Galaxy. (This phrase was used in the episode "The Man Trap.") He was a noted speaker who toured college campuses and conventions bringing with him copies of "The Cage" and the famous *Star Trek* blooper reel. He was the first writer ever nominated for a star on Hollywood Boulevard, and the ceremony was held on September 4, 1985. The star is number 1,810 and is located at 6683 Hollywood Blvd. A building on the Paramount lot is also named after Gene. He suffered several strokes during his last years with *TNG*, before dying of a heart attack in 1991 at the age of 70. Of Gene's vision, Rick Berman says, "Gene felt strongly about the goodness of mankind. He knew there were rotten things also, but he liked to think of the future where wonderful things would continue and man could enhance the quality of his life."

Rodent — homeless man who is killed by a phaser he stole from McCoy in Classic episode "The City on the Edge of Forever." He was played by John Harmon.

rodinium — hardest known substance, used to shield outposts, though the Romulan attacks pulverize it in Classic episode "Balance of Terror."

Rodriguez, Esteban, Lieutenant — Angela Martinez Teller's friend on the recreation planet in Classic episode "Shore Leave." He was played by Jerry Lopez.

Rodriguez, Marco — played Paul Rice in *TNG* episode "The Arsenal of Freedom" and Glin Telle in "The Wounded."

Rodriguez, Percy — played Commodore Stone in Classic *Trek* episode "Court-Martial." Born in 1924, his TV appearances include *Tarzan* and *Planet of the Apes*, as well as a regular role on *Peyton Place*, *The Silent Force*, and *Executive Suite*. He also appeared in Roddenberry's *Genesis II*.

Roebuck, Daniel — played Romulan #1 in *TNG* episode "Unification, Parts I and II."

Roeves, Maurice — appeared in *TNG* episode "The Chase."

Rogers, Elizabeth — played Lt. Palmer in Classic *Trek* episodes "The Doomsday Machine" and "The Way to Eden." Her film credits include *Something Evil* and *An Officer and a Gentleman*.

Rogers, Amanda — young woman who interns

aboard the *Enterprise* but who is actually, according to Q, a member of the Q Continuum. The Q Continuum killed her biological parents and she was adopted and raised by humans. She has had strange powers all her life, but hid them, not understanding what she was. She decides to join the Q Continuum, determined to do good with her powers. Amanda was played by Olivia D'Abo in *TNG* episode "True Q."

Rojan — Kelvan (see entry) in charge of the expedition to invade the Milky Way in Classic episode "By Any Other Name." He was born in intergalactic space, so has never known his homeworld in the Andromeda galaxy. He has taken human form, though his actual shape is large with many tentacles. He was played by Warren Stevens.

Rojay — companion of Devinoni Ral in *TNG* episode "The Price."

***rokeg* blood pie** — one of Worf's favorite Klingon dishes, mentioned in *TNG* episode "Family."

Rolfe, Sam — scriptwriter of *TNG* episode "The Vengeance Factor." He also wrote *DS9* episode "Vortex."

Rollman, Admiral — Kira calls her in an attempt to go over Sisko's head in *DS9* episode "Past Prologue." She was played by Susan Bay (Leonard Nimoy's wife).

Rolls, Dana Kramer — author of Classic *Trek* novel *Home Is the Hunter*.

Rom — Quark's brother who has a recurring role on *DS9*. He is rather weasellike and cowardly. He has a son named Nog.

Romaine, Jacques — mentioned as Mira Romaine's father in Classic episode "The Lights of Zetar." He is a retired Starfleet engineer.

Romaine, Lydia — mentioned in Classic episode "The Lights of Zetar" as Mira Romaine's mother.

Romaine, Mira, Lieutenant — she is supervising the transfer of equipment to Memory Alpha, via the *Enterprise,* when Scotty falls in love with her in Classic episode "The Lights of Zetar." Her parents are Jacques and Lydia Romaine. She was played by Jan Shutan.

Roman, Ron — scriptwriter of *TNG* episode "Booby Trap."

Romanis, George — composer of incidental music for *TNG* episode "Too Short a Season."

Romas — felicium-addicted Ornaran seen in *TNG* episode "Symbiosis." He was played by Richard Lineback.

Romboi Dronegar Sector 006 — location of the Pakled vessel when it signals the *Enterprise* in *TNG* episode "Samaritan Snare."

Romero, Ned — played Krell in Classic *Trek* episode "A Private Little War." His TV appearances include regular roles on *The D.A.* and *Dan August.* Film credits include *Winchester 73, I Will Fight No More Forever,* and the 1984 miniseries *George Washington.*

Romii — sun in the Romulan system, mentioned in Classic episode "Balance of Terror."

Romulan ale — Kirk gets some of this blue drink from McCoy for his birthday in *The Wrath of Khan.* It is also served to the Klingons in *The Undiscovered Country.* It is mentioned as not reproducible by the *Enterprise* replicators in *TNG* episode "The Defector."

Romulan Commander — commander of the *Bird-of-Prey* warship which attacks outposts using a cloaking device in Classic episode "Balance of Terror." He destroys his ship rather than allowing himself to be taken prisoner. He was played by Mark Lenard.

Romulan Empire — nation of Romulans, and enemy of the Federation. This empire changes little from Classic

Trek through *TNG* and *DS9*. They continue to be enemies of the Federation, a very warlike, territorial race of beings who trust few other races.

Romulan execution — involves torture before death, as mentioned in Classic episode "The *Enterprise* Incident."

Romulan Female Commander — commands a flagship of three Romulan vessels that surround the *Enterprise* and demand its surrender. Her strong attraction to Spock causes her downfall. The *Enterprise* takes her prisoner. She is played by Joanne Linville.

Romulan Neutral Zone — see entry for Neutral Zone.

Romulan War — referred to in Classic episode "Balance of Terror" as a war fought 100 years before. The ships were less advanced and neither side saw the other's face. The struggle resulted in the establishment of the famous Neutral Zone. Entry into the Neutral Zone could start a war.

Romulans — pointy-eared race who resemble Vulcans and are, in fact, their distant cousins. They are militaristic, but beyond that little is known about them. They appear in both Classic *Trek* and *The Next Generation*. In "Unification," Spock is working hard on bringing about peace between the Federation and the Romulans, apparently a very difficult task.

Romulus — twin to Remus, the double-planet homeworld of the Romulans. The secondary star of the binary Romulan sun is also sometimes called Romulus by the Federation. In *TNG* episode "The Defector," Jarok, a Romulan, mentions the firefalls of Gal'Gathong and the Apnex Sea on this world.

Ron, Tiny — appeared in the *DS9* episode "The Nagus."

Rondell, R. A. — stunt coordinator on *The Voyage Home*.

Rondon — in *TNG* episode "Coming of Age," he is a Zaldan who insults Wesley. He was played by Daniel Riordan.

Root, Stephen — played K'Vada in *TNG* episode "Unification, Parts I and II."

Rose — one of the children kidnapped from the *Enterprise* in *TNG* episode "When the Bough Breaks."

Rose, Christine — appeared in *TNG* episode "Birthright."

Rose, Margot — played Eline in *TNG* episode "The Inner Light."

Rosenberg, Grant — scriptwriter of *TNG* episode "New Ground."

Rosenman, Leonard — composer of the score for *The Voyage Home*. He also wrote the music for *Rebel Without a Cause, Beneath the Planet of the Apes, Lord of the Rings,* and the unsold pilot for *Alexander the Great* (starring William Shatner). He was born September 7, 1924.

Ross, Chief — *Enterprise* officer in *The Motion Picture*. He was played by Terrance O'Connor.

Ross, David L. — actor/extra who played a security guard in Classic *Trek* episodes "Miri," "The Return of the Archons," "The Trouble with Tribbles," and "Turnabout Intruder"; Galloway in "A Taste of Armageddon," "The City on the Edge of Forever," and "The Omega Glory"; Lt. Johnson in "Day of the Dove," and the transporter officer in "The Galileo Seven."

Ross, Jane — played Tamoon in Classic *Trek* episode "The Gamesters of Triskelion."

Ross, Steven — producer of *The Final Frontier*.

Ross, Teresa, Yeoman — appears in Classic episode "The Squire of Gothos," played by Venita Wolf.

Rossa, Connaught, Admiral — Jeremiah Rossa's human grandmother in *TNG* episode "Suddenly Human." She was played by Barbara Townsend.

Rossa, Jeremiah — human boy found on board a Talarian ship in *TNG* episode "Suddenly Human." He had been missing for ten years after the Talarians raided the colony on Galen IV. He was assimilated into Talarian society and loves his Talarian adoptive father, Endar. He goes by the name Jono and does not want to return to Earth or his human heritage, stabbing Captain Picard to prove to him that he is no longer human. Admiral Connaught Rossa is his grandmother. He was played by Chad Allen.

Rossilli, Paul — played the Klingon Kerla in *The Undiscovered Country*.

rostrum — beam on Statos to which prisoners are tied in Classic episode "The Cloud Minders." When the prisoner answers a question incorrectly, a painful beam of light enters the prisoner.

Rousseau V — in *TNG* episode "The Dauphin," Wesley takes Salia here via the holodeck. This broken world is held together by neutrino clouds that sing.

Rowe, Douglas — played Debin in *TNG* episode "The Outrageous Okona."

Rowe, Stephen M. — music editor in *DS9*.

Rowe, Lieutenant — security officer in Classic episode "I, Mudd." He is played by Mike Howden.

Royale, The — hotel and casino, in *TNG* episode "The Royale," built to resemble a hotel out of a pulp-fiction book called *The Royale*. The place was created by aliens on Theta VIII as a home for Colonel Stephen Richey, who was taken from his ship, *The Charybdis*.

"Royale, The" — second-season *TNG* episode written by Keith Mills and directed by Cliff Bole. Data, Riker, and

Worf become trapped in a hotel that is taken from the novel *The Royale* and made real by aliens on Theta VIII. There they find the wreckage of a NASA shuttle. Guest stars: Noble Willingham, Sam Anderson, Jill Jacobsen, Leo Garcia, Gregory Beecroft, and Colm Meaney.

Roygas, Michael — played Lt. Cleary in *Star Trek: The Motion Picture.*

Roykirk, Jackson — creator of Nomad or, at least, the person Nomad thinks is its creator in Classic episode "The Changeling." He did create the original Nomad probe, a machine supposedly capable of independent thought.

Rozhenko, Alexander — Worf's son. See entry for Alexander.

Rozhenko, Sergey and Helena — Worf's adoptive parents who adopted him after his parents died on Khitomer. They are Russian natives but raised Worf on the farm world Gault. They are seen in *TNG* episode "Family" and are played by Theodore Bikel and Georgia Brown.

Ruah IV — mentioned as a class M world that Professor Galen recently visited in *TNG* episode "The Chase."

Ruben, Paul — scriptwriter of *TNG* episode "Power Play."

Rubenstein, Paul — played one of the garbagemen in *The Voyage Home*. He had a regular role in the series *Working Stiffs*. His film credits include *Contract on Cherry Street*, *The Last American Virgin*, and *Getting Physical*.

Rubenstein, Scott — story editor of *TNG*'s second season and scriptwriter of *TNG* episode "The Dauphin."

Rubicam III — paradiselike homeworld of the Edo in *TNG* episode "Justice."

Rubin, Richard — property master in *Star Trek: The Motion Picture.*

rubindium crystals — seen in Classic episode "Patterns of Force" as part of the subcutaneous transponders Kirk and Spock have embedded in their arms.

Rubinek, Saul — played Kivas Fajo in *TNG* episode "The Most Toys."

Rudman, Commander — mentioned in *TNG* episode "Birthright" as an officer aboard the *Merrimac*.

Rugg, Jim — special effects coordinator for Classic *Trek*.

Ruginis, Vyto — played Logan in *TNG* episode "The Arsenal of Freedom."

Ruk — very tall, male android and one of Dr. Korby's helpers in Classic episode "What Are Little Girls Made Of?" Created by the "old ones" of Exo III, he was the only one of the old androids left when Dr. Korby arrived. He was played by Ted Cassidy.

runabout — shuttle capable of warp drive used in both *TNG* and *DS9*. Runabouts on *DS9* look small, but in *TNG* episode "Timescape" one had a conference room, bunk sections, and an aft engineering section.

Rush, Marvin V. — director of *TNG* episode "The Host" and director of photography on *TNG*.

Rushton infection — mentioned in *TNG* episode "The Bonding" as the disease Jeremy Aster's father died of five years before.

Ruskin, Joseph — played Galt in Classic *Trek* episode "The Gamesters of Triskelion." His TV credits include *Voyage to the Bottom of the Sea*, *Planet of the Apes*, and *The Bionic Woman*. Film credits include *Panache*, *Captain America*, and *The Munsters' Revenge*.

Russ — one of the engineers who beams aboard the *Constellation* with Kirk in Classic episode "The Doomsday Machine." He is played by Tim Burns.

Russell — *Enterprise* engineer in *TNG* episode "The Tin Man."

Russell, Mark — played a Vulcan litterbearer in Classic *Trek* episode "Amok Time."

Russell, Mauri — actor who played a Vulcan bell, and banner carrier in Classic *Trek* episode "Amok Time."

Russell, Randee — scriptwriter of *TNG* episode "Qpid."

Russell, Toby, Dr. — in *TNG* episode "Ethics," she is a neurologist who comes aboard the *Enterprise* to help treat Worf. She tries an experimental technique on him that has previously failed. She was played by Caroline Kava.

Russo, Barry — played Lt. Commander Giotto in Classic *Trek* episode "The Devil in the Dark" and Commodore Wesley in "The Ultimate Computer."

Ruth — Kirk's old flame who appears to him on the shore-leave planet in Classic episode "Shore Leave." She is played by Shirley Bonne.

Rutia IV — in *TNG* episode "The High Ground," the homeworld of the Ansata and the Rutians, who are fighting each other. The Ansata believe the Federation is aiding the Rutians, which is why they kidnap Dr. Crusher and Picard.

Rutledge, USS — Chief O'Brien served aboard this ship under the command of Benjamin Maxwell in *TNG* episode "The Wounded."

Rutter, George A. — script supervisor of Classic *Trek*.

R'uustai — Klingon ritual that translates to "The Bonding." It can make brothers of those who are not related. Jeremy Aster and Worf share this ceremony after the death of Jeremy's mother, Marla Aster, in *TNG* episode "The Bonding."

Ryan, Lieutenant — he takes over the helm for Sulu in Classic episode "The Naked Time."

Ryan, Mitchell — played Kyle Riker (William Riker's father) in *TNG* episode "The Icarus Factor."

Rydbeck, Whitney — played Alans in *TNG* episode "Pen Pals."

Ryder, Alfred — played Professor Robert Crater in Classic *Trek* episode "The Man Trap." His TV credits include *Voyage to the Bottom of the Sea* and *One Step Beyond*.

Ryder, Richard — played a Bajoran deputy in *DS9* episodes "Past Prologue" and "A Man Alone."

Ryen, Adam — played Willie in *TNG* episode "Brothers."

ryetalyn — only known cure for Rigelian fever which plagues the *Enterprise* in Classic episode "Requiem for Methuselah." A deposit is found on Holberg 917G, Flint's planet. It has to be pure to effectively cure the fever.

Ryusaki, Kimberly L. — stand-in in the film *The Search for Spock*.

Sabaroff, Robert — scriptwriter of Classic *Trek* episode "The Immunity Syndrome" and *TNG* episodes "Home Soil" and "Conspiracy."

Sabre, Richard — hair stylist on *DS9*.

Sackett, Susan — assistant to Gene Roddenberry on *Star Trek: The Motion Picture* and all the other movies as well as *TNG*. She wrote the *TNG* scripts "Ménage à Troi" and "The Game" and is also the author of *The Making of Star Trek: The Motion Picture* with Gene Roddenberry, and the books *Letters to Star Trek* and *Star Trek Speaks*. She nominated Gene Roddenberry's name to the Walk of Fame committee for a star on Hollywood Boulevard, which they awarded him.

Sackman, Gerry — incidental music composer for *TNG*.

Sage, David — played Tarmin in *TNG* episode "Violations."

Sage, Willard — played Thann in Classic *Trek* episode "The Empath." His TV credits include *The Man from U.N.C.L.E.*, *Voyage to the Bottom of the Sea*, *Perry Mason*, and *The Young Rebels*. His films include the 1958 *Timbuktu* and the 1971 *A Step out of Line*.

Saint Louis Academy — dance school Dr. Crusher attended and mentions in *TNG* episode "Data's Day."

Sakar of Vulcan — mentioned in Classic episode

"The Ultimate Computer" by Dr. Daystrom as a genius along the lines of Einstein.

Sakharov — Pulaski uses this *Enterprise* shuttle in *TNG* episode "Unnatural Selection." Picard and Wesley use it in "Samaritan Snare."

Sakkath — Sarek's Vulcan assistant in *TNG* episode "Sarek." He helps to shield Sarek's emotions and enhance his mental discipline. He is played by Rocco Sisto.

Sakuro's Disease — the disease Nancy Hedford is suffering from in Classic episode "Metamorphosis." It resembles leukemia and exists on Epsilon Canaris III. It is deadly unless properly treated.

Salia — an allasomorph whose form is pure light. She has lived on Klavdia III for her entire life, 16 years, and is the future leader of Daled IV. She is played by Jamie Hubbard in *TNG* episode "The Dauphin."

Salish — medicine chief who fights Kirk in Classic episode "The Paradise Syndrome." He is supposed to know how to make the asteriod deflector work in the obelisk but his predecessor died before he could learn how. He is in love with Miramanee. Rudy Solari plays him.

Sallin, Robert — producer of *The Wrath of Khan*.

salt vampire — name for the M–113 creature in Classic episode "The Man Trap." It is the last of its kind and is killed at the end of the episode when it tries to feed on Kirk by sucking out all his body's salt through his face. Sharon Gimpel played this horrible creature.

saltzgadum — a material, one of five such substances, that can alter glass, as mentioned in *TNG* episode "Hollow Pursuits."

Sam — ship's officer who is in the gymnasium when Kirk tries to teach Charlie about wrestling in Classic episode "Charlie X." When Sam laughs at Charlie, Charlie makes him disappear. The Thasians later return him to the ship.

"Samaritan Snare" — second-season *TNG* episode written by Robert L. McCullough and directed by Les Landau. Picard is forced to have surgery on his artificial heart that could kill him, and Geordi is kidnapped by a Pakled vessel. Guest stars: Christopher Collins, Lycia Naff, Leslie Morris, Daniel Banzali, and Tzi Ma.

Sampson, Robert — played Sar 6 in Classic *Trek* episode "A Taste of Armageddon." His TV credits include *Voyage to the Bottom of the Sea* as well as regular roles on *Bridget Loves Bernie* and *Falcon Crest.* Films include *Fear No Evil* ('68), the *Shell Game* ('75), and the 1984 film *The Jerk, Too.*

Samurai — Japanese warrior Sulu thinks about on the recreation planet in Classic episode "Shore Leave." When the warrior appears, he attacks Sulu and others. He is played by Sebastian Tom.

San Francisco Navy Yard — mentioned in animated episode "The Counter-Clock Incident" as the place where the original components for the *Enterprise* were built.

Sanchez, Ralph — scriptwriter of *TNG* episode "Home Soil."

Sanchez, Dr. — medical officer on the *Enterprise* mentioned in Classic episode "That Which Survives." He does the autopsy on Ensign Wyatt, who was killed by Losira's touch.

Sanction — Ornaran freighter destroyed when its control coil malfunctions in *TNG* episode "Symbiosis."

Sandara — original home of the Platonians mentioned in Classic episode "Plato's Stepchildren." Its sun went nova.

sandbats of Maynark IV — mentioned in Classic

episode "The Empath" as creatures who look like rock crystals when at rest.

Sandor, Steve — played Lars in Classic *Trek* "The Gamesters of Triskelion." He had a regular role in *Amy Prentiss* (1974–75), and guest starred on *Alias Smith and Jones*. Film credits include *The Young Country, Stryker,* and *Fire and Ice.*

Sandoval, Elias — the leader of the colony on Omicron Ceti III who is affected by the spores. When the spores leave him, he wants to move to another world and start over. He is played by Frank Overton.

Sands, Serena — played a Talosian in Classic *Trek* pilot "The Cage" and "The Menagerie."

Sanford, Gerald — scriptwriter of *DS9* episode "A Man Alone."

saplin — mentioned in Classic episode "The Apple" as a substance comparable to what tips the poison thorns of the Gamma Trianguli VI pod plant. The Saplin thorns, however, are a thousand times more deadly.

Sar, Galek — in *TNG* episode "The Booby Trap," he is captain of the Promellian battlecruiser *Cleponji*. He was played by Albert Hall.

Sar 6 — Anan 7's aide in Classic episode "A Taste of Armageddon." He is played by Robert Sampson.

***Saratoga,* USS** — ship seen in *The Voyage Home*. This ship is also the ship Benjamin Sisko, commander of *DS9*, served on as first officer under the command of a Vulcan, Captain Storil. Storil dies when the ship is attacked by the Borg at Wolf 359, along wtih Sisko's wife, Jennifer. Sisko escapes the ship with his son, Jake, in a shuttle, as seen in a flashback in *DS9* episode "The Emissary."

"Sarek" — third-season *TNG* episode written by Peter S. Beagle, Marc Cushman, and Jake Jacobs, directed by Les

Landau. Spock's father, Ambassador Sarek, comes aboard the *Enterprise* to meet with a reclusive alien race, the Legarans. He is suffering, however, from a rare Vulcan disease, Bendii Syndrome, which affects the brain and makes him unable to control his emotions. His telepathic output, as a result, affects those around him. There is no cure for the disease and it eventually kills him. Guest stars: Mark Lenard, Joanna Miles, William Denis, Rocco Sisto, John H. Francis, and Colm Meaney. Of note: The music recital in this episode contains a sextet (not a quartet) by Brahms, not Mozart, as misstated in the script.

Sarek, Ambassador — Spock's father in Classic *Trek* episode "Journey to Babel," who also appears in *The Search for Spock, The Voyage Home,* and *The Undiscovered Country,* as well as in *TNG* episodes "Sarek" and "Unification." He was married to a human, Amanda Grayson, in Classic *Trek* and the movies, and to another human woman, Perrin, in *TNG.* An astrophysicist, he acts as a Vulcan ambassador to many different worlds, often working for the Federation. In Classic *Trek* he is 102.437 years old. (Vulcans' normal life span is 250 years.) He stopped talking to Spock for 18 years after Spock chose a Starfleet career over one of distinguished repute working and teaching at the Vulcan Science Academy. Both Sarek and Spock have t-negative blood. In *The Final Frontier,* Spock encounters his older brother, Sybok, previously unknown in the Vulcan's biography. Spock intimates that Sarek was once married, when he was very young, to a Vulcan princess but apparently the marriage was dissolved. In "Sarek," Sarek is suffering from Bendii Syndrome, a Vulcan form of Alzheimer's that causes a breakdown in his Vulcan mental disciplines, making his emotions uncontrollable. There is no cure for this disease and Sarek dies from it in "Unification." Sarek is played by Mark Lenard.

Sargent, Joseph — director of the Classic *Trek* episode "The Corbomite Maneuver." Born in 1925, his work includes *The Man from U.N.C.L.E.* and the films

Colossus: The Forbin Project and *McArthur*. He won an Emmy in 1973 for *The Marcus-Nelson Murders*.

Sargent, William — played Dr. Thomas Leighton in the Classic *Trek* episode "The Conscience of the King." He also made guest appearances in TV shows such as *The Immortal*, *Barnaby Jones*, and *The Man from U.N.C.L.E.*

Sargon — one of three energy beings that survived for millennia after a devastating war on Arret 500,000 years before. His wife is Thalassa. Henoch, the third survivor, was Sargon's enemy. Sargon uses Kirk's body to move around in Classic episode "Return to Tomorrow," and James Doohan's voice to speak.

Sarjenka — Dremian girl who calls for help on a transmitter. Data picks up her distress signal and breaks the Prime Directive to help her and her world from being destroyed by massive seismic activity. Dr. Pulaski clears her memory of the *Enterprise* and Data from her mind. She has parents and brothers who are unseen. She appears in *TNG* episode "Pen Pals" and is played by Nikki Cox.

Sarlatte, Bob — played the waiter in *The Voyage Home*.

Sarona VIII — destination of the *Enterprise* in *TNG* episode "We'll Always Have Paris." They planned to take shore leave there before they were diverted to Vandor IV.

Sarpeidon — world whose sun is going nova. All the inhabitants have escaped into their world's past through the atavachron in Classic episode "All Our Yesterdays."

Sartaarans — a reptilianlike race and longtime enemies of the Lysian Alliance as seen in *TNG* episode "Conundrum."

Sarthong V — in *TNG* episode "Captain's Holiday," Vash says she wants to visit the archeological ruins here but Sarthongians don't like trespassers.

Sasek — Spock claims to be the son of Sasek and T'Pel, when he goes back in time to meet himself in animated episode "Yesteryear."

Sasheer — name of a Kelvin flower made of crystals that grow very quickly, mentioned by Kelinda in Classic episode "By Any Other Name."

Satak, Captain — name of the commander of the Vulcan ship *Intrepid*, lost with all hands when it encountered the galactic amoeba in Classic episode "The Immunity Syndrome."

Satelk, Captain — Vulcan who is on the inquest panel looking into the death of Cadet Joshua Albert in *TNG* episode "The First Duty." He is played by Richard Fancy.

Satie, Norah, Admiral — she investigates the sabotage to the *Enterprise* warp core and believes there is an alien infiltration. Her investigation becomes a witch hunt as she obsesses on everyone's darker motives in *TNG* episode "The Drumhead." Her father was Judge Aron Satie, a famous Federation judge. She is played by Jean Simmons.

Sattler — a member of the team trying to steal trilithium from the *Enterprise* in *TNG* episode "Starship Mine." He is killed by the baryon sweep.

Saurian brandy — McCoy's favorite drink, as seen throughout the Classic series. Kirk seems to like it too; his negative self demands this kind of brandy from McCoy in "The Enemy Within." It is served in Ten Forward on *TNG*.

Saurian virus — Dramia II was hit by this virus which McCoy cured nineteen years before in animated episode "The Albatross."

"Savage Curtain, The" — written by Gene Roddenberry and Arthur Heinemann, directed by Herschel Daugherty, this third-season Classic *Trek* episode aired 3/7/69. The *Enterprise* is surveying a planet where there is thought to be no intelligent life when suddenly a patch of Earth-like conditions appears on the planet, and Abraham Lincoln beams aboard. Lincoln invites them back down to the planet where Kirk, Spock, and McCoy meet up with Surak of ancient Vulcan lore, and four notorious villains—Colonel Green, Kahless, Genghis Khan, and Zora—and are ordered by a rock creature, Yarnek, to fight it out to the death. Guest stars: Phillip Pine, Carol Daniels Dement, Lee Bergere, Barry Atwater, Nathan Jung, Robert Herron, and Arell Blanton.

Savar, Admiral — Vulcan Starfleet officer controlled by parasites in *TNG* episode "Conspiracy."

Saviola, Camille — appeared in *DS9* episode "Emissary."

Sawaya, George — played Chief Humbolt in Classic *Trek* episode "The Menagerie" and Second Klingon Lt. in "Errand of Mercy." TV credits include *Perry Mason*, *Branded*, *The Man from U.N.C.L.E*, and *Barnaby Jones*. Film credits include *Moon of the Wolf*, *The Red Badge of Courage*, and *Dead Men Don't Wear Plaid*.

Saxe, Carl — stunt double for Korob in Classic *Trek* episode "Catspaw."

Sayana — young woman of Gamma Trianguli IV who is in love with Makora in Classic episode "The Apple." She is played by Shari Nims.

Scalos — planet located in an outer quadrant of the galaxy where a beautiful city is all that is left of the dying inhabitants' civilization, in Classic episode "Wink of an Eye." Radiation killed the world's children and left the adult males sterile. When the *Enterprise* answers their distress call, the few remaining survivors try to kidnap fertile men from the ship to impregnate their women. They are also difficult to detect, since they live in an accelerated time frame compared to the *Enterprise* crew. The substance responsible for the Scalosians' acceleration, and later, that of some of the *Enterprise* crew, is found in the water on Scalos. (Also see entry on Deela.)

Scanlan, Joseph L. — director of *TNG* episodes "The Big Goodbye," "Skin of Evil," and "Time Squared."

Scarabelli, Michele — played Jenna D'Sora in *TNG* episode "In Theory."

Scarfe, Alan — played Mendak in *TNG* episode "Data's Day," and appeared in "Birthright."

Schafer, Ken — scriptwriter of *TNG* episode "The Mind's Eye."

Schaffer, Sharon — stunt woman who appeared in *The Voyage Home.*

Schallert, William — played Nilz Baris in Classic *Trek* episode "The Trouble with Tribbles." He has been a familiar face on TV and recently was a regular on the sitcom *The Torkelsons.*

Scharf, Sabrina — played Miramanee in Classic *Trek* episode "The Paradise Syndrome." She has also made guest appearances on such TV shows as *Hunter* and *The Man from U.N.C.L.E.*

Scheerer, Robert — director of *TNG* episodes "The Measure of a Man," "Peak Performance," "The Price," "The Defector," "Tin Man," "Legacy," "New Ground," "The Outcast," and "True Q."

Schenkkan, Robert — played Dexter Remmick in *TNG* episodes "Coming of Age" and "Conspiracy."

Schiavelli, Vincent — played the Peddler in *TNG* episode "The Arsenal of Freedom."

Schiffer, Paul — scriptwriter of *TNG* episode "Conundrum."

"Schisms" — sixth-season *TNG* episode written by

Brannon Braga, Ronald Wilkerson, and Jean Matthias, directed by Robert Wiemer. Riker has not been sleeping well, while other crewmembers, including Worf, are having strange reactions to things, such as barber scissors. It is discovered that aliens from another dimension are kidnapping, experimenting on, and torturing crewmembers while they sleep.

"Schizoid Man, The" — second-season *TNG* episode written by Hans Beimler, Richard Manning, and Tracy Torme, directed by Les Landau. The dying Dr. Ira Graves transfers his personality into Data. Guest stars: W. Morgan Sheppard, Barbara Alyn Woods, and Suzie Plakson.

Schkolnick, Barry M. — scriptwriter of *TNG* episode "Conundrum."

Schmerer, James — scriptwriter of the animated episode "The Survivor." His other writing credits include the series *Chase*.

Schmidt, Folkert — played a doctor in *TNG* episode "Contagion."

Schmidt, Georgia — played a Talosian in Classic *Trek* pilot "The Cage" and "The Menagerie." Film credits include *A Killing Affair* ('77) and *Terror at Alcatraz* ('82).

Schmitter — a miner on Janus VI killed by the Horta in Classic episode "Devil in the Dark." He is played by Biff Elliott.

Schneider, Paul — scriptwriter of Classic *Trek* episodes "Balance of Terror," "The Squire of Gothos," and the animated "The Terratin Incident."

Schoenbrun, Michael P. — unit production manager of *The Search for Spock*.

Schofield, Sandy — author of *DS9* novels and the pen name for the married science-fiction writing/editing team Kristine Kathryn Rusch and Dean Wesley Smith.

Kristine Rusch currently edits *The Magazine of Fantasy and Science Fiction* and has had several horror and fantasy novels published. Dean Smith is the current publisher of the magazine *Pulphouse*.

Scholar, Yang — old man who is keeper of the records on Omega in Classic episode "The Omega Glory." Among the documents are a United States Constitution, a Bible, and an American flag. He is played by Morgan Farley.

Schone, Reiner — played Esoqq in *TNG* episode "Allegiance."

Schuck, John — played the Klingon ambassador in *The Voyage Home* and *The Undiscovered Country*. Born in 1944, his TV work includes roles on the series *McMillan and Wife*, *Holmes and Yoyo*, *Turnabout*, and *The Odd Couple*. He was also in the movies *M*A*S*H* and *Earthbound*. He is also the ex-husband of Susan Bay (see entry), Leonard Nimoy's wife.

Schultz, Dwight — played Lt. Reginald Barclay in *TNG* episodes "Hollow Pursuits," "The Nth Degree," "Realm of Fear" and "Ship in a Bottle." He has also appeared in many TV movies.

Schultz, Joel — played a Klingon in *Star Trek: The Motion Picture*.

Scorza, Philip A. — scriptwriter of *TNG* episode "Disaster."

Scott, Judson — played Joachim in *The Wrath of Khan* and guest starred as Sobi in *TNG* episode "Symbiosis." He was unbilled in the movie due to a misunderstanding between his agent and the studio. He also starred in the short-lived TV series *The Phoenix* and appeared in the film *I, The Jury* ('82).

Scott, Renata — played an admiral in *TNG* episode "Realm of Fear."

Scott, Ted — played Eraclitus in Classic *Trek* episode "Plato's Stepchildren."

Scott, Tryla, Captain — captain of the *Renegade* who was controlled by parasites in *TNG* episode "Conspiracy." She was played by Ursaline Bryant.

Scott, Montgomery, Lieutenant Commander — chief engineer on the *Enterprise* in Classic *Trek*. The resident miracle worker, he always seems to be able to call up more power out of the ship's maxed-out engines. He is played by James Doohan. Scotty, which is the nickname his friends use, had a nephew, Peter Preston, who died in *The Wrath of Khan*. Born in Aberdeen, Scotland, his serial number is SE197514. He likes to read technical manuals for recreation. He appears in *TNG* "Relics," awakened after being held in stasis by a transporter beam for 75 years.

Scotter, Dick — played Painter in Classic *Trek* episode "This Side of Paradise."

Seago, Howie — played Riva in *TNG* episode "Loud As a Whisper."

Seales, Franklyn — played a bridge crewman in *Star Trek: The Motion Picture* and had a recurring role on *Silver Spoons*. Film credits include *Beulah Land* and *Southern Comfort*.

"Second Chances" — sixth-season *TNG* episode written by René Echevarria and Michael A. Medlock, directed by LeVar Burton. The *Enterprise* discovers a duplicate Riker who has been stranded, through a transporter accident, for eight years on Nervala IV. He is Riker in every way, a complete being, but still in love with Troi. Guest star: Mae Jemison.

Sector 001 — Earth's sector mentioned in *TNG* episodes "The Best of Both Worlds" and "Time's Arrow."

Sector 23 — region closest to the Neutral Zone, as mentioned in *TNG* episode "The Measure of a Man." Philipa Louvois is the representative of this region's JAG office.

Sector 30 — located in the Neutral Zone, as mentioned in *TNG* episode "The Neutral Zone." The Federation had two outposts that were destroyed in this sector.

Sector 31 — in *TNG* episode "The Neutral Zone," this sector had two outposts with which all communication was lost on Stardate 41903.2. It is located near the Neutral Zone.

Sector 39J — location of the Gamma 7A system. It is in this system that the *Intrepid* is destroyed by the galactic amoeba in Classic episode "The Immunity Syndrome." The *Enterprise* later meets up with the amoeba here and destroys it.

Sector 63 — in *TNG* episode "Conspiracy," the *Horatio* was destroyed here.

Sector 108 — in *TNG* episode "Where Silence Has Lease," this sector is located in the Void.

Sector 396 — the Selimi Asteroid Belt is located here in *TNG* episode "The Offspring."

Sector 2520 — near the Klingon-Federation border, mentioned in *TNG* episode "Aquiel."

Sector 9569 — in *TNG* episode "Transfigurations" the *Enterprise* meets the Zalkonian ship here.

Sector 21305 — where the *Enterprise* conducts surveys in *TNG* episode "Ensign Ro."

Sector 21459 — where the Rahm Izad system is located, and where Crusher believes Professor Galen's micropaleontology clue can be found in *TNG* episode "The Chase."

Sector 21947 — on the border of Talarian space in *TNG* episode "Suddenly Human."

Sector 37628 — destination of the *Enterprise* in *TNG* episode "Ethics."

security guards — the *Enterprise* has many, and they appear in dozens of episodes. Often called "red shirts" by the fans of *Trek*, they often do not last long. They are the first to be killed on landing parties, etc.

Seel, Charles — played Ed in Classic *Trek* episode "Spectre of the Gun." His TV credits include *One Step Beyond, The Guns of Will Sonnett,* and *Griff.* He also had a regular role as Barney on *Gunsmoke* and another regular role on *The Road West.* He also appeared in the 1983 film *Duel.*

Seeley, Eileen — played Ard'rian MacKenzie in *TNG* episode "The Ensigns of Command."

Segall, Pamela — played Oji in *TNG* episode "Who Watches the Watchers."

sehlat — Vulcan animal which resembles a giant teddy bear with six-inch fangs. Spock had one for a pet, named I'Chaya, according to Amanda in Classic episode "Journey to Babel." I'Chaya dies while defending Spock during his *kahs'wan* in animated episode "Yesteryear."

Sela, Commander — half-Romulan daughter of Tasha Yar, played by Denise Crosby, who brainwashes Geordi in *TNG* episode "The Mind's Eye," aids Klingon rebels in "Redemption," and captures Picard, Spock, and Data in "Unification."

Selar, Lieutenant — *Enterprise* medical officer who is Vulcan. She appears in *TNG* episode "The Schizoid Man," "Tapestry," "Remember Me," and "Yesterday's Enterprise." She is played by Suzie Plakson.

Selay — planet located in the Beta Renor system which is inhabited by reptile people who eat live prey. They are at war with Antica, a neighboring world, in *TNG* episode "Lonely among Us."

Selburg, David — played Whalen in *TNG* episode "The Big Goodbye," and appeared in "Frame of Mind."

Selcundi Drema Sector — sector whose systems are plagued with seismic disturbances in *TNG* episode "Pen Pals."

Selek — Vulcan name Spock gives himself when he meets his young self on Vulcan in animated episode "Yesteryear." He claims to be a cousin to the family, the son of Sasek and T'Pel.

Seleya, Mount — Mount Seleya, located on Vulcan, is a special place for mysticism and healing which can be reached by climbing an endless curve of stairs carved into the mountain's side. It is also where people bring the *katras* of their loved ones to the Hall of Thought. Seleya is seen in *The Search for Spock*. It is here that a Vulcan priestess rejoins Spock's body with his *katra* (the *katra* was held by McCoy) at the end of the film. It is at the temple at the top of this mountain where they give Spock the white monk's robe with a hood which he wears throughout his healing and on into *The Voyage Home*. He regains his uniform by the end of *The Voyage Home*.

selgninaem — substance that can alter glass, one of five such substances, mentioned in *TNG* episode "Hollow Pursuits."

Selimi Asteroid Belt — in *TNG* episode "The Offspring," the *Enterprise* is en route to this location to chart the area.

Selmon, Karole — played Yareena in *TNG* episode "Code of Honor."

Selodis IV Convention for the Treatment of Prisoners of War — mentioned in *TNG* episode "Chain of Command." Picard demands his rights under this treaty when the Cardassians capture him, but they do not abide by the convention.

Selsby, Harve — played a guard in Classic *Trek* episode "The Cloud Minders." He was in the 1978 movie *Sergeant Matlovich vs. the US Air Force*.

Seltris III — where Picard is captured by Cardassians while attempting to ascertain if it is the location of a secret underground base in *TNG* episode "Chain of Command."

Senensky, Ralph — director of Classic *Trek* episodes "This Side of Paradise," "Metamorphosis," "Obsession," "Return to Tomorrow," "Bread and Circuses," "Is There in Truth No Beauty?" and "The Tholian Web." TV directorial credits include episodes of *Planet of the Apes*. Films include *A Dream for Christmas*, *Death Cruise*, and *The New Adventures of Heidi*.

sensor web — Miranda Jones wears one of these, which allows her to "see" and move about without aid in Classic episode "Is There in Truth No Beauty?" She is blind, but the web allows her to ascertain the shapes of objects and the distance they are from her body.

Sentinel Minor IV — destination of the *Lalo* when it was attacked by the Borg in *TNG* episode "The Best of Both Worlds."

sentinels — the guards in Stratos City are called sentinels in Classic episode "The Cloud Minders."

Septimis Minor — in *TNG* episode "The Ensigns of Command," the *Artemis* was en route to this location but ended up on Tau Cygna V.

Septimus — a former senator of Planet 892 IV in Classic episode "Bread and Circuses." He is an older man who leads the worshippers of the Son. He is played by Ian Wolfe.

servo — Gary Seven's weapon which resembles a pen in Classic episode "Assignment: Earth."

Setal, Sublieutenant — false name used by Romulan Admiral Jarok in *TNG* episode "The Defector."

Seti, Mr. — the barber's assistant on the *Enterprise* in *TNG* episode "Schisms."

Setlik III — O'Brien killed a Cardassian on this world, which was massacred by Cardassians in *TNG* episode "The Wounded."

Setznick, Albie — played the juggler in *TNG* episode "Cost of Living."

Seurat, Pilar — played Sybo in Classic *Trek* episode "Wolf in the Fold." TV credits include *The Man from U.N.C.L.E.* and *Voyage to the Bottom of the Sea*.

Seven, Gary — twentieth-century Terran who was born on another planet and a member of a highly advanced, secret society interested in helping Earth survive its nuclear age and develop into a peaceful society. He is also known as Supervisor 194. His 20th-century human assistant, inadvertently drawn into his mission, is Roberta Lincoln. In Classic episode "Assignment: Earth," is it intimated at the end that the two will marry. Gary is played by Robert Lansing.

Sevrin, Dr. — leader of a group of space hippies in Classic episode "The Way to Eden." Once an engineer in acoustics, electronics, and communications on Tiburon, he is a carrier of *Synthococcus novae*, a disease contagious to indigenous peoples of primitive worlds. He dies when he eats poisoned fruit on the so-called Eden world. He is played by Skip Homeier.

Seymour, Carolyn — guest starred in *TNG* episode "Face of the Enemy" and played Taras in *TNG* episode "Contagion" and Mirasta Yale in "First Contact."

"Shades of Gray" — second-season *TNG* episode written by Maurice Hurley, Hans Beimler, and Richard Manning, directed by Rob Bowman. A parasite invades Riker's body and to save him Pulaski must stimulate the memory center of his mind, forcing him to relive in flashbacks certain periods of his life. Guest star: Colm Meaney.

Shahna — Kirk's drill thrall who is to teach him the

games in Classic episode "The Gamesters of Triskelion." She is actually from Triskelion, born as a slave. Her mother was killed in the games. She is played by Angelique Pettyjohn.

ShaKaRee — home of the god Sybok says he seeks and to whom he has a personal channel. He searches for ShaKaRee using the *Enterprise* in *The Final Frontier*. ShaKaRee turns out to be a dead world imprisoning an evil, omnipotent being.

Shankar, Naren — scriptwriter of *TNG* episodes "The First Duty," "Face of the Enemy," "Suspicions," and "The Quality of Life." He also wrote the *DS9* episode "Babel" and worked as the science consultant on *TNG* and *DS9*.

Shanklin, Douglas Alan — played a prison guard in *The Search for Spock*.

Shanthi, Fleet Admiral — she orders Picard to command the blockade fleet on the Romulan–Klingon border during the Klingon civil war, in *TNG* episode "Redemption." She is played by Fran Bennett.

Sharee, Keith — author of *TNG* novel *Gulliver's Fugitives*.

Shatner, Leslie — extra in Classic *Trek* episode "Miri," when she was around age seven. She is the eldest daughter of William Shatner.

Shatner, Lisabeth — extra in Classic *Trek* episode "Miri," when she was around age five. She also wrote the book *The Making of Star Trek V*. She has worked on other projects with her father, William Shatner, and did some writing for the show *T.J. Hooker*.

Shatner, Melanie — played Kirk's yeoman in *The Final Frontier*. She is the youngest of William Shatner's three daughters and has also done a car commercial, which had a *Star Trek* theme, with her father. Her other TV credits include *T.J. Hooker*.

Shatner, William — starred as Captain James Tiberius Kirk in *Star Trek,* the subsequent six movies, in the animated series, and directed the fifth *Trek* movie, *The Final Frontier.* He also had a cameo appearance as Kirk on the sitcom *Mork and Mindy.* Born March 22, 1931, in Montreal, Canada, Shatner intended to follow in his father's footsteps and take over the family company. He studied business in college, but his problems with math caused him to start studying acting. He moved to New York in 1956 and landed jobs on stage as well as in live television. His first film, *The Brothers Karamazov,* in which he played Alexei Karamazov, received critical praise in 1957. In his stage and screen work in the late fifties and early sixties, Shatner won critical acclaim for just about everything he did, winning numerous acting awards. He single-handedly saved the play *The World of Suzie Wong* from turning into a disaster by playing it as a comedy when audiences started walking out. Because of his imaginative performance, the play was not cancelled but went on to a successful two-year run on Broadway. He starred in the films *The Intruder* (also called *I Hate Your Guts!* and *Shame*) and *Judgment at Nuremberg.* He did two very famous *Twilight Zone* episodes before acting in the *Star Trek* pilot "Where No Man Has Gone Before" in 1965. The series ran for three years and was a bittersweet experience for Shatner. During the series, he was going through many emotional ups and downs: He was in the process of separating from his first wife, Gloria, and he was also concerned that it had not been the right decision to work in Hollywood on a television series when his dream had actually been the pursuit of film and theatre. Gaining fame, recognition, and notoriety did not necessarily mean success to him. When *Star Trek* was cancelled, he was forced to take almost any role he could get just to pay the bills. During this time he starred in such films as *White Comanche, Sole Survivor, Pray for the Wildcats,* and *The Andersonville Trial* (where he met his second wife, Marcy Lafferty). He made many guest appearances on TV shows of the 1970s such as *The Sixth Sense, Barnaby Jones, The Magician, The Six Million Dollar Man, Police*

Woman, Columbo, Mission: Impossible, and dozens of game shows including several appearances on *The 20,000 Dollar Pyramid* with Leonard Nimoy. He did some stage work as well, such as *Otherwise Engaged* (starring with his second wife, Marcy Lafferty, see entry). When the *Star Trek* movies were made, he found new financial success. He was hesitant, at first, upon hearing that Nimoy would be directing the third movie; unsure of how their professional relationship would affect their personal one. But their friendship survived and strengthened, and of Nimoy's directing Shatner says, "Leonard is an outstanding director, very sure of himself but also receptive to ideas." Shatner finally got the chance to direct his own *Star Trek* movie, *The Final Frontier.* Prior to the movie, he became the star of the series *T.J. Hooker* and had directed some of its episodes. The show lasted four seasons, mostly on the strength of Shatner's popularity, since the series was not especially notable in any other way. Leonard Nimoy guest starred in one episode, however, reuniting with Shatner for the first time outside their *Star Trek* roles. Shatner now hosts the very popular *Rescue 911* series, which has run, to date, for four years. He also cowrote, with Ron Goulart, the action science-fiction novels *Tekwar, Teklords,* and *Teklab,* with more novels in the series scheduled to be published. The books have been sold to Universal for a possible movie and TV series. Shatner will direct the series and Greg Evigan will star. Also currently in progress is a play called *Believe* (based on a novel by Shatner and Michael Tobias), which William Shatner and Leonard Nimoy are working on together. They are also interested in producing movie projects together and recently toured the U.S. in a two-man show discussing their *Star Trek* days. In 1993, Shatner's memoirs were finally released, *Star Trek Memories,* and *Star Trek Movie Memories* followed in 1994. These are not his first. The book *Shatner: Where No Man* (cowritten by Shatner, Sondra Marshak, and Myrna Culbreath) came out in the early 1980s, but has never been re-released. Shatner, unhappy with the book, bought all reprint rights and buried it. He continues to work hard as an actor, writer, director, and producer, has a great love of horses, and rides in professional horse shows in his spare time. He has three daughters from his first wife, Leslie, Lisabeth, and Melanie. Despite earlier setbacks during the 1970s, he has enjoyed continuing success, much of it due to the cult popularity of *Star Trek*, and much of it to his own energy and spirit. Of *Star Trek*, he says, "It's been something that has given me great opportunities that I wouldn't have had otherwise." His star on Hollywood Boulevard is only one of the many awards he has received for his work.

Shaw, Larry — director of *TNG* episode "Loud As a Whisper."

Shaw, Katik — in *TNG* episode "The High Ground," he is a Rutian waiter attacked by the Ansata. It turns out he was probably the person who set off the bomb, and is a terrorist himself. He is played by Marc Buckland.

Shaw, Areel, Lieutenant — an old lover of Kirk's, she is a lawyer in the judge advocate's office on Starbase 11 who is hired to prosecute him in Classic episode "Court-Martial." She is played by Joan Marshall.

Shawn, Wallace — played Zek in *DS9* episode "The Nagus."

Shea, Ann — played Nellen in *TNG* episode "The Drumhead."

Shea, Lieutenant — *Enterprise* officer who is tortured by the Kelvans when they reduce him into a block of white powder and threaten to crush him. He is played by Carl Byrd in Classic episode "By Any Other Name."

Shearer, Hannah Louise — scriptwriter of *TNG* episodes "When the Bough Breaks," "Skin of Evil," "We'll Always Have Paris," "Pen Pals," and "The Price." She also wrote the *DS9* story "Q Less."

Shearman, Alan — played Inspector Lestrade in *TNG* episode "Elementary, Dear Data."

Shegog, Clifford — played a Klingon officer in *The Undiscovered Country*.

Shelby, Lieutenant Commander — Starfleet tactical officer who helps the *Enterprise* fight the Borg in *TNG* episode "The Best of Both Worlds." She is played by Elizabeth Dennehy.

Sheldon, Jack — played the piano player in *TNG* episode "11001001."

Sheldon, Lee — scriptwriter of *TNG* episode "Remember Me."

Sheliak Corporate — group of beings who are crystalline in appearance and have refused contact with the Federation for 111 years. They do not see humanity as an intelligent race, merely an "infestation." In *TNG* episode "The Ensigns of Command," they threaten to destroy the colony on Tau Cygna V.

Sheliak vessel — this ship is en route to Tau Cygna when Picard stops it in *TNG* episode "The Ensigns of Command." The Sheliak commander of the ship is played by Mart McChesney.

Shelius — location of the Sheliak Corporate in *TNG* episode "The Ensigns of Command."

Shelyne, Carole — played the Metron in Classic *Trek* episode "Arena." TV credits also include *The Man from U.N.C.L.E.*

Shepard, Dodie — costume designer for *The Final Frontier* and *The Undiscovered Country*.

Shepherd, Jim — stunt double for Thelev in Classic *Trek* episode "Journey to Babel."

Sheppard, W. Morgan — played Dr. Ira Graves in *TNG* "The Schizoid Man."

Sherman's Planet — located near Space Station *K–7*

in Classic episode "The Trouble with Tribbles" and the animated episode "More Tribbles, More Troubles." Both the Federation and the Klingon Empire claim rights to this world, which will go to whoever can best develop it, according to the precepts of the Organian Peace Treaty. It suffers from a famine in the animated episode.

Sherven, Judi — played a nurse in Classic *Trek* episode "Wolf in the Fold."

Shika Maru — ship which first encounters the "Children of Tama" in *TNG* episode "Darmok." It is commanded by Captain Silvestri.

ShiKahr — Vulcan city where Spock was raised. It is seen in the animated episode "Yesteryear."

Shimerman, Armin — stars as the Ferengi bartender Quark in *DS9*. Born in Lakewood, New Jersey, he was 17 when he moved to Los Angeles, not to act but to practice law. He got into acting, however, when he joined a drama group, and moved to New York where he starred in productions on Broadway. His TV credits include *Beauty and the Beast*, as well as appearances in *L.A. Law*, *Who's the Boss?*, *Married with Children*, *Alien Nation*, and *Cop Rock*, as well as a recurring role in *Brooklyn Bridge*. He had many appearances in *TNG*, including unbilled performances as voices or aliens. His *TNG* credits include: Letek in "The Last Outpost," the voice of the "wedding box" in "Haven," and Bractor in "Peak Performance." The makeup team for both *TNG* and *DS9*, responsible for the Ferengi makeup, won an Emmy for their work.

Shimoda, Jim — in *TNG* episode "The Naked Now," he is the assistant chief of engineering who removed all the chips from the computer. He was played by Benjamin W. S. Lum.

"Ship in a Bottle" — sixth-season *TNG* episode written by René Echevarria and directed by Alexander Singer. Barclay returns, this time to fix a malfunctioning holodeck, only to discover a secret memory file that includes Professor Moriarty, who appears to have achieved consciousness. Moriarty wants to figure out a way to leave the holodeck without disintegrating, and he takes over the ship in an attempt to make Data and others work on a solution. Guest stars: Daniel Davis, Dwight Schultz, and Stephanie Beacham.

Shireleus VI — the Parallax Colony in *TNG* episode "Cost of Living" is located here.

Shirriff, Cathie — played Valkris in *The Search for Spock*. Her other roles include *Today's FBI* and cohost of *Ripley's Believe It or Not*. Film credits include *Friendships, Secrets and Lies*, *She's Dressed to Kill*, and *One Shoe Makes It Murder*.

Shor, Dan — played Dr. Arridor in *TNG* episode "The Price."

"Shore Leave" — written by award-winning science-fiction author Theodore Sturgeon, this first-season Classic *Trek* episode was directed by Robert Sparr and aired 12/29/66. It involves a world where thoughts and wishes can become real and, in some cases, dangerous. Guest stars: Barbara Baldavin (who appeared in "Balance of Terror"), Emily Banks, Oliver McGowan, Perry Lopez, Bruce Mars, and Shirley Bonne. Of note: Theodore Sturgeon based this plot on a short story he wrote titled "Case and the Dreamer." In one scene of this episode, you can see a collar on the terribly "vicious" tiger.

Shore Leave Planet — on this world, whatever you think or wish for can come to life, since it is a planet embedded with sensors that can read or overhear your desires. It is run by the Caretaker, a friendly old man who appears human in Classic episode "Shore Leave."

Shras — an Andorian ambassador to the Babel Conference in Classic episode "Journey to Babel." He is played by Reggie Nalder.

Shugrue, Robert F. — film editor on *The Search for Spock*. He also worked with Harve Bennett on *The Gemini Man*.

Shutan, Jan — played Lt. Mira Romaine in Classic *Trek* episode "The Lights of Zetar." Film credits include *Message to My Daughter*, *Senior Year*, and *This House Possessed*. She was also a regular in *Sons and Daughters*.

Shuttle 6 — Q takes this shuttle in *TNG* episode "Q Who."

Shuttle 10 — shuttle from the USS *Repulse* which brings Pulaski on board the *Enterprise* in *TNG* episode "The Child."

Shuttlecraft — small spacecraft on the *Enterprise* which can comfortably seat seven. In Classic *Trek* the *Enterprise* has two, the *Galileo* and the *Columbus*. In the animated series, it has one called the *Copernicus*. In *TNG*, the *Enterprise* has both shuttlecraft and runabouts of various names including the *El Baz*, *Onizuka*, *Pike*, *Sakharov*, *Magellan*, *Feynman*, *Hawking*, *Goddard*, *Fermi*, *Famen*, *Cousteau*, *Aries*, and the *Justman*.

Shuttlecraft 13 — destroyed by Armus on Vagra II in *TNG* episode "Skin of Evil."

sick-bay — ship's hospital, overseen by Dr. McCoy in Classic *Trek* and Dr. Crusher in *TNG*. It is headed by Dr. Pulaski in *TNG*'s second season only. It is the most protected area of the ship.

Sierra VI, Outpost — this outpost tracks the Romulan ship heading for the borders of the Federation in *TNG* episode "The Defector."

Sigma Draconis — G9 type star with nine planets where the ship that took Spock's brain ends up in the Classic episode "Spock's Brain."

Sigma Draconis III — another inhabited world of the

Sigma Draconis system, with a technology rating of 3, equivalent to Earth's development in 1485. It is mentioned in Classic episode "Spock's Brain."

Sigma Draconis IV — a world in the Sigma Draconis system with a G rating, equivalent to Earth's 2030 technology. This world is scanned in Classic episode "Spock's Brain."

Sigma Draconis VI — an ice world in the Sigma Draconis system where the Morgs live. The Eymorgs of "Spock's Brain" live under the surface with advanced technology, but no knowledge of how it works. A computer runs their society.

Sigma Draconis VII — planet in the Sigma Draconis system, mentioned in Classic episode "Spock's Brain."

Sigma Erani System — in *TNG* episode "The Most Toys," this system is mentioned as the only source of hytritium.

Sigman Survivor — a mining accident survivor played by Elaine Nalee in *TNG* episode "Hide and Q."

Sikking, James B. — played Captain Styles in *The Search for Spock*. He has been a regular in the TV series *Turnabout, Hill Street Blues,* and *Doogie Howser,* M.D., and has guest starred in numerous series and TV movies. He also appeared in the 1983 film *The Star Chamber*.

Silarian Sector — location of the dead world Katan in *TNG* episode "The Inner Light."

"Silicon Avatar" — fifth-season *TNG* episode written by Lawrence V. Conley, Nancy Bond, Peter Allan Fields, and Jeri Taylor, directed by Cliff Bole. The return of the Crystalline Entity occurs while Dr. Kila Marr, whose son was killed by the creature, is on board the *Enterprise*. Under the auspices of studying it, she deliberately murders it just as the *Enterprise* crew might be on the verge of learning how to communicate with it to get it to voluntarily stop destroying worlds. Guest stars: Ellen Geer and

Susan Diol. Of note: Dr. Marr holds her tricorder upside-down during a conversation with Data.

Silver, Spike — stunt man in *The Voyage Home.*

Simmons, Jean — played Admiral Nora Satie in *TNG* episode "The Drumhead."

Simoco III — in *TNG* episode "Conundrum," a technician strains her shoulder while diving off the Cliffs of Heaven located on this world in a holodeck simulation.

Simpson, Billy — played voice of young Spock in the animated "Yesteryear."

Simpson, Jonathan — played young Sarek in *The Final Frontier.*

Singer, Alexander — director of *TNG* episodes "Relics" and "Ship in a Bottle."

Singer, Raymond — played the young doctor in *The Voyage Home.* His TV credits include *Remington Steele, The Feather and Father Gang, Operation Petticoat* (on which he was a regular), and *Mama Malone.* He also appeared in the 1983 film *The Entity.*

Singh — *Enterprise* engineer killed by the cloud creature in *TNG* episode "Lonely among Us." He is played by Kavi Raz.

Singh, Khan Noonian — a superman, the result of genetic enhancement, who came to power on Earth briefly during the Eugenics Wars of the late 1990s. He is found by the *Enterprise* on a sleeper ship, the *Botany Bay,* along with 80 of his people, and is awakened into the 23rd century. He attempts to take control of the *Enterprise* and when he fails, Kirk condemns him to exile on Ceti Alpha V. *Enterprise* officer Marla McGivers goes with him to be his wife. Ricardo Montalban played Khan in Classic episode "Space Seed" and in the film *The Wrath of Khan.*

Singh, Lieutenant — an *Enterprise* crewmember who

is briefly in charge of Nomad in Classic episode "The Changeling." He is played by Blaisdell Makee.

Singh, Reginald Lal — played Board Officer Chandra in Classic *Trek* episode "Court-Martial."

"Sins of the Father" — third-season *TNG* episode written by Ronald D. Moore, W. Reed Moran, and Drew Deighan, directed by Les Landau. Worf and his younger brother challenge a ruling against their dead father, who is thought to have been involved in high treason, in the Klingon high courts. Guest stars: Tony Todd, Charles Cooper, Patrick Massett, Thelma Lee, and Teddy Davis.

Sirah — Cloud William's Yang woman on Omega in Classic episode "The Omega Glory." She is played by Irene Kelley.

Sirius IX — in the animated episode "Mudd's Passion," Mudd relocated here with the money he made from selling Starfleet Academy to the people of Ilyra VI.

Sirrie IV — the vase owned by Fajo in *TNG* episode "The Most Toys" was carved by Mark Off'Zel on this world.

Sirtis, Marina — stars as Counselor Deanna Troi in *The Next Generation*. Born on March 29, 1964, she is a British actress of Greek descent, who worked in England before coming to Hollywood. Six months after arriving, she landed the *Trek* series. She only had a six-month visa and it was running out when she got the call that she had the job. She originally auditioned three times for the part of Tasha Yar, when the producers decided to have her read for the part of Troi. While working in England, her roles included British TV and musical theatre. She appeared in the films *The Wicked Lady* (with Faye Dunaway), and *Deathwish III* (with Charles Bronson). She is a soccer fan (her brother is a professional soccer player) and an avid animal rights activist. Marina is married and lives in Los Angeles.

Sisko, Benjamin, Commander — commander of *Deep Space 9* and played by Avery Brooks. He had a wife, Jennifer, who died at Wolf 359 when the Borg attacked the USS *Saratoga*, on which he served as first officer. His son, Jake, lives with him on *DS9* and it is obvious that Sisko is a highly devoted parent. Sisko is a likable man who has few prejudices, save against the Borg who killed his wife. A firm leader who does not allow his orders to be questioned, he is also open minded and fair. He has great compassion for the Bajorans and what they have gone through at the hands of the Cardassians. He himself was discovered to be the "emissary" the Bajorans were waiting for, who would help them solve the riddle of the Bajoran Orbs they worship, which can tell some people their future. Before commanding *DS9* Sisko worked for three years at the Mars Utopia Planetia Shipyards where the *Enterprise* was built. Ben's best friend is Dax, whom he knew when Dax was Curzon. Now that "he" is Jadzia, he has some trouble with the fact that he's a beautiful young female, but still talks about old times with his old friend, whose memories are retained within Jadzia. Sisko is one of the few people who has held communication with the aliens living within the wormhole that leads to the Gamma Quadrant. It is thanks to him that ships now have safe passage through the wormhole.

Sisko, Jake — Benjamin Sisko's son who survived the Borg attack and lives with his dad, commander of *DS9*, on the station, and attends the school there, taught by Keiko O'Brien. His best friend is Nog, Rom's son and Quark's nephew. They enjoy hanging out on a balcony, their legs swinging over the side, watching all the people on *DS9* come and go (especially the girls). Jake, at fourteen, gets into some trouble, but is really a good kid, guided by intelligence and conscience, and has a very strong bond with his father. Jake is played by Cirroc Loften.

Sisto, Rocco — played Sakkath in *TNG* episode "Sarek."

Sito, Cadet Second Class — Bajoran female cadet in Wesley's Nova Squadron in *TNG* episode "The First Duty." She is played by Shannon Fill.

"Skin of Evil" — first-season *TNG* episode written by Joseph Stefano and Hannah Louise Shearer and directed by Joseph L. Scanlan. An evil being with great power causes a shuttle with Deanna Troi on board to crash on its world, Vagra II. When the *Enterprise* crew comes to Troi's rescue, the slimy creature, named Armus, kills Tasha Yar. It is the first time in the series that a major player is killed, and the crew mourns her death for a long time. Guest stars: Walker Boone, Brad Zerbst, Raymond Forchion, Mart McChesney, and Ron Gans (voice of Armus). A blooper in this episode has Geordi dropping his phaser into Armus; in the next scene he has it back in his hands.

Skorr — planet with winged humanoids in the animated episode "Jihad."

Sky, Kathleen — author of Classic *Trek* novels *Vulcan!* and *Death's Angel*.

Slack, Ben — played K'Tal in "Redemption, Part I."

Slater, Christian — played a Starfleet officer in *The Undiscovered Country*. As a *Star Trek* fan, he asked for this cameo role. His film credits, which are numerous, include *Pump Up the Volume*, *Heathers*, *Kuffs*, *Young Guns II*, and *True Romance*.

"Slaver Weapon" — written by renowned science-fiction author Larry Niven, this animated Classic *Trek* episode aired 12/15/73. A Slaver stasis box found on the planet Kzin is being shuttled to Starbase 25 for inspection. Spock, Uhura, and Sulu are on board the *Copernicus* with the box en route to the starbase when they get readings from a nearby planet that another stasis box is there. They investigate and discover Kzin, who takes them prisoner. In the box is a Slaver weapon that talks and has settings none of them understands. The weapon finally self-destructs.

Slavin, George F. — scriptwriter of Classic *Trek* episode "The Mark of Gideon." He also wrote the script for the 1959 film *Son of Robin Hood*.

slingshot effect — the *Enterprise* uses this procedure to travel backward and forward in time, in Classic episode "Tomorrow Is Yesterday" and in *The Voyage Home*. They use the gravitational pull of a star to sling them at high warp speed through time.

Sloyan, James — played Admiral Jarok in *TNG* episode "The Defector."

Slutsker, Peter — played Nibor in *TNG* episode "Ménage à Troi" and appeared in "Suspicions."

Small Boy — the boy who assists Kirk and Spock in Classic episode "A Piece of the Action" and is played by Sheldon Collins.

Smith, Eve — played the elderly patient in *The Voyage Home*.

Smith, Frank Owen — played Curzon in *DS9* episode "Emissary."

Smith, Fred G. — played a policeman in *TNG* episode "The High Ground."

Smith, K. L. — played a Klingon in Classic *Trek* "Elaan of Troyius." Film credits include *Battle of the Coral Sea*, *Incident in San Francisco*, and *The Delphi Bureau*.

Smith, Keith — director of photography for Classic *Trek* episode "By Any Other Name."

Smith, Kurtwood — played the Federation president in "*Star Trek* VI: The Undiscovered Country."

Smith, Patricia — played Sara Kingsley in *TNG* episode "Unnatural Selection."

Smith, Sandra — played Dr. Janice Lester in Classic *Trek* episode "Turnabout Intruder." She had a regular role on the TV series the *The Interns* and also appeared in *Iron Horse*.

Smith, Yeoman — a yeoman Kirk keeps calling Jones in Classic episode "Where No Man Has Gone Before." She is played by Andrea Dromm.

Smithers, William — played Merikus or Captain R. M. Merik in Classic *Trek* episode "Bread and Circuses." His TV credits include *Voyage to the Bottom of the Sea*, *Barnaby Jones*, and regular roles in *Peyton Place*, *Executive Suite*, and *Dallas*.

Snodgrass, Melinda M. — scriptwriter (and story editor/executive script consultant for fourth and fifth seasons) for *TNG* episodes "The Measure of a Man," "Pen Pals," "Up the Long Ladder," "The Ensigns of Command," and "The High Ground." A science-fiction novelist, she is also the author of the Classic *Trek* novel *The Tears of the Singers*.

Snyder, John — played Bochra in *TNG* episode "The Enemy" and Aaron Conor in "The Masterpiece Society."

Snyder, Michael — played a Starfleet communications officer in *The Voyage Home*. He also played Quol in *TNG* episode "The Perfect Mate" and appeared in "Rascals."

Sobelman, Boris — scriptwriter of Classic *Trek* episode "The Return of the Archons." Other writing credits include *The Man from U.N.C.L.E.*

Sobi — leader of the Brekkan sales team, who is trapped on the *Sanction* and is brought aboard the *Enterprise* in *TNG* episode "Symbiosis." He is played by Judson Scott.

Soble, Ron — played Wyatt Earp in Classic *Trek* episode "Spectre of the Gun." TV credits include a regular role on *The Monroes* and appearances in the films *The Daughters of Joshua Cabe*, *The Beast Within*, and *The Mystic Warrior*.

Sofaer, Abraham — played the Thasian in Classic

Trek episode "Charlie X" and the Melkotian voice in "Spectre of the Gun." Born October 1, 1896 in Burma, he has been acting in the U.S. since the fifties. Film credits include the 1951 movie *Quo Vadis, Captain Sinbad*('63), and *Journey to the Center of Time.*

Sohl, Jerry — scriptwriter of Classic *Trek* episodes "The Corbomite Maneuver," "This Side of Paradise," and "Whom Gods Destroy." A science-fiction novelist who has written *The Time Dissolvers* and *The Odious One*, he also wrote under the pen name Nathan Butler (see entry).

Solar System L370 — ingested by the device in Classic episode "The Doomsday Machine."

Solari, Rudy — played Salish in Classic *Trek* episode "The Paradise Syndrome." TV credits include *The Bionic Woman* and *Voyage to the Bottom of the Sea*. He also had regular roles on *The Wackiest Ship in the Army, Garrison's Gorillas,* and *Redigo*. He appeared in the 1982 film *The Boss's Son.*

Solarion IV — Federation colony attacked by the Cardassians, but they made it look like the Bajorans did it in *TNG* episode "Ensign Ro."

Soleis V — in *TNG* episode "Loud As a Whisper," this planet houses two warring groups of a race called the Solari. Riva is sent to help them.

Solis — *Enterprise* bridge officer in *TNG* episode "The Arsenal of Freedom." He is played by George de la Peña.

solition wave — new propulsion method invented by Dr. Jidar in *TNG* episode "New Ground"; it doesn't work.

Solok, DaiMon — this Ferengi gives Picard, Worf, and Crusher passage on his ship to Seltris III in *TNG* episode "Chain of Command."

Solomon, Gerald — hair stylist on *DS9.*

Solow, Herbert F. — executive in charge of production for first and second seasons of *Star Trek.* He also worked on the films *Heatwave!*, *Get Crazy*, and the TV series *The Man from Atlantis*.

Son, The — the son of God and the deity the people of planet 892 IV worship. Kirk mistakenly thinks they mean their planet's sun, in Classic episode "Bread and Circuses."

Sonak — Kirk's new Vulcan science officer who is going to meet him on the *Enterprise* in *The Motion Picture*. He dies at the beginning of the film in a terrible transporter accident along with Admiral Lori Ciani.

Songi, Chairman — head of Gamelan V in *TNG* episode "Final Mission." She was played by Kim Hamilton.

sonic disruptor field — Klingon invention that acts as a door on the brigs of Romulan ships, as mentioned in Classic episode "The *Enterprise* Incident."

sonic separator — medical device McCoy uses to put Spock's brain back in its rightful place in Classic episode "Spock's Brain."

Soong, Noonian, Dr. — father and creator of Data and Lore as seen in *TNG* episode "Datalore" among others. Soong created Data in his own image. He was played by Brent Spiner.

Sorel, Louise — played Reena (or Rayna) Kapec in Classic *Trek* episode "Requiem for Methuselah." Her TV credits include *Iron Horse*, *The Survivors* (in which she was a regular), *The Don Rickles Show*, *The Curse of Dracula*, and *Ladies' Man*. She also appeared in the 1982 film *Airplane II: The Sequel*.

Soren — a member of the androgynous race, the J'naii, she thinks of herself as female, which is against the law on her world. She has an affair with Riker in *TNG* episode "The Outcast." She is played by Melinda Culea.

Sorensen, Paul — played a merchant ship captain in *The Search for Spock*. TV credits include *Iron Horse*, *The Guns of Will Sonnett*, and *Barnaby Jones*.

Sorenson, Cindy — played Furry Animal in *TNG* episode "The Dauphin."

Soul, David — played Makora in Classic *Trek* episode "The Apple." Born August 28, 1943, he was the star of the TV series *Here Come the Brides*, *Owen Marshall, Counselor at Law*, *Starsky and Hutch*, *Casablanca*, and *The Yellow Rose*. He has also starred in numerous TV movies and had a hit single song in the late seventies, "Don't Give Up on Us."

Sovak — Ferengi on Risa who is looking for the *Tox Uthat* and thinks Picard and Vash can lead him to it. He is played by Max Grodenchik in *TNG* episode "Captain's Holiday."

Sowards, Jack B. — scriptwriter of *The Wrath of Khan*. He also wrote the *TNG* episode "Where Silence Has Lease" and the films *Deliver Us from Evil*, *Cry Panic*, *Death Cruise*, and *Desperate Woman*, as well as episodes of *Barnaby Jones*.

space normal speed — slower than the speed of light (which is also known as impulse power), as mentioned in Classic episode "The Galileo Seven."

"Space Seed" — written by Gene L. Coon and Carey Wilbur, directed by Marc Daniels, this first-season Classic *Trek* episode aired 2/16/67. The *Enterprise* encounters a sleeper ship, the SS *Botany Bay* from the late 1990s, and awakens the people on board only to have them take over the *Enterprise* and threaten the crew's lives. This episode led to the movie sequel, *Star Trek II: The Wrath of Khan*. Guest stars: Ricardo Montalban, Madlyn Rhue, Blaisdell Makee, Mark Tobin, and John Winston. Of note: Chekov does not appear in this episode but in the movie Khan recognizes him from the past.

Spano, Charles A., Jr. — coauthor of Classic novel *Spock Messiah!*

Sparks, Dana — played a weapons officer in *TNG* episode "Contagion."

Sparr, Robert — director of Classic *Trek* episode "Shore Leave." He also directed episodes of *Voyage to the Bottom of the Sea*.

"Spectre of the Gun" — written by Lee Cronin and directed by Vince McEveety, this third-season Classic *Trek* episode aired 10/25/68. Finding a Melkot buoy in space that warns them away, the *Enterprise* crew insists on a meeting with the aliens on their mission of peace, and find itself victim of a great illusion wherein Kirk, Spock, McCoy, Scotty, and Chekov are the Clanton gang that must fight the Earps and Doc Holliday. The only problem is, history dictates that the Clanton gang will lose and no matter how hard they try to escape the strange, half-built town or reason with its inhabitants, they find themselves at a face-off at the O.K. Corral. Guest stars: Bonnie Beecher, Rex Holman, Ron Soble, Charles Maxwell, Sam Gilman, Bill Zuckert, Charles Seel, Ed McReady, and Gregg Palmer. Of note: James Doohan provides the voice for the Melkot buoy.

spectro readings — used by the *Enterprise* to detect disease and contamination on alien worlds. It is mentioned in Classic episode "The Naked Time."

Spellerberg, Lance — played the transporter chief in *TNG* episode "We'll Always Have Paris" and Ensign Herbert in "The Icarus Factor."

Spencer, Jim — played the air policeman in the Classic *Trek* episode "Tomorrow Is Yesterday."

Spican flame gems — Cyrano Jones tries to sell these on Space Station *K–7* in Classic episode "The Trouble with Tribbles." He is still selling them in the animated episode "More Tribbles, More Troubles."

Spielberg, David — actor who guest starred in *TNG* episode "Starship Mine."

Spies, Adrian — scriptwriter of Classic *Trek* episode "Miri." He also wrote for the TV show *The Man from*

U.N.C.L.E. and the films *Hauser's Memory*, *The Family Kovack*, and *Hanging by a Thread*.

Spinelli, Lieutenant — *Enterprise* navigator seen on the bridge in Classic episode "Space Seed." He is played by Blaisdell Makee.

Spiner, Brent — stars as Commander Data on *The Next Generation*. He also plays Lore, Data's brother, and Dr. Noonian Soong, Data's creator. Because of the nature of his character, he has played several multiple roles on *TNG*. Born in Houston, Texas, Spiner did a lot of acting work on and off Broadway and even drove a cab for six months when he was just starting out. He hates the fact that he can still hear his Texas accent in the voice of Data when he watches the show. He watched the original *Star Trek* series when he was in college (which perhaps hints at his age, which he does not like to divulge), but says his hero when he was young was Jock Mahoney, the Range Rider. He does, however, believe in beings from other planets. Interested in comedy, he appeared in *The Little Shop of Horrors* at the Westwood Playhouse in Los Angeles. His film credits include *Stardust Memories* as well as some TV movies. He has also guest starred on *The Twilight Zone*, *Hill Street Blues*, *Cheers*, and *Night Court*.

Spinrad, Norman — scriptwriter of Classic *Trek* episode "The Doomsday Machine." A science-fiction novelist who has penned such titles as *The Void Captain's Tale*, *The Iron Dream*, *Bug Jack Barron*, and others, he currently has a review and science-fiction criticism column in the magazine *Asimov's SF*. He also sells his short stories to various magazines, and has been nominated for, and won, many writing awards.

spiny lobefish — served at the Tilonus Institute for Mental Disorders to Riker in *TNG* episode "Frame of Mind." Riker does not like it.

Spock, Commander — first officer of the *Enterprise* and the ship's science officer, who starts out as Lt.

Commander in the show's first season and is Captain Spock by the second *Trek* film, later becoming an ambassador in *TNG*. He is played by Leonard Nimoy. Spock is half-Vulcan, half-human, and was raised by his parents, Amanda Grayson and Sarek, on Vulcan. He had a pet *sehlat* (see entry) named I'Chaya when he was a child. His service record, as quoted from Classic episode "Court-Martial," reads: "Serial no.: S179 276 SP; rank: Commander; commendations: Vulcan Scientific Legion of Honor, Award of Valor, and twice decorated by Starfleet Command." He has adopted his Vulcan heritage but finds it often difficult to come to terms with his human half. He is reserved, claims he has no emotions (though he is often really suppressing them), and is a vegetarian. In Classic episode "The Cage," he was only a lieutenant when he served under Pike. Spock has an A–7 computer rating, meaning he has very strong computer capabilities. He can memorize things in an instant, calculate odds while performing other, non-related tasks, and is a genius at math, science, and computer programming. He also appears interested in literature, and quotes often from literary works by humans. He plays the Vulcan lyre (and many other musical instruments, including the piano) with great skill. He had not spoken to his father for 18 years prior to "Journey to Babel," and was betrothed to a woman, when they were both seven years old, named T'Pring. T'Pring divorces Spock during their "wedding" when Spock was in the midst of *Pon farr* (see entry). He never married again during the series, although in the 24th century Picard mentioned attending Spock's wedding when he was a cadet at the Academy. At the beginning of the original series, Spock had been in service to Starfleet for 15 years and has served 11 years on board the *Enterprise*. Spock shows an unswerving loyalty to Captain Kirk and despite Spock's aloof nature, they become "brothers" (according to Spock in "Whom Gods Destroy") and "family" (as mentioned in *The Final Frontier*). McCoy and Spock often spar verbally, but are actually good friends as well. Spock even refers to Kirk as *T'hy'la* (see entry) in the novelization of *The Motion Picture* by Gene Roddenberry. Spock has had a lot of experiences, including dying and coming back to life (in *The Wrath of Khan* and *The Search for Spock*, respectively). Over the years his devotion to emotional discipline has relaxed, allowing him to reveal very deep emotions and a quick sense of humor.

Spock, Mirror — seen in Classic episode "Mirror, Mirror," this Spock is less compassionate but no less intelligent. Also played by Leonard Nimoy, he is not afraid to show anger, and though he, too, is a scientist, he has few loyalties to the Empire he serves, and to the Captain Kirk for whom he works. He inflicts pain upon Transporter Chief Kyle for a supposed error committed during the act of beaming up the landing party. He also sports a beard and mustache and a more rugged appearance than that of the real Spock. Kirk appeals to him to try to change the future of his Empire at the end of the episode, and Spock's reply is that he will think about it.

"Spock's Brain" — written by Lee Cronin and directed by Marc Daniels, this third-season Classic *Trek* episode aired 9/20/68. A woman is transported aboard the *Enterprise*, attacks the crew, and surgically removes Spock's brain while the rest of the crew is unconscious. Kirk and the crew trace her advanced ship to a world populated by women, where they find Spock's brain in time to return it to Spock before he dies. Guest stars: Marj Dusay, James Daris, and Sheila Leighton. Of note: This episode also helped supply the plot for an X-rated parody film, only it wasn't Spock's brain that was stolen.

spores — plants found on Omicron Ceti III that can enter a human's system and heal any illness, but also make an individual placid and lazy. Violent emotions will overcome and destroy the spores in the human (or Vulcan) system, as seen in Classic episode "This Side of Paradise."

Spot — Data's cat. Spot does not get along well with

Riker. He likes to jump on Data's keyboard when Data is working at the computer. He eats Feline Supplement 127.

"Squire of Gothos, The" — first-season Classic *Trek* episode written by Paul Schneider and directed by Don McDougall. It aired 1/12/67 and involves a powerful creature, Trelane, who captures the *Enterprise* crew to "toy" with them. Guest stars: William Campbell, Richard Carlyle, Michael Barrier, and Venita Wolf. Of note: William Campbell returns later as Koloth in "The Trouble with Tribbles." Also, Campbell dislocates his shoulder in a fight with Kirk (you can see this toward the end where he ends up not using the arm at all and holding it close to his side). The voices of Trelane's parents are Barbara Babcock (who guest stars in "A Taste of Armageddon" and "Plato's Stepchildren") and James Doohan.

Stacius Trade Guild — Fajo belongs to this guild in *TNG* episode "The Most Toys."

Stader, Paul — stuntman in Classic *Trek* episode "Bread and Circuses."

Star Cluster NGC 321 — where Eminiar and Vendikar are located in Classic episode "A Taste of Armageddon."

star desert — part of space with few stars. The *Enterprise* encounters Gothos in a star desert, as mentioned in Classic episode "The Squire of Gothos."

Star Station *Earhart* — where Picard, as a cadet, was stabbed through the heart by Nausicaans, as mentioned in *TNG* episode "Tapestry" and "Samaritan Snare."

Star Station *India* — in *TNG* episode "Unnatural Selection," the *Enterprise* is en route here when they receive a message from the *Lantree*.

Star System 611 — Landru's planet, Beta II, is located here, as mentioned in Classic episode "Return of the Archons."

Star Trek: The Motion Picture — this first feature-length film of the Classic *Star Trek* series had a record-breaking premiere at theaters in December, 1979. Directed by Robert Wise, it reunites the old crew of the *Enterprise* after a separation of over two years since their original five-year mission ended. Spock lives on Vulcan while attempting to achieve *Kolinahr* at the Gol temple, and Kirk has become an unhappy desk-bound admiral. McCoy is in retirement on Earth, but all are called back to pilot the *Enterprise* on a mission to discover the mystery of a cloud that is destroying ships and planets. The cloud, a machine entity calling itself Vejur, is actually what remains of the Voyager One spacecraft launched from Earth in the late twentieth century. The craft apparently entered a machine-dominated universe, and encountered an intelligence that reprogrammed it and sent it back on a new mission to seek out and destroy inferior, non-machine infestations. The *Enterprise* crew rushes to stop it. Guest stars include: Stephen Collins and Persis Khambatta, as well as brief appearances by previous *Trek* stars Grace Lee Whitney (reprising her role as Rand) and Mark Lenard (playing the Klingon captain). Of note: Marcy Lafferty, William Shatner's wife, also appears. Gene Roddenberry returns as producer, and science-fiction author Alan Dean Foster created the story, which was in turn scripted by Harold Livingston. The special effects team of Douglas Trumbull and John Dykstra, along with the musical score by Jerry Goldsmith, made the movie a landmark epic in the industry. The movie broke both production cost records (with a budget of over $40 million spent) and box office totals. Though pronounced too long and boring by many fans, the film remains a classic, with added footage augmenting the video release.

Star Trek II: The Wrath of Khan — released in 1982, directed by newcomer Nicholas Meyer, this movie details the characters in their later years, and pays little if any homage to *The Motion Picture*. It is, instead, a sequel to an episode from the original series, "Space Seed." The antagonist is Khan, who has escaped from exile and is seeking out Kirk to take his revenge. Kirk is now serving as a desk-bound admiral. Spock is an instructor, using the docked *Enterprise*, under his command, to educate his trainees. While Kirk is on board inspecting a new group of cadets, the emergency call comes in to investigate distress signals from a science team on Regula I. The *Enterprise* is the closest ship, and Spock ends up turning over command to Kirk. Once in flight, they discover that Khan has appropriated a valuable device containing a Genesis Wave which can obliterate entire planets and then create new life in their wake. While battling Khan's insanity, the *Enterprise* becomes the target for the terrible device. Spock gives his life to save the day and the movie ends with a funeral service for the heroic Vulcan. Though many people consider this movie to be "real" *Trek*, accurate in areas of characterization, and involving a people-oriented plot which was one of the things that made *Trek* work, demands for Spock's return in a third movie were made worldwide. Guest stars include some famous names: Bibi Besch, Merritt Butrick, Paul Winfield, Kirstie Alley, Ricardo Montalban, and Ike Eisenmann. John Winston reprises his role from the series as Kyle, and Teresa Victor, Leonard Nimoy's long-time assistant from the original series, provides the voice of the Bridge. Harve Bennett was the film's executive producer as well as the writer (with Jack B. Sowards). James Horner scored the film and Lucasfilm's Industrial Light and Magic team directed the special effects. This film's budget was substantially less than *The Motion Picture*'s, but it also broke box office receipt records on opening day. It remains critically and financially the most successful of all the *Trek* movies.

Star Trek III: The Search for Spock — in Leonard Nimoy's feature directorial debut, the characters put their lives and careers on the line to recover Spock's body and *katra*, only to discover that the Genesis Wave has somehow given Spock life. Spock goes through a rapid aging process (from babyhood to adulthood) as the crew battles vengeful Klingons on its way to save him. The *Enterprise* is destroyed and Klingons murder Kirk's son in the battle. Kirk, who has disobeyed Starfleet orders, faces a court-martial, but they recover Spock, discover McCoy has been the receptacle for his *katra* all along, and end up on Vulcan where a high priestess performs a kind of psychic surgery that puts Spock's *katra* back in its place. The end is bittersweet, with a Spock who has little memory of his friends, and fans called immediately for a sequel. Guest stars include James B. Sikking, Miguel Ferrer, Merritt Butrick, Robin Curtis, Christopher Lloyd, John Larroquette, and Robert Hooks. Grace Lee Whitney returns in a cameo appearance and Mark Lenard returns as Sarek. Musical score was written by James Horner. Harve Bennett wrote the script and produced the film with Gary Nardino. Special effects were produced by Industrial Light and Magic.

Star Trek IV: The Voyage Home — again directed by Leonard Nimoy, this fourth *Trek* movie is the third in the so-called "Wrath of Khan" trilogy, giving fans the sequel to *The Search for Spock* which they so adamantly demanded. It was released during Christmas of 1986. The crew, flying from Vulcan back to Earth to face criminal charges, is hurtled back in time to Earth's 20th century to capture a humpback whale in order to save a future Earth from a probe which is disrupting the atmosphere when it doesn't get an answer to its summons. The probe is apparently calling out to humpback whales, which are extinct in the 23rd century. The crew find their whales, George and Gracie, at a water park near San Francisco, and Chekov runs into trouble when he is caught aboard the aircraft carrier *Enterprise*. They all get out alive, however, and hurtle forward in time with the whales in the cargo bay of a Klingon ship to save Earth. They are then put on trial but the charges are dropped against everyone but Kirk, whose punishment is to be reduced in rank to captain. Guest stars include: Jane Wyatt as Amanda, Mark Lenard as Sarek, Catherine Hicks, Robin Curtis, Robert Ellenstein, and John Schuck. Majel Barrett returns as Dr. Chapel and there is an appearance by Grace Lee Whitney. Though the plot of this movie sounds somewhat ridiculous, fans loved it, and it proved to be the second-highest grossing *Trek* film, after *The Wrath of Khan*. Executive producer: Ralph Winter. Screenplay: Steve Meerson, Peter Krikes, Harve Bennett, and Nicholas Meyer. Story by: Leonard Nimoy and Harve Bennett. Music: Leonard Rosenman. Producer: Harve Bennett. Director of photography: Don Peterman.

Star Trek V: The Final Frontier — directed by William Shatner, this June 1989 release introduces Spock's half-brother, Sybok, who journeys to Nimbus III, the planet of intergalactic peace, to recruit followers in his quest to locate ShaKaRee, a god with whom he says he has contact. To fulfill his quest, he kidnaps the *Enterprise* and crew, imprisons Kirk, Spock, and McCoy, and heads to the center of the galaxy. This movie has some interesting aspects, though many fans consider it inconsistent with the *Star Trek* universe (mainly because Spock's half-brother pops up like the proverbial Vulcan inner eyelid). The best parts of this movie, however, are the characters, their actions, and their sense of humor. In no other movie does the crew relate so much like a family, a result of their deep faith in, and experiences with, each other. Uhura and Scotty appear to have developed a very close relationship, and Spock has greatly mellowed since his *The Voyage Home* problems with assimilating his human half. Melanie Shatner, William Shatner's daughter, plays yeoman to his captain. Guest stars: Laurence Luckinbill and David Warner. Executive producer: Ralph Winter. Producer: Harve Bennett. Special visual effects: Brad Ferren. Story by: William Shatner, Harve Bennett, and David Loughery. Script by: David Loughery. Music: Jerry Goldsmith.

Star Trek VI: The Undiscovered Country — directed by Nicholas Meyer, this December

1991 film is dark, with an unmistakably claustrophobic feeling as it follows Spock on a Sherlock Holmes–type investigation into the assassination of a high Klingon commander, and follows the journey of Kirk and McCoy when they are sentenced to a cold, Klingon prison world, wrongly convicted of the assassination. There they meet a shapechanger who says she can help them escape. Guest stars: Iman, Christopher Plummer, David Warner, Michael Dorn, Kim Cattrall, René Auberjonois, Kurtwood Smith, and Brock Peters. Christian Slater has a cameo, as does Grace Lee Whitney, who plays Commander Rand on Sulu's ship, *Excelsior*. This movie tried to tie in with *The Next Generation*, and in fact, the references to Khitomer do accomplish that. Executive producer: Leonard Nimoy. Producers: Ralph Winter and Steven Charles Jaffe. Written by: Nicholas Meyer and Denny Martin Flinn (screenplay), Leonard Nimoy, Lawrence Konner, and Mark Rosenthal (story). Music: Cliff Eidelman.

Starbase 2 — located between Beta Aurigae and Camus II. The *Enterprise* is headed here in Classic episode "Turnabout Intruder."

Starbase 4 — base near Triacus where the *Enterprise* is headed in Classic episode "And the Children Shall Lead." This is also the *Enterprise*'s destination at the end of "Let That Be Your Last Battlefield."

Starbase 6 — destination of the *Enterprise* before it is diverted to Sector 39J to find the *Intrepid* in Classic episode "The Immunity Syndrome." Also mentioned as a destination in *TNG* episode "The Schizoid Man."

Starbase 9 — where the ship was headed in Classic episode "Tomorrow Is Yesterday." Also mentioned in "Catspaw."

Starbase 10 — commanded by Commodore Stocker as mentioned in Classic episode "The Deadly Years." It is located near Gamma Hydra IV and the Neutral Zone.

Starbase 11 — visited by the *Enterprise* in Classic episodes "Court-Martial" and "The Menagerie."

Starbase 12 — located on a planet in the Gamma 400 system, as mentioned in Classic episode "Space Seed." Also mentioned as being nearest to the planet Pollux in "Where No Man Has Gone Before." In *TNG* episode "Captain's Holiday" the *Enterprise* is en route here after dropping Picard off on Risa. This starbase is also where an unexplained evacuation took place in *TNG* episode "Conspiracy."

Starbase 14 — in *TNG* episode "Code of Honor," a subspace message comes from here telling the *Enterprise* the extent of a plague which has hit Styris IV.

Starbase 22 — ship's destination in animated episode "How Sharper Than a Serpent's Tooth."

Starbase 23 — Dr. Crusher is to meet Admiral Brooks here before a formal Starfleet inquiry into Dr. Reyga's death in *TNG* episode "Suspicions." Also mentioned as being nearest to the Arachna supernova in animated episode "The Terratin Incident."

Starbase 24 — where Kahlest was brought by the *Intrepid* after the Khitomer Massacre in *TNG* episode "Sins of the Father."

Starbase 25 — where the shuttle *Copernicus* is headed in animated episode "The Slaver Weapon."

Starbase 27 — near Omicron Ceti III mentioned in Classic episode "This Side of Paradise."

Starbase 29 — in *TNG* episode "Frame of Mind," Admiral Budron of this base supposedly denied that Riker was a Starfleet officer.

Starbase 39 Sierre — in *TNG* episode "The Neutral Zone," Picard takes humans from an Earth satellite to this base.

Starbase 45 — Admiral Jameson's last medical was taken here in *TNG* episode "Too Short a Season."

Starbase 55 — *Enterprise* destination in *TNG* episode "Relics."

Starbase 67 — destination of the *Enterprise* for repairs in *TNG* episode "Disaster."

Starbase 73 — the *Enterprise* makes stops here in *TNG* episodes "Up the Long Ladder" and "Time Squared." Riker gets some Owan eggs (see. entry) here. Worf meets his parents there in "Reunion."

Starbase 74 — it orbits Tarsus III where the Bynars take over the *Enterprise* in *TNG* episode "11001001."

Starbase 83 — in *TNG* episode "Q Who," the *Enterprise* sets a course here after encountering the Borg.

Starbase 84 — after leaving the Klingon ship *Kartag* in *TNG* episode "Heart of Glory," the *Enterprise* heads here.

Starbase 97 — mentioned by Hutchison as being an "awful place" in *TNG* episode "Starship Mine."

Starbase 103 — in *TNG* episode "The Arsenal of Freedom," the saucer section separates from the ship and is ordered to head to this base.

Starbase 105 — mentioned in *TNG* episode "Yesterday's Enterprise."

Starbase 112 — where the *Enterprise* picks up supplies for Tagra IV in *TNG* episode "True Q."

Starbase 118 — the *Enterprise* is to pick up personnel on this base in *TNG* episode "A Fistful of Datas."

Starbase 121 — in *TNG* episode "Hollow Pursuits," Geordi tells Picard the ship needs to be bio-decontaminated to rid the ship of invidium. He suggests they go to Starbase 121.

Starbase 123 — in *TNG* episode "The Tin Man," this base detects two Romulan cruisers on their way to Beta Stromgren.

Starbase 133 — the *Enterprise*'s destination after they leave Rana IV in *TNG* episode "The Survivor."

Starbase 152 — destination of the *Enterprise* for inspection and repairs after leaving Beta Stromgren in *TNG* episode "The Tin Man."

Starbase 153 — in *TNG* episode "The Emissary," K'Ehleyr is from here.

Starbase 157 — the *Lalo*'s distress signal was received by this base in *TNG* episode "The Best of Both Worlds."

Starbase 173 — located on the border of the Neutral Zone, this is a new post commanded by Admiral Nakamura. It is mentioned in *TNG* episodes "The Measure of a Man" and "Q Who."

Starbase 179 — Ensign Mendon is picked up by the *Enterprise* from here in *TNG* episode "A Matter of Honor."

Starbase 185 — mentioned in *TNG* episode "Q Who" as being two years, seven months, three days, and eighteen hours away at maximum warp from where the Borg are.

Starbase 211 — the *Phoenix* returns here after Captain Maxwell has been relieved of command in *TNG* episode "The Wounded."

Starbase 212 — where Lt. Uhnari will be taken, mentioned also as Starbase 12, in *TNG* episode "Aquiel."

Starbase 214 — where Rasmussen is taken in *TNG* episode "A Matter of Time."

Starbase 218 — Nella Daren and Nurse Beck come aboard ship from here in *TNG* episode "Lessons."

Starbase 220 — the *Enterprise*'s destination in *TNG* episode "Night Terrors."

Starbase 234 — Fleet Admiral Brackett relays a message from here to the *Enterprise* about Spock's defection to the Romulans in *TNG* episode "Unification."

Starbase 260 — the *Enterprise*'s destination in *TNG* episode "In Theory."

Starbase 301 — destination of the *Enterprise* in *TNG* episode "Conundrum."

Starbase 313 — the *Enterprise* picks up scientific materials from here to take to the Guernica Colony in *TNG* episode "Galaxy's Child."

Starbase 324 — Admiral Hanson arrives here to discuss strategy on the Borg threat with Starfleet Command.

Starbase 336 — this base received the SOS from the T'Ong in *TNG* episode "The Emissary."

Starbase 343 — in *TNG* episode "The Vengeance Factor," the *Enterprise* takes shore leave here after seeing to the Gatherer treaty.

Starbase 416 — Willie Potts is to be taken here for emergency treatment in *TNG* episode "Brothers."

Starbase 440 — where the *Enterprise* takes the Ullian historian delegation in *TNG* episode "Violations."

Starbase 513 — this starbase lost contact with the *Vico* in *TNG* episode "Hero Worship."

Starbase 515 — Wesley is traveling here to take his Academy exam in *TNG* episode "Samaritan Snare."

Starbase 718 — a meeting is held here to discuss the destroyed outposts in the Neutral Zone in *TNG* episode "The Neutral Zone."

Starbase Armus 9 — in *TNG* episode "Datalore," Picard is to take the *Enterprise* here for upgrading.

Starbase *G6* — in *TNG* episode "Hide and Q," Troi was dropped off here to catch a shuttle home.

Starbase *Montgomery* — Kyle Riker boards the *Enterprise* from this station in *TNG* episode "The Icarus Factor."

Starbase *Scylla 515* — a branch of Starfleet Academy is located here in *TNG* episode "Samaritan Snare."

Starbase *Zendi 9* — located in the Zendi Sabu sector, the *Stargazer* is headed here in *TNG* episode "The Battle."

stardate — consisting of four numerals (the year) along with one or two after a decimal (or point) mark. In *TNG* it consists of 5 numerals and one numeral after the point. The one (or two) numerals after the point supposedly denote the time.

stardrive — another term for warp drive.

Starfleet — also known as Starfleet Command, they run defense and exploration missions for the Federation. They answer only to the Federation.

Starfleet Academy — where Starfleet hopefuls learn about life in space. The Academy is in San Francisco, California, and has apparently very high standards students must meet in order to graduate.

Starfleet Cybernetics Journal — in *TNG* episode "Birthright," Dr. Bashir wants to write an article for this publication on Data's newly discovered ability to dream.

Starfleet orders — there are many. General order number one is also known as the Prime Directive, and forbids interference in naturally developing alien societies. According to Classic episode "The Doomsday Machine," order #104, section B, paragraph Ia states: "In the absence of the commanding officer, the highest ranking officer, even if not of that ship's command, may take command." In section C, it reads: "The highest ranking officer may be relieved if medically or psychologically unfit to command." Starfleet order #2 prohibits Starfleet officers from taking the life of intelligent beings.

Stargazer, USS — Picard's first command. Jack Crusher served as his first officer and died when Picard sent him on an away team. The ship was lost at Maxia Zeta, then was presented by the Ferengi nine years later to Picard in the Zendi Sabu system in *TNG* episode "The Battle."

starithium ore — ore which interferes with Vash's sensor readings on Risa in *TNG* episode "Captain's Holiday."

Starnes, Professor — led the science expedition on Triacus and commits suicide under the Gorgon's influence in the Classic "And the Childern Shall Lead." He leaves behind a son, Tommy. He was played by James Wellman.

Starnes, Tommy — the oldest of the surviving children from Triacus, influenced by the Gorgon in Classic episode "And the Children Shall Lead." He is played by Craig Hundley.

"Starship Mine" — this sixth-season *TNG* episode was written by Morgan Gendel and directed by Cliff Bole. The *Enterprise* is docked at the Remmler Array to go through a cleansing sweep to rid the ship of baryon particles. All personnel are transported off the vessel, since the sweep is harmful to life, but Picard goes back at the last minute to retrieve his personal saddle in the hopes that on leave he can go horseback riding. Just as he is about to leave, he realizes he is not alone. There is a group of thieves on board stealing trilithium from the ship to sell to terrorists on the black market. Guest star: David Spielberg.

Starships — in Classic *Trek*, the fleet includes: The *Constellation* NCC 1017 (destroyed in "The Doomsday Machine"), the *Constitution* NCC 1700, the *Defiant* NCC 1764 (destroyed in "The Tholian Web"), the *Enterprise* NCC 1701, the *Excalibur* NCC 1664 (destroyed by the M-5 computer in "The Ultimate Computer"), the *Exeter* NCC 1672, the *Farragut* NCC 1647 (Kirk first served aboard this ship), the *Hood* NCC 1703, the *Intrepid* NCC 1631 (all-Vulcan ship, destroyed by the galactic amoeba in "The Immunity Syndrome"), the *Lexington* NCC 1709, the *Potemkin* NCC 1702, the *Republic* NCC 1373, and the *Yorktown* NCC 1717.

Statier, Mary — stunt double for Edith in Classic *Trek* episode "The City on the Edge of Forever."

Station Nigala IV — destination of the *Enterprise* in *TNG* episode "Déjà Q."

Station Salem I — this station is the locale for a preamble to war in *TNG* episode "The Enemy."

Staton, Joi — played a servant in *TNG* episode "Qpid."

Steele, Karen — played Eve McHuron in Classic *Trek* episode "Mudd's Women." Her TV credits include: *Voyage to the Bottom of the Sea, Branded,* and *The Wackiest Ship in the Army.* She also appeared in the 1959 film *Ride Lonesome.*

Steele, Tom — stunt man in Classic *Trek* episode "Bread and Circuses."

Steelplast — a material mentioned in *TNG* episode "Too Short a Season." It can be cut by phasers.

Stefano, Joseph — scriptwriter of *TNG* episode "Skin of Evil."

Stein, Mary — played the alien nurse in *TNG* "Time's Arrow, Part II."

Steiner, Fred — composer for dozens of episodes of Classic *Trek*, all seasons, as well as for *TNG*. He also wrote music for the series *Lost in Space* and the well-known *Perry Mason* theme.

stellar core fragment — a dense chunk of star matter that threatens Moab IV in *TNG* episode "The Masterpiece Society."

Stellrecht, Skip — played an engineering crewman in *TNG* episode "The Naked Now."

Sten — artist mentioned in Classic episode "Requiem for Methuselah." Flint owns some of his work.

sterilite — used during surgery to prevent infection, as mentioned in Classic episode "A Private Little War."

Sternbach, Rick — senior illustrator/technical consultant on *DS9*.

Steuer, Jon — played Alexander in *TNG* episode "Reunion."

Steven, Carl — played Spock, age 9, in *The Search for Spock*. He has also appeared in the 1982 movie *Rosie: The Rosemary Clooney Story*, *Appearances*, and the 1983 *Wait Till Your Mother Gets Home!*

Stevens, Warren — played Rojan in Classic *Trek* episode "By Any Other Name." Born in 1919, his films include the 1956 *Forbidden Planet*. He has made guest appearances on the TV series *I Spy*, *Griff*, and *Voyage to the Bottom of the Sea*, as well as regular roles on *Tales of the 77th Bengal Lancers*, *The Richard Boone Show*, *Bracken's World*, and *Behind the Screen*.

Stewart, Bryan — scriptwriter of *TNG* episode "Family" (he helped write the premise).

Stewart, Charles J. — played Captain Ramart in Classic *Trek* episode "Charlie X."

Stewart, Patrick — stars as Captain Jean-Luc Picard in *The Next Generation*. Stewart was born on July 13 in the English town of Mirfield. He appeared in such BBC productions as *I, Claudius*; *Smiley's People*; and *Tinker, Tailor, Soldier, Spy*. He was also in the American-made films *Dune*, *Excalibur*, and *Lifeforce*. He has done a lot of stage work, and is considered one of the leading talents on the British stage where he has played such notable characters as Shylock, Henry IV, Leontes, King John, and Titus Andronicus.

Stewart has also done directing on *TNG*, including the episodes "Hero Worship," "In Theory," and "A Fistful of Datas." Stewart was very surprised to learn, in 1992, that *TV Guide* readers voted him "sexiest man of the year." He only wished it had happened before he lost his hair at the age of 19. He has worn wigs most of his life, but the *Star Trek* producers decided he looked fine without and apparently that didn't deter the voters either. He lives in Los Angeles. Stewart's son, Daniel Stewart, appeared with him in the episode "The Inner Light" as his (and Kamin's) son, Batai.

Stiers, David Ogden — played Dr. Timicin in *TNG* episode "Half a Life." He is best known for his role on the TV comedy *M*A*S*H*.

Stiles, Andrew, Lieutenant — an *Enterprise* navigator seen in Classic episode "Balance of Terror." He is a bigot who hates the Romulans because they killed his father. He soon learns to hate Spock when he finds out Romulans and Vulcans are very much alike, until he learns his hatred is irrational when Spock saves his life. He was played by Paul Comi.

Stillwell, Eric — scriptwriter of *TNG* episode "Yesterday's Enterprise."

Stimson, Viola — played the lady in the tour on *The Voyage Home*.

Stovo Kor — Klingon afterlife where Kahless is, mentioned in *TNG* episode "Rightful Heir."

Stocker, George, Commodore — he takes over command of the *Enterprise* from Kirk when Kirk, due to accelerated aging, can no longer function as captain. He is inept at command, and needs to be pulled out of a dilemma with the Romulans when Kirk recovers in Classic episode "The Deadly Years." Stocker is played by Charles Drake.

stokaline — in Classic episode "By Any Other Name,"

McCoy gives this to Spock to cure his faked Rigelian Kassaba fever. Stokaline is actually a vitamin compound.

Stone, Commodore — port master of Starbase 11 in Classic episode "Court-Martial." He heads Kirk's trial board. He is played by Percy Rodriguez.

Stonn — T'Pring's preferred Vulcan champion, before she ends up choosing Kirk to fight Spock, in Classic episode "Amok Time." T'Pring wants to divorce Spock so she can marry Stonn. Stonn is played by Lawrence Montaigne.

Strangis, Greg — creative consultant on *TNG*.

strategema — in *TNG* episode "Peak Performance," this is a three-dimensional electronic tabletop game of skill.

Stratos — the cloud city that floats high above Ardana as seen in Classic episode "The Cloud Minders." The city's inhabitants devote themselves to art and education and violence is unheard of. Stratos is subsidized by the hard, blue-collar labor of Ardana's "lower class" citizens, the Troglytes. The city is sustained by antigravity elevation.

Stratton, Albert — played Kushell in *TNG* episode "The Outrageous Okona."

Streleb — located in the Medina system. It has a neighbor, Atlek, from which it is divided. Its inhabitants believe Captain Okona stole the Jewel of Thesia in *TNG* episode "The Outrageous Okona."

Streleb ship — captained by Kushell and seen in *TNG* episode "The Outrageous Okona."

Stringer, Ken — second assistant director on *The Search for Spock*.

Strnad — in *TNG* episode "Justice," mentioned as a new Federation colony located near Rubicam.

Strong, Brenda — played Rashella in *TNG* episode "When the Bough Breaks."

Strong, Michael — played Dr. Roger Korby in Classic *Trek* episode "What Are Little Girls Made Of?" His TV credits include *Planet of the Apes*, *The Man from U.N.C.L.E.*, *Cannon*, and *Barnaby Jones*. Film credits include *Vanished*, *Queen of the Stardust Ballroom*, and *This Year's Blonde*.

Struycken, Carel — Mr. Homn in *TNG* episodes "Haven," "Manhunt," "Ménage à Troi," "Half a Life," and "Cost of Living." His other roles include the giant in *Twin Peaks* and Lurch in the films *The Addams Family* and *Addams Family Values*.

Stuart, Norman — played the Vulcan Master in *Star Trek: The Motion Picture*. He also appeared in the 1977 movie *79 Park Avenue*.

Stubbs, Paul, Dr. — he is an astrophysicist studying the Kavis Alpha explosion in *TNG* episode "Evolution." He is a fan of baseball. Ken Jenkins played him.

Sturgeon, Theodore — scriptwriter of Classic *Trek* episodes "Shore Leave" and "Amok Time." He was born in 1918 and died on May 8, 1987. He is a well-known science-fiction writer who wrote such novels as the Hugo award–winning *More Than Human*, as well as *The Dreaming Jewels*, *Venus Plus X*, and many more. His story "Case and the Dreamer" is the one upon which "Shore Leave" is based. He has many wonderful short-story collections, and has won numerous writing awards.

Sturgeon — an *Enterprise* crewman killed by the salt vampire (the M–113 creature) in Classic episode "The Man Trap."

Styris IV — this world is plagued by Anchilles Fever in *TNG* episode "Code of Honor."

styrolite — sterile barrier that resembles thick, clear plastic seen in *TNG* episode "Unnatural Selection."

subhadar — a Tarsian War rank to which Danar is promoted, as mentioned in *TNG* episode "The Hunted."

sublight speed — attained using impulse power and mentioned in Classic episode "Elaan of Troyius." (See also "space normal speed.")

subspace radio — used to talk to ships and places far away. Often the *Enterprise* is out of range even for this extended communication. It uses a warp effect so the radio waves can travel even faster than ships in warp.

Subspace Relay Station 47 — Starfleet installation near the Klingon border to which Aquiel Uhnari and Keith Rocha are assigned in *TNG* episode "Aquiel."

Subspace Relay Station 194 — in *TNG* episode "Aquiel," Station 47 receives this station's communications load.

"Suddenly Human" — fourth-season *TNG* episode written by John Whelpley, Jeri Taylor, and Ralph Phillips, directed by Gabrielle Beaumont. The *Enterprise* encounters a Talarian freighter with five boys on board, one of whom is human and has been missing for years, ever since his world was attacked by Talarians. His rescue suddenly puts him in the position of having to leave the only family he's ever known to regain his human heritage. Guest stars: Chad Allen, Sherman Howard, and Barbara Townsend.

Sullivan, Kevin — played March in *The Wrath of Khan*.

Sullivan, Liam — played Parmen in Classic *Trek* episode "Plato's Stepchildren." TV credits include *Voyage to the Bottom of the Sea* and *Lost in Space*. He also had a regular role on *The Monroes*. Film credits include the 1979 *The Best Place to Be* and the 1984 *Ernie Kovacs: Between the Laughter*.

Sullivan, Susan J. — played the woman in the transporter in *Star Trek: The Motion Picture*.

Sulu, Hikaru — the *Enterprise* helmsman, he ends up

captain of the *Excelsior* by the sixth film, *The Undiscovered Country*. Sulu can pilot anything, and is fascinated by botany, old guns, and fencing. His ancestry is Japanese, and he exhibits a great love for life. He is good friends with Chekov (they took shore leave together in *The Final Frontier*). He was underused in the series and so his character is less developed than the rest of the crew. He is played by George Takei. In the mirror universe, Sulu is a very sinister man with a long scar down the side of his face. He has aspirations to be captain of the *Enterprise* one day, even if he has to kill to do so, and has a "thing" for Uhura.

Summers, Jaron — scriptwriter of *TNG* episode "The Child."

Summers, Jerry — stunt double for Chekov in Classic *Trek* episode "The Trouble with Tribbles."

Sun Tzu — mentioned in *TNG* episode "The Last Outpost" as a Chinese philosopher who wrote about war. One of his strategies, still taught in Starfleet, is "He will triumph who knows when to fight and when not to fight."

Suna — person responsible for Riker's hallucinations in *TNG* episode "Frame of Mind." He is a scientist working with Tilonus IV rebels trying to get secret information from Riker's mind using a neurosomatic process.

Sunad — Zalkonian in command of a ship that threatens the *Enterprise* in *TNG* episode "Transfigurations." He is played by Charles Dennis.

Supera, Max — played Patterson on *TNG* episode "Disaster."

Supervisor 194 — Gary Seven's title in Classic episode "Assignment: Earth." (See entry for Seven, Gary.)

Surak — the legendary Vulcan who brought ultimate peace through logic to the Vulcan society thousands of years before. He was a great philosopher. An image of him is conjured up by Yarnek in Classic episode "The Savage Curtain." He is played by Barry Atwater.

Surata IV — in *TNG* episode "Shades of Gray," Riker is infected by microbes from this world.

Survey on Cygnian Respiratory Disease — name of the tape Nurse Chapel used to threaten Ensign Garrovick into eating. She says McCoy's voice is on the tape, ordering Garrovick to eat, in Classic episode "The Immunity Syndrome."

"Survivor, The" — written by James Schmerer, this animated Classic *Trek* episode aired 10/13/73. The *Enterprise* rescues a man, Carter Winston, who has been missing for five years. Winston is really a Vendorian, however, an alien that can assume the form of other humanoids. He assumes the form of Kirk and orders the ship into the Neutral Zone. A battle with the Romulans ensues. Guest voices: Ted Knight (Carter Winston/Allen), Nichelle Nichols (Lt. Anne Nored), Majel Barrett (Lt. M'Ress, computer), and James Doohan (Romulan Commander/Gabler).

"Survivors, The" — third-season *TNG* episode written by Michael Wagner and directed by Les Landau. 11,000 inhabitants of Delta Rana IV have been wiped out, except for two humans, an older couple, who have mysteriously survived. Troi is going insane from hearing music in her mind, which is connected to the survivors. Guest stars: John Anderson and Anne Haney.

"Suspicions" — sixth-season *TNG* episode written by Joe Menosky and Naren Shankar, directed by Cliff Bole. Dr. Crusher is relieved of duty and about to be tried for violating medical ethics for conducting an illegal autopsy on a Ferengi scientist who was responsible for a metaphasic field discovery and committed suicide on board the ship. She believed he was murdered but the autopsy reveals nothing and the Ferengi are furious. Guest stars: Peter Slutsker, James Horan, Joan Stuart Morris, and Tricia O'Neil.

Sutherland, Keith — voice of young Sepec in animated "Yesteryear."

Sutherland, USS — Data briefly commands this ship during the Klingon civil war in *TNG* episode "Redemption." Its first officer is Christopher Hobson.

Sutter, Clara — Ensign Daniel Sutter's daughter who encounters her imaginary friend in the flesh in *TNG* episode "Imaginary Friend." Her friend, Isabella, is actually an alien studying the crew. Clara is played by Noley Thornton.

Suvin IV — location of an archeological dig mentioned in *TNG* episode "Rascals." Dr. Langford and his team have offered Picard an open invitation to join them at the dig.

Swahili — the native language of the United States of Africa in the 23rd century. Uhura is Bantu and speaks Swahili fluently in Classic episode "Man Trap."

Swanson, Jandi — played Katie in *TNG* episode "When the Bough Breaks."

Swensen, Edithe — scriptwriter of *TNG* episode "Imaginary Friend."

Swenson — Yar is supposed to compete against him in the ship's martial arts tournament in *TNG* episode "Skin of Evil."

Swetow, Joel — played Gul Jasal in *DS9* "Emissary."

Swift, Joan — played Aurelean Kirk in Classic *Trek* episode "Operation: Annihilate!"

Sybo — wife of Prefect Jaris of Argelius II. An empath, she forms a psychic link with the Jack the Ripper entity during a kind of seance in order to find out more about it in Classic episode "Wolf in the Fold." She dies when the entity kills her. Sybo is played by Pilar Seurat.

Sybok — Spock's older half-brother, slipped into Spock's personal history in the film *The Final Frontier*.

Played by Laurence Luckinbill, Sybok is searching for the legendary ShaKaRee, and claims to have a personal, mental channel to the mystical Vulcan god. He gathers followers interested in peace using a special Vulcan mind control on them, beginning his quest on Nimbus III, the planet of Galactic Peace. Sybok renounced logic and left his homeworld of Vulcan decades before the film. Spock says he barely knew him. When he thinks he's found ShaKaRee, it turns out to be a prison housing an omnipotent, evil entity, and Sybok gives his own life to try to kill it and save the *Enterprise*. Before dying, he transfers his *katra* to Spock.

Sylvia — blond woman Chekov meets in the Melkot simulation of the gunfight at O.K. Corral. She was played by Bonnie Beecher. Another Sylvia, played by Antoinette Bower, appears human but in her native form is actually a crablike, frail creature in "Catspaw." She is ultimately destroyed by her own warped powers.

Symbalene blood burn — a swift-acting plague mentioned in Classic episode "The Changeling."

"Symbiosis" — first-season *TNG* episode written by Robert Lewin, Hans Beimler and Richard Manning, directed by Wi Phelps. Ornara and Brekka are two worlds involved in a trade dispute which the *Enterprise* is trying to resolve. It is learned, however, that the Brekkians are selling useless drugs for profit to the Ornarans who are addicted to them and believe they need them to keep from succumbing to a terrible disease. Guest stars: Merritt Butrick, Judson Scott, Kimberly Farr, and Richard Lineback. Of note: both Merritt and Judson had major roles in *The Wrath of Khan*. Merritt played David Marcus, Kirk's son. Judson was Khan's protege, Joachim.

synchronic meter — tool used to check out the transporter in Classic episode "The Enemy Within."

synthehol — drinks in Ten Forward aboard the *TNG Enterprise* are made of this substance. It is nonalcoholic and was invented by the Ferengi.

Syrus, Dr. — doctor at the Tilonus IV medical asylum who tells Riker he fell and hit his head in *TNG* episode "Frame of Mind."

System J-25 — in *TNG* episode "Q Who" the *Enterprise* first sees the Borg here. It is 7,000 light years away from their position when Q causes the ship to materialize here.

System L374B — where the planet-eating device is when the *Enterprise* encounters it, in Classic episode "The Doomsday Machine."

Synthococcus novae — a deadly bacillus strain which Dr. Sevrin carries in Classic episode "The Way to Eden." Primitive people on a world which has not known this disease can catch it very quickly and die if they are not immunized. All Federation citizens are immunized, so Dr. Sevrin can move freely among them, but he is a murderer if he sets foot on a new world that has not known the disease. It was discovered in the 21st century, and an immunization vaccine was discovered by Dr. J. Pearce.

T-9 converter — in *TNG* episode "The Last Outpost," this is an energy system stolen by the Ferengi from Gamma Tauri.

Taar — Ferengi leader (his title was DaiMon), who fought Picard at Delphi Ardu in *TNG* episode "The Last Outpost." He is played by Mike Gomez.

tachyon web — one of these is erected between the blockading Starfleet ships in *TNG* episode "Redemption."

T'Acog — the *Batris* destroyed this ship in *TNG* episode "Heart of Glory."

Taggart, Captain — commander of the *Repulse*, the ship Pulaski served on before coming to the *Enterprise*, and mentioned in *TNG* episode "Unnatural Selection." Taggart is played by J. Patrick McNamara.

Tagra IV — the *Enterprise* is carrying relief supplies to a colony on this world when they pick up Amanda Rogers in *TNG* episode "True Q."

Tagus III — Federation world with famous billion-year-old ruins mentioned in *TNG* episode "Qpid." The Tagians have closed off their world to outsiders.

Tajor, Glin — Cardassian aide of Gul Lemec in *TNG* episode "Chain of Command."

Takaki, Russell — played Madison in *The Wrath of Khan.*

Takaran — race that can simulate death in *TNG* episode "Suspicions." They have bluish skin.

Takei, George — starred as Lt. Hikaru Sulu in *Star Trek* and all the movies (in which his rank rose to captain), as well as the voice of Sulu in the animated series. Born in Boyle Heights, Los Angeles, his family was forced to relocate to Japanese detention camps in Arkansas and Tule Lake, California, during World War II. Although only a small child at the time, the traumatic experience affected him for years afterward. He graduated from UCLA with a theater arts degree and made his debut on *Playhouse 90*. His TV credits include *Hawaiian Eye, Perry Mason, Alcoa Premiere, Checkmate, The Islanders, The Wackiest Ship in the Army, Mr. Novak, The John Forsythe Show, I Spy, Bob Hope Chrysler Theatre, Felony Squad, Bracken's World, Ironside, Mr. Roberts, My Three Sons, It Takes a Thief, Voyage to the Bottom of the Sea, The Twilight Zone, Kung Fu, The Six Million Dollar Man, Baa Baa Black Sheep, Chico and the Man, Hawaii Five-0, Miami Vice*, and the PBS movie *Year of the Dragon*. He first appears in *Star Trek* in the second pilot, "Where No Man Has Gone Before." He also appeared in *Mission: Impossible* during the filming of *Trek*, and in the movie *Green Berets*. His other film credits include *A Majority of One, Ice Palace, Red Line 7000, Hell to Eternity, An American Dream, Walk Don't Run, Never So Few, Josie's Castle, The Loudmouth, The Young Divorcees, Pt 109, Which Way to the Front,* and most recently, *Return from the River Kwai* and *Prisoners of the Sun*. Always politically active during his career, Takei ran for the Los Angeles City Council but came in second. He has also cowritten a novel, *Mirror Friend, Mirror Foe* with science-fiction author Robert Asprin. He also loves to run and has competed in many long-distance marathons.

Takemura, David — visual effects associate on *TNG*.

Tal, Subcommander — the Romulan Commander's second officer in Classic episode "The *Enterprise* Incident." He is played by Jack Donner.

tal shaya — Vulcan form of execution which involves quickly breaking the neck of a victim. It is the way the Tellarite Gav dies in Classic episode "Journey to Babel."

Tal Shiar — greatly feared Romulan intelligence agency with a lot of power over the Romulan military. In *TNG* episode "Face of the Enemy," Troi masquerades as Major Rakal of the Tal Shiar.

Talarians — humanoid and warlike, Talarians attacked Galen IV ten years before the *Enterprise* encounters a ship with a human teenage survivor from the colony on board. The Talarians are suspicious, wear gloves around strangers, and are very family-oriented. The human boy, Jeremiah Rossa, who has been adopted by the captain of the ship, does not want to return to his own kind. A Talarian freighter, the *Batris*, is stolen by Klingon rebels and is destroyed in "Heart of Glory."

Talos IV — one of eleven planets circling a binary star, it is the home of the Talosians, beings with mental superpowers in Classic episode "The Menagerie." The Talosians moved underground when their surface world could no longer support them. They keep a zoo full of various creatures on this world, including a female human named Vina. After Pike visited this world, it was declared off-limits to all under General Order #7, an order that carries the death penalty if disobeyed.

Taluno, Kai — the Bajoran predecessor to Kai Opaka in *TNG* episode "Emissary." Two centuries earlier, when he was in the region of the Denorios Belt (where most of the Bajoran Orbs were found) he was stranded in space and claimed the "heavens opened up and swallowed him."

Tama, Children of — race of beings whose communication involves metaphor and allusion, making it very difficult for the Federation to communicate with them, in *TNG* episode "Darmok."

Tamar — a member of the underground movement on Landru's planet who is killed by the lawgivers in Classic episode "The Return of the Archons." He is played by Jon Lormer (who also appeared in "For the World Is Hollow and I Have Touched the Sky").

Tamoon — drill thrall on Triskelion assigned to Chekov in Classic episode "The Gamesters of Triskelion." She was played by Jane Ross.

Tamura, Yeoman — member of the landing party to Eminiar in Classic episode "A Taste of Armageddon." She was played by Miko Mayama.

Tan ru — the machine Nomad met and joined with in space, in Classic episode "The Changeling."

Tango — name of Pike's horse, left behind in the city of Mojave, California, and seen in Classic episode "The Menagerie."

Tango Sierra — located in the Rachelis system, this is a Federation medical facility mentioned in *TNG* episode "The Child."

Tankris, Yeoman — an *Enterprise* recorder at Scotty's hearing in Classic episode "Wolf in the Fold." She was played by Judy McConnell.

Tantalus field — dangerous weapon found in Kirk's quarters in the mirror universe in Classic episode "Mirror, Mirror." It can spy on a person and make him or her disappear or die with the touch of a button.

Tantalus Penal Colony — hospital for the violently mentally ill headed by Dr. Tristan Adams and his associate, Dr. Simon Van Gelder. Dr. Adams invents a neural neutralizer that can brainwash patients, but starts using it to control others and make them obedient only to him. He uses it on Dr. Van Gelder in Classic episode "Dagger of the Mind," as well as on Kirk.

Tantalus V — location of the Tantalus Penal Colony in Classic episode "Dagger of the Mind."

Tanuga IV — location of the Tanuga Research Station. The Tanugans, who are humanoid, have a rule that men are guilty until proven innocent. The Tanuga Research Station which orbits the planet explodes in *TNG* episode "A Matter of Perspective."

Tao classical music — Rishon Uxbridge composes this type of music in *TNG* episode "The Survivors."

Taos lightning — type of whiskey served in Tombstone in Classic episode "Spectre of the Gun."

"Tapestry" — sixth-season *TNG* episode written by Ronald D. Moore and directed by Les Landau. When Picard is knocked unconscious, while Crusher works desperately to save his life, he finds himself standing in a room filled with light. Q, wearing long robes, approaches him, and tells him he is in the afterlife. Picard is forced to relive segments of his life at Q's behest and finds himself back at the Academy when he was stabbed through the heart by Nausicaans. Because he is reliving the episode with full foreknowledge, things happen differently, but he learns that without some of his brash decisions, he would not be the man he is today. Guest stars: John deLancie and Ned Vaughn.

Taras, Subcommander — she commands the Romulan ship *Harkona* in *TNG* episode "Contagion." She is played by Carolyn Seymour.

Tarbolde, Phineas — author of the poem "Nightingale Woman" from which Gary Mitchell quotes in Classic episode "Where No Man Has Gone Before."

Tarbuck, Barbara — played Leka in *TNG* episode "The Host."

Tarchannan III — home of parasites that have infected Geordi and Susanna Leitjen in *TNG* episode "Identity Crisis."

Tarcher, Jeremy — scriptwriter of Classic *Trek* episode "The Lights of Zetar" (with Shari Lewis).

Tarella — where the people from planet Haven are from. They are survivors of a biological war that happened on Tarella many years before in *TNG* episode "Haven."

targ — Klingon animal Worf once had as a pet when he was a child. It is mentioned in *TNG* episode "Where No One Has Gone Before."

Tark — father of the dancer Kara, who was killed by the Jack the Ripper entity in Classic episode "Wolf in the Fold." He is an Argelian and is played by Joseph Bernard.

Tarkesian razor beast — Guinan uses this phrase in *TNG* episode "Rascals." When she is reverted to her child form, she wants to jump up and down on the bed like one of these beasts.

Tarmin — an Ullian historian going to Kaldra IV via the *Enterprise* in *TNG* episode "Violations." He is a mind rapist and is played by David Sage.

Tarod IX — in *TNG* episode "The Neutral Zone," this outpost on the Romulan border was destroyed.

Tarrant, Newell — played a CDO in *The Voyage Home.*

Tarrigan, Ensign — *Enterprise* security officer in *TNG* episode "Rightful Heir."

Tarsec aperitif — tricky concoction Guinan makes in Ten Forward in *TNG* episode "Time's Arrow."

Tarses, Simon — medical technician on the *Enterprise* whose grandfather was a Romulan, which makes the prejudiced Admiral Satie suspect him of treason in *TNG* episode "The Drumhead." He was played by Spencer Garrett.

Tarsian War — for this war, the Angosians altered their soldiers biologically to fight for them, then abandoned them in prison camps in *TNG* episode "The Hunted."

Tarsus III — the location of Starbase *74* where the *Enterprise* was when the Bynars stole her in *TNG* episode "11001001."

Tarsus IV — it was on this world that Kodos the Executioner murdered half the population (4,000 less desirable colonists), so that the rest of the colony could survive a famine. Kirk and Kevin Riley were children at the time and witnesses to the atrocity, as mentioned in Classic episode "The Conscience of the King."

Tartares V — mentioned as the location of some newly discovered ancient ruins. Q tells Vash she should go there in *DS9* episode "Q Less."

Tarver, Milt — played a scientist in *TNG* episodes "Time's Arrow, Parts I and II."

Tasmeen — Vulcan month mentioned in animated episode "Yesteryear." In an alternate timeline, Spock died on the 20th of this month during his *kahs'wan*.

taspar egg — the Cardassian Gul Madred gives one of these to Picard, whom he has tortured nearly to death in *TNG* episode "Chain of Command." It is moving and still alive, but Picard eats it anyway.

"Taste of Armageddon, A" — written by Robert Hamner and Gene L. Coon, directed by Joseph Pevney, this first-season Classic *Trek* episode aired 2/23/67. The *Enterprise* gets caught between two warring planets, Eminiar VII and Vendikar, who are using computers to fight their battles. Guest stars: Gene Lyons, David Opatoshu, Robert Samson, Barbara Babcock, Miko Mayama, and Sean Kenney.

Tate, Nick — played Dirgo in *TNG* episode "Final Mission."

Tatro, Richard — played Norman in Classic *Trek* episode "I, Mudd."

Tau Alpha C — Riker thinks the Traveler is from here, in *TNG* episode "Where No One Has Gone Before."

Tau Ceti — star near where the *Enterprise* used the Cochrane deacceleration maneuver to outwit a Romulan ship. This event is mentioned by Spock to Garth in Classic episode "Whom Gods Destroy."

Tau Ceti III — in *TNG* episode "Conspiracy," Picard first met Walker Keel here in a bar.

Tau Cygna V — the crew of the *Artemis* settled here in *TNG* episode "The Ensigns of Command." This world, located in the DeLaure Belt, is bombarded by hyperonic radiation and is owned by the Sheliak Corporate. The colony has a population of 15,253.

Taurus II — where the shuttlecraft *Galileo* crash lands in Classic episode "The Galileo Seven." The natives are large, furry humanoids who attack the shuttle crew and kill several of them. This planet is also used in the animated episode "The Lorelei Signal" as a planet whose inhabitants lure men to their world so they can drain them of their emotions. The men then age rapidly and die.

Tava, Dr. — medical aide at the hospital Riker is taken to on Malcoria in *TNG* episode "First Contact." Sachi Parker plays Tava.

Tayar — Borg killed by the away team on Ohniaka III in *TNG* episode "Descent."

Tayback, Vic — played Jojo Krako in Classic *Trek* "A Piece of the Action." He was a regular on the TV series *Griff, Khan,* and *Alice*; his film credits include *Bullitt* and *The Choirboys.* An owner of race horses, he died in the early 1990s.

Taylor, Deborah — played Zaheva in *TNG* episode "Night Terrors."

Taylor, Jeri — scriptwriter of *TNG* story for the episodes "Descent," "Aquiel," "Final Mission," "The Wounded," "Night Terrors," "The Drumhead," "Silicon Avatar," "Unification, Part I," "Violations," "The Outcast," and "Time's Arrow." Taylor also wrote the novelizaton of *Unification.*

Taylor, Jud — director of Classic *Trek* episodes "The Paradise Syndrome," "Wink of an Eye," "Let That Be Your Last Battlefield," "The Mark of Gideon," and "The Cloud Minders." His other directing credits include episodes of *The Guns of Will Sonnett* and *The Man from U.N.C.L.E.*, and the films *Future Cop* and *Return to Earth*.

Taylor, Keith — played Jahn's friend in Classic *Trek* episode "Miri." He also guest starred in *Lost in Space* and was a regular on *McKeever and the Colonel*.

Taylor, Mark L. — played Haritath in *TNG* episode "The Ensigns of Command."

Taylor, Gillian, Dr. — an expert on whales, played by Catherine Hicks, and a marine biologist who works at the Cetacean Institute in Sausalito in *The Voyage Home.* She works for Bob Briggs, who transports the whales to the sea in the middle of the night without notifying her in order to set them free. She helps Kirk and Spock find the whales and transport them to the 23rd century. She tags along and becomes a new resident of the 23rd century, immediately finding work on a science vessel as a marine biologist.

Tayna — Dr. Apgar's assistant in *TNG* episode "A Matter of Perspective" who claims Riker tried to rape her. She is played by Juli Donald.

T'Bok, Commander — Romulan commander who helps Picard in *TNG* episode "The Neutral Zone." He is played by Marc Alaimo.

Tchar — prince of the Skorr in Classic animated episode "Jihad." The Skorr are avian creatures. Tchar steals his own people's valuable relic in the hopes of starting a religious war.

Teacher, The — machine placed over the head of an individual that instantly gives him or her all knowledge contained within the computer brain that runs Sigma Draconis VI, in Classic episode "Spock's Brain." The knowledge is only temporary, however. The Eymorg, Kara, uses it when she steals Spock's brain.

Teer — title of a leader of the Ten Tribes on Capella IV in Classic episode "Friday's Child." The original Teer was Akaar, but he was killed and replaced by Maab, who was then killed and replaced by Eleen's newborn son, Leonard James Akaar.

telemetry probe — device shot into the galactic amoeba by the *Enterprise* to gather more information in Classic episode "The Immunity Syndrome."

Tellarites — aggressive species with piglike faces. They are members of the Federation and appear in Classic episodes "Journey to Babel" and "Whom Gods Destroy." A Tellarite ship is caught in the Delta Triangle in animated episode "Time Trap."

Telle, Glin — Cardassian member of a delegation on the *Enterprise* in *TNG* episode "The Wounded." He is played by Marco Rodriguez.

Tellun star system — on the border of Klingon space, this system contains Troyius and Elas, two warring worlds who are to make peace when the Dohlman of Elas, Elaan, and the leader of Troyius marry in Classic episode "Elaan of Troyius."

Tellurian spices — Andorians want to bid for these spices, owned by Fajo, in *TNG* episode "The Most Toys."

Temarek — tastes a drink Marouk offers Brull in *TNG* episode "The Vengeance Factor." He is played by Elkanah J. Burns.

Temple, Nurse — *Enterprise* nurse in *TNG* episode "Transfigurations." She is played by Patti Tippo.

Templeman, S. A. — played John Bates in *TNG* episode "The Defector."

temporal rift — a time displacement.

Ten Forward — bar and lounge on the *TNG Enterprise* where the crew can relax while off duty and be served synthehol drinks as well as exotic foods.

Tepo — one of the lesser bosses on Iotia in Classic episode "A Piece of the Action."

Terkim — Guinan's uncle, her mother's brother. Guinan says he was the family misfit but the only one in the family with a sense of humor, in *TNG* episode "Hollow Pursuits."

Terraform Command — Federation agency mentioned in *TNG* episode "Home Soil."

Terra Ten — an original Earth colony sent to colonize a distant world and mentioned in animated episode "The Terratin Incident." The name "Terra Ten" has been, over the years, changed to "Terratin."

"Terratin Incident, The" — written by Paul Schneider, this animated Classic *Trek* episode aired 11/17/73. After the *Enterprise* is hit by a bolt of energy from a planet orbiting the star Cepheus, the crew begins to shrink. A tiny city on the planet is responsible for the attack, and the transporter is the key to restoring the crew. Guest voice: James Doohan (Lt. Arex, Mendant of the Terratins).

Terratins — people of the original Terra Ten Earth colony who colonized a world they call Terratin. Spiroid waves are responsible for shrinking them to the point that other ships could never find them. They built their own miniature cities, but are on an unstable planet and must now be moved in animated episode "The Terratin Incident."

Terrell, Clark, Captain — commander of the *Reliant* when it is taken over by Khan in *The Wrath of Khan*. Chekov is his first officer. He kills himself when the parasite in his brain tries to force him to shoot Kirk. He was played by Paul Winfield.

Territorial Annex of the Tholian Assembly — what the Tholians call the unknown region of space into which the *Enterprise* and the *Defiant* have traveled. They claim the area as their territory.

Tessin III — an asteriod threatens this world in *TNG* episode "Cost of Living."

tetralubisol — white, liquid poison Lenore uses to try to kill Kevin Riley in Classic episode "The Conscience of the King."

tetryons — subatomic particles which pass through Dr. Reyga's shield in *TNG* episode "Suspicions."

Texas — name of a man from Texas who is in the Royale in *TNG* episode "The Royale." He is played by Noble Willingham.

Thalassa — an energy entity, one of three who have survived for thousands of years after a war destroyed her world in Classic episode "Return to Tomorrow." She is Sargon's wife. She enters the body of Dr. Anne Mulhall in order to build an android body for herself. Anne Mulhall is played by Diana Muldaur.

thalium compound — compound found in Mintakan strata that disrupts sensor probes in *TNG* episode "Who Watches the Watchers."

Thalos VII — mentioned in *TNG* episode "The Dauphin" as the "home of Thalian chocolate mousse."

Thandaus V — mentioned in *TNG* episode "Loud As a Whisper" as a world where the people are born with no limbs.

Thann — one of the Vians who tortures Kirk, Spock, and McCoy in Classic episode "The Empath." He is played by Willard Sage.

Tharn — leader of the Halkans in Classic episode "Mirror, Mirror." He refuses the *Enterprise* permission to mine dilithium on Halka. He is played by Vic Perrin.

Thasian — an alien entity, one of many, who rescued Charlie Evans from his crashed ship on their world, Thasus, in Classic episode "Charlie X." They are energy beings with great mental powers. The Thasian who appears on the bridge to take Charlie away is played by Abraham Sofaer.

"That Which Survives" — written by John Meredyth Lucas and Michael Richards, directed by Herb Wallerstein, this third-season Classic *Trek* episode aired 1/24/69. When Kirk, McCoy, Sulu, and D'Amato beam down to investigate a Class M planet riddled with earthquakes, they find it inhabited by Losira, a woman whose touch can kill life. Guest stars: Lee Meriwether, Naomi Pollack, Arthur Batanides, Brad Forrest, Kenneth Washington, and Booker Marshall. Of note: This is Dr. M'Benga's second appearance.

Thatcher, Kirk — actor/associate producer/musician who appeared as the punk on the bus in *The Voyage Home*. He wrote the song "I Hate You" which is loudly playing on the tape player on the bus. He was also the associate producer of *The Voyage Home*. Kirk is former British Prime Minister Margaret Thatcher's son and the creator/producer/writer of the popular sitcom *Dinosaurs!*

Thatcher, Torin — played Marplon in Classic *Trek* episode "The Return of the Archons." Torin was born in Bombay on January 15, 1905, and died in 1981. He was a teacher before he took up acting. His roles include the films *Great Expectations*, *The Seventh Voyage of Sinbad*, and *Mutiny on the Bounty*. TV credits include *Lost in Space*, *Voyage to the Bottom of the Sea*, *One Step Beyond*, and *The Guns of Will Sonnett*.

Theela — leader of the females on Taurus II in animated episode "The Lorelei Signal." Majel Barrett plays her voice.

Thei — Romulan subcommander in *TNG* episode "The Neutral Zone." He is played by Anthony James.

Theiss, William Ware — costume designer for *Star Trek*. He also did work on the film *Heart Like a Wheel* and is the costume supervisor on *The Next Generation*.

Thelev — an Andorian who is actually an Orion spy in Classic episode "Journey to Babel." He is the murderer of the Tellarite Gav and stabs Kirk in the back during a fight in the ship's corridor. He commits suicide through slow poisoning when he is caught. He is played by William O'Connell.

Thelka IV — Picard mentions that a dessert he is especially fond of is made on this world. He wants Nella to try it some time in *TNG* episode "Lessons."

Thelusian flu — a mild flu that mutates and then causes accelerated aging in *TNG* episode "Unnatural Selection."

theragen — a Klingon nerve gas that, when diluted with alcohol by McCoy, is the cure for the madness that plagues the *Enterprise* when it is trapped in Tholian space in Classic episode "The Tholian Web."

thermoconcrete — used for building temporary shelters for landing parties, it is also used by McCoy to bandage the wounded Horta in Classic episode "The Devil in the Dark."

Theta VII — the inhabitants of this planet are waiting for the *Enterprise* to deliver medical supplies to them, but the *Enterprise* is delayed when it goes after the vampire cloud in Classic episode "Obsession."

Theta VIII — the *Charybdis* was taken here in *TNG* episode "The Royale." It is located in the Theta 116 system. The atmosphere contains nitrogen, methane, liquid neon, and ammonia tornadoes and the temperature remains at 291 degrees centigrade.

Theta Cygni XII — this world's inhabitants were destroyed by the flying rubbery parasites on Deneva in Classic episode "Operation: Annihilate!" The parasites also attacked Ingraham B two years before reaching Deneva.

"This Side of Paradise" — written by D. C. Fontana and Nathan Butler, directed by Ralph Senensky, this first-season Classic *Trek* episode aired 3/2/67. On the planet Omicron Ceti III, spores from an alien plant protect the colony inhabitants from deadly Berthold rays but also give them an extreme feeling of peace and harmony that makes them never want to leave the world. The spores infect the *Enterprise* crew, causing everyone to abandon the ship to go live on the planet. Guest stars: Eddie Paskey, Jill Ireland, Frank Overton, and Grant Woods. Of note: The late Jill Ireland's husband, Charles Bronson, was on the set to make sure Leila's love scenes with Spock did not get out of hand.

Tholian Web — web spun around the *Enterprise* by the Tholians to capture them in Classic episode "The Tholian Web." This special effect was created by Mike Minor.

"Tholian Web, The" — written by Judy Burns and Chet Richards, directed by Ralph Senensky, this third-season Classic *Trek* episode aired 11/15/68. The *Enterprise* finds the missing ship *Defiant* in a part of space that is unstable. They board to investigate and discover that the ship is phasing out into another dimension. Kirk stays behind as the transporter malfunctions, then disappears with the ship and is feared dead. The crew then starts seeing his ghost. Apparently he was half-caught in a transporter beam, and at the next interphase in space when the *Defiant* again becomes visible, they beam him back on board. Meanwhile, the Tholians are disturbed by the ship's presence and begin building a web around the ship because it will not leave. Of note: Barbara Babcock's voice is used for the Tholians.

Tholians — Kyle Riker is the only survivor of an attack by the Tholians in *TNG*. Kirk first encountered them in Classic episode "The Tholian Web." They are an unfriendly, territorial race who will kill to keep people away from them. The leader, who shows himself to Kirk, is named Loskene. He looks as if he's made of crystal and light. Tholians supposedly live on a hot planet. They may have little individual identity, instead submerging themselves in the group

Tholl, Kova — Mizarian who is held captive with Picard, Esoqq, and Mitena Haro in *TNG* episode "Allegiance." He is played by Stephen Markle.

Thomas, Craig — played a Klingon in *Star Trek: The Motion Picture*. He also appears in the 1983 movie *Spring Fever*.

Thomas, Sharon — played the waitress in *The Search for Spock*. She also appears in the 1982 movie *Portrait of a Showgirl*.

***Thomas Paine*, USS** — Captain Rixx commands this frigate in *TNG* episode "Conspiracy."

Thompson, Brian — played Klag in *TNG* episode "A Matter of Honor."

Thompson, Garland — played the second crewman in Classic *Trek* episode "Charlie X," and Technician Wilson in "The Enemy Within."

Thompson, Leslie, Yeoman — *Enterprise* junior officer who is killed by the Kelvans in Classic episode "By Any Other Name." She is played by Julie Cobb.

Thompson, Scott — played DaiMon Goss in *TNG* episode "The Price."

Thompson, Susanna — played Varel in *TNG* episodes "The Next Phase" and "Frame of Mind."

Thorley, Ken — played Mot in *TNG* episode "Ensign Ro," and Seaman in *TNG* episode "Time's Arrow, Part I."

Thorne, Dyanne — played Girl #1 in Classic *Trek* episode "A Piece of the Action."

Thorne, Worley — scriptwriter of *TNG* episode "Justice." He has written scripts for *Paper Chase*, *Sesame*

Street, Barnaby Jones, Cannon, Apple's Way, Dallas, Fantasy Island, and *The Adventures of Grizzly Adams.* He currently writes film scripts.

Thorne, Ensign — an *Enterprise* junior officer in *TNG* episode "In Theory." She was played by Pamela Winslow.

Thornton, Colleen and Maureen — twin actresses who played the "Barbara" series in Classic *Trek* episode "I, Mudd."

Thornton, Noley — played Clara in *TNG* episode "Imaginary Friend."

Thorson, Lynda — appeared in *TNG* episode "The Chase."

Thrett, Maggie — played Ruth Bonaventure in Classic *Trek* episode "Mudd's Women."

Throne, Malachi — played Commodore Mendez in Classic *Trek* episode "The Menagerie." He also played Pardek in *TNG* episode "Unification, Parts I and II." TV credits include *Iron Horse, Lost in Space,* and *Voyage to the Bottom of the Sea,* as well as a regular role in *It Takes a Thief.* Film credits include *The Doomsday Flight, Assault on the Wayne* (with Leonard Nimoy), and *The Sex Symbol.*

t'hy'la — Vulcan term of friendship defined in Roddenberry's novel *Star Trek: The Motion Picture.* It can mean, depending on the context, "friend, brother, or lover." Spock uses this term in his mind to describe his relationship with Kirk. On a talk show, William Shatner mispronounced it as *t-ha'la.* Some fans have been known to pronounce it *t-hee-a.* It is actually pronounced *t-high-la.* It is a popular word with fans and often appears in fan fiction, but the word, Roddenberry's invention, has never been used on screen.

***Tian An Men,* USS** — ship which took part in the blockade between the Klingons and Romulans in *TNG* episode "Redemption."

Tibella Minor — Dr. Crusher recommends this world to Nurse Ogawa as a nice place to vacation in *TNG* episode "The Icarus Factor."

Tiburon — mentioned as Dr. Sevrin's homeworld in Classic episode "The Way to Eden." This world is also mentioned as the site of Zora's horrible experiments on native tribes in "The Savage Curtain."

Tierney, Lawrence — played Cyrus Redblock in *TNG* episode "The Big Goodbye."

Tiffe, Angelo — played the electronic technician in *The Voyage Home*. He also appeared in the 1984 film *The Dollmaker*.

Tigar, Kenneth — played Ornaran Leader in *TNG* episode "Symbiosis."

Tilonus IV — the government of this world collapses into anarchy while a Starfleet team is on the planet. The team hides and Riker poses as a merchant to find them, but is abducted and hallucinates that he is confined in the asylum located on this planet.

Tilonus Institute for Mental Disorders, Ward 47 — where Riker finds himself confined in *TNG* episode "Frame of Mind."

"Time Squared" — second-season *TNG* episode written by Kurt Michael Bensmiller and Maurice Hurley, directed by Joseph L. Scanlan. One of the *Enterprise*'s own shuttlepods with a twin Captain Picard on board is encountered. It comes from six hours in the future, a future in which the *Enterprise* is destroyed. Guest star: Colm Meaney.

"Time Trap" — written by Joyce Perry, this animated Classic *Trek* episode aired 11/24/73. In a triangle of space where ships have disappeared, the *Enterprise* meets up with the Klingon ship *Klothos*. They enter an alternate universe where all the other ships that vanished previously now drift. The place is called Elysia and is inhabited by the Elysians, the people of all races from the other ships who have made a peaceful society for themselves. They tell Kirk and the Klingon captain that there is no way out. The two ships must work together to escape.

"Time's Arrow, Part I" — fifth-season *TNG* episode written by Joe Menosky and Michael Piller, directed by Les Landau. Data's head is discovered in a cave on Earth, a clue that aliens are going into Earth's past and killing people. Guest stars: Whoopi Goldberg, Jerry Hardin, Michael Aron, Barry Kiven, Ken Thorley, Sheldon Peters Wolfchild, John M. Murdock, Marc Alaimo, Milt Tarver, and Michael Hungerford.

"Time's Arrow, Part II" — sixth-season *TNG* episode written by Joe Menosky and Jeri Taylor, directed by Les Landau. Picard and his crew are stranded in Earth's past in San Francisco, where Picard meets a woman who looks exactly like Guinan. Meanwhile, aliens are feeding off human life forces. Guest stars: Whoopi Goldberg, Jerry Hardin, Alexander Enberg, Van Epperson, Pamela Kosh, Michael Aron, James Gleason, Bill Cho Lee, William Boyett, and Mary Stein.

"Timescape" — sixth-season *TNG* episode written by Brannon Braga and directed by Adam Nimoy. While Picard, Geordi, Data, and Troi are en route to the *Enterprise* via a shuttle, they start experiencing periodic time freezes, and discover the *Enterprise* is frozen in space in the midst of a Romulan attack. Time has stopped, and they must figure out a way to start it again without causing their ship to be destroyed by the frozen phaser beams directed at it.

Timicin, Dr. — a Kaelon astrophysicist specializing in research aimed at re-energizing dying stars. His theory fails on the star Praxillus but he wants to try again. However, his death is scheduled for his 60th birthday, an involuntary ritual he cannot refuse to carry out. Lwaxana

Troi becomes briefly involved with him in *TNG* episode "Half a Life." Dr. Timicin is played by David Ogden Stiers.

Timothy — friend of Kirk's who gives him the cold shoulder on Starbase 11 in Classic episode "Court-Martial." He is played by Winston DeLugo. Another Timothy appears in the *TNG* episode "Hero Wars." He imitates Data and is played by Joshua Harris.

Tin Man — organic creature born in space, also known as a Gomtuu in *TNG* episode "The Tin Man." It is actually a live spaceship which can be run telepathically by a crew. It had been alone, without a crew, for thousands of years.

"Tin Man, The" — third-season *TNG* episode written by Dennis Putman and David Bischoff, directed by Robert Scheerer. A Betazoid named Tam Elbrun and a corporeal entity, which is actually also a space vessel, come together in this story of loneliness and telepathy. Guest stars: Harry Groener, Michael Cavanaugh, Peter Vogt, and Colm Meaney.

Tippo, Patti — played Temple in *TNG* episode "Transfigurations."

Tirellia — world mentioned in conversation to Data by Commander Hutchinson as being one of three inhabited worlds without a magnetic pole. Data says five Tirellians serve aboard the *Enterprise*. It is also one of seven inhabited worlds with no atmosphere. All this trivia is discussed in *TNG* episode "Starship Mine."

Titus IV — O'Brien got his pet tarantula, Christina, from this world, as mentioned in *TNG* episode "Realm of Fear."

T'Jon — an Ornaran who is captain of the *Sanction* in *TNG* episode "Symbiosis." He is played by Merritt Butrick.

T'Kon Empire — ruled the galaxy 600,000 years ago. Their leftover outposts are encountered in *TNG* episode "The Last Outpost."

T'lli Beta — the *Enterprise* encounters these two-dimensional life-forms while en route to this world in *TNG* episode "The Loss."

T–negative — blood type of both Spock and his father, Sarek, as mentioned in Classic episode "Journey to Babel."

Tobin, Marc — played Joaquin in Classic *Trek* episode "Space Seed," and a Klingon in "Day of the Dove."

Tochi, Brian — played the child, Ray, in Classic *Trek* episode "And the Children Shall Lead." He also played the helmsman Kenny Lin in *TNG* episode "Night Terrors." He had regular roles in the series *Anna and the King*, *Renegades*, and *Space Academy*. He also appeared in the 1981 film *We're Fighting Back*.

Todd, Hallie — played Data's daughter Lal in *TNG* episode "The Offspring." She is best known for her recurring role on the sitcom *Brothers*.

Todd, Tony — played Kurn in *TNG* episodes "Sins of the Father" and "Redemption, Parts I and II."

Toff, Palor — alien with three nostrils who is Kivas Fajo's rival. He appears in *TNG* episode "The Most Toys" and is played by Nehemiah Persoff.

Tog, DaiMon — Ferengi captain of the *Krayton* who falls for Lwaxana and kidnaps her along with Deanna and Riker in *TNG* episode "Ménage à Troi." He is played by Frank Corsentino.

Tokath, Commander — commands the Romulan prison colony on Carraya IV in *TNG* episode "Birthright." He married a Klingon, Gi'ral, and fathered a half-Romulan, half-Klingon daughter, Ba'el.

Tokyo Base — in *TNG* episode "The Icarus Factor," Kyle Riker worked on Ferengi tactics here.

Tolaka, L. Isao, Captain — captain of the *Lantree* who rapidly ages in *TNG* episode "Unnatural Selection."

Tolstoy, USS — one of the ships destroyed by the Borg at Wolf 359 according to Shelby in *TNG* episode "Best of Both Worlds."

Tom, Sebastian — played the samurai in Classic *Trek* episode "Shore Leave."

Tomalak — commander of the Neutral Zone security force for the Romulans in *TNG* episodes "The Enemy" and "The Defector." He is played by Andreas Katsulas.

Tomar — Scotty drinks this Kelvan literally under the table with his "green" drink in Classic episode "By Any Other Name." He is played by Robert Fortier.

Tomid Incident — the last encounter with the Romulans, 53 years, 7 months, 18 days before *TNG* episode "The Neutral Zone."

Tomlinson, Robert, Specialist — his wedding vows to Angela Martine are interrupted in Classic episode "Balance of Terror." He worked in the phaser room and was killed by phaser coolant fumes that leaked during a Romulan attack. He was played by Stephen Mines.

"Tomorrow Is Yesterday" — written by D. C. Fontana and directed by Michael O'Herlihy, this first-season Classic *Trek* episode aired 1/26/67. The *Enterprise* is thrown back in time to the year 1969 where they are mistaken for a UFO. They must erase evidence of their presence before they can leave, but Kirk gets captured by Air Force personnel. Guest stars: Roger Perry, Sherry Townsend, Hal Lynch, Ed Peck, John Winston, and Mark Dempsey. Of note: This episode introduces the slingshot time-travel effect, and shows food processors in the transporter room.

Tompkins, Paul — played Breville in *TNG* episode "Identity Crisis."

Tondro, Anina — widow of General Tondro, who was killed on Klystron IV before Dax became Jadzia Dax.

Curzon Dax was best friends with the man, and in *DS9* episode "Dax" Jadzia is accused of killing the general. Dax, however, is in the clear because he was the general's widow's lover and with her at the time of the murder. It is Tondro's son, who did not know of this fact, who pursues Dax to avenge his father's murder.

T'Ong — Klingon ship, class D–7, commanded by Captain K'Temoc. Its crew had been in cryonic suspension for 75 years.

"Too Short a Season" — first-season *TNG* episode written by Michael Michaelian and Dorothy Fontana, directed by Rob Bowman. The *Enterprise* brings aboard an admiral who is taking a youth serum that is killing him. They are headed to Mordan IV to negotiate a hostage situation. Guest stars: Clayton Rohner, Marsha Hunt, and Michael Pataki.

topaline — mineral used in life support systems on sealed colony worlds, as mentioned in Classic episode "Friday's Child."

Toq — a young Klingon in the prison colony on Carraya in *TNG* episode "Birthright." He wants Worf to teach him how to become Klingon.

Torak, Governor — Klingon official who oversees the region of space near Subspace Relay Station 47 where Aquiel is stationed in *TNG* episode "Aquiel."

Toral — Klingon boy and Duras's bastard son, whose aunts, Lursa and Batur, intend to help him claim the title of the Head of the High Council in *TNG* episode "Redemption." He was played by J. D. Cullum.

Toreth, Commander — commands the Romulan warbird *Khazara* in *TNG* episode "Face of the Enemy." She hates the Tal Shiar because she believes they killed her father. Troi relieves her of command once she convinces her Troi is Major Rakal of the Tal Shiar.

Torg — second-in-command under Kruge, this Klingon is killed when he boards the *Enterprise* in *The Search for Spock.* He is played by Stephen Liska.

Torme, Tracy — scriptwriter of *TNG* episodes "Haven," "The Big Goodbye," "Conspiracy," and "The Schizoid Man." He was also the creative consultant on the show.

Tormolen, Joe — this *Enterprise* crewman is the first to catch the Psi 2000 virus when he beams down to the station with Spock in Classic episode "The Naked Time." He stabs himself in the rec room and later dies in sick-bay, though not of the wound itself, but of "despair" according to McCoy. He is played by Stewart Moss.

Torona IV — planet located in the Jarada sector with which Picard establishes diplomatic relations in *TNG* episode "The Big Goodbye."

Torres — an *Enterprise* ensign frozen by Q in *TNG* episode "Encounter at Farpoint." He is played by Jimmy Ortega.

Torsek, Dierk — played Dr. Bernard in *TNG* episode "When the Bough Breaks."

Tosk — in *DS9* episode "Captive Pursuit," Tosk is an alien from the Gamma Quadrant who was raised to be prey in a deadly hunt.

Toussaint, Beth — played Ishara Yar in *TNG* episode "Legacy."

Tovin III — according to Gul Madred, this is the closest neutral world to Seltris III in *TNG* episode "Chain of Command."

Towers, Robert — played Rata in *TNG* episode "The Battle."

Towles — *Enterprise* security officer stationed at the command post on the world which the now aggressive Borg command in *TNG* episode "Descent."

Townes, Harry — played Reger in Classic *Trek* episode "The Return of the Archons." TV credits include *Rawhide*, *Voyagers!*, and *Planet of the Apes*. He also appeared in the 1959 film *Cry Tough* and the 1983 film *Agent of H.E.A.T.*

Townsend, Barbara — played Admiral Rossa in *TNG* episode "Suddenly Human."

Townsend, Sherri — played a crewmember in Classic *Trek* episode "Tomorrow Is Yesterday."

Tox Uthat — device which can halt nuclear reaction in a star. It was invented by Kal Dano in the 27th century and resembles a small crystal cube. It is hidden on Risa in the past, when Picard and Vash, with people from the future, are drawn into the intrigue in relocating it in *TNG* episode "Captain's Holiday."

Toya — Alexandra's mother in *TNG* episode "When the Bough Breaks." She was played by Connie Danese.

Toyota, Vic — stunt double for Sulu in Classic *Trek* episode "Catspaw."

T'Pan, Dr. — director of the Vulcan Science Academy who is married to a human, Dr. Christopher, in *TNG* episode "Suspicions."

T'Pau — Vulcan matriarch who turns out to also be Spock's grandmother in Classic episode "Amok Time." She is the only person to ever turn down a seat on the Federation High Council. She is played by Celia Lovsky. Also, the name of a Vulcan ship dismantled and left at Qualor II in *TNG* episode "Unification."

T'Pel, Ambassador — secretly a Romulan, Subcommander Selok, who is posing as a Vulcan in *TNG* episode "Data's Day." In "The Drumhead," Admiral Satie accuses Picard of being in league with her spy mission. She is played by Sierra Pecheur.

T'Pel — Spock mentions her as his mother when he pretends to be Selek in animated episode "Yesteryear."

T'Pring — Spock's betrothed. They were promised to each other in a ceremony at the age of seven on Vulcan. Spock is drawn to return to her when he enters *Pon farr* in Classic episode "Amok Time." She, however, does not want Spock. She wants Stonn, and challenges Spock for the right to divorce. This means Stonn must fight Spock, but T'Pring chooses Kirk as her champion instead, forcing the two friends to fight to the death. T'Pring is played by Arlene Martel.

Tracey, Ronald, Captain — captain of the *Exeter* in Classic episode "The Omega Glory." His crew dies of a terrible disease they caught on Omega, but Tracey survives when he stays on Omega, because the planet's atmosphere provides a natural immunity to the plague. He ends up breaking the Prime Directive and interfering with the planet's natural progression because he thinks he has found the answer to immortality, since the Omegans live for centuries. He tries to kill Spock and Kirk when he discovers they won't help him discover the planet's properties or keep his secret about breaking the Prime Directive. He is played by Morgan Woodward.

Tracy, Karen, Lieutenant — an *Enterprise* officer who beams down to Argelius to give Scotty tests in Classic episode "Wolf in the Fold." She is killed by the Jack the Ripper entity. She was played by Virginia Aldridge.

Trager — Gul Macet's Cardassian *Galor,* class warship in *TNG* episode "The Wounded."

Trainor, Saxon — played Larson in *TNG* episode "The Nth Degree."

Tralesta Clan — clan massacred by their enemies, the Lornacks of Acamar III, in *TNG* episode "The Vengeance Factor." Five of the Tralestas survive. In the episode, Yuta, the last survivor, tries to kill Chorgon, the last of the Lornacks.

transceiver — long-range communication device found on Thelev, the Orion spy, in Classic episode "Journey to Babel."

"Transfigurations" — third-season *TNG* episode written by René Echevarria and directed by Tom Benko. The only survivor of a wrecked ship is aided by the *Enterprise*. His amnesia hinders him from relating his experience but some very strange qualities, such as an ability to heal very rapidly, make him appear not quite human. He is really a Zalkonian evolving into a higher being, who is being pursued by his own people who fear this transfiguration of their species. Guest stars: Mark La Mura, Charles Dennis, Julie Warner, Patti Tippo, and Colm Meaney.

transmuter — device which amplifies Sylvia and Korob's power in Classic episode "Catspaw."

transparent aluminium — Scotty gives the matrix for this unique man-made substance to the head of a polymer factory in *The Voyage Home*. It is apparently a very strong, clear substance that can be used in space, underwater, etc.

transporter — a matter/energy conversion device on the *Enterprise* that can move people and objects by scrambling matter and then rematerializing it at its destination. In *TNG*, intership beaming is common, whereas during Classic *Trek* time, it was considered very dangerous. A transporter cannot be used when the shields of the ship are up. Biofilters in transporters automatically screen out harmful bacteria from alien worlds. Scotty survives into the 24th century because his pattern is held in stasis in a transporter beam.

Transporter Code 14 — in *TNG* episode "Captain's Holiday," Picard gives Riker this code with which Riker then transports the *Tox Uthat* into space where it is disintegrated.

transtater — device on which much of Federation technology is based, including the transporters, phasers, and communicators as mentioned in Classic episode "A Piece of the Action."

Tra'nusah — Klingon world mentioned in *TNG* episode "A Matter of Honor."

tranya — drink offered to Kirk, Spock, McCoy, and Bailey by Balok in Classic episode "The Corbomite Maneuver."

Traveler, The — appears in *TNG* episode "Time Squared." In "Where No One Has Gone Before," he was played by Eric Menyuk. He travels through time using his mind power.

Travers, Commodore — leader of the Earth colony on Cestus III that is attacked by the Gorns, as mentioned in Classic episode "Arena."

Treaty of Algeron — treaty that ended the Romulan war 200 years before. It forbids any ships from either side to enter the Neutral Zone as mentioned in *TNG* episode "The Defector."

Treaty of Armens — treaty that established peace between the Federation and the Sheliaks, as mentioned in *TNG* episode "The Ensigns of Command." The treaty took 372 experts to negotiate and is more than 500,000 words long. The humans on Tau Cygna V are in violation of the treaty and the Sheliak want them off the world.

Treaty of Sirius — treaty that forbids the Kzin to possess any weapons beyond police vessels in animated episode "The Slaver Weapon."

Trefayne — clairvoyant member of the Organian Council in Classic episode "Errand of Mercy." He is played by David Hillary Hughes.

Trelane — an omnipotent energy being who acts like a spoiled brat and plays deadly games with the *Enterprise* in Classic episode "The Squire of Gothos." He appears in human form to toy with them (much like Q in *TNG*) until his parents show up, also energy beings, and make him stop. He is played by William Campbell.

Trent — Beate's servant on Angel One in *TNG* episode "Angel One." He is played by Leonard John Crowfoot.

triox compound — McCoy says he's giving this to Kirk during his fight with Spock in Classic episode "Amok Time" so Kirk can breathe easier in the thin atmosphere. He actually slips him a neural paralyzer to simulate death and save his life.

Triacus — located in Epsilon Indi, the Starnes expedition runs into the Gorgon on this planet in Classic episode "And the Children Shall Lead." Spock says that according to legend Triacus was the site of a band of marauders who made war throughout Epsilon Indi and were themselves destroyed in the war. However, the evil power that caused these marauders to war still waits on Triacus for a catalyst which will set the evil in motion throughout the galaxy again. The Gorgon of Triacus is possibly the last of these marauders who survived.

Triangulum System — mentioned in *TNG* episode "The Survivors." Renegade Andorians hid a ship here by dismantling it.

tribble — a ball of fur that purrs. Thousands are seen in Classic episode "The Trouble with Tribbles" and the animated "More Tribbles, More Troubles." If they eat too much, they get pregnant and have more tribbles. Their breeding gets out of control on the *Enterprise*. In the animated episode, it is learned that the glommer is the tribble's natural predator.

tricobalt satellite explosion — in Classic episode "A Taste of Armageddon," Anan 7 tells Kirk the *Enterprise* has been destroyed by a tricobalt satellite explosion.

tricorder — device that is a computer, sensor unit, and recorder in one; it is taken on landing parties. It is a small box on a strap. In *TNG*, tricorders are smaller, fitting in the palm of the hand, and feature a little screen.

tricordrazine — Pulaski uses this on Riker to slow the absorption of the microbes in his system in *TNG* episode "Shades of Gray." Probably related to cordrazine (see entry). It is also mentioned in "Yesterday's Enterprise" and "Who Watches the Watchers."

tricyanate — element which has contaminated the water on Beta Agni II in *TNG* episode "The Most Toys." Fajo used this on the water deliberately to lure the *Enterprise*. Hytritium is the only known substance that can negate tricyanate poisoning.

Trieste, USS — ship closest to Starbase 74 when the Bynars steal the *Enterprise* in *TNG* episode "11001001."

trilaser connector — medical device McCoy uses during surgery to restore Spock's brain to his body in Classic episode "Spock's Brain."

trilithium — substance a team of thieves is trying to steal from the *Enterprise* in *TNG* episode "Starship Mine."

Trill — symbiont race first encountered in *TNG* episode "The Host." Not all Trills receive symbionts. Jadzia of *DS9* trained all her life for the opportunity to be chosen to host a symbiont. Jadzia's symbion is Dax whose previous host was Curzon. Trills who are symbionts can remember their previous body's memories because, though the humanoid bodies wear out from old age, the symbiont's life span lasts hundreds of years. Therefore, a symbiont Trill can draw on the experiences of several lifetimes, as does Jadzia Dax. Trills in "The Host" have a kind of ridge structure on their foreheads and the bridge of their noses. This look was changed for Jadzia in *DS9* who has very human features. Her only physical differences include small horseshoe-shaped markings like light freckles that cover the sides of her forehead and temples, curve against her ears to her neck, and disappear under her uniform down her back. They are barely noticeable except when Jadzia is filmed in a close up shot. If she wore her hair down, they would not be seen at all.

trillium 323 — in *TNG* episode "The Price," a Caldonian mineral for which Riker tries to make trade agreements in order to offer it to the Barzans during the wormhole negotiations. In Classic episode "Errand of Mercy," Spock pretends to be a Vulcan merchant selling kivas and trillium. Trillium is never defined.

trimagnesite — fuel used in the satellites that create the light flares which destroy the parasites in Classic episode "Operation Annihilate!" It was also called trivium.

triolic waves — form of radiation harmful to humans that Geordi can see with his visor. These waves are produced by the power source used by the aliens who historically preyed upon humans in *TNG* episode "Time's Arrow."

Trioma System — in this system, Keith Rocha was absorbed by a coalescent organism, according to Dr. Crusher in *TNG* episode "Aquiel."

Trion, Leka, Governor — leader of the world Peliar Zel. She asked Ambassador Odan to mediate a dispute between her world's two moons, Alpha and Beta, in *TNG* episode "The Host."

Tripoli, USS — ship that found Data on Omicron Theta IV in *TNG* episode "Datalore."

tripolymer composites — Data is composed mostly of this, as mentioned in *TNG* episode "The Most Toys."

trisec — time unit used on Triskelion in Classic episode "The Gamesters of Triskelion."

Triskelion — planet with a trinary sun called M24

Alpha to which Kirk, Chekov, and Uhura are taken when they are kidnapped by a powerful transport beam in Classic episode "The Gamesters of Triskelion." The Providers live here, enslaving the people they have kidnapped and forcing them to participate in deadly games for the Providers' entertainment. The Providers gamble on the outcome of the games.

tritanium — alloy which the weapons of Minos are powerful enough to melt, as mentioned in *TNG* episode "The Arsenal of Freedom." It can be found on Argus X, as mentioned in Classic episode "Obsession."

trititanium — element used on the hulls of starships, as mentioned in Classic episode "Journey to Babel."

Trivers, Barry — scriptwriter of Classic *Trek* episode "The Conscience of the King."

trivium — see entry for Trimagnesite.

Troglytes — the blue-collar workers and miners on Ardana who are basically slaves to the upper-class citizens of Stratos in Classic episode "The Cloud Minders."

Troi, Deanna, Lieutenant Commander — regular in *TNG*, played by Marina Sirtis. She is the ship's counselor, a half-human, half-Betazoid with empathic powers that allow her to read the emotions of others (except for Ferengi). She has full telepathy with her Betazoid mother, Lwaxana Troi, who is an eccentric aristocrat of Betazed's fifth house, one of the oldest and richest families on the planet, and holder of the sacred chalice of Riix. Lwaxana is a woman steeped in tradition, outspoken, and somewhat of an embarrassment to her daughter, but she loves Deanna very much. Deanna's father was a Starfleet officer named Ian Andrew, who died when she was a baby. In the seventh season of *TNG* it is discovered that Deanna had an older sister who drowned on a picnic at about the age of seven. Deanna was too young to remember her. Deanna and Will Riker knew each other before either one was posted to the *Enterprise*. They had a love affair and almost married, but Riker was called away by his career. She still refers to him as her *Imzadi* (see entry). She once gave birth to an alien child, whose conception was mysterious and whose life was very brief. She named him Ian Andrew after her father. She now helps Worf care for his son, Alexander, and as a result she and Worf have become very close friends. In alternate universes (seen in the *TNG* seventh-season episode "Parallels"), Deanna and Worf are married and have children. Deanna loves chocolate more than any other food.

Troi, Ian Andrew — Deanna's human father, who Deanna named her son Ian Andrew after in *TNG* episode "The Child."

Troi, Lwaxana — Deanna Troi's mother who has made several appearances on *TNG* and one on *DS9*. She is played by Majel Barrett. She is a Betazed aristocrat of the fifth house, the holder of the sacred chalice of Riix, heir to the holy rings of Betazed. She was married to Ian Andrew, Deanna's father, and they had another daughter who drowned at age seven when Deanna was a baby.

Trose, Kalin — a representative from the moon Alpha, orbiting Peliar Zel, in *TNG* episode "The Host." He stopped Ambassador Odan from being killed in an assassination plot 30 years before. Trose is played by Franc Luz.

Trost, Scott — played a Bajoran officer in *DS9* episode "A Man Alone," and an ensign in *TNG* episode "Unnatural Selection."

"Trouble with Tribbles, The" — written by now noted science-fiction author David Gerrold and directed by Joseph Pevney, this second-season Classic *Trek* episode aired 12/29/67. Tribbles, little purring balls of fur that multiply if fed too much, become a pest problem for the *Enterprise* and the Space Station K–7. Klingons are another problem, especially for Scotty when they insult his ship.

Guest stars: William Schallert, William Campbell, Stanley Adams, Whit Bissel, Michael Pataki, Charlie Brill, Ed Reimers, and Guy Raymond. Of note: David Gerrold penned an entire book called *The Trouble with Tribbles*, which narrates the autobiographical story of the creation of this episode. Also, a sequel to this was made into an animated episode, "More Tribbles, More Troubles." It is said David Gerrold patterned his tribbles after Robert Heinlein's Martian flat cats. This episode was nominated for the Hugo Award for Best Dramatic Presentation of 1967 but placed second.

Troupe, Tom — played Lt. Harold in Classic *Trek* episode "Arena." TV credits include *Griff* and *The Young Rebels*. He also appeared in the 1959 film *The Big Fisherman* and the 1973 film *The Alpha Caper*.

trova — drink offered to Kirk by Anan 7 on Eminiar in Classic episode "A Taste of Armageddon."

Troy, David — played Lt. Matson in Classic *Trek* episode "The Conscience of the King."

Troyius — located in the Tellun star system (see entry) on the border of Klingon space. The monarch of this world is to be married to Elaan of Elas in Classic episode "Elaan of Troyius." Troyius has been at war with Elas for centuries. The marriage is supposed to bring peace.

"True Q" — sixth-season *TNG* episode written by René Echevarria and directed by Robert Scherrer. An eighteen-year-old girl joins the *Enterprise* crew as an intern after winning a student competition. It is soon discovered that she has incredible mental powers that she has been hiding from everyone because she doesn't want to be seen as different. Then Q arrives, dropping the bombshell that she is not really human, but a Q herself, born of a Q couple who left the Continuum to be human. The couple was killed for their "treason" and Amanda was adopted by human parents. Q gives her the opportunity to be a part of her true race but Amanda has other aspirations for her life. Guest stars: Olivia D'Abo and John deLancie.

Trumble, Doug — special photographic effects supervisor on *Star Trek: The Motion Picture*. He has also worked on the films *Close Encounters of the Third Kind* and *2001: A Space Odyssey*. He also directed the movies *Silent Running* and *Brainstorm*.

Tsingtao, Ray — one of the children of the Starnes party rescued from Triacus in Classic episode "And the Children Shall Lead." He is played by Brian Tochi (who also had a small role in a *TNG* episode; see entry for Tochi).

T'Shalik — in *TNG* episode "Coming of Age," she is a Vulcan girl from another ship who takes the Academy Exam with Wesley. She is played by Tasia Valenza.

Tsiolkovsky, USS — freighter, *Grissom* class, infected by the Psi 2000 virus in *TNG* episode "The Naked Now." Its crew committed suicide.

T'su, Lian — *Enterprise* ensign tested by Geordi in *TNG* episode "The Arsenal of Freedom." She is played by Julia Nickson.

Tsu, Tan — survivor of the *Arcos* in *TNG* episode "Legacy." He is played by Vladimir Velasco.

T Tauri–type star system — single star with only one satellite, which is extremely rare according to Data in *TNG* episode "Clues."

Tubert, Marcelo — played Jared Acost in *TNG* episode "Devil's Due."

Tula — Reger's daughter in Classic episode "The Return of the Archons." She was attacked by Bilar during the Festival. She is played by Brioni Farrell.

Tumen, Marion — script supervisor on *The Final Frontier*.

turbolift — elevator on the ship that transports people to the various levels and moves sideways as well as up and down. They are verbally commanded to their destinations.

Turing Test of Sentient Ability — test given to Data by Starfleet, which he passed.

Turkana IV — Tasha Yar's world where the society is split into two factions, the Alliance and the Coalition. They fight constantly, as seen in *TNG* episode "Legacy." The planet no longer belongs to the Federation (as of 15 years earlier).

"Turnabout Intruder" — written by Arthur H. Singer and Gene Roddenberry and directed by Herb Wallerstein, this last third-season Classic *Trek* episode aired 6/3/69. Kirk's old friend Janice Lester discovers a device that allows her to switch bodies with him. Now she is Captain Kirk, and he is Janice, and no one will believe him except Spock (who can tell with a mind meld who is who). Guest stars: Sandra Smith, Harry Landers, Barbara Baldavin, and Roger Halloway. Of note: While filming this episode, William Shatner had a flu which weakened him, and when he was required to pick up Janice Lester (Sandra Smith) and place her on the bed, he dropped her several times before he got the shot right. This episode has some of the best acting ever seen in the series.

Twenty-first Street Mission — where Edith Keeler works to feed the homeless in Classic episode "The City on the Edge of Forever." It is located in New York City in 1930.

Tycho IV — where the vampire cloud attacked the *Farragut* eleven years before the *Enterprise* encounters it. It has returned there to breed when the *Enterprise* destroys it.

Tyken's Rift — a rift or rupture in space that traps the *Enterprise* and another ship in *TNG* episode "Night Terrors."

Tyler, José — also called Joe, he is Pike's navigator in Classic episode "The Menagerie" and "The Cage" and is played by Peter Duryea.

Typerias — mentioned in Classic episode "A Private Little War" as a world where coagulating sand can be found, which can be used to stop the flow of blood.

Typhon Expanse — in *TNG* episode "Cause and Effect," the *Enterprise* is the first to explore this region of space.

Tyree — Kirk's friend on Neural whose wife, Nona, is a Kanutu woman. He is the head of the hill people and met Kirk 13 years before when Kirk was a lieutenant on a landing party studying Neural. He does not know Kirk is an alien until, on their second meeting, when Kirk is in command of the *Enterprise*, it is discovered that the Klingons are interfering with the world's natural progression.

Tyrus VIIA — a mining station orbits this world, directed by Dr. Farralon, who is experimenting with a particle fountain for excavation in *TNG* episode "The Quality of Life."

Ugly Bags of Mostly Water — phrase the micro-brains of Velara III use to refer to humans in *TNG* episode "Home Soil."

Uhnari, Aquiel, Lieutenant — a young lieutenant assigned with Lt. Keith Rocha to Subspace Relay Station 47 in *TNG* episode "Aquiel." She is a Hahliian, and has a sister, Sheana, to whom she often sends messages. Rocha went crazy and attacked her, then killed himself, but Aquiel is suspected of murdering him. She also falls for Geordi, who is one of the few people who believe she's innocent. She has a dog, Maura. Aquiel is played by Renée Jones.

Uhura, Lieutenant — a regular on *Star Trek,* the animated series, and the films, she is played by Nichelle Nichols. Uhura, the communications officer on the *Enterprise,* eventually rises in rank to "commander" in the movies. Uhura has been a role model for women everywhere, proving to the 1960s audience (and on into the '90s) that women can be as effective as men in their careers. She was born in the United States of Africa, as mentioned in the animated "Counter-Clock Incident." She is Bantu and speaks Swahili fluently (which has become the main language in the United States of Africa). Uhura means "freedom" in Swahili. She is a talented singer, musician, and dancer, performs often in the rec room to entertain others, and has played duets with Spock. She also knows how to play the Vulcan lyre. Uhura loves animals, as seen in "The Trouble with Tribbles." She buys a tribble to take back to the ship, not knowing it is already pregnant (from eating too much). In *The Final Frontier*, it appears that Uhura and Scotty have, after many years, discovered a mutual affection for each other that could lead to more. Uhura and Sulu also appear to be very good friends. Uhura has one of the best scenes in *The Search for Spock* when she locks "Mr. Adventure" in the closet. Another priceless moment in *Trek* is when she and Chekov are looking for nuclear "wessels" in San Francisco in *The Voyage Home*. She also performs an erotic dance in *The Final Frontier* to distract some men away from their camp and horses. Uhura has no trouble melding both her feminine, softer side with the strict regimen of a Starfleet career. She can be tough while retaining her grace, beauty, and charm.

Uletta — name of Isak's fiancée, who was shot down in the street, where she lay for five hours before dying, in Classic episode "Patterns of Force."

Ullians — telepathic race of people, three of whom board the *Enterprise* to go to Kaldra IV in *TNG* episode "Violations." They all have white hair and indentions at their temples.

"Ultimate Computer, The" — written by D. C. Fontana and Lawrence N. Wolfe, directed by John Meredyth Lucas, this second-season Classic *Trek* episode aired 3/8/68. The *Enterprise* is equipped with a new computer that can not only run the ship on a skeleton crew, but can replace the captain by making all necessary decisions. Guest stars: William Marshall, Barry Russo, and Sean Morgan. Of note: The M–5 computer voice is performed by James Doohan.

ultrasonics — sound weapon used by Dr. Sevrin to try to kill the *Enterprise* crew in Classic episode "The Way to Eden."

ultretie pae — an explosive which lines the Antedians, robes in *TNG* episode "Manhunt."

ultritium — an explosive substance. Traces of it are found in the wreck of a Romulan vessel in *TNG* episode "The Enemy."

undari — means "coward" in the Nausicaan language from *TNG* episode "Tapestry."

"Unification, Parts I and II" — fifth-season *TNG* episode written by Rick Berman, Michael Piller, and Jeri Taylor, directed by Les Landau (part I) and Cliff Bole (part II). The Federation suspects that Ambassador Spock, who has been working closely with the Romulans, has defected. Picard is sent to find out what is going on, meets with a dying Sarek in the process, then heads into Romulan space with Data. In part II, we learn Sarek has died from Bendii Syndrome while Picard and Data meet with Spock, who is a member of the Romulan underground on Romulus. Sela gets involved to undermine it all. Guest stars: Leonard Nimoy, Denise Crosby, Malachi Throne, Norman Large, Stephen Root, William Batiani, Susan Fallender, Vidal Peterson, Daniel Roebuck, and Harriet Leider. Of note: After Data neck pinches Sela, you can see a camera man chewing gum in the glass pyramid on the table.

Uniform Code of Justice — Picard cites this in *TNG* episode "The Drumhead." Chapter Four, Article 12 gives him the right to make a statement before being questioned by Admiral Satie.

uniforms — in Classic *Trek*, the uniforms consist of black pants, boots, and tunics in gold, red, and blue. Gold is for command personnel, blue for science, red for security and engineering. (At times Kirk has been known to wear a variation of the gold shirt, which is green. He has two styles of green command shirts.) The women have an option of wearing pants or dresses in "Where No Man Has Gone Before;" however, they wear short dresses throughout the rest of the series. Dress uniforms involve simply a change of tunic to one made of a shiny satin material. All uniforms have the ship's insignia sewn above the left breast. Gold braid on the sleeve denotes rank, depending on how many rows or broken rows there are. One row indicates Lieutenant; one and half rows indicate Lt. Commander; two rows denote the rank of Commander; two and a half rows the rank of Captain; three rows designate a Commodore; and four rows stand for Admiral.

Unit XY 75847 — a unit of ships exploring the Organian system for Klingon ships, mentioned in Classic episode "Errand of Mercy."

United Earth Space Probe Agency — term used in Classic episode "Tomorrow Is Yesterday." Kirk tells Christopher the *Enterprise* is part of this organization in the future.

United Federation of Planets — also known as UFP, it is a large organization to which many alien worlds in the galaxy belong. Starfleet is under the jurisdiction of the Federation. The UFP symbol is a circle with star systems within it, and on the outside of the circle are the silhouetted partial profiles of a human male and female. There is a constitution called "The Articles of the Federation." Its ultimate goal is peace in the galaxy. (All of the "Articles" are published in *The Starfleet Technical Manual* by Franz Joseph.) The main currency in the Federation is the credit. The Federation came into being in 2161. The capital of the Federation is San Francisco on Earth, which is also the home of Starfleet Command and Starfleet Academy.

United Nations — mentioned as having been dissolved in 2079 in *TNG* episode "Encounter at Farpoint."

United States of Africa — Uhura's birthplace, as mentioned in animated episode "The Counter Clock Incident." Swahili is the main language.

universal gravitational constant — Q refers to altering this as a way of solving the problem of Bre'el's moon in *TNG* episode "Déjà Q," but Geordi and Data don't understand him.

universal translator — this device is seen in Classic episode "Metamorphosis." Spock uses a hand-held version to talk to the Companion, the cloud entity who has befriended Cochrane. It can translate unknown alien languages into Federation Standard. All ships' computers are equipped with this device. By the time of *TNG* and *DS9*, it appears to be a device that works in conjunction with each person's brain or thought waves.

"Unnatural Selection" — second-season *TNG* episode written by John Mason and Mike Gray, directed by Paul Lynch. A genetic experiment goes awry and the entire crew of the *Lantree* dies from accelerated aging. Pulaski is affected when she tries to help the afflicted children on a station. Guest stars: Patricia Smith, J. Patrick McNamara, Scott Trost, George Baxter, and Colm Meaney.

"Up the Long Ladder" — second-season *TNG* episode written by Melinda M. Snodgrass and directed by Winrich Kolbe. The *Enterprise* encounters a dying race of clones when they rescue a colony in the Ficus Sector from solar flares. Guest stars: Rosalyn Landor, Barrie Ingham, Jon de Vries, and Colm Meaney. Of note: While Picard is looking at a list of ships, one appears on the list by the name of *Buckaroo Banzai,* captained by John Whorfin and built by Yoyodyne Propulsions.

Ursulian neopoppy — mentioned in Classic episode "A Private Little War" as a plant with antihallucination pollen.

Utopia Planetia — shipyards on Mars where the *Enterprise* was built in orbit. This is mentioned in *TNG* episode "Booby Trap."

uttaberries — Deanna, Lwaxana, and Riker are kidnapped when Homn leaves them while he picks these berries in *TNG* episode "Ménage à Troi."

Ux Mal — Ux Mal prisoners on the moon of Mab Bu IV take over Troi, Data, and O'Brien in *TNG* episode "Power Play." They are noncorporeal beings.

Uxbridge, Kevin — a Douwd, an immortal being, who disguises himself as the human Kevin Uxbridge. His wife is Rishon, a human woman to whom he has been married for 53 years. In *TNG* episode "The Survivor's" Kevin uses his mental powers to destroy all Husnocks everywhere because some of them invaded and killed all the people in the colony in which he lived, an action that killed billions of people. He is played by John Anderson.

Uxbridge, Rishon — Kevin's human wife of 53 years. She is 82, a botanist, a composer, and she has lived with Kevin on Rana IV in the colony for the past five years. She was killed when the Husnocks attacked the colony. She is played by Anne Haney.

Vaal — a computerlike "god" that rules the people of Gamma Trianguli VI in Classic episode "The Apple." The Vaal temple looks like a giant cave formed like the mouth of an animal, with red eyes on the side of the cave. The mouth has fangs.

Vagh, Governor — leader of the Klingon colony Kreos in *TNG* episode "The Mind's Eye." LaForge, who is brainwashed, almost kills him. He is played by Edward Wiley.

Vagra II — located in the Zed Lapis sector, this is the world on which Armus lived. He killed Tasha Yar in *TNG* episode "Skin of Evil."

Valenza, Tasia — played T'shanik in *TNG* episode "Coming Of Age."

Valeris, Lieutenant — Vulcan protégée of Spock's seen in *The Undiscovered Country.* She is a traitor who is in league with Chang to keep the Klingons from making peace with the Federation. She is mind-raped by Spock because she will not give much-needed information to save the Federation president's life. She is played by Kim Cattrall.

Valiant, USS — this ship's recorder was retrieved by the *Enterprise* in Classic episode "Where No Man Has Gone Before." It had encountered the galactic energy barrier 200 years before and one of the crew became so dangerous with his accelerated psi powers that the captain destroyed the ship to keep the galaxy safe. Another ship named the *Valiant* was the first to contact the planet

Eminiar in "A Taste Of Armageddon" fifty years before the *Enterprise* came along. That *Valiant* was never heard from again.

Valkris — Klingon agent used by Kruge in *The Search for Spock* to get information on the Genesis device. Kruge kills her when he gets the information from her. She is played by Cathie Sherriff.

Vallis, Elizabeth — Wilson Granger's chief aide and chief of staff on the *Mariposa* in *TNG* episode "Up the Long Ladder."

Vallone, John — art director on *Star Trek: The Motion Picture*. He also worked on the movies *Southern Comfort*, *48 Hours*, and *Brainstorm*.

Valo System — Ensign Ro introduces Picard to the rebel leader Orta on the third moon of this system in *TNG* episode "Ensign Ro."

Valt Minor — in *TNG* episode "The Perfect Mate," this planet has long been in a conflict with Krios.

vampire cloud — in Classic episode "Obsession," this is what the cloud entity that feeds off red blood cells is called. Its home is the planet Tycho IV. It can travel through space using gravitational fields. Kirk met up with this creature once when he was a lieutenant on the *Farragut*, and it killed his captain, Garrovick. He meets it again on Argus X.

Van Der Veer, Frank — creator of the special optical effect in the Classic *Trek* episode "The Immunity Syndrome."

Van Gelder, Simon, Dr. — assistant director to Dr. Tristan Adams of the Tantalus Penal Colony in Classic episode "Dagger of the Mind." He has been subjected to a device called the neural neutralizer, which has drained his will and his brain of knowledge because Dr. Adams doesn't want him telling people he is using this device at the colony. Spock uses the Vulcan mind meld on him to get information the man cannot communicate by speech. This is the first time the mind meld is seen in Trek. Van Gelder was played by Morgan Woodward.

Van Hise, Della — author of Classic *Trek* novel *Killing Time*. This novel was pulled off the shelf in its first edition for reediting, since the unedited manuscript inadvertently went to the typesetter. The changes in the final edition were minor, but the mistakes make the first edition a collector's item.

Van Meyter, Lieutenant — in *TNG* episode "In Theory," she is an *Enterprise* officer who is killed when she falls into a partially dematerialized deck up to her waist.

Van Zandt, Billy — played the alien ensign in *Star Trek: The Motion Picture*. He also appeared in the 1981 film *Taps*.

Vanderberg, Chief Engineer — the administrative head of the mining colony on Janus VI in Classic episode "The Devil in the Dark." He learns to work with the Horta and its babies by the end of the episode. He is played by Ken Lynch.

Vandor IV — one planetoid in a binary star system which has a B-class giant star and a pulsar. Dr. Paul Manheim experiments with time here in *TNG* episode "We'll Always Have Paris."

Vanessa — young woman helped out by Texas and Data in *TNG* episode "The Royale." She is played by Jill Jacobsen.

Vanna — Troglyte woman who has been educated to serve Plasus in Stratos, though she is still considered to belong to a lesser class in Classic episode "The Cloud Minders." Vanna heads an underground movement called the Disruptors (like terrorists). It is actually the zienite gas that makes her fellow Troglytes less intelligent, as Vanna realizes when she is removed from the influences of the gas to live on Stratos. Exposure to the gas makes a person sluggish and slow, but it is not a permanent condition if they are removed from exposure. Vanna is played by Charlene Polite.

Vantakar — prisoner who comes to *DS9* with a guard in *DS9* episode "The Passenger." He is a scientist who kills to prolong his own life and is very dangerous, but Bashir enters his cell anyway. Vantakar appears to be dead, but he has really transferred his consciousness into Bashir.

Vardeman, Robert E. — author of Classic *Trek* novels *The Klingon Gambit* and *Mutiny on the Enterprise*.

Vargas, John — played Jedda in *The Wrath of Khan*. His TV credits include a regular role on *At Ease*, and he has appeared in the films *Only When I Laugh*, *Emergency Room*, and *My Tutor*.

Varley, Donald, Captain — commander of the USS *Yamato* in *TNG* episode "Contagion." He is killed when the *Yamato* self-destructs. He is played by Thalmus Rasulala.

Varon T Disruptor — Kivas Fajo owns four of these banned weapons in *TNG* episode "The Most Toys." He kills his aide, Varria, with one. It disrupts the body from inside out and is an extremely painful way to die.

Varria — Zibalian who is Kivas Fajo's aide in *TNG* episode "The Most Toys." Fajo kills her. She is played by Jane Daly.

Vash — a woman Picard meets in *TNG* episode "Captain's Holiday." She is passionate about archeology, and she and Picard immediately discover a mutual rapport which leads to an affair. She appears in future episodes, and ends up in "Qpid" traveling into the Gamma Quadrant with Q, who is very fond of her. She shows up in *DS9* in "Q Less." Vash is played by Jennifer Hetrick.

Vassey, Liz — played Kristin in *TNG* episode "Conundrum."

Vaughn, Ned — appeared in *TNG* episode "Tapestry."

Vaughn, Reese — played Latimer in Classic *Trek* episode "The Galileo Seven." TV credits include *Dan August*.

Vault of Tomorrow — what the Horta calls her nest of eggs in Classic episode "The Devil in the Dark." She also calls the nest The Chamber of the Ages.

Vaytan — the name of the star where Dr. Reyga's experiment is tested successfully in *TNG* episode "Suspicions."

Vedala — a catlike creature and a member of the oldest spacefaring race seen in animated episode "Jihad." They live on an asteroid within a globe or dome.

Vega IX — destination of the *Enteprise* in Classic episode "The Menagerie" before it is called to Talos IV.

Vega IX Probe — probe of this sort is sent to the Beta Stromgren system in *TNG* episode "Tin Man."

Vega Omicron Sector — the *Ares* is patrolling this sector, as stated in *TNG* episode "The Icarus Factor." Intelligent life has been reported here.

Vegan choriomeningitis — an inflammation of the brain tissues that causes fever. Kirk had this a long time ago, and is still a carrier of the microorganisms used by the Gideons to infect Odona in Classic episode "Mark of Gideon."

Vejar, Michael — director of *TNG* episode "Coming Of Age."

Vejur — what the cloud being in *The Motion Picture* calls itself. It is actually a variation of the word "Voyager." Vejur is actually part of the Voyager VI, which was launched by NASA in the 20th century. The machine passed into an alternate machine universe, was changed, and then sent back into the galaxy of its origin to seek out all knowledge and its creator. Decker and Ilia merge with

Vejur at the end of the film in order to help it rise to a higher level of being when it destroys itself.

Vekma — Klingon officer who taunts Riker on the *Pagh* in *TNG* episode "A Matter of Honor." She is played by Laura Drake.

Velara III — planet being terraformed in *TNG* episode "Home Soil." It is home to the microbrain, a life-form that is intelligent but was undiscovered until it killed a person on the terraforming project to make itself known.

Velasco, Vladimir — played Tan Tsu in *TNG* episode "Legacy."

Veltan sex idol — in *TNG* episode "The Most Toys," Fajo says he has four of these rare items with pearls intact.

vendor — he gave Picard a free newspaper in *TNG* episode "The Big Goodbye." He is played by Dick Miller.

Vendikar — the planet that has been at war for 500 years with Eminiar, in Classic episode "A Taste of Armageddon." They fight their war by computer since it is a cleaner and cheaper method.

Vendorian — they are a race who can rearrange their molecular structures into anything with the same mass as themselves. Carter Winston's form is actually a Vendorian in animated episode "The Survivor."

vendurite — Ferengi renegades mine this mineral found on Ligos VII in *TNG* episode "Rascals."

"Vengeance Factor, The" — third-season *TNG* episode written by Sam Rolfe and directed by Timothy Bond. The Acamarians and the Gatherers have had a long-standing dispute, and the *Enterprise* steps in to assist in keeping the ceasefire. There are people, however, who don't want to see peace. Guest stars: Lisa Wilcox, Joey Aresco, Nancy Parsons, Stephen Lee, Marc Lawrence, and Elkanah J. Burns.

Ventanin — in *TNG* episode "The Perfect Mate," Kamala recognizes one of Picard's artifacts as being from this world.

Ventax II — in *TNG* episode "Devil's Due," this world struck a bargain with a being named Ardra, who is equivalent to the devil, in exchange for a thousand years of peace and prosperity. The deadline, however, is up and Ardra returns.

Venton, Harley — played Collins in *TNG* episode "Ensign Ro."

Venturi Chamber — power is rerouted through this channel to the main engines on the *Mondor*, in *TNG* episode "Samaritan Snare."

Venus drug — Harry Mudd gives this to the three women he is traveling with in Classic episode "Mudd's Women." It makes women more curvaceous and gives them more allure, or "more of what they already have." Given to men, it makes them more masculine, stronger, and more handsome. It is a highly illegal substance.

Verdanis — the planet to which the *Enterprise* relocates the Terratins in animated episode "The Terratin Incident."

verul — Romulan word for an uncultured or rude person used by Riker in *TNG* episode "The Defector."

Verustin infection — in *TNG* episode "The Bonding," it is mentioned that Jeremy Aster's father died of this five years before.

Veto, Ron — played an Eminiar technician in Classic *Trek* episode "A Taste of Armageddon," and a security guard in "The Alternative Factor."

Vians — humanoid race who are from one of the worlds of Minara. They are testing Gem's empathic people to see if they are worth saving. The Minara sun is going nova and the Vians have the power to save only one race from one planet in the fully inhabited system. They tortured the science team which preceded the *Enterprise*, killing them, and then torture Kirk, Spock, and McCoy in Classic episode "The Empath."

Vickery, John — played Hagan in *TNG* episode "Night Terrors."

Vico, USS — *Grissom*-class research ship lost while investigating the Black Cluster in *TNG* episode "Hero Worship." Timothy is the only survivor.

Victor, Teresa E. — played an usher in *The Voyage Home*. She is also the bridge voice in *The Wrath of Khan* and the *Enterprise* computer voice in *The Search for Spock*. She was the assistant to Leonard Nimoy for over 20 years, from the early days of *Trek* in the 1960s through the fourth movie. She currently lives in Los Angeles with her husband.

Victory, USS — ship of the *Constellation* class which the *Enterprise* is to meet in *TNG* episode "Elementary, Dear Data."

Vignon, Jean-Paul — played Edouard in *TNG* episode "We'll Always Have Paris."

Vigo — *Stargazer* weapons officer in *TNG* episode "The Battle."

Vilmoran System — a system with seven worlds. It does not belong to the Federation, but it is thought that this world holds the final clue to Professor Galen's micropaleontology mystery in *TNG* episode "The Chase."

Vina — the only survivor of a crash on Talos IV, she was rescued by the Talosians and put back together wrong so that she looks horribly deformed. She lives in a fantasy world of illusion they have created for her, in which she remains forever young and beautiful in Classic episode "The Menagerie." Spock ends up bringing the injured Captain Pike back to stay with her. She is played by Susan Oliver.

Vinci, Frank — played a stunt double in Classic *Trek*

episode "The Galileo Seven," an Eminiar technician in "A Taste of Armageddon," and a Vulcan banner carrier in "Amok Time." He was also the stunt double for Spock in "Catspaw."

"Violations" — fifth-season *TNG* episode written by Shari Goodhartz, T. Michael Gray, Pamela Gray, and Jeri Taylor, directed by Robert Wiemer. The *Enterprise* escorts the highly telepathic Ullians to Kaldra IV, but in the process Troi, Riker, and Beverly experience a form of mind rape, a crime the Ullians abhor. Picard must discover who the culprit is, at the risk of offending these people. Guest stars: Ben Lemon, Eve Brenner, David Sage, Rosalind Chao, Doug Wert, Rick Fitts, and Craig Benton.

Virgo, Peter, Jr. — played Lumo in Classic *Trek* episode "The Paradise Syndrome."

Visitor, Nana — stars as Major Kira Nerys on *DS9*. Raised in New York, she has studied dance since the age of seven. Her stage career began after high school, when she appeared in many Broadway productions before landing regular roles on the soap operas *One Life to Live* and *Ryan's Hope*. She was also in the 1977 movie *The Sentinel* and has guest starred on such TV shows as *Jake and the Fatman*, *Baby Talk*, *Murder, She Wrote*, *L.A. Law*, *Empty Nest*, *In the Heat of the Night*, *Matlock*, and *Thirtysomething*. She also had a regular role on the TV series *Working Girl*. Nana is a *Star Trek* fan who watched the show regularly in reruns and is thrilled to now have a place in its chronicles.

V.I.S.O.R. — Geordi wears one of these to "see." It looks like a silver headband worn about the eyes and fits into red, blinking nodes at Geordi's temples. It allows him to access visual information better than a human, but he still cannot "see" as a human. The word is an acronym for Visual Instrument and Sensory Organ Replacement and it covers the spectrum from 1 hertz to 1 terahertz, which covers radio, microwave, and infrared frequencies. It is said to be constantly painful for the wearer.

visor — used by Spock when he deals with the Medusan Ambassador Kollos in Classic episode "Is There in Truth No Beauty?" The visor is silver with a transparent red stripe around it that allows the wearer to see.

visual acuity transmitter — attached to Geordi's Visor in *TNG* episode "Heart of Glory." It allows the bridge crew to see objects as Geordi sees them. They are able to see the *Batris* and Data's aura.

vitalizer beam — this is a medical "field" of energy used to keep the patient from using more blood in Classic episode "A Private Little War."

Vogt, Peter — actor in *DS9* episode "A Man Alone." He also played the Romulan commander in *TNG* episode "Tin Man."

Vollaerts, Rik — scriptwriter of Classic *Trek* episode "For the World Is Hollow and I Have Touched the Sky." His TV writing credits include *Voyage to the Bottom of the Sea*.

Volnoth — a member of the Lornack species who is killed when Yuta transmits a microvirus to him. He is one of the last Lornacks alive in *TNG* episode "The Vengeance Factor." He is played by Marc Lawrence.

Voltera Nebula — the *Enterprise* is to study this "stellar nursery" in *TNG* episode "The Chase."

Von Puttkamer, Jesco — special NASA advisor on *Star Trek: The Motion Picture*. He also wrote an introduction to one of the stories appearing in the book *The New Voyages*.

Vorgons — a race from the future, the 27th century, who come to Risa to find the *Tox Uthat* in *TNG* episode "Captain's Holiday." They are actually criminals who the inventor of the device feared would get hold of it. He hid it in the past hoping they would never find it.

Vornholt, John — author of *TNG* novels *Masks*, *Contamination*, *War Drums*, and Classic *Trek* novel *Sanctuary*.

Vortex — in *DS9* episode "Vortex," this is an area where Crodon tells Odo he found a colony of changelings.

"Vortex" — first-season *DS9* episode written by Sam Rolfe and directed by Winrich Kolbe. Miradorns, who are twin beings, are chasing a man visiting *DS9* named Crodon. He attacks them and kills one, leaving his twin alone, but pleads self defense. Odo arrests him but while en route to Miradorn to deliver the criminal, he learns the truth about the man's life and helps him rescue his daughter and escape. He also comes a step closer to learning about his own heritage as Crodon gives him a device that, though inanimate, has the same metamorph properties as Odo himself. Guest stars: Cliff DeYoung, Randy Oglesby, Max Grodenchik, Kathleen Garrett, Leslie Engelberg, and Gordon Clapp.

Vortis — a Klingon ship in *TNG* episode "The Defector."

V'Sal — played by Shelly Desai in *TNG* episode "Data's Day."

Vulcan — class M planet that is a member of the Federation. It has a sister planet, T'Khut, but no moon. It is a desert world with thin air, red skies, and a very bright sun. Spock grew up on this world in the city of ShiKahr. Vulcan is seen in Classic episode "Amok Time" and in *The Motion Picture, The Search for Spock,* and *The Voyage Home.* Picard visits Vulcan briefly in *TNG* episode "Unification."

Vulcan — a native of the planet Vulcan. They revere logic and are very unemotional because they believe logic is the answer to the philosophy of life. They have green, copper-based blood and pointed ears, and they resemble Romulans. They have low blood pressure, a high pulse and respiration, and a body temperature higher than humans. Their heart is where the human liver is located. They can heal themselves mentally when they enter a Vulcan healing trance. Vulcans are vegetarians and have an inner eyelid to protect them from the harsh glare of the Vulcan sun. Every seven years, the Vulcan male goes into

Pon farr, during which he must mate or die. There is no indication that that is the only time a Vulcan mates, however. They are touch telepaths, but can sometimes sense thoughts over a distance if the sender is strong. In Classic episode "Where No Man Has Gone Before," the obsolete term *Vulcanian* is used for *Vulcan*. 5000 years ago, Vulcans were a barbaric race with warrior clans who constantly fought until Surak, the father of logic, came along and introduced order. The Vulcans have a quasi-religious ritual called *Kolinahr* which is used by Vulcans to purge all emotion from their minds. Very few people who attempt it succeed. Spock tries and fails.

Vulcan Academy of Sciences — Sarek wanted Spock to attend school here and eventually teach, but Spock chose a career in Starfleet, a decision which created a rift between father and son for 18 years, as mentioned in Classic episode "Journey to Babel." The director of the Vulcan Science Academy visits the *Enterprise* in *TNG* episode "Suspicions." Her name is T'Pan and she is married to a human.

Vulcan death grip — Spock uses this on Kirk to kill him in Classic episode "The *Enterprise* Incident." There is really no such thing, Kirk simply fakes unconsciousness, but the Romulans buy it. Vulcans do have a form of a death grip, however, called *Tal shaya*. It snaps the neck very quickly. Gav the Tellarite in "Journey to Babel" is killed this way.

Vulcan kiss — also a Vulcan embrace. Two people extend their first two fingers, and place them against each other. Romulans kiss this way, as seen in "The *Enterprise* Incident," as do Sarek and Amanda in Classic episode "Journey to Babel."

Vulcan mind fusion — see entry for Vulcan mind meld.

Vulcan mind meld — also called the Vulcan mind fusion (ultimate joining) or mind touch (a light joining), or mind link, it involves joining two minds together mentally with a telepathic touch. Spock proves he can do this over short distances in Classic episode "By Any Other Name" when he influences a Kelvan to believe they have escaped their prison. He uses the meld many times throughout the series. It is first introduced when he uses it on Dr. Van Gelder to open his mind in "Dagger of the Mind." The mind "fusion" is used by Spock on Kirk in "The Paradise Syndrome" to bring Kirk's memories back. He also uses a mind touch on Kirk to help him forget his grief over Reena in "Requiem for Methuselah." He melds several more times with Kirk, once while he is in the body of Janice Lester in "Turnabout Intruder" and once in "Spectre of the Gun." (In that episode he also melds with Scotty and McCoy.) Spock melds with the Horta in "Devil in the Dark" and with Nomad in "The Changeling." His empathic powers also allow him to feel the deaths of 400 Vulcans when the *Intrepid* is destroyed in "The Immunity Syndrome." Spock also melds with Vejur in *The Motion Picture*, which nearly kills him. Spock uses the mind touch on McCoy in "Mirror, Mirror" and *The Wrath of Khan* (to pass his *katra* on to him.) He also uses the mind touch on the humpback whale Gracie in *The Voyage Home*, learning she is pregnant. Saavik uses the mind touch on a teenage Spock in *The Search for Spock* to calm him when he goes into his first *Pon farr*. Sarek uses a mind touch on Kirk in *The Search for Spock* to see if he carries Spock's *katra*. Sarek also uses it on Picard to help Sarek maintain control of his emotions in *TNG* episode "Sarek." The mind touch is an ultimately personal thing, and Vulcans rarely use it unless it is an emergency. It can be forced on an individual, as Spock does to Valeris in *The Undiscovered Country*, but it is considered akin to rape and hurts the attacker as much as the victim. Sybok uses it to control his subjects by forcing them face their fears and griefs in *The Final Frontier*. He also uses the mind touch on Spock to give him his *katra* toward the end of that movie.

Vulcan mind touch — see entry for Vulcan mind meld.

Vulcan neck pinch — invented by William Shatner and Leonard Nimoy in Classic episode "The Enemy Within," it involves placing the fingers on the side of the neck, thumb on one side, fingers on the other, and pressing. It knocks a person out. Spock uses it often and has tried to teach it to Kirk, but Kirk still can't do it. It is also called the Vulcan nerve pinch. Spock teaches Data this technique in *TNG* episode "Unification," and Data performs it flawlessly.

Vulcan salute — the right hand is raised with the fingers spread only between ring finger and middle finger. Thumb is extended outward. It is accompanied with the words "Live long and prosper" or "Peace and long life."

Vulcana Regar — Vulcan colony world where T'shalik is from, in *TNG* episode "Coming of Age."

Waddi — beings who come aboard *Deep Space 9* in *DS9* episode "Move Along Home." They introduce Quark to a new game, in which the players are actually the crew of *DS9*. It puts them in seemingly real danger, forcing them to play out extremely dangerous scenarios without realizing it is only a game.

Wagner, Lou — appeared in *DS9* episode "The Nagus."

Wagner, Michael — scriptwriter of *TNG* episodes "Evolution," "The Survivors," and "Booby Trap."

Wagnor — Angosian pilot in *TNG* episode "The Hunted." He is played by Andrew Bickell.

Walberg, Gary — played Commander Hansen in Classic *Trek* episode "Balance of Terror." He had a regular role on *The Odd Couple* and *Quincy*. Film credits include *The Challenge*, *Man on the Outside*, and *Rage*.

Walker, Robert, Jr. — played Charlie Evans in Classic *Trek* episode "Charlie X." Born April 15, 1940, in New York, his film credits include *Ensign Pulver*, *Easy Rider*, and *The Passover Plot*. His parents are Robert Walker and Jennifer Jones.

Walking Bear, Dawson, Ensign — an *Enterprise* helmsman in animated episode "How Sharper Than a Serpent's Tooth." He is a Comanche.

Wallace, Art — scriptwriter of Classic *Trek* episodes

"Obsession" and "Assignment: Earth." His other writing credits include *Dark Shadows*, *Planet of the Apes*, and the films *Dr. Cook's Garden*, *She Waits*, and *Charlie and the Great Balloon Race*.

Wallace, Basil — played a Klingon guard in *TNG* episode "Reunion."

Wallace, George D. — played an admiral in *TNG* episode "Man of the People."

Wallace, Janet, Dr. — an endocrinologist who is aboard the *Enterprise* when the radiation that makes people rapidly age hits Kirk, Spock, McCoy, and others of the landing party on Gamma Hydra IV, in Classic episode "The Deadly Years." She is an old girlfriend of Kirk's who married Dr. Theodore Wallace, who has died prior to the episode. She was played by Sarah Marshall.

Wallace, William A. — played the adult Wesley in *TNG* episode "Hide and Q."

Waller, Phillip N. — played Harry in *TNG* episode "When the Bough Breaks."

Wallerstein, Herb — director of Classic *Trek* episodes "Whom Gods Destroy," "The Tholian Web," "That Which Survives," and "Turnabout Intruder." His other credits include assistant director of *Father Knows Best* and the films *The Tingler* and *Snowbeast*, and unit production manager of *Iron Horse*. His other directing credits include *Petrocelli*.

Walsh, Gwynyth — actress in *DS9* episode "Past Prologue." She also played Batur in *TNG* episode "Redemption, Parts I and II."

Walsh, Leo Francis — Harry Mudd's alias in Classic episode "Mudd's Women." Walsh was once a spaceship captain, now deceased, and Harry goes about impersonating him. Harry is played by Roger C. Carmel.

Walston, Ray — played Boothby in *TNG* episode "The First Duty." He is best known for his role as Uncle Martin in the series *My Favorite Martian*.

Walter, Tracy — played Kayron in *TNG* episode "The Last Outpost."

Warburton, John — played the centurion in Classic *Trek* episode "Balance of Terror." Born in Ireland in 1903, he died on October 27, 1981. His credits include the films *A Study in Scarlet*, *Tarzan and the Huntress*, and *City Beneath the Sea*, as well as many TV appearances.

Ware, Herta — played Picard's mother in *TNG* episode "Where No One Has Gone Before."

Warhit, Doug — played Kazago in *TNG* episode "The Battle."

Warner, David — played St. John Talbot in *The Final Frontier* and Chancellor Gorkon in *The Undiscovered Country*. He is a British-born actor whose many credits include *The French Lieutenant's Woman*, *Holocaust*, *Time Bandits*, and *The Omen*. He also appeared in *TNG* episode "Chain of Command."

Warner, Julie — played Christy Henshaw in *TNG* episodes "Booby Trap" and "Transfigurations."

warp core — vital mechanism of the warp drive in which matter and antimatter are combined. A warp core breach can destroy an entire ship. According to *TNG* episode "Booby Trap," the dilithium crystal chamber on the *Enterprise* was designed at Outpost Seran T One.

warp drive — drive on a starship that bends space so ships can travel faster than the speed of light. Every starship is equipped with warp drive. The warp engines run on dilithium crystals and the propulsion is a matter/antimatter mix of delicate proportions. The ships theoretically cannot exceed warp ten, but under special circumstances some have. Usually a ship traveling faster than warp 10 will break up.

Warren, Mary, Dr. — scientist injured in the Mintaka station explosion in *TNG* episode "Who Watches the Watchers." She later dies. She was played by Lois Hall.

Warrior/Adonis — member of Riva's chorus who is also the romantic representing passion and lust. He talks alone with Troi. He is killed by a Solari gunman in *TNG* episode "Loud As a Whisper." He is played by Leo Damian.

Washburn — an *Enterprise* engineer who beams aboard the *Constellation* with the landing party in Classic episode "The Doomsday Machine." He is played by Richard Compton.

Washburn, Beverly — played Lt. Arlene Galway in Classic *Trek* episode "The Deadly Years." TV credits include regular roles in *Professional Father* and *The New Loretta Young Show*, as well as a guest star role in *Adventures of Superman*.

Washington, Kenneth — played John B. Watkins in Classic *Trek* episode "That Which Survives." TV credits include a regular role in *Hogan's Heroes*. He was also in the TV movies *Climb an Angry Mountain*, *Cry Rape!*, and *Money on the Side*.

Wasson, Suzanne — played Lethe in Classic *Trek* episode "Dagger of the Mind."

Watkins, James Louis — played Hagon in *TNG* episode "Code of Honor."

Watkins, John B. — *Enterprise* engineer who is killed on the ship by Losira when she appears out of thin air and starts asking him questions about the ship in Classic episode "That Which Survives." He was played by Kenneth Washington.

Watson, Bruce — played Crewman Green in Classic *Trek* episode "The Man Trap." His TV movies include *Dragnet*, *Judge Horton and the Scottsboro Boys*, and *Billy: Portrait of a Street Kid*.

Watson, Technician — *Enterprise* engineer who discovers sabotage and tries to prevent Kryton from transmitting a message to the Klingon ship in Classic episode "Elaan of Troyius." Kryton kills him. He was played by Victor Brandt.

"Way to Eden, The" — written by Arthur Heinemann and Michael Richards, directed by David Alexander, this third-season Classic *Trek* episode aired 2/21/69. A group of young rebel adults comes aboard the *Enterprise* when their shuttle, the *Aurora*, explodes. They are led by an insane alien named Dr. Sevrin and are looking for the mythical planet Eden. When Spock finds a planet that might fit the description, they steal a shuttle to go there. As they leave, Sevrin sets up a trap to murder the entire crew of the ship. Guest stars: Skip Homeier, Mary-Linda Rapelye, Victor Brandt, Charles Napler, Deborah Downey, Phyllis Douglas, and Elizabeth Rogers. Of note: Spock plays a musical duet with a young woman playing an instrument that looks like a bicycle wheel.

"We'll Always Have Paris" — first-season *TNG* episode written by Deborah Dean David and Hannah Louise Shearer, directed by Robert Becker. A scientist named Dr. Manheim, who married an old girlfriend of Picard's, set the universe into a time loop with one of his experiments, and Picard and Janice Manheim must correct the problem. Guest stars: Michelle Phillips, Rod Loomis, Isabelle Lorca, Dan Kern, Jean Paul Vignon, Kelly Ashmore, and Lance Spellerberg.

weather modification net — device that regularizes Earth's weather patterns, as mentioned in *TNG* episode "True Q." Since Amanda's parents were killed in a freak tornado, Picard suspects the Q Continuum actually had something to do with their deaths.

Webb, Richard — played Lt. Commander Benjamin Finney in Classic *Trek* episode "Court-Martial." TV credits include *Voyage to the Bottom of the Sea* and *The Guns of Will*

Sonnett. He also appeared in the 1959 film *On the Beach.* He played Captain Midnight in the series of the same name.

Webb, Technician — one of the Air Force personnel who sights the *Enterprise* over the Omaha Air Base in Classic episode "Tomorrow Is Yesterday." He is played by Richard Merrifield.

Webber, Barbara — played the young woman in Classic *Trek* episode "The Return of the Archons."

Weber, Paul — played one of the Vulcan masters in *Star Trek: The Motion Picture.*

Webster, Joan — played a nurse in Classic *Trek* episode "Space Seed."

weeper — plant Sulu keeps in the botany room in Classic episode "The Man Trap." It must be hand fed.

Weinstein, Howard — scriptwriter of the animated episode "The Pirates of Orion." Born in 1954, this script was his first professional sale. He is the author of the *TNG* novels *Power Hungry, Exiles, Perchance to Dream,* and Classic *Trek* novels *The Covenant of the Crown* and *Deep Domain,* as well as three novels based on the series *V.*

Weiss, Erick — played a crewman in *TNG* episode "Conundrum," and Kane in "Relics."

***Wellington,* USS** — the Bynars worked on this ship before coming to work on the *Enterprise* in *TNG* episode "11001001."

Wellman, James — played Professor Starnes in Classic *Trek* episode "And the Children Shall Lead."

Werntz, Gary — appeared in *TNG* episode "Frame of Mind."

Wert, Doug — played Jack Crusher in *TNG* episodes "Family" and "Violations."

Wesley, Katie — Commodore Robert Wesley's eleven-year-old daughter mentioned in animated episode "One of Our Planets Is Missing."

Wesley, Robert, Commodore — appearing in Classic episode "The Ultimate Computer," Wesley commands the USS *Lexington*. He leads the war game attack, which becomes a real attack, against the *Enterprise* that has Dr. Daystrom's M–5 computer on board. He mentions he has a daughter named Katie in animated episode "One of Our Planets Is Missing." He and Kirk are old friends, which explains why Wesley senses that Kirk lowers his shields as a message that the computer has been put out of commission and holds his fire, thus saving the *Enterprise* and the skeleton crew aboard her. Wesley is played by Barry Russo.

Westerfield, Karen — makeup artist on *TNG* and *DS9*. She was part of the team that won an Emmy for make up on *TNG*. She now does Quark's makeup on *DS9*.

Westervliet, Admiral — Starfleet officer who forbids the *Enterprise* to plot a parallel course with the spaceship world Yonada in Classic episode "For the World Is Hollow and I Have Touched the Sky." He is played by Byron Morrow.

Westmore, Michael — makeup design supervisor on *DS9*.

Weston, Brad — played Ed Appel in Classic *Trek* episode "The Devil in the Dark."

Weyland, Phil — stand-in on *The Search for Spock*.

Whalen — *Enterprise* historian almost killed by Felix Leech in *TNG* episode "The Big Goodbye." He is played by David Selburg.

"What Are Little Girls Made Of?" — written by horror writer Robert Block and directed by James Goldstone, this first-season Classic *Trek* episode aired 10/20/66. The story involves Christine Chapel and her fiancé, Dr. Roger Korby, who has been missing for some time. On Exo III, Korby has discovered a way to transplant the human mind into android bodies, a discovery which offers virtual immortality. Guest stars: Michael Strong, Sherry Jackson, and Ted Cassidy.

Wheaton, Wil — starred as Wesley Crusher in *TNG* on the first 83 episodes, then in recurring episodes thereafter. He is most famous for his theatrical film roles, including the award-winning *Stand by Me* and *Toy Soldiers*. His first break was a Jell-O pudding commercial with Bill Cosby when he was just seven years old. He also appeared in the TV movie *A Long Way Home* and the afterschool special *The Shooting*. Other feature length films include: *The Buddy System, The Curse, Hambone and Hillie, The Last Starfighter,* and *The Secret of N.I.M.H.* (in which he was the voice of the rat Martin). He has also guest starred on the TV shows *Family Ties, St. Elsewhere,* and *Highway to Heaven*. Since starring in *TNG*, he's appeared in the movies *Young Harry Houdini, The Last Prostitute,* and *A Deadly Secret*. He left the show during its fourth season in order to pursue more theatrical film roles and to attend college. He has a younger sister named Amy who is also into acting. He likes to surf, is an avid *Star Trek* fan, and dreams of one day owning a Malibu beach house.

Wheeler, John — played Gav in Classic *Trek* episode "Journey to Babel." Film credits include *Rescue from Gilligan's Island* and *The Wild, Wild West Revisited*.

Whelpley, John — scriptwriter of *TNG* episode "Suddenly Human." He also worked on the shows *Trapper John, M.D., Kay O'Brian,* and *The Wizard,* and as producer/writer of *MacGyver*. He currently has feature-film screenplays making the rounds.

"When the Bough Breaks" — this first-season *TNG* episode was written by Hannah Louise Shearer and directed by Kim Manners. *Enterprise* children are kidnapped by beings on the planet Aldea in an attempt to repopulate their dying world. Guest stars: Dierk Torsek, Michele Marsh, Dan Mason, Philip N. Waller, Connie Danese, Jessica and Vanessa Bova, Jerry Hardin, Brenda Strong, Jandi Swanson, Paul Lambert, and Ivy Bethune.

"Where No Man Has Gone Before" — aired during first season on 9/22/66, this was the second pilot for the original *Star Trek* series, and it has a slightly unfinished look and feel compared to other first-season episodes, mainly because the uniforms are different (Spock wears a gold shirt) and the props are cruder. Written by Samuel A. Peeples and directed by James Goldstone, the story deals with extrasensory perception powers in humans and how that power, expanded, creates a monster out of Kirk's friend and first officer, Gary Mitchell. Dr. McCoy had not yet been conceived in the *Star Trek* canon during the filming of this episode. Instead, a Dr. Piper, played by Paul Fix, appears. Guest stars: Gary Lockwood, Sally Kellerman, Paul Carr, and Lloyd Haynes. Of note: In this episode, Mitchell quotes from a futuristic poem called "Nightingale Woman," Kirk and Spock play tri D chess, and the newly discovered energy barrier around the galaxy sets a standard for future *Trek* episodes.

"Where No One Has Gone Before" — this first-season *TNG* episode was written by Diane Duane and Michael Reaves. Directed by Rob Bowman, this episode introduces the character of the Traveler, who enhances the ship's engines and sends the ship hurtling into an alternate reality where thought becomes reality. Guest stars: Eric Menyuk, Stanley Kamel, Herta Ware, Biff Yeager, Charles Dayton, and Victoria Dillard.

"Where Silence Has Lease" — this second-season *TNG* episode was written by Jack B. Sowards and directed by Winrich Kolbe. The *Enterprise* is trapped in a black void by an advanced life-form who is studying them. Then the alien sentences half the crew to death, to everyone's shock and outrage. Guest stars: Earl Boen, Charles Douglass, and Colm Meaney.

whip — Ferengi energy weapon seen in *TNG* episode "The Last Outpost."

White, Callan — played Krite in *TNG* episode "The Outcast."

White, Diz — played the prostitute in *TNG* episode "Elementary, Dear Data."

White Rabbit — this creature from *Alice in Wonderland* is the first strange apparition/sighting McCoy sees on the recreational planet in Classic episode "Shore Leave." The rabbit is followed by a young girl with blond hair.

Whiting, Arch — played an engineering assistant in Classic *Trek* episode "The Alternative Factor." He played Sparks on *Voyage to the Bottom of the Sea* and has also guest starred on *Cannon* and *Barnaby Jones*.

Whitman, Parker — played a Cardassian officer in *DS9* episode "Emissary."

Whitney, Grace Lee — starred as Yeoman Janice Rand during the first half of *Star Trek*'s first season. She also reprised her role as Rand in *Star Trek: The Motion Picture* (in which she played the transporter chief), *The Search for Spock*, *The Voyage Home*, and *The Undiscovered Country* (in which she was Commander Rand under Captain Sulu on the ship *Excelsior*). Born in Detroit, Michigan, on April 1, 1930, her first role was as the mermaid in the Chicken of the Sea commercials. She appeared in the 1959 film *Some Like It Hot* and guest starred in *The Twilight Zone*, *Batman*, and *One Step Beyond*. She is a singer and has recorded some singles, a couple of which have *Star Trek* themes. She is a recovered alcoholic and gives lectures in women's prisons to inspire people who have similar problems.

Whitney, Michael — played Tyree in Classic *Trek*

episode "A Private Little War." His TV credits include *Cannon* and *Iron Horse*.

"Who Mourns for Adonais?" — written by Gilbert Ralston and Gene L. Coon, directed by Marc Daniels, this second-season Classic *Trek* episode aired 9/22/67. The *Enterprise* encounters a powerful alien being who claims to be Apollo and demands the crew beam down to his world to worship him. Guest stars: Michael Forest, Leslie Parrish, and John Winston.

"Who Watches the Watchers" — third-season *TNG* episode written by Richard Manning and Hans Beimler, directed by Richard Wiemer. Riker and Troi disguise themselves as Vulcans to infiltrate a somewhat primitive Vulcan colony in order to search for a missing Federation anthropologist. Guest stars: Kathryn Leigh Scott, Ray Wise, James Greene, Pamela Segall, John McLiam, Lois Hall, and James McIntyre.

"Whom Gods Destroy" — written by Lee Erwin and Jerry Sohl, directed by Herb Wallerstein, this third-season Classic *Trek* episode aired 1/3/69. On Elba II, a penal colony for the criminally insane, inmate Garth of Izar, a once famous starship captain, takes over and uses his morphing powers to try to trick Kirk and Spock into giving him access to the *Enterprise*. Guest stars: Steve Inhat, Yvonne Craig, Keye Luke, Richard Geary, and Tony Downey.

Widen Dairy — company name printed on the side of the horse-drawn buggy in New York in the 1920s in Classic episode "The City on the Edge of Forever."

Wiedlin, Jane — played the alien communications officer in *The Voyage Home*. She is a singer in the group The Bangles.

Wiemer, Robert — director of *TNG* episodes "Who Watches the Watchers," "Data's Day," "Violations," "Schisms," and "Lessons."

Wilber, Carey — scriptwriter of Classic *Trek* episode "Space Seed." His other writing credits include *Lost in Space, Bonanza,* and *The Wackiest Ship in the Army.*

Wilcox, Lisa — played Yuta in *TNG* "The Vengeance Factor."

Wilder, Glenn R. — stunt coordinator on *The Final Frontier.*

Wilderson, Ronald — scriptwriter of *TNG* episode "Imaginary Friend."

Wiley, Edward — played Governor Vagh in *TNG* episode "The Mind's Eye."

Wilkerson, Ronald — scriptwriter of *TNG* episodes "Lessons" and "Schisms."

Wilkins, Professor — one of the first archeologists to find and explore the Gorgon's cave before the Starnes expedition showed up on Triacus in Classic episode "And the Children Shall Lead."

Williams, R. J. — played Ian in *TNG* episode "The Child."

Williams, Ensign — member of Picard's art class in *TNG* episode "A Matter of Perspective." According to Data, his style of painting is influenced by geometric constructivism.

Williams, Michael — character in Data's Henry V holo simulation in *TNG* episode "The Defector." The cameo role is played by Patrick Stewart.

Williamson, Fred — Anka in Classic *Trek* episode "The Cloud Minders."

Willingham, Noble — played Texas in *TNG* episode "The Royale."

Willis, Mirron E. — played a Klingon guard in *TNG* episode "Reunion."

Willrich, Rudolph — played Reittan Grax in *TNG* episode "Ménage à Troi."

Wills, Ralph — scriptwriter of *TNG* episode "Justice."

Wilson, Starr and Tamara — twin actresses who played the "Maisie" series in Classic *Trek* episode "I, Mudd."

Wilson — on the USS *Enterprise* in Classic episode "Mirror, Mirror," he saves Kirk's life when Chekov tries to assassinate Kirk in the hopes he'll get on the captain's good side. Kirk punches him in the mouth for it. Wilson is played by Garth Pillsbury.

Wilson, Technician — transporter technician on duty when two Kirks beam up in Classic episode "The Enemy Within." The evil Kirk beats him up and steals his phaser. He is played by Garland Thompson.

Wincelberg, Shimon — scriptwriter of Classic *Trek* episodes "Dagger of the Mind" and "The Galileo Seven." He also writes under the pen name S. Bar David (see entry). He wrote the pilot for *Lost in Space,* as well as episodes of *Voyage to the Bottom of the Sea* and *Planet of the Apes*.

Wind Dancer — in *TNG* episode "Cost of Living," the wind dancer is the Parallax colony's sentinel, who challenges all who wish to enter. He has a clown face and is balloonlike.

Windom, William — played Commodore Matt Decker in Classic *Trek* episode "The Doomsday Machine." Born in New York on September 28, 1923, his TV credits include *The Feather and Father Gang, Iron Horse,* and *The Bionic Woman*. He starred in the series *The Farmer's Daughter, My World and Welcome to It* (for which he won an Emmy), *The Girl with Something Extra,* and *Brothers and Sisters*. He appeared in the 1962 movie *To Kill a Mockingbird* and the 1978 film *Mean Dog Blues*.

Winfield, Paul — played Captain Terrell in *The Wrath of Khan*. He also played Captain Dathon in *TNG* episode

"Darmok." Born in Los Angeles in 1940, Winfield's films include *Damnation Alley* and *The Terminator.* He has had many TV appearances, including a regular stint on *Wiseguy* during a series of episodes about a record company. He is a UCLA alumnus.

Wingreen, Jason — played Dr. Linke in Classic *Trek* episode "The Empath." TV credits include *The Man from U.N.C.L.E., Voyage to the Bottom of the Sea,* and *The Guns of Will Sonnett.* He also had regular roles in the series *The Rounders* and *All in the Family.*

"Wink of an Eye" — written by Arthur Heinemann and Lee Cronin, directed by Jud Taylor, this third-season Classic *Trek* episode aired 11/29/68. Beings who exist in a different time frame (in the wink of an eye) use a potion to accelerate Kirk and another crewman to their speed of existence, where Kirk finds out they plan to take over his ship and put his crew into deep freeze storage. Guest stars: Kathie Brown, Geoffrey Binney, Eric Holland, and Jason Evers.

Winslow, Pamela — played an ensign in *TNG* episodes "Clues" and "In Theory."

Winston, John — played Transporter Chief Kyle in Classic *Trek* episodes "Tomorrow Is Yesterday," "Space Seed," "The City on the Edge of Forever," "Who Mourns for Adonais?," "Mirror, Mirror" (in which he also played the voice of the mirror universe computer), "The Apple," "The Doomsday Machine," "Catspaw," "Wolf in the Fold" (in which he played the bartender), "The Immunity Syndrome," "The Lights of Zetar," and in the movie *The Wrath of Khan.* His other TV appearances include *The Man from U.N.C.L.E.* and *The Young Rebels.*

Winston, Carter — in animated episode "The Survivor," he is a famous space trader who was engaged to *Enterprise* security officer Anne Nored but mysteriously disappeared. The *Enterprise* finds him after five years, but he is not who he seems to be. He is actually a Vendorian shape changer who has taken Winston's form. The real Winston died on Vendor, despite the Vendorians' attempts to save his life. His voice is played by Ted Knight.

Winter, Ralph — associate producer of *The Search for Spock*, and executive producer of *The Voyage Home*.

Winters, Time — played Gen Daro in *TNG* episode "The Wounded."

Wintersole, William — played Abrom in Classic *Trek* episode "Patterns of Force." His TV credits include *The Young Rebels*, as well as a regular role on *Sara*. Film credits include *Pray for the Wildcats* (with William Shatner), *Son Rise: A Miracle of Love*, and *The Day the Bubble Burst*.

Wirt, Kathleen — played an aphasia victim in *DS9* episode "A Man Alone."

Wise, David — scriptwriter of the animated episode "How Sharper Than a Serpent's Tooth."

Wise, Doug — second assistant director on *Star Trek: The Motion Picture* and first assistant director on *The Voyage Home*, *The Final Frontier*, and *The Undiscovered Country*. He was also an assistant director on the 1981 film *Private Eyes*.

Wise, Ray — played Liko in *TNG* episode "Who Watches the Watchers." He is most famous for his role as Leland Palmer on *Twin Peaks* and in the film *Twin Peaks: Fire Walk with Me*.

Wise, Robert — director of *Star Trek: The Motion Picture*. Born September 10, 1914, he was a film editor for *Citizen Kane* and *The Magnificent Ambersons*. His first directorial debut was *Curse of the Cat People*. He went on to direct *The Day the Earth Stood Still*, *West Side Appearances*, *The Haunting*, *The Sound of Music*, and *The Andromeda Strain*, among others.

Wistrom, Bill — sound editing supervisor on *DS9*.

Witches — there are three witches encountered by the landing party on Pyris VII, in Classic episode "Catspaw." They are like the three witches in *Macbeth*, and try to warn the *Enterprise* away. They are played by Rhodie Cogan, Gail Bonney, and Maryesther Denver.

Woden — this unmanned, automated freighter is destroyed by the M–5 computer against orders, in Classic episode "The Ultimate Computer."

Wolf, Venita — played Yeoman Teresa Ross in Classic *Trek* episode "The Squire of Gothos."

Wolf 359 — the battle of Wolf 359 is where many Federation Starfleet vessels were destroyed by the Borg, including the *Saratoga*, Benjamin Sisko's ship, on which he served as first officer. Nearly 11,000 people were killed in the battle, including Sisko's wife, Jennifer. The battle is shown briefly at the beginning of *DS9* episode "Emissary." This was the battle in which Locutus/Picard, who was part of the Borg hive mind at that point, led the Borg in *TNG* episode "The Best of Both Worlds."

"Wolf in the Fold" — written by horror writer Robert Bloch and directed by Joseph Pevney, this second-season Classic *Trek* episode aired 12/22/67. A rewrite of the old Jack the Ripper tale, Kirk and crew must find the identity of a brutal killer on Argelius II. Guest stars: John Fiedler, Charles Macaulay, Pilar Seurat, Joseph Bernard, Charles Dierkop, Judy McConnell, Virginia Aldridge, Judi Sherven, and Tania Lemani.

Wolfchild, Sheldon Peters — played a Native American in *TNG* episode "Time's Arrow, Parts I and II."

Wolfe, Ian — played Septimus in Classic *Trek* episode "Bread and Circuses" and Mr. Atoz in "All Our Yesterdays." Born in Canton, Illinois, in 1896, his films include *The Scarlet Claw*, *The Lost World*, and *The Terminal*

Man. He had guest appearances in the TV series *The Feather and Father Gang* and had a regular role in *Wizards and Warriors*.

Wolfe, Lawrence N. — scriptwriter of Classic *Trek* episode "The Ultimate Computer."

Wolfe, Robert Hewitt — scriptwriter of *DS9* episodes "Q Less" and "The Passenger" and *TNG* episode "A Fistful of Datas."

Wolvington, Jim — sound effects supervisor on *DS9*.

Woman — part of Riva's chorus, she represents harmony, balance, and wisdom. She is killed by Solari gunmen in *TNG* episode "Loud As a Whisper." She is played by Marnie Mosiman.

Wong, Lieutenant — *Enterprise* officer mentioned in *TNG* episode "Angel One." She repairs climate control systems.

Wong, Nancy — played the personnel officer in Classic *Trek* episode "Court-Martial."

Wood, Eugene — assistant editor of *DS9*.

Wood, Laura — played the old lady in Classic *Trek* episode "Charlie X," and Elaine Johnson in "The Deadly Years."

Woods, Barbara Alyn — played Kareen Brianon in *TNG* episode "The Schizoid Man."

Woods, Beth — scriptwriter of *TNG* episode "Contagion."

Woods, Grant — played Lt. Commander Kelowitz in Classic *Trek* episodes "The Galileo Seven," "Arena," and "This Side of Paradise." His TV credits include a regular role on the show *Custer*, as well as guest spots on *The Wackiest Ship in the Army* and *The Man from U.N.C.L.E.*

Woodville, Kate — Natira in Classic *Trek* episode

"For the World Is Hollow and I Have Touched the Sky." Her TV credits include *The Avengers* (she was married to star Patrick MacNee at the time). She moved to the U.S. from England where she appeared in the films *Fear No Evil*, *Widow*, and *Keefer*, and she guest starred on *Kolchak: The Night Stalker*.

Woodward, Morgan — played Dr. Simon Van Gelder in Classic *Trek* episode "Dagger of the Mind," and Captain Ronald Tracey in "The Omega Glory." He had regular roles on *The Life and Legend of Wyatt Earp* and *Dallas*, as well as guest appearances on the shows *Iron Horse*, *Planet of the Apes*, and many others. He appeared in the films *Yuma*, *The Last Day*, and *A Last Cry for Help*.

Worf — regular on *The Next Generation*, he is played by Michael Dorn. He is the *Enterprise*'s resident Klingon and chief of security (after Yar's death), raised by human, Russian parents on the farming colony Gault from a very early age, along with a foster brother. His Klingon father, Mogh, and mother were killed in the Khitomer massacre. His brother, Kurn, is alive because he was not present at Khitomer. Kurn was an infant when their parents died and Worf was about six. Worf was the first Klingon to attend Starfleet Academy. He has a young son, Alexander, by K'Ehleyr. Worf makes up for his lack of a true Klingon upbringing by trying to be a super-Klingon, but has mellowed out some as the series progresses, showing a deep loyalty to Riker and Picard, and an ability to be a good friend, especially to Troi, who is like a godmother to Alexander. Lwaxana Troi often calls Worf "Woof." He likes prune juice, calling it a "warrior's drink." His quarters are on Deck 7, Section 25 Baker.

Worf, Colonel — said to be the grandfather of *TNG* Worf, he is played by Michael Dorn in the film *The Undiscovered Country*. He is the defense attorney for Kirk and McCoy when they are tried in the Klingon courts for high treason and murder. He defends them honorably, but loses.

World War III — mentioned by Spock as occurring in the late 20th century on Earth. Mentioned by Q as a war that happened in the middle of the 21st century and that nearly destroyed Earth.

Woronicz, Henry — played J'Ddan in *TNG* episode "The Drumhead."

Wortham units — unit of power of a ship's engines or on a phaser, mentioned in Classic episode "The Apple."

"Wounded, The" — fourth-season *TNG* episode written by Stuart Charno, Sara Charno, Cy Chermak, and Jeri Taylor, directed by Chip Chalmers. The *Enterprise* engages a Cardassian ship in mutual fire, only to learn that a Federation ship destroyed a Cardassian vessel against orders and Picard must investigate the matter. Guest stars: Bob Gunton, Rosalind Chao, Marc Alaimo, Time Winters, John Hancock, and Marco Rodriguez.

Wrenn — leader of the last of the Tarellia in *TNG* episode "Haven." He is played by Raye Birk.

Wright, Gary — played a Vulcan litterbearer in Classic *Trek* episode "Amok Time."

Wright, Herbert J. — scriptwriter of *TNG* episodes "The Last Outpost," "The Battle," "Heart of Glory," and "Power Play." He is also a producer.

Wright, Lieutenant — officer who is in Picard's art class in *TNG* episode "A Matter of Perspective." According to Data, her art suffuses surrealism with Dadaism.

Wu — one of the Kohm leaders in Classic episode "The Omega Glory." He has seen 42 years of the redbird, who only makes an appearance once every eleven years. This makes him 462 years old, a fact which convinces Tracey that he has discovered a world with the answer to immortality. In reality, it's just natural for the Omegans to live long lives. Wu is played by Lloyd Kino.

Wyatt, Ensign — an *Enterprise* transporter technician killed by Losira in Classic episode "That Which Survives." He is played by Brad Forrest.

Wyatt, Jane — played Amanda, Spock's mother, in Classic *Trek* episode "Journey to Babel." She reprised the role in *The Voyage Home*. Born August 12, 1911, in Campgaw, New Jersey, her film credits include *Lost Horizon* and *Gentleman's Agreement*. She also starred, and won three Emmy awards for her role in, *Father Knows Best*, which lasted nine years. Her TV credits include guest appearances in *Wagon Train*, *Going My Way*, *Alcoa Premiere*, *The Virginian*, *Alfred Hitchcock Hour: The Monkey's Paw*, *Love, American Style*, *Here Come the Brides*, *Men From Shiloh*, *Alias Smith and Jones*, *Marcus Welby, M.D.*, *Medical Center*, *Fantasy Island*, *Quincy*, and many others. She has done dozens of TV movies, including *Tom Sawyer*, *Amelia Earhart*, *Superdome*, *The Nativity*, *The Millionaire*, and *Missing Children: A Mother's Story*. She is married to Edgar Ward and has a passion for poodles.

Wyllie, Meg — played the Keeper in Classic *Trek* pilot "The Cage" and "The Menagerie." TV credits include regular roles in *Hennessey* and *The Travels of Jaime McPheeters*. She also appeared in the TV movies *Death Sentence*, *Elvis*, and *The Thorn Birds*. Guest star spots include *Perry Mason*, *The Man from U.N.C.L.E.*, and *Alias Smith and Jones*.

Xanthras System — the *Enterprise*'s destination at the end of *TNG* episode "Ménage à Troi."

Xelo — former valet to Lwaxana Troi who had pornographic thoughts of her. She dismissed him for it, as mentioned in *TNG* episode "Haven."

xenopolycythemia — disease McCoy is dying from in Classic episode "For the World Is Hollow and I Have Touched the Sky." It is characterized by too many red blood cells in the blood stream. Before the Fabrini knowledge cures him, McCoy figures he has about a year to live.

Xerxes VII — on this world, the Neinmann civilization simply disappeared, much like Atlantis, in Classic episode "When the Bough Breaks."

Xylo Eggs — Data paints these in *TNG* episode "11001001."

Yacobian, Brad — first assistant director of *TNG*.

Yale, Mirasta — minister of science on Malcoria III with whom the *Enterprise* makes first contact, via Picard and Troi, in *TNG* episode "First Contact." Though Chancellor Durken decides his world is not ready to know alien life, Mirasta has permission to leave the world and travel with the *Enterprise* among the stars, as she's always dreamed of doing. She is played by Carolyn Seymour.

Yamato, USS — *Galaxy*–class sister ship to the *Enterprise* with the call letters NCC 1305 E, commanded by Captain Donald Varley. It is destroyed by a transmitted computer virus in *TNG* episode "Contagion."

Yanar — daughter of Debin of Atlek in *TNG* episode "The Outrageous Okona." She is pregnant and believes Captain Okona is the father but is supposed to marry Benzan of Streleb. She is played by Rosalind Ingledew.

Yang Tse K'ien — runabout from *Deep Space 9* in *DS9* episode "Emissary."

Yangs — group of people fighting the Kohms in Classic episode "The Omega Glory." They are a human species, with a culture so parallel to Earth's they could actually be Earth descendents.

Yar, Ishara — sister of Tasha Yar whom the *Enterprise* meets in *TNG* episode "Legacy." She is a soldier of the Coalition faction on Turkana IV, and uses the *Enterprise* without their knowledge to get close to her enemy, the Alliance, in order to fatally attack them. She is played by Beth Toussaint.

Yar, Tasha ("Natasha"), Lieutenant — series regular in the first season of *TNG*. Yar is played by Denise Crosby, and was the *Enterprise*'s security chief at the young age of 28. She and Data have a very close relationship; in fact, she seduced Data successfully in "The Naked Now." She dies on Vagra II in "Skin of Evil," murdered for no apparent reason by a slimy-looking creature named Armus. Data has a holoimage of her, and always remembers her with fondness. Yar grew up in hostile conditions in an Earth colony, Turkana IV, that deteriorated into anarchy. The colony no longer belongs to the Federation. She left her colony to attend Starfleet Academy, leaving behind one sister, Ishara. Yar reappears in "Yesterday's Enterprise," still living in the altered timeline. The timelines merge in the past, and Yar goes to the *Enterprise* C where she will survive in the past and ends up having a half-Romulan daughter, Sela, who shows up in "Redemption" at the same age Yar would have been if she had not escaped into the past. Sela is a high-ranking Romulan official who tries to outwit Picard.

Yareena — in *TNG* episode "Code of Honor," she challenges Tasha to a death duel. She is the wife of Lutan of Ligon and the former First One. She is played by Karole Selmon.

Yari — a Mintakan in *TNG* episode "Who Watches the Watchers."

Yarnek — name of the rock creature encountered on Excalbia in Classic episode "The Savage Curtain." He is a master of illusion, creating a place on his boiling, burning planet where humans can survive and breathe. The creature itself is portrayed by Janos Prohaska, and its voice is played by Bart LaRue.

Yarnell, Celeste — played Yeoman Martha Landon in Classic *Trek* episode "The Apple." Film credits include

In Name Only, Ransom for a Dead Man, and *The Judge and Jake Wyler.* TV credits include *The Man from U.N.C.L.E.*

Yashima, Momo — played a bridge crewwoman in *Star Trek: The Motion Picture.* Film credits include *Charlie Chan and the Curse of the Dragon Queen, V,* and *The Return of Marcus Welby, M.D.* She also had a regular role in *Behind the Screen.*

Yasutake, Patti — played Nurse Ogawa in *TNG* episodes "Future Imperfect," "Identity Crisis," "The Host," "Ethics," "Imaginary Friend," "The Inner Light," and "Realm of Fear."

Yeager, Biff — played Argyle in *TNG* episodes "Where No One Has Gone Before" and "Datalore."

Yellow Alert — a standby alert. The ship could be in danger, and all hands should be ready to move if this is so.

Yep, Laurence — author of the Classic *Trek* novel *Shadow Lord.*

"Yesterday's Enterprise" — third-season *TNG* episode written by Trent Christopher Ganino, Eric Stillwell, Ira Stephen Behr, Hans Beimler, Richard Manning, and Ronald D. Moore, directed by David Carson. A rare phenomenon, a temporal rift (see entry), causes timelines to shift. In the new timeline, Yar is still alive and the Federation is at war with the Klingon Empire. Guest stars: Denise Crosby, Christopher McDonald, Tricia O'Neil, and Whoopi Goldberg.

"Yesteryear" — written by D. C. Fontana, this animated Classic *Trek* episode aired 9/15/73. On the planet of the Guardian of Forever, somehow Vulcan timelines have changed and no one recognizes Spock. An android first officer works on the *Enterprise,* and Spock must go back in time and find out what went wrong. He visits his home city of ShiKahr and meets himself at seven years of age. Guest voices: Mark Lenard (Sarek), Majel Barrett (Amanda), Billy

Simpson (young Spock), and James Doohan (The Healer, Thelin the Andorian, Guardian of Forever).

Yonada — spaceship world traveling off its course and endangering the inhabitants of Daran V. The people on Yonada do not know they are on a manufactured vessel in Classic episode "For the World Is Hollow and I Have Touched the Sky." It is constructed to look like an asteroid, 200 miles in diameter. It was built by the Fabrini, whose sun went nova, and is run by an Oracle. Priestess Natira rules the world.

Yorktown, **USS** — the *Enterprise* is supposed to rendezvous with this ship in Classic episode "Obsession." They are delayed by the vampire cloud.

Yosemite, **USS** — in *TNG* episode "Realm of Fear," the *Yosemite* is found badly damaged with its crew of five missing. In "Frame of Mind," when Riker is in the Tilonus Institute for Mental Disorders, he meets a woman who says she is Commander Bloom of the *Yosemite*. She claims two other inmates are also from the *Yosemite*.

Young, Dey — played Hannah Bates in *TNG* episode "The Masterpiece Society."

Young, Tony — played Kryton in Classic *Trek* episode "Elaan of Troyius." TV credits include *Iron Horse, Get Christie Love!,* and *Barnaby Jones*. He was also a regular in *Gunslinger*. He was in *He Rides Tall* ('63) and *Charro* ('69).

Youngblood, Ensign — an *Enterprise* officer and science specialist, seen in several *TNG* episodes. He is played by James Becker.

Yridian — in *TNG* episode "Birthright," a Yridian named Jaglom Shrek tells Worf he knows where his father, Mogh, is. Yridians are blue, with large ears and no thumbs. In "The Chase," Professor Galen's shuttle is destroyed by a Yridian ship.

Yuricich, Richard — special effects producer of *Star*

Trek: The Motion Picture. He also did work on the film *Brainstorm.*

Yuta — the last survivor of the Tralesta Clan in *TNG* episode "The Vengeance Factor." She is the chef and taster for Sovereign Marouk of Acamar III. She is also the chosen assassin, whose cells have been restructured to age slowly, to destroy the last Lornack, Chorgon, but Riker kills her to prevent her from doing so. She is played by Lisa Wilcox.

Yutan — one of Tyree's men, a hill person from Classic episode "A Private Little War." He is played by Gary Pillar.

Zabo — hood who works for Krako and captures Kirk in Classic episode "A Piece of the Action." He is played by Steve Marlo.

Zaheva, Chantal R., Captain — captain of the USS *Brattain* in *TNG* episode "Night Terrors." She is played by Deborah Taylor.

Zakdorns — master strategists mentioned in *TNG* episodes "Unification," "Peak Performance," and "Ménage à Troi." They have wavy lines on their cheeks but, apparently, no sense of humor.

Zaldan — humanoids of this world are insulted by courtesy and have webbed hands, as seen in *TNG* episode "Coming of Age."

Zalkon — John Doe's homeworld in *TNG* episode "Transfigurations." Located in the Zeta Gelis Cluster. The Zalkonian ship is equivalent in speed and armaments to the *Enterprise*.

Zalkonian weapon — an invisible device that chokes the crew on the *Enterprise* in *TNG* episode "Transfigurations."

Zambrano, Jacqueline — scriptwriter of *TNG* episode "Loud As a Whisper."

Zan Periculi — species of the Ferengi flower Pericules, indigenous to Lappa IV. Tog gives one to Lwaxana in *TNG* episode "Ménage à Troi."

Zanza Men's Dance Palace — in *TNG* episode "We'll Always Have Paris," this place is mentioned as located right across from the Blue Parrot Café.

Zapata, USS — the *Enterprise* is to rendezvous with this ship when it leaves Betazed in *TNG* episode "Ménage à Troi."

Zarabeth — young woman trapped in the past on Sarpeidon, who lives a lonely life in that planet's ice age in Classic episode "All Our Yesterdays." She lives in a cave and was sent there as punishment by a leader named Zor Kahn. Spock and McCoy run into her and, because she wants them for companions, she lies to them, telling them they will die if they ever try to return to the future. She is played by Mariette Hartley.

Zaslow, Michael — played Darnell in Classic *Trek* episode "The Man Trap," and Ensign Jordan in "I, Mudd."

Zatteral Emerald — in *TNG* episode "Devil's Due," Picard tells Ardra he knows where to find the fabled Zatteral Emerald lost among the Ruins of Ligilium.

Zatucke, Donald W. — played first Lt. USMC in *The Voyage Home.*

Zaynor — Prime Minister Nayrok's aide in *TNG* episode "The Hunted." He is played by J. Michael Flynn.

Zed Lapis Sector — Vagra II is located here in *TNG* episode "Skin of Evil."

Zedak IV — an *Enterprise* boy named Harry Bernard used to live on this world, as mentioned in *TNG* episode "When the Bough Breaks." It is made up largely of oceans.

Zegov — Klingon female on board the *Pagh* in *TNG* episode "A Matter of Honor."

Zek — the Ferengi Grand Nagus in *DS9* episode "The Nagus." He is an ancient ruler who has hair growing out of his ears, which his aides comb. Disgusting and crude, he is motivated by profit and is played by Wallace Shawn.

Zembata, Captain — mentioned in *TNG* episode "Elementary, Dear Data" as the captain of Geordi's old ship, the *Victory*. Geordi served under him as an ensign.

Zena — she is chosen to be Alexandra's mother on Aldea in *TNG* episode "When the Bough Breaks."

Zendi Sabu System — it is in this system that the *Enterprise* encounters the lost *Stargazer* and DaiMon Bok's ship in *TNG* episode "The Battle."

Zenga, Bo — played Asoth in *DS9* episode "Babel."

Zeon — neighboring world to Ekos and involved in a war with that world. Zeon's star is M43 Alpha. The Zeons are peaceful people who were first attacked by the Ekosians, who want to dominate and rule them in Classic episode "Patterns of Force."

Zera IV — in *TNG* episode "Realm of Fear," O'Brien mentions he was on a Starbase here that was infested by Talarian hook spiders. He still shivers when he thinks about cleaning them out.

Zerbst, Brad — played a nurse in *TNG* episodes "Heart of Glory" and "Skin of Evil."

Zeta Alpha II — where the *Lalo* disembarked to fight the Borg in *TNG* episode "The Best of Both Worlds."

Zeta Gelis Cluster — place where the *Enterprise* finds John Doe's ship in *TNG* episode "Transfigurations." It contains several pulsars and G-type stars.

Zetar — whirlwind of lights calling themselves the "lights of Zetar" appears in Classic episode "The Lights of Zetar." They speak through Mira Romaine and try to take over her body. They destroy the files and all personnel on Memory Alpha. They say they are what is left of the desires, hopes, and dreams of the Zetars, whose world was destroyed long before, and that they have searched for a body to take over ever since. Their morality ignores murder, so they are deemed insane by the *Enterprise* crew, who must kill the Zetars to survive.

Zhukov, USS — ship on which Barclay previously served, commanded by Captain Gleason, mentioned in *TNG* episode "Hollow Pursuits."

Zibalia — Kivas Fajo of *TNG* episode "The Most Toys" is from this world.

Zicree, Mark Scott — scriptwriter of *TNG* episode "First Contact."

Zienite — substance mined by the Troglytes on Ardana in Classic episode "The Cloud Minders." It produces an invisible gas that temporarily affects a person's thinking and retards his brain functions.

Zimmerman, Herman — production designer of *DS9* and set designer of *TNG*.

Zor Kahn the Tyrant — tyrant in Sarpeidon's past who exiled Zarabeth to that world's ice age in Classic episode "All Our Yesterdays." Her punishment is to live alone. He apparently killed all her family except for her as some sort of revenge for a plot to overthrow him. The ice age in which she lives is 6000 years in the past from the time when the *Enterprise* discovers Sarpeidon.

Zora — an infamous scientist of a previous age who experimented with body chemistry on Tiburon tribes and is brought back into being to face off against Kirk, Spock, McCoy, Lincoln, and Surak in Classic episode "The Savage Curtain." She is played by Carol Daniels Dement.

Zorn, Groppler — leader of the Bandi on Deneb IV in *TNG* episode "Encounter at Farpoint." He held an alien entity hostage. He is played by Michael Bell.

Z particles — according to Geordi, these particles jump every time Armus uses his powers in *TNG* episode "Skin of Evil."

Zuckerman, Ed — scriptwriter of *TNG* episode "A Matter of Perspective."

Zuckert, Bill — played Johnny Behan in Classic *Trek* episode "Spectre of the Gun."

Zweller, Corey, Ensign — one of Picard's two best friends from the Academy, along with Marta Batanides, seen in *TNG* episode "Tapestry." He got revenge on a Nausicaan who cheated him in a game of dom-jot. He is eventually posted to the USS *Ajax*.

Zytchin III — mentioned in *TNG* episode "Captain's Holiday" as a place where Picard spent four lovely days. He says he lied about enjoying those four days, however.

NUMBERS

"11001001" — this first-season *TNG* episode was written by Maurice Hurley and Bob Lewin and directed by Paul Lynch. In this episode, Bynars working on repairing the computer on the *Enterprise* steal the ship with Picard and Riker on board trapped on the holodeck. Guest stars: Carolyn McCormick, Gene Dynarski, Ron Brown, Abdul Salaam el Razzac, Jack Sheldon, Alexandra Johnson, Katy Boyer, Iva Lane, and Kelly Ann McNally.

498th Air Base Group — where Colonel Fellini interrogates Kirk and Sulu in Classic episode "Tomorrow Is Yesterday." It is located on the Omaha Air Force Base.

829–IV — world that has evolved a culture that looks like 20th-century Rome, in Classic episode "Bread and Circuses."

APPENDIX A

A List of All Series Episodes in Order of Appearance and Season

STAR TREK

PILOT

"The Cage"

FIRST SEASON

"The Man Trap"

"Charlie X"

"Where No Man Has Gone Before"

"The Naked Time"

"The Enemy Within"

"Mudd's Women"

"What Are Little Girls Made Of?"

"Miri"

"Dagger of the Mind"

"The Corbomite Maneuver"

"The Menagerie, Parts I and II"

"The Conscience of the King"

"Balance of Terror"

"Shore Leave"

"The Galileo Seven"

"The Squire of Gothos"

"Arena"

"Tomorrow Is Yesterday"

"Court-Martial"

"The Return of the Archons"

"Space Seed"

"A Taste of Armageddon"

"This Side of Paradise"

"The Devil in the Dark"

"Errand of Mercy"

"The Alternative Factor"

"The City on the Edge of Forever"

"Operation: Annihilate!"

SECOND SEASON

"Amok Time"

"Who Mourns for Adonais?"

"The Changeling"

"Mirror, Mirror"

"The Apple"

"The Doomsday Machine"

"Catspaw"

"I, Mudd"

"Metamorphosis"

"Journey to Babel"

"Friday's Child"

"The Deadly Years"

STAR TREK: THE ANIMATED SERIES

FIRST SEASON

SECOND SEASON

"The Counter-Clock Incident"

STAR TREK: THE NEXT GENERATION

FIRST SEASON

"Encounter at Farpoint, Parts I and II"
"The Naked Now"
"Code of Honor"
"The Last Outpost"
"Where No One Has Gone Before"
"Lonely among Us"
"Justice"
"The Battle"
"Hide and Q"
"Haven"
"The Big Goodbye"
"Datalore"
"Angel One"
"11001001"
"Too Short a Season"
"When the Bough Breaks"
"Home Soil"
"Coming of Age"
"Heart of Glory"
"The Arsenal of Freedom"
"Symbiosis"
"Skin of Evil"
"We'll Always Have Paris"
"Conspiracy"
"The Neutral Zone"

SECOND SEASON

"The Child"
"Where Silence Has Lease"
"Elementary, Dear Data"
"The Outrageous Okona"
"Loud As a Whisper"
"The Schizoid Man"
"Unnatural Selection"
"A Matter of Honor"
"The Measure of a Man"
"The Dauphin"
"Contagion"
"The Royale"
"Time Squared"
"The Icarus Factor"
"Pen Pals"
"Q Who"
"Samaritan Snare"
"Up the Long Ladder"
"Manhunt"
"The Emissary"
"Peak Performance"
"Shades of Gray"

THIRD SEASON

"Evolution"
"The Ensigns of Command"
"The Survivors"
"Who Watches the Watchers"
"The Bonding"
"Booby Trap"
"The Enemy"
"The Price"
"The Vengeance Factor"
"The Defector"
"The Hunted"
"The High Ground"
"Déjà Q"
"A Matter of Perspective"
"Yesterday's Enterprise"
"The Offspring"
"Sins of the Father"
"Allegiance"
"Captain's Holiday"

"Tin Man"

"Hollow Pursuits"

"The Most Toys"

"Sarek"

"Ménage à Troi"

"Transfigurations"

"The Best of Both Worlds,
Part I"

FOURTH SEASON

"The Best of Both Worlds,
Part II"

"Family"

"Brothers"

"Suddenly Human"

"Remember Me"

"Legacy"

"Reunion"

"Future Imperfect"

"Final Mission"

"The Loss"

"Data's Day"

"The Wounded"

"Devil's Due"

"Clues"

"First Contact"

"Galaxy's Child"

"Night Terrors"

"Identity Crisis"

"The Nth Degree"

"Qpid"

"The Drumhead"

"Half a Life"

"The Host"

"The Mind's Eye"

"In Theory"

"Redemption, Part I"

FIFTH SEASON

"Redemption, Part II"

"Darmok"

"Ensign Ro"

"Silicon Avatar"

"Disaster"

"The Game"

"Unification, Parts I and II"

"A Matter of Time"

"New Ground"

"Hero Worship"

"Violations"

"The Masterpiece Society"

"Conundrum"

"Power Play"

"Ethics"

"The Outcast"

"Cause and Effect"

"The First Duty"

"Cost of Living"

"The Perfect Mate"

"Imaginary Friend"

"I, Borg"

"The Next Phase"

"The Inner Light"

"Time's Arrow, Part I"

SIXTH SEASON

"Time's Arrow, Part II"

"Realm of Fear"

"Man of the People"

"Relics"

"Schisms"

"True Q"

"Rascals"

"A Fistful of Datas"

"The Quality of Life"

"Chain of Command, Parts
I and II"

"Ship in a Bottle"

"Aquiel"

"Face of the Enemy"

"Tapestry"
"Birthright, Parts I and II"
"Starship Mine"
"Lessons"
"The Chase"
"Frame of Mind"
"Suspicions"
"Rightful Heir"
"Second Chances"
"Timescape"
"Descent, Part I"

Star Trek VI:
  The Undiscovered Country

STAR TREK: DEEP SPACE NINE

FIRST SEASON

"Emissary"
"Past Prologue"
"A Man Alone"
"Babel"
"Captive Pursuit"
"Q Less"
"Dax"
"The Passenger"
"Move Along Home"
"The Nagus"
"Vortex"

STAR TREK: THE FILMS

Star Trek:
  The Motion Picture
Star Trek II:
  The Wrath of Khan
Star Trek III:
  The Search For Spock
Star Trek IV:
  The Voyage Home
Star Trek V:
  The Final Frontier

APPENDIX B

A List of Series Novels in Order of Appearance

(Note: Listings in the encyclopedia are by author only.)

BANTAM BOOKS

Spock Must Die!
by James Blish

Spock Messiah!
by Theodore R. Cogswell
and Charles A. Spano, Jr.

The Price of the Phoenix
by Sondra Marshak and
Myrna Culbreath

Planet of Judgment
by Joe Haldeman

Vulcan! by Kathleen Sky

The Starless World
by Gordon Eklund

Trek to Madworld
by Stephen Goldin

World Without End
by Joe Haldeman

The Fate of the Phoenix
by Sondra Marshak and
Myrna Culbreath

Devil World
by Gordon Eklund

Perry's Planet
by Jack C. Haldeman II

The Galactic Whirlpool
by David Gerrold

Death's Angel
by Kathleen Sky

Star Trek: The New Voyages,
vols. 1 and 2 (short
stories), edited by Sondra
Marshak and Myrna
Culbreath

Star Trek 1–12 by James
Blish, with #12 by J. A.
Lawrence and James Blish

Mudd's Angels by J. A.
Lawrence, Blish's wife

DEL REY BOOKS

STAR TREK LOGS 1–10
by Alan Dean Foster

POCKET BOOKS

Star Trek: The Motion Picture
by Gene Roddenberry

The Entropy Effect
  by Vonda N. McIntyre

The Klingon Gambit
  by Robert E. Vardeman

The Covenant of the Crown
  by Howard Weinstein

The Prometheus Design
  by Sondra Marshak and
  Myrna Culbreath

The Abode of Life
  by Lee Corey

Star Trek II: The Wrath of Khan
  by Vonda N. McIntyre

Black Fire by Sonni Cooper

Triangle
  by Sondra Marshak and
  Myrna Culbreath

Web of the Romulans
  by M. S. Murdock

Yesterday's Son
  by A. C. Crispin

Mutiny on the Enterprise
  by Robert Vardeman

The Wounded Sky
  by Diane Duane

The Trellisane Confrontation
  by David Dvorkin

Corona by Greg Bear

The Final Reflection
  by John M. Ford

*Star Trek III: The Search for
  Spock* by Vonda N.
  McIntyre

My Enemy, My Ally
  by Diane Duane

The Tears of the Singers
  by Melinda Snodgrass

*The Vulcan Academy
  Murders* by Jean Lorrah

Uhura's Song
  by Janet Kagen

Shadow Lord
  by Laurence Yep

Ishmael by Barbara Hambly

Killing Time
  by Della Van Hise

Dwellers in the Crucible
  by Margaret Wander
  Bonanno

Pawns and Symbols
  by Majliss Larson

Mindshadow by J. M. Dillard

Crisis on Centaurus
  by Brad Ferguson

Dreadnought!
  by Diane Carey

Demons by J. M. Dillard

Battlestations!
  by Diane Carey

Chain of Attack
  by Gene DeWeese

Deep Domain
  by Howard Weinstein

Dreams of the Raven
  by Carmen Carter

Romulan Way
  by Diane Duane

*How Much for Just the
  Planet?* by John M. Ford

Bloodthirst by J. M. Dillard

POCKET'S SPECIAL *TREK* SERIES

The Romulan Prize
  by Simon Hawke

POCKET BOOKS: *DEEP SPACE NINE*

Emissary by J. M. Dillard

The Siege by Peter David

Bloodletter by K. W. Jeter

The Big Game
  by Sandy Schofield

BIBLIOGRAPHY

Files Magazine Focus on Star Trek: The Voyage Home by John Peel, published by Pop Cult, Inc., 1987.

Files Magazine: Star Trek IV The Voyage Home by Edward Gross, published by Psi Fi Movie Press, 1986.

New Voyages: The Next Generation Guidebook by Edward Gross and Mark A. Altman, published by Image Publishing, 1991.

Star Trek Concordance by Bjo Trimble, published by Ballantine, 1976.

Star Trek Deep Space Nine published by *Starlog*, May 1993.

Star Trek Files: The Search For Spock by Edward Gross, published by Psi Fi Movie Press, 1985.

Star Trek Starfleet Technical Manual by Franz Joseph, published by Ballantine 1975.

Star Trek: The Next Generation official magazine published by *Starlog*, June 1993, April 1993, August 1993, June 1992, February 1992.

Star Trek: The Next Generation 18, published by *Starlog*, 1992.

Star Trek: The Next Generation 25th Celebration, published by *Starlog*, 1993.

Star Trek V: The Final Frontier official movie magazine, published by *Starlog*, 1989.

Star Trek: Deep Space Nine, vol. 1, published by *Starlog*, 1993.

Star Trek: The Next Generation—The Armchair Viewer's Guide by Jim Shaun Lyon, October 1992. Not published in book form but available for computer.

Star Trek: The Next Generation First, Second and Third Season Encyclopedia by Jim Shaun Lyon. Not published in book form, but released on computer network.

Starlog #1, August 1976.

The Classic Trek Crew Book by James Van Hise, published by Pioneer Books, 1993.

The Making of Star Trek II, The Wrath of Khan by Allan Asherman, published by Pocket, 1982.

The Making of Star Trek, The Motion Picture by Susan Sackett and Gene Roddenberry, published by Pocket, 1980.

The Man Who Created Star Trek: Gene Roddenberry by James Van Hise, published by Pioneer Books, 1992.

The Star Trek Files: Star Trek III: The Search for Spock by John Peel, published by Psi Fi Movie Press, 1987.

The Star Trek: The Next Generation Encyclopedia by William F. B. Vodrey, published by Kearsarge Press, 1993 in fanzine format.

The Trek Encyclopedia Second Edition by John Peel with additional material by Hal Schuster and Scott Nance, published by Pioneer Books, 1992.

Trek 25th Anniversary Celebration by James Van Hise, published by Pioneer Books, 1991.

Trek Deep Space Nine: The Unauthorized Story by James Van Hise, published by Pioneer Books, 1993.

Trek The Next Generation by James Van Hise, published by Pioneer Books, 1992.

Trek The Next Generation Crew Book by James Van Hise, published by Pioneer Books, 1993.

⬛ HarperPrism

SMALL GODS by Terry Pratchett.
International bestseller Terry Pratchett brings
magic to life in his latest romp through Discworld, a
land where the unexpected always happens—usually to the
nicest people, like Brutha, former melon farmer, now The
Chosen One. His only question: Why?

0-06-109217-7 — $4.99

MAGIC: THE GATHERING™—ARENA
by William R. Forstchen. Based on the
wildly bestselling trading-card game, the first novel
in the *MAGIC: THE GATHERING™* novel series features wizards and warriors clashing in deadly battles. The book also
includes an offer for two free, unique MAGIC cards.

0-06-105424-0 — $4.99

SEAROAD:Chronicles of Klatsand by
Ursula K. Le Guin. Here is the culmination
of Le Guin's lifelong fascination with small island cultures. In a sense, the Klatsand of these stories is a modern
day successor to her bestselling *ALWAYS COMING HOME*. A
world apart from our own, but part of it as well.

0-06-105400-3 — $4.99

CALIBAN'S HOUR by Tad Williams. The
bestselling author of *TO GREEN ANGEL TOWER*
brings to life a rich and incandescent fantasy tale of
passion, betrayal, and death. The beast Caliban has been
searching for decades for Miranda, the woman he loved—the
woman who was taken from him by her father Prospero. Now
that Caliban has found her, he has an hour to tell his tale of
unrequited love and dark vengeance. And when the hour is
over, Miranda must die.... Tad Williams has reached a new
level of magic and emotion with this breathtaking tapestry in
which yearning and passion are entwined.

Hardcover, 0-06-105204-3 — $14.99

and Tomorrow

WRATH OF GOD by Robert Gleason.
An apocalyptic novel of a future America about to
fall under the rule of a murderous savage. Only a
small group of survivors are left to fight — but they are
joined by powerful forces from history when they learn how
to open a hole in time. Three legendary heroes answer the
call to the ultimate battle: George S. Patton, Amelia Earhart,
and Stonewall Jackson. Add to that lineup a killer dinosaur
and you have the most sweeping battle since *THE STAND*.
Trade paperback, 0-06-105311-2 — $14.99

THE X-FILES™ by Charles L. Grant. America's
hottest new TV series launches as a book series with
FBI agents Mulder and Scully investigating the cases
no one else will touch — the cases in the file marked X.
There is one thing they know: The truth is out there.
0-06-105414-3 — $4.99

THE WORLD OF DARKNESS™: VAMPIRE—
DARK PRINCE by Keith Herber. The ground-
breaking White Wolf role-playing game Vampire: The
Masquerade is now featured in a chilling dark fantasy novel of
a man trying to control the Beast within.
0-06-105422-4 — $4.99

THE UNAUTHORIZED TREKKERS' GUIDE
TO *THE NEXT GENERATION* AND *DEEP SPACE
NINE* by James Van Hise. This two-in-one
guidebook contains all the information on the shows, the characters, the creators, the stories behind the episodes, and
the voyages that landed on the cutting room floor.
0-06-105417-8 — $5.99

HarperPrism
An Imprint of HarperPaperbacks

The tapes are terrific entertainment anywhere. Pop them into your car stereo, plug in your headphones, or listen while at home—these fabulous tales will intrigue and entertain you for hours!

— — — — — — — — — — — —

ORDER TODAY!
MAIL TO: HarperCollins Publishers
P.O. Box 588, Dunmore, PA 18512-0588
TELEPHONE: 1-800-331-3761 (Visa/Mastercard)

Yes, please send me the audios indicated below:

____**Star Trek® Memories** • 1-55994-783-7, $22.50
     4 cassettes, 4.5 hours, abridged
____**Star Trek® Movie Memories** • 0-69451-480-2, $22.50
     4 cassettes, approx. 6 hours, abridged
     (available 10/94)
____**William Shatner and Leonard Nimoy Read Four
     Science Fiction Classics** • 1-55994-884-1, $25.00
     4 cassettes, 4 hours, abridged

SUBTOTAL..._____
POSTAGE AND HANDLING... 2.50 _____
SALES TAX (Add applicable sales tax).........................._____
TOTAL.._____
(Remit in U.S. dollars, do not send cash.)

Name_____

Address_____

City_____State_____Zip_____

Allow up to six weeks for delivery. Prices subject to change.
Valid in U.S. and Canada only.   G00811